Adventures of the First Woman Mountie IV

The Fourth Omnibus

LAURIE SCHRAMM

Adventures of the First Woman Mountie IV. The Fourth Omnibus

An Inimitable Mountie. Book 13
An Inside Mountie. Book 14
An Interrupted Mountie. Book 15
An Inveterate Mountie. Book 16

This book is a work of historical fiction, set in the early 1980s. Although most of the historical references are accurate, a few are not, and names, characters, places, and incidents are either the product of the author's imagination or are used fictitiously. Any resemblance to actual persons, living or dead is entirely coincidental.

Print ISBN: 978-1-0690565-8-0
ePub ISBN: 978-1-0690565-9-7

Laurie Schramm

DEDICATION

Dedicated to the present and past Members of the Royal Canadian
Mounted Police and its forebears, the Royal North-West Mounted
Police and the North-West Mounted Police.

Dedicated also to the countless sled-dogs and Police Service Dogs
that have been part of the Force since the 1890s.

Laurie Schramm

CONTENTS

Omnibus Dedication   vii

Acknowledgements   xi

An Inimitable Mountie. Book 13   1

An Inside Mountie. Book 14   147

An Interrupted Mountie. Book 15   291

An Inveterate Mountie. Book 16   419

Adventures of the First Woman Mountie   579

Summaries of Books 1 - 16   581

About the Author   585

Laurie Schramm

ACKNOWLEDGMENTS

I am extremely grateful to the growing number of friendly readers that that have provided encouragement, comments, and suggestions based on drafts of these books: Ann Marie, Katherine, Victoria, William, Dawson, Al, Peter, Jayme, Karen D., Karen F., and Ernie.

Special thanks also to three real-life veterans of the RCMP, all of whom have supplemented their encouragement with background, advice, and factual reference materials on the Force: Chief Superintendent William Schramm (Ret.), who also kindly allowed my main character to borrow his Regimental Number, Assistant Commissioner Dawson Hovey (Ret.), Deputy Commissioner Peter German, KC, Ph.D. (Ret.), Constable Karen Frost (Ret., one of the trailblazing women Mounties who joined-up when women represented only 2% of the total uniformed complement), and especially Staff Sergeant Al Lund (Ret., author of Mounties on the Cover and probably the world's leading authority on Mountie fiction).

Laurie Schramm

"I demand that neither hardship, suffering, privation, nor fear of death should move you by a hair's breadth from carrying out your duties."

Attributed to:
Sir George Arthur French,
First Commissioner of the NWMP, 1873

Laurie Schramm

An Inimitable Mountie

Adventures of the First

Woman Mountie. Book 13

LAURIE SCHRAMM

in·im·i·ta·ble

adjective: impossible to imitate

The Canadian Oxford Dictionary,
Oxford University Press, 1998

Laurie Schramm

DEDICATION

To Chipper

Laurie Schramm

BOOK 13 CONTENTS

Dedication 5

List of Characters 9

List of Acronyms and Abbreviations 10

1 Prelude 11

2 A Chance Discovery 19

3 More Surprises 39

4 Vacation's Over 55

5 In the Gulf 73

6 Another Attack 89

7 Progress 107

8 Who Knows What Evil Lurks 119

9 Loose Ends 127

10 Epilogue 131

Book 9 Endnotes 135

Shediac's Flying Boats Historical Society 145

Laurie Schramm

LIST OF CHARACTERS
(IN ORDER OF APPEARANCE)

- Captain Healey, British Overseas Airways (BOAC) pilot
- Corporal Alexandra (Alex) Houston, RCMP Security Service
- Silver, an Alaskan Malamute; Alex's police-dog-service (PDS) partner
- Sharon Sanders, Research Scientist, Bedford Institute of Oceanography (BIO)
- Jean Friend, owner of The Lobster's Brew, Parlee Beach, N.B.
- Abe Strong, lobster-boat skipper, Pointe-du-Chêne, N.B.
- Marlea Becker, lobster-boat skipper, Pointe-du-Chêne, N.B.
- Chipper, an American-shorthair calico boat cat
- Major Donald (Don) Harrison, Military Intelligence, Canadian Armed Forces
- Special Agent Vivian Rule, FBI
- Constable John Hardisty, RCMP, Shediac, N.B.
- Dr. Bruce Solinsky, Family physician, Shediac, N.B.
- Sergeant Mike Morrison, RCMP, Shediac, N.B.
- Staff Sergeant Robert (Bob) Simpson, RCMP Security Service
- Noah Campbell and Marcel Bourque, small-time criminals
- Wade Kean, Curator, Shediac Museum, N.B.
- Dr. Levi Murray, retired college professor, Shediac, N.B.
- Dr. Odette Billon, Family physician, Shediac, N.B.
- Coralie Lessoile, Receptionist/secretary at ABC Shediac Import and Export
- Duncan Moray, local resident, Cap-Pelé, N.B.

LIST OF ACRONYMS AND ABBREVIATIONS

aka — Also known as
CFB — Canadian Forces Base
CRS — Central Records System (FBI, Washington)
HQ — Headquarters
JP — Justice of the Peace
NASA — National Aeronautics and Space Administration (U.S.)
NBC — Nuclear, biological, and chemical
NCO i/c — Non-commissioned officer-in-charge
nmi — Nautical miles
NRC — National Research Council of Canada
PDS — Police Dog Service
PEI — Prince Edward Island
PSD — Police Service Dog
RCAF — Royal Canadian Air Force
RCMP — Royal Canadian Mounted Police

1 PRELUDE

April 9, 1945

Cruising at a speed of 300 km/h (160 thousand knots) and an altitude of just over 3.3 km (11,000 ft.) above the ocean's surface, the flying boat *Atlantic Sky Queen* was crossing the Atlantic Ocean, with its four, 14-cylinder 1,600 hp Twin Cyclone engines putting out a constant roar. The aircraft itself was a Boeing 314A Clipper[1].

When the first such Clipper made its inaugural test-flight on June 7, 1938, it had been a flying boat like the world had never before seen. Now, seven years later, their flights had become routine but the aircraft still stood out. Huge in size, the *Atlantic Sky Queen* had a wingspan of 46 m (152 ft.), weighed as much as 14 metric tonnes (42 tons) and, for such as large aircraft, had a revolutionary flying range of nearly 6,000 km (3,000 nmi).

In peacetime, one of the airliner's main routes had been the northern route: from Southampton to New York via Foynes, Ireland, Botwood, Newfoundland, and Shediac, New Brunswick. In those times, the Clipper had routinely carried a crew of 10, most of whom were occupied looking after the 74 daytime or 40 nighttime passengers in luxurious first-class style. The hazards of the Second World War, however, had almost immediately put an end to the northern transatlantic service. Due to their huge range and carrying capacity, most of the Clippers – even those flying other routes - had been pressed into service with either the US Navy or the US Army

Air Force.

Now, the *Atlantic Sky Queen* was flying the old northern route once again, albeit with a scaled-back crew and solely military passengers and cargo. Although the aircraft now belonged to the U.S. Navy, most of the flight crew was made up of civilian Pan Am employees, due to their specialized experience taking these huge flying-boats over long-distance trans-ocean flights.

At the front of the flight deck, on the upper deck, sat Captain Healey. To his right sat the first officer and co-pilot. Immediately behind the captain was a navigator, standing at his plot table and poring over his charts and updating his calculations. Behind the co-pilot, on the right-hand side of the cabin was a radio operator, seated at his large, angled station, and behind him was the flight engineer, seated at his own large console. None of these crew members felt crowded. On the contrary, an aviator from any other kind of aircraft would have been astonished to the point of disbelief at the size of the flight deck.

It had already been a long journey. They had left Southampton at 2 pm the previous day, but not before loading a few military passengers and nearly 10,000 pounds (4,000 kg) of cargo. Although it was clear that the war in Europe would soon be over[2], it seemed that there was still a steady stream of passengers and cargo to be ferried in both directions across the Atlantic.

Once finally free of Southampton it only took an hour and half to reach Foynes, Ireland where they had a one-hour stop to take on additional passengers and cargo. Then came the nearly 16-hour transatlantic leg to the North American coast, during which the first officer had handed over the controls to the captain and gone for a rest, while the navigator and radio operator had similarly switched over to their alternates as well. The plane was only carrying one flight engineer, who had to take periodic naps while remaining on-call.

It was tiring work. Other than the occasional course adjustment there was only the unrelenting drone of the engines and a complete absence of anything to see in the dark sky around them. That made boredom a more dangerous enemy for the crew than the small change of an errant enemy fighter plane. Halfway across the ocean, the crew did another swap.

The Boeing 314 Clipper

Seventeen hours into this leg of the journey, and about 100 miles from the Newfoundland coast, Captain Healey yawned. He was getting tired again. Giving the gauges a routine scan, his gaze shifted to peering out through the windscreen. Although it was getting lighter, there was nothing to see in the pre-dawn skies around them. Then, something registered in his brain and he scanned the gauges once more. This time he spotted what he should have seen before. The portside fuel gauge reading was lower than it should be. Much lower.

"Wake up the first officer and engineer, would you," he said to the navigator, "and then see if you can get a good fix on our position."

"Trouble?" asked the first officer as he slipped into the right-hand seat. He was joined by the flight engineer, who leaned in from just behind their seats.

"See for yourself," said the captain, pointing to the gauge for the portside fuel tank.

"I'll go take a look," said the engineer, who walked back along the flight deck to where there were two hatches, one on each side of the aircraft. Grabbing a flashlight from its spring-clip mount, he opened the portside hatch and crawled inside the wing. Near the leading edge of each wing there was just enough room for a person to crawl along a catwalk that allowed some inflight access to the engines. This had been designed to enable some kinds of repairs to the engines while in flight. This time, though, the engineer was headed for the large fuel tank.

The smell of aviation fuel that had been unmistakeable when he first opened the hatch, became stronger as he approached the tank. Persevering, he inspected as much of the tank as he could, then crawled back to the cabin, resealed the hatch, and walked forward to report.

"We've got a major fuel leak somewhere underneath the tank," he said to the two pilots, leaning over their shoulders. "Must be either a fitting or the fuel pump, but there's no way to get underneath and do anything about it while we're in the air."

"All right," said the captain, sharing a long look with the first officer. The portside tank was rapidly emptying. They were not going to make it to New York on the fuel remaining in the starboard tank.

While the engineer had been checking on the fuel tank, the navigator had gone to a small set of metal stairs that led him to the astrodome: a small turret with windows mounted on the roof of the upper deck. From the turret, he could use a sextant to determine their position. When that was done, he returned to his plot table and marked the position on the chart. His subsequent report to the captain and first officer was not good news.

"We're 55 nautical miles from the Newfoundland coast."

Having flown this route many times before, all of them knew that the nearest two seaports capable of handling the huge aircraft were Botwood and Shediac.

"Advise Botwood we're low on fuel and diverting to them," said the captain to the radio operator.

That resulted in more bad news. "Botwood advises they have limited visibility due to fog, with occasional periods of brief clearing."

"We may as well give it a try," said the captain. "Declare an emergency and tell them we're coming in." Then, to the navigator "Better go below and bring our passengers up to speed."

With dawn rapidly approaching, the sky was lightening as they began a gradual descent through a thick layer of dense clouds. Flying blind, time seemed to slow while they were in the clouds but, eventually, they broke through at 10,000 feet. The sea below them looked rough, but they had good visibility. Up ahead, they could see nothing. It was as if the cloud bank extended all the way down to the surface of the ocean.

After a while, the horizon resolved into three layers: a bank of heavy cloud, the ocean, and a thick band of dense fog in between.

As they continued to head towards it, the radio operator had an update. "Botwood reports zero visibility. No sign of clearing."

They couldn't approach much closer so, taking care to remain clear of the fog bank, the Clipper flew in two very broad circles while both pilots looked for any signs of clearing or movement. There was nothing. Meanwhile, their fuel level continued to decline. After their third circuit, the captain gave up.

"OK. That's enough," he said to the radio operator. "Tell Botwood we're diverting to Shediac, then declare an emergency with Shediac."

The air harbour at Pointe-du-Chêne on Shediac Bay was going to be their last hope, but to get there they would have to cross most of the breadth of the Gulf of St. Lawrence, then fly over Prince Edward Island (PEI), to reach the Northumberland Strait and Shediac Bay. That meant their fuel would have to hold out for another 500 nautical miles. It was going to be close.

Taking the Clipper back up above the clouds, they flew on. An hour later, visibility began to drop and, of course the fuel-level was still dropping. When he judged that they couldn't risk losing more visibility, nor any more fuel, Captain Healey said "Advise Shediac we're ditching[3] and give them our latest position."

The Clipper began its descent.

Down below, it was a grey and stormy morning.

At an altitude of one-hundred feet, the captain circled a few times so he could try to judge the waves. The ocean, with up to 10 m (30 ft.) waves, looked vicious, especially considering that the Clipper was only certified for sea states up to 1.2 m (4 ft.)

Had there been another option, Captain Healey would never have attempted to land there, but they were out of options. He turned into the 30-knot wind, which enabled them to approach at much less than their usual landing speed, and tried to land. Unfortunately, he mistimed the waves and had to circle around for another try.

On the second attempt, he again turned into the wind. This time, while approaching the rough sea he was able to just barely pass over the crest of a wave, after which the aircraft stalled and went nose-first into the trough. The following wave surged over most of the length of the body of the aircraft, after which it rose up and rode high on the water.

They were down!

As the Clipper bobbed and weaved with the waves, the captain kept the engines running in order to keep the Clipper heading into the wind. Meanwhile, he sent the navigator and radio operator to check up on the health of the passengers and relief crewmembers, and he sent the engineer to check for damage and leaks.

The news regarding the passengers wasn't too bad, considering there were no seatbelts for passengers. There had been a few minor injuries when the plane landed, but not serious. The news from the engineer was much worse. The force of the landing had caused cracks along the junction between the fuselage and one of the stabilizer wings, which were stubby sea-wings mounted at the water-line on each side.

"Two problems," the engineer summarized. "One: the cracks are leaking seawater. Two: if the damaged stabilizer wing separates completely from the fuselage, you may not be able to keep us upright on the water. We aren't likely to capsize considering our full load of cargo, but we're going to sink. The only questions are how soon and how quickly."

The captain considered attempting to launch their 5-person life-rafts, of which they had nine, but decided to continue to keep the aircraft pointed into the wind and stabilized until they were rescued or their fuel ran out.

Meanwhile on the lower deck, with so much water sloshing around, no one had noticed that a second major leak had developed. Nor, for a while, did anyone notice that the water level was, on average, beginning to rise rather rapidly. This second leak came from the second stabilizer wings, right where it was attached to the fuselage. The only signs of impending disaster were the screeching and tearing sounds as the waves crashed, over and over again, into the Clipper. These sounds were enough to force Captain Healey to his next decision.

"Inform Shediac we're sinking," he ordered the radio operator. "Were you able to give them our position?"

"I gave them the best estimate I had, but it was only a rough estimate."

To other crew members, the captain said "Break out the rafts and get them ready to launch when I give the word."

The crew were in the process of complying when eventually, inevitably, the repeated stresses had become too much and both sponsons tore away, enabling so much water to flow into the plane, at such a great rate, that the Clipper sank within three minutes. It sank in the shallows, some 80 nautical miles east of the northern tip of PEI.

No one escaped.

An aerial search was launched, of course, despite the poor weather. When the search plane flew over the location where the Clipper had sunk, however, its spotters were unaware of it because there was nothing left floating on the surface.

2 A CHANCE DISCOVERY

Sunday May 4, 1980
New Brunswick

Vacation time!

I still had the big red and white '76 Chevy Cheyenne, 4-door crew-cab, pickup truck that I'd purchased when posted to Alberta four years earlier. My treasured truck and a beautiful Sunday morning found Silver and I driving from Fredericton to Point-du-Chêne, New Brunswick, which meant driving east along a long highway, most of which (over 200 km) had been simply cut out of the forest. It was like driving along a huge hallway whose walls comprised a dense mixture of red and Norway maples, white pines, red oaks and fir trees and the Spring air was full of the scents of the forest. Here and there were road signs warning drivers to beware of crossing moose or deer, and the walls of forest were only occasionally broken when we crossed rivers, including the broad expanse of the Saint John River, plus a large break in the forest when we passed the city of Moncton.

With such nice weather I had opened the crew-cab's back windows so that Silver could engage in his usual practice of sticking his head out of the window on one side and then the other, with his nose raised into the slipstreams along the vehicle. This still entertained him and amused me. I could only imagine the range of forest smells that his hypersensitive nose could detect.

I see that I have gotten ahead of myself here, so I will pause for

introductions. My name is Corporal Alexandra Houston, Royal
Canadian Mounted Police (RCMP) Security Service. My friends call
me Alex. Within the Security Service, I worked in K Section: Special
Operations[4] which I loved, partly because my immediate boss, and
also his boss, were so great to work for, and partly because the
'special operations' nature of our work meant that my assignments
crossed the boundaries between straightforward crimes, intelligence,
and counter-intelligence and frequently took me from coast-to-
coast-to-coast in Canada. As if that weren't enough, I'm also a dog
master and everywhere that I go, I travel with Silver, an Alaskan
Malamute, my friend and partner. Whether for security reasons, or
because we were a police-dog-service (PDS) team, or both, Silver
and I were essentially always on call, which is why I generally brought
my tactical uniform and gear with me. Even when I was on holiday.
OK, back to my story.

We were on our way to meet a friend I'd made on a previous
case. When we first met[5], Sharon Sanders had been a graduate
student in biochemistry, at Dalhousie University in Halifax. I had
been sent to the department to establish an undercover persona as a
university researcher so I could snoop around an area on Cape
Breton Island where Sharon had discovered a German Second-
World-War-era automatic weather station that appeared to still be
transmitting - more than thirty years after the end of the war. Along
the way, Sharon and I had become friends and had done quite a bit
of SCUBA diving together. When Sharon had later graduated to
become a Research Scientist at the Bedford Institute of
Oceanography (BIO), she had maintained her interest in SCUBA
diving, as had I.

Although I was based in Ottawa, having a boyfriend (later fiancé)
living in Halifax meant that I visited the city as often as I could,
which had helped me stay in touch with Sharon as well. Now I was
looking forward to another such visit, but this time we were meeting
in New Brunswick. It had been some time since I'd last seen her, so
we had some catching-up to do and we were planning to do some
more diving.

When I reached the small community of Pointe-du-Chêne, I
turned off the highway and followed a series of narrow roads and
lanes, some of which were paved, some gravel. Although Sharon had
sent me a sketch-map, the lanes were so narrow and some of the
turns looked so much like people's driveways that I went right past

them and had to make U-turns to get back on track. The distances involved were short, however, so it didn't take long to find the cottage she had rented. When I did, there she was, sitting out on the front deck.

After greeting both me and Silver, who always remembered her, the next order of business was for her to give us a quick tour of the cottage. It wasn't huge, but it had the porch out in front, of course, then a kind of great room at the front, which encompassed the kitchen, dining area, and living room. Behind that were two modest bedrooms and a bathroom, all in a row, plus a door to a back deck and the back yard. In the back yard was a nice fire pit, and then a row of shrubs and trees. Behind the trees was Parlee Beach. All-in-all it had everything we needed and more, including being just steps away from the beach, which would be a great place to take Silver for walks and runs.

Being late in the afternoon when I'd arrived, the sun had swung around to the front of the cottage, so we sat out back to relax and share our latest news while Silver found a nice corner from which he could keep an eye on everything and laid down to snooze. It didn't take long for the conversation to come around to diving.

"What's the diving like around here?" I asked. "All you told me was that you'd rented a boat and you thought it would be fun."

"The ocean's quite warm right here. In fact, Parlee Beach prides itself on having the warmest saltwater in Canada. On the other hand, the bottom drops off at such a shallow angle that you have to go way out to get to any real depth at all. That's partly why I engaged a boat and a skipper to take us out. We can actually go almost anywhere the boat can get to in a reasonable time, but I'm hoping we can do some diving off North Cape, PEI, which is the northernmost tip of the island. There are reported to be hundreds of shipwrecks around there."

"Why so many?"

"Well, lots of people built fishing schooners around here, then some built or bought larger ships so they could sail to other countries to sell and buy goods. Between storms and uncharted rocks and reefs, many of them eventually didn't make it home. Then there were ships that got lost and accidentally ran too fast into shallow waters when they thought they were much further out in the middle of the Gulf of St. Lawrence. Here, look at this list from a shipwreck book I found."

"Wow, they're all pretty old," I commented as I perused the list. "Do you think there'll be much left of them?"

Shipwrecks of PEI

Off Cape North

- Fishing schooner *E. Attwood*, 1858
- Barque *Alfred*, 1882,
- Sailing ship *Undine* 1873 gale
- Fishing schooner *Carrie P. Rich*, 1873 gale,
- Fishing schooner *Charles C. Dame*, 1873 gale

"They'll be broken-up and partly buried, but I'm told there's usually enough exposed that you can tell they're shipwrecks. But that's not all," she said with a grin.

Ah ha, I thought, *here it comes.*

Sharon saw my expression. "Yes. When I was doing some research on shipwrecks in the area, I came across several accounts of people seeing a German U-boat being sunk by navy Corvettes off North Cape on May 7, 1943. Since then, there have been stories about it 'regularly snagging the nets of local fishing vessels.' There were several U-boats sent to this area during the war, and there are two that never returned home, U-184 and U-376. They're assumed sunk, but no knows for sure where. Now, before you ask, other people are quite skeptical about all this and some think that what was seen was just gunnery practice. No one seems to know for sure[6]."

"Sounds like fun."

"Great, if you're not too tired we'll go meet the captain tomorrow and make our first dive."

With that we left the topic of diving and went on to other subjects while I helped ferry things outside for a backyard barbeque. When I saw Sharon place a huge pot on the barbeque and fill it with salty water, I knew what the main course was going to be.

"Lobster!"

"You bet. I bought four nice-size lobsters right off the fishing boats this afternoon. The potato salad is in the fridge, and I've got butter and fresh buns warming in the oven. What else could we possibly need?"

"Wine!" we both said, in unison.

"Right, that's chilling in the fridge too."

We continued to visit while the water for the lobsters heated and then sat down to one of my favourite Atlantic Canada feasts.

"Too bad for Silver," said Sharon, looking over at him. In response, Silver managed to look up at us with a slightly martyred-looking expression.

"He can eat almost anything but he doesn't care for lobster so he'll actually prefer his dog food. He does pretty well in general though, so I wouldn't feel too sorry for him."

"Because you spoil him!"

I didn't deny the charge.

After dinner we went for a walk along Parlee Beach, which was beautiful. Sharon suggested we first stop for coffee at The Lobster's Brew, a coffee shop and café located on the edge of the long row of sand dunes that ran along the landward side of the beach. In addition to being on top of the sand dunes, it was also raised up about another metre on thick-looking pilings. It had an outdoor deck so we secured a table there and I marvelled at the view.

There were quite a few people walking along the beach, many with children and dogs, but it wasn't too crowded. A few brave people had waded out in to the ocean, and they'd had to go quite far from the shore just to be waist-deep. I decided that I'd be far happier waiting until the next day when I could venture into the ocean wearing a full wetsuit.

When a woman came to take our order, I mentioned what a perfect spot I thought it was for a café.

"Thank you," she said, introducing herself as Jean Friend, the owner.

"Why is the café up on pilings?" I wondered. "It seems like the view would be just as good from the tops of the sand dunes."

"The view, yes, but the pilings are to protect us from storm surges."

"Really?" I said, impressed. "Those must be some storms!"

"Believe it. Sometimes, we can get hit by some powerful storms around here. You can see where the high tides are reaching," she said, pointing to the beach. "A few years ago, there was a big storm with a surge that raised the water level nearly 2 m higher than the high-tide level you can see. That's an ocean rise of nearly 3 m from the low tide mark[7]. You'd have to be here and see it to believe it."

The owner had to bustle off to deal with other customers, leaving us to sip our coffees and enjoy the view, then we left and went down to walk along the beach.

By this time, the sun was dropping below the horizon to produce a beautiful warm-orange sunset and a number of beach fires were being lit. We kept walking, however, and when we'd returned to the cottage, we were able to have our own private fire in the back-yard fire-pit. We didn't stay up late though, so we'd be rested for an early start the next day.

In the morning, the weather forecast called for a mix of sun and cloud, and little to no wind. We hoped that boded well for our prospects of experiencing calm seas.

It was a short trip to the Pointe-du-Chêne wharf, which we could have easily walked were it not for the bulk and weight of our diving gear, so we drove. After we'd parked and unloaded some of our gear, Sharon pointed out a Cape Islander-style boat painted bright orange with white trim that was docked among several other colourful lobster-fishing boats, all of them sheltered by a stone breakwater. That was our destination.

Lugging our gear along the dock we encountered a man and a woman standing in front of another Cape Islander, this one with a white hull and a royal blue superstructure. As introductions were conducted, the man was revealed to be Abe Strong, the skipper of the blue and white boat. He was of medium height and build, with brown eyes and hair, and sported a full but nicely trimmed beard. Between the beard and his sailor's toque and sea boots, he looked every bit the mariner, and with his hearty manner he sounded like it too.

Abe's boat was moored directly in front of our destination and as we were standing right between the two boats, I was able to read the name of Abe's. It was *April Rose*.

The woman turned out to be the skipper of our destination, Marlea Becker. Her boat was the *Atlantic Grace*. Marlea was of similar height and build to Abe but had curly dark – almost black – hair and hazel eyes.

"Going diving, I see," offered Abe, looking at our pile of gear. "Not looking for lobsters I hope?" he asked, but with a twinkle in his eye to suggest he was joking[8].

"They're hoping we can find the famous U-boat," put in Marlea. "I'm going to take them out and give them a chance."

"Well, no one has been able to find it yet, assuming it even exists, although many have tried. Good luck to you I say. It would be good for the charter business if you actually found it!"

With Abe and Marlea's help we loaded our gear onto the deck of the *Atlantic Grace*, then Sharon and I made a second trip back to my truck for the remainder of our gear and loaded it all onto the boat. Then Abe said good-bye and Marlea gave us a tour of the boat, of which she was obviously proud. It was rigged for lobster fishing and seemed to be well organized.

Marlea seemed to have an interest in technology, as the wheelhouse (she referred to it as the 'cuddy') was packed with electronics. I wasn't surprised, as when Sharon had first pointed to the boat, I'd noticed a profusion of antennas rising up from it, including the usual marine radio masts, but also the tell-tale rotating antenna of a marine radar.

While we were being shown all the electronics, we were joined by Marlea's First Mate, an American-shorthair calico cat who was white with large orange and black patches. For his part, Chipper ignored us completely and settled onto a cushion by one of the front windows, from which vantage point he proceeded to stare at us.

"I thought cats hate the water," said Sharon.

"I suppose most do. Chipper certainly does," replied Marlea. "But he loves being with me and he loves being with me on the boat. Besides, cats are considered to be good luck on a boat or ship[9]. When it's raining outside, he simply retreats in here and stays put until the weather clears and, unlike some cats, he never seems to get seasick so it works out fine." Marlea then showed us where two cupboards in the wheelhouse had been set-up, with the doors removed, one for a high-sided litter box and the other for high-sided food and water dishes. At the rear of the wheelhouse, attached to the chart table, was a tall scratching/climbing post.

I kept an eye on Silver, but he seemed merely curious about the cat. Chipper, on the other hand, tended to glare accusingly at Silver.

Marlea was solidly built, but she moved around her boat with a surprising agility and she demonstrated an outgoing, cheerful disposition that I found quite engaging.

We'd planned for an early start because we had a long way to go, and we left the dock as scheduled, at 7 am.

Leaving the protection of the harbour's breakwater we cruised past the big white and red lighthouse into Shediac Bay, then Marlea headed approximately north, almost immediately passing to the east of Shediac Island, then turned north-northeast making a diagonal crossing of the Northumberland Strait.

After cruising about 25 miles (21 nm) we were approaching the west coast of PEI, so Marlea changed course again and basically followed that coast all the way around, sailing first northwest and then northeast. This continued until we were off the most northerly part of the island, North Cape and the nearby town of Tignish. Somewhere, off in the distance, was Channel-Post aux Basques, the most westerly town in Newfoundland and Labrador. In between, was a huge expanse of ocean.

To this point, we'd made good time. Marlea had a larger than usual engine installed in her boat, enabling it to cruise at 13 knots. As a result, we'd covered just over 50 nautical miles in four hours, making it 11 am.

As we continued heading northeast into the Gulf of St. Lawrence Marlea divided her time between scanning the horizon and watching the compass. At noon we had a simple lunch of sandwiches, after which Marlea explained to us how side-scan sonar works.

"Basically, the system consists of three units," she said, "a torpedo-shaped 'fish' containing a pair of transducers that send out short sonar pulses, a steel wire reinforced cable that acts as transmission- and tow cable simultaneously, and a dual channel chart recorder to show us the results."

Reducing the engine speed to 'slow,' she showed us the sonar torpedo and we helped by putting it into the water while she paid out the cable. Returning to the wheelhouse, she showed us where the sonar signal was fed into a sweeping pen-plotter that burned the signal image into a scrolling paper recorder. Then she increased speed somewhat, but not as fast as we had previously been cruising, and resumed instructing.

"The 'fish' has two transducers that send short sonar pulses to port and starboard. Then, the returning signals come here and are amplified and fed to the electrode-pens which sweep out from the centre of the recording drum. The current passing through the paper produces marks that are lighter or darker depending on the strength of the incoming signals. That way, they give us an idea of the nature of the sea-bed. Any questions?"

"How accurate is it?" asked Sharon.

"We're doing six knots right now. At this speed, we can pick-up 2-metre objects if they aren't too far away, and 10-metre objects as far away as 400 metres[10]."

As we looked at the moving sonograph image, Marlea must have noted that we looked confused.

"OK. Look here," Marlea continued. "The two dark, parallel lines that you see running vertically down the centre are the port and starboard transmission marks. Think of them like the 'road' we just went along. The lighter vertical lines are 50-foot (15 m) range marks. They show distance out to each side. Everything else is signal. The rippled wave-looking areas are sand ripples, the white areas are smooth, silty seafloor, the dark dots are fish, and the very dark splotchy areas are rocks and rocky outcrop."

Watching the sonograph, I could accept the dots as fish and the wavy lines as sand, but the rest looked like just noise to me.

Once again, Marlea must have read my expression. She sighed. "OK. Look," she said, "I know that all of this probably looks to you like a bunch of random ink blotches, but once you've looked at enough of these, and then tested out what's really there, then you start to get pretty good at reading the charts."

"Now then. See this kind of torpedo-shaped dark mass here?" She pointed to a spot on the starboard side where some kind of dark mass seemed to be angling upwards from the ocean floor. "Right there, is something large, and long, and dense."

"Could it be a submarine?" asked Sharon.

"Possibly, I suppose, if part of the sub is buried or if this is just a section of a sub. Otherwise its too short for that. Besides, we're still some distance from the spot where some people claim there's a sunken U-boat snagging their fishing nets."

"Maybe that's why no one has been able to find the U-boat," said Sharon, undeterred and getting excited. "Maybe it's right here."

"What else could it be?" I asked.

"Well, an unusual rock formation, or possibly a barge."

"Could it be an aircraft?"

"Yes, actually it could. If the wings are buried in silt or sand then only the fuselage would show up like this. But it's most likely..."

"A shipwreck," all three of us said in unison.

"How deep is it?" I asked.

"Well look here. The distance from the starboard transmission mark to the first vertical line gives us the distance from the sensor position to the surface. Looks like about 30 feet. The distance from the same transmission mark to the second vertical line gives us the distance from the sensor position to the bottom. Looks like about 40 feet. surface. That means the water depth is about 70 feet. Now look at the torpedo shape. Part of it lies on the bottom and part is angled upwards, with the highest part being at about 30 feet or so."

"Can we dive on it? Here? Now?" asked Sharon.

"Sure. You're paying the bill. We can stop wherever you want."

"What do you think?" Sharon asked me.

"It's fine with me," I replied. "I'm happy just to get into the water."

"OK then," said Marlea. "Let me see how close I can get you to it."

First, she led us up onto the deck by the bow and showed us the anchor she wanted to use and where to wrap the anchor rope so we could belay it when she gave us the word. Then, she went back to the wheelhouse, swung the boat around and headed back to where we'd passed the blob on the bottom, as I thought of it, but this time going a bit slower, presumably with her attention focused on the sonograph. Then, she took the boat on yet another loop and, when she judged the time was right, wound the engine down to dead slow and called for us to drop the anchor. Once the anchor had touched down, we called out and she stopped the engine and joined us on deck. As the boat swayed in the swell, Marlea watched the angle of the rope for a while then, when satisfied, she tied it off.

"There you are," she concluded. "I've placed it as close as I can. The rest is up to you."

It didn't take us long to change into our wetsuits and sort out our equipment, then we took a few moments for dive planning. We agreed that we'd follow the anchor rope down together, then remain within sight of each other while we looked around. Assuming that the water depth really was 70 feet, our dive table showed that our maximum no-decompression[11] bottom time would be 50 minutes[12]. Accordingly, we planned to limit our bottom time to 40 minutes, and to make a safety-stop for five minutes at a depth of 15 feet. If we followed our plan, we would have plenty of air for this.

Each of us had an 80 cubic-foot-capacity aluminum SCUBA tank filled to, or at least very close to its rated maximum pressure of 3,000 psi. Mine, when I checked the gauge, was at 2,950 psi.

When we were fully ready Sharon and I sat, with our backs to the water, on the gunwale at the stern of the boat, one of us to each side. Then, with a wave to Marlea and Silver, we simply leaned back until we dropped into the water.

I gasped. The thing about SCUBA diving in Canadian waters is that the water is cold. It's worse in winter, but even in May it was still cold. My thermometer read the water temperature as 1.9°C (35.4°F) and the creeping flow of that cold water into my wetsuit was a shock. All I could do for a few moments was float there, gritting my teeth until my body was able to warm the thin layer of water that the wetsuit allowed to cover me from head to toe.

When the shock was over, Sharon and I met up at the anchor line and, following nods of readiness, we each bent sharply at the waist and jackknifed down below the surface to began our descent. Watching our depth gauges, we stopped at a depth of 15 feet where I securely tied a length of white cloth[13]. This would serve as a marker – and a reminder – for our decompression safety-stop when we later ascended.

At a depth of 15 feet, there was lots of sunlight and the water was a light blue colour. As we continued our descent, the amount of light diminished and some of the colours disappeared, due to absorption by the water. By 25 feet, the reds and oranges had disappeared, followed by yellow by 45 feet. Much of the green would also be gone by the time we reached our target depth of 70 feet.

We didn't get there right away because we found the wreck first. Amazingly, Marlea had managed to have the anchor catch onto the wreck itself, so we couldn't have missed it if we'd tried!

Sharon's eyes were wide as she turned to me and spread her arms and hands out as if to say 'look at the size of it!'

'It,' whatever it was, was huge and it was clearly an aircraft of some kind. As we swum around it, we could see that it lay at an angle from the bottom, nose up, with the engines and wings resting on a broad mound of rock. This front part was easily twenty feet tall and I couldn't begin to guess the wingspan, but there were four large engines lying on the rocks, with the rest of the wings sticking out beyond the limit of the water visibility to each side. Judging the visibility to be about 25 feet, that made the wingspan something more than 50. *An airliner or a bomber*, I guessed.

Having completed a circuit of the plane's nose, we next moved to the side of the plane and continued to descend down towards the tail-end. As we moved over and past the broad wings I looked back and noticed that the nose was no longer visible. Turning back again in the direction we were swimming, I could just make out the plane's huge vertical stabilizer, except that it was angled sharply and no longer vertical. Looking back again, I could no longer make out the wings and quickly estimated that the plane must be something like a hundred feet in length.

We took a quick look at the tail-end, enough to see that the registration number was G-AG(something)(something). The last two letters were difficult to make out. Otherwise, the tail-end didn't look too interesting so we didn't descend deeper than 65 feet and instead swum back over to the top of the fuselage and made a slow ascent along the centerline of the plane. As we did, we got a shock. At about the trailing edge of the wings, there was a huge opening in the top of the plane. The opening was just about the full width of the plane, which looked to be about 12 feet, and about the same distance lengthwise.

We'd brought diving lights with us, which we now switched on. Our lights produced narrow, rather than wide beams which was perfect for peering into things like we did now. We found ourselves looking down into what had obviously been a cargo compartment. I say cargo, rather than baggage, because this one was partly filled with metal cannisters.

They looked like oil drums, but smaller, and there were a couple dozen of them at least. Because some were clearly missing, we could see that they'd been stacked three high. The cargo nets that had been used to keep them from moving around in flight had been undone, or more likely cut, and were lying in tangles on the deck. A few individual drums were also lying about on the deck.

Curious about what the drums might represent, I was tempted to enter the compartment for a closer look. Sharon must have noticed a slight movement on my part, or perhaps a look in my eyes when we turned to look at each other mask to mask, but whatever the reason, she shook her head signalling negative. She was right of course, we didn't have the time nor the equipment and planning needed to explore inside a wreck, so I reluctantly agreed.

As we pulled back from the huge opening in the fuselage, I happened to play my dive light over the broad wing that extended out to the port side. There, lying behind one of the huge engines was what looked like one of the small drums. I motioned to Sharon so she could see my interest, then I checked our elapsed diving time and showed her. We were still in pretty good shape for time, so she nodded and we moved across the wing for a look. It was lying on its side and appeared to be one of the drums from the cargo hold. It seemed clear that someone had been removing the drums from the plane and this one had been dropped. Curiosity rising, I passed my light to Sharon and reached out to pick up the drum. As I did so, a slight motion caused me to look to one side where there was a pile of large pieces of aircraft fuselage – presumably pieces that had been cut or broken out from the top to create the large opening we had just been peering into.

As soon as I realized what had attracted my attention my heart gave a lurch and, for a moment, it felt like my entire body had leapt out of my skin. There, nestled into a space between sheets of fuselage was the most menacing head I've ever seen in my life! In mottled shades of dark grey and blue, it was very nearly the size of a volleyball, with dark eyes and a large, wide mouth with protruding teeth. Even as I write these words, the memory makes my heart pound.

I'd heard about wolf eels[14] before, but this was the first time I'd ever seen one and chance had brought my face way too close to it for my comfort. In Nova Scotia, the fishers referred to them as oarfish because they were reputed to be able to bite through a full-size wooden oar with their powerful jaws and grinding teeth. When I noticed it, I'd involuntarily shrunk back, and I realized that my pulse and breathing rate had skyrocketed. When I looked more carefully at the wolf eel - all the while trying to get my pulse and respiration rates down - I could see that, although it still looked intimidating, it was simply lying in place watching.

Trying hard not to think about the four to five feet of body that was somewhere behind that head, I reached back for the steel drum and picked it up. It felt heavy, but not quite as heavy as my 19-pound weight belt[15], so maybe 15 pounds (7.5 kg), and it appeared to be dented a bit where it struck the wing. But it seemed otherwise intact. As I backed away with the drum in my hands, it crossed my mind that the wolf eel might be guarding the drum but it just lay there staring and occasionally opening its huge mouth a bit.

With Sharon shining the two dive lights on it I rotated the drum in my hands. There was rust on the surface but the metal seemed to be in good shape. In the illumination of the dive lights, the drum seemed to be more or less the same dark grey-blue colour as it did without them, and there seemed to be some markings stencilled on the side, but I couldn't make out what they were.

One thing about shipwreck diving, if you're lucky enough to even find the wreck, is that once you're there exploring it becomes very easy to lose track of your depth, time, and air pressure. I knew our depth, but checked time and pressure. My air tank, that had started out at 2,950 psi was now dropping below 1,000 psi. That was OK, but my diving watch indicated that we'd been down for about 37 minutes. Already! I would have liked to look around more, but there wasn't time, so I motioned upwards with my index finger and Sharon nodded agreement. Time to begin our ascent.

The two of us swam back to the fuselage and retraced our route towards to the front of the plane and found the spot where the anchor rope ran upwards from whatever the anchor had caught onto lower down. With one hand each placed loosely on the rope, we ascended together – slowly – following the diver's tradition of watching the rise of our exhaled bubbles and making sure that we rose no faster than the smallest ones we could see[16].

Oh, and the small drum? I brought it with me, of course. Someone seemed to have collected a bunch of them; more than the single souvenir that a diver might normally take, and I was curious, and even a little bit suspicious given the strangeness of the large hole in the top of the plane's fuselage. I couldn't imagine that happening naturally.

Anyway, when we reached the white cloth at a depth of 15 feet we stopped there and, holding firmly to the rope, spent five minutes waiting-out our decompression safety-stop. After that, we resumed our slow ascent to the surface and, with Marlea's help, got our fins, weight-belts, and tanks into the boat and then climbed up and into the boat ourselves.

We described our dive to Marlea as we stripped off our wetsuits, towelled-off, and changed into dry clothes, followed by welcome cups of hot coffee (and I got more than a few licks of welcome from Silver, of course).

We also described the aircraft as best we could, based on our very limited survey of it, and Marlea said she'd never heard of a large plane going down in this area. I also gave an account of my wolf eel encounter, which made her laugh.

"Scared you, did it?"

"Scared isn't the word. I now know what people mean when they say they've nearly jumped out of their skin!"

"Well, they're ugly alright, and they look vicious, but they're generally quite sedentary and don't bite unless provoked. Some people fish for them – they're supposed to be good eating – but there's no commercial fishery for them around here. If you ever go to England though, some of the fish and chip shops sell them under the names Scotch halibut or woof."

Naturally, we also talked about the small drum I'd brought up. It was shaped like a fuel drum but smaller, having a diameter of about 14" (36 cm) and a height of about 18" (46 cm). Marlea said it was a standard ten U.S. gallon (30 litre) size. Hefting it, we agreed that it weighed something like 15 or 16 pounds. The lid was secured by a ring that went all the way around the top and had been secured by tightening a screw-clamp. Marlea immediately went for a screwdriver with which to open it, but when she returned with it, I suggested caution.

I'd been looking at the stencilled letters and could make out two different sets, one in black and one in a dark blue, each set having been produced with differently-shaped letters. The older-looking, black set read PRODUIT DU CONGO, and the newer-looking dark-blue set read TUBE ALLOYS PROJECT.

"There's something familiar about these labels," I said, thinking hard. Then I remembered.

"I took a course in nuclear and radiochemistry in my third year of university," I related. "One of the historical things was that most of the uranium production in the 1930s and early 1940s came from the Belgian Congo[17] and from Canada. I think Tube Alloys was a codename for a secret atomic energy project that the U.S., U.K. and Canada ran during the Second World War[18].

"So, you think there's a bomb in there?" asked Marlea.

"Not a bomb, no. Not pure uranium metal either. But it might contain uranium ore from a mine, or uranium oxide – what they used to call black oxide – from an early uranium refinery."

"Is it radioactive then?" asked Sharon.

"Probably, but if it's uranium ore or uranium oxide then it shouldn't be too bad. Natural uranium isn't actually very radioactive, but I think it would be safest for us if we don't open the drum because we shouldn't get any on our skin or breath any particles into our lungs. Beyond that, we'll have to get some advice from someone who knows more about these things."

I could see that Sharon and Marlea were disappointed but they didn't argue the point and I placed the drum on the deck in the stern of the boat, and arranged our weight belts around it to keep it from rolling around.

Before raising the anchor and departing, I asked Marlea to show me the wreck's location on her hydrographic chart and I noted the latitude and longitude in my diving logbook.

As we began the long journey back to the Pointe-du-Chêne wharf I found myself staring at the steel drum. I was naturally curious about the huge sunken airplane and its cargo, but I found my spider-sense tingling when I thought about the drum's probable contents. It's been said that police officers are naturally suspicious. If so, I certainly qualify, and my suspicions were already aroused.

Although I'd disapprove, I could understand someone breaking into the aircraft to 'see what's there,' and I could understand someone taking one of the drums – like we had – to 'see what's in it.' But there was more to it than that. My limited view had indicated that many drums had been taken. How many, I didn't know but it could easily have been a dozen. My mind leapt to questions: *Why? What would, or could, someone do with, say, a dozen drums of uranium oxide?*

I thought of a few possible answers, and I didn't like any of them.

Laurie Schramm

3 MORE SURPRISES

Although long, our return journey to Pointe-du-Chêne and Shediac was uneventful, aside from some lively swells. When we reached the dock and tied up, we unloaded everything and thanked Marlea for an exciting trip. Before driving away, I promised to come back and tell her whatever I was able to learn about the mystery plane and its even more mysterious cargo.

Sharon and I were both tired by the time we'd reached the cottage and unloaded everything. We'd docked at just after 8 pm and it was approaching 9 pm. A very full day. It wasn't too late, however, to phone my fiancé Don in Halifax. Ours was a long-distance relationship, with me living in Ottawa. When apart, we tried to phone each other at least every second night and it was always reassuring just to hear his voice.

He was almost as amazed as Sharon and I had been, when I told him about the diving, the sunken plane, and the mysterious steel drums. Of course, he laughed at me when I'd told him about my wolf eel encounter.

"How much do you know about Canada's atomic energy history?" I asked him.

"I know a little from a couple of cases I worked on a few years ago," he replied, cautiously. Don was in Military Intelligence.

"Same here," I said. "I learned a bit in university and then a bit more when I worked on that heavy water plant case a few years ago."

"That was a great case!" said Don. "It led to us being introduced and working together for the first time."

There was a pause while we each reflected on some of the old memories that came back. The case had been interesting, my meeting Don had been exciting, and we'd found that we worked well together, but there had been a couple of life-threating episodes as well[19]. It had been good just to survive... I had to shake myself from my reverie.

"The reason I ask is this. I seem to recall that the first big producer of uranium was Shinkolobwe in the Belgian Congo, followed by Port Radium in Canada, both in the 1930s."

"I think so, yes."

"OK, then fast-forward to the Second World War, and the U.S., U.K. and Canada had a secret project in which they all cooperated on atomic-weapons development. Right?"

"They called it Tube Alloys, right. Then it got merged into the Manhattan Project."

"OK, we're both remembering the same things. So, what would you think would be in a bunch of steel drums with labels marked product of Congo and Tube Alloys?"

"Nothing highly refined or enriched or it would be in lead containers. That leaves uranium ore, yellow cake, or black oxide[20]."

"Agreed. Next question: what would it have been doing on a plane that sunk in the Gulf of St. Lawrence? If we're talking 1930s or '40s Canada wouldn't have needed it. We had our own big uranium mine in the Northwest Territories. I can think of two possibilities: it was heading for Port Hope, Ontario to be further refined, or else it was heading for the stockpiles in the U.S."

"Sounds reasonable to me."

"If it was lost enroute to the U.S. then the FBI would know about it. I can check that out. Would your people know about it if it was coming to Canada?"

"Maybe. If not, NRC[21] was a leading agency for things nuclear back then, so someone there might know. I'll make a few calls."

Tuesday May 6, 1980
Pointe-du-Chêne, N.B.

In the morning, I phoned the FBI. Special Agent Vivian Rule and I had worked on previous cases together[22],[23] and had become friends as well. When I'd filled her in, she said "In those days, gathering up as much uranium as we could from around the world was a big deal so we'd surely have someone keeping track of any shipments into or around the country. How much do you think the plane was carrying?"

"Hard to say, but I'd guess three to five dozen drums."

"OK. So, let's say 50 10-gallon drums at, say, 15 pounds each. That's 750 pounds. If that much uranium went missing, we'd have had someone investigating, so there should be a file in the archives. Give me a day or two and I'll call you back."

"Thanks Viv."

"No problem. By the way, is this an official case or just you and Silver with your trusty noses for trouble?"

"Nothing official, and just my nose. For the moment."

"OK. Call you back."

Following my call to Vivian, Sharon and Silver and I went for a sightseeing drive. First, we drove around the town of Shediac, then we drove north, across the Shediac Bridge, and then we continued to drive more-or-less north along a succession of scenic, secondary roads that hugged the coast. These took us by a number of beaches, villages, points, and great scenic views of the ocean. When it felt like we'd seen enough for one day we picked a likely-looking place to stop for lunch and then drove back to the cottage for a walk along the beach and then some quiet time in the backyard.

That evening, I received a call from Don.

"I found a contact at NRC in Ottawa who referred me to one of their retired people that was involved in NRC's nuclear research of the 1940s and '50s. He confirmed our recollections about the secret U.S.-U.K.-Canada project code-named Tube Alloys, and described a bunch of things they were up to at the time including the fact that the NRC team developed what was at the time the best and most efficient nuclear reactor in the world: the NRX reactor, which in turn was used to produce a range of useful radioactive isotopes[24]. This guy mostly wanted to talk about nuclear reactors, but I was able to

41

steer him back to the question of uranium supplies.

He confirmed that, especially in the 1940s, there was a great push on by the British and Americans to gather together as much of the world's supply of uranium as possible. He said that for quite some time the two main miners of uranium ore were the Belgian Congo and Canada, and that Canada also had one of the world's few operating uranium refines: the one at Port Hope, Ontario. Apparently, Canada's uranium went to three places: NRC for Canada's work on nuclear reactors and isotopes, the British, and to the Americans. Of these, he said the Americans had the most unquenchable thirst for uranium as they wanted it for their own programs and also to keep it away from countries they thought were, or might become, unfriendly to their interests. On that note, he said the Americans tired to secure as much as possible of the uranium materials originating in the Belgian Congo, quite a lot of which had gone to Belgium before, and possibly during, the Second World War.

Beyond that, he either couldn't remember or wasn't willing to give me any specifics, but he said Canada wouldn't have had any need for European uranium so if it came here, it would have been enroute to the U.S., possibly after further refining at Port Hope but more likely simply in transit."

"Wow. I wonder of that means the sunken plane has been sitting there since the Second World War – that's more than 30 years."

"Maybe. If it was on its way to the U.S., I'm pretty sure the FBI would have been monitoring its progress."

Don's call seemed to confirm our original thinking, but it didn't get me any further. I resigned myself to waiting for a return call from Vivian.

***

Meanwhile that morning at the Pointe-du-Chêne Wharf, Marlea Becker had been conducting some minor maintenance on her boat when a voice hailed her from the dock. She emerged to find two men standing there, one rather tall and one quite short. The shorter one asked whether she'd be willing to take them on a sight-seeing tour.

"How long?" she asked, looking them over.

"Two hours?" the shorter one said, questioningly. "Up towards Bouctouche and back?" That meant travelling more or less north-

northwest, up along the coast.

"Might take nearly two hours just to get there," she replied.

"How about just going in that direction then. When we're an hour out, just turn back wherever we are and bring us back. If it takes two-and-a-half hours that's OK by us, and we'll pay for three hours worth anyway."

Marlea considered it. The two men seemed like a strange pair, and not tourists either. Their clothing, general manner, and the shorter man's slightly Acadian-sounding accent made them seem more like locals, although she didn't recognize either of them. Oh well, *she thought,* no point in turning away paying customers. *She named a price, for which the shorter man nodded acceptance and pulled out a wallet from which he withdrew a number of bills.*

That decided her. "Hop aboard," she said. Reaching out a hand to help them step into the boat should they need it. They didn't but the shorter man put the cash into her outstretched hand instead.

"In advance," he said.

"Have a seat anywhere you like," she said, as she went to the wheelhouse to start-up the engine. A few minutes later, she untied and cast off, and took them out of the harbour.

When she had taken the two women divers out the day before, she had headed directly into the strait but, since this was to be a sight-seeing tour, she instead motored close to the coastline, taking them first through the protected waters between Shediac Island and the mainland. As she did so, she noticed that the men didn't seem to be too interested in the scenery. Maybe later, she thought.

When they had passed the island and moved further out into the strait, in preparation for rounding the point that led to Cap-des-Caissie (Cassie Cape), the swell picked up noticeably. The two men still didn't seem very interested in the scenery, and they both began to look uncomfortable.

Uh oh, *Marlea thought.* Not cut out to be sailors if they're feeling queasy already. Good job we're heading all the way to the gulf. *Partly to distract them, and partly to try to get them interested in where they were she pointed out a few of the landmarks — and some of their history — along the way, but it didn't seem to do any good, so she gave it up. As they passed Cap-des-Cocagne, she steered a direct course for the Bouctouche Bar Lighthouse, which took them still further from shore.*

As they approached the lighthouse, Marlea steered even further from shore, in order to give the lighthouse — and its rocks — a wide berth. Although the water was calm by her standards, over an hour of constant rolling in the swell had taken a toll on her two passengers, who were beginning to look a bit greenish.

The lighthouse was positioned at the tip of a long, narrow strip of rocky land that projected out and ran almost parallel to the mainland for some 10 km.

"It looks pretty barren," said the shorter man, somewhat surprisingly as it was the first time either man had spoken since they'd left the harbour.

"Yes," said Marlea, trying to encourage some interest. "It's essentially an extremely thin peninsula, but it shelters the entrance to Bouctouche Bay. Way over there across the strait," she pointed across the open water to the east is PEI's North Point Lighthouse."

"Really?" said the shorter man, showing some real interest for the first time. "I can't see it. Can you show me where to look?"

"Sure," replied Marlea, grabbing her binoculars and moving to the stern of the boat where the two men were standing. As she approached, she moved to the starboard gunwale and, standing beside the shorter man, pointed in the direction of North Point, PEI. As she did, so she sensed more than felt, something come over her head and down. At first it blocked her sight, but after a moment she felt something clingy cover what seemed like her whole face. Whatever it was formed an effective seal over her mouth and nose. As she instinctively dropped the binoculars and tried to raise her hands to her face, she found that someone was behind her tightly pinioning her arms to her sides.

She couldn't breathe, she couldn't scream, and she couldn't move her arms. With a rising sense of panic, she tried twisting her body; then she tried kicking backwards with her right leg and foot, but she wasn't able to move enough to get free, nor to contact her assailant's legs. As her panic increased, it began to feel as if her head was going to explode. Her rushing adrenaline enabled her to keep struggling for a few extra seconds but it wasn't enough and she lost consciousness. At this point the taller man, who was the one holding her, felt her body relax but he maintained his grip while the shorter man consulted his watch.

Eventually, the shorter man said "Ten minutes. You can take the hood off." At this, the other man released Marlea, whose body slumped to the deck. Bending over, he carefully removed the hood and stuffed into one of his pockets. Then the two men lifted her up and unceremoniously eased her over the side, into the ocean.

Next, the shorter man waved to a boat that had first approached, and then remained on station some distance behind them. At this, the boat approached and came alongside. As the taller man moved into the second boat, the other first went to the wheelhouse and shut-off the engine, then he followed his companion into the other boat.

As the second boat pulled away, Marlea and the Atlantic Grace *were left swaying in the ocean swell. As they did, the wind began to pick up.*

It was perhaps appropriate that a storm was moving into the area.

The easterly storm winds blew at an average speed of 20 knots, causing Marlea's body and the Atlantic Grace *to drift towards, and then come to rest on the shore of the peninsula at Bouctouche. This took about three and a half hours[25], and led to the body being washed up about a hundred metres north of the lighthouse, and the boat a few hundred metres further north of that. At about 6 pm that evening a passing fishing boat spotted the* Atlantic Grace *and, while moving in close for a look, spotted Marlea's body as well. By 7 pm, RCMP Constable John Hardisty from the Shediac detachment was on the scene, followed by Dr. Bruce Solinsky, a physician who happened by, and then an ambulance with paramedics.*

"What do you think doc?" asked Hardisty after the physician had carefully examined the body.

"She drowned," Dr. Solinsky replied, motioning to the paramedics to take the body away. "Must have fallen overboard and not been able to get back on board. No bruises on her head. No sign of foul play. No lifejacket either. I guess she should have learned to swim."

"That's what it looks like to me too," agreed Hardisty. "I checked all around the body and came up empty. Well, thanks for lending a hand anyway."

"Happy to help. See you later."

Dr. Solinsky left to resume his walk along the shore. As soon as the ambulance was loaded and had left, Const. Hardisty left as well.

***

Wednesday May 7, 1980

The following day began quietly enough, but several kinds of news came in as the day wore on. In mid-morning I received a call back from Vivian, but it was just a progress report. She'd talked to a colleague familiar with things nuclear and learned what the FBI's role had been in the early days, and what classifications to look for when she went to the Bureau's Central Records System in Washington. She said she'd be going there the next day.

Sharon had been out shopping for groceries when I was on the phone. When she returned, she looked pale and seemed upset. Before I could ask what was the matter, she blurted it out. "Marlea's dead!"

"Dead? We were just out on her boat two days ago."

"I know, but when I was shopping, I heard people talking. She drowned and was found washed up on shore north of here last night. Not far from where we drove yesterday in fact. Her boat was washed up on shore too."

"Any idea what happened?"

"No. One of the people talking about it in the store was a fisher. He said that it was a bit stormy yesterday afternoon but nothing that should have threatened her or her boat."

"Did she know how to swim?"

"No idea. There's kind of a stereotype about fishery people not being able to swim, but I think it's more of a historical myth than reality."

The news was a shock and we both felt bad for poor Marlea, but we went on with our morning activities and then, after an early lunch, we went on a long walk with Silver along the beach. We were well along with our walk when Sharon abruptly realized that she had been doing all the talking while I'd barely been listening.

"What's the matter?" she asked. "You seem distracted."

"Sorry. I guess I'm still thinking about Marlea and wondering what really happened to her."

"Policewoman's instincts again?" she asked.

I shrugged. "Maybe. I'm just struggling with the coincidence of us making a once-in-a-lifetime discovery on a more-or-less random dive and then her dying the very next day."

"You think the two are connected?"

"No… well, I don't know what to think. Maybe that's why it's bugging me."

Sharon thought about for a few moments while we continued to walk, then said "If it's bothering you, why not go talk to the local police. They're bound to have been called about it. Maybe they'll be able to put your mind at ease."

"Yes…" I said, drawing the word out as I thought about it. "I think you're right."

An hour later Silver and I walked into the Shediac RCMP Detachment where I identified myself and asked to speak with the NCO (non-commissioned officer) in-charge about the recent drowning incident. The woman at the main desk didn't ask a bunch of questions but simply said "Follow me please," and led me to one of two chairs located beside the closed door of an office. We could hear someone shouting on the other side of the door.

"He'll be with you in just a moment," she said, rather cryptically, and then walked back to her desk.

The sign on the door read NCO i/c. As I sat there, with Silver sitting beside me, I couldn't help but hear some of the words from what was obviously a very one-sided 'conversation.' Someone, I assumed it must be a young constable, was getting an angry dressing-down from someone with a loud, parade-ground voice. The latter was presumably the NCO in charge. The gist of it seemed to be that the defaulter had been spending all their time with a girlfriend when they were on duty and supposed to have been out in a patrol car roving around and watching for Motor Vehicle Act offences. The tone and loudness of the male voice providing the dressing down reminded me of my training days at Depot Division in Regina, when all of us inevitably received something like this, for something or other. Still… there was something vaguely familiar about this particular voice…

It wasn't long before the door opened and an ashen-faced male constable marched out of the office and down the hall. As he did so, a phone rang in the office, there was a pause, and then the male voice said "Enter."

As Silver and I got up and walked into the office, I got no further than "Good afternoon…" when the male voice, still loud but no longer angry-sounding boomed "Alex and Silver! It's a small world after all!"

There getting up from his desk to greet us was Sergeant Mike Morrison. With his strong features and thick handlebar moustache, he still looked like he could have been the model for a turn-of the century recruiting poster. Mike, when a Corporal, had been my boss for my very first posting after basic training[26], way up north in Radium City, Saskatchewan. At first, he hadn't taken well to having a woman Mountie foisted onto him but to be fair, as time went on, he turned out to be a good boss and colleague and we eventually got along very well together. It had helped that he'd turned out to be a good person underneath his tendency to bark and growl.

"Congratulations on making Corporal," he said, after shaking hands, saying hello to Silver and motioning me to a chair.

"Thank you," I said. "I see that you gained another stripe as well."

"I did." He smiled. "We should find some time to catch up on things, but first tell me what's brought you here?"

I explained about the odd coincidence and had wanted to discover whether Marlea's death had been accidental.

"Seemed like it, but having you and your intuition show up is giving me second thoughts. Hang on a minute." He lifted his phone, pressed a button, and waited for a second. "Helen, call Hardisty back here, would you?

"Hardisty's the misfit that was just in here before you."

Sgt. Mike Morrison

Constable Hardisty couldn't have been far away, as he was standing in the doorway within a matter of seconds.

"Hardisty, this is Corporal Houston. She has a few questions about the woman whose body washed up on shore yesterday."

"Did you see the body? Was there anything unusual about it?" I asked.

"Yes, I saw the body. There was no obvious sign of damage to either her body or clothing. Rigor mortis had set-in on her face and arms and legs, although I can't say for sure whether it had fully set-in or not. Dr. Solinsky happened to be walking along the shore and came over to see what I was doing. When he saw the body, he examined her himself."

"That's one of four doctors we have here in town," said Mike, for my benefit. Then to Const. Hardisty: "Did he give an opinion?"

"Yes. He concluded that the woman had drowned." Hardisty consulted his notebook. "Specifically, he said 'No bruises on her head. No sign of foul play.' He concluded that she had probably fallen overboard and not been able to get back on board the boat. It was him that declared the woman deceased and directed the paramedics to remove the body from the scene. The ambulance took her to the Moncton Hospital."

"How about the boat?" asked Mike.

"Once the body had been removed, I went to look at the boat. It was only a few hundred metres further up the shore. North, that is. I went aboard to look around and everything seemed to be in order. The boat didn't seem to be damaged in any way. There was no sign of it having been in a collision or anything like that, and it didn't even seem to take any damage when it washed up on the shore. I had one of the local fishers take a look at it too."

"Where is it now?"

"The key was still in the ignition, so the same fisher tried starting the engine. It caught immediately, so I had him run it back to the harbour and tie it up. When I drove there to pick him up and bring him back into town, he gave me the keys."

There was silence in the office for a few moments. After which Mike raised an eyebrow to give me an inquiring look. I hesitated, then said "Look. I'm just here on vacation and I have no intention of butting-in or second-guessing but… would you mind if I had a look at the boat for myself?"

Constable Hardisty knew better than to say anything, so it was Mike who paused for a moment's thought then said. "Let's all go have a look. It will do me good to get out of this chair for a while if nothing else."

So that's what we did. Mike joined Silver and I as we drove to the harbour in my truck, while Constable Hardisty drove one of the detachment's police cars. It was a very short drive to the harbour. When we parked, I could see the bright colours of the *Atlantic Grace* at her usual mooring.

"Alex," I said to Const. Hardisty, putting my hand out to shake. "John," he replied with the first smile I'd seen from him. As we boarded and walked to the wheelhouse, I asked whether it looked like anything had been disturbed.

"Not that I can see," he said, after looking around.

As we looked around the wheelhouse, I asked if I could borrow the key for a moment and used it to switch on the engine ignition. The engine fired up right away. As it was idling, I glanced at the instrument panel then motioned to Mike.

"The fuel gauge is still reading full," I said.

"So?"

"Well, what do you think happened to her? Say she's out by herself, cruising around the strait for some reason. Then she sees something in the water maybe. She wouldn't turn the engine off; she'd throttle it back so that the boat could more or less maintain its position. That's what she did when Sharon and I were out with her on Monday. Anyway, then maybe she goes to look over the side, maybe even reaches for whatever it is, and then she falls in the water. Maybe she can't swim and can't get a grip to climb back in to the boat, especially when she's being dragged down by the weight of her clothing. Is that how you see it?"

Mike shrugged and looked at Hardisty, who said "Yes, I guess it must have been something like that."

"OK then. In that case the body gets pushed to shore where it's later discovered. But the boat should have kept on maintaining its position, more or less, until the fuel ran out. Maybe the wind continued to pick up and eventually became too strong and pushed it as well, but in that case, it should have ended up further away from Marlea's body than it did. And even if I'm wrong about that, why didn't it run out of fuel – or at least run low on fuel?"

Silence.

While we pondered all that, I continued to look around the wheelhouse. Something seemed wrong but I couldn't figure out what it was. Then, finally, it hit me. "Where's the chart?"

"What chart?" asked Mike.

"Well, look here." I motioned to the chart table at the rear of the wheelhouse. "There are charts here, but not the Northumberland Strait chart. It was here on Monday. It covered the whole area around here and out past PEI."

"If someone took it, it would have been Paul, the fellow that found the boat, and that we had bring it back here," said Hardisty.

"You think it's important?" asked Mike, looking at me.

"Marlea marked the position of the sunken plane on that chart."

"And you think there's a connection – that someone murdered

the woman and stole the chart to keep the crash site secret?"

I nodded. "I didn't make the connection at first, but the coincidences are piling up too fast for me to ignore them now."

Mike looked at me for a long moment, then turned to Hardisty. "How did you get on with the fisher?"

"Fine. He's pretty outgoing and we chatted about various things while the paramedics were dealing with the body."

"Fine. I want you to go find him and ask him whether he noticed anything was missing or looked out of place on the boat. Tell him it's just routine but try to work the conversation around to the chart. Don't get his back up by making accusations, just find out whether he noticed anything and get a sense of whether he might have taken it himself. Go now. I'll get a ride back with Corporal Houston." He looked at me for confirmation, and I said "Happy to."

When Hardisty had departed, he said "How about a cup of coffee? There's a place with an outside deck here on the wharf."

I agreed, appreciating the fact that he chose a place that would be dog-friendly.

Just before we left the boat Silver's ears twitched and he went down the steps to the door leading to what was probably a sleeping compartment in the bow. The door was shut.

I paused, seeing Silver sniff at the door. He turned to gaze at me and I watched him carefully for a moment. "He obviously thinks there's something interesting in there, but he's not acting like he senses a threat," I said, "Let's take a look." Calling Silver to stand behind me, I went down and opened the door. Standing there mewing was Chipper. After a cautious look at Silver, he dashed up the stairs to the wheelhouse, where we found him in one of the open cabinets eating.

"He must be hungry and thirsty if he's been shut up in there since last night," said Mike, "let's give him some time while we have our coffee then figure out what to do with him."

Leaving the boat, we made for the coffee shop on the wharf that Mike had recommended. When we were settled at an outside table with our mugs of coffee and a bowl of water for Silver, I said "You may think I'm crazy, but it looked all along like someone has been removing those drums from the plane wreck. When I hear back from the FBI, I think it's going to turn out that the drums do contain some form of uranium oxide and that it was enroute to them when the plane went down."

"So, we might be looking at murder to cover-up whatever someone's up to with the uranium."

"Maybe. It feels like it."

"Hmmm. Why?"

"Why does it feel like it?"

"No. I mean why steal uranium in the first place? Beyond grabbing a couple of samples as curiosities, I mean."

"I don't know. Money maybe, or there could be a connection to someone that wants uranium but can't get it legally, or both."

Mike gave me a rueful look. "It's usually quiet and boring here. Most of the year it's just another small town in a rural, seaside setting. It picks up somewhat during the tourist season, when the population more than doubles with all the beach-goers and so forth. That's why I have six constables here instead of the usual three, but even so most of the troubles are minor traffic and liquor offences, plus some small thefts and the odd assault to liven things up. In any case it's all just routine."

"Meaning?"

"I was just thinking, that's all. When you arrived on my threshold in Radium City five years ago, I seem to recall telling you that nothing much ever happened around there – and it was true, at least until you arrived. Something tells me that your arrival means life is going to get interesting here too now." He smiled, to show that he wasn't angry. If anything, he seemed amused.

I wasn't sure how to respond to that, so I stuck to business. "You may be more right than you know. I think that before the week is out, the Americans are going to be calling Ottawa to demand that we get to the bottom of things and get the plane's cargo back to them."

"And catch the thieves, no doubt," added Mike.

I nodded again. "I'm sorry the heat is going to drop in your lap. If it's any consolation, I suspect that my vacation is going to be over by tomorrow."

Leaving the current situation aside for the time being, Mike and I turned to catching-up with each other's news of the previous couple of years and had a good chat over coffee. Before we left, I said "What about Chipper the cat?"

"Well," said Mike, rubbing his chin thoughtfully, "we can't just leave him there, and the nearest animal shelter is in Moncton, so I think for now we'll look after him at the detachment until we find out whether Ms. Becker had any relatives."

So, we went back to the boat for Chipper who, now fed and watered, seemed quite content to let Mike pick him up. I found some cans of wet cat food and a bag of kitty litter, which we brought with us, along with his cushion, so he'd have some familiar things around in his new temporary lodging.

When we arrived back at the detachment, Constable Hardisty was there waiting for us.

"How'd it go?" asked Mike.

"We had a relaxed conversation. He said that he didn't need a chart just to bring a boat back to the harbour since he's sailed the local waters all his life. For the same reason, he didn't pay any attention to the chart table at all so he didn't notice what was or wasn't there."

"You believe him?"

"Yes, I do. He seemed relaxed, forthright, and genuinely disinterested."

Mike turned back to me then. "And you still think the woman was murdered and her chart stolen?"

"You could call it a working hypothesis. But since you ask, yes, I have a feeling it was murder. At the very least I think it should be treated as a suspicious death."

Mike sighed. "OK, there's a regional coroner for the Moncton/Miramichi area. I'll call her, explain what we know and ask for an autopsy. I'll also ask her for a verbal, preliminary report as soon as possible."

I thanked Mike, and gave him the address and phone number of the cottage Sharon had rented. Before I took my leave, Mike gave Hardisty a thoughtful look and said "Do you like cats?"

"I suppose so," he said, slowly.

"Well, this is Chipper. He was Ms. Becker's ship's cat. Look after him for now until we learn whether she had any next of kin."

4 VACATION'S OVER

Thursday May 8, 1980

Late the next morning, I received another call from Vivian.

"Were you able to check the records?" I asked eagerly.

"I'm at CRS right now," she replied. "Sorry, that means Central Records System. I struck gold, or maybe I should say uranium. In the early 1940s, there were a lot of shipments of uranium ore and uranium oxide coming to the U.S. Almost all of it came from either the Belgian Congo, some of which was partly refined in Belgium, or from Canada's Eldorado mine, after processing at Port Hope. Quite a lot of the Belgian materials had been moved out of the country before Germany invaded in 1940. Everything that arrived in the early years went to the U.S. Army and was stored at Staten Island... You with me so far?"

"Yes. Keep going."

"OK, this is where it gets interesting. Late in 1944, when Allied forces finally carried out the liberation of Belgium, they were able to recover more than a thousand tons of Congolese uranium that had been refined and stored at the Olen refinery. Under the U.S.-U.K.-Canada Tube Alloys agreement, the British began moving the uranium to Southampton, and then overseas to the army in New York. They seem to have used whatever ships and planes were available in those days. One of those was the overseas flights of the Boeing Clippers, which were huge, four-engine flying boats built for overseas transport of people and cargo. The British had taken over three of them from BOAC, given them registration numbers beginning with the letters G-AG, and were using them to ferry some of the uranium over, half a ton at a time – or, 400 kg to be exact."

"And it was one of those that we found," I interjected, excitedly.

"Right you are. One of those planes, the *Atlantic Sky Queen*, was flying from Southampton to New York in April 1945 but was lost along the way. They made it across the Atlantic, but reported they were running low on fuel. They tried diverting to Botwood, Newfoundland, which was one of the commercial harbours they had used before the war, but it was completely fogged in. They re-routed to the air harbour at Pointe-du-Chêne on Shediac Bay, which was another of their pre-war harbours but they never made it. The last radio report that was received indicated that their fuel status required them to ditch in the ocean somewhere just east of North Cape, PEI. To answer your next question: no, they never found it. A search was launched, of course but nothing was found, no survivors, no wreckage, nothing. According to the file I'm reading, the army decided that if the RCAF couldn't find it, then no one else would either, which seems to have suited them just fine. By 1945 they had enough for the weapons program and were just acquiring everything else to keep it away from unfriendlies."

"So that's it. That's got to be the plane we found." I paused for a moment, bringing my mind back to more serious matters. "How much uranium was it carrying?"

"The manifest says 55 ten-gallon drums of refined uranium black oxide. I asked a colleague who works on the nuclear security side, and he says that in those days the term black oxide could have meant uranium trioxide or uranium dioxide. From our point of view, it doesn't matter. Anyway, each ten-gallon drum would have weighed 16 pounds. In your units that would be 30 litre drums weighing 7.2 kg each."

"That matches the drums I saw and the one I brought up."

"Good. My nuclear colleague says don't open it and don't cuddle-up with it, and the amount of radiation you'll be exposed to won't be a health concern."

"Great. Everyone's a comedian."

Vivian chuckled. "One more thing. As far as the FBI is concerned that uranium is American property, so the Bureau will be sending a request for assistance to your HQ in Ottawa and it will be requesting you in particular, with me to serve as liaison officer."

"Yes," I sighed. "I could see that one coming. So much for my vacation."

"Sorry about that." She didn't sound sorry. "Serves you right for always sticking your nose into things. Almost literally, in this case." She chuckled again.

"All right then, smarty-pants, tell me why someone is going to the trouble of stealing the drums."

"I asked my nuclear colleague about that too. As far as the Bureau knows, none of the uranium from this shipment has turned up anywhere. If it's being salvaged and sold, then he says it's probably being sold on the black market and then ending up in the hands of someone that has a secret nuclear program. The prime suspects from the Bureau's point of view – and the CIA's too – would be the Soviet Union, China, India, and South Africa[27].

"We'll look after the nuclear threat side of things. At your end, it's most likely just money. My colleague says that up until the early seventies, uranium was quite cheap at around US$16 per kilogram (C$19) but since then the price has gone up exponentially. He says it's now about US$111 per kilogram (C$130). That means the uranium on your plane is worth about $44 thousand Canadian dollars[28]. He figures that on the black market it would easily fetch a hundred thousand dollars, maybe more depending on who the ultimate buyer is."

"OK, so we have motive. I'll keep sniffing around."

"Fine, we'll keep in touch. Good luck. Stay safe."

Given Vivian's confirmations, and her warning about a pending FBI request for assistance, it was clear that it was time to call my boss in Ottawa, Staff Sergeant Bob Simpson, who was in charge of the Special Operations section in the Security Service.

When I reached him by phone, I filled him in on what had been happening and the news that there would be an FBI request coming in. The line went silent for a while. I was used to this; it meant that he was thinking. Eventually, he asked a few questions and then said "What's the local NCO i/c like?"

"No problems there. Sergeant Mike Morrison. I worked for him for a while in the Radium City detachment. That was five years ago; my first posting. He's tough and crusty – very old school – but we learned to get along in the end. He actually listens to my crazy ideas."

"Hmmm. I bet he learned that the hard way."

"No comment," I chuckled.

"All right then. Consider yourself assigned to the case. I can tell from your voice that you don't want to let it go anyway. I'll brief Uncle George and recommend he work the chain of command and get an official 'render assistance' memo telexed or faxed[29] to your Sergeant Morrison."

'Uncle George' was Bob's and my unofficial and top-secret codename for Assistant Commissioner George MacLeod, the head of the Security Service and Bob's boss.

That afternoon, I phoned Mike.

"Good timing," he said. "Anything new on your end?"

I related the news from Vivian and told him I was now officially attached to the case.

"Welcome aboard. Meanwhile, I just got off the phone with the coroner in Moncton. We won't get the official autopsy report for a few weeks, of course, but he gave me his very unofficial conclusions." He paused for effect.

"And?"

"And your boat skipper did die from asphyxiation, but she didn't die from drowning."

"Really?"

"No water in the lungs, no seawater in the stomach, no indication of asthma or seizure, or anything like that."

"Murder, then."

"Seems like it, but no indication of strangling or even a struggle. No cuts or bruises. They've ordered a bunch of lab tests, so we won't get anything more definitive out of them for a while. Meanwhile, I had Hardisty go out and check around and try to find out what she'd been up to between the time you left her boat and when we found her." There was another pause.

"He found something?"

"He did. Hardisty's actually pretty good if you can just get him to focus on his work instead of his extracurricular interests. Turns out there's a bar in town that the fishers, men and women, particularly go to in the summer because it isn't a favourite of the tourists. It seems she was there that night, talking about how she'd taken out some divers that wanted to try for the fabled sunken U-boat, but that instead they found an old sunken plane carrying nukes."

"Nukes!"

"That what the fisher Hardisty talked to claimed, and it was confirmed when he talked to the bartender. Apparently, it sparked a big debate about whether Canada should have nuclear weapons or not, and then ended up where it usually does: with a consensus that there's a conspiracy and we're all being lied to by our politicians."

"So that's what she took away from it, that we'd found a plane carrying tiny nuclear mines or something. All I said was that I thought the drums might contain uranium ore or uranium oxide, but I suppose one thought must have led to another and she ended up at bombs."

"And then broadcast it. Which might be what got her killed."

"Mmmm. Word spreads, and then it must have reached the ears of someone that wants the plane's location kept secret."

"That's why you were worried about the missing chart yesterday." It was a statement not a question.

"Yes. I'd asked her to mark the plane's location on the chart. If there's no Marlea, and no more chart, then maybe no one knows where to find the plane and our mystery person is safe."

"Maybe, but if whomever it is was taking no chances with the woman or the chart, they may wonder about the two divers."

"You mean the two silly women divers, both of whom are 'from away' and probably don't know the local waters at all?"

"I'm serious Alex. I'm glad you phoned rather than coming to the office because I've gone from humouring you to worrying about you."

"Well... thank you. What do you suggest?"

"First of all, if you must be on the case then stay undercover and stay the hell away from the detachment. Secondly, alert your friend to be on her guard if strangers show up asking about the rumours of a sunken plane and its cargo, whatever innocent-sounding reasons are given. Third, make sure you let as many people as possible know that you don't know where the plane is other than somewhere out past PEI."

"OK. I agree."

"You don't, do you?"

"Don't what? Know where it is? Of course I do, that's why I asked Marlea to mark in on her chart, so I could make a note in my dive log."

Mike groaned. "How about I have someone drop by to pick up your log book and we'll lock it up here for now? That way you can honestly tell anyone you like that the police confiscated it as part of their investigation."

"OK. Good idea… I do have one other thought. How would you feel about setting a trap?"

Another groan. "You mean like the one you used back in Radium City?"

"Sort of. Besides, you might recall that that one actually worked. Anyway, what if we were to 'donate' the drum we salvaged to the local museum? They might like to put it on display."

"And when the word goes out, someone might get the bright idea of breaking-in and stealing it?"

"Exactly."

"I like the idea of moving it away from you and your friend, but I don't have the resources for a full-time surveillance exercise." He paused, obviously thinking about it. "I do, however, have a brand-new videotape surveillance system I've been wanting to try out. I suppose we could try that. All right, send in the drum with your diving log and I'll talk to the museum curator, Wade Kean about putting it on display."

"Fine. Talk to you soon."

After my conversation with Mike, I needed to have a long talk with Sharon. I suggested a walk along the beach. As we strolled, I brought her up to date on what had been learned so far and why I thought she would be in danger if she stayed.

Not surprisingly, she wanted to stay but I argued that someone was willing to strike and kill without warning to keep their activities secret, and that they might try to kill her based only on the suspicion that she might remember the location of the sunken plane.

She tried arguing that I was in danger too, but gave up when I insisted that I'd be better able to look out for myself if I wasn't also trying to also guard her.

When we got back to the cottage Sharon telephoned the owner, who lived in Fredericton, explained that she suddenly had to return home, and asked her to shift the rental over to me.

When Sharon had packed up and was ready to leave, I promised to let her know how things turned out, and extracted a promise from her to phone me if she got worried or if anything suspicious happened when she was back in Halifax. That got Sharon out of harm's way – I hoped.

Mike didn't waste any time sending someone to pick up the steel drum and my diving log, as Const. John Hardisty promptly dropped by to get them. John didn't have any news on the case per se but, when I asked about Chipper the cat, he told me that he had discovered he was allergic to it and had to take him back to the detachment.

"What happens to him now?" I asked.

"The Sarge is going to look after him," he said, with a straight face, but his eyes were twinkling.

That should be interesting, I thought. I had eventually learned that Mike's bark was worse than his bite, I wondered whether Chipper was going to be able to break through his gruff exterior as well. Time would tell.

When John left, I had two more calls to make. One to Don in Halifax, and one to Vivian in Washington. I had the same question for each of them: If I gave them the latitude and longitude of the sunken plane, could they arrange for someone to look for satellite images to see what kind of boat had been going to the site. I was thinking of historical images, as I imagined that whomever was taking the drums would lie low for a little while, and perhaps even keep the site under observation to see whether news of its location had gotten out.

I called Don first. On the satellite angle, he said he could get a colleague to see if there was any useful imagery to be obtained from earth observation satellites.

"We can easily get at the images from Landsat[30] but they won't have the resolution needed to see a fishing boat, much less identify or track it," he replied after a moment's thought. "Our only hope would be to ask the CIA for help. They aren't likely to give us images, but they might be willing to have someone go through them themselves and give us a summary of anything they find. The problem is that the level of resolution they can achieve is a closely guarded secret[31]."

"Do you think they'd be willing to help?"

"I'll see if I can get the Admiral to call the head of the CIA directly." By 'the Admiral' he meant his boss, Rear-Admiral Peter White, the head of the Canadian Forces Security Branch, which included Military Intelligence. "Since nuclear power is a strategic area for them, I think they'd be willing, especially if the FBI make the same request."

"OK. I can take a hint. Vivian is next on my list to call anyway." I didn't get off the phone quite that easily however, as Don made me promise to call him immediately if I was approached by anyone, or if there was any sign that I was being watched or followed.

My final call of the day was to Vivian, to bring her up to date and ask her the same question about satellite imagery.

"Well, I agree with Don that NASA's imagery won't have the resolution needed to help you," was her first response. "Hypothetically speaking, the CIA might be able to help, but like Don said, even then you'd only get sanitized results – most likely verbal only. I don't think they'd be likely to commit the resources needed to do active monitoring for you, but I think there's still enough Cold War hysteria that they'd be willing to have someone go through the archival imagery, especially since you have the exact coordinates. I'll see if I can get my boss to persuade the Director to make the request personally. His voice and that of your Admiral White should be more than enough." By 'boss' she meant Deputy Director Jonathan Wheeler of the Bureau.

"What will you do next?" asked Vivian. "You're not going to go running around searching for radiation like we did in the north two years ago[32] are you?"

"No," I said. "The drums won't be giving off enough radiation for that to work, and I'd look pretty conspicuous running around with a Geiger Counter in my hands. I'll have to think of something else."

"OK. Be careful then, and call out if you need backup."

"OK," I agreed. "Don told me the same thing and the local Sergeant is a former boss of mine. I can count on him too, if I need help."

With Sharon out of harm's way - I hoped – and my calls to Vivian and Don made, it wasn't obvious what else to do so I drove downtown intending to take Silver for a walk around town. We had just begun our walk when we came across the town's small museum. Glancing at the front windows I noticed a sign indicating that they had on display:

'Drum of uranium recently recovered from a wreck in the Gulf of St. Lawrence. Could this have come from the fabled sunken German U-boat of 1943?'

That was quick work on Mike's part, I thought to myself. The museum had taken an interesting approach to getting people's attention, one that explained why a rusty barrel might merit being on display. The mention of uranium, which was surely Mike's idea, would be intended to interest anyone that was actually taking the drums from the sunken plane.

I decided to go in for a quick look. Since I didn't want to advertise my true identity, I had to leave Silver outside which I did, with instructions to sit and wait for me.

Although the museum was open, there didn't seem to be anyone around, simply a sign indicating that visitors were welcome to walk around and that, although there was no entry fee, donations would be gratefully accepted. A small box was conspicuously positioned nearby, for such donations.

Walking through the museum there were quite a few exhibits relating to the area's lobster fishing history, and a couple relating to the harbour's fame as a safe landing place for seaplanes, including having hosted a famous visit by a squadron of 25 large Italian military seaplanes of the Royal Italian Air Force in 1933[33], and the harbour's role as a stopover point for transatlantic Boeing 314 Clipper flights flown by Pan American between 1939 and 1946. As I read some of the museum's posters at the latter display, I realized that it must have been one of these Boeing Clippers that Sharon and I had discovered lying on the ocean floor. The pictures and cutaway diagram of the plane certainly matched the wreck we had swum around, and the upper deck cargo bay was depicted as being exactly where we'd peered at the drums through the large opening that had been made at the top of the airframe.

Tucked into a corner at the back of the museum was the steel drum I had recovered. The poster beside it gave the same brief statement as had the one in the museum's window, and two adjacent posters described the Second World War occurrences of U-boats in the Gulf of St. Lawrence and, of course, the possible sighting off the coast of PEI of the mystery U-boat and associated gun action of Canadian and American naval forces in sinking it. In reading it all over, I realized that Mike must not have been very specific about the nature of the wreck from which we had recovered the steel drum, allowing the museum curator to naturally assume that it must have been a shipwreck or, in this case, a submarine wreck. I found it ironic that it had been in the hopes of finding the possible U-boat wreck that Sharon had wanted to do our dive in the first place.

The U-boat posters must have already existed somewhere in the museum, or else in storage, to have been able to place them with the steel drum so quickly.

Having examined the display, I turned and glanced around wondering where the hidden video camera and recorder might be, but couldn't see any indication, which was good.

I had just turned back for another look at the images of the Boeing Clipper when I heard or sensed something come up behind me. I was just about to turn around to see if it was the curator when some kind of bag came down over my head, something pushed, or was pushed, against my mouth, and my arms were tightly pinioned against my chest.

I had vaguely become aware that one or more other people had entered the museum but, being busy reading about the Clippers and submarine, I hadn't paid much attention. I tried to yell but couldn't with something so firmly pushed against my mouth, and I tried to struggle but couldn't do much when I was so tightly held. Even my attempts to shift my body to throw my assailant off balance failed, as did my attempts to kick backwards in hopes of connecting with my assailant's legs.

It quickly became clear that there were two assailants, because a second person picked up my struggling legs while the first maintained their hold on my arms. Presumably the second person was the one with the bag and whatever was against my mouth, the latter presumably having been firmly tied into place.

I could breathe through my nose and I could struggle, which I did, but that was about all as I was carried off to – somewhere. Between not being able to see and focused on struggling, I couldn't judge time or distance very well but it seemed to me that I wasn't carried far and, from the sounds and the jostling, a lot of it involved going down stairs.

Eventually the grip on my arms changed and I both felt and heard my wrists being handcuffed behind me, after which I was unceremoniously – and rather thoroughly – searched, then pushed down onto a hard-backed chair. Then, thankfully, whatever had been held against my moth was removed, as was the hood.

"*Mais pourquoi diable me fait ça?* " ("Why the hell did you do that?") said a short, stocky man in a rough-sounding voice.

"She was having trouble breathing in there. She can't tell us anything if she's dead," replied a tall, slender man in thin, reedy male voice.

"*C'est pas possible comment que t'es cave!*" ("There's no way you can be this stupid!")

The tall man said something in reply, in a lower voice and with his head turned, so I couldn't make out what he said. The shorter man similarly turned his head and lowered his voice, so I couldn't hear him clearly either, but it was clear that an argument was taking place.

While they argued I glanced around. I was in a large but rather dingy-looking room with cement walls and only a couple of small windows, placed high up. There was a rough set of stairs behind me. *A basement?* I wondered. In front of me was a plain table with a few more hard-backed chairs, and the two men. Seeing me looking around the two men stopped arguing and shorter one took charge.

"We removed the gag and hood so you can breathe and answer questions," he said, "but no yelling or screaming or we'll just put them both back on again. OK?"

I nodded. I'd figured that part out for myself already.

"You're one of the women divers, aren't you?"

I didn't answer, but it may have been a rhetorical question as he continued on without pause. "You saved us a lot of work, trying to figure out how to separate you from that wolf of yours."

Great, I thought. I'd already wished that I hadn't left Silver sitting outside the museum. If dogs could talk, he'd have something to say about this when we were together again… *if we were together again.*

On the table was the meagre result of their search. I hadn't been carrying much. A set of keys and a belt pouch. When in civilian clothes I normally wore a belt pouch – kind of like a miniature fanny-pack – rather than carry a purse. It was to the latter that they turned their attention as the tall one opened and emptied it out. There was a pen, a short pencil, a pad, some tissues, lip balm, my wallet and some coins.

When the tall one opened the wallet, he exclaimed in the thin, reedy voice "She's a cop – a Mountie!"

"*Tabarnak!* [34]"

"Are you two crazy?" I asked. "Kidnapping a cop? If you don't release me, my colleagues will hunt you down to the ends of the earth."

The two men looked at each other, then the short one said "Keep an eye on her. I'll go talk to you-know-who."

The tall one just nodded.

The short one then stomped up the stairs, muttering a mixture of English and French words under his breath, after which I heard a door open and then slam shut. My initial sense was that the shorter man was the brighter of the two, so with him out of the way for the moment I wondered if there might be a way to take advantage of the taller one's slower brain. If there was, it wasn't yet obvious to me.

While I racked my brain for ideas, the tall one took an interest in the pen he'd found in my belt pouch. That wasn't surprising. It did look unusual with its home-made-looking body of blued aluminum metal and finished with a knurled surface, making it easy to grip.

"What's this?" he asked in a taunting voice. "I suppose it's some kind of James Bond spy pen that shoots gas or bullets?"

"Darts, actually," I replied.

He snorted derisively, then growled. "Think I'm stupid, do you? How do you fire it then?"

'How do you fire it, the man says,' I thought to myself. "See the pocket clip near the thicker end? Push the bottom of the clip into the barrel."

As I said this, he'd been holding the pen up to a light bulb that hung suspended over the table. He was looking at the thin end!

I held my breath and tried not to stare as he actually began pushing on the bottom of the clip. As he did so, the clamshell closure on the thin end opened so that the pen was pointing directly towards... *Whisk...* there was the soft sound of the dart being ejected from the pen.

"Ouch. What the hell?" The tall man lifted his free hand and pulled the dart out from where it had lodged in his upper chest, just to the left of his sternum.

Better and better, I thought. *Have to keep him talking.* "I told you," I said, in as conversational a tone as I could manage. "It really is a kind of pen gun. It was given to me by a Soviet spy I once worked with[35], and it shoots anesthetic darts."

"Anesthe..." he seemed to have trouble forming the word.

"It means that you'll begin to feel sleepy in a moment. Maybe even right now, as the drug is very fast acting. You might want to sit down so you don't fall down and get hurt."

"Yeth, I think I'll thit down…" he said, in a slow voice that was slurring and fading. He dropped the pen, reached for the back of the nearest chair and, almost in slow motion, he made to sit down but only made it to the edge of the chair. From there he slumped to one side, slid off, and collapsed onto the floor.

These two remind me of Mutt and Jeff[36], I thought to myself. *If this character is Mutt, then I need to get out of here before Jeff returns.* Easy to say but, of course, I was still handcuffed. The question was whether they'd used cheap handcuffs, or authentic police ones. I wasn't able to simply stand up from the chair I was in, but by throwing myself forward and bending forward at the waist, I was able to get the chair angled up on its two front legs. From there, I was able to slither forward so that the back of the chair slipped down my back and, eventually, past my arms to fall on the floor.

I dropped to my knees and then sat down on the floor myself. From there, it was a case of bending forward at the waist again, but this time as far as I possibly could, while attempting to slip my bound wrists underneath me and around my butt – that was the hard part – with the aim of getting them under my legs, and then around my feet and up in front of me.

It was at this point that I wished I was as flexible as I'd been when I was younger.

In any case, miracle number one was that persistence and adrenaline somehow enabled me to get my arms up in front of me. Miracle number two was that they'd actually used authentic police handcuffs rather than the cheaper kinds.

I didn't need a third miracle. It was already hanging around my neck. Most police officers carry a second handcuff key. Sometimes, for example, they'll have one on their regular key ring and the other tucked inside their handcuff pouch. Some handcuff pouches even have a special sleeve for this exact purpose. In my case, I kept a slightly unusual one that was shorter and had a wider bow than the standard kind. The wider bow allowed the shorter key to be turned with enough torque to lock or unlock the cuffs. The small size and shape of the key meant that it fit into a round, sterling silver locket. When opened the locket was designed to hold two oval photos, but instead I was able to just barely fit my key, which was no longer than a dime and slightly less wide. The locket hung on a thin silver chain that had a breakaway clasp so it couldn't strangle me in a struggle.

Removing the key from the locket, and taking care not to drop it, it took some fiddling to get the key and cuffs properly aligned so I could get the key in the lock of one cuff and release it. The second one was easy. Then I went to check on Mutt. His pulse and breathing seemed OK, so I recovered the pen and the spent dart, and put them and the rest of my stuff in my belt pouch and reattached it. A quick search of his clothing produced a wallet and some loose change. Then, I did a quick survey of the room I was in. It was definitely a basement, as I could now see a furnace and water pipes and so on.

Dragging Mutt over to where the main water line entered the basement, I used the same handcuffs to attach Mutt to the pipe by locking one cuff to the pipe and the other to one of his wrists. He hadn't had a key in his clothing, so I assumed Jeff must have one, but at least it would immobilize Mutt until his partner returned.

I decided to confiscate Mutt's wallet and took a last look around. Not seeing anything interesting, I quickly but carefully made my way up the stairs. I was still in the museum!

I would have liked to hang around in hopes of catching Jeff as well but, the Soviet dart pen had been the only weapon in my possession. Being alone and unequipped, it seemed like a better strategy to look for Silver and find a way to call for backup.

Making my way to the front of the still deserted museum, I looked out the front windows to make sure there was no returning Jeff in sight – there wasn't – then went out the front door. Thankfully, Silver was still where I had left him. He'd obviously been watching for me, and looked quite anxious, so I knelt to give him a quick hug saying "Good boy Silver. Let's get some help."

I looked around. There was a small drugstore almost directly across the street from us so I made for it figuring that it would have a phone. When we entered and went to the back, I identified myself to the pharmacist, asked to use his phone, and called the detachment. Fortunately, Mike was in his office, which was a time-saver as all I had to do was give him the gist of what had happened, tell him where I was and ask for backup so we could watch for Jeff's return and hopefully arrest both him and Mutt.

The pharmacist had heard my side of the conversation, so I asked whether he was familiar with a pair of men that would frequently have been seen together around town, one tall and one short, and added as much other description of the pair as I could remember.

He said that it sounded like a pair of small-time hustlers named Campbell and Bourque that generally spent the summer months trying to defraud or even rob unsuspecting tourists.

"Nothing sophisticated, you understand," he explained. "More like constantly looking out for crimes of opportunity. Sergeant Morrison will be familiar with their names, I'm sure."

Thanking him, Silver and I left the pharmacy and went and sat in my truck, which was parked on the same side of the road as the pharmacy and in sight of the museum entrance. We didn't have to wait long before an unremarkable sedan pulled in and parked behind me. Through my rear-view mirror I saw Mike get out of it and walk around to the passenger side of my truck, get in, and take his hat off.

"Are you OK?" he asked. "Not injured or anything?"

"I'm OK," I replied. "I feel stupid for getting caught like I did, and my modesty took a beating when they searched me, but I'm mostly just feeling lucky to have gotten away and lucky to have a chance to maybe learn something useful from these two goons."

"That's a relief.... Are they armed?"

"I don't know. Mutt wasn't but I'm not sure about Jeff."

"OK then. I didn't want to be too obvious, so I drove my own car," he said. "I've sent Hardisty to take up position in the alley, using his personal car as well, and I've called in another constable that was out on highway patrol. As soon as he gets back to town, he's to stay back a couple of blocks and wait for me to call. Let's see where they are." He removing his Motorola hand-held VHF radio from his belt and held it up.

"Hardisty. What's your twenty?" By 'twenty' he meant 10-20, the code for location.

"10-23" was the reply, giving the code for 'At scene.'

"C237?" I assumed this was directed at the other constable. The letter C prefix was commonly used to denote highway patrol and traffic services cars.

"C237, ten minutes out," came the acknowledgment.

"So. Now we wait," said Mike. "You said there were two men?"

"Yes, one tall and one short." I gave him the same descriptions I'd given the pharmacist, concluding with "I've been thinking of them as Mutt and Jeff. The Mutt fellow isn't too bright. The pharmacist said you'd know them."

"Hmmm. Sounds like Noah Campbell and Marcel Bourque. They're generally up to some kind of trouble, but usually petty thefts and frauds. Kidnapping is pretty big league for these two to be involved."

"I think the person we're really after hired them. They were surprised to find my badge in my wallet. I think it threw them for a loop, and I suspect Jeff went off the report to Mr. Big and get instructions." I remembered then, that I'd confiscated Mutt's wallet and took it out for a look. "You called it. Mutt's driver's licence reads Noah Campbell," I said.

Mike just grunted and we spent the next few minutes just sitting quietly.

The radio crackled. "C237, two minutes."

Several minutes later came "C237, 10-23."

"10-12," said Mike, into his radio, giving the code for 'Stand by.' We both looked forward and back as best we could, trying to spot the highway patrol car.

"Got him," I said. "A little more than two blocks behind us, on our side of the road."

"OK, I think we should wait a little longer before we... aha! Look ahead, other side of the street, just coming onto the block and heading our way."

I looked. "That's Jeff.... Seems to be in a hurry."

"Hmmm hmm."

Walking quickly, Jeff soon made it to the museum, took a quick look all around and then went in the front door.

"Suspect has entered the building," said Mike into his radio. "Hardisty, give us two minutes, then go in. C237, come now, 10-33." The latter being the code for 'Help me quickly."

Mike, Silver, and I got out of my truck and walked briskly across the street and then stopped one of us on each side of the museum's front door. We each looked for signs of trouble, then Mike looked at me, and I nodded and motioned towards Silver. Mike nodded back. Telling Silver to precede me, I opened the door and the two of us walked in, followed by Mike, who had his gun out.

Just like before, the museum seemed deserted and I motioned Silver towards the back. Still nothing. As we moved towards the rear door and the stairs to the basement, Constable John Hardisty opened the back door, saw Silver and I and nodded. Coming up from behind us, Mike motioned that John should go first.

John tried going down the stairs without making a sound, but the building was old and the stairs creaked under his weight so he abandoned that approach and went for speed instead, his boots making a racket in the confined space. As we followed, we heard him exclaim "Police. Freeze!"

When Silver and I had made it to the bottom I could see that John had moved well over to one side and was pointing his revolver at the corner where I had handcuffed Mutt - Noah Campbell – still apparently unconscious and still attached to the water pipe and Jeff - Marcel Bourque – rising up from where he had presumably been checking on Mutt.

While John had Jeff raise his hands and stand by a side wall to be frisked, the other constable called out from the top of the stairs. When Mike yelled out "Clear!" he came down the stairs, and Mike had him release Mutt from the pipe.

"How long does the anesthetic last?" asked Mike.

"I don't really know," I said, "a couple of hours I think, but it must vary with people of different body sizes."

Mike used his portable radio to call the detachment's radio room for an ambulance.

When the ambulance arrived, Mike had John accompany Mutt to the town's medical clinic and the other constable take the disarmed Jeff – a Smith & Wesson revolver had been found concealed in the waistband of his pants - into custody and put him in a cell at the detachment.

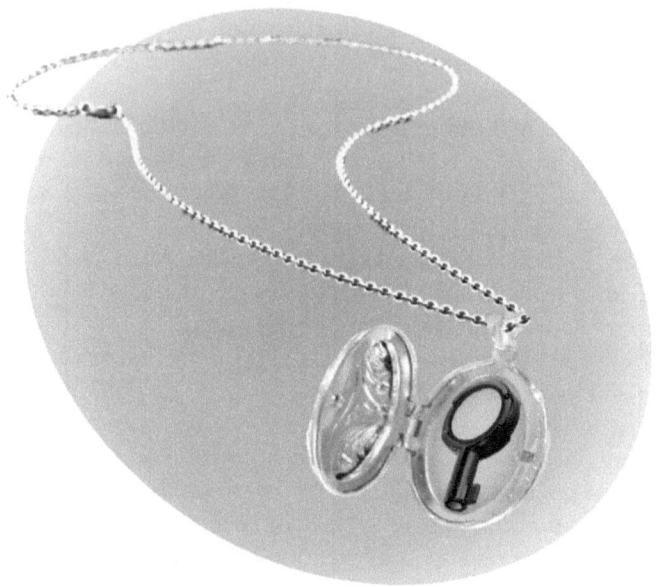

5 IN THE GULF

Friday May 9, 1980

In the morning, I awoke to a beautiful sunrise and discovered that I had actually been able to get a good night's sleep. Although I had to assume that whomever had been after me might try again, I'd had Silver and his keen senses watching over me and my gun under my pillow. Either that had been enough to give me a feeling of reasonable security or else I'd been too exhausted to do anything else but fall into a deep sleep. *Probably both*, I decided.

My first priority was to warn Sharon, so I phoned her first and filled her in. She was naturally horrified to hear about my experience and I did my best to remind her to keep her guard up without alarming her unduly. In addition to my earlier offer that she should call me if she got worried, I now extended that to my fiancé Don who lived nearby, saying that I would relate all this to him as well.

Don, when I called him, naturally wanted to come out and protect me but he was tied-up with a case of his own for the time being, forcing him to remain in Halifax. He did say that the soft signals he was getting indicated that the CIA had agreed to have someone go through their recent satellite imagery for the region I was in and that he expected to hear from them whether they found anything or not.

Mike, when I called him, filled me in on the latest news regarding my 'Mutt and Jeff' characters, also known as (aka): Noah Campbell and Marcel Bourque. Campbell had been transferred to cells once he'd regained consciousness at the medical clinic and the attending physician had determined that he was fit to be transported. When interviewed, individually of course, each had refused to say anything other than wanting to get a lawyer. Each had been allowed to make a phone call and a single lawyer had appeared at the detachment that morning saying that he was representing both clients. Mike assumed the lawyer was being paid by whomever had hired the two.

"By the way, our surveillance camera at the museum did its job, but not in the way we expected. The camera caught our two friends jump you and carry you off, so there's more than enough evidence on those two.

"There's more news about you too. We can assume that Bourque went flying off to inform their boss about your identity, so there's a leak right there. More than that, this morning half the town is talking about the undercover woman Mountie spy and her huge 'wolf.' I imagine that means that Campbell probably told everyone at the medical clinic about it, and from there it spread. It's a small town after all."

"Great," I groaned.

"It's kind of a 'laugh or cry' thing too, because the story has shifted as it's been retold and there are rumours circulating about a small nuclear weapon and radiation hazards, and there's already a petition going around with the aim of having the 'nuclear weapon' removed from the museum display."

"All that since last night?"

"I'm afraid so. With your cover blown, it might be safest for you to go in uniform from now on. That way you'll be conspicuously armed and it will be obvious that you have a police dog with you."

"Yes," I said slowly, "I think you're right, especially now that Mr. Big knows enough that he'll probably lie low for a while anyway."

"Fine. In that case, drop by the detachment and we'll loan you a portable radio so we can reach each other if you go out prowling around."

Before doing anything else, I took Silver down to Parlee Beach for a walk. When we reached The Lobster's Brew, we popped in and sat out on the deck for a moment. When Jean Friend, the owner, came to take our order I asked for coffee for me and a bowl of water for Silver.

Whatever else Jean was, she wasn't shy. "I hear you're a Mountie, but that's no wolf you have there," she began.

"Yes, I'm a vacationing Mountie, and no Silver's not a wolf, although he does look wolfish. He's an Alaskan Malamute, and he was even born in Alaska. I see you're up to speed on the local town gossip," I said, smiling to show that I wasn't criticizing.

"Small town, small community," she said. "Terrible what happened to Marlea Becker... did you hear about it?"

"Yesterday," I confirmed. "I heard that she was out in her boat, fell overboard and drowned. Horrible. I'd met her but didn't get to know her at all."

"I heard she took you and your friend out diving the day before it happened?"

"Yes. We were hoping to find the German U-boat people talk about, and we did find a wreck, but it wasn't a submarine."

"I hear it was a big airplane and it had nuclear bombs on board."

"We don't really know what we found," I said, trying to keep a straight face and sound nonchalant. "It looked like a big plane of some kind and we found a small barrel. It certainly doesn't look like a bomb, but we don't actually know what's inside it. We didn't open it. It's in the town museum right now."

"Yes, so I hear... where's your friend, by the way?"

"Oh, she left yesterday. Had to go back home."

"That's too bad. She left a sweater behind when she was last here. I was going to give it to her."

"I can take it if you like, and give it to her when I see here next."

"Actually, I'd like to send it to her. I'm trying to build up the business here, and that kind of service gets people talking. Would you be able to give me her address?"

I wasn't entirely sure that I believed her story, and I wanted to try to cover Sharon's tracks anyway, so I said "That would be very good of you. Her name is Paula Doyle."

"Paula? I thought her name was Sharon and she lived in Nova Scotia somewhere?" It sounded like a direct question, and her eyebrows were inquisitorially raised.

"That sounds like someone else. My friend's name is Paula, and she lives in Newfoundland. You may have noticed her soft accent when we were here on Sunday." I'd given a fictitious surname that's common in Newfoundland, so I extended my lie with a made-up address on a well-known street, saying "She lives at 301 Water Street, apartment 22, in St. John's, Newfoundland. I don't know the postal code, but the post office can give you that."

I could tell she wanted to probe for more information but she was called to the front register by one of her staff and had to leave us. When she'd left, I exhaled a big breath. I rarely lie, preferring to instead limit what I say to people, but I'll lie to protect someone from harm and I was determined to protect Sharon's name and domicile at all costs.

After I'd finished my coffee, Silver and I walked back to the cottage so I could shower and change clothes.

Later, with my tactical uniform on and Silver wearing his police vest – our brief vacation was over - we drove into town and went for a stroll. Our first stop was the museum, where we found that Wade Kean, the curator, was in this time. He'd heard that there'd been some kind of an incident the previous day, but none of the details beyond the fact that a man had been taken to the medical clinic. He'd also heard the story making the rounds about a woman Mountie and a large wolf but a single glance had enabled him to correctly identify Silver as an Alaskan Malamute. He was much more interested in the steel barrel now and, although he'd dismissed the bomb rumour as nonsense, he was worried about whether there was a radiation hazard. I explained that the hazard would be very low as long as no one opened the drum, which seemed to satisfy him.

Not surprisingly, given his job, Wade had a keen interest in anything and everything to do with Pointe-du-Chêne and the local area's history, including boats, flying boats, and underwater shipwrecks, particularly the fabled sunken U-boat.

I asked him about the 'Mutt and Jeff' characters Campbell and Bourque and he was aware of them, but only superficially, and wasn't able to tell me anything more about them.

One of my last questions for Wade was whether anyone had showed particular interest in the steel drum since it had been put on display.

"Not really. Quite a few folks came for a look, but they all seemed pretty disappointed to find that it just looks like 'a rusty beer keg,' as one of them put it." He paused, in thought for a moment. "The professor was quite interested, of course."

"The professor?"

"Levi - Levi Murray. He's 'come from away' you know," he said, with a knowing look[37]. "He's a retired college professor that moved in the community a few years ago."

"Do you know what he used to teach?"

"Oh sure. He taught physics and chemistry at the College of Cape Breton[38]."

I smiled to myself. The College of Cape Breton was in Syndey, Nova Scotia so their 'come from away' professor hadn't come from very far away. I made a mental note to look him up.

After the museum, I next tried the pharmacist that had helped me the previous day. He was pleased to hear that I was OK and that we'd caught Campbell and Bourque. I already knew that he was somewhat familiar with the two men and tried probing further about any associates, frequent haunts, and whether they were known or thought to do jobs for other people, but he said he didn't know.

It turned out that Dr. Levi Murray, 'the professor,' lived in a heritage house one street back from Main Street, so we went there next. Although he humoured me and my questions, his demeanor was very reserved - even haughty – and I couldn't help wondering whether it was his normal manner, or whether he resented being questioned by the police, by a woman, or by someone he didn't perceive to be an intellectual equal, or all three. Even Silver noticed his manner and signalled his displeasure by a series of low growls. That seemed to put Murray off even more of course.

For all that, he was courteous enough in his replies, although I sensed condescension. However, he told me essentially nothing beyond admitting that he'd been interested to go see the 'atomic bomb' that was on display on the museum. He said that he'd fully expected it to be nothing of the kind and pronounced the find to be a "worthless old steel drum."

When I asked him if the stencilled markings seemed a little unusual, he shrugged and replied that anyone could stencil anything on drum. If it did come from the Belgian Congo then it may have contained copper ore which, he explained, was once a major export for them after demand for their natural rubber had declined.

This struck me as difficult to believe since they would surely have refined copper ore to produce copper metal before exporting it and in any case wouldn't have shipped copper ore in such small barrels, nor by airplane, but he was steadfast in his pronouncement that the drum must contain copper ore or something of the sort, and said that when it was eventually opened and analyzed it would be clear to everyone.

I felt sure that he wasn't helping me as much as he could have, but not so sure about his motivations, so I simply thanked him for his time and took my leave, for the time being.

Once back on Main Street, I also tried a few other places where the staff might know something about other members of the community, like the two banks in town, the post office, and so on without learning much. Among the questions I asked everyone I encountered were whether there were particular cafes and bars that were favoured by the locals and, in particular, fishers and boat skippers. The consensus identified two cafes and one bar, so I went to speak with the managers of all three. From the cafes I heard that Campbell and Bourque were known to them and that they were frequently low on cash.

The bar mentioned was the same one that Mike had told me Marlea went to on the evening after she'd taken us out diving, so I'd planned to go there anyway. The bar manager was familiar with Campbell and Bourque, but said the two of them tended to drink alone together and he didn't recall them tending to associate with anyone else in particular.

"Were they in the bar last Monday evening, the evening Marlea Becker was there telling stories about the two women that she'd taken out SCUBA diving that day?"

"Not that I remember, no," he'd said, "but I remember her being here and talking about the sunken airplane and the uranium."

Further questioning brought out the information that the bar had been quite full that evening and that anyone that cared to might have heard her story. "I went over and listened to her for a while myself as I was curious about whether the phantom U-boat had finally been found. It was certainly the first I'd ever heard of a large airliner crashing anywhere near here!"

As it was approaching noon by the time I exited the bar, I decided to make the medical clinic my last stop of the morning. I asked to see Dr. Bruce Solinsky and after a moderate wait was ushered to his office.

"I knew who you must be, but not your name," he said after I'd identified myself, "I'm Bruce Solinsky."

"I want to ask you a few questions about Marlea Becker, but I have to ask about those unusual-looking plane models up there." There were actually quite a few airplane models on display in his office, all of which appeared to be vintage. While some were sitting on shelves in a bookcase, the two most unusual were suspended from wires from the ceiling. One was clearly a Boeing Clipper, but I had no idea about the other.

"They're both flying boats," he said, clearly pleased at my interest. The older model is a an Italian Savoia-Marchetti S.55. It flew in the 1920s through to the mid-1940s. As you can see, it's got some unusual features: two large hulls for passengers and cargo, a central cockpit that sits in the thicker section of the wing between the two hulls, and two in-line propellers mounted up high and rotating in opposite directions."

"It looks like two large airplanes tied together. I've never seen or heard of anything like that."

"Well, it's part of the local history. In 1933, 25 of these Italian Air Force flying boats left Italy on their way to a World's Fair Exhibition in Chicago. At that time there hadn't been a lot of successful transatlantic flights yet, so it was amazing that 24 of the 25 actually made it to North America. They actually stopped right here in our harbour[39]. Here, let me show you." He went to one of several well-filled bookcases in his office and selected a binder. After riffling through the pages for a moment he found the one he wanted. "Here's a photograph of one of them taking off from the harbour. Like you said, it looks a bit like two airplanes attached side-by-side. Anyway, they went on from here to the world's fair and then a few weeks later, the same planes took off to fly back to Italy. Once again, they stopped here, among other places to rest and refuel. On their way home, they lost another plane, but 23 of the original 25 made the entire transatlantic crossing, in each direction. An amazing feat that involved over a hundred pilots and crew! Can you imagine?"

"No, I really don't think I can," was all I could say. "It must have been considered highly risky."

A Savoia-Marchetti S.55

"You bet your life it was risky, but it was a unique opportunity, and it paved the way for transatlantic airliners, the first of which was this other flying boat, the Boeing 314 Clipper, which Pan Am and BOAC flew between 1939 and 1948. Pan Am was running three regularly scheduled flights a week from New York to Europe and, of course, three back, and every time they made a stopover right here."

I'd already learned some of the Boeing Clipper background on my own but didn't want to divulge any special interest, so I encouraged him to continue on with his story. Eventually, however, he ran out of steam, ending with "… but you didn't come here to learn about vintage airplanes."

"No. You're right of course. I understand you were one of the first on the scene when Marlea Becker's body was found?"

"Not the first," he shook his head, "I was walking along the shore and came across John - Constable John Hardisty, that is - kneeling by the head of someone that was lying stretched out on the sand. When he saw me, he waved me over and said the body was stone cold and he didn't think he could feel a pulse.

"So, I went to check, of course. It was a woman, later identified as Marlea Becker, one of our lobster-boat skippers, and she was deceased."

"I understand that you examined the body."

"Yes, in a cursory fashion – not a complete examination of course – but to check for any obvious signs of injury. I found none and speculated that perhaps she had fallen overboard and drowned. By that time, the paramedics had arrived, so I declared the woman deceased and left the rest to them."

"Did you know her?" I asked.

"No, not really. We must have been introduced at some time or other because right away I knew who she was, but I don't know anything more about her. It's more than likely that she comes to our clinic because we're the only game in town, but if so, I haven't myself seen her as a patient as far as I can remember."

I asked if he could check to see if she had been a particular patient of one of his colleagues and he agreed and went out to check their records. When he returned it was with a Dr. Odette Billon, who said that Marlea had been a patient of hers. Upon more questioning from me I learned that no, there were no pre-existing medical questions that would have made Marlea susceptible to falling overboard or drowning. My final question was: did she knew whether Marlea could swim.

"Yes, she did. I know that because she was learning to SCUBA dive a few years ago and she wanted a tetanus vaccination to protect her in case she ever cut herself while exploring a shipwreck."

One more reason to consider her death suspicious, I thought to myself as Silver and I left the medical clinic. Not that we needed any more reasons given everything else we'd learned.

As Silver and I were walking back to where I'd parked my truck, we passed an antique store. On a whim, and unrelated to my investigation, I went inside for a look around. Like many such stores in Atlantic Canada they had a nice assortment of furniture, collectibles, and other pieces dating from the 1960s all the way back to the late 1800s. Near the section featuring fine china and other pieces of plate- and tableware was a display cabinet featuring a selection of pieces of uranium-glass tableware and several collections of uranium sea glass, all illuminated by a black light[40]. The ultraviolet light made the pieces strongly fluoresce in a bright green colour. I'd heard of uranium glass but I'd never seen uranium sea glass before and as I looked at the oddly-shaped and well-worn pieces of the latter, it occurred to me that I should perhaps rethink my earlier decision not to try to find a Geiger counter. My identity was already known, and if I was ever able in a position to look over boats that might have been used in the recovery of the steel drums, or places where they may later have been stored, it could be possible to identify them as such if the salvagers had opened a drum to check the contents and possibly spilled some. It would be a long-shot, of course, but I could now see where a Geiger counter could possibly come in handy and I made a mental note to see if I could borrow one somewhere. I was musing over this when my radio crackled. It was Mike asking if I'd like to meet him for lunch. I said yes and, since it was such a nice day, he suggested a nearby restaurant with a nice outdoor patio.

When we reached the restaurant, Mike was already there and had secured a corner table where, with care, we'd be able to converse without much risk of being overheard.

"How was your morning," Mike asked as we were perusing our menus.

"Not very productive." I gave him a summary of the people I'd spoken with, concluding that "I met a lot of townsfolk but didn't really learn much."

"Mine wasn't very productive either, I'm afraid," groaned Mike. "The local Justice of the Peace (JP) was tied up last night, so it was only this morning that we had Campbell and Bourque up in front of him for a bail hearing."

"Hmmm. How did that go?"

"Not well. The JP wasn't convinced that they should remain in custody, and agreed that their lawyer can be their surety. Among the standard bail conditions, the JP ordered the two not to contact or approach you and added the requirement that they not use or possess firearms, alcohol, or drugs. So, part of the reason I'm here is to warn you that they've been released."

"I don't suppose you have the resources to put them under surveillance either."

"No, but I've instructed everyone in the detachment to keep a lookout for them and report times and places when they're spotted. There's one more thing I'm going to try after lunch. Like most detachments, we don't record prisoners' calls to their lawyers but I am going to visit the phone company and ask them to give me a list of the times and phone numbers that were dialed from the phone Campbell and Bourque used to call their lawyers yesterday. The local office has been good about volunteering that kind of information when we ask, so I'm pretty sure they'll agree in this case too."

"What are you after? You must know who their lawyers are since the bail hearing."

"We do, and it turns out they both have the same lawyer, but it's not that. It occurred to me that these two probably can't afford lawyers yet they didn't choose to rely on duty counsel like they've done for smaller crimes in the past. This time, they somehow got the best and most expensive lawyer in town. That makes me curious, and I'd like to know whether they were dumb enough to call your Mr. Big for help, thinking that whomever that is would be willing to pay for a fancy lawyer rather than risk them squealing to us."

Once we'd caught up on things and finished our lunch, we each went our separate ways. In my case, it was back to the cottage to try checking in with Don and Vivian.

My first few calls were actually to the chemistry and physics departments at the *Université de Moncton* but in each case, I was told that they didn't have active teaching or research programs underway in nuclear physics or radiochemistry so they didn't have any Geiger Counters on campus, as far as they were aware.

When I phoned Don, he had news. "We've heard back from the CIA. They're obviously taking this case seriously, because that's pretty fast work on their part. Anyway, they've refused to send anything in writing but gave me a verbal rundown on what they've found so far. First of all, they have imagery of your target site on the day of your dive there showing a boat with white hull and the gunwales and superstructure of some other light colour. Their imagery is black and white, sometimes enhanced with infrared, but they can't do colour. Anyway, that's clearly when you and Sharon were there.

"They haven't spotted any activity there since then, but going backwards they've found several images of a different boat at the same site over the previous two months. They can't be sure, but it may have been the same boat each time. They say it looks to be essentially the same size and shape as the one you were on, but this one has a white hull and a darker-coloured superstructure, not black but darker than the one you were on. Possibly a deep blue, dark green, or a purple colour."

"That's something anyway," I said, encouraged. "Were they willing to give you the times and dates?"

"I have the dates and the times, yes, but the times are UTC[41] so you'll have to convert them to local times." Don read them out to me and I wrote them down.

"I've saved the best for last," Don continued when I had everything written down. "They have images from two satellite passes per day. In the morning satellite passes they have images of what they think is the same boat making its way to the crash site. The boat is in a different position each time but that's good because they plotted each sighting on a chart to see if they could get an idea of where it had been coming from."

"Yes?" I exclaimed.

"This assumes the boat took the same route each time, and it's a bit rough, but it seems to have been originating from somewhere in the Northumberland Strait. That probably means eastern New Brunswick or the west side of PEI. Definitely not Newfoundland or Labrador, and it would only include Nova Scotia if the boat went all along the strait before turning north and heading around the tip of PEI."

"That's more than I expected. Please pass on my thanks to your CIA colleague."

"Will do."

"By the way, I'd like to borrow a Geiger Counter from someone but there don't seem to be any in Moncton. Would there by any military bases around here that might?"

There was a pause as Don thought about it. "The army has a support base at Gagetown[42]. That's near the town of Oromocto, which is close to Fredericton – about a two-hour drive from you."

"Yes. I drove through Fredericton on my way out from Ottawa. I must have driven right by it."

"Well, Gagetown has huge training capabilities and grounds. It's possible they might have NBC-defence[43] equipment there."

"OK. I'll bite. What's NBC?"

"Oops. Sorry. It's a life of acronyms around here. I should have said nuclear, biological, and chemical warfare and terrorism defence. What I mean is, they might have Geiger Counters. I'll make a few calls and find out."

The first thing I did when I got off the phone with Don was to convert the UTC times Don had provided into local times. They were all afternoon times.

After that, I made update calls to Vivian in Washington and Bob, my boss, in Ottawa. Vivian was aware of the CIA information and was pleased to hear that it was helpful, other than that she had nothing to report. Bob was concerned about the attack on me and asked if I wanted him to get me some backup independent of the local detachment. I said not yet. Both Vivian and Bob advised caution, of course.

I'd no sooner finished my calls with Vivian and Bob when Don called back to say that he'd arranged for me to borrow a Geiger Counter and that it would be sent out the next day on an army truck that was going to be travelling to nearby Moncton anyway. He gave me the designation of a building at CFB Moncton[44] where I could pick it up.

Later that afternoon, Silver and I went shopping as I was running low on supplies, and I'd invited Mike to come over when he got off work for a barbeque dinner in the back yard. That was actually a bit time consuming because a number of kids, with their parents in tow, approached us on our way in and out of the store. For the kids its was invariably that they wanted to meet a police dog, and for some of the parents it was more the relative novelty of meeting a woman Mountie. Even then, in early 1980, women represented only about one-and-a half percent of the total uniformed complement in the RCMP[45].

When I wasn't pressed for time, I actually found these informal public-relations opportunities to be quite pleasant and, in this case at least, they gave me a mental break from the stress of trying to figure out what I should be doing next in pursuit of my investigation.

By the time we were back at the cottage and I had changed out of uniform and gotten things organized, there was a knock at the door. It was Mike. As we settled into the back yard, we had two pre-dinner orders of business: a couple of cold beers and shop-talk.

"How are you making out so far?" Mike wondered.

I told him about the information that had been relayed to me about the satellite imagery then tried to organize my thoughts. "So far, everything seems to be pointing in the direction of right here in the Shediac area:

o   Marlea got a number of people's attention with her story about divers finding a sunken airliner and drums of uranium. News travelled, gaining the attention of someone

I've provisionally labelled as Mr. Big, although it could be a man or a woman,

o   Mr. Big got worried news might leak out about the wreck site and either he or his agents tracked down Marlea, purposely killed her without a struggle and threw her overboard, then stole her chart and left her boat adrift,

o   Putting the uranium drum in the local museum almost immediately got the attention of Mr. Big, whom I suspect hired the Mutt and Jeff characters to grab me, presumably to find out whether I knew the location of the crash site,

o   I think I got Sharon out of here in time, and I don't think they'll know her name or address as I got the woman we're renting the cottage from to erase it from her records,

o   Mutt and Jeff are locals, and they might be Marlea's murderers,

o   One or more boats have been seen at the crash site over the past several months. Let's assume for the moment that there was just one boat and that it has a white hull and a darker-coloured superstructure. Not black but something like blue, green, or purple maybe. That boat seems to have been coming from somewhere in the strait but probably not from much further south than where we are right here or else the travel time would be so long that they'd have based the boat in a more convenient location to avoid overnight trips."

"Sounds reasonable so far. I have a little bit of news for you," supplied Mike. "The phone company looked up the numbers that were called from the detachment phone yesterday, at the time when Campbell and Bourque were allowed to make their calls. Bourque – that's the brighter one - called an unlisted number. The phone company looked up who it's assigned to, and it's not a law firm, it's called ABC Shediac Import and Export. It has an address in the old Tait & Melanson Block on Main Street. The building is a shopping mall now, but there are a bunch of offices on the upper floors."

"Do you know anything about it?"

"No. I'll send someone over in the morning but I have a feeling we'll find a small office with a receptionist who 'doesn't know anything.' We'll also contact Corporate Registry in Fredericton to see if there's another address and to learn who the owner or owners are. One way or another, I'll bet it's being used by someone local."

"Hmmm. Who did Campbell call?"

"Oh right, I forgot about him. Well," Mike chuckled, "that was even less helpful. He called his girlfriend. I sent someone over to talk to her but she just clammed up and won't say a thing. I think he knew that Bourque was going to arrange for a lawyer for both of them, so he was able to use his call to talk to whomever he felt like."

Since neither of us had any other news to speak of, we migrated to other topics and got down to the serious business of grilling burgers and searing scallops on the barbeque. After Mike left, I cleaned up, made my regular evening call to Don, and then settled down to another evening habit: I almost always read for a while before going to sleep – usually novels.

It wasn't exactly a case of history repeating itself, but they came after me again that night.

Laurie Schramm

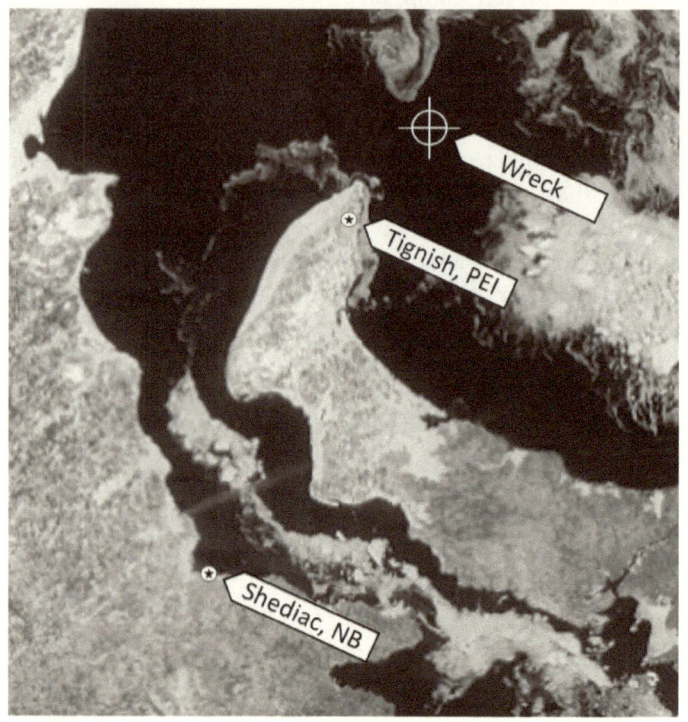

6 ANOTHER ATTACK

"Grrr... grrr."

I awoke to the sound of growling. It was the kind of low, back-of-his-throat growling that meant Silver sensed something he thought might be a threat but wasn't yet sure. It was pitch dark so I knew it was late.

I retrieved my snub-nosed revolver from under my pillow and sat up. Silver was also sitting up right beside me, with his ears peaked, concentrating and continuing his low growling. I put my free hand on his shoulder and told him to stay quiet. That wouldn't stop him from growling, I knew, but I didn't want him to bark.

As I quietly got out of bed and went to the door, I told Silver to remain beside me. The bedroom door wasn't closed and I stopped there for a moment, listening. After a few moments I heard a noise at one of the front windows, then both heard and saw it slide upwards. It was one of the older-style two-pane windows for which one half could be opened. When the lower half was open, I could hear a rustling sound, then something was pushed through the window. It dropped with a kind of *plop* sound.

Silver twitched at that and I knelt down, still in the bedroom doorway, and pressed my hand on his shoulder to remind him to stay with me and be quiet.

Silence.

I also found it hard to stay put and remain silent with my mind running through possibilities. In triage order, the plop could have been a bomb, firebomb, noxious emitter, or... *what?* I wondered, but there was only silence. Whether wisely or foolishly, my instinct was to remain silent and still.

After what seemed like forever, but couldn't really have been more than more than a few minutes, there was a new noise. This time the noise came from the back door. It was a standard cottage door with only a simple lock and I recognized the sound: someone was using a jimmy to force the lock. That is, something like a crowbar was being used to increase the gap between the door and the frame to the point where the latch or bolt came free.

A moment later, there was a slight creak and then the door swung open.

My hand tightened on Silver's shoulder as a shadowy form softly stepped into the cottage. The figure quietly walked further in and continued right past me on its way to where the *plop*-thing had been dropped.

"*Merde*," said a gruff voice.

"Did you get it?" asked another voice as a second shadowy figure came in the back door, *possibly the same person that had opened the front window*, I thought.

"*Tais-toi, imbécile.*" ("Shut-up, you fool.")

I grimaced. It sounded like my Mutt and Jeff pair had returned, their bail restrictions notwithstanding.

Still crouched low, I waited while the second figure reached the first. There was a hushed conversation, and I figured that if they hadn't heard Silver growl then they'd either head for the bedroom where I was or else give up and leave.

While the two continued to whisper I slowly rose up and reached around the doorframe for the light switch. As I did so, the two figures seemed to come to a decision and each took two careful steps in my direction.

I turned on the lights and used both hands to aim my gun.

"Looking for something?" I asked, conversationally.

It was Campbell and Bourque alright, aka Mutt and Jeff.

The tall one, Mutt, immediately dropped a crowbar to the floor and raised his hands.

The short one, Jeff, raised a handgun of some kind and took a shot at me. There was loud bang followed by a *crack* as the bullet hit the brick of the kitchen wall, followed by the even louder bang of my heavier-calibre revolver. Jeff yelled out in pain and I heard, as much as saw, his gun hit the floor.

"Alex?"

A male voice called from outside the back door. It sounded like Const. John Hardisty.

"Clear!" I yelled back.

A second later John burst in, gun in hand, and gave a loud sigh of relief when he saw that I looked intact. "You hit?" he asked.

"No. He missed me. We'll need an ambulance for Bourque though."

John used his portable radio to call the detachment for help, then went kick to the dropped handgun aside and give first aid to Bourque while I covered Campbell.

"Haven't you two had enough?" I asked the latter while keeping a firm grip on Silver, who was practically vibrating with his instinct to attack.

"It's not our fault!" said a scared-looking Campbell. "We were told to finish the job, and that if we didn't..."

"*Ta guele*" ("Shut up"), interrupted Bourque.

The sound of an approaching siren told us that help was on the way, reinforced by the different notes of a second siren coming from further away. In short order, there were engine sounds and doors opening and closing, followed by the entrance of another constable and two paramedics.

With the second constable on the scene, I was finally able to lower my gun and go for a robe to put on over the t-shirt and running shorts in which I'd been sleeping.

Mike himself arrived soon after, dressed in civilian clothes. After I'd related the night's events, he told me that he'd assigned John and another constable to take turns watching the cottage overnight, for which I thanked him.

John, for his part, explained that he'd seen one of the men approach the front window, fiddle with it for a few moments, then leave the window to go around to the back. John had first called in what he'd seen by radio, then he himself had crept to the cottage and around the back.

At that point, I suddenly remembered the *plop* thing and we all went for a look. It was a fairly large-sized piece of raw meat. Mike had John carefully put it in a plastic bag, saying "I think the lab will tell us that it's either laced with a quick-acting anesthetic or poison."

I felt like growling myself at that point. I've always found it emotionally easier to deal with an attack on me than one on Silver.

91

Once everyone else had finally left, Mike surprised me by suggesting that I go back to bed while he would stay and sleep on the couch in the great room; not that either of us would get much more sleep that night.

"You think someone else will come?" I asked.

"No. I don't, but let's not get complacent. Your Mr. Big seems to be quick to act and quite ruthless, and I don't think we should take the chance that he or she sends someone more professional than these two idiots you keeping running into." And with that, he began rummaging around for blankets while I went to find him a spare pillow.

Before settling in, he too pulled a snub-nose revolver from a holster concealed under his large and wildly-coloured Hawaiian shirt saying "There are still two marked police cars parked out front. I think that between that and you, Silver, and I in here we'll be able to 'hold the fort' for the night."

Saturday May 10

I suppose I must have gotten some sleep, although it didn't feel like it. In the morning, I made breakfast for Mike and I and thanked him for staying-over to watch out for me.

"My pleasure," said Mike, with a smile. "I seem to recall you looking after me when I nearly killed myself a few years ago[46]."

"Seems like a long time ago," I replied with a smile of my own. "A lot of 'water under the bridge' since then, for both of us."

He nodded at me over his coffee cup, remembering.

"By the way," he said, changing the subject, "yesterday, we had a look at the videotape from the museum. It has a pretty good clip of the two men grabbing you, and their faces became visible when they turned to carry you out. Between the mounting pile of evidence against them, and the fact that they just breached their bail conditions, I'm sure the JP will revoke their bail and they'll remain locked up for a while now."

I wondered what Mr. Big would do next, and why whomever it was had been so rash.

After breakfast Mike went to get dressed for work, while Silver and I took my truck for a drive to CFB Moncton to get the Geiger Counter. This was only about twenty minutes away and was very scenic and relaxing, which helped me wind down from the excitement of the previous night's activities and the trauma of having shot someone (no matter how well deserved).

At the Canadian Forces Base, one of the guards at the main entrance gave me precise directions for the building Don had told me to go to so I had no trouble finding it. Inside, we were met by an army sergeant in combat uniform which, at the time consisted of olive-drab shirt and pants – each with two large cargo pockets - and black combat boots. He had the Geiger Counter ready for me. It was packed in a green canvas shoulder bag, and he took everything out to show me that it contained one Geiger Counter, one manual, two types of detector wands (on in the classic cylinder-style and the other in a pancake-style[47]), a set of batteries, plus a spare set of batteries.

I was familiar with this kind of instrument, so I thanked the sergeant, signed for the equipment, and left.

Since I was already out on the road, I decided to drive to the marinas in the area to see how many fishing boats might have white hulls and a dark-coloured wheelhouses. There were more than a dozen marinas and yacht clubs on the Northumberland Strait that hosted such fishing boats. It took most of the rest of the day but I visited most of them, ranging from Pointe-du-Chêne to as far north as Caraquet. As I did so, I looked at fishing boats of vaguely similar size to Marlea's but ignored the much bigger boats: the ones in which the fishers would go out into the ocean for days at a time. Most of the 'standard' fishing boats were about 38 to 44 feet (11.5 to 13.5m) in length, and I also looked at the ones that were in the lower 30s (9m) and upper 40s (12m) and 50s (15m).

I knew that the boats would be painted in a variety of colours, but the distribution of colours I saw was a surprise. Out of 196 boats, nearly half - 97 - had substantially white hulls and nearly another half – 95 – had substantially white wheelhouses with fairly dark hulls (mostly blue, black, dark yellow, turquoise, and so on). Only two had dark wheelhouses and dark hulls, and only two had dark wheelhouses and white hulls.

That meant that, of the boats I saw, only two matched the description from the satellite imagery. One was quite far north, at Bathurst, for which I made a note of its number, searched out the owner and had a pleasant chat but didn't learn anything that seemed useful beyond the fact that the owner agreed that his boat's colour scheme was rare in those parts.

Laurie Schramm

The other boat of interest I'd seen before: it was Abe's *April Rose*, the boat that had been moored right in front of Marlea's the day we went diving. I'd already met Abe and had seen his boat up close without noting anything suspicious there either. So far, then, this lead was getting me nowhere. Of course, I knew that some boats would have been out at sea and not moored when I went by, but it was somehow reassuring to find that there weren't going to be a massive number that matched the CIA's description.

Since my journeys had taken me back to the Shediac area in the afternoon, I also went to the town's fire station. The chief happened to be in and I asked whether they had any commercial or sport SCUBA divers in the area, and whether they filled air tanks for SCUBA divers. He said that the nearest commercial diving companies were based in Fredericton and St. John, and that there was another one on PEI. As far as sport divers, yes, they did fill tanks for sport divers. I asked if they kept a log for these, and if I could see it.

The log was by their air compressor station. Having myself had air tanks filled many times at dive shops and fire stations, I was impressed with their operation at this station. Their log documented both maintenance and tank-filling usage, so I could see that their modern-looking compressor and filters were being well maintained. The log entries for tank fills were quite detailed as well, noting the date, size and type of tank (that is, whether steel or aluminum), the date of the tank's last hydrostatic test, and the final filling pressure. This was done regardless of whether they were filling the firefighters' breathing-apparatus tanks, or sport divers' SCUBA tanks. In the latter case, they also noted the customers' names, addresses, and certification types and numbers.

They clearly didn't fill tanks very often, as the binder had entries for the previous six months. Scanning the sheets, and ignoring the firefighters' tank fills, I could see several instances in which pairs of divers had brought their tanks in to be filled once or twice, in each case within a period of a week, and mostly in April and May. That would be consistent with visiting sport divers. I only found one name that recurred many times and that also involved dates in each month. In fact, someone named Duncan Moray seemed to be regularly diving several days a week, using up two tanks at a time, in most weeks of each month going all the way back to December. I made a note of the diver's name and address.

94

"Looks like you have a regular here," I said to the deputy chief, pointing to the entries. "Do you know anything about the diver?"

He didn't, but he took me to the firefighter that did the regular maintenance on the compressor system and also did much of the tank filling.

When questioned, he said that he didn't really know the diver but that he said that he was searching for a lost wreck somewhere out in the strait. The only things he was able to add were that the diver dove alone and that he didn't live far away, but was not a resident of Shediac or Pointe-du-Chêne.

Mike and I had planned to meet and compare notes that afternoon, so I put off going to see the diver and went to meet Mike instead.

"Well, bail was revoked for Campbell and Bourque, your Mutt and Jeff characters," Mike began, when we were together in his office. "They breached their original bail conditions by coming after you, and we've added more charges now too so they'll stay locked up for a while."

"That's good," I said. "Did you get anywhere on Mr. Big's local company?"

"Yes and no. Someone's being tricky. ABC Shediac Import and Export is provincially incorporated, and it's owned by a numbered company that's federally incorporated. So, I had someone call Ottawa to check into it. Turns out the federally-registered company lists two principals, both of whom live in Montréal. Both people are known to the local police as being connected with organized crime, but both have been able to avoid being of convicted of anything by having intermediaries do their dirty work for them. Obviously neither of them is going to volunteer anything to us."

"So. A dead end then."

"Yes, but I've asked the JP for a warrant to put a wire-tap on the company's phone here in town. If we get the warrant, I'll have the tap installed tonight."

After my meeting with Mike, Silver needed a walk and I felt too tired to cook supper so we went for a walk along the beach and stopped in at The Lobster's Brew to see what the café had in the way of food. They had fresh croissants and their own take on the classic Lox bagel. In this case it was a croissant filled with smoked salmon and cream cheese, plus red onions, capers, and a touch of dill. It was so good I ordered a second one and gave Silver some of the smoked salmon from each one. The owner, Jean Friend, came over to our table at one point, ostensibly to see if we were enjoying our meal but clearly trying to tease out more information about Sharon and my diving trip.

"I hear it was you and your friend that brought up the rusty steel drum that's in the museum," she began. "Marlea told me all about it before she went to the bar downtown to tell the rest of the town about it."

Great, I thought. There seemed no point in denying it, so I didn't. To the next series of probes, I confirmed that it was from some kind of large aircraft, said that no, I didn't know what kind, nor what was in the drum, and that I expected that Wade, the museum curator would find some kind of expert to have a look at it. After a bit more verbal fencing she was called away and I gratefully took the opportunity to pay the bill and slip back to the beach.

As Silver and I walked back to the cottage, I mused about our conversation, unable to decide whether Jean was just nosy or something more than that.

When we reached the cottage, I noticed a marked police car parked out front. It was empty – left there as a signal to discourage any more break-in attempts. Mike had taken to parking police cars in front of the cottage, sometimes with a constable present and other times simply left standing empty in a seemingly random pattern. This was his way of trying to protect me when he didn't have the resources for a full-on security detail.

After Campbell and Bourque, my Mutt and Jeff characters, had been arrested for the second time, following their break-in to my cottage, Mike's investigators had been able to prod the less intelligent one – Campbell, aka Mutt – into blurting out that no one had told them to come after me that night, it had been their idea to make up for their failure when they'd kidnapped me the previous day. Sensing victory, the investigators had tried to pry further but apparently Mutt had abruptly realized what he had just said, came to his senses and clammed-up other than asking for a lawyer. Mike said that he wasn't convinced, hence his caution about protecting me from another attack, but to me it sounded like exactly the kind of thing these two clowns might have done in order to get some kind of forgiveness from whomever was paying them.

***

Meanwhile, earlier that day:

Ringgg… ring. *"Good morning, ABC Shediac Import and Export,"* said Coralie Lessoile, *ABC's receptionist and secretary.*

"It's me, Coralie," said a male voice.

"Ohhh! Good morning, sir."

"Any messages today?"

"No sir but… well, the police were here."

"The police? What did they want?"

"They wanted to know about the company and its business, and who owned it."

"What did you tell them?" asked the voice, in a lower tone.

"I gave them the same import and export description I give to everyone, and I told them I have no idea who owns it. When they asked who my boss is, I explained that I was hired through an agency and that I don't know who he is."

There was a short laugh. *"Then they asked how we communicate. Right?"*

"Yes, sir. I told them the truth, that you call in at intervals for messages and to give me instructions, that you pick up or drop off packages when I'm not here, and that anything else you need is usually in our files."

"Good. Anything else?"

"Oh yes, they also asked whether we have ever had any dealings with Marcel and Noah. I said that I wasn't sure, but that Marcel sometimes called to leave messages for you. They asked what kind of messages, and I said that I didn't pay any attention to the details so I don't remember."

"Fine. You just keep it up and eventually the police will go snoop somewhere else. I'll call you again tomorrow."

"OK Sir, thank you."

Later that evening:

Knock, knock… knock. *Coralie went to her apartment door to see who was knocking.* "Oh, it's you sir!" *she said in surprise.*

"Evening Coralie. I know it's unusual for me to come here, but I just wanted to make sure the police snooping around hasn't upset you."

"No sir. It's fine. Really. I was a little worried at first, but I guess it's all just routine."

"That's right. When they go around questioning everyone, it's because they have no idea what they should be looking for. Besides, you haven't done anything wrong and I haven't done anything wrong, so there's no need for you to worry. Right?"

"Yes sir. I understand that reason you do things in such secrecy is to make sure your competitors can't get ahead of you. That's just good business."

"Exactly. Now, as long as I'm here do you mind if I come in for a moment and we discuss what you should say if the police come back trying to dig for more? It might set your mind at ease."

"Yes sir, that would be helpful. Please come in."

As the man entered the apartment, he paused for a moment and coughed. "My throat must be a little dry. Do you mind getting me a glass of water Coralie?"

"No, of course not. I'll get it."

Coralie walked to the kitchen, opened a cupboard and selected a glass, then moved to the sink to fill it. As she did so, she didn't notice that the man had followed her into the kitchen. So it was a surprise for her to suddenly feel something come down over her head that completely blocked her sight and covered her face. As she reflexively dropped the glass and put both hands to her face, her first impressions were: cloth, clingy, can't breathe! Have to remove the cloth!!

Unfortunately, she couldn't remove the cloth because someone stronger had placed their hands over hers and used them to keep the cloth pressed firmly against her mouth and nose. Panicking, she tried twisting, rocking, and even bending her body in an attempt to get away but, even with her adrenalin surging, she was no match for her assailant.

It wasn't long before she lost consciousness, after which the man released his grip, allowing her body to slump to the floor. Dragging her body to the bathroom, he began to fill the bathtub with water.

Other than the running bathwater, the only significant sound during the entire encounter had been that of the water glass breaking when it fell into the sink.

***

Sunday May 11

The next morning, I woke up to a beautiful red sunrise that immediately made me think of the sailors' maxim[48]:

Red sky at night. Sailors delight.
Red sky in the morning. Sailors take warning.

I'm not superstitious by nature, but it did make me wonder whether there might be more trouble ahead. In any case, my plan for the day was to go looking for the diver, Duncan Moray, whom I'd identified with the help of the fire department. His address was listed as being in Cap-Pelé a coastal village[49] about 22 km (13.5 mi) to the east of Shediac, so it was a short drive.

There was no answer when I knocked on his door, but a neighbour told me that he was usually to be found on his boat down at the docks. *Interesting that he has a boat*, I thought. Unfortunately, this wasn't one of those small villages with a single dock. There was no mistaking the fact that fishing is the big industry there, as Cap-Pelé had a large number of fish-processing plants that I later discovered produced smoked herring. What it meant for me was that there were a number of docks and quite a few boats coming and going.

It wasn't too difficult for all that, as I simply went from boat to boat until I found a local resident that knew who Duncan Moray was and where his boat was usually tied up. As I approached the indicated dock, there was a Cape Islander with a dark blue wheelhouse and a white hull with blue gunwales. I had a feeling that would be the boat, and I was right.

There was a young man working on something in the stern, who looked up when I approached the boat and called his name.

"Yes, that's me," he said after what might have been a moment's hesitation.

"That's a nice-looking boat you have there. Would you mind taking a moment and showing it to me?"

"OK," he said, then he paused for sure and, looking meaningfully at my uniform, added "Is this an official visit?"

"Only in the sense that I'd like to ask you a few questions... and I really am interested in your boat."

He seemed fine with that, but he had paled a little, I thought. In any case, he invited me aboard and took some pride in showing me around. There were two interesting things in the wheelhouse, a rack holding two aluminum SCUBA tanks, and a dual-pen strip-chart recorder. "What's that?" I asked, pointing to the recorder.

"Side-scan sonar," he said proudly, and proceeded to explain how it worked and what it did, although not as well as Marlea had done.

"So, you use it to search for shipwrecks?" I asked.

He nodded.

"And dive for them yourself?" I asked, pointing to the SCUBA tanks.

"Yup."

"Have you found the sunken U-boat I keep hearing about?"

He smiled at that? "If it exists you mean? No, I haven't found it, but I'm going to! I do diving jobs for the local boat owners: propellor replacements, hull cleaning, searching for lost underwater moorings, whatever. Every penny of the money I make goes into this boat, my gear, and the search for the U-boat." He pointed to a stack of books, files, and charts. "I've been doing my research too, and I know pretty well where it should be."

"So, you do think it really exists?"

"I do. Too many people saw the battle that sunk the sub for it to be a myth, and their descriptions don't match anything as simple as gunnery practice, like some people claim."

"Cool, I hope you find it," I said, truthfully, then changed the subject. "Did you hear that a couple of divers found some kind of drums on the wreck of a sunken airplane?"

He didn't say anything for a moment but had instantly turned white as a sheet, then he recovered himself and said "Yes, I did. A couple of women that Marlea Becker took out. They were supposedly looking for the U-boat too."

"Competition for you then?" I asked.

"Not really," he laughed, "from what I heard they were looking in the wrong place if that's what they were after."

"Did you happen to also hear what happened to Ms. Becker?"

He shook his head no.

"She drowned... curious, don't you think?"

He'd turned pale again but only said "What do you mean?"

"Only that she didn't seem to have any injuries and she was a good swimmer. I wonder what happened to her?"

Silence. I could see that he was thinking, but he didn't say anything. Leaving him to think, I thanked him for the tour of his boat, wished him well with his search for the U-boat, and left.

Reflecting on my visit, as I drove away, it seemed to me that I had found both the boat and the diver involved in recovering the steel drums from the sunken airplane. Whether he was involved any deeper remained to be seen. The fact that he'd visibly paled twice during our conversation could be a sign of guilt, but I suspected it was more a sign of fear and I wondered whether he was afraid of Mr. Big.

I decided to head for the Pointe-du-Chêne wharf and see if I could talk to Abe Strong. Having arrived and parked nearby, Silver and I walked along the wharf. Most of the way along the main wharf, in its usual berth, was Abe's blue and white Cape Islander, the *April Rose*. As we approached, Abe gave us a wave from inside the wheelhouse, then came outside to the stern to greet us.

"How're our two newest Mounties doing?" he asked, in his usual hearty manner.

"We're doing fine. Looks like all or most of the boats are in today," I said, gesturing to the various docks, all of which appeared to be filled to capacity.

"Yeah. There's a storm brewing out in the gulf and the water's getting rough. It's still pretty easy going here in the strait but no one's going further out than that without good reason until the storm blows over."

"Red sky in the morning?" I asked.

"You might say that," he said, sounding surprised. "Those old sailors' adages are worth bearing in mind. Far too often they turn out to be right."

"Kind of like farmer' almanacs?" I ventured.

"Mebbe. I wouldn't know about that, I'm just a plain old fisherman."

"I suppose you know most of the fishers and their boats around here?"

"The working boats, yes, but not the pleasure craft. I've lived and fished here all my life. It's not often I pass a lobster, crab, or herring boat I don't know."

"Would you happen to know of anyone in the area that spends a lot of time SCUBA diving? Maybe a wreck or treasure hunter even? Someone I could talk to about the wreck that my friend and I found when Marlea took us out."

"That would be Duncan Moray, has a blue and white Cape Islander. He's a fanatic, always out looking for interesting wrecks and treasures. Has a bee in his bonnet about that U-boat too. Swears he'll be the one to find it and prove the rumours true. He's the only one like that around here, although I don't know about Nova Scotia or the island[50]."

"Duncan stops over here all the time, sometimes for fuel, and sometimes to deliver packages and things. He's a great one for odd jobs – anything that will help finance his next diving trip."

"Do you know what kind of things he delivers?"

"Not really. Someone drives in with a plain-looking van, and he uses a hand-truck to wheel big cardboard boxes down to it." He gestured with his hands to indicate something about two feet (0.6 m) wide and maybe three feet (1 m) tall."

Just large enough to hide one of those steel drums, I thought. "Can you describe the van?"

"Sure. It's a cube van; the kind rental companies offer for people that want to do their own moving. This one used to belong to a rental company too." He mentioned the name of a moving and storage firm that was well-known across North America for its trailer and van rentals. "The name and advertising have been painted out but it has the original colour scheme."

"Thanks," I said. "About the diver. Do you know where he lives? It sounds like I should go talk to him."

"Cap-Pelé. Ask anyone there and they'll direct you. Be warned though. If you admit you're a diver and interested in shipwrecks, he'll talk your ear off!"

I laughed. "Thanks, but I'm interested in shipwrecks too. Maybe I'll be the one to talk his ear off."

There was a pause in the conversation, after which Abe gave me a very direct look. "Found Marlea's killer yet?"

Surprised, I riposted "What makes you think Marlea was killed?"

"Arrgh. All that bilge about her falling overboard and drowning.... Even if she fell overboard, which I would rate as extremely unlikely, she was a strong swimmer and she'd have to have been knocked out to have drowned in the water."

"And you don't think she was knocked out?"

"I know she wasn't, and so do you. Doc Solinsky told me that there wasn't a mark on her anywhere when he examined her."

I sighed. Apparently, there were few secrets in this town. "You're right, I don't believe it either but please keep it to yourself. Whether she was killed accidentally or on purpose, until Sergeant Morrison says otherwise, we're investigating an accidental death."

"You mean, you don't want to spook her killer."

I nodded. "Nor panic him or her either. At least not yet."

"And the reason you're in uniform all of a sudden means you're involved too."

It was a statement, but I nodded.

He stared at me for a moment, then gave a warm smile. "Well, all right then. How can I help?"

"For now, I have a few questions. For starters, did you happen to see Marlea's boat go out last Tuesday?"

"Matter of fact, I did, now that you mention it." He scratched his beard while he thought. "We passed each other in the strait. She was going out and I was coming in."

"Can you remember when and where that was?"

"Mmmm, well, it was late morning but not yet noon, and we passed just the other side of Shediac Island."

I copied this down in my pocket notebook. "Could you see if there was anyone else on board at the time?" I asked, making my voice sound as casual as possible.

"She wasn't alone but I really didn't pay much attention. I only remember thinking that she must be taking someone sightseeing, or maybe fishing. I can't be sure, but I have the impression there were two people on board with her."

"OK," I said, continuing to write. "Can you remember anything about them: male, female, tall, short, light or dark hair, clothes, that kind of thing?".

"Mmmm, not really. They were sitting in the stern, on the port side, with their backs towards me. Nothing stood out about their clothes that I remember... Oh, yes, one was taller than the other. Not saying the taller one was tall, mind, just taller than the other."

"Thanks," I said, continuing to write. *Mutt and Jeff, I'll bet,* I thought to myself.

***

Meanwhile that same day:

Ringgg... ring. *"Hello?"*

"I have another little job for you."

"No. It's too dangerous. There was a Mountie here this morning asking a lot of questions. I didn't say anything, but they might be watching me now and I don't want to get arrested."

"Relax, I'm not asking you to take your boat out and dive on the plane again... Not yet, anyway. I want you to steal the drum that's on display in the Shediac Museum. No one's watching there and there's no security. All you have to do is force a simple lock in the back door, walk in, and carry it out. Right?"

"No! It's too dangerous. I don't want anything more to do with this."

"It isn't wise to anger me you know. Look what happened to Marlea Becker..."

"What do you mean?" said Duncan, sounding really afraid now.

"Well, you don't think she just fell overboard and drowned all by herself, do you?"

Duncan didn't speak, but he made a choking sound.

The caller let it hang in the air between them for a few moments, then continued in a gentler voice. "Look. I know what I'm doing, and it's all been going very well for everyone, right up to this little hitch. Right? I've gotten what I want, and you've been getting the money to put into your boat so you can search for that U-boat of yours. Right? All I need you to do right now is get the drum from the museum for me. I don't care how you do it, just get it. Since you don't need to take your boat out and dive it won't even cost you anything and, I'll tell you what, I'll pay you double for this one. How's that sound? Then, when all this blows over, we'll go back to getting the rest of the drums and you'll have lots more money to show for it. Right?"

An agonized groan could be heard over the line, followed by "All right. You win. I'll get it... leave it in the usual place?"

"The usual place. And your money will be in the usual place too."

Much later that night or, more precisely, 3 am the next morning a shadowy figure walked down an alley behind Main Street. The bars had all closed and the last of the lagging drinkers had finally made their way to wherever they were going to 'sleep it off.' A few doors from the museum, the silence was broken by a sudden shuffling sound, followed by the sight and sound of a stack of cardboard boxes falling over.

The figure froze... and waited, hardly daring to breathe.

Finally, after what seemed like forever but was only a few moments, there was a "Mrrow" and a black cat bolted out from under the boxes, across the alley, and into the narrow space between two buildings.

With a slow exhalation of breath, the figure visibly relaxed, then continued on to the back door of the museum. The door had a locking knob and a deadbolt, but the figure had a crowbar. It was only an ordinary door and a short-throw deadbolt, and they yielded to the crowbar with surprisingly little noise. The figure walked right in.

With the aid of a flashlight, the figure made its way to the section where the recently recovered steel drum was displayed. A single glance assured the figure that this was in fact the intended target. Without further hesitation, the drum was picked up and carried out. On the way out, the figure unlocked the deadbolt from the inside, made sure the doorknob lock was still set, and then closed the door. If the police happened by making door-to-door checks, they would find a door that seemed to be locked as usual.

The figure strode away, carrying the drum and crowbar.

The only living witness was the black cat.

Laurie Schramm

7 PROGRESS

Monday, May 12

"I'm amazed that you kept the surveillance system running" I said to Mike, when Silver and I got to the detachment.

He gave me a Cheshire Cat smile that reminded me so much of my boss, Bob, who frequently did the very same thing. "It was already in place, and we didn't need it for anything else, so we left it where it was and I had someone go over in civvies[51] at intervals to put fresh tapes in. When Wade Kean called to report the theft of the drum from the museum, I was glad we did."

"Did anything show up on tape?"

Another grin. "Come see." He led me down a hallway to a meeting room in which stood a tall, wheeled cart bearing a large Sony U-matic[52] videorecorder and a colour monitor

"Morning John," I said to Const. Hardisty, who was advancing a tape while consulting a notebook.

"Morning Alex. Come see what we caught." He continued while Mike and I took our seats. "I've been reviewing the latest tape. There's nothing to see until just after 3 am, then the action begins." With a flourish, he hit the play button.

The first thing we saw was the steel drum on display, together with the posters about the rumoured U-boat. Although the main museum lights were off, the drum was illuminated by the beam from some kind of dedicated display light that was coming from somewhere high up and to the right of the camera. After a moment, we could see a flashlight beam waving around, followed by the appearance of a figure moving towards the display. The intruder had their back to us and had a hood pulled up over their head. Without delay, the intruder picked up the drum, turned, and started to move away.

"Stop!" said Mike.

John must have been waiting for this and had his finger on the pause button, because he immediately pushed it, freezing the image.

"Bingo!" I said.

The still image showed the figure turned almost directly towards the camera, with the drum cradled in his hands and his almost fully visible within the raised hood.

"You recognize him?" asked Mike.

"Duncan Moray. He lives in Cap-Pelé. He's a SCUBA diver, has a boat matching the description I was given, and apparently does freelance diving jobs for boat owners around the area. I just talked to him yesterday morning. I think it was him that brought the missing steel drums up from the plane wreck. It might even have been him that found the wreck in the first place. He seems to be on shipwreck research to guide his dives."

"Well, we have enough to pick him up and it might be safer for him if we did."

"What do you mean?"

"I didn't have a chance to tell you yet, but Coralie Lessoile was found dead in her apartment this morning."

"Who's that?"

"She was the receptionist/secretary at ABC Shediac Import and Export, the office on Main Street that Bourque – that's the one you've been calling Jeff – phoned to get a lawyer. Anyway, she was supposed to have met her sister for an early breakfast before work today. When she didn't show up, her sister went to her apartment. When no one answered her door, she got worried and had the building manager open the door.... They found her floating face-down in her bathtub."

"Not an accident?" I asked.

"It looked like it, but there were no signs of injury."

"Just like with Marlea Becker."

"Right. We had Dr. Solinsky examine the body before it was moved. He said that it looked like she might have slipped in the tub, hit her head and drowned. I don't buy that because, as I said, there were no signs of injury. We'll know more after the autopsy, but it does explain something else. We got that wiretap I wanted on the office phone but there were no more calls in or out since then. I was beginning to suspect that someone had somehow found out about the wire tap but now I think there were no more calls because your Mr. Big decided to silence Coralie."

I nodded. "And it we don't move fast Duncan Moray will be the next victim."

"Yes," Mike agreed. "Hardisty, take someone with you and arrest this Duncan Moray before he disappears on us, or worse."

"Quite a crime-wave our little town is having this summer," he said after John Hardisty had left.

"Hmmm, but there's a pattern. We just need to figure out a little bit more. I think we should search Moray's house and boat. I doubt we'll find anything linking him to Mr. Big, but we might find evidence linking him to the other barrels from the plane wreck. In fact, there might even be a barrel or two tucked away there besides the one from the museum."

"Agreed. I'll ask for the warrant and radio you when we're on our way over there."

I had a feeling it might be a busy day ahead so, since I had a bit of time, I decided to take Silver for a walk along the beach since I was going to have to return to the cottage anyway in order to collect the Geiger Counter I'd borrowed from the military.

Having taken the walk from the cottage down to, and along the length of, Parlee Beach we arrived at the Lobster's Brew where we sat out in my favourite spot on their deck for coffee, realizing as we did so that I was risking another fencing match with the owner, Jean.

As it happened, I was barely able to get my first sip of coffee in before she came over to my table.

"I just heard about the nuclear bomb being stolen from the museum. What are you people doing about it?" By 'you people' I presumed she meant the police.

"Yes," I confirmed, "it seems to have been stolen from the museum last night but it's not a nuclear weapon. It's too small, for one thing. What we are doing about it is trying to find the thief and also the steel drum."

"Do you know who did it?"

"I can't comment on an ongoing investigation, but we have some ideas of our own that are being pursued." I tried, probably unsuccessfully not to sound mysterious.

She tried a few more approaches, but eventually realized that I wasn't going to give her any interesting tidbits and abruptly returned to the inside of the café.

When Silver and I left the café, I decided we should walk a bit further before turning back so we went on the Pointe-du-Chêne Wharf. As we strolled along the wharf, looking at the fishing boats, I was hailed by Abe Strong.

"You remember that cube van I was telling you about yesterday?" he began.

"Sure. The former moving van, right?"

"That's the one. Thought you might like to know that I saw it again early this morning."

"Really. Here at the wharf?"

"No, it was parked at the back of the Lobster's Brew."

"When was that?"

"Mmmm, must have been about 5:30 in the morning, give or take. I happened to see it when I drove by on my way to park here. I come at about the same time every day so I can get the boat out to my traps in the gulf."

"Did you see anyone?"

"No. It just struck me as odd because it's not Jean's van and the café doesn't open anywhere near that early in the morning."

We chatted briefly about general things, but he didn't seem to have any other news related to my investigation so I eventually thanked him and Silver and I left to walk back to the cottage.

As we were walking, the radio crackled. It was Mike advising me that he had the warrant and he and Const. Hardisty were on their way to Duncan Moray's house. I said that I was just a few minutes walk from my cottage and that I'd meet them there.

"Did you manage to pick Moray up?" I asked.

"Yes, we did. He's in cells now. Probably the safest place he could possibly be right now and I suspect he knows it."

There were two police cars parked at Duncan's when I got there, and both Mike and John Hardisty were already inside searching. When I found them, they said that they'd found exactly nothing in the house. There was a garage in the back yard, which turned out to be a combination workshop/garage. There was a fair amount of diving gear there, including the things you'd expect a wreck hunter to have: large and small crowbars, marker floats, polypropylene rope for anchoring floats and lifting things from the bottom, and so on, but nothing for the kind we were looking for. I even went over the garage with my borrowed Geiger Counter, but it only ever registered background radiation at about 0.21 microsieverts per hour, which is essentially the average across Canada[53].

"No barrels anywhere, not even the one from the museum," said Mike, disgustedly. "That was fast work. Where could it have gone already?"

"Maybe he quickly handed it over to Alex's Mr. Big," said John.

"Unless Duncan Moray is Mr. Big," added Mike.

"I considered him a suspect too," I said, "but I have some new information from just this morning." I told them about my conversation with Abe Strong.

"So, you think the café is being used the way spies use a blind drop," said Mike.

"Could be. The Lobster's Brew is in a very convenient location, and a van backed-up there while someone moves large cardboard boxes around with a hand-truck is going to look pretty natural, even outside of their opening hours."

"Well, let's go look at Moray's boat before we make that leap," said Mike.

Duncan Moray's blue and white Cape Islander was still tied up at the same dock I'd seen it before. It was gently swaying in the water and there was no one there. When we boarded the boat Mike and John disappeared inside to search the wheelhouse, engine, and other cabin spaces while Silver stayed with me while I surveyed the deck for radiation. Up near the bow the Geiger Counter registered only background radiation again, as did the wheelhouse. The open deck area in the stern was another matter entirely.

The Geiger Counter, which inside the boat had given off a slow series of clicks and a dial reading of about 0.20 microsieverts per hour, began to click a bit faster around the edges of the deck at the rear of the stern. The dial reading moved up to 2.1.

Aha, I thought.

"Find something?" asked Mike, as if he'd read my mind.

"Yes. The radiation level is ten-times the background back here. He probably opened up the first drum he recovered and dumped a couple of kilograms out to see what it was."

"Is the level dangerous?"

"No. It's elevated. No mistake there. But it's not at a safety concern level."

"OK. Well, we're finished here then. When I get back to the office, I'll have someone check with motor vehicle records for vans of the type you described."

"Right, I'll join you after I finish making notes and a sketch of where the radiation levels are high."

By the time I got back to Shediac the morning had almost disappeared and Mike suggested we chat over lunch. Since it was on the early side of lunch-time we were able to find a quiet table on an outdoor patio so we'd be able to continue discussing the case.

"We just received the preliminary autopsy report before you arrived," he said, passing over a thin file folder. He gave me a summary as I flipped through his notes.

"We already knew that she was last seen late Monday afternoon. The pathologist puts the time of death at some time that evening. Subject to the results from the lab tests that won't be available for a while, the rest of the news is basically the same as we got for Ms. Becker. Coralie Lessoile died from asphyxiation, but she didn't drown. Her lungs were dry, no abnormal water in the stomach, no indication of any other health problems, no cuts, no bruises, no needle marks, nothing."

"So, like we thought: our Mr. Big struck again."

"Seems like it. Where are you at on suspects?"

I took out my notebook and selected a page.

"OK. Motive is probably as simple as money, so from that point of view it could be anyone. Here's my list, in no particular order:

o   Campbell and Bourque, aka Mutt and Jeff, seem like underlings. I think they murdered Marlea Becker on Mr. Big's orders, but I believe them when they claim that they came after me of their own volition in order to make amends with Mr. Big. With them in jail, I wonder whether Mr. Big murdered Coralie Lessoile personally. He might have been the only one she'd open her door to that late at night.

o Abe Strong has a boat matching that from the satellite surveillance imagery, and he's fully capable of taking divers to the wreck site. On the other hand, he seemed quite open when interviewed, and he volunteered the information on spotting the cube van at the café, although that could have been misdirection.

o Dr. Bruce Solinsky is interested in aviation and has airplane models in his office, including one of a Boeing Clipper. Also, he keeps showing up at deaths and suggesting they're accidents,

o Jean Friend has been quite nosy about the name and whereabouts of my friend Sharon, and also about what I know about the steel drum that was in the museum. On top of that, we now have Abe's sighting of the cube van outside her café very early in the morning after the theft from the museum,

o Wade Kean has an interest in Pointe-du-Chêne's flying boat history and has posters on it in his museum and he's also interested in sunken shipwrecks in the area including the fabled U-boat. On the other hand, you'd expect that kind of interest from a museum curator. On the other hand, would he have sent Duncan Moray to steal the drum from his own museum knowing you had video surveillance set up?"

"He might not be aware of that," Mike interjected. "I may have given him the impression that we removed all the video equipment after you were attacked. Unless he actually went into the closet to check, he may not know it was still there and running when the theft occurred."

"You're becoming devious in your old age," I teased.

He smiled. "Let's just say that while you were learning from me, way back on your first posting, I learned some things from you too. Deviousness was one if them. But I interrupted. Please continue."

"OK. Here's the rest:

o Dr. Levi Murray, aka The Professor, has an interest in science and technology and I have a feeling he may be involved somehow, but it might only be peripherally. When

I interviewed him, he seemed to be holding things back, but I don't know what or why,

o Finally, Duncan Moray is a wreck- and treasure-hunting SCUBA diver. He's out diving a lot according to the fire department, he has a boat that matches the satellite surveillance images, and the deck at the stern of his boat has radiation levels consistent with spilled uranium oxide. He's been seen at the Pointe-du-Chêne wharf delivering boxes of about the right size from his boat, and now he's stolen a drum from the museum."

"But you don't think Moray's the murderer?" Mike prompted.

"No," I sighed. "He stole from the museum and he stole the drums from the plane wreck, which belong to the U.S. government. But no, you're right, I see him as just another underling."

"Hmmm. And now?"

"Now? Well, unless Duncan Moray decides to co-operate, I suggest we look for the cube van, and ask for a search warrant for the Lobster's Brew to see if we can find radiation or a drum or two."

Mike agreed to have someone get the registration information for vans matching our description and also to ask for the search warrant. I could have made the warrant request myself, but it seemed better to have Mike do it since he had an existing good relationship with the local JP whereas I was a visiting stranger.

"What are you going to do next?" he asked.

"I think I'm going to take Silver for a drive to CFB Chatham."

He nodded. I didn't have to explain why. As I turned to leave, a thought suddenly struck me. "Who has the contract to deliver meals to the prisoners in cells?"

Mike's eye widened as the implication struck him. "I don't know. It moves around each time we put it up for bids. I'll check as soon as I get back to the office."

During the Second World War, there had been an RCAF Station near Chatham[54], the forerunner to CFB Chatham. The base was just over 120 km (76 mi), so an hour-and-a-half's pleasant drive had us checking-in at the main gate. I'd called ahead to ask for a brief chat with the base commander (a colonel), so I was given directions and then waved in.

After parking to the side of the indicated office building, the first thing I had to do after getting out of my truck was put my hands over my ears as a formation of three CF-101 Voodoo fighter jets screamed overhead at an uncomfortably low altitude. I decided I'd quickly tire of trying to get any work done in an environment where that was happening all the time.

Anyway, sitting in the colonel's office I explained my interest in the 1945 downing of a Boeing Clipper, on a military mission, some 80 nautical miles east of the northern tip of PEI. Since the airbase would have been the closest to that location plus the fact that the plane was attempting to reach Pointe-du-Chêne, I wondered whether it would have been their search-and-rescue aircraft that were sent out.

"Sounds logical," said the colonel, as he went to pull a file from one of the many filing cabinets located in an adjacent office. "During the Second World War, the station here was home to two bomber-reconnaissance squadrons, a flight training school, and an air observer school," he said, reading from the file. "Air observers were what we now call navigators.

"Anyway, the bomber-reconnaissance squadrons were only here in 1942 and 1943, and the flight training school ran from 1941 to 1942, but the No. 10 Air Observer School operated here between 1941 and the end of April, 1945. So, if any search aircraft were sent out from here, they'd probably have been Avro Ansons[55] from the air-observer school."

"Is that likely?" I asked.

"Could be. If there was bad weather like you say, then it would have come down to which air stations were close enough, had pilots and aircraft available, and had enough visibility to conduct air operations."

"Is there a way to check?"

He nodded. "The military never throws anything away. Sergeant?" he called out. There was a creaking sound as someone rose from a desk chair in the adjoining office, then a Sergeant appeared in the doorway.

"This is Corporal Houston. Take her to the archives and see if you can find the daily diaries for No. 10 Air Observer School in 1945."

"Yes Sir," she said.

Thanking the colonel, I got up to leave and motioned Silver to follow.

"Happy to co-operate. Good luck," he said.

As the Sergeant led me down the hallway, she turned to face me and put out her hand to shake, saying "Helen."

"Hi. I'm Alex and this is my partner, Silver."

"Our older records are in the basement of the next building. There are gaps in some of the files, but we'll see what we can find."

The basement of the next building didn't just have records; it had a LOT of records. There were rows of multi-tiered shelving units that seemed to extend forever.

"Are you looking for a specific date?"

I gave her the exact date in April of 1945 that I was interested in.

"OK, that helps." She led me down one of the aisles, glancing at the boxes from time to time until finally she stopped at a particular shelf and began reading the box labels more carefully. Eventually, she pulled a box out and led me down a side aisle at the end of which were several plain tables and chairs. Placing the box onto one of the tables, she opened it and began riffling through the index tabs on the thick file folders it contained, then pulled one out and began flipping through the pages.

"Here it is."

The page was headed:

<u>SECRET</u>

DAILY DIARY

OF <u>No. 10 Air Observer School, Chatham, N.B.</u>

Underneath, in neat rows, were typed brief summaries of the daily activities for about a week and a half, spanning the date I wanted[56]. For that date, I read: "Flying details cancelled due to bad weather. Exception granted for search-and-rescue flight in A.M.; F/Lt. D.G. Murray...." It went on to give Bale's service number, but otherwise that was the entire entry for the day.

"Thank you. Is there any chance you'd have the log books of Flight Lieutenant Murray?"

"That's a bit more iffy. Some pilots kept the briefest logs they could get away with, some kept extensive logs, and others kept two logs – a brief official one and a more detailed personal one. To make matters worse, some of the logs were lost or destroyed, for various reasons, before making it into the archives.... But don't give up," she added, seeing my disappointed expression. "We'll take a look."

After replacing the box of Unit Diaries back where it belonged, she led me to a different row of shelving units and briskly walked down the row until she came to the section she wanted. Then she went more slowly along a row of boxes mouthing letters as she did so. "La to Li, Lj to Lr, Ls to Lz... here we are, Ms to Mz." Slipping the latter box from its shelf we went back to the same table as before.

"Let's have a look. Morgan, Morris, Morton, Muir, here we are, Murray, D.G. – Dennis George. Hmmm, looks like we have just three of his logs. Of course, he may only have been posted here for a short period of time. Let's check the dates. What was the date you were looking for?"

"April 9, 1945," I told her.

"Yes, here we are, it should be in this one." She lifted one out and moved the box aside so we could leaf through the log together. "Let's see now, yes, April, 1945, and the day..." She stopped flipping pages at the Flight Lieutenant's entry for the 9th of April, the day the Boeing Clipper ditched into the ocean.

We read the entry together, which succinctly outlined the mission, serial number of the Avro Anson flown, names of the other crewmembers, takeoff time and meteorological conditions, and the search.

"That's it!" I said excitedly. "He actually gives the latitudes and longitudes of the best estimate of the plane's location plus those for the grid squares they actually searched."

"That's what you were looking for?" Helen asked.

"That's half of it. The other half begins like this: how often in the past couple of years, say, would someone have come here wanting to root through old logs and diaries like I just did?"

"Probably never. It's certainly very rare."

"OK. If a person does come, and you agree to let them look, do you log it somewhere?"

"I see where you're heading. Yes, we do. Come back to the office and I'll show you."

After replacing the logs in the box and the box on its shelf, we walked back to the main building. Back in her office, Helen went to another of the ubiquitous filing cabinets and opened a drawer and extracted a ring-binder. The she opened it up on her desk, saying

"We log records in and out, and visits to view records. I'll be recording yours after you leave for example."

"If you have what I'm after it would be a civilian, if that helps."

"Yes. That will eliminate most of the visits actually. Now then, let's see. The last time a civilian came to view records was'..." There was a delay as she scanned page after page. "Ah. Here's a series of visits from last year. It was a military historian from Ottawa."

"No. Not those."

"OK, then." Another pause while more pages were scanned and flipped. "Actually, that takes us back eighteen months. A Professor Levi Murray – that's the same last name as your pilot. The professor's from the College of Cape Breton."

"That's it, but his address wasn't in Cape Breton, was it?"

"No, you're right. It lists an address in Shediac. How did you know?"

I smiled grimly. "I've met him."

8 WHO KNOWS WHAT EVIL LURKS[57]

By the time I got back to the Shediac detachment things were beginning to move quickly. I filled Mike in on the results of my trip to Chatham, and he had news of his own.

"We got a break on the cube van," he began. "According to motor vehicles there are eleven vans of that type registered in the area. Four of them are registered to an outfit that rents moving vans and trailers, and one to a more traditional moving and storage company. I think we can cross those off the list, but I've sent a constable out to track them down and make sure they don't look like the one Abe Strong described. The other six are registered to people or companies. None of the names match anything we know about, but I have another constable out tracking them down."

"Great. Anything else?"

"Yes. Who do you think has the current contract to deliver meals to the prisoners in cells?"

"No…"

"Yes. The Lobster's Brew."

"My God! The lunch that was brought in for the prisoners!"

"Don't worry. There are four people in cells right now, Campbell and Bourque, Moray, and a thoroughly disreputable-looking constable who's been 'arrested' so he can sit there and listen if the other three start talking to each other. We haven't let Moray make any phone calls yet so we can be fairly confident that no one knows he's here yet."

"Hmmm. Unless someone saw him being arrested or brought

in."

"Right, which is why the meal that was delivered for him has been sealed and is sitting in our fridge, where it's going to stay for a while. Instead, I had someone buy similar dishes from a nearby restaurant and we gave them those."

"Ah ha. When are you going to let him make his call?"

"It's probably just been done, and this time we got a warrant and recorded the call."

We were interrupted by a knock at Mike's office door. It was a constable I hadn't yet met. After introductions, Mike waved him in and he shut the door behind him as he did so.

"He made his call Sarge, and it was to the same law firm that Campbell and Bourque used. He asked specifically for the same lawyer too."

"That's interesting," Mike reflected. "He didn't call the office downtown that Campbell and Bourque called but went straight to the lawyer."

"Sounds like he knows Mr. Big well enough to know who his lawyer is. Maybe he knows more than that," I hazarded.

"I wouldn't be at all surprised. Anything else?" the latter was directed at the constable.

"Not really. Once he got the lawyer, he basically just told him what had happened. Here's a copy of my notes." He handed over a couple of photocopy pages.

Thanking the constable, Mike let him go, then caught me staring off into space. "Penny for your thoughts?"

"I'm not sure they're worth a penny, but let's say the lawyer calls Mr. Big to get instructions. Mr. Big suddenly knows that Duncan Moray has been arrested for stealing the drum from the museum. He's going to be worried, and we already know that when he gets worried, he doesn't lose any time trying to make sure people are silenced."

"I agree," Mike said. "I suggest we..." He was interrupted by Const. Hardisty.

"Sorry to interrupt you, but I thought you'd like to know that only one van registered in the area matches the description – and we just found it!"

***

Later that afternoon, a cube van drove into the Pointe-du-Chêne parking lot adjacent to Parlee Beach. It approached the short walkway that led to the rear of the Lobster's Brew, turned around, and backed up to the curb.

A familiar figure stepped out from the driver's side of the van, reached back to retrieve a small bag, then walked purposefully to the back door of the café. The door was apparently locked, because the figure removed a key ring from a pocket, chose a key, unlocked the door, and went in.

After about ten minutes the door opened again and the figure, still carrying the small bag, exited the café, strode back towards the van, and stopped to unlock the driver-side door.

"Hi Doc!" I said, having stepped out of my own truck, which I'd parked nearby after he'd disappeared into the café.

His head turned sharply at my greeting, but if he was startled or worried, he hid it well.

"Oh, hello," he replied. "Are you two still sniffing around for information on Marlea Becker?"

"No. I think we've got her death figured out – she was murdered."

"Murdered! You must be kidding. I examined her myself, right where she washed-up on the beach."

"Yes, and you were right that she asphyxiated, but wrong about her drowning. It was caused by someone blocking-off her breathing. You can read the autopsy report sometime if you like."

"Yes. Thank you. I'd definitely like to do that." He was a cool one all right. His voice and demeanor sounded normal and even his skin tone hadn't changed.

"Turns out she died almost exactly the same way that Coralie Lessoile was."

"Who's that?"

"You don't know her?"

"I don't think so." He furrowed his brow, as if in thought. "Should I?"

"I would think so. She was your receptionist/secretary at the ABC Shediac Import and Export office in the old Tait & Melanson Block on Main Street downtown."

"I think this conversation's about over," he said, opening the door to the van and tossing his bag in.

"I'm afraid not. You're under arrest Dr. Solinsky. You're going to have to come with me."

"I think not," he said, turning back towards me. As he did so, several things happened at once.

I motioned to Silver to sweep-out to one side and flank him.

Solinsky pulled a handgun from inside his sport jacket.

I had wondered whether he'd bring a gun, so I was ready to draw my own at the same time he drew his.

By this time each of us was pointed out guns directly at each other - he standing tall and holding a snub-nosed revolver in a casual, one-handed manner, and me from a crouch with both hands on my own gun. It looked like a .38 or .45 calibre; difficult to hold steady, especially in a one-handed grip. If he fired at me, he might or might not miss, but my return shot wasn't going to miss.

"Drop the gun!" I commanded. "You're just going to make things worse."

"Tell you what," he countered. "Why don't we both drop our guns and you let me drive away?"

"I think not," I said, repeating the words he'd just used on me.

"I'm willing to gamble that I'm a better shot than you are..."

"Really Bruce?" interrupted Mike, who had come up from behind him and was standing on the other side of the van's cab.

Solinsky began to turn his head towards Mike, then obviously decided I was the principal threat and looked back at me. This time his expression was angry.

He used his thumb to cock the hammer on his pistol.

I gave Silver the command to go for his gun. He was already poised and waiting for it so he took off like a shot.

Solinsky turned towards him, gave an involuntary half-step back, then caught himself and made as if to aim at the onrushing Silver, but that one slight hesitation had given Silver all the time he needed. It was still astonishing to me how fast Silver could accelerate when he wanted to, and almost literally in the blink of an eye there was an anguished yell from Solinsky as Silver's powerful jaws clamped down hard around his gun hand. Solinsky was pulled right over, almost to the ground as Silver used his body weight to pull the gun hand down as far as he could. Silver is big, even by sled dog standards, so when he puts his whole body into dragging something down, he's using his full 39 kilograms (86 lb). Dr. Solinsky didn't have a chance.

While I kept Solinsky covered, Mike came around the front of the van and approached him. As he did so, I gave Silver the command to release the gun hand. Unable to even hold the gun any more, Solinsky had to let it drop.

Using one hand to pick up the gun, he used the other to trigger the switch on the radio microphone that was attached high up on his left shoulder. "Hardisty?"

"Here."

"How'd you make out?"

"I got it all."

"Come on out then."

After a moment, the back door to the café opened and John Hardisty came out carrying their fancy video camera and a shoulder-slung, portable videotape recorder. That made Doc Solinsky turn pale.

"I'm going to sue you for false arrent! You've got nothing on me," he blustered, trying to put a brave face on.

"Bring a first aid kit from your car would you please, John?"

He's slipping, I thought. It was the first time I'd heard him refer to Const. Hardisty by his first name.

"You'd be surprised what we have on you," he said, turning to face Doc Solinsky. "And when we analyze the food trays that are in the café waiting to be delivered for the prisoners in our detachment, I think we might find we have a bit more on you, especially after we see what you've got in your medical bag there."

Solinsky flinched at that, as if to try to get to the medical bag we'd seen him toss back in the van, but Mike had a firm grip on his uninjured arm and he used his superior body weight to force the doctor from crouching to being seated on the ground.

John drove his police car right up to us, then got out carrying the first aid kit. Opening it up, he let the doctor guide him through dealing with the bite wounds. Once the hand was bandaged, Solinsky was handcuffed and put in the back of the police car.

"What was it like in there?" I asked him.

"Almost perfect," he said, with a smile. "I was hidden off to one side where it was dark. The other side of the back room was well lit, and the food trays for the detachment were sitting out on a small table. When the Doc came in, he didn't even look around. He spotted the table and trays right away, went over to them. He paused for a moment – I think he was reading the name labels that were on the plastic film covering the trays. He carefully pulled the film back on one of the trays, then he put his medical bag on the table, took something out and did something – I couldn't see exactly what, but I was holding the camera up at a better angle so it might be on tape. Then he put something back in his bag, replaced the plastic wrap on the tray, and I had to lower the camera and go back to hiding after that, as he turned and walked back out."

"Nice work John. Take him in. We'll be there shortly." *That's twice he's used John's first name*, I thought, *his stock with Mike is rising.*

Mike had a search warrant for the café, so after he'd carefully released the hammer on the pistol and placed it in an evidence bag, we confiscated all four of the food trays that had been waiting to go to the detachment. Then I got my borrowed Geiger Counter and we searched the café, focussing mainly on the back rooms. While Mike prowled around, poking in to things, I used the Geiger Counter to scan everything that looked like it could hold one of the salvaged steel drums – mostly large cardboard boxes, of which there were many.

For almost everything I checked, the Geiger Counter gave a slow series of clicks and a dial reading of about 0.19 microsieverts per hour. Just natural background radiation. Almost everything, that is. There was one cardboard box sitting on the floor just to one side of the back door. The stencilling on the box read PAPER TOWELS.

"Mike," I called out. He came over right away.

"Find something?"

"Right here." I said, pointing to the box.

He came closer and gave it an experimental push. It didn't move. "Too heavy to be paper towels," he pronounced.

"Yes." I held up the Geiger Counter so he could hear the more rapid clicking sounds. "I'm reading 7 microsieverts per hour. That's probably about right for 7 kg of uranium oxide partly shielded by the steel wall of the drum, and the reading is 35 times the background level and more than three times the level we found on Moray's boat, so it's nothing trivial."

"Dangerous?"

"No. It's still well below the 'Turn-Back and Re-evaluate' level[5radiation8]." I used a knife to open the top of the box. "There it is, another drum like the one I brought up."

"A bomb!" said Jean Friend, who had been hovering as we did our search.

"Not a bomb," I explained. "I've told you before. What I couldn't tell you then was that it's uranium oxide – kind of like a concentrated version of uranium ore. It's not dangerous as long as we don't open it up. We're going to have to take it with us though."

"Please do," she said, "the sooner the better. I might have known Bruce was up to no good."

"You know Dr. Solinsky then?"

But she'd obviously realized what she'd said, paled, and flung a hand up over her mouth.

"It's OK," said Mike. "We'd like to get a statement from you, but tomorrow will do. You can just come down to the detachment, or I can send someone here. Talk to a lawyer first, if you wish. In the meantime, I'll write you a receipt for the box."

Laurie Schramm

9 LOOSE ENDS

As they say, hindsight is perfect, and Mike and I were eventually able to put most of the puzzle together.

Even once Dr. Solinsky had been arrested, Noah Campbell and Marcel Bourque – my 'Mutt and Jeff' characters – had decided to take their chances with the justice system and refused to open up. Frankly, I don't think Campbell even knew much more, but I would have liked to learn from Bourque what Dr. Solinsky's instructions to him regarding me were. Perhaps it's just as well I'll never find out.

Duncan Moray seemed genuinely horrified to learn of the murders, and the attempted murders, and once Dr. Solinsky had been arrested, he agreed to plead guilty to the uranium drum thefts, and to tell everything he knew in hopes of being treated leniently by the courts.

Dr. Levi Murray – 'The Professor' – opened up once we explained some of what had really been going on. He had learned about the aerial search for the ditched Boeing Clipper from his brother, F/Lt. Murray, D.G. (Dennis George), who must also have learned about the uranium, or at least heard rumours about it. All professors know how to do background research, so Murray had researched where the plane had likely gone down and the area searched, just like I did. He said that he told Dr. Solinsky about it because they shared an interest in the old flying boats and they were both interested in the fact that the Boeing Clipper had apparently crashed so near to them.

When Dr. Solinsky brought him a sample of the black powder from the first drum, he agreed to send it to a friend at the University of New Brunswick for analysis. When he received the results, he had passed them on to Solinsky and agreed to keep it secret as a favour between friends.

Dr. Bruce Solinsky then took the information a step further and hired Duncan Moray, who was a second-cousin of his, to search for the plane, saying he wanted to keep it quiet because it was a competition among history buffs to find it. Moray admitted to searching for it, mostly as a way to earn money to pay for the searching he really wanted to do, which was for the U-boat. The original 1945 search was conducted by aircraft, and they were looking for a downed plane on the surface or at least floating wreckage. In comparison, Moray's 1979 search was beneath the waves and using a modern side-scan sonar. All he needed was the approximate location, a grid search pattern, and patience. He had all three and he succeeded.

Once Moray had found the plane, broken into the fuselage, and lifted one of the steel drums up to his boat, he'd immediately opened it. When he reported to Dr. Solinsky that it was some kind of black power, Solinsky told him it was a new kind of battery material developed by the Nazis during the war, and that he'd pay him $150 for each drum he recovered as long as it was all kept secret. I thought that was pretty cheap considering Solinsky was probably getting something like $1,500 per drum, and his underworld contact in Montreal (yet another relative of his; in this case one with connections to the black market) was probably selling them to an unfriendly foreign nation for twice that. In any case, Solinsky had arranged for Moray to deliver the drums to the rear of The Lobster's Brew, where envelopes of cash would also be left for him. It was done the way spies use dead-drops, and each delivery and payment cycle was pre-arranged by a series of phone calls.

Jean Friend was a first-cousin of Dr. Solinsky, and she had been willing to help her cousin by letting him use her café for pick-ups and deliveries for the 'import/export business' he ran on the side of his medical practice. Her café had provided a convenient place from which to move goods in and out, and even for short-term storage, because food delivery trucks were always coming and going anyway. That meant that the barrels could be placed into cardboard boxes and loaded onto a plain-looking truck or van at the dock and then driven to the café where they could be stored until it was time to deliver them onwards. Jean had also been willing to make enquiries about the two women divers, but she wasn't willing to go to jail for him, so she opened up to us about the roles she and her café had played.

Incidentally, we learned that virtually everyone else in the community knew about the first- and second-cousin relationships among Solinsky, Jean Friend, and Duncan Moray. Almost everyone, that is, except for the RCMP personnel – myself included - all of whom were posted to parts of Canada that were far removed from wherever they grew up. This is standard practice in the Force, and it meant that every one of us had 'Come From Away.' Outsiders, in other words. Very frustrating.

Not that we didn't already have enough evidence on Dr. Solinsky, but exercising the search warrant on his home turned up two more of the steel drums, in cardboard boxes, in his garage. All three of the steel drums were ultimately delivered to the U.S. Energy Research and Development Administration. Later that summer, a dive team from the Royal Canadian Navy recovered the remainder of the drums on the Boeing Clipper and delivered them to the Americans as well. Meanwhile, the FBI continued to investigate the black-market uranium smuggling business.

And the meal trays? Mike had correctly guessed that the lunchtime trays were uncontaminated, although it was wise of him to quarantine them, just in case he was wrong. We weren't wrong about the suppertime trays though. The forensic analysis determined that the food in each of the trays contained small amounts of botulism. 'Small amounts' that were sufficient to have caused death in an average-sized human within six to twelve hours. The toxicologist told us that none of the men would have tasted anything different or wrong about the food, but four men – including one undercover Mountie – would have been murdered.

Mike had taken the toxicologist to look around Solinsky's house, and the latter had discovered that part of a greenhouse in the backyard had been turned into a mini botulism factory. He had found an entire row of opaqued Mason jars filled to the brim with a concoction of meat, vegetables, and garden soil. The toxicologist had explained that two-to four-weeks ageing in those jars, warmed by the sun, but blocked from receiving any sunlight, would have produced the brown-coloured mold known as Clostridium botulinum, the bacterium that produces the neurotoxin botulinum. Something about that still gives me the creeps.

On the lighter side, you may have wondered whatever happened to Chipper the cat. It turned out that the late Marlea Becker had a brother, but he was allergic to cats and asked Mike to please find him a home or else hand him over to the local animal shelter. Unable to find him a home, and having looked after Chipper for a week, *Mike decided to keep him!* Mike, the old-school, often gruff, occasionally parade-square-loud Sergeant Mike Morrison has a soft side after all. Of course, I've known that ever since I worked for him so many years earlier, but his colleagues in the detachment would be unlikely to let him live it down.

10 EPILOGUE

Sometime in June, 1980
Embassy of the Union of Soviet Socialist Republics,
Ottawa, ON

"What is it?" asked Major Emilis (Emi) Matulis, Chief Military
Attaché, Embassy of the Soviet Union, as he entered the embassy's
mail room on the main floor of the building.

"See for yourself, Comrade Major," said the security officer,
pointing to the monitor of the X-ray scanning machine through
which all envelopes and parcels entering the embassy were screened.

On the monitor, Emi could see that there was a large box
containing twelve bottles, and that the bottles appeared to be full of
some kind of liquid.

"The box came addressed to you personally care of the embassy.
It was dropped off by a courier, and it has no return address or any
other indication of who may have sent it."

"Looks like a case of liquor," said Emi, felling a sudden sense of
déjà vu.

"Could be Molotov Cocktails," said the security officer.

"I don't see any detonators or wicks though. Do you?"

"No, but it is not correct to take any risks here. You know that."

"Yes…" said Emi, looking closely at the monitor. Then he smiled
a quiet smile. "All right. Release it to me on my own responsibility.
I will take it out back to the outside parking lot. You will keep people
from leaving the embassy for the few minutes it will take me to open

the box and check the contents. If it blows up, you will have done your duty, and only I will be injured or killed."

"If you are sure, Comrade Major," said the security officer, relieved to be insulated from possible repercussions.

As agreed, Emi carried the box to the outside parking lot at the rear of the embassy, and set it down between two huge steel garbage dumpsters, and next to a high, steel-reinforced concrete wall that formed part of the perimeter of the embassy. He looked around. There was no one else in the lot and no vehicles parked nearby. Then, he looked back at the security officer who stood in the embassy doorway, physically blocking it.

The security officer, having noted all of the same things, gave an ironic bow and motioned Emi to proceed.

Opening the box, Emi quickly noted that it did indeed seem to contain 12 liquor bottles. He lifted one up for inspection. In large white letters on a red background, the label read STOLICHNAYA RUSSIAN VODKA, it bore a red-bordered, white label, bearing four gold award seals, and an image of the famous Hotel Moskva.

Twisting off the gold-coloured screw cap, Emi angled his head back and took a swig, then re-capped the bottle and put it back in the case.

"It's Stoli," he yelled with a grin, "a whole case of it."

Feeling foolish, the security officer retreated back into the embassy.

Alone in the lot, Emi, gave the case a closer inspection and discovered that a letter-sized envelope had been slipped into the box alongside one of the bottles.

Inside the envelope was a plain white card with a few handwritten words. It read: "Thank you once again. The pen was mightier than the sword[59], and it probably saved my life." It was signed simply: Alex. Beside Alex's name was a small drawing of a dog's paw-print.

"Alex and Silver," said Emi, in a low voice, shaking his head in disbelief.

I should never have given her that dart-pen, he thought to himself, *but I'm glad I did.*

… Alex and Silver return in
"An Inside Mountie."

Laurie Schramm

BOOK 13 ENDNOTES

1. Although this specific aircraft is fictional, the Boeing 314 and 314A Clippers did exist as described. Only 12 were ever made. The Clippers flew from 1939 through 1948, with a few surviving until 1951, by which times they had been made obsolete by the introduction of the Lockheed Constellation and Douglas DC-4. None of the Clippers have survived although it may someday be possible to resurrect two that were sunk. See J.A. Zichek, "A Detailed Look at the Fabulous Boeing B-314," *Airpower*, **2005** (*Jan.*) 14- 27.

2. The European part of the Second World War concluded on May 8, 1945; the Pacific part on September 2 of the same year.

3. In 1947, one of the real-life B-314A Clippers, the *Bermuda Sky Queen*, ran out of fuel while crossing from England. It had to ditch in the Atlantic Ocean about 800 km (430 nmi) east of Gander, Newfoundland.

4. In the Security Service, at this time in history, the sections were denoted with letters A through L: 'A', for security screening, 'B', for counter-espionage, 'C' for administration, 'D', for counter-subversion (or anti-communism), 'E' for electronic surveillance, 'F' for files, 'G' for counter-terrorism (absorbed into D Section in 1976), 'H' for China, 'I' for physical surveillance, 'J' for bugging, and 'L' for informants. According to Sawatsky (See

endnote #7): "*As far as is known, there is no K Section. For some reason the letters jump from J to L. One Security Service member theorized that K Section may exist but plays such a minor role that nobody knows about it. 'Either that,' he joked, 'or it exists and is very important'.*" Other accounts suggest that this section was for research. Since there is some mystery about whether 'K' Section actually existed, or it's purpose if it did exist, I have made it 'Special Operations,' hence very important, in these novels. See: J. Sawatsky, *Men in the Shadows. The RCMP Security Service*, Doubleday, Toronto, 1980.

5.   See *An Indestructible Mountie* (ISBN: 978-1-9994940-4-9).

6.   U-184, a Type IXC/40 U-boat, was reported missing since November 21, 1942, with its last known position being in the North Atlantic east of Newfoundland. Some months later, two U-boats were actually sent directly to PEI. In April, 1943, U-376 set out for PEI where they were to pick up German Naval officers who planned to escape from Camp 70, a prisoner-of-war camp in Fredericton, N.B., and make their way to North Point in P.E.I. When U-376 failed to transmit a regular report, it was declared missing and another submarine, U-262, was sent to out. Enroute from Norway, U-262 was fired-on and depth-charged by escorts from convoy HX 233, but survived the attack and made it to PEI. There was no one there to meet it because the escape was either unsuccessful or not attempted. As a result, U-262 ultimately returned to Germany where it was captured in 1945. It is unclear whether U-376 ever made it to PEI, with some researchers concluding that she sunk in the Bay of Biscay. Others believe that one of the lost submarines, either U-184 or U-376, was sunk on May 7, 1943 off PEI and may lie in shallow waters off North Cape, PEI, "regularly snagging nets of local fishing vessels." This theory was bolstered in 1989, when a diver claimed to have found a submarine wreck at a depth of about 95 feet and just over a mile from shore: the same location identified by the witnesses. The wreck was described by the diver as "covered with debris, lots of nets… with a large deck gun, a 20

mm anti-aircraft gun, [and] periscopes."

According to naval records, three Canadian-built corvettes: USS Intensity, USS Alacrity, and USS Haste left Quebec City on May 5, 1943, on their maiden voyages to Boston, and had apparently agreed to escort the Canadian merchant ship Essex Lance to Halifax, N.S. On May 7, they found themselves in heavy fog off North Cape, P.E.I., consistent with the time and date for which eyewitnesses said the submarine battle occurred. What is less certain, even in view of studies of the ships' logs, seems to be whether the gun and depth-charge action was a battle or a drill. An aircraft observed at the time is thought to have been an RCAF Lockheed Hudson from 119 Squadron (Chatham, N.B.), but that aircraft apparently made no report of spotting the surface ships, let alone a submarine engagement.

Numerous attempts have been made to find the possibly sunken U-boat, but without success as of the time of writing this book. For more information see: "U-184," "U-262" and "U-376," www.uboat.net; Mary MacKay, "Back to the Battle," SaltWire News, June 14, 2010 (updated Sept. 30, 2017), www.saltwire.com/prince-edward-island/lifestyles/back-to-the-battle-108625/; and Richard O. Mayne, "The Great Naval Battle of North Point: Myth or Reality?" *Canadian Military History*, **2007**, *16(3)*, article 2.

7. In later years (in real life), there was an even larger storm on January 21, 2000 that raised the ocean level at Pointe-du-Chêne by 3.6 m from the low tide mark (i.e., storm surge plus tide). See: "Impacts of Sea Level Rise and Climate Change on the Coastal Zone of Southeastern New Brunswick," Report EPSM-753, Environment Canada, Ottawa, 2006, pp. 123-127.

8. commercial fishing for lobsters is legal in Atlantic Canada, and the limited number of commercial lobster fishing licences makes them very expensive. The legal consequences for catching lobsters without such a licence can be severe.

9. Shipboard cats, particularly calicos, have been thought to bring good luck, in addition to their value in dealing with mice and

rats. In some countries, male calicos have been considered to be particularly lucky because they are rare.

10. Typical of a sonar of 1970s vintage.

11. When SCUBA-diving with compressed air, a diver's body absorbs into its tissues more and more nitrogen than usual from the breathing-air as the depth and time-at-depth increase. Then, when the diver ascends and the pressure decreases, the absorbed nitrogen is slowly released but the diver has to ascend soon enough, and slowly enough to expel the released (and expanding) nitrogen quickly enough to prevent decompression sickness ('the bends'). Every depth has its own no-decompression limit, which is the maximum time that a diver can spend swimming to - and at - that depth and still be able to ascend directly to the surface without the need for decompression stops along the way.

12. The cited values correspond to the no-decompression dive tables of the 1970s, when Alex and Sharon would have trained. More modern dive tables list the maximum no-decompression time for a dive to 70 feet as 40 minutes.

13. White is among the most visible colours underwater, when viewed against the blue background of open water

14. More properly the Atlantic wolffish, *Anarhichas lupas.*

15. SCUBA diving while wearing a wetsuit or dry-suit, the suit itself adds considerably to a person's buoyancy. To counter this a diver uses weights, generally made of lead, that are fitted to a waist belt and/or to the back plate that also holds the SCUBA tank(s). The amount of weight needed depends on several factors including whether one is diving in fresh water or seawater.

16. That corresponds to an ascent rate of about 60 feet (18 m) per minute, which was the basis for the no-decompression dive tables in the 1970s, when Alex and Sharon would have trained. Some organizations now recommend a slower ascent rate, especially from depths shallower than 60 feet.

17. Now the Democratic Republic of Congo.

18. This part of the story is true. By August 1943 the U.S., U.K., and Canada had merged their atomic weapons development programs under a cooperation agreement called "The Articles of Agreement on Tube Alloys," and Tube Alloys became the code name for this project. The Tube Alloy Project was later folded into the Manhattan Project, led by the U.S. but still in cooperation with the U.K. and Canada. The world's first nuclear fission reactors were built in the U.S. and Canada.

19. See *An Indestructible Mountie* (ISBN: 978-1-9994940-4-9).

20. Uranium ore from the Shinkolobwe mine was about 65 percent uranium, as U_3O_8, yellowcake concentrate from early uranium mills was about 80 percent uranium as U_3O_8, and black oxide from early uranium refineries was about 96 percent U_3O_8.

21. National Research Council of Canada. NRC built Canada's first laboratory-scale nuclear-fission reactor in Ottawa in 1940, using uranium from Eldorado's Port Radium mine and the Port Hope refinery.

22. *An Inseparable Mountie* (ISBN: 978-1-7772424-0-4).

23. See *An Intrepid Mountie* (ISBN: 978-1-7772424-6-6).

24. See W. Eggleston, *National Research in Canada. The NRC 1916-1966*, Clarke, Irwin & Co., Toronto, 1978.

25. The rate of drift for a remarkably wide range of floating objects in open water is approximately 3% of the prevailing wind velocity relative to the water. See T.J.W Wagner et al., "How Winds and Ocean Currents Influence the Drift of Floating Objects," *J. Phys. Oceanogr.*, **2022**, *52*, 900–916, DOI: 10.1175/JPO-D-20-0275.1

26. See *An Inconvenient Mountie* (ISBN: 978-1-9994940-0-1).

27. South Africa had a nuclear weapons program for some time, but then halted it and dismantled their nuclear-fission weapons in the 1990s. Other countries, like Pakistan and North Korea began their own nuclear weapons programs after the time span of this novel.

28. About C$150 thousand in 2024 dollars.

29. By the end of the 1970s, fax machines had become standard

business equipment in North America.

30. NASA's Landsat-2 earth observation satellite was in operation between 1975 and 1982.

31. In late 1976, the U.S. launched the first of a revolutionary series of reconnaissance satellites, the KH-11, that could transmit high-resolution images back to earth in near real-time. Five such KH-11 satellites had been launched by 1982. The images they captured were converted to electronic signals and relayed through higher-orbit communications satellites back to a ground station, where the images were recreated by laser writing on film. Compared with earlier satellites that had to eject film canisters for retrieval on earth, this dramatically reduced the lag time from several weeks to 90 minutes or less. The theoretical resolution for this series of satellites was two inches, although in practice it is thought not to have been quite this good. The KH-11s could produce images day or night, including through clouds. The KH-11s orbited in pairs, enabling them to cover the same target area twice a day: once in the in the morning and once in the afternoon. See J.D.T. Severance, "Proposed Design of a Tactical Reconnaissance Satellite System," M.Sc. Thesis, Air Force Institute of Technology, Wright-Patterson Air Force Base, Ohio, December, 1990.

32. See *An Indispensable Mountie* (ISBN: 978-1-7772424-2-8).

33. See "Italian Air Fleet Alights at Shediac. Balbo Armada Flies 800 Miles from Labrador to New Brunswick Town," *The New York Times*, July 14, 1933, p. 1.

34. Literally "tabernacle." A common *sacre*, or profane term relating to the Catholic Church.

35. See *An Ineradicable Mountie* (ISBN: 978-1-7387599-2-7).

36. Bud Fisher's "Mutt and Jeff," was a long-running comic strip in United States' newspapers between 1907 and 1983. It featured 'two mismatched tinhorns,' one tall and one short.

37. The expression "come from away" (CFA), has long been used throughout the Atlantic Canadian provinces to refer to people that were not born in the given province, but who moved in later

in life, or even just came to visit.

38. Originally a satellite campus of St. Francis Xavier University, it was known as Xavier College in the 1960s. In 1974, it was merged with the Nova Scotia Eastern Institute of Technology to form the College of Cape Breton. Subsequent to the time of this story, it became known as the University College of Cape Breton in 1982.

39. See Ian Andrews, "Shediac on the World Aviation Scene." Feature article #3 / Heritage Week 2009, News Release, Government of New Brunswick, 11 February 2009, www2.gnb.ca/content/gnb/en/news/news_release.2009.02.01 43.html

40. Uranium glass is yellow-green to green coloured glass that gets its colour from the inclusion of uranium oxide. The amount of uranium in such glass usually varies from trace levels up to about 2% uranium by mass, and it was added to various kinds of glass tableware between the 1800s and the Second World War. Uranium sea glass is one of several kinds of fluorescent (or 'ultraviolet') pieces of broken and eroded glass found washed-up on beaches. Although uranium glass generally glows in natural light, it fluoresces bright green under ultraviolet light. Although the amounts of uranium in the mix were small, it can usually be detected with a Geiger counter.

41. Historically Greenwich Mean Time (GMT) was standard, this being the local time at the Royal Observatory in Greenwich, London, but over the years it has not always been calculated in a consistent way. Since 1972, GMT has been replaced by Coordinated Universal Time (UTC) as the international time standard. The UTC standard is maintained by series atomic clocks around the world.

42. 5th Canadian Division Support Base Gagetown

43. The Canadian Forces has been developing and maintaining nuclear, biological, and chemical (NBC) counter-terrorism defence capabilities through their Canadian Forces Nuclear Biological Chemical School (CFNBCS) since 1976. Since 2002,

a joint NBC Defence Company has been given the mission of providing chemical, biological, radiological, and nuclear (CBRN) support and response capabilities for the forces.

44. Canadian Forces Base (CFB) Moncton was active, and attached to Maritime Command, at the time of this story. Later (in 1996) it was stood down and replaced by a smaller detachment that is organizationally part of CFB Gagetown.

45. Calculated based on information from the Solicitor General of Canada's Annual Reports for the years 1974-75 through 1979-80 (Supply and Services Canada, Ottawa) and L. Comeau, "Womens' Struggle to Gain Equality Status in the RCMP," M.A. Thesis, Carleton University, Ottawa, July 1990.

46. See *An Inconvenient Mountie* (ISBN: 978-1-9994940-0-1).

47. The classic cylinder style Geiger–Müller tube has the detector window at one end, while the pancake style has a handle leading to an angled thick, disc-shaped detector having a larger detector window. The latter gives a faster response.

48. When it works, this bit of sailing lore has a scientific basis. Due to its shorter wavelength, a dilute aerosol of fine particles or droplets in the atmosphere will scatter much more blue light than red light, which has a longer wavelength. This is why the sky can appear blue overhead while the sun appears yellowish-red when viewed across the horizon as it is rising or setting. In the mid latitudes of the Northern Hemisphere, storm systems generally follow the jet stream from west to east. A red sky over the setting sun at night can be due to light being scattered by dust particles in the air to the west, indicating dry weather approaching. A red western sky in the morning can indicate a sun rising in clear eastern skies illuminating storm clouds approaching from the west. See: L.L. Schramm, *Emulsions, Foams, Suspensions, and Aerosols: Microscience and Applications*, 2nd Ed., Wiley - VCH, Weinheim, Germany, 2014.

49. At the time of this story, Cap-Pelé was a village in its own right, but in 2023 it became part of the town of Cap-Acadie.

50. Prince Edward Island.

51. Civilian clothes.
52. The Sony U-matic used ¾-inch videotape and was one of the first videocassette systems, as opposed to the previous reel-to-reel systems. It was popular among professional users in the 1970s through 1990s.
53. The fictional radiation-dose reading attributed here works out to be 1.8 millisieverts per year, which is the real-life Canadian average for radiation from natural sources. The average in the United States is 3.0 and for the entire world is 2.4, in the same units. See CNSC, "Radiation Doses," Canadian Nuclear Safety Commission, Ottawa, 2023, www.cnsc-ccsn.gc.ca/eng/resources/radiation/radiation-doses/
54. CFB Chatham was a Canadian Forces Base located near Chatham, N.B. Active at the time of this story, it operated between 1941 and 1989.
55. The Avro Anson was a twin-engine reconnaissance aircraft. It nominally carried a crew of three: pilot, navigator/bombardier, and a radio operator/gunner. For maritime reconnaissance missions it generally carried an additional crew member to assist with spotting. Over 4,000 of them were flown by the RCAF and the RCN between 1940 and 1952.
56. For real-life examples see RCAF.Info, "Daily Diary – Links – No. 10 Air Observer School," https://rcaf.info/rcaf-stations/new-brunswick-rcaf-stations/rcaf-station-chatham/#operational-record-book-links-no-18-service-flying-training-school
57. From "Who knows what evil lurks in the hearts of men? The Shadow knows!" which was the introduction to each episode of the classic radio program *The Shadow*, which was broadcast from 1930 to the mid-1950s.
58. Turn-back dose guidance is designed for emergency workers that respond to a radiological emergency. It is actually a series of dose levels designed to balance radiation exposure risk against the urgency of the responder's task, such as life-saving vs. evacuation of the public vs. sample collection.

59. The phrase "The pen is mightier than the sword" comes from the 1839 play *Richelieu; Or the Conspiracy*, by English playwright and novelist Edward Bulwer-Lytton.

Laurie Schramm

An Inside Mountie

Adventures of the First Woman Mountie. Book 14

LAURIE SCHRAMM

Laurie Schramm

Espionage Rules

TOP SECRET
SECRET
CONFIDENTIAL

1. Betrayal may come from within,
2. Assume nothing,
3. Stay consistent over time,
4. Keep your options open,
5. Never go against your gut,
6. Don't look back, you are not alone,
7. Go with the flow; blend in,
8. Use misdirection and deception,
9. Do not harass the opposition,
10. Lull them into complacency,
11. Pick the time and place for action,
12. Remember Murphy's Law.

(See Book 14 Endnote 1)

Laurie Schramm

DEDICATION

To the women and men of Canada's real-life security-intelligence services (1864 - Present).

Laurie Schramm

BOOK 14 CONTENTS

	Dedication	151
	List of Characters	155
	List of Acronyms and Abbreviations	156
1	Theirs Not to Reason Why	157
2	A Very Odd Call	165
3	The Investigation Begins	183
4	A Secret Meeting	197
5	Her Majesty's Secret Service	215
6	A New Assignment	235
7	Convergence	249
8	Aftermath	263
9	Epilogue	269
	Book 14 Endnotes	279

Laurie Schramm

BOOK 14 LIST OF CHARACTERS
(IN ORDER OF APPEARANCE)

- Major Jack Evans, Defence Attaché, British High Commission
- Corporal Alexandra (Alex) Houston, RCMP Security Service
- Silver, an Alaskan Malamute; and Alex's friend and police-service-dog partner
- Staff Sergeant Robert (Bob) Simpson, RCMP Security Service
- Deputy Commissioner George MacLeod
- Mary MacLeod, George's wife
- Rear-Admiral Peter White, head of the Canadian Forces Security Branch.
- Captain Donald (Don) Harrison, Military Intelligence, Canadian Armed Forces
- Staff Sergeant Avery Blunt, RCMP Security Service
- Special Agent Vivian Rule, FBI
- Staff Sergeant Alexander Demeniak, RCMP Security Service
- Sergeant Frank Wilson, Military Intelligence, Canadian Forces
- Lieutenant Sandy Moore, Military Intelligence, Canadian Forces
- Ginger Brandt, Canadian TV and film actress
- Major Emilis (Emi) Matulis, Chief Military Attaché, Embassy of the Soviet Union, Ottawa
- 'C,' head of the British Secret Intelligence Service (MI6)
- Constable Jack McDonald, RCMP
- Constable Chris Williams, RCMP

LIST OF ACRONYMS AND ABBREVIATIONS

AECL   Atomic Energy of Canada Limited
CANDU CANadian Deuterium Uranium (nuclear reactor system)
CFB   Canadian Forces Base
HMCS   Her Majesty's Canadian Ship
HQ   Headquarters
IDENT   Identification (or Forensic) Services
MI6   Military Intelligence Sect. 6 (the UK's Secret Intelligence
        Service)
OPP   Ontario Provincial Police
PDS   Police Dog Service
PSD   Police Service Dog
RCAF   Royal Canadian Air Force
RCMP   Royal Canadian Mounted Police
USAF   Unites States Air Force
USCGC   United States Coast Guard Cutter

1 THEIRS NOT TO REASON WHY[2]

'Black Friday'
February 20, 1959
Ottawa, Ontario

The Right Honourable John G. Diefenbaker, Prime Minister of Canada, rose in the House of Commons to give a speech[3]:

> "Mr. Speaker, with the leave of the house I should like to make a somewhat lengthy statement on the subject of one facet of the national defence of Canada.... The announcement I wish to make has to do with the decision regarding our air defence.... The government has carefully examined and re-examined the probable need for the Arrow aircraft and Iroquois engine known as the CF-105.... The conclusion arrived at is that the development of the Arrow aircraft and Iroquois engine should be terminated now."

With that simple announcement, Canada's program to build a nuclear-weapon capable, long-range, all-weather, supersonic interceptor came to an abrupt end. The plane was named Avro Arrow, and the new engines that would propel it to speeds of Mach 2 (twice the speed of sound), were named Iroquois. The Arrow had been conceived in response to growing apprehensions about the probability of the Soviet Union developing a supersonic, intercontinental bomber coupled with an assessment that no other country, at the time, had a jet fighter capable of intercepting such aircraft with the speed and range needed to protect Canada's vast land mass.

As soon as the Prime Minister's announcement had been made, the Department of Defence Production notified Avro Canada, the primary contractor on the program, that the program was cancelled and that they were to immediately cease all work. With all funding cut off, the company had little choice but to shut down its operations that same afternoon, throwing more than 25,000 people out of work: 14,000 Avro Aircraft and Orenda Engines employees, and more than 11,000 at various sub-contractors.

The news media, of course, launched into a frenzy of questions, assertions, and speculations about the wisdom of the government's decision, and the reason(s) it had been made. The latter ranged from budgetary considerations (the official reason), to undue influence from the United States (whether due to politics, their own defence policies, or simply pride)[4]. Not the least of the concerns expressed was whether there would be any return from the over $300 million[5] that had already been spent on the Avro program by the time of the cancellation order.

From *The (Toronto) Telegram*, February 21, 1959.

Within months, orders were given to scrap the five flyable aircraft plus those under construction[6], all but three of the engines, and the rest of the parts, jigs, documents, and so forth, saving only one complete set of drawings, specifications, manuals, and the like[5].

By January of 1960, Avro had been ordered to destroy the balance of the documentation[5]. For security reasons, the government wanted to make sure that no other country would be able to make the Arrow either (although in later years several countries 'reinvented' some of the Arrow's most advanced features, including the internal weapons carriage, and the fly-by-wire power-assist for the controls while in supersonic flight).

> In the fields of observation chance favours only the prepared mind.
>
> Louis Pasteur, French microbiologist/chemist,
> During a lecture at the University of Lille,
> 7 December 1854

Sunday, May 10, 1959
Mississauga, Ontario

In a rented aviation-hanger on Airport Road, not far from the manufacturing facilities of Avro Aircraft and Orenda Engines, all the lights were still on despite it being late in the evening. Inside the nearly empty hangar were stacks of irregularly-sized cardboard boxes. Next to the boxes was a large and disorderly pile of documents. That the documents had been unceremoniously dumped from other boxes could fairly be deduced from the third pile, which comprised empty boxes that had been flattened and tossed aside.

Beyond the boxes and documents, the only noteworthy things were in a noisy corner where two men toiled away. Other than that, the hanger was empty and quiet: it was the night shift on a Sunday, and there was no one else around except the security guards at the front door.

The noise in the corner where the men were working and the pervading, almost intolerable smell of machine oil, came from two sturdy-looking industrial paper shredders[7]. The men were hand-feeding documents to the shredders which, notwithstanding the machine oil, frequently overheated and jammed. When this happened, the machines had to be turned off, opened-up, and allowed to cool, while the men used pliers to free the cutting blades from the jammed tangles of paper.

There was a recurring debate between the two men about which was the more tedious: the monotonous feeding of documents into the jaws of the shredders or the frustrating job of freeing the jammed blades.

It would be an understatement to say that the men were unenthusiastic about their work. They were surrounded by piles of documents from the cancelled Avro Arrow program; mostly test reports, drawings, specifications, manuals, and the like. A few were stamped CONFIDENTIAL, others were stamped SECRET, and most of them were stamped TOP SECRET.

It was boring, menial work, and they had been at it for hours with no end in sight. Since the documents were being destroyed for security reasons, they could only be handled by people with Top Secret, or higher, security clearances. In this case, both men had Top Secret security clearance, and both men acutely felt the indignity of having to do a job they felt was beneath them.

"Look at this," said one of the men, in a tone of disgust. "The government spends over 300 million dollars developing the best fighter jet in the world, and now we're helping to destroy it all. What a waste!"

"Well, it's all pensionable time, as they say," replied the second, more philosophical of the two.

"But why? That's what I don't get. Even if the program became too expensive, there are rumours that the British offered to buy the design from us. Why not just sell it to them instead of all this?"

The second man, who had been about to say 'Ours not to reason why,' stopped himself to instead say: "The British are interested? I didn't know that."

"That's what I heard. You know Frank over in B Section[8]? He told me yesterday that the British called and were interested in buying or licensing Arrows for long-range defence over the North Sea[9]."

"Huh. What do you know about that?" said the second man, thoughtfully. As this was a purely rhetorical expression, the first man didn't say anything further, and the two men went back to their shredding.

After another hour of relentless shredding, a telephone rang and they switched off the shredders so the first man could answer it.

"Hello? Yes, that's me, put her on.

"Hi Honey, what's up? No, no, slow down. Stop and take a breath; I can't understand a word you're saying.

"Ok. Yes, that's better…. What!! Now? You're sure? Ok, ok, I get it. I'll be there as fast as I can. You get your coat on and get that bag you packed. I'll be right there."

"Trouble?" asked the second man, after the first had hung up the phone and taken a deep breath.

"Yes and no. That was my wife. She says she's gone into labour. She keeps saying something about water breaking."

"Your first?"

"Yes…. Look, I need to ask a big favour."

"You want to go take her to the hospital and you want me to cover for you. Right?"

"Yes. Look, I know we were ordered to only do this together, with each of us watching the other for security reasons, but it's stupid, for God's sake. I mean, look at us, we're on the same side – we're both Mounted Policemen, so we're even on the same team. It won't take me long to slip out, go pick her up, drop her off at the hospital[10], and then come straight back here. Two hours at the most. Then, if you keep on shredding while I'm gone, and the two of us keep going after that, we'll still get enough done on this shift and no one will be the wiser."

"Sure. Go ahead. I'll cover for you," said the second man, "but make sure you go out the back way so the front-desk people don't see you."

"Thanks. I owe you one," said the first man gratefully, as he headed for the door.

Alone in the room, the second man picked up one of the manuals. "January 1959. AIRCRAFT OPERATING INSTRUCTIONS – ARROW 1. Avro Aircraft limited," read the label on the cover[11]. It was over 140 pages. *Everything a pilot needs to know to fly one of these*, he thought, as he flipped through it

He picked up another manual, then another. *Everything someone would need to build and maintain one of these*, he thought, as he flipped through several of the specification books and manuals. When he reached over to pull another manual out of the pile, a box of technical reports that was sitting on top fell over to reveal a very thick wad of blueprints, held together on one edge by a wooden frame. As he flipped through the blueprints, his jaw dropped, and he paused to gaze around the various piles.

There's enough material here to build, operate, and maintain a fleet of Avro Arrows, he thought.

Structural Drawing of the Arrow Mk. I, Avro Canada

***

Two weeks later.
Ottawa, Ontario

In a large, eight-story building, directly across the street from the National Arts Centre in downtown Ottawa the morning routine was just getting started when a call was received on the main telephone line.

"Good morning, British High Commission," said a woman's voice belonging to one of the main switchboard operators.

"Major Evans, please," said man's voice. The voice sounded muffled, and there was crackling on the line, but it was possible to understand his request.

"One moment please. I'll connect you."

There was a click on the line, a pause, and then another click.

"Defence Liaison," said a new woman's voice.

The caller repeated his request.

"Who may I say is calling?"

"Just tell him it's a *friend*[12]," said the voice, with heavy emphasis on the last word.

"One moment please. I'll see if he can take your call."

There was a another click on the line as it was put on hold, a longer pause this time, and then another click as a handset was picked up.

"Major Evans speaking."

"You can call me Smith, Major Evans. I have something that I think will interest you very much."

"What might that be, Mr. Smith?"

"Just Smith, if you please. I understand that you have an interest in long-range, supersonic jet fighters for use over the North Sea and elsewhere."

"Possibly. We do try to keep abreast of things you know," Major Evans, said, cautiously.

"Indeed. What if I could supply you with the plans for the Avro Arrow and its supersonic engines?"

"The Arrow was cancelled. Didn't I read somewhere that everything was being destroyed?"

"Possibly, but you shouldn't believe everything that you read, you know."

"Well, then, what do you have?"

"Everything but the planes themselves. Materials lists, assembly instructions, blueprints[13], maintenance instructions, service manuals, wind-tunnel test results, weapons systems specifications... even operating instructions."

"I see, and am I to assume that these are all for sale?"

"You are."

"Hmmm. What do you want?"

"Not much. Let's say five-hundred thousand. That wouldn't be much to pay for three-hundred-million worth of technology. Not when there's enough information to build as many jets as you want. It would be worth it just for the engines alone. Wouldn't it?"

There was a pause. Then, "I'll have to get approval, and we'll need some kind of evidence."

"Of course. Across the street from you is the National Arts Centre. In the box office lobby is a wire-frame news-stand with free neighbourhood and religious newspapers. At the back of the papers in the upper-left corner, you will find three samples. Get one of your experts to look over the samples, get approval for the money, and I'll phone you again in a week."

A week later, another call was received at the High Commission for Major Evans.

"Well?"

"The documents check out. We're interested."

"All right. We won't meet. We'll use dead drops[14]. Put 150 thousand into a briefcase. Used, unmarked bills, in small denominations. I'll phone in two days with instructions. When I get the money, I'll phone again and tell you where to get the first large batch of documents. They will be in two large suitcases. After that we'll repeat the process. Then, for the last cycle, it will be the remaining 200 thousand dollars, in return for which you'll get the only surviving, complete set of original blueprints."

Over the next two weeks, the three rounds of exchanges of money and documents took place. Every exchange took place at a different pair of dead drops. A few days after the final exchange, Major Evans received another call at the High Commission.

"You have everything?"

"Yes."

"And you are satisfied?"

"Yes. Do you have anything else for us?"

"Not now, but sometime in the future, I may call you again."

"Cheers."

That went well, thought the security man.

2 A VERY ODD CALL

> *Quis custodiet ipsos custodes* (who watches the watchers)?
>
> From *Satires of Juvenal*, (Satire 6, 346-348)
> Rome, *Circa*. 100

October, 1980
Ottawa, Ontario

"E007, 10-21," the radio in my truck crackled to life.

My name is Corporal Alexandra Houston, Royal Canadian Mounted Police (RCMP) Security Service. My friends call me Alex. E007 was the call-sign assigned to my radio. The letter E designated my unit as operational support. This prefix was assigned to unmarked police-dog-service (PDS) or forensic (IDENT) units. In my case I'm also a dog master and I always travel with Silver, an Alaskan Malamute, my friend and partner. The number '007' showed that my boss, Staff Sergeant Robert (Bob) Simpson, Bob had a sense of humour (he often jokes that I'm like a female James Bond). As if my Security Service posting didn't give me enough variety, we were often called out in our capacity as a PDS team.

"E007," I acknowledged.

"Message for you from Staff Sergeant Simpson. Message reads: 'Phone in when convenient. Not urgent.'"

That was odd. My boss Bob wouldn't have gone through the radio room to contact me if it wasn't important, so I took his message to mean fairly urgent but not an emergency.

"E007, 10-4," I responded over the radio, meaning that I was acknowledging receipt of the message and that I would handle it 'as requested.'

I was driving along an Ottawa street, heading for one of the main highways at the time. Looking ahead, I spotted a phone booth in the corner of a service station's parking lot and pulled in to make the call.

Pushing a coin in to the appropriate slot, I received a dial tone and punched in the number for the RCMP's Ottawa radio room. When it was answered, I identified myself, read-out the number on the pay phone, and explained that I'd received a radio message to phone in. The duty officer replied that he'd pass my message on and we hung up. I didn't expect to be kept waiting long, and I was right. Within a few minutes the phone rang.

"Alex?" came a familiar voice over the phone.

"Hi Bob. What's up?"

"Where are you now and what are you doing today?"

"Well, I was working on the Strangways case until a request came in from the OPP[15] for me to help them on a search. Their own dog teams are either fully engaged or out of the area. I was just on my way out of town, heading for Highway 416 and Kemptville."

"Ah. Good. So, you won't be far away." Kemptville was about 60 km (36 miles) south of Ottawa, so about a 40-minute drive.

"I have news," he continued. "Uncle George was on today's promotion list. He's being bumped up to Deputy Commissioner." Uncle George was Bob's and my unofficial and top-secret codename for (formerly) Assistant Commissioner George MacLeod, the head of the Security Service and Bob's boss. Others on the staff referred to him as 'The Old Man,' the same as if he was the CO of a Division, but Bob and I referred to him as Uncle George. We always figured that if we were ever found out, we'd claim it was a code name for security reasons, but it was really because he looked after us like family.

"Deputy Commissioner! That's great. It's overdue, but it's great."

"Right. His job title is still Director General of the Security

166

Service, but it's always been a Deputy Commissioner-level position[16]. He was pretty young when he came into the role, so this is a kind of recognition that he's been doing a good job. Anyway, he's having a few people over this evening for come-and-go cocktails at his house and you're invited."

I hesitated. "Isn't that a bit high-brow? I imagine his friends in the Force are senior officers. The Ottawa ones anyway."

"Well, that's true enough, quite a few of the top brass and their wives will be there, but there'll be a few token non-comms[17] like you and I there as well."

I hesitated again. "I'm not sure when I'll be able to get back into town, you know."

"Yes, I mentioned that possibility to him but he said he'd be particularly pleased if you'd come, and that when you go off duty just head over to his house dressed as you are – no need to clean up, and no need to change into civilian clothes."

That sounded suspicious to me but, in practice, a politely-phrased request from a senior officer wasn't much different from a direct order, so I agreed. "What about Silver?" I asked.

"Well, I asked him that too, and he said, 'Tell her to bring Silver too. She never goes anywhere without him anyway'"

I had to chuckle at that. He'd said more or less the same thing to me more than once in the years I'd been indirectly working for him. "OK," I relented. "I'll be there, but I'll still clean up and change clothes first if there's time."

"Fair enough," said Bob. "I'll see you there. In the meantime, good luck with the OPP and your search."

As I rung off it still seemed odd to me, to be invited to a Deputy Commissioner's promotion party. I had a huge amount of respect for 'Uncle George,' and I was pleased to be invited, but it still seemed… odd. I forced it to the back of my mind as I went back to my unmarked police SUV and resumed course for Kemptville and its OPP detachment.

The search, turned out to be for the escape route used by a thief who'd broken into a farmhouse and stolen a pair of valuable handguns. This wasn't the sort of thing we'd normally be called out to, except for some unusual circumstances. The break-in had been very recent, perhaps only an hour or two earlier, the pistols were both functional and loaded, and the thief had left a piece of clothing behind. Apparently, the thief had gotten their jacket caught in the barbs of a barbed-wire fence while getting away, and the local police thought there might be an opportunity to catch the thief while still in possession of the guns.

We'd done this kind of searching many times before, so after letting Silver get a good sniff of the jacket, I simply set him off to search. In company with us were an OPP sergeant and two constables. Silver set about doing his thing, and we followed along as his zig-zagging sniffing led us to a wind-break stand of trees, then along a narrow creek-bed, and finally to a neighbouring field and a rough, narrow dirt road that could have been the wagon-road of a hundred years earlier. The scent trail ended at a spot to one side of the road, where fresh-looking tire tracks indicated a vehicle had been parked. From the size of the tread marks and the spacing between them, the sergeant concluded that a full-size pickup truck had been parked there. While these were being examined, Silver had meandered off to investigate some nearby bushes, after which he gave a sharp bark, sat down on his haunches, and looked expectantly at me.

"What'd you find Silver?" I asked, as I walked over. He looked pointedly down to one side, and there, in the scrub, was a cheap backpack. Closer investigation showed that it contained a rather heavy, polished mahogany box.

"Find something?" asked the sergeant, who had noticed us and come over to see for himself.

"Were the guns in a presentation case, by chance?" I asked.

"They were, and that looks like the description we were given." Pulling on a pair of gloves, he carefully removed the box from the backpack and eased open the two latches. There was nothing inside but the moulded depressions in the felt that would have held the two guns: revolvers from the shape of the depressions. Closing the case, he turned it this way and that, looking at the outer surfaces. "Looks like some nice prints here. We'll get them taken and run through your database. Maybe we'll be lucky and get a hit."

The other officers had more work to do, but it was clear that Silver and I had done all we could so, with their thanks for our help, we walked back to the original farm and our truck where I wrote everything up in my notebook in case we should be called sometime later to testify in court.

That done, I sighed and checked my watch. I was pleased that we'd helped enough to give the officers some clues, and a fighting chance to eventually catch their thief, but it was pretty routine and hardly qualified as one of our more exciting cases. It was, however, getting late. Uncle George's promotion social was scheduled for 7 to 10 pm, and it was already past 8. There was no way I'd be able to get home, clean up, change clothes and get over there in time. If I was going to go at all, I would have to drive straight there. As I looked down at the tactical uniform I was wearing, it brought new meaning to the term 'come as you are.' My boots were dirty, of course, but beyond that my uniform still looked pretty clean. *Oh well*, I thought, *he asked for it.* And I did want to honour his invitation and congratulate him.

Deputy Commissioner George MacLeod lived in Rockcliffe Park, a very historic and prestigious neighbourhood that is quite close to the centre of Ottawa. It was originally a small village, having been established in the mid-1800s, but eventually became amalgamated into the city of Ottawa. It contains many stately homes, with beautiful yards and mature trees and, of course, was inhabited by some of Ottawa's elite, and I slowed down a bit as I drove past Stornoway, a beautiful three-story period home owned by the federal government and operated as the residence of the leader of the Official Opposition. As I passed it, I couldn't help wondering whether Joe Clark[18] was in residence at that moment. The MacLeods lived a few blocks away, in a smaller but otherwise similar 19th-century house.

"Well Silver, this should be an experience for us," I said, as we got out of the truck and walked up to the front door.

When I rang the doorbell, I wasn't sure quite what to expect, but I was surprised when the door was opened by the Deputy Commissioner himself.

"Alex!" he said, with a big smile, "and Silver too, I see."

I instinctively stiffened to attention and saluted even though, strictly speaking, I needn't have as he was dressed in civilian clothes.

He nodded in acknowledgement, but said: "Now, now. At ease Alex. That's more than enough formality for tonight, thank you. I'm pleased you could come. Welcome to our home." Turning to look back into the house, he bellowed in a full, parade-ground voice: "Mary! Come see who's here!"

"I'm sorry about my appearance, Sir, but Staff-Sergeant Simpson said to come straight from work if necessary, and Silver and I just finished a search near Kemptville then came directly here."

"Don't worry about it, I'm just glad you were able to make it. Mary, I'd like you to meet someone." This last was directed at a woman who'd arrived at his shoulder. As he stepped aside, he said: "This is Alex Houston and her partner Silver. Alex, my wife Mary."

"How do you do Ma'am," I said, tipping my head deferentially.

"Alex?" she said, raising an eyebrow.

"Short for Alexandra Ma'am."

"Well, it's a pleasure to meet you Alexandra," she said, offering a hand to shake, "and you too Silver," she said, looking directly into his eyes.

"*Grruph*," said Silver, gazing directly back at her with a slightly inquisitive look. That broke the ice, and had everyone chuckling.

"You must call me Mary," she said, "none of that Ma'am stuff. It makes me feel old and stuffy. Now come inside and let's get you freshened up before you have to meet anyone else."

As we stepped inside, I paused to remove my boots and leave them – and my hat - in the entrance vestibule. Then, I was whisked upstairs to what was clearly Mary's bedroom, which had a beautiful Victorian-era makeup desk and mirror, and an attached bathroom.

"Don't worry about your uniform, but if you'd like to wash your face and run a comb through your hair, I'll see if I can find a pair of slippers for you that won't clash too much with your uniform trousers."

Thanking her, I set about to make 'emergency repairs' which didn't amount to much because my hair is fairly short, I don't normally wear any makeup, and didn't have any with me anyway. It did feel good to wash my face in warm water and run a comb through my hair though.

I'd just finished when Mary returned with a pair of handmade leather moccasins and pulled out a chair to sit on. The moccasins actually fit me reasonably well. "Very appropriate," I commented and thanked her.

"Well, you look better already," she commented, looking me over. Then, she reached out a hand towards my hair, saying: "may I?"

I nodded, and she gently ran her fingers through my red hair.

"It's too bad, your job won't let you grow it out," she said. "I'd give anything to have rich, thick hair like yours. It's your natural colour too, isn't it? It matches your green eyes and fair complexion beautifully. Your appearance isn't what I'd imagined at all.

"I know a lot about you, you see. George told me all about convincing you to leave the Toronto Police and join the Force, and how you and Silver first met – it must have been terrifying – and some of your adventures. He doesn't tell me the really secret parts, of course, but he hints at them, and the parts he has shared sound like they could have come out of adventure novels."

"Well, I've been very lucky," I replied. "I wanted adventure, I've been able to do the kind of work I love, and I've been able to survive too. So far, at least."

"Yes, you seem to have experienced more action in the past six or seven years than most officers see in an entire career. George is very proud of you, you know. He might not ever tell you to your face, but you can take it from me."

I blushed. "That's very kind."

"Well now," she said, deftly changing the subject. "Before we go and mingle, I'd like to explain a little bit about a side of the Force's culture that you may not have encountered before."

As I nodded, she pulled up another chair.

"You know better than I that the Force is still a male-dominated, paramilitary organization. Even with new women coming in each year, only one in ten of the new constables are women. That means culture change is coming, but it will take decades before there is any kind of gender equality within the ranks. Naturally, many of our friends are within the Force, and of our own generation. That means, when we go downstairs to mingle, you're going to find that all of the other women are spouses from an earlier generation, leaving you as the only woman who is a serving Member.

"On top of that, most of the men downstairs are senior officers. That's OK, you already know how to deal with them. But there's a kind of society among the wives that has its own hierarchy determined by the ranks of the women's husbands. Understand?"

"I suppose so. Presumably, it's the same in the military."

"Probably so. It's tempered a bit here in Ottawa, because our circle merges with those of the rich, and the politicians, and the diplomats, but it still exists. My only point is that you will be something of a novelty, and a very junior novelty in terms of rank. Everyone will be superficially nice tonight because of the setting but, underneath, some of them will be uncomfortable because they won't quite know where you fit in."

"Yes. Or if I fit in at all," I mused.

"I'm afraid so. I just thought I should warn you in advance."

"All right. Thank you. I think I'm as ready as I'm going to be, if you'd like to go down."

So, we went down, and Mary walked me over to a small group of people, introduced me, and then moved on to complete other hostly duties.

Then, periodically, after a few minutes she would come rescue me and introduce me to another group, and so on. Before long, I had met most of the people there and I was amazed at how efficiently, yet discreetly, she had managed it all. Everyone was very polite, and in many cases asked where I had grown up, and where I had been previously posted. I soon learned that almost everyone was originally from other parts of the country and that I was one of the few that had actually grown up in Ontario.

As Mary had predicted, everyone was polite and friendly. At least on the surface. But it wasn't exactly enjoyable and certainly not relaxing. A fair number of the women seemed rather condescending and, behind my back I heard a few whispering words to the effect that the Force had been crazy to begin letting women in. I did my best to pretend not to hear them, and to ignore them. Silver, perceptive as always, was tense and I had no doubt that he detected the unstated moods, and my reactions to them.

I reminded myself that I'd faced worse on my cases, like being shot at and nearly drowning or crashing in aircraft, and so on, but that didn't help as much as it should have. I guess we all share an inner desire to be liked. Having Mary move me around from group to group did make it easier for me, though, and I survived.

It was probably around 9:30 pm when the tinkling of a glass bell was used to call for order, and a distinguished looking man wearing a dark suit asked for a moment of everyone's attention.

"The Commissioner himself, no less," said a voice behind me. Although I turned to look, I'd immediately recognized the voice of Bob, my immediate boss.

"Hi Bob," I whispered, "when did you get here?"

"Just now. I was detained."

The Commissioner offered just a few remarks, in which he praised the new Deputy Commissioner's career and recent work leading the Security Service and said he looked forward to future great things from him. Although brief, I thought that his remarks carried a sense of genuineness and conviction.

For his part, Uncle George followed up with some nice words of thanks and appreciation for the opportunities he'd been given, reminded us that no one accomplishes great things all by themselves, and said some very complimentary things about the men and women it had been his pleasure to work with, and his honour to lead. His final words were: "The military have a saying: 'look after your troops, and your troops will look after you.' I've always felt it is quite appropriate."

"And *that*, is why most of us would follow him to the gates of Hell and back," said Bob, *sotto voce*.

I nodded in agreement. I felt that way too.

"By the way," continued Bob in a whisper, "don't rush off at ten o'clock with everyone else. Uncle George would like a quiet word with you before you go, but not while everyone else is still here."

I looked at him in surprise, but all he did was tip his head slightly down and tap the side of his nose with a forefinger.

"Corporal Houston, I believe," said a new voice behind me. This one, I did not recognize. When I turned, I was surprised to see who it was.

"Commissioner, Sir," I said, coming to attention.

"Relax, Houston. We're off duty here, although I see that you've been on duty more recently than the rest of us," he said, looking at my uniform with a chuckle. "No, no, you don't need to explain," he added, correctly discerning that I was about to apologize for having showed up in uniform. "George told me that you were off lending a helping hand to the OPP and only recently escaped to join us here." He looked down. "And this must be your partner, Silver. Hello Silver!" He carefully knelt down on one knee, held out a hand for Silver to sniff, and looked him straight in the eye.

Silver, having given him a sound sniffing, and a penetrating stare, decided the Commissioner was OK and relaxed.

"I think I just passed an inspection there," said the Commissioner. "It's probably just as well. I don't think I'd like to meet him alone on a dark night if he took an active dislike to me."

"No Sir. The first time I met him, it was in the dark, and I thought he was a wolf. When he snarled at me, it felt like every hair on my body was standing on end!"

"I don't doubt it. Is it OK if I offer him a dog treat?" he asked, rummaging in one of his suit pockets.

"Yes Sir, but please don't be offended if he doesn't take it. I've only seen him accept food from a stranger once and that was from my future fiancé."

"Ah yes, the good Captain Harrison. I've been hearing about him lately too…. Ah, here we go. I have two dogs myself, so I usually have a little something for them in my pockets. Used to carry a few lumps of sugar around with me too, in the old days, for the horses." He gave another low chuckle. "It took a while for my old troop-mates to figure out why the horses we were training with seemed to like me so much, but it was simple. I bribed them with sugar. Worked like a charm…. Here Silver. Would you like a dog biscuit?"

Silver, for his part, stunned me by gently grasping the dog biscuit with his front teeth, devouring it in a flash, and then looking up at us both with his mouth open and his tongue out in a wolfish grin.

"See what I mean?" said the Commissioner. "The Force is like one very large family. It was a pleasure to meet you Houston, George has told me quite a lot about you over the past couple of years, so I wanted to take the opportunity to meet you for myself."

As I thanked him, he strolled away, still chuckling quietly to himself.

"What do you think?" said a familiar voice. Bob had quietly materialized behind me again.

"Interesting. I sensed power and humanity at the same time. I think Silver did too. How can he possibly even know I exist? And he even seemed to know something about Don."

"Well, he can't know everything about everybody, of course, but he keeps up-to-date on the things he believes are important…. Excuse me, I see someone over there I need to speak with before this evening wraps up. Don't forget to stick around."

And with that, he was gone again, before I could ask him any more questions.

It wasn't much later that people began leaving, and soon there was a steady stream of people saying good-night and leaving. Mary came by to ask whether Silver might like some water, and led us to the kitchen for that purpose, so that by the time we re-entered the living room, everyone seemed to be gone.

Mary took this as a cue, saying "I have a confession to make. I delayed you purposely while everyone else left. George would like a word with you in his study, if you don't mind."

"Of course not," I replied, and she led me down a short hallway to the study, which was in a back corner of the house. She opened the door for me, and then closed it behind us after Silver and I had walked in.

The Deputy Commissioner was there, of course, looking more relaxed now that he'd removed his suit jacket and untied his tie and collar-button. With him was another man who was standing in one corner with his back to me, looking out one of the windows into the back yard. This second man was older, thinner, and not quite as erect in his bearing. I didn't recognize him from the back, but I could tell from his manner that Silver did. *Stranger and stranger,* I thought.

Before I could say anything, the study door opened again to admit a young man in a suit, who closed it behind him, and then walked in. He first gave a nod to Bob, and then looked at the Deputy Commissioner and said: "I just made the rounds of the whole security detail. All clear, Sir."

"Thank you," he said, and the man left, again shutting the door behind him.

"Thank you too, for staying behind for a moment, Alex. Please have a seat and get comfortable."

I sat with, perhaps, a hint of a frown.

If I did give a hint of a frown, he caught it immediately. "You've deduced that there's something unusual afoot, of course, and you're wondering why we would have a security detail covering the house and, in short, what the hell this is all about."

It was a statement, not a question, but I answered anyway. "Yes, Sir."

"It's a matter of national security, my dear," said the man in the corner.

I *did* know that voice!

"Admiral. Sir. I didn't see you out there tonight."

"No, you didn't, because I wasn't out there, and as far as anyone is ever going to know, I'm not here right now, either," said Rear-Admiral Peter White, head of the Canadian Forces Security Branch. We had met before, and I knew him to be a close friend of Uncle George and the boss of my fiancé Don, who was a Captain in Military Intelligence.

"Nice to see you again," he continued. "I hear you're going to marry one of my best intelligence operatives."

"Yes Sir."

"Good for you. He's a fine young man…. Now then, to business." He began rubbing his hands briskly, as he collected his thoughts. "I won't mince words. We have a problem."

I waited, but it was the Deputy Commissioner that spoke next.

"You've survived some extremely dangerous assignments in the past, but this one could make them look like a walk in the park. My conscience tells me that I can't ask you to take this one on, but my sense of duty says that I have to ask you exactly that, if you know what I mean."

"It's OK, Sir. If you really believe that it's me, that is, Silver and I that you want to send in, then whatever it is, the answer is yes. We'll take it on and do our best."

Uncle George looked so relieved that I immediately asked: "Did you really think I'd turn you down, Sir?"

"Well. Things have changed, haven't they? You're engaged now. I understand that you and Don each have inheritance income coming in from Don's late grandmother, so you probably don't need to work at all anymore, at least not because of the money. Besides, let's face it, you've cheated death more than once in some of the cases you've been on, Silver too. No one could blame you – no one could say you haven't done your bit and then some – if you decided to call it quits or wanted to shift to a desk job."

"Quits! Desk job!" I laughed and sat up straight. "Look, Sir, I was the one that left the Toronto force because I wanted to do some real policing – in the field! You gave me that opportunity. Then, when Silver and I found each other, it was you that cleared the path for us to get Silver in as a PSD, and I'll bet that took some doing on your part. And then, when you offered us the chance to transfer into the Security Service, and we took it, I found that Silver and I could take on things that I could never have previously even imagined. Silver was made for this kind of work. He loves it. And so do I. And all along you and Bob have had our backs…. So, now there's a new challenge? Count us in." I paused for a moment, and no one said anything; no one moved, and then I continued more quietly.

"You're right about one thing, of course. I can't keep on doing this forever. I don't want to die. I do want to get married. I want to have a family. I'll even want to retire someday – maybe even soon, when Silver does, because he's irreplaceable – to me anyway.

"But that day, is not today, Sir. If you want us for this, then count us in. A mutual colleague of ours recently commented that we'd follow you to the gates of Hell and back if you wanted." I avoided looking at Bob, who seemed to have found something interesting in the ceiling to look at. "I think our colleague was right."

Uncle George said... nothing. It was the first and the last time I ever saw him left speechless. It was Admiral White, that came to the rescue, with his trademark brisk manner.

"Well spoken, young woman. So," he said in anticipation, "let's get on with the planning, shall we?" He was rubbing his hands together again.

"Right," said Uncle George, regaining his composure, although it seemed to me that his eyes were a little moist.

"Have you ever heard of the Avro Arrow program?" asked the Admiral.

"Yes," I nodded, "it was going to be a supersonic fighter jet but the program was cancelled, wasn't it?"

"Indeed, in 1959 the program was scrapped and everything was ordered destroyed for security reasons. No one wanted the Soviets to be able to learn its secrets and use them against us. We weren't even allowed to transfer the know-how to the Americans, although they managed to get it all anyway, or the British, or the French, both of whom were interested. BUT," he said, smacking his hands together for emphasis, "someone acquired a complete set of the designs and manuals and sold them to the British."

There was silence in the room for a moment.

"We don't know who it was," continued the Admiral. "Both of our services knew the British got the plans, and the British knew that we knew, but it was never spoken of directly and we were ordered not to pursue it from the highest levels. They're our allies after all, it's not as if the secrets went to an unfriendly power, and our government wanted to avoid an embarrassing diplomatic incident. So, our predecessors followed orders and dropped it. But we have long memories in the intelligence business, and we never forgot that there was an insider threat somewhere. Since then, there have been a few other incidents – security breaches involving leaks of secret information - that our services were not able to quite get to the bottom of."

"You'll remember the Second World War weather station and the two East German agents you and Don caught in Nova Scotia a few years ago?" asked the Deputy Commissioner, picking up the tale.

"Vividly," I said. "1977. It involved the technology behind the plants in Cape Breton that were making heavy water for our CANDU nuclear reactors[19]."

"Right. Well, you broke up the information pipeline but we never discovered how the information was obtained in the first place."

"I remember now. Bob told me that he suspected an agent in-place somewhere, like in the plants, or at AECL[20] maybe."

"Very likely, but there may have been someone in the security and intelligence community as well, that put the pieces together, established the connections, and possibly even directed the operation. There were a few hints along those lines, but nothing actionable.

"There was also a case in the 1960s, in which an entire file disappeared that had been confiscated from a document forger. The file contained a half dozen 'legends,' complete fake identities and supporting documents that could be used to obtain Canadian passports[21]. They were sold to a broker, who was later apprehended, but the original source was never discovered.

"Well, there were a few other incidents but you get the idea. Now, it's possible that there's no connection between these incidents, but Admiral White and I think there is. The common thread is some kind of connection in either the Security Service or Military Intelligence[22]."

"A mole, then, do you think?"

"Not in the usual sense, because the consistent theme is money, and the beneficiaries of the security breaches are so varied: enemies, allies, crooks, and even organized crime. More likely it's a lone-wolf working for himself, and only when he wants, or when opportunities present themselves every few years.

"We even had Bob here try putting out bait a few times. Bits of real intelligence, but not critical intelligence, to see if we could expose the source." He paused and looked at Bob, who gave an unhappy-looking shrug.

The Deputy Commissioner sighed, and suddenly looked very tired. "In each case, we failed. In some cases, our mysterious agent managed to outwit us and take off with the bait. In other cases, they simply didn't even try for it, as far as we know. Whether the bait was too subtle and didn't come to the agent's attention, or the agent somehow smelled a trap and steered away, well, we don't know that either.... In fact, I'm beginning to wonder some days whether we really know anything at all." He seemed to be lost in thought for a moment, then his attention snapped back and his manner became a bit more brisk.

"There's another thing. This person's motivation might not be primarily money. We're coming to the conclusion that it might just be the challenge, and possibly even the opportunity to prove to himself that he's smarter than everyone else."

"He?"

"If we're right, then the first job was in 1959. At that time, only men were highly enough placed for this kind of work. Gender equity is only beginning to creep into our culture now, twenty years later, as you well know."

"So. Someone in security and intelligence, with a high security clearance as far back as 1959," I said.

"Top Secret or better. Yes. That someone would now be in his forties, if not older."

"There can't be all that many possibilities then, can there?" I asked.

"There are at least twenty people that could possibly have had access to the various materials over the years and who are still on active duty in high-security positions. Some are in the Security Service; some are in Military Intelligence; others are in the diplomatic service. All of them have Top Secret, or better, security clearances, and all of them are supposed to be above suspicion, including Bob here and even the Admiral himself."

I think my jaw must have dropped, as the implications set in. "So. You suspect none of them, but you have to suspect all of them," I whispered.

They both nodded.

"My God! What a mess," I said, trying to think. "But... why me? I'm not in counter-intelligence, or a spy catcher, except by accident."

"Really?" challenged the Admiral. "I understand that you caught a pair of East German agents in Nova Scotia[23] in 1977, and an international arms dealer operating on the West Coast[24] later the same year, and earlier this year there was that rogue, former CIA agent in Newfoundland and Labrador[25]. Am I right?"

"Yes sir, but I didn't always know who I was chasing, or exactly what they were up to…" I trailed off, and both men smiled at me as I realized that I was inadvertently making their case for them. "And, besides," I finished, rather weakly, "I had lots of help."

"You're selling yourself short, as usual Alex," said the Deputy Commissioner. "Besides, things seem to happen around you. I don't know how you do it, but you seem to fall into the middle of things, and you've been remarkably successful so far. Look at Silver there beside you. He's astoundingly perceptive. Sometimes, I think he can actually understand what we're saying. He has done things that don't make any logical sense, that science tells us are impossible, and yet he does them over and over again, and I have no qualms about using his talents either."

"Besides," put in the Admiral, in a quiet voice. "We've tried the conventional approaches. Gone by the book, you might say. We've done it very carefully; very quietly. Bob here was part of it when he was in B Section[26]. But we've gotten nowhere. As a result, we've decided it's past time we tried something unconventional."

I couldn't repress a chuckle. "And Silver and I are still the most unconventional team in the Force?"

"Yes," said the Deputy Commissioner, with a smile, "no contest. As for help, we'll try to get you anything you need, within reason, and this time you pick your own team. OK?"

"Yes Sir."

"Fine. When you communicate with Bob, assume you are being monitored. If you need to reach me, don't go through channels, call Mary here at home. It's simple and as secure as anything else we might dream up. This house is regularly swept for bugs and wiretaps. I'd set you up with a STU phone[27], except that they're so large it would raise questions by its very presence, and they're not portable yet either.

"I suggest that you ask Bob here for a few days leave to go visit your fiancé in Halifax. The Admiral will give Don a set of detailed notes containing a *précis* of the suspicious incidents and our attempts to get more information. Read; think; talk to Don. After that you can still back out. I won't hold it against you.

"If you're still in, then phone Bob and Mary separately, and tell them 'the game is on.' Then, pick your team and think up a cover story that will let you go off from time to time without arousing anyone's suspicions…. Any immediate questions?"

Millions, I thought. "Can I have Don?"

The Admiral nodded. They'd foreseen this, of course. "I'll give him a secure way to reach me as well," he said.

"Like I said, whomever you want, within reason. Just let us know. But don't take too long about it. All right?"

"Yes, Sir," and that was it. They thanked me, and Silver and I took our leave, pausing on the way so I could thank Mary again, for her hospitality, on the way out.

Then, having done that, Silver and I walked out in to the night air. Before we'd gone far, Bob caught up with us.

"You think Don will be OK with this?" he asked.

"Well, he'll understand at least, that's for sure."

"He's going to want to be involved, you know, if for no other reason than to try to keep an eye on you."

"Yes. I'm counting on that."

"I might have known. You're going to argue with him a bit, and then 'surrender' and agree that he can join the team. Aren't you?"

"Maybe.... Yes," I said, with a smile. "After all, Uncle George said I can pick the team."

Then, I stopped and faced him. "Seriously, Bob, you're not going to be happy with some of my choices."

"Some of your choices." He paused in thought for a moment, and from the change in his expression I could detect the exact instant that he realized what I was hinting at. "You don't mean...?"

"That's right. I don't have anything like a plan yet, but I think I'm going to need your niece, Ginger. Don't worry, her role will be advisory and well away from the action."

"Hmmm. That's what we all thought the last time...."

Laurie Schramm

3 THE INVESTIGATION BEGINS

Early November, 1980
Halifax, Nova Scotia

"How's it going?" asked Don, as we walked along the Halifax harbourfront. We didn't discuss my case when we were at Don's place for fear that it might be bugged, despite Don's periodic electronic sweeps to try to identify such things. We didn't use his phone for sensitive conversations either, for the same reason.

"Arrgh. I've gone through all the files the Admiral gave you for me, and it's like I was told. There have been serious leaks, but the only patterns in them seem to be that it was always information sold to various different parties: friends, foes, or criminals, and that they seem like crimes of opportunity. Like the Avro Arrow information all coming together at once and just when other countries were interested in getting their hands on it. Or the set of false identities all happening to become available at one time and in a single file."

"That's pretty much what the Admiral said to me when he handed me the files. How about the summaries of the investigations that were done?"

"None of the investigations turned up any clues, and in each of the cases there was enough police – military cooperation that the information could have been hijacked from either service.

"As far as the possible suspects go, every one of their background checks was gone over with a fine-tooth comb by Uncle George's and the Admiral's predecessors, and they found nothing. If any of them has been living beyond their known sources of income, taking expensive vacations, or racking up big gambling debts, then they've kept it well hidden."

"So they're all very clean or at least one of them is very, very careful," mused Don.

"Yes, but I think we could have assumed that from the start, given that whomever it is hasn't slipped up and been caught."

"Yes, that makes sense. Any other thoughts?"

"One thing that struck me after reading all the files was that there was another incident that wasn't even mentioned."

"What?"

"Yes. Remember when our government was trying to negotiate offshore mineral-rights access and secure a future strategic-mineral development, while I was running around Ottawa trying to protect Dr. MacKay's daughter from an international mercenary group that was trying to thwart us?[28]"

"Of course, that's when you got into that big shoot-out that still gives me nightmares!"

"Well, that's another time when, despite everyone's best efforts to maintain secrecy, information was getting to the bad guys that should have been nearly impossible to obtain. Information that nearly got me killed several times over. Everyone naturally suspected the Soviets in that case, with some justification I might add, but it wasn't from them that the mercenaries got their information. So who?"

"Good question, but look, whatever you do this could be the most dangerous thing you've ever attempted."

"More dangerous than accepting your proposal of marriage?" I teased.

"Alex! This is serious," he protested.

"OK. I know."

"At a minimum, you're going to have to be on your guard and assume that the leak knows that you're on the hunt. Depending on the person and how well placed they are, they may also try to interfere, misdirect, or even come after you directly."

"I know. That's going to really complicate things. I can't trust anyone but I'll have to trust some people in order to make any progress."

"Welcome to the world of espionage. It means only trusting people as far as you have to, and always bearing in mind that whomever you're dealing with at any given time could betray you."

I shuddered. "Maybe it's time to go back to regular police work."

"You can, you know."

"I know." I sighed. "But I said I'd take this case on and now I have to see it through."

Don turned and looked into my eyes for a few moments, as if to test my resolve. Whatever he saw there must have convinced him, because he sighed in return and I knew he was resigned to it.

"What next then?" he asked.

"Next, is to check in with Bob when I'm back in Ottawa,

***

When I returned to Ottawa, one of the first things I did was to check-in at the office and ask Bob for his advice.

"You've read all the file summaries?"

"Yes. When I was in Halifax. There really didn't seem to be anything there to follow up on."

"I agree. That's what I discovered when I went through them myself."

"Can you think of anything that might have been missed, or anything I should try?"

Bob sighed. "I been thinking about that, but I don't have anything specific to suggest. There have been a whole series of people that have looked into this already: my predecessor, Uncle George's predecessor, and the military intelligence people. Everyone has drawn a blank."

"Do you think there really is anyone to find then? Could it have been just be a series of isolated incidents over the years?"

"Possibly, but I doubt it. Maybe I've been in this game too long to believe in coincidences, but I think Uncle George and the admiral are probably right that someone has been playing games. If so, they've been very smart about it, and very careful not to overdo it."

"So, what do you suggest, then?" I asked.

Bob shrugged. "Just do what Uncle George asked you to do: bring a fresh perspective, question everything, challenge our assumptions, and think outside the box. In the meantime, you'll still be getting other assignments as usual. Is there anything you need?"

"No. Not right now. Not until I get some ideas, at least."

"Well, you know where to find me if you need anything, or even if you just want to talk things over."

So that was that. Since I didn't have any 'out of the box' ideas, I decided to pursue the one incident that had affected me, and which everyone else seemed to have overlooked: the leaks that had almost gotten me killed in the Diefenbunker[29].

One of the advantages of working in K Section: Special Operations[30], was that my assignments crossed the boundaries between straightforward crimes, intelligence, and counter-intelligence. As a result, people were used to me sticking my nose into all kinds of things, and it wouldn't have seemed out of the ordinary when I signed myself into the files room of F Section: Files. First, I searched for the file on the two East German agents I had exposed and helped to catch back in 1977[31], but that was just to provide cover in case anyone did get to wondering what I'd been looking for in the files. Before I left, I would even sign the file out to add to my cover story.

Next, I went after what I was really looking for: my file, and the files on the twenty 'possibles' that had been listed for me by the Uncle George and Admiral White.

When I found the Security Service's file on me, I flipped it open and gave the contents a cursory glance. Nothing seemed amiss. I was about to move on to other files when it dawned on me that it was strange that nothing should seem amiss, so I looked over my file once more. That time it hit me. It was on the page stapled to the inside cover: the sign-out list. What was interesting was what wasn't there. No one had signed it out in the days before the Diefenbunker episode, yet someone had passed information about me to both the as-yet unidentified international criminal organization and also to Soviet intelligence. That suggested that our leak was someone working in the Ottawa sections of the Security Service, as anyone else would have had to get the file signed out just to be able to read it – either that, or our leak didn't need the file because they already had the information in their head.

Although I wasn't surprised, it was both disappointing and frightening to realize that our leak was probably within the Force rather than within military intelligence.

Next, I drew the files of the twenty possibles. Although I'd read the summaries provided by Admiral White, I was curious to see whether there was anything different in our own service's files. For the most part, the two sets of files matched well with two exceptions. One of the twenty was a fellow in the diplomatic service for whom there had been an accusation that he could be a security risk with a communist past. This person had then been subjected to exhaustive investigation by the RCMP and also by the Department of External Affairs, and had been pronounced 'safe' by both. Although the conclusion was the same in each file, the Security Service one had more details concerning the investigation. Those details, although interesting, didn't seem to leave any questions unanswered. Although the poor fellow would probably be under a shadow of suspicion forever, I didn't see anything for me to follow-up on.

The second person of interest, Staff Sergeant Avery Blunt, actually worked in the Security Service and had been suspected of having communist leanings based on his days (in the 1950s) as a university student in the United States, where one of the things he studied was Marxism. It was probably doubly unfortunate for him that his last name was the same as that of one of the members of the infamous Soviet spy ring, the Cambridge Five[32]. Blunt, for his part, had consistently denied having ever done more than study the subject in his student days and apparently no one, including the RCMP, the FBI, MI5, or MI6 had come up with any real evidence to the contrary. This I already knew from reading the corresponding file I had been given by Admiral White. I also found it hard to believe that much suspicion remained, given that S/Sgt. Blunt was now head of B Section, Counter-Intelligence.

What was not in the Admiral's file, however was a somewhat rumpled, hand-written note that read "Might be worth checking to find out why subject was placed on the FBI Index." The note was unsigned. I had heard of the FBI Index. It was basically a blacklist established by J. Edgar Hoover[33] that contained the names of people the FBI considered to be highly suspicious or worse. Given the paranoia of the times, I had the impression that it was a very long list, but my curiosity was piqued and I made a mental note to check with my friend in the FBI.

On my way out, I did sign out the file relating to the East German agents' case, just to maintain my ruse, but I didn't bother to read it. I'd written most of it myself.

My next step was to call Mary to get Uncle George to call the Deputy Director of the FBI, to get approval for Special Agent Vivian Rule to help me secretly, when asked. Vivian and I had worked on previous cases together[34,35] and were both colleagues and friends. My request was quickly accomplished, and the next day found me using a downtown, public pay-phone to call her at her office.

"What's up Alex? The Deputy Director says to give you whatever help you need. You're not on a mole-hunt, are you?"

"It's a bit more complicated than that, but essentially, yes."

"Jeez. I was only kidding…. OK. What do you need."

"For now, just information. Is the FBI Index still active?"

"Sure. We don't call it that any more, but all the old files have been retained."

"Can you check a name for me: Avery Blunt. He's a Staff Sergeant in the Security Service, and I'm interested in anything you might have on him, including why you might have a record of him at all. Also, can you check for a file on him without anyone knowing about it?"

"Whew. You don't ask for much, do you?"

"Sorry. If it makes you feel any better, I just pulled the same kind of stunt with our own administration section."

"OK. Leave it with me. Where are you anyway? I can hear the sounds of vehicles going by."

"I'm calling from a pay phone. My phones might be bugged."

"Even your office!" Vivian exclaimed. Then, more thoughtfully, "you think your mole, or leak, or whatever might be well enough placed to be aware of your assignment."

It was a statement, rather than a question, but I answered it anyway. "Yes. I'm assuming so anyway. If you want to reach me at home or in the office, ask for Cathy or leave a message for Cathy if you get an answering machine. I'll phone you back when I can."

"Who's Cathy?"

"I don't know. It's just the first name that popped into my head."

"OK. Cloak and dagger stuff! Sounds like fun."

"Maybe, but watch out for daggers heading for you. I'm probably going to upset more than a few people before I'm done."

The next day, I received a call on my office phone. A muffled, man's voice asked to speak to Cathy, and when I said they had the wrong number the man swore rather graphically and hung up. It took me twenty minutes to leave the office and drive to a suitable public pay-phone to call Vivian in her office.

"Who was it that made the phone call for you?" I asked when Vivian came on the line.

She chuckled. "I asked a colleague here in the office to do it, not to ask any questions, and not to sound like an FBI agent. Here's what I found out. There is a file on your person of interest, but there's not much in it. The file was started back in '50s because in his student days he took a university course in Marxism down here."

"And?"

"And it was given a cursory check, but he didn't actually join any of the Marxist, communist, or fascist movements, and it seemed that he didn't even participate in any of the campus rallies. So, his file was simply retained as a possible person of interest in case other information came to light later."

"But nothing did?"

"Not much. There are several notes on the file that show when requests for information on him were received from your Security Service and MI6. That's the kind of thing that can make people suspicious, but the requests could have been simply part of Canadian or NATO checks for security clearances.... There is one other thing though. There is an old-looking, hand-written note stapled to the inside cover of his file saying 'Could be Gideon,' with a large question mark."

"Gideon. A cryptonym[36]?"

"Yes. We have an index file for cryptonyms, so I looked it up. The name Gideon has been used quite a few times over the years to refer to people or projects. Assuming that in this case the reference is to a person then there are still quite a few references, but only one to someone operating in Canada."

"Yes?"

"In 1959, someone contacted the U.S. Air Force offering to sell us classified information on the Avro Arrow jet fighter you people had developed. His code name was Gideon. The Air Force person contacted us to see whether we were familiar with the name, but we weren't. In the end, the Air Force decided that they already knew as much about the project as they needed to, so the contact wasn't pursued and the matter was dropped. The name Gideon was flagged though; in case it ever came up again."

"Thanks Vivian. I'll keep digging on my end."

After thinking about it a bit, I decided to keep the name Gideon to myself for a while, rather than run around asking whether anyone recognized it. Even at the time, I realized that I was becoming paranoid, but I didn't know how best to proceed and decided to keep as low a profile as possible until I knew more.

The next time I entered Bob's office, he said "I can tell from the look in your eyes that you have questions."

"Always," I said with a laugh. "In this case I have a few. Do we keep a master list of cryptonyms?"

"Like the FBI does? No, but we probably should. I have one of my own, and I'm positive that the heads of A and B Ops[37] each have their own."

"And do they share with each other?"

Bob chuckled. "Officially, yes, but probably not. It all depends on the circumstances and the personalities of the people involved at any given time."

"Need to know only?"

"Always. But beyond that, there are some things that the heads would probably keep to them selves even in the face of a direct order from the Commissioner himself. What are you after?"

"Well, I was wondering how readily accessible such information would be, and I'm also interested in the cryptonym Gideon."

"Gideon." Bob's eyes lit up. "Go ahead and ask the heads about it if you want. Use Uncle George's name if you have to, but I can tell you a little bit about it myself because I also came across it when I was walking in your boots.

"In the Avro Arrow incident, someone got hold of everything needed to build the Arrow. I mean everything: blueprints, parts lists, assembly instructions, manuals… everything, and then tried quietly shopping them around. He approached the British and the Americans for sure; possibly also the French. We got wind of this through the British, who said that he identified himself as Gideon. From the FBI, we learned that Gideon made the same offer to the USAF."

"And he really did sell to the British."

"Right. So much had already been shared between the RCAF and the USAF that the Americans didn't need to buy anything, and as far as anyone knows the French didn't pursue the matter at all."

"Did the name Gideon ever turn up again?"

"A few times, over the years, but only as speculation. It became kind of a joke after a while. People would say 'maybe it was Gideon' meaning that they really had no idea."

For the next few weeks, I worked on other cases while I waited for inspiration or opportunity. I got the latter, one day, when Bob mentioned that there was going to be a two-day information sharing conference involving the heads of all of the RCMP and military intelligence sections. The idea was to pool information and to make sure that the 'left hand' knew what the 'right hand' was doing, as the old saying went. The first day of the two-day conference would involve briefings on the domestic intelligence situation, while the second day would have briefings on the international intelligence situation. Since the sessions were open to anyone with Top Secret, or better, security clearance, I simply had to sign-up to get in as an observer. For me, this would be an opportunity to put faces to the names of the people on the watch-list that Admiral White had given me because I had only previously met some of them.

The conference was held in a secure meeting room in our headquarters building and comprised about 45 people, including all of the 20 that I was interested in, and I already knew about half of the 20. I focused about half of my attention on the intelligence briefings, particularly the ones on international security since I hadn't had much exposure to that side of the business. I was well acquainted with our close relationship with the FBI, since I'd worked with them myself several times, but was interested to see how closely we worked with the intelligence community of the rest of the Five Eyes[38] nations.

I focused the other half of my attention on the 'people of

interest,' particularly those that I had not previously met. In this area, there were no startling revelations, of course, but I did come away with first impressions and a better feeling for what everyone looked like than I'd been able to gather from mere photographs. That made me feel a bit better, for some reason, possibly because unknown demons are scarier than known ones.

Two people whose personalities did stand out somewhat seemed, at first glance, to be polar opposites. Staff Sergeant Avery Blunt, whose name had come to my attention through our files, as well as those of the FBI, came across as one of the nicest people you'd ever want to meet. I had to remind myself that dark things could lurk under the guise of an outwardly friendly manner. The other one, Staff Sergeant Alexander Demeniak, who was the head of A Section, Security Screening, came across as cranky, narrow-minded, and one of the fossils, as I thought of them, that regularly let it be known that there was no place in policing or the military for women. For him, I had to remind myself that he wasn't necessarily guilty just because I didn't like him or his mannerisms. Unfortunately, since one was the head of counter-intelligence and the other security screening, I was going to have to talk to each of them.

I didn't think the technical side of the event advanced my case at first, but in subsequent days an idea began to percolate. One of the presenters at the conference had discussed attempts – thus far unsuccessful – to identify an arms dealer that was operating in Canada and was somehow able to gain access to Canadian Forces weapons. That gave me the idea for a sting operation in which it might be possible to tempt our leak into action and at least show how the information flowed. This too, I kept to myself until an opportunity arose.

My next steps were going to be trying to meet with each of the 'possibles.' This took some time to arrange, and required a cover story. After talking it over with Bob, we arranged that he would 'assign' me to work on an old, unresolved case from 1959. It wasn't a particularly important case, but it had the virtues of being real, dating from the same time period as the Avro Arrow incidents, and unimportant and non-threatening enough to amuse people with the fact that I'd been stuck with such a dead-end task. "If people jump to the conclusion that you're being punished for something," commented Bob, "then so much the better. They might let something slip."

I won't go through the details of each of my meetings with these people, except to summarize those with Staff Sergeants Blunt and Demeniak.

Staff Sergeant Blunt was friendly and accommodating, insisting that I call him by his first name, but he was nobody's fool and immediately dismissed my cover story.

"That case is dead and cold, where it belongs. What are you really after?" he asked.

That shook me, so I admitted that he was right and that I really had been assigned to look into an old case that dated back to 1959, but that my orders came from the Deputy Commissioner, and I couldn't tell him what it really was.

"OK," he said, leaning back in his chair. "That makes a bit more sense. How can I help?"

"Can you tell me what cases stand out in your memory from that time?" I asked.

He thought in silence for a few moments. "Well, in 1958 there was a nuclear reactor incident at Chalk River[39]. This had been the second significant nuclear accident at Chalk River and we were called in to assess security measures and make recommendations.

"Then there was the Gouzenko affair[40] of course. The Royal Commission brought a bunch of things to the surface that we had to chase down, not to mention things that came up during the various trials. All together that kept us pretty busy until at least 1962."

"Was there ever any indication there might have been leaks in the security or intelligence communities?" I asked.

"Ah ha," he pounded. "So that's what you're really after is it?"

"Look," I tried again. "I'm sorry, but I'm not allowed to tell you anything specific. Not yet, at least."

"Fine." He smiled. Genuinely, I thought. "Ask your questions and I'll answer as best I can. No, there were no indications or accusations of leaks from the intelligence community. There were some university professors, some scientists from the National Research Council, a few people from the Department of Munitions and Supply, and some low-level administrative people in places like External Affairs, the Bureau of Statistics, the Bank of Canada, and even the National Film Board."

"External Affairs?" I asked.

"Yes, a cipher clerk, I think. I don't remember the name, but it will be in the files."

I made a note to follow that one up.

"Anything else?"

"Well, the only other big deal was the cancellation of the Avro Arrow program."

"And?" I prompted.

"Well, we were involved in helping to round up all the secret material: files, reports, and drawings - that sort of thing – and make sure they were all destroyed."

"And were they?" I tried to keep my face blank and my voice neutral.

"No. Now that you mention it, some of the material was either not handed over or diverted away from destruction. It was quite embarrassing for everyone at the time, because the British actually contacted us to tell us that someone had offered to sell them a complete set of plans, drawings and manuals for the Arrow, and that they had gone ahead and bought them."

"What happened?"

"Well, the British returned everything to us of course. They even said they'd tried to discover who the source was but failed. It was damn embarrassing I can tell you. It made us look like fools regardless of whether it was a leak, a mole, or just plain incompetence somewhere along the line.

"If you dig hard enough, you'll discover I was peripherally involved, so I'll just tell you straight out. I was a young Corporal at the time, helping shred Arrow documents. It was tedious work, but when the dam burst all of us went from boredom to panic in a hurry! We were all afraid we'd be fired even if we hadn't done anything wrong."

"Had you?"

"You're very direct."

"I'm not dumb enough to play games with the head of counter-intelligence, and I'm no psychologist," I responded.

"From what I hear, you're not dumb at all, and you don't have to be a psychologist as long as you have your dog with you." He looked pointedly at Silver, who was lying on the floor beside my chair, watching everything.

"What have you heard?"

"About you? That you're the Director's rising star. About your dog? People are saying you think he's part psychic."

"And that I'm crazy?"

"No, I haven't heard that," he chuckled. "But you'd be smart to assume people think it."

"Why do I get the feeling that you don't?" I asked.

"I've read your case files, and Bob's notes on them. The people you've put away seem to be absolutely convinced that you and your dog are both part psychic. For myself, I don't believe in that kind of stuff, but one way or the other you always seem to get the job done and that's what counts the most around here."

"So, if I asked what you know about Gideon, you'd tell me the truth?"

"With him watching me with that intent stare of his?" He looked at Silver again. "No. Normally, I'd tell you nothing at all, but in this case, I'll make an exception because I want Gideon caught too."

I raised an eyebrow.

"No, it isn't me, but I don't expect you to take my word for it. In fact, I know that there's still a shadow over a bunch of us old-timers because Gideon was never identified and it could be any of us. I also know that the FBI suspected me, and probably still does, although they have a tendency to suspect everyone of everything anyway. Naturally, I'd like to get my name cleared, but I tried to find out who Gideon is, or was, and failed, so if you can do it, you'll have my blessing, and my thanks too."

"Do you know who it was on the British side that raised the alert? I read the file, but couldn't find it."

"That's because it isn't there to find. He was basically a source trying to help us out so, to protect him, his name was never mentioned; never written down.'

"But you know who it was?"

"I know who it had to have been." He paused and stared at me for a while, then seemed to make a decision. "Don't write this down, but the name you want is Major Jack Evans. In 1959, he was the Defence Attaché, at the British High Commission here in Ottawa. I don't know whether he's still in the service, or even if he's still alive."

"I think I'll go see if I can find out. Thank you for your help, I really appreciate it," I said as I stood up to leave.

"Just do me two favours: find the bastard for us, and always remember that if anyone asked, I told you...."

"Nothing. You told me nothing at all."

He nodded in appreciation as we left.

Meeting with Staff Sergeant Demeniak, the head of A Section, Security Screening, was completely different. In the first place he refused to see me at all, claiming that he was too busy. When I got Bob to go to bat for me Demeniak gave him exactly the same treatment. Bob didn't take that lightly and got the Deputy Commissioner to call him, after which Demeniak ungraciously consented to "spare me a few minutes."

Unsurprisingly, he was hostile, vulgar, and sexist in his comments. This produced a low warning growl from Silver that actually prompted him to tell me to "get that dog" out of his office before he shot him. I was in full tactical uniform at the time, as we had just returned from a call, and when I stood up, I could see in his eyes when it dawned on him that I was armed and he wasn't. Not that he'd have shot Silver anyway, of course, nor I him, but it did put him on the defensive for the first time.

For my part, I avoided calling him an asshole to his face – barely – and simply smiled sweetly, said "Thank you Staff," and left. "Smile," a sergeant had once advised me. "It makes people wonder what you're up to." I've always liked that one and have used it a few times to good effect.

I continued smiling as I walked down the corridor, but my teeth were grating and my jaw was clenched. Even Silver looked up at me from time to time trying to judge my mood.

So, I hadn't learned anything useful from Staff Sergeant Demeniak and, in the end, I didn't learn much I didn't already know from any of the others I interviewed, whether they were in the RCMP, Department of External Affairs, or the military. Some of the latter I'd had to travel to Halifax to see, and it was in Halifax that I got wind of another opportunity. Strangely enough, it came from a news report I heard on the radio.

4 A SECRET MEETING

January 22, 1981
Halifax, NS.

"Don, would you take me to a hockey game?" I asked as Don, Silver, and I were walking along the Halifax harbourfront.

Although it sounds un-Canadian to say it, I wasn't a huge hockey fan but I knew that Don was. So, in the pause that followed, I imagined him doing a mental double-take.

"Uh, sure," he said. "Did you have a particular game in mind?"

"Actually, I do. On the news today I heard that after postponing it twice[41], they've finally settled on a schedule for the Canada Cup and I want to see one of the games." This much anticipated hockey tournament was finally going to get underway between teams from the six 'best hockey countries' in the world: Canada, Soviet Union, United States, Sweden, Czechoslovakia, and Finland. Games and the various rounds were going to be held at arenas in Edmonton, Winnipeg, Montreal and Ottawa.

"Any particular reason for this sudden interest in hockey?"

"Well, it's the talk of the town. Around the office, everyone seems to think that the series will come down to Canada against either the Soviets or the Americans."

"Probably. What game do you want to see?"

"I want to see the championship final between Canada and the Soviets. It's going to be on September 13 at the Montreal Forum[42]."

"What makes you so sure those will be the two finalists?

Anything can happen in a hockey tournament, you know. Unexpected injuries, even, can make a big difference."

"Yes, I know. I guess I'm playing the odds. Maybe we should get tickets for the two semi-final games as well, just in case. Besides, I think I should learn more about our national game and this is in the nature of *homework*."

I didn't place heavy emphasis on the last word, but we had arranged to use a code word for my mission in the course of our personal conversations: homework.

Don picked up on our codeword and stopped probing.

"OK. Let me see what I can do."

"Thanks. I'll try from my end too, but it will improve our odds if we both try."

"Sounds good to me."

My next call was to Mary MacLeod, the Deputy Commissioner's wife.

"Mary, this is Alex Houston. We met at your husband's promotion party at your house."

"I remember it well Alex, how are you?"

"Just fine, thank you. I have a special request, but it's going to sound frivolous."

"I'm sure it will be fine dear. What is it you need?"

"I'd like to get two tickets for each of the semi-final games and also for the final game of the Canada Cup hockey tournament. The final's going to be at the Montreal Forum on September 13th."

"You want to go to three hockey games?"

"Well, not really, but I think there's going to be someone at one or two of them that I'd like to have a quiet talk with. Someone that I don't want anyone to know I'm speaking to. Not even Bob."

"All right dear. I understand. I'll talk to George about it, but I don't know whether he can help or not, I heard on the news that all of those games are selling out fast."

"I know, that's why I'm asking for help. If it helps, I don't need good seats, I just need a pair of seats anywhere in the building, even if it's in the nosebleeds[43]."

"Give us a few days and then call me back."

Thanking her, I said goodbye and hung up. Now, I just had to wait and hope for two lucky breaks: one that I could get tickets, and the other that the Soviet team would actually make it to one of the final games.

Once again, it was hurry-up and wait. I never liked the waiting part but, with me back in Ottawa, my regular duties kept me busy with routine things until the fall, and I did do a few things related to what I now thought of as my Gideon Case. One of the latter that later turned out to be important was tracking down the British Military Attaché from the Avro Arrow incident.

Don and I spent so much time apart that we normally had a nightly phone chat no matter where our respective jobs took us. I have already mentioned our choosing a personal code word for my mission (homework). We'd also come up with a list of places that had a public pay phone Don could go to if I ever said that I'd like to discuss my 'homework' with him sometime. In such a case, he would go to the next place on the list, and I would call him there from a randomly chosen pay phone wherever I was. In this way, we'd never use the same phone combination twice. I kept my copy of the list in a hidden compartment in Silver's collar.

The first place on the list was just outside the Dartmouth fast-food restaurant in which Don and I had first met. When I phoned Don there, it was to ask him to quietly see if he could find out what had happened to the Major Jack Evans that had been Defence Attaché at the British High Commission in 1959 when Gideon had made contact about selling the Avro Arrow plans.

Several days later, a call to my office phone yielded a muffled male voice asking for Cathy. When I explained that he must have dialed the wrong number, the voice said: "Are you sure? It's pretty important I talk to her. It's about her homework." I repeated "Sorry, but you must have dialed the wrong number." The voice then grumbled something I couldn't make out and hung up.

Reaching for Silver's collar, I removed it to access the second list I had hidden there. This one had a list of Ottawa pay-phone locations at which Don could call me. Silver and I left the office to drive to the next unused one on my list.

I was starting to feel conspicuous loitering around public pay-phones by this time, so I was relieved when this latest one began to ring. It was Don, of course, and he had the information I'd asked for.

"It's Colonel Jack Evans now, but retired. He's now a widower, and living in England."

"Do you have an address for him?"

"An address but no phone. It's in Bath."

"Hmmm. I suppose it doesn't matter. He'd hardly be willing to talk to a stranger on the phone about intelligence matters. Even ancient ones. I may need to go pay him a visit. We'll see."

While we had each other on the phone, we chatted about a few other things, but they weren't related to the case. My first instinct turned out to be right though: I was going to have to go look him up later on.

**

Early September, 1981

"Have you been watching the series?" Bob asked me one day when we ran into each other at the office coffee machine. He didn't need to identify what he meant by 'series,' almost everyone in Canada had been watching the hockey series and it was the main topic of conversation in coffee shops across the country, even to the point of beating-out Canadians' favourite topic: the weather.

"A bit. Mostly on TV. I saw Canada beat Finland during the first round, and I watched Canada beat the Americans in the second round. I missed the third and fourth round games, but Don and I actually got to go to the semi-final game here in town and watched the Soviets beat the Czechs 4 - 1."

"Lucky you. Are you going in on the office pool for the final game?"

"You bet." I didn't tell him, or anyone, that I'd gotten my real wish already: the final game was going to be between Canada and the Soviets, and Don and I had tickets for the game, which would be at the Montreal Forum.

September 13, 1981
Montreal, QC

Don and I flew to Montreal and, since I was on duty, I was able to bring Silver on the plane with us. When we arrived at the Montreal Airport on the morning of game day, we were met outside the terminal building by an unremarkable-looking sedan. When the driver got out to help us with our luggage, my first impression was that he looked like he could have been a defensive lineman for a professional football team: large, well muscled, but with a spring in his step that suggested remarkable agility. A second glance revealed that I had met him before on an earlier case[44]. Silver, of course, had recognized him right away and didn't react to him at all.

"Sergeant Wilson!" I exclaimed. "The last time we met you were in full battledress, armed to the teeth, and bundling me into a 5-ton army truck."

He gave me a huge smile. "I'm surprised that you remember me Ma'am, and I'm sure glad you survived that one. The scuttlebutt is that you did some real damage with that shotgun you were carrying."

"Well, I was very lucky and I feel fortunate to have been able to walk away more or less intact, Sergeant."

"Frank Ma'am – remember?"

"Only if you call me Alex – remember?"

"Fair enough," he said, chuckling as he helped us load our bags and get in.

As we drove away, I noticed that we didn't have to tell him where we were staying. Don had obviously given him the address already.

When we had travelled the main highway from the airport and exited into the downtown core, I glanced behind us from time to time and was just about to make a comment when I noticed Frank looking at me in the rear-view mirror.

"Don't worry Ma'am... I mean Alex, that car following us is one of ours."

"Do you remember meeting Lieutenant Sandy Moore a few years ago[45]?" asked Don.

"The helicopter pilot? Yes, he picked me up in Alaska, flying one of those giant helicopters of yours."

"Well, that's him back there. He's following us to make sure no one else does, if you know what I mean."

"I do, but what's a helicopter pilot from the Pacific Fleet doing driving a car here?"

"Well, Sandy works for us. He's a very capable fellow, just like Sergeant Wilson here. You'd be amazed at some of the things they can do, but their most important qualification right now is that I'd trust them with my life – and yours."

It seems that no one else was following us so, without the need for evasive maneuvers, we were efficiently deposited at our hotel, where we checked into a very nice suite – using false names and addresses. Don even had a credit card and an Ontario driver's licence made out in the false name he was using.

We had arrived in time for lunch and a nice walk around town with Silver, and hadn't been back in our suite long before there was a knock on the door. When I went to open the door, there was a loud squeal of delight.

"Alex!" said Ginger Brandt, the famous Canadian TV and film actress. We had met several years earlier when she helped me with a case[46], at the suggestion of her uncle, who was also my boss, Bob.

"Ginger! It's been too long." We exchanged a longish and heartfelt hug, after which I led her into the room. "Don, come see who's here." Don came in from the other room, but Silver beat him to Ginger, having rushed up and stood on his two back legs so he could get a few licks in.

Don had to look at her quite intently before he realized who she was. "Ginger!" he exclaimed. "But you don't look like Ginger Brandt."

"Elizabeth Peterson is my real name," she corrected. "Ginger Brandt is my stage name, and this" – she pointed to herself with a sweeping motion – "is the disguise I use when I want to get away from my fans and the media." As she stood there in our suite, she appeared to be two or three inches shorter than Ginger the actress (who wore high heels), had hazel-coloured eyes (instead of Ginger's blue contact lenses), lustrous, medium-brown hair cut short (instead of Ginger's long blond wig), wore no makeup (which Ginger would never do), and had glasses (which Ginger didn't). I'd seen her dress like this before, but the effect was still remarkable. The one thing she couldn't hide was her brilliant smile.

"I still can't get over how effortlessly you pull this off," I said.

"Well, I'm an actress, so it's kind of like another role. Besides, I do it so often that I can switch personalities almost without thinking, and it does me good to spend some time as the real me every once in a while."

After catching up a bit on things since we'd last seen each other, Ginger brought our meeting to order, saying: "All right Alex. What are you really up to?"

"As you know, the big hockey game is tonight. The Soviets are going to have two big things on their minds: winning the game and, more importantly, making sure none of their players try to defect after the game. Because of that, their intelligence people are going to be watching everything and everybody very closely. I want to have a quiet chat with one of those intelligence people."

"Are you sure the person you want will be there?"

"Not for sure, no. But he's pretty senior over there, and I think they'll have everyone out in full force. In any case, it's a chance I have to take, but I don't want their watchers to recognize me if they see me talking to him. That's where you come in. Did you bring everything?"

"You bet," she said, lifting the medium-sized suitcase she was carrying. "Are you ready to get started?"

'Yes," I said, excitedly.

"OK then. Don, if you wouldn't mind taking Silver for a long walk, we have some things to do. Give us at least 45 minutes and then come back. You'll be the judge and jury."

When Don and Silver had left, Ginger got down to business. Opening her suitcase, she first removed two cases. One was a makeup case and the other contained a blond wig.

"Is that one of yours?" I asked. "Sure is," she replied. "I have a room full of duplicates so we can switch them out as fast as they get damaged or worn out, but let's start with makeup."

"But I don't wear makeup and, anyway, I only need to look different from a distance. I don't expect to get very close to any of the watchers, just the man I want to talk to."

"The makeup isn't so much a part of the physical disguise. It's to help make you feel the new look. The more you feel different, the more your body language will fit the disguise rather than the real you. Trust me, OK?"

"You know I do."

"Good. Then sit down and relax. This is going to be fun."

So, I tried to suffer in silence while Ginger gave me the full treatment: lotions, powders, eyebrow pencil, mascara, false eyelashes, the works. So much so, that I fully expected to look quite garish, but when she had me look into a mirror, I was astonished to see that everything had been done very subtly. It was me, but it wasn't me.

"Amazing," I exclaimed. "After all that work, you've only changed everything a little bit, but it changed everything."

"Exactly. If I paint you up like an actor on stage and give you monstrous eyelashes, it would produce exactly the wrong effect. We're not trying to make your *face* stand out, we're just trying to make it difficult to recognize."

Something about the way she said the word face caught my attention, and she noticed.

"Yes. We will be a little more drastic with some other parts of you, beginning with these. Since you aren't used to wearing contact lenses, we'll use glasses." She then had me try on several pairs of glasses (with plain glass lenses) before deciding on one. "And now the hair." She had actually brought two blond wigs with her, and had me model each before deciding on one. Then she brought up the mirror again. "Look" she said, expectantly.

I gasped, then giggled. "I can't believe it!"

"Neither will Don, but we aren't finished yet. Let's try some clothes. I'd like to put you in high heels to change your height but, since you aren't used to them, you'll just wobble around and be lucky not to fall over and draw attention to yourself – the wrong kind of attention. So, once again, we're going to be a bit more subtle. A nice top and skirt that you can wear with the shoes you already have on."

"Ugh. Do I have to wear a skirt?"

"Let's not go through that again. I want you to do almost everything except what you usually do. That means almost nothing you're comfortable with. Right?"

"Fine," I grumbled. I wasn't looking forward to this as much any more.

"My goodness," she said, "trying to get you looking feminine is like trying to get Silver to go near water. Now, suck it up and try these on."

Once again, she had brough a couple of skirts and a couple of tops. The skirts were short – not miniskirts, but close, and the tops were more revealing than anything I was used to wearing. After modelling every possible combination for her, Ginger selected one. She certainly had a good eye and a good memory, as everything fitted me quite well.

"Not bad," she decided. "Now try the top with one of these." She reached into her suitcase and brought out a couple of bras.

"But I already have… push-up bras? Oh no. That's going too far."

"Humour me," she said. "See which one fits best. It needs to be comfortable or you'll be fidgeting and readjusting everything all the time."

So, I clamped my jaw and tried those on too. Surprisingly, I found one that wasn't anywhere near as uncomfortable to wear as it looked.

"OK, now one more thing." Out from her suitcase came pantyhose, quite sheer and natural in colour, but in slightly different shades. Now that my outfit had been selected, she picked one out right away, saying: "These should do nicely. Just enough colour to warm-up your pale skin."

Once I had everything on, Ginger made me practice walking around the suite until I relaxed a bit, then said: "Fine. Let's go down to the lobby. We'll surprise Don when he and Silver walk in and see what he thinks."

"OK. Wait a minute." I felt around the top of the skirt. "There aren't any pockets. Where am I going to put everything?"

"Ah yes, I thought of that." Back in to her suitcase she went and brought out a small, tan-coloured leather purse that would go with almost anything casual. "I thought you might feel undressed without that little derringer of yours," she said, handing it over.

Sure enough, there was just enough room for my wallet, a few tissues, and the fancy-looking, double-barreled silver derringer that I often wore concealed when I was working undercover. "It looks like a toy, doesn't it? But it takes .38 Special rounds and is deadly at close range."

Ginger looked at it, shuddered, and said "Let's go."

A few minutes later, we were in the hotel lobby where we found a couple of comfortable chairs with a good view of the main entrance. Not too comfortable however, as I couldn't just flop down in the softest looking easy chair like I would have with pants on. While we waited, Ginger and I continued to catch up on things, trading stories of some of my recent cases for her accounts of recent film sets, TV episodes, and a new movie she was going to be filming soon. Before I knew it, there were Don and Silver coming in the front door.

"Don! Over here!" Ginger called out, with a wave.

Silver immediately spotted us and led Don to where we were sitting. As he approached, I stood up and watched as he spotted me, looked me up and down with a quizzical expression on his face. Then he looked at me again and did a gratifying double-take. "Alex!?" It was half exclamation, half question.

"That's me. Same old Alex," I replied, with a wink.

"It's amazing," said Don. "I would have walked right past you.

It's only up close that your face and your green eyes give you away."

"Yes, well almost no one is going to get that close, and it's not her eyes they're going to be looking at, is it?"

"I'll say," said Don, looking me up and down again.

"Don!!" I exclaimed, and he had the grace to blush. Very cute.

"So, does she pass?" asked Ginger, with a complacent smile on her face.

"She passes all right. I think she'll fool everyone except Silver."

So, now we had the disguise; we just had to wait for game time and see if it was all going to be worthwhile. When it was time to walk to the Montreal Forum, which was less than a kilometre from our hotel, I wasn't shocked to spot two men walking about a block behind us.

"A bit of an unusual looking pair wouldn't you say?' I asked Don. Sergeant Wilson, as I've already mentioned looked like he could have been a linebacker from the Montreal Alouettes, his muscles straining the fabric of his civilian clothes. He was dark-haired, and exuded a sense of rough toughness. Lieutenant Sandy Moore, in contrast, was fair-haired, a bit taller, and much thinner. He looked more like a cowboy in street clothes.

"Just a couple of friends taking in a hockey game," said Don.

"They have seats too?" I asked, surprised.

"They do. In fact, they'll be sitting almost directly behind us, but a few rows back."

"I'm amazed. How did you pull off getting an extra two seats? I can still hardly believe that Uncle George even got seats for us."

"Miracle workers. That's us. You make a wish; we'll try to make it happen."

"I wonder whether Admiral White fully appreciates the kind of talent he has on his team."

"That's what we think. Maybe you should tell him some time."

"I will, but he may think I'm just a tiny bit biased."

Our walk to the Forum was uneventful. Apparently, we weren't followed. So, all seemed well as we went in and found our seats. It was a sellout crowd of over 17,000 people. They were excited but quiet. It was almost as if the crowd was holding its collective breath.

"You still think he'll be here?" Don asked quietly, with his mouth close to my ear.

He knew in advance, of course, but Ginger didn't know, that the point of this whole exercise was that I wanted to meet 'the enemy.' Although the Soviet Union was normally the arch foe of the Western Allies, especially when it came to international intelligence work, there were times when we worked as allies again, almost like we were back in the days of the Second World War. There weren't many such times, to be sure, but one of them intersected with a case I'd fallen into in which we had a common enemy and the Soviets had contributed the services of a man named Emi, who was really an intelligence officer of their Foreign Intelligence Service (as distinct from the KGB or the GRU).

Without Emi's help I really doubt that we could have resolved the case, nor that I would have survived[47] and, as it turned out, we worked well together and became respectful colleagues even though we worked for opposing governments. At that time, he'd been Captain Emilis (Emi) Matulis and, officially, an Assistant Military Attaché at the Embassy of the Soviet Union in Ottawa. Since then, he'd been promoted to Major and made Chief Military Attaché at the embassy.

To Don's question, I replied: "After last year's defections of the Šťastný brothers from the Czechoslovakian team[48], I'll bet every intelligence officer they have will be here watching to make sure there are no Soviet defections. I'm pretty sure he'll be here too."

Although we didn't have terrific seats by hockey-fan standards, they suited my purpose admirably. We were about two-thirds of the way up the stands, but almost in line with the centre-line, and we were directly across the rink from the players' benches. I had brought a compact pair of binoculars with me – not an uncommon sight in the higher-up seats, and was using it to scan the seats on the other side, looking for Emi.

This was the most stressful part of the evening for me. I had gambled that the Soviet team would be in the series final and doubled-down by gambling that Emi would be in the crowd as part of the Soviets security force. I think Don was aware of the exact moment I spotted Emi as, with a whoosh, I released the breath I hadn't realized I was holding.

"See something?" asked Don, as nonchalantly.

"Directly behind the Soviet team's bench, about ten rows up."

"So, you can relax and watch the game now."

That made me laugh. "As I look around, I don't think there's a relaxed person in this whole building." I'd been to an NHL game in the Montreal Forum in the early 1970s, and compared with that experience the Montreal Forum was strangely quiet. Perhaps it was because so much national pride was riding on this one last game, but it was the players that were really under pressure. The Soviet team had entered the tournament as the favourite, with a mixture of seasoned and younger players and was led by the famous 'KLM Line' of Vladimir Krutov, Igor Larionov, and Sergei Makarov. The Canadian team, in comparison, was much younger, although it boasted such rising young stars as Wayne Gretzky and Ray Bourque. Both teams had done extremely well during the earlier rounds, and now they would face off against each other for the final, big game.

The first period was a nail-biter, with Canada on the offensive throughout the entire period but unable to get the puck past the Soviet's star goaltender Vladislav Tretiak. As the period ended with the score tied 0 – 0, Don and I, like almost everyone else in the arena, found ourselves sitting on the edges of our seats, still holding our breath.

"Wow," said Don. "I think it's going to be a close one. Either that, or the first goal for either side will trigger a shoot-out."

"A shoot-out, I think," I replied. "There's so much talent and energy out there, just waiting to be released."

During the first intermission, Emi seemed content to remain in his seat, so I did the same while Don went to secure some hot dogs and pop for us.

It was the Soviet team that dominated the second period, scoring a goal within the first five minutes. Although Canada quickly scored to even the score, the Soviets responded in kind with another goal to retake the lead. At that point I got up to make the long walk around to the other side of the Forum. When I got there, I stood at one of the two nearest doorways to Emi's section, to keep watch to see whether he would get up to find either a restroom or refreshments. I'd no sooner arrived at my vantage point than the crowd gave out a huge, collective groan as the Soviet team scored a power-play goal, giving them a 3 – 1 lead. Although there were still a few minutes left in the period, I saw Emi rise up from his seat and make his way to the other side of his section from the side I was on. As he did so, I quickly moved to the door on the far side of his section and waited for him to make his way up the steps.

Noticing that he seemed to be headed for one of the concession windows, I came up from behind him and said, "Buy you a hot dog, Comrade Major?"

He was too experienced to show any sign of being startled, and without breaking stride he simply said "I know that voice, and yes, I do like your decadent hot dogs."

After another couple of paces, he causally glanced at me and I saw his eyes widen as he took in my appearance.

"You're changed your hair colour since I saw you last, and grown it longer too."

"All the better to not be recognized speaking to you," I replied.

"Ah ha," he responded. "I would have had a difficult time believing that meeting you here was pure coincidence."

"No. I took a chance, hoping you'd be here helping ensure there are no embarrassing defections."

"Quite correct. A distasteful, but unavoidable assignment, I am afraid."

"May I have a brief word with you after we get our hot dogs?"

"Of course, but only if they are, as you say, 'on me' tonight."

Once we'd obtained our hot dogs, we moved to one of the many places where fans could stand and chat while eating and drinking, before returning to their seats. I congratulated him on his promotion to Major, for which he thanked me, then, after a moment he stopped talking and just looked at me, expectantly. That was my cue.

"You remember when you penetrated what we call the Diefenbunker to help me in the underwater minerals case?"

"Of course. It was not an experience easily forgotten."

"Well among all the other strange aspects of the case were the fact that you somehow knew where I would be, and you seemed to know all about me, some of my earlier cases, and Silver, too, for that matter. Much more than anyone should ever have been able to find out."

"Yes. I was hoping you'd overlook that given the other pressures we faced."

"You're half right. I noticed and chose to overlook it. I meant to ask you about it later, but the right time never seemed to materialize and I was so grateful for your help that I didn't pursue it."

"Something is telling me that you intend to pursue it now though. No?"

"Yes, because now I have a 'need to know,' as we say. I realize that if you have a mole in the Security Service or our Military Intelligence that you're not going to admit it, but I'm hoping that if you got your information from some kind of leak or information broker that you might be able to throw me a bone... Excuse me, I mean give me some kind of lead."

"Yes, I understand your 'throw me a bone,' although from where you get these strange expressions I cannot imagine. As to your question...." He paused, as if searching his memory. "I will tell you frankly that my service has no mole in your system, however I cannot speak for the KGB or the GRU. In the case where we worked together, it was much simpler. We had an intermediary – a broker, if you will – that had a source that could gain access to your service's files."

"OK. I won't ask you who your intermediary is, or was, but can you tell me anything about the source?"

He looked at me intently for a few moments, then took a bit of his hot dog – probably to buy more time – and for an instant, I didn't think he was going to say anything more. But then he did.

"You wouldn't approach me in public and ask me this unless it was very important." It was a statement, but I answered it anyway.

"Very important, and what I'm after is purely defensive, no threat to your country."

"Hmmm. Well then, for the sake of our former comradeship-in-arms together I will tell you the only things I have ever learned about this so-called source in Ottawa. First, my interpretation is that this is no ideological traitor but most likely a highly-placed opportunist motived by money and perhaps even 'the game' as our business is sometimes termed. Such people are completely untrustworthy, but can be useful if handled carefully. Secondly, the person's name – man or woman I don't know – appears to be Gideon. I am not certain of it, you understand, but I believe it is likely to be the case.... I see that the name is not unknown to you."

"No, the name is not unknown to me. It has been used before. Many years before, in connection with another incident."

"You are going to try to find this Gideon?"

"Yes."

"Even though you are neither a trained nor experienced intelligence officer?"

"Even though," I nodded. "Several experienced professionals have tried, without success. I am what is being called a fresh approach."

"Yes. I understand. Someone who sees things differently, thinks about them differently, without the usual preconceptions…. It could work. Sometimes this approach works, but this is dangerous. It sets the amateur against the professional." He raised his hands immediately. "I mean no disrespect. In other fields you are the professional and I would be the fish that is out of water. Yes? But in this case, you are…."

"Expendable."

"I was going to say vulnerable."

"I can't help that," I countered. "I can only do my best and hope it works out."

"Yes, well, in spite of what I just said, I would not like to have you coming after me. I think you would be imaginative and relentless, that makes you dangerous too."

I smiled my best feral smile.

"Thank you, Emi. I appreciate your help."

"You are welcome, and I will let you 'owe me one' for it. Now, would you like another hot dog?"

I laughed. "You know, I think I would."

When we walked back to the concession stand, Emi ordered two more hot dogs, but when presented with the bill took out a pen and wrote something on it. Then, the pen seemed to jam or run out of ink because he cursed, threw it into a nearby garbage bin and took out a second pen. This pen he laid down on the receipt, then turned to me saying; "Please excuse me, but I seem to have run out of your currency. May I ask you to pay the bill instead?"

"Of course," I replied, taking a couple of bills from my purse and handing them to the server. Then I picked up the pen and receipt and turned towards Emi.

"Keep them. Please. As a small favour to me. A souvenir, if you will."

Odd, I thought, but I thanked him and tucked them into my purse. And with that we gave each other a smile; said 'until the next time,' or something to that effect; then turned and went our separate ways.

It took me a while to walk all the way back around the Forum and down to my seat, but I was able to meld with the crowd and gain my seat just moments before the third period commenced.

"Have a nice walk?" asked Don.

"Very," I replied, but I knew he could hear the concern in my voice. While part of my brain wrestled with how Emi's information fit into the larger jigsaw puzzle, I spared a bit of attention for the third period. The latter wasn't difficult since, if the first and second periods had been rather quiet, this final period was raucous in the extreme as the fans, most of whom were cheering for Team Canada, were doing their best to inspire the players to catch up to the Soviets. Unfortunately, nothing worked, as the Soviets scored five unanswered goals, including a natural hat trick of three goals in a row by Sergei Shepelev. Final score: 8 – 1.

Although the crowd was fairly polite, by hockey standards at least, it was a disappointed crowd that filed out of the Forum that night. Canada had done well overall, of course, having played well throughout the series and finishing in second place, and we found some solace in having the young Wayne Gretzky emerge as the overall scoring leader of the series with 12 points to his credit. The Soviets, for their part, came away as the champions and the best hockey team in the world – for the moment, at least – and I don't think anyone seriously questioned the selection of the Soviets' star goaltender, Vladislav Tretiak, as the Canada Cup's Most Valuable Player (MVP). Tretiak had been outstanding; almost miraculous, and stunning to watch, even if he had been playing for 'the other side.'

After we'd returned to our hotel and said good-night to our shadows: Frank and Sandy, I changed out of my costume and washed most of the makeup off. Then, after first taking Silver outside for a short walk and 'pee break,' Don and I took Ginger out for dinner at a nearby restaurant. All I had told Ginger was that there was someone at the game I'd wanted to meet, and that it had gone well.

It was sometime during dinner, when Ginger had gone off to the ladies' room, that I reached into my purse for a tissue and came up with the receipt Emi had wanted me to keep from the Forum. I looked at it, and thought it was odd that there seemed to be no writing on it. Yet I had seen him writing on it. Then I turn the receipt over. There on the back he'd printed a few words: "For average size and build male, about 2 hours, APPROXIMATELY!!" Frowning, I searched around in my purse and brought out the pen. This time, I looked at it carefully. It was not an ordinary pen.

"Trouble?" asked Don, seeing me frown.

"No. A gift. In fact, a very unexpected gift." I showed him the note. "From Emi" I said. Then, I handed him the pen. "Careful," I warned. "This is no ordinary pen."

Don gave the pen a close inspection, then whistled under his breath. "If this is what I think it is, then this is an extraordinary gift. It appears to be some kind of spy pen, like the on you used to have. Is it lethal?"

"No. It's like the one he gave me after the Diefenbunker case. The one I used in my escape after I'd been captured in Point-du-Chêne last summer[49]. It ejects a dart with a fast-acting tranquilizer. I've seen Emi use them in action. They're very effective."

"He took a big risk giving it to you."

"Yes, he did, and another big risk giving me a new one."

"Exactly the kind of thing 'Jane Bond,' double-oh-one, of Her Majesty's Secret Service would carry with her if there was ever a female Bond movie made."

"Funny you should mention Her Majesty's Secret Service," I said, thoughtfully, looking unfocusedly off in the distance.

"Oh oh. I know that look," said Don. "What crazy thing are you considering now?"

I spotted Ginger returning to our table, so all I said was: "I think it's time I met a real MI6 intelligence officer, so we're going to need your Admiral's help."

After Ginger had returned to our table and taken her seat, I said: "I've been scheming again, and I'm going to want you to help me destroy that blonde wig of yours."

Laurie Schramm

5 HER MAJESTY'S SECRET SERVICE

With our Montreal adventure completed, Ginger flew to Vancouver for a screen-test for a new movie, Don flew back to Halifax where he would meet with his admiral, and Silver and I flew back to Ottawa.

It took a few days for Don to meet with Admiral White, and a few more for the admiral to place a few calls to England but, eventually, a path had been cleared and there were two meetings arranged for me in England. I requested a couple of days leave for this, and for something so short no-one bothered to ask me why. This time I would have to leave Silver behind, which I did, in care of a friend in Ottawa.

Getting overseas was somewhat convoluted. I'd been told to pack no more than a medium-sized duffel bag plus a shoulder bag or small backpack. I'd been told I'd be issued new clothes along the way, so I packed only a very few things plus the glasses I'd worn in Montreal, and Ginger's blonde wig, which we had cut short to the point where it would just cover my own hair.

It was a Saturday morning, when I dropped Silver off at my friend's house. With luck, I would be back on the Tuesday evening. I left my truck at my friend's house as well, and was picked up by a black sedan of the type driven by countless senior civil servants in Ottawa. The main differences were that this was a military car, with a military driver, and it was followed at a discreet distance by another such car. Our little convoy took me to the Ottawa Airport, where we went to a medium-sized government terminal building that was off to one side of the much larger public terminal. Inside, I was met by Lieutenant Moore and Sergeant Wilson. I was in civilian clothes, but they were both in uniform. The former in his Air Force blues with wedge cap[50], and the latter in army green and wearing the scarlet beret of the military police.

"Good morning, Ma'am," said Sandy. "We're the security detail for your trip."

"I'm grateful," I said, "but I'm sorry you two seem to be stuck babysitting me again."

"No problem, Ma'am," replied Sandy. They both grinned. "In fact, the chance to fly to England and see the sights isn't exactly rough duty."

"Will I be able to get you two to just refer to me as Alex, at least?"

"Only in private, Ma'am, especially since once we get to Trenton, you're going to outrank us."

"What do you mean?"

"Trust us. We wouldn't want to spoil the surprise." Both grins were switched on again.

"Fine. Are we flying on that monster out there?" There was a huge C-130 Hercules[51] aircraft sitting on the tarmac with its loading doors open.

"Yes Ma'am. It will take us to Trenton[52], where we'll have a short layover, then we'll be travelling by jet to London-Heathrow."

I'd flown on a Hercules before. The noise and vibration were incredible, but it wasn't a long flight, and I'd at least taken the precaution of packing a pair of acoustic earmuffs[53].

When we arrived at the Trenton Air Force Base, it was about 1 pm, so lunch was the next order of business. Following that, we were escorted to a large, warehouse-type building and introduced to a quartermaster sergeant.

"Ah yes," he said, "we have some things for you to try on. Please come with me."

He led me through a part of the building that was packed full with military clothing of all kinds, and for all seasons. Off to one side was an area equipped with chairs, tables, and several doors in proximity. Changing rooms, I presumed.

There was clothing laid-out on one of the tables. "Captain Harrison sent us sizing suggestions, but if you would please try these on, we can change anything that doesn't fit properly." He picked up one of the piles that had been set out on the table.

"A uniform? But I'm not in the service! I was expecting identity papers, not uniforms."

"This is what we were told to issue you with Ma'am. The requisition for the clothes came from Captain Harrison, but they were authorized by Admiral White."

I overheard sniggers from Sandy and Frank, who had followed along to watch the show.

"Look at the epaulettes," said Sandy

I'd been handed what they called No. 3C Service Dress – Sweater, which comprised an open-neck light-blue shirt, a V-neck sweater and dress pants, both in Air Force-blue, black shoes, and all of it topped off with an Air Force-blue wedge cap. On the sweater someone had already attached epaulettes with Captain's bars. This was getting weird!

"We can practice saluting later," said Frank, with a broad grin. Rather than being offended, Sandy and Frank seemed more intent on enjoying my discomfort.

"Admiral's orders, eh?" I grumbled. But I went into a change room and tried everything on, including the shortened blonde wig and the fake glasses. Not surprisingly, since my measurements had been provided by my fiancé, everything fit very well – even the shoes - as the others agreed when I stepped out to look at myself in one of the full-length mirrors that was provided for the purpose.

"Very nice," said the Quartermaster Sergeant approvingly. "I don't think you'll need to try the rest," he said, pointing at the other piles on the table. There were more shirts and socks, a second pair of trousers, a second sweater, a second wedge cap, and an overcoat. The sergeant also gave me a military duffel bag to use for my new uniforms and also everything I had brought with me in my own suitcase. The duffel bag was made of heavy-duty green canvas, and was cylindrical in shape, with a large zippered main compartment, button-down zipper flap, and transparent ID windows on each end. When I had stuffed everything in, I left my own case with the sergeant, to be picked up when I returned.

"Now for your papers," said the sergeant. "Identification tags, NDI-20, and passport."

The identification tags were what were historically called dog tags; the NDI-20 was a National Defence, Canadian Forces Identification card with my actual photo – except that it was me as a blonde - and listing me as regular officer named MacLerie,

Wilhelmina; and the passport wasn't the usual blue one, but a green Special Passport[54]. These had been 'issued' in the name of Wilhelmina MacLerie. There was also a pin-on nametag with white lettering on an air force blue background, that read MacLERIE, but I was advised that this was only provided as a contingency, and not to be affixed to the sweater.

As I put the dog tag chain around my neck, and the nametag in my shirt pocket, I showed the rest of the ID to Sandy and Frank, who had come over for a closer look. "Don's grandmother was Wilhelmina MacLerie. Everyone called her Willie. I guess you'll have to get used to calling me Willie from now on."

"Yes Sir, Captain," they both said. Smiling.

"Is all this really necessary?" I asked.

"Security!" said Sandy, trying to keep a straight face. "Seriously, it was the Admiral's idea. Even if there was a watcher on this base, or at the other end, all they'll see is a bunch of military personnel boarding and deplaning air transport, and customs and passport control in both countries will only know that someone named MacLerie went to England and back."

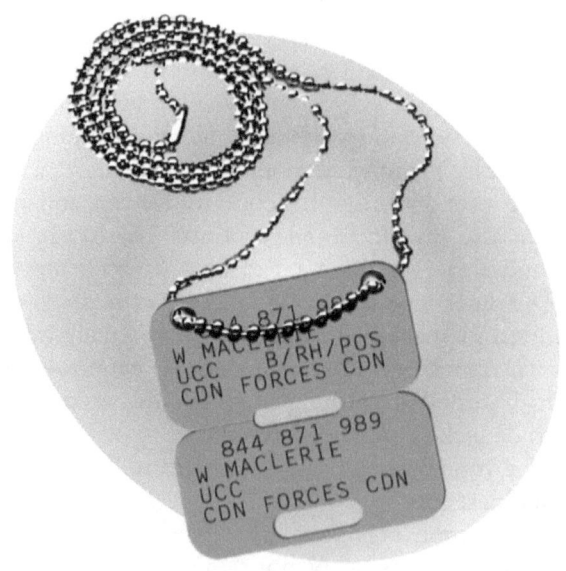

Next, came saluting practice. The Canadian Forces salute is what is sometimes called the 'naval salute' and involves having the palm of the hand turned slightly down and inwards, so the palm is not seen. This is different from the RCMP salute, in which the hand is vertical, with the palm facing directly outwards. We had to practice this several times, before Sandy and Frank were satisfied.

Now feeling more than ever like an actress in dress-rehearsal for a play, I thanked the Quartermaster Sergeant, insisted on carrying my own shoulder bag and duffel, and the three of us went to check-in for our flight. Sandy had all of the paperwork for that, and we checked our duffles, then went for coffee while we waited for departure time, which was about 7 pm.

For the overseas part of our trip, we flew on a Canadian Forces Boeing CC-137, which was a large, four-engine passenger jet[55]. It was quite comfortable and incredibly quiet compared with the noise and vibration aboard a C-130 Hercules.

This time, it was a long, overnight flight and, although I rested, I wasn't able to sleep much. They served us coffee and a light breakfast just before landing though, which helped me focus on the next part of our trip. That and the anticipation of my upcoming meeting.

We landed at a military airport, operated by the RAF, that was located very close to Heathrow Airport. Once we'd cleared security, an RAF Sergeant in plain clothes met and guided us to a BMW full-size sedan, in which he drove us almost due west to the city of Bath.

Of course, I knew that they drove on the left side of the road in the UK, but it was still unnerving to see us being driven on what seemed the wrong side of the road, especially when we had to turn at intersections. The most unsettling of all, however, was when we came to a traffic circle and had to go around in what felt like the wrong lane and in the wrong direction. I was glad I wasn't driving! Had I been driving, I didn't like to think about how many times I'd have had to go around the full circle, before being able to successfully - and safely – navigate the exit.

Most of the trip was on the M4 motorway, which felt very much like being on a divided highway in North America, making it easier to sit back, relax, and enjoy the scenery.

Visiting Bath was like stepping back in history. Named for the famous hot-spring-fed baths built by the Romans *circa.* 60 CE, the older parts of the city have the distinctive narrow streets and many buildings constructed from 'Bath stone,' a creamy-gold coloured limestone.

Major (later promoted to Colonel) Jack Evans (RAF, Ret'd.) lived in Weston, just to the northwest of Bath, a community favoured by retirees. Our driver took us to a very nice-looking two-story, stone apartment building that was surrounded by trees and bushes and bounded on one side by beautiful communal gardens – much like a small park, in fact. He remained in the car while we got out.

Evans was clearly expecting us as he promptly met us at the front door and, following the usual introductions, ushered us through a nicely furnished, large, ground-floor apartment. One wall had floor-to-ceiling windows and windowed-doors looking out on the garden, which was where he ultimately led us.

Immediately outside the door was a small courtyard with some comfortable chairs for us to sit in, while Sandy and Frank went for a stroll in the adjacent communal gardens.

"How about a brew?" he asked. There was a beautiful tea service laid out on a small table between our chairs.

"Yes, please!" I found that I was thirsty after the drive from the airport.

"Standard NATO?" he asked. "Milk and two sugars?"

"No. Just black, if you don't mind." Then: "Would it be possible to get tea for Lieutenant Moore and Sergeant Wilson as well?"

"Take care of the troops and they'll take care of you. Is that it?" It sounded like a test.

"Yes, Sir. We have the same expression."

He seemed to approve and went for two more cups and saucers, waved Sandy and Frank over to a separate table and poured tea for them. Then, as he was pouring the tea for the two of us, I said: "Thank you for agreeing to see me, Colonel."

"My pleasure," he said, handing me my cup. Then, continuing in a lower voice: "Got a call from C himself[56]." He stared at me as if daring me to take the bait.

I didn't. If I didn't already know what 'C' stood for, I think he'd have clammed-up and shown us the door.

When I simply nodded in understanding, he continued. "Special request," he said. "Told me I can tell you anything, within reason of course. There are still a few secrets we don't even tell ourselves," he quipped. "You don't get a call from him unless its damned important, I can tell you, so I agreed. Naturally." He paused, and looked at me rather shrewdly from under a set of very busy eyebrows. "Don't mind telling you it got my curiosity up too. So. What's it all about, eh?"

"Well, Sir," I began. "I want to ask you about something that happened a long time ago, when you were a Military Attaché at the British High Commission."

"Yes. I enjoyed that posting."

"My understanding, is that you received a call in 1959 from someone who offered to sell you the complete plans for the Avro Arrow Jet Fighter."

"Avro Arrow," he mused. "Yes. Your government had just rubbished the whole program and everything was being destroyed to keep it from getting into unfriendly hands. Then, from out of the blue I got a call. A man's voice. Didn't identify himself, naturally, but said he had a set of everything: blueprints, drawings, manuals; the whole lot, in fact. Asked whether we wanted to buy them. I had no idea, of course, but he expected that and said he'd call again in a few days for an answer."

"And you did want to buy them?"

"Yes. After a series of coded cyphers back and forth from higher authority, it was decided that we'd try to buy them. For two reasons, I understood. One was so our people could see the details and possibly incorporate them into a project that was already underway to design a high-altitude, long-range, supersonic fighter that could cross the North Sea to intercept Soviet bombers. That's basically the mission the Arrow was designed for, except across your own northern territories."

"Makes sense. And the second reason."

"Well, to make sure no one else got their hands on them, of course."

"Did you tell our people about all this?"

"Eventually, yes, but not right away. You see our boffins[57] wanted to have a good look at them first. We've always been allies, but there's a limit, what? So, I was instructed to manage the deal, then send everything back home, which is what I did."

"Did any of it actually help you back here?"

"Haven't the foggiest. Probably wouldn't be allowed to tell you even if I did, what? But I believe that everything seemed genuine enough. The source would send us some of the material, for which we'd pay, then call us later to see if we wanted more, and so on. Since everything he gave us was examined and I was always told to go buy the next allotment, I assume it must all have been pretty good stuff."

"And you did eventually tell us about it all."

"Oh yes. Not me. Someone higher up handled all that. I heard that your government didn't even want the plans back. Just asked us to destroy them ourselves so no one else could get at them."

"And did you?"

"I've no idea. I don't think I'd have been told if I'd asked, which I didn't. It was 'need to know' in those days."

"That's one thing that hasn't changed much," I laughed. "Almost no one seems to trust almost anyone."

"Ah, but it was worse in my day, my dear. Much worse."

"What about the source? Did you ever learn anything about who it was?"

"No. Nothing."

"But you must have been curious?"

"Not just curious. I did my damnedest to find out who it was. Would have been quite a feather in my cap if I'd succeeded too. But I didn't."

"Can you tell me about that part of it?"

"I don't see why not. Nothing worth hiding there I don't think.... Let me think for a moment. We used dead-drops for the exchanges. He'd phone me and specify a time and place, and where to look for the latest batch of documents. He wouldn't give me much lead time, so we could arrange stakeouts or anything like that, but we did try having several colleagues travel independently of me, but at the same time, if you take my meaning, to the locations. Then, while I went to pick-up the documents and leave behind an envelope full of money, my colleagues would stick around and take pictures in hopes of photographing whomever went to pick them up later."

"And did you?"

"Who knows?" he said, pounding his fist on one knee for emphasis. "He always picked crowded places, so we ended up with thousands of pictures in which you could make out the faces of some hundreds. We went through them all looking for repetitions at the various drops, but didn't find any."

"So. Everything came to dead-ends then?"

"Everything except the Arrow materials. He delivered everything he said he would, and we paid for all of it. Financially, it was quite a bargain, really. Cost only a tiny fraction of what you chaps would have paid to get all the work done."

"Yes. I've never quite understood why the program was killed-off in the first place. The public story is plausible, but it feels like it may only be a part of the truth."

"Quite likely. Government pronouncements are frequently like that here too." He paused, and looked at me rather shrewdly again.

"On a mole hunt, are we?"

"Sort of. I think of him as a leak. There have been several such leaks spaced out over the years, and my superiors think they – or at least many of them – have come from the same source. It's probably not a mole though. More likely someone out for money, or revenge, or both, rather than anything ideological. As far as we know the Arrow incident was the first of the series."

"Hmmm. Yes, it would have to be something like that to get C to call me and clear the way for you."

"Has no one contacted you before to ask questions like I have, Sir?"

"No," he replied. "You're the first."

"I'm surprised. It seemed so obvious to me."

"Not so surprising if you understand that times were different back then. Look, there have been others before you, who tried to track down your leak, right?"

"Right. Several times, I've been told."

"Well then. In the middle of the Cold War, your predecessors would have been looking for an ideological traitor. Someone with Communist sympathies, that sort of thing. We all were. And they were there too. Right here in Britain, in your country, in the US, in Australia – no one was immune…. Your people must have a list of possible suspects?"

"Yes."

"Well, I won't ask you about it, but it has to be a list of limited size. Your counter-intelligence people of the time may have been looking for the wrong kind of person."

"Yes. No one said so in so many words, but it was kind of implied when I was given the case."

"There you are then. Fresh eyes. New ideas. That kind of thing."

"Yes." I smiled. "That's almost exactly what I was told."

"Thought so." He turned on 'the gaze' again. "And you're not really a Captain in the RCAF are you?"

"What makes you say that?" I asked, involuntarily stiffening a bit.

"I'm not sure." He sat back in his chair and peered at me. "Something about your manner. The way you hold your body. Your way of phrasing things, I think. In fact, now that I think about it, you look and sound more like someone from Scotland Yard than the service. I can't explain myself better than that. It's just a feeling, you see. But I learned to trust my instincts over the years. Seldom let me down if I paid attention to them you know."

Well, I had to hand it to him. After all our precautions, I sit down with him for fifteen minutes and he penetrates my disguise just like that. "Well," I replied. "Since it isn't you that I'm disguised from, I'll admit it."

"Hmmm hmmm. Mounted Police, I'll bet. Security Service maybe?"

"Please never ask me to play poker or chess with you, Sir" I replied. "I'd never be able to afford it."

That brought out a chuckle. "So. You're afraid that your source may be well enough placed to know that you've been set on his trail." It was a statement, not a question.

I nodded yes.

"That explains the security detail." He nodded towards Sandy and Frank, who had returned from their reconnoitre and were standing some distance away, trying to look nonchalant.

"Military intelligence?" he asked.

"That I can neither confirm nor deny," I said, with a smile.

He nodded; his question answered.

"Is there anything else you can remember from the Arrow incident that might help me?"

This time he didn't answer me right away, and I waited while he either searched his memory or mused about how much he could tell me, or both. To be fair, I think it was mostly the former. Eventually, his eyes came back in to focus and he looked directly at me with a gleam in his eyes.

"I asked his name once. Abruptly. Without warning. Figured it was worth a try to see if he'd make a slip. But he didn't. He actually seemed amused ay my clumsy attempt."

"So, it didn't work."

"Yes and no. He said I could call him... let's see now, it was something biblical...."

I didn't start suggesting names, for fear of derailing his thinking. I just waited.

"Not exactly biblical," he mused, "but close." Then, "I have it," he said, clapping his hands. "Gideon[58]. He said I could call him Gideon." He looked at me closely, watching for a reaction, and he got one. "You've heard the name before, haven't you?"

"I have," I confirmed. "Around the same time, someone using the codename Gideon contacted the USAF offering to sell them the Arrow plans."

"Bollocks! The Yanks had the Arrow secrets all along."

"Yes, so I understand. Apparently, Gideon's offer was simply ignored by the Americans, although the FBI kept the name on file and even had some suspicions about his identity."

The Colonel snorted. "The FBI! They suspected everyone of everything back in Hoover's era."

I nodded.

"Well, there you are. Any more questions?"

I tried to think quickly, but there was only one more question on my mental list. "Just one, I think. All those pictures that were taken at the dead-drops in 1959: is there any chance they still exist?"

"Good question," he replied, approvingly. "We kept everything in those days. The older stuff was boxed-up and stored chronologically. After a certain point it would have been shipped here to headquarters."

"And then?"

"Then? Well, I can't really say for certain…. What I mean is, I don't know. It's possible they were shredded, or burned, at some point, of course. You'd have to ask someone at headquarters, I suppose." He paused, at gave me a significant look. "You do know which headquarters I mean?"

I smiled. "Yes Sir. I think I know exactly which one. I'll go where James Bond would have gone."

"If you can get in, of course."

"I think it can be arranged, Sir," I said with more confidence than I actually felt.

"Yes, I have a feeling you might just pull it off at that." He gave me another penetrating look and then, surprisingly, gave me a conspiratorial grin. "I think you might indeed."

After taking out leave of the Colonel, our driver took us to our hotel in London where we checked in. My first task was to call Don at his office in Halifax. It was just after 5 pm London time, so just after the lunch hour in Halifax.

"How's you day been?" he asked, meaning that plus how my trip overseas had gone.

"A few surprises, but it's been good. I'm calling for some help with my homework."

He caught the code-phrase right away. "I'm tied up right now. Can you call me back in twenty minutes."

I agreed and rung-off. I'd brought my list of phone numbers to use for secret calls to Don, looked up the next unused one, waited twenty minutes and dialed the number. He was right there.

"Hi," came Don's voice on the line.

"Hi yourself. I feel like a fraud in this uniform but the meeting went really well."

"That's great. Did you get anything you can use?"

"Maybe, I don't know. That's why I'm calling. Do you think the Admiral can get me into MI6 to see someone in records or archives, or whatever they call their file storage over here?"

"I have no idea, but I'll ask him. He'll want to know why."

I told him why.

Don whistled. "Talk about a long-shot! But it makes sense since you're over there anyway. I'll try to get in to see him right away. I'll call you as soon as I know something, either late tonight your time, or early tomorrow morning. OK?"

I agreed, and we chatted about more personal things for a while before saying goodbye.

Don's return call to my hotel room came late at night and was circumspect. "It's a go for your homework research tomorrow. No need to dress up, but bring the documents you brought with you."

That meant that I could go visit MI6, that I wasn't to go in uniform, but that I was to use the MacLerie persona and its passport and military ID.

The next morning, after breakfast, the same car and driver picked us up and took us to the headquarters of Britain's Secret Intelligence Service, popularly known as MI6[59]. It was less than a block away from the Lambeth North Tube Station, but Sandy and Frank had vetoed my idea of taking The Tube[60] on security grounds.

Taking our cue from Don, we were all in business-casual clothes, although I still thought that Frank looked like a sergeant in somebody's army in any kind of clothes. I supposed that in this case, it didn't really matter. I retained the blonde wig and glasses of my disguise from the previous two days.

Our identities were carefully checked against a list twice, once at the main gate, and again just inside the main entranceway. From there we were given visitor passes to wear and someone escorted us to a bank of elevators and up to the 21st floor, which was the second highest. This floor had unusually high ceilings and seemed to comprise a reception area and a number of large meeting rooms.

In the centre of the floor, to one side of the elevators, was a staircase, and beside that, an ornate desk that could have been from the Victorian era. At it sat an alert-looking, middle-aged woman. *Shades of Moneypenny*[51], I thought to myself, and had to concentrate to avoid grinning. The whole thing seemed so surreal to me.

The woman at the desk didn't identify herself, but once again carefully checked our identities against a list, which I suspected contained physical descriptions in addition to ID and passport identification numbers. While she did that, I glanced around wondering about enhanced security, and I noticed that there were a couple of offices facing us that had a clear view of the elevators, the staircase, and the desk at which we were standing. The fronts of the offices had floor-to-ceiling glass windows and glass doors, with the glass doors standing open. Sitting inside each office was a heavily-built man that looked reminiscent of Sergeant Wilson. Both men seemed to find us fascinating, as they never seemed to take their eyes off of us.

My thoughts in this direction were interrupted by the woman at the desk who, having completed her identity checks, picked up her phone, dialed a number and whispered something we couldn't hear. Then she said: "Captain MacLerie, the Chief would like a word with you."

"Of course," I replied.

"I'm sorry, but the Lieutenant and the Sergeant will have to wait here for you."

I glanced at the two men, who both nodded and strode over to some comfortable-looking chairs to settle-in and wait.

The woman from the desk nodded to the person that had escorted us up from the main entrance, who left, and then led me up the staircase to the top floor. At the top of the stairs, and set back only a few metres, was a solid wall with large, glass double doors. Sitting at desks on either side were two more heavily-built men, with the same intent look and lack of facial expression that the two in the offices a floor below wore. Presumably, the body language of the woman guiding told them that nothing was amiss, because neither of the men seem to move a muscle as we went through the doors.

On this floor, there were windows right in front of us, and a solid wall, each with a solid door, on each side of us. It was to one of these doors that I was led and, after a discreet knock on the door, I was ushered in.

It was silly of me, I know, but having read my share of spy novels I actually expected to see a dimly lit alcove with an old, greying man hunched over a small desk, surrounded by piles of files and papers. Possibly even smoking an old pipe. This was completely wrong, of course.

The first thing that caught my attention was the man himself. He wasn't old. *Middle-aged*, I judged. Even sitting, he appeared tall and somewhat on the slender side. He had blond hair and ice-blue eyes.

His office was far from my imagined image too. The office I really entered was large and bright, with two of the walls being completely glass, offering stunning views of the city. There was a very modern desk just off-centre, and in one corner there was a small meeting table with four comfortable-looking chairs around it. A quick glance around his office showed the remaining walls were covered by bookcases, with souvenirs or ornaments on some of the shelves, but mostly just books. Lots of books, in fact. I would have liked to look at them to see their titles, or if they were even real. The bookcases, like the rest of the office furniture were made of gleaming chrome and glass. Everything, in fact, seemed bright and clean. New, even.

Although I tried to take everything in, my attention was focused on the man himself. Rather than waiting for our approach, he sprung up from his desk and came round to greet me, saying: "Welcome, please come and take a seat." He motioned to the small meeting table. "Can we offer you something to drink?"

"Yes, thank you. Tea would be nice."

He was dressed in a fashionable business suit that would not have looked out of place if he was walking around the business and financial district of the city.

He gazed at me with a smile. "You don't have to drink tea just to be accommodating, you know. We do have such things as coffee around here... somewhere."

I smiled in return. "Actually, I am a dedicated coffee drinker, but I've been enjoying the change so I really would prefer tea if that's OK."

"Of course." He nodded to his assistant who left to get my tea. She obviously didn't have to ask him for his own preference.

"Now then. Captain MacLerie. Or, should I say Corporal Houston?"

"Either Sir. I can't say I'm surprised that you know who I really am."

"No. Peter White had a lot to say about you." He motioned to a small cabinet beside his desk, that had just one thing on it: an ordinary looking telephone set.

Appearances can be deceiving. That cabinet, I knew would be filled with racks of electronics. "A scrambler phone."

"Indeed. What the Americans call a STU phone."

"Yes, Sir. My Deputy Commissioner has one in his office; I'm sure the Admiral has one too."

"Just so. Very handy for frank conversations, I find."

We were interrupted by his assistant, who softly knocked and brought us our tea, then discreetly left.

"I'll refer to you as Captain, to keep things simple. No one else in this building knows anything else about you or why you're here, except that you're Canadian. If they harbour any suspicions about why you have a Lieutenant and a Sergeant following you around like guard dogs, well, it wouldn't be the first time someone has come for a meeting here accompanied by a security detail. Right?"

"Yes, Sir."

"Now then, how was your meeting with Colonel Evans?"

"It went well, I think, although he mostly just confirmed what I already suspected. The same codename – Gideon - seems to keep popping up for our leak, which could be helpful. Our meeting did reassure me that I may be going in the right direction, which is always a help, too."

"And now I understand that you want to delve into our archives."

"Yes, Sir. Your Consulate people in Ottawa took a huge number of pictures at the dead-drops. I know that nothing came from that exercise but…."

"You think you might actually recognize one of the faces in the pictures, don't you? Something our chaps would never have been able to do."

"That's my hope, Sir. Yes. Now that I know what all of our 'possibles' look like, I'm hoping I'll get lucky and spot one of them in the pictures. If they still exist, and if we can find them in your archives, that is."

"Do you know how many pictures were taken at the time?"

"Thousands, the Colonel estimated."

His eyebrows went up. "A tall order then, I'm afraid." He looked at me, as if weighing things in his mind, then he seemed to reach a decision. "Right then. I agree it's worth a try. We don't let people into our files and archives lightly, of course[62], but I think we'll let you have a go."

He got up, and walked over to his desk and reached inside the knee-hole, presumably to press a button. Before long, his assistant knocked and entered.

"Take Captain MacLerie down to meet our librarian, would you? Tell him to call me if he has any questions."

"Yes, Sir," she replied and went to the door to wait for me.

"Nice to have met you, Captain. I'd most likely have honoured Peter White's request in any case, but I wanted to meet you in person first. Take your measure, as we say." He offered his hand, which surprised me.

"Thank you very much, Sir," I acknowledged, shaking his hand with a firm grip.

He noticed that too.

"Good luck," he said, but he'd already turned back to his desk, his mind having shifted to other things.

As we walked down the stairs, C's assistant told me that it wasn't really a library to which we were heading, but that they tended to refer to their massive collection of files and documents as the library, rather than its official designation. The Head of Section, was similarly referred to as "L," their librarian.

At the bottom of the stairs, I went to check-in with Sandy and Frank, telling them that I had one more stop, and that it might take me several hours. They replied that they were "doing just fine, Ma'am."

C's assistant then guided me to the main elevators, one of which took us down several floors. As we exited the elevator, we entered a floor that reminded me of a large university library. Most of the floor seemed to be taken up by floor-to-ceiling shelving on which were arranged books, document cases, and even file boxes. Closer to where we were standing, to one side, was a bank of desk-stations that seemed to be hybrid computer terminals and scanning stations. At each sat an operator scanning files and documents page-by-page. *Digitizing paper records*, I thought. To the other side was a bank of more conventional-looking computer terminals at which operators seemed to be busily alternating between typing things and then peering intently at the computer monitors. *Digital search and document retrieval*, I thought.

Directly in front of us were a couple of desks that looked exactly like librarian's desks in a conventional library. Just past the computer stations, was a glass-enclosed office, and it was to this that I was led.

"Good morning, L," said C's assistant to the man who was seated at a desk in the office. He was elderly, I thought, probably well past the normal retirement age, and he was definitely not dressed as fashionably as the other I had met that morning. In fact, he reminded me very much of the retired chemistry professors that had volunteered their time to help my student colleagues and I grapple with the concepts and laws of thermodynamics, in my university days. Old, soft-looking shirts, corduroy trousers, topped off with a sleeveless, V-neck sweater had been our mentors' dress code, and this man seemed to have come from the same mold. He even had a shock of unruly white hair, with bushy white eyebrows to match.

I tried hard not to stare.

"This is Captain MacLerie" said C's assistant. "C asks that you try to help her out, and to call if you have any concerns."

"How do you do, my dear," said the man, as he got up from his seat and came around the desk to shake hands.

"How do you do, Sir," I replied.

"Now, now. No need for formality down here. People call me L. It's not my real title, but that's not important."

"L for librarian?" I asked, as C's assistant silently glided away.

"Of course," he said, as if surprised that anyone would ask. "You probably noticed the scanning stations and computer terminals as you walked in?" He peered over the tops of his glasses inquisitively.

I nodded.

"Right. Everything's going digital these days, and of course we're scanning the most current records first and then working backwards, so it will be many years before we get to the old stuff. That's why I'm still here, and why they call me L." He tapped his head significantly. "Until the computers make me obsolete, I'm the retrieval system, especially for the really old stuff. It's all filed away in me. Been here through every C we've ever had, I have. Right back to the original one."

"How do you manage to keep it all straight," I asked, "besides being able to remember it all?"

"Well, I can't really remember everything, can I?" he asked, with a twinkle in his eyes. "But I have a good memory for most things, and a pretty good feeling for dates and events, so I'm usually pretty close, and then it's the old method of sifting through papers by hand after that. I'm a bit of a ferret once I get started, and I usually find what people are looking for in the end. Not always on time, you understand, but I do generally get there…. Let's put me to the test, shall we? What might it be that you're after?"

"I'm hoping you will have retained a large collection of photographs," I said, and I launched into a description.

"Canada, you say… 1959… Avro Arrow and the Consulate. Hmmm. Major Jack Evans. Yes, I remember him all right, the young puppy. Hmmm. Well, they may have been shredded or burned long ago, you understand?"

"Yes, I know. But I'm hoping they weren't."

"Well, if they still exist then we have them, but not here. Come with me." With that he led me back to the elevators and we went down, way down, to one of several basement levels.

When we arrived and exited the elevator, it was like we'd left one world and entered another. This world was only dimly lit and consisted almost entirely of row upon row of floor-to-ceiling racks containing storage boxes. Although the building was quite modern, this level smelled old.

Noticing me take it all in, L said: "Yes, you can feel the age of things down here, can't you? It puts some people off, especially the ones with allergies, but not me. This is where I feel most at home. Have a seat," he pointed to a couple of old desks and equally old-looking hardwood chairs, "and let me nose around a bit. I'll call you when I find something."

So, I took a seat and waited. I didn't expect him to find anything right away, but it was at least 45 minutes before he came back carrying an old file box.

"You found them?" I asked.

"Could be. Could be. We'll see in a moment." He placed the box on the desk, switched on the desk lamp and opened it up. At the front was a file folder, which he extracted and quickly perused. "Report of Surveillance, Source: Gideon, Location: Ottawa, June, 1959," he said, and then handed the file to me. As I read the brief report, L looked through the rest of the box. "Photographs!" he said, "hundreds and hundreds of them."

"Fantastic!" I said. "I'm looking for a face."

"Description?"

"I have no idea," I responded. Then, "I'm looking for a face that I recognize."

"Ah. I see. You'll be here for a while then." He opened a drawer and took out a large magnifying glass. "This might help. While you start on these, I'll go back for the other boxes."

"Other boxes?"

"There are two more. I would say you're going to be looking at more than 3,000 photographs."

It didn't go quite as slowly as I first thought. Some of the photos didn't show any clear facial details, some didn't show people at all, and some were so poorly focused that I wondered why they had been kept at all. It took me an hour to go through everything in the first box and, since the photos were numbered, I knew that I had looked at over 900 of them.

L had brought back two more boxes for me to go through, and I was about to start on the second when someone arrived with a thermos of tea and some paper cups.

"Take frequent breaks," L advised. "I know what it feels like when the hunt is on, but if you push too far you can't help but lose focus and before you know it, you're glossing over the very things that should be getting your most careful attention."

This sounded like good advice to me, so I thanked him and poured myself a cup. "Would you care to join me?" I asked.

"Don't mind if I do, actually. I'm not allowed to leave you alone down here anyway. Never know what you colonials might get up to, what?"

I didn't take offense. His smile could have been misinterpreted, but his tone told me he was joking.

So, I did take breaks, during which he told me some hair-raising stories of old cases that had been completed due, in no small part, to his ability to 'ferret-out' valuable intelligence from their massive 'library' collection.

I took periodic breaks after that, but by the time I'd gone through the second box, I was getting tired and hungry. L offered to take me upstairs for lunch, but I was in a groove, of sorts, and wanted to see the whole collection first. L just nodded. He understood, and he settled back companionably enough, to wait.

I was probably about halfway through the third box, when I gasped and my whole body stiffened.

"Found something, have you?" queried L.

"Maybe. It's out of focus, and only part of the face is visible, but it reminds me of someone."

"Often the case," muttered L. "Your Gideon has been through multiple dead-drops, multiple exchanges, the money's adding up, and he's beginning to relax. The one thing an agent must never do. But they all do, sooner or later, otherwise we'd never catch them. Not the smart ones, anyway. Keep going, but carefully now. If he's slipped up once, he'll do it again."

Nothing could have stopped me at that point. I'd come too far. As I finished scanning each photo, I'd eagerly reach for the rest, but it was probably a hundred photos later that my body froze again as I came across what appeared to be the same face, partly obscured and from a different angle, but it looked like the same face.

"Another hit?' L asked, but I simply nodded as I continued on.

It took another two hundred photos, before I found it – he must have chanced to look in exactly the direction of the camera. He was wearing a hat, but otherwise his whole face could be clearly seen, and it was in sharp focus.

"Here it is," I said, passing the photo to L and pointing out the face I'd recognized out of the thousands of others.

"You don't look very happy," L observed.

"I'm not at all happy," I agreed.

"You know who this is?"

"Yes. I know who it is."

6 A NEW ASSIGNNMENT

I'd had lots of time to think on the way home, and had devised and discarded quite a few convoluted schemes for getting Gideon into the open and compromised. As we landed, I still hadn't come up with anything that seemed realistic and I tried to put it out of mind for a while, hoping that my subconscious mind would eventually produce inspiration.

I did, however, drop by Staff Sergeant Blunt's office for a quiet chat one day and I told him that I was still working on the case.

"But it wasn't me that...."

"I know," I interrupted.

"I can't prove it, but I assure you that... wait a minute. What do you mean you know?"

"I mean, I know who it is, and it's not you, OK?"

He looked at me. "What do you want then?"

"I'm asking for your help. To play along with this, when the time comes, so we can catch the real Gideon."

"Who is it?"

"Trust me? Please? If you know who it is, you'll react differently to things, and our quarry will bolt. OK?"

"He made a sour face. "I suppose I don't have much choice, do I?"

"Look, I'm not threatening you. You can just walk away. Right? I'll still try to prove it wasn't you and catch the real Gideon."

He looked at me again, but this time as if I'd just passed some kind of test. "No, no. Not on your life. Count me in… Alex."

Now, again, I needed to wait for an opportunity, so I worked on a number of routine cases that came up. Not all of them were exactly routine, however.

Several weeks later, for example, I was in my office typing reports when Bob called me into his office.

"Uncle George got a call from the FBI," he began. "Last week, there was a break-in at a National Guard armory near Houston, Texas. Whomever it was got away with a load of weapons crates. The crates contain M203 under-barrel grenade launchers[63] designed to be mounted on the U.S. M16 rifle, or the Canadian C7. The FBI traced them as far as the Port of Houston, but by the time they arrived in force, it was too late: the goods had vanished. They think the weapons were loaded onto an unregistered ship that was anchored out in the harbour, then taken out through the Gulf of Mexico.

"They have a general description, but not a positive ID on the ship, which was last seen disappearing into a storm that covered most of the Gulf of Mexico in dense cloud. A couple of days ago, they found three unidentified cargo ships passing the southern tip of Florida and heading for international waters. The three ships seem to have been heading more-or-less north along the west coast, all of them outside of the 12-nautical-mile territorial limit, and the US Coast Guard has been watching out for them."

"OK," I said. "What do they want from us?"

"Today, one of the ships has been spotted off the New England coast, but still in international waters, and they think it may be intending to cross into Canadian waters."

"Sounds like a job for our Coast Guard and maybe a few people from H or B Division[64]."

"Normally yes, but here's where it gets interesting. Apparently, the CIA think that one of the crates is a dummy and really contains some kind of new, experimental explosive shells that were stolen from a research lab at the armory at the same time."

"How big is this thing?"

"The crate contains two specially modified M549[65] rocket-assisted howitzer rounds," said Bob, reading from a sheet of paper in his hand. "Each round is 155 mm (6.1") diameter, nearly a metre (33") in length, and weighs about 40 kg (88 lbs). That means the crate weighs more than twice that.

"No one will admit anything, but the FBI think that the bomb-in-a-crate thing was actually a CIA operation. The suspicion is that they were intending to ship it somewhere for experimental use, but someone got wind of it and stole the whole shipment."

"If that were true, why not steal just the one important crate? It would have been a lot easier to disguise and transport."

"I asked the FBI that. They suspect that the thieves were hired to steal the weapons by an arms dealer, or someone posing as one, and that they don't know anything about the special crate."

"Sounds like a plot from a James Bond novel."

"I agree, but Deputy Director Wheeler called Uncle George directly over this. He has his reservations too, but the CIA is apparently major-league cranky over this, despite denying any involvement of course. The U.S. Army is doubly upset, partly because the shipment was stolen from their facility and partly because they also think they were being used as dupes by the CIA. The U.S. Coast Guard is under pressure to find the right ship, and the FBI is under pressure to reel it in. If that isn't enough, the FBI doesn't want to get caught in the crossfire of a nasty inter-service battle between the CIA and the U.S. Army."

"OK," I said, "That part makes sense at least."

"Right. So. If the ship crosses into our waters, then it's like you said. Our Coast Guard will take over, backed-up by the navy if necessary, and H Division will put someone on the Coast Guard ship."

"And..." I prompted, waiting for the punch-line.

"None of them are allowed to know anything about the possibility of a secret cargo in one of the crates, nor anything about its contents, and especially nothing about any possible CIA involvement. In fact, the CIA asked – ordered is more like it – the FBI to keep us in the dark too, but Director Wheeler told Uncle George anyway. Said he'd never send one of his own Special Agents in half-blind and he wasn't about to start doing it to us either."

"Ah ha. And you want me to go."

Bob smiled his Cheshire Cat smile. "Everybody wants you and Silver to go: Uncle George, Director Wheeler, me, and the Special Agent they're sending in." He paused for a moment, to make sure I had it all straight in my mind.

"Let me guess."

"Right. Special Agent Vivian Rule."

"All right. I suppose Silver makes some sense since we're looking for explosives again. You realize, of course, that if it's a really new kind of explosive then Silver might not be able to detect it or recognize it for what it is. Can we get a sample, or some information on the chemical components?"

"No. For two reasons. One, that we're not supposed to know anything about it. The FBI wasn't supposed to tell us. Secondly, the CIA won't tell the FBI anything about it either, nor the U.S. Army, nor their own Coast Guard."

"Makes you wonder who's side they're on, doesn't it?"

"I'll pretend I didn't hear you say that," said Bob, with a straight face. The he switched his smile back on again. "Any other questions?"

"Tons. I suppose we also don't know how the thing is supposed to be triggered or detonated, or handled for that matter, or its explosive power?"

"Nope, but it's a safe bet the thing is powerful. Everyone is way too upset for it to be anything less."

"Great."

"OK. Uncle George says to ask…."

"I know, 'Will I do it?'"

Bob smiled.

"Why me?" I asked, rhetorically, as I raised my hands in surrender.

"Fine," said Bob. He'd expected my answer. He waited until I'd stood up before adding: "One more thing Alex," he said. "With the CIA this upset, and everyone running around in circles, we have to assume it's all pretty important. That means other parties may take an interest as well. Our usual opponents, anarchist groups, real arms dealers, extremists. Any or all of them might be just as anxious to get their hands on the thing, whether for its own sake or the money that could be made by selling it."

"If they know about it."

Bob sighed. "We have to assume they do. You know that. Look how many people know about it already that aren't supposed to. It's only a matter of time before rumours begin to expand and travel."

"Riiight."

I started for the door, then paused and turned back towards Bob's desk as I realized I'd missed something. "If the CIA's in such a snit and pushing everyone around so much, don't you think they'd send in one of their own agents as well?"

"I wouldn't be the least bit surprised," said Bob, approvingly. "Great."

"You're going to be out in the open on this one, so keep me informed as best you can, and call out if you need anything. Right?"

"Right."

Our next steps saw Silver and I fly to Halifax where we boarded a navy destroyer, the *HMCS Assiniboine*[67]. I was told that a local constable from H Division was already aboard.

It turned out to be Constable Jack McDonald. This was good news, but I wasn't completely surprised as it wasn't the first time Uncle George and/or Bob had arranged for Jack to be close at hand when I was going into something that could be unusually dangerous.

A Chief Petty Officer showed me to my quarters so I could stow my gear. It turned out that one of the ship's officers had been moved to make a cabin available for Silver and I. When that was done, he escorted me to the bridge so I could make a courtesy call on the ship's captain. Silver and I had been on Canadian destroyers before, so Silver and I were then set free to roam about the ship, and I'd found Jack playing cards, cribbage in this case, with some sailors in the Chiefs' and Petty Officers' Mess.

"What's going on, Alex?" asked Jack. "I've been briefed, but something tells me there was more going on than meets the eye, and now 'the penny drops[67]' with you showing up!"

"Like a bad penny?" I asked, with a grin. Then, more seriously: "when you've finished your game, let's take a walk."

"I've already lost this one," he said ruefully, standing up and tossing a five-dollar bill onto the board. "Besides, I don't get paid enough to be able to play crib with these sharks."

The two petty officers he'd been playing with tried to put innocent expressions on, but there were telltale gleams in their eyes.

"What's that all about? You almost never lose at crib," I said as we walked down several passageways, heading for the stern of the ship.

He smirked. "I thought that if I lost a game or two, it might make me less of an intruder and more of a colleague onboard."

"Ah ha. So speaks the real shark. Even I know better than to play crib with you for money."

Jack chuckled. Then, more soberly asked: "So, what's up?"

I waited until we were out in the open, on the helicopter landing pad, which was also our primary location for Silver to pee because it was so easy to clean-up after him there. Then, I turned to him and picked up the tale.

"Well, you're right," I began. "There is more going on than meets the eye, and everything is on a 'need to know' basis."

"That's the case for almost everything in your line of work!"

"Almost," I agreed, "and I'm not supposed to admit anything to anybody except in case of emergency. But!" I held up a hand to forestall the protests that were making their way to Jack's lips. "I want you to know. So, what I'm NOT telling you is…." I told him some of what I knew to be going on, and quite a bit of what I suspected. But I didn't tell him everything. Maybe if I had, he'd still be alive today. I'll never know, and it will haunt me for the rest of my life.

After our confidential chat, and with the help of a passing sailor, we were able to find the executive officer, who took us to see the ship's captain.

The captain had been briefed on the three mystery ships, the possibility that one of them was carrying stolen armaments from the American armory, and that the U.S. Coast Guard had been trying to locate them.

"Isn't there some kind of tracking device for large ships?" I asked.

"No[68]. Even if there was, this kind of ship would simply switch it off."

"I suppose. Can the ships be followed by a spy satellite then?"

"Not easily. The Americans have a number of Big Bird[69] satellites up, but even if one passes our target and photographs it, we won't know about it until the film is dropped on one of the satellite's four recoverable re-entry vehicles, then caught by an aircraft in mid-air while it parachutes down, then analyzed back on earth. Instead, the U.S. Navy has been using Vigilante reconnaissance aircraft[70].

A U.S. Navy RA-5C Vigilante Reconnaissance Aircraft

"Until recently, the cloud cover was too dense for the aircraft to spot the ships except sporadically. Now that the weather has begun to clear, they have found one of the ships in international waters due east of New York and heading north-north-east."

"Heading towards us, you mean," I said.

"As of the latest aerial photos, yes. The Americans have sent the *USCGC Decisive*[71] to find it and keep it under observation. Initially they'll use their radar but the ship carries a helicopter, like we do, so they'll use that to make a visual confirmation that it matches the description provided by the FBI in Texas. Once they've located and identified the ship, they have been ordered to keep well back, out of sight, and follow it on radar."

"Will the freighter be able to use their radar to figure out that they're being followed?"

"Not if the *Decisive* is careful. Their radar is more powerful than the freighter's."

"What are your orders, Captain?"

"We are to cast-off at dawn tomorrow and head south on an interception course, except that we won't be intercepting them. Instead, we are to remain out of sight and off their radar and help keep an eye on them. We can do that because our radar will have at least twice the range of the freighter.

"If the ship stays in international waters and heads for Europe or Africa, say, then we return to port. Same thing happens if they turn around and head for the southern states or South America. If, on the other hand, it looks like they are going to head for our waters and make for one of our ports, then an FBI liaison agent will be transferred to us and we'll follow them in."

As announced, we cast-off at dawn the next morning with Jack, Silver, and I up to sightsee as we made our way out of the harbour. At this point, we were nearly 600 nautical miles from the mystery freighter, with us cruising roughly southeast at about 12 knots and the freighter heading toward us at about 11 knots. Depending on reports from the U.S. Coast Guard, the captain therefore expected that it would be sometime on the second day before we learned much new about the probable destination of the freighter.

By the next morning, the freighter was still on a direct heading for Nova Scotia, or perhaps Newfoundland, and we were getting close, so the destroyer swung out towards the open sea in order to avoid being spotted. By mid-day, we were summoned to the bridge where the captain explained he had been advised that the freighter was southeast of Lunenberg, Nova Scotia, and that it was still in international waters but beginning to turn towards Halifax.

"Assuming that they are heading for Halifax," he said, "my orders are to rendezvous with the *Decisive*, and bring the FBI Agent onboard. Once they cross into our waters, law enforcement will be up to you and the FBI Agent will serve as liaison. The *Decisive* has a helicopter, and will use that to transfer the agent."

"OK. Thank you," I said. "I know the agent. It will be Special Agent Vivian Rule. May I ask what are your orders are regarding the freighter?"

"You may ask. Perhaps you can even explain them to me," he said, with a growl. "I'm to continue to stand off, remain out of their radar range, and observe while rendering you all possible assistance short of endangering the ship. Seems crazy to me, but I'm just the captain. No one has explained anything to me," he complained. His tone and expression made it clear that he wasn't joking.

I didn't want him to be too grumpy because I needed that assistance he was supposed to provide, so I said: "May we have a word in private, Captain?"

He nodded brusquely and led Jack and I to the back of the bridge.

"OK," I began. "You know that the freighter is suspected of carrying crates of military weapons that were stolen from an armory in Texas."

He nodded.

"So it is, but what I'm not allowed to tell you is that at least one of those crates may contain some kind of new, top-secret explosive mounted in howitzer shells. It has something to do with the CIA, and apparently, they're upset and crawling all over the FBI. Whatever this new thing is, the CIA don't want the freighter to toss it overboard when they see a coast guard or navy ship approaching. Instead, they want the ship to be able to dock and offload it. Then it will be our job to find out who it's being shipped to and then recover it before anyone else can."

"Sounds like a tall order to me, but someone must think it's important to take the risk of the thing blowing up in the harbour!"

I nodded, soberly.

"OK then," he sighed. "What do you need from me?"

"Once it's clear that it's heading for the harbour, would you have your helicopter take us up, get ahead of the freighter, drop Jack off on Georges Island[72], and then drop Vivian, Silver, and I at the berth we cast-off from at the dockyard?"

"That's all?"

"Well, I'd also like to make a couple of radiotelephone calls, but otherwise that's all."

The captain agreed, I made my calls, and then we all had to wait.

Within an hour, as Jack, Silver, and I stood by the helideck near the stern of the destroyer, we could hear the sound of a large Sikorsky helicopter approaching. It was from the *Decisive*, and touched down just long enough for Vivian to disembark and grab her duffel bag. Then, with an increasing roar, it lifted off again, angled back and away from the destroyer, then turned and headed back to its own ship.

When the noise from the helicopter had abated a bit, Silver and I were able to greet Vivian properly. We had worked together on three previous cases, but she and Jack hadn't crossed paths yet, so I introduced them. With that done, we went off to find a quiet place to catch up on any new details regarding the case.

It seemed like no time before we were called to the bridge and advised that the *Decisive* had radioed to say that the freighter was entering the outer reaches of the harbour. The captain seemed relieved to be nearing the end of this particular assignment, for him at least, and even managed a smile when we offered our thanks and goodbyes.

As we left, I heard him say: "Helmsman, stay alert when we enter the harbour. We don't want to run aground again[73]."

Maybe he has a sense of humour after all, I thought.

As soon as we had piled into the *Assiniboine's* helicopter, along with our gear, the pilots started it up and we were soon in the air. When we arrived at the mouth of the harbour, the pilots remained over water, but kept to the northeast shore (the Dartmouth side) and tried to look like just one more military helicopter flying toward the dockyard and other military facilities known collectively as CFB Halifax.

"There she is. Directly to port," came the voice of the co-pilot over the headphones that we'd all been given. As we peered out and down, we could see an older-style freighter in the sea-lane. Any cargo that it was carrying was stowed below decks because there was nothing to see up top, just streaked, fading paint and lots of rust.

We passed the freighter, landed Jack on the northern tip of Georges Island, out of sight of the freighter, and then continued to the naval dockyard where Vivian, Silver and I, and our gear were deposited. With a wave, the pilots took off and headed back to their ship, while the rest of us went and stored our gear in the unmarked police SUV that I had parked there previously. Then, we walked back to the *Assiniboine's* empty pier and I tried calling Jack on the hand-held VHF radios we each had. We were each equipped with powerful binoculars, as well.

"Great visibility from the old fort," said Jack. "The freighter is just passing McNabs Island now." This, I knew, was the larger island, which was positioned near the mouth of the harbor.

"She's still headed my way, and is about two kilometres from my position."

About 15 minutes later came another update. "She's just at my position now. Can't be doing much more than about 6 knots. Obviously not heading for the Ocean Container docks."

After another 15 minutes: "Must be just about at your position now. Looks like she may be heading for the Bedford Basin. The police boat is here for me now. We'll follow her, but keep about 2 kilometres back."

At this point we all got into my SUV and drove to the North Marginal Road, which passes underneath the A. Murray Mackay Bridge, the most northerly of the two bridges that connect Halifax to its sister city of Dartmouth. There was a bit of a park there, that afforded us a great view of the bridge, the most northerly part of The Narrows, and the expanse of the Bedford Basin.

The freighter must have slowed down even more, because it was half an hour before we received another radio report from Jack.

"It's approaching the Mackay Bridge. If you're where I think you are, you should see it any minute."

"Got it," I acknowledged. "It's coming under the bridge now. Maybe it's going to anchor out in the basin. That will sure complicate things for us."

As I watched the freighter through my binoculars, thoughts of trying to deal with the ship at anchor were flying through my head. I was just wondering whether we'd be able to get approval for an armed boarding party when I realized that the ship was turning towards me.

"Careful Jack. The ship is turning. If they're not heading for the Fairview Docks behind me, then they might be turning completely around so they can get to the Richmond Docks[74]."

As I watched in fascination, the ship came about an entire 180 degrees and headed back towards the bridge.

"They're definitely heading back towards the bridge, Jack. It's got to be making for the Richmond Docks. If you can keep an eye on them from the water, we'll drive as close as we can. We'll need to know the exact dock they tie-up at."

"Right," he said.

Before long, we were able to radio H Division headquarters, downtown, with the exact position of the freighter and also to make arrangements to have it closely watched as it began unloading its cargo. With those arrangements made, we drove back to the naval dockyard to pick up Jack and head for an office from which we could plan our next steps.

When we got there, the first thing I did was phone my boss, Bob to update him. He wasn't in the office, but I was able to leave a detailed message for him before I went back to our meeting.

While we were discussing tactics, the first watchers were sent out. The ideal observation position for the cargo unloading was up on the Mackay Bridge, but there were no pedestrian or bike lanes on that bridge. For that reason, a large highways truck made its way up onto the eastbound lane and wasn't far along the bridge before it pulled over to the curb and parked, with its two flashing amber lights operating and an illuminated highways sign carrying an arrow that indicated to other traffic that they should move over and pass on its left-hand side.

As most of the following traffic moved over to comply, a plain van passed and then turned in to park just ahead of the highways truck. This was an unmarked police van, with no emergency lights switched on at all. The two plainclothes officers inside simply opened the rear doors and set up - within the van but looking towards the Richmond Docks – two reasonably comfortable folding chairs, one of each mounted behind a tripod-mounted spotting scope and a tripod-mounted camera. That done, they settled in to take turns watching the freighter until the next shift would come to relieve them. This went on for some time, because the freighter began unloading cargo and continued to do so well into the evening.

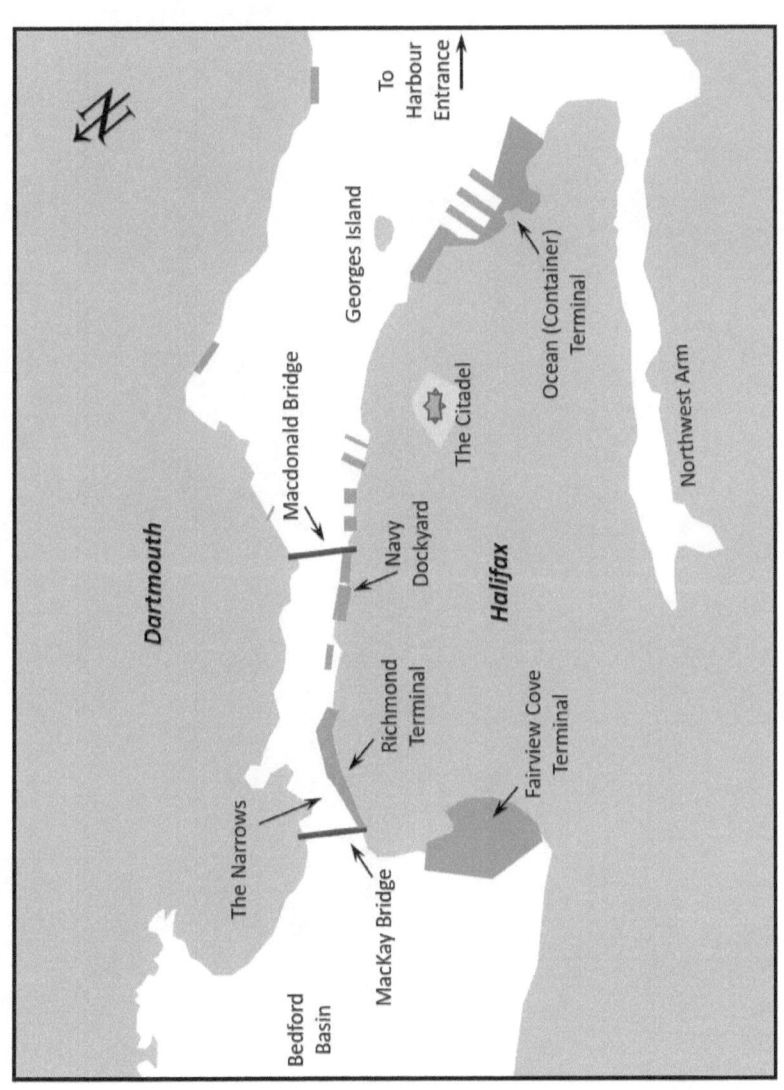

Laurie Schramm

7 CONVERGENCE

Betrayal may come from within.

Moscow Rules (see Book 14 Endnote 1).

A phone began to ring in a Halifax hotel room. It was just past midnight, but the occupant was awake. He'd been waiting for this call.

"Hello?"

"Hi Avery. Bob here. I just got word on the crates from the freighter." *There was noise on the line, but the words could be understood.*

"You know where they are?'

"I think so. We had to wake up a lot of people at the terminal authority, and they did a lot of complaining, but we finally got what we need. Unless somebody screwed-up, the crates should be in the northeast corner of Warehouse A. That's the north one. Got it?"

"I think so," said Staff Sergeant Blunt, writing on a pad beside the phone. "Northeast corner, north building, which is Warehouse A. You think someone will try for it tonight?"

"Hard to say from all the way back here in Ottawa," Bob paused for a moment, as if in thought. "But the FBI seem to think the receiver is

going to be in a hurry. That might mean it's the CIA that thinks that, or maybe it means it's the CIA that's nervous. Who the hell know? You're the counter-intelligence expert, not me."

"Thanks a lot. You're saying you don't think we should take any chances." It was a statement, not a question.

"Well, no, I don't. Do you?"

"No... I suppose not," said Blunt, considering. Then he came to a decision. "All right. I'll go out and take a look around. I'm probably not going to be able to get back to sleep anyway."

"Sorry. I'd have come out there for this one, but I'm still tied to my desk back here.... By the way, if you stop by H Division on your way, there should be a search warrant waiting for you at the front desk. I made the request in your name as soon as I got the latest news from the FBI to show probable cause."

"Right. Thanks."

"No problem. Good luck."

"Good luck, the man says," muttered Blunt after hanging up the phone. No rest for the wicked[75], *he thought, as he got up. He'd been asleep in bed, but fully dressed while he waited for the possible phone call. Now he reached for his gun and his jacket and got ready to head out and get that search warrant.*

***

At an all-night doughnut shop near the waterfront, a uniformed RCMP constable was seated at a table sipping on a cup of black coffee that he hoped would keep him awake through the rest of the graveyard shift. Chris Williams wasn't paying much attention to the few other customers in the restaurant, but his police instincts caused him to glance up and take a second look at the man that walked in the door.

The man was of average height. He was somewhat stocky in build, but moved with ease, suggesting that he wasn't in bad physical condition. He wore glasses, had greying hair cut reasonably short, and a well trimmed but greying mustache. After a quick survey of the restaurant, the man immediately walked over to the constable's table.

As Constable Williams looked up, the man removed and opened his wallet to display a badge and identification card.

"Staff Sergeant Avery Blunt, Security Service, Counter-Intelligence," he said.

"What can I do for you Staff?' asked the constable after he'd taken a close look at the proffered ID.

"I'm on a national security case, Williams. I need to take a quick look at some crates in a warehouse near here, and I need backup." He held up a hand to forestall questioning as he continued. *"Normally, I'd go through channels and arrange everything properly, but this case is breaking too quickly for that. I only recently learned where the things I'm after have been placed, and I had to use what time I had to get a search warrant. Here it is."* He handed the warrant over for the constable's inspection.

"I'd use your radio to call for backup, but our frequencies are being monitored. Understand?"

"Sure Staff," said the constable, barely keeping up. *"What do you want me to do?"*

"Simple. Just follow me over to the Richmond Terminal. We'll be going to Warehouse A. That's the north one. We'll park out of sight somewhere, then I'll go in and look for the crates I'm after. All you need to do is stand at the door and make sure no one comes in to interfere while I'm in there. If I find what I think I'm going to find, I'll bring it out and then you escort me while I drive it over to headquarters. That's all. OK?"

"OK Staff," said the constable, taking a last sip of coffee and rising up.

"Let's go then."

There was a large parking lot surrounding the warehouse buildings of the Richmond Terminal, but the two cars parked on the street and both men got out.

"Do you want to just go straight in?" asked Constable Williams.

"Yes, but now that I've thought it over, we're going to change the plan just a bit. The doors to the warehouses are on the harbour side, so we'll walk over there. When we get there, we'll find a spot from which you can remain hidden but still watch the doors to Warehouse A. I'll go in, but you watch.

"Now. If a single man comes along in a bit and follows me in, let him do it but you stay put. It will be the suspect I'm after, and I'll be ready for him. If it's more than one person, then let them go, but follow them in. I'll

have a better chance of dealing with them if you're there backing me up from behind. Got it?"

"OK Staff, I've got it. What's it all about though?"

"I can't tell you that now. If everything goes according to plan and I can wrap this thing up tonight, then I'll be able to tell you later because secrecy won't matter any more at that point. That's the best I can do.... Ready?"

"Ready."

"Let's move. Keep your eyes open"

Constable Williams was fully awake now, as the two men walked across the parking lot, taking some care to avoid walking in the better lit portions that surrounded the several lamp-posts on the lot. When they reached the harbour side, it was easy to find a stack of empty pallets, behind which the constable took-up station.

"How long do you think you'll be in there?" asked Williams.

"If I'm right, and the crates I'm looking for are in there, then an hour. Two hours at the most. If I'm wrong, then we'll have to stake the place out until dawn. After that I'll use your car radio to get another team out here to relieve us."

"OK Staff. Good luck."

***

Everything seemed quiet as Staff Sergeant Blunt walked cautiously to the main double-doors on the harbour-facing side of Warehouse A. It's quiet... too quiet, he thought, grimly, remembering the trite line used in so many old Western and war movies. Reaching the doors, he withdrew a slim case containing lock-picking tools, took a good look at the deadbolt lock and selected a pair of picks. Working with one pick in each hand, he used a very slender one to pick each pin in succession, and an L-shaped tension wrench to hold the picked pins in place. Once he had successfully picked all of the pins, he used the tension wrench to turn the key-cylinder and open the lock.

Blunt quietly opened the door and went in, closing the door behind him. Gazing around, he could see that only about half of the warehouse lights were turned on, providing just enough illumination for a person to be able to navigate around the cavernous space. His rubber-soled shoes enabled him to move very quietly as he chose an indirect route to the northeast corner of the building. As he approached the indicated corner, he couldn't hear anything but there was one location from which a bit more light was emanating. Slowing down, and watching and listening even more carefully – if that was possible – he approached the light.

As he rounded the corner of a stack of crates, he found the source of the additional light. A 12V, 'Big Jim' style hand lantern was sitting on top of a large crate, with its swivel-head lamp aimed towards the cement floor where several crates had been pulled down and opened. One of the opened crates revealed two shiny projectiles of the kind that might be fired from a large cannon. Like howitzer projectiles, *he thought. Approaching the crate, and kneeling down for a better look, he could see some unusual features: each projectile had a gleaming casing that might have been stainless-steel or brushed aluminum, and an odd-looking access hatch of some kind near the base. There was also a small, black-plastic box that appeared to be a remote control. In the upper half of the face, there was a small red indicator light and a large, oblong, grey push-button switch. The red light was on.*

He only had time to frown, before he felt a sharp pain in the side of his neck, a cloth bag came over his head, and he was thrown to the floor.

Although Blunt struggled, he was disoriented by the bag which made it almost impossible to breathe, and his attacker had the advantage of being on top of him. As the seconds went by, he not only couldn't breathe but became quite dizzy, making his struggles weaker and weaker.

Drugged, *he thought, as he lost consciousness.*

His assailant knelt and crouched overhead, positioning Blunt's arms so he could handcuff him.

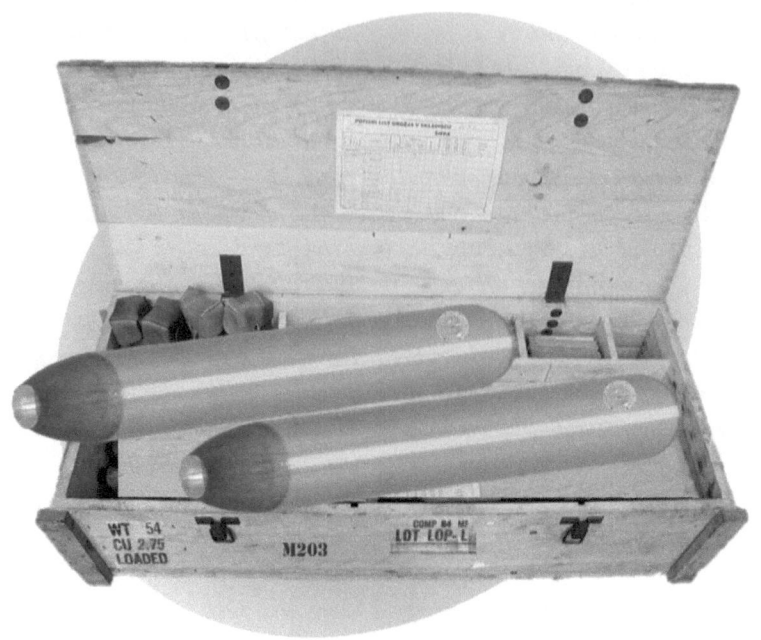

The Modified M549 Rocket-Assist Projectile

"I think that's enough Bob," I said as I emerged, with Silver by my side, from my place of concealment behind a stack of crates. At the sound of my voice, Jack emerged from another stack a few metres to one side, and Vivian did the same from a stack that was a few metres to the other side of me.

Bob, who had frozen in-place at the sound of my voice, slowly rose from his crouch over Avery and turned. As he did so, I gasped. It was Avery, but then it wasn't either. The man facing me either wore a wig or had his hair dyed to match Avery's greying dark brown. His eyebrows had been similarly treated or attached, as was the moustache. Bob, however, had blonde hair and was clean shaven. Despite the glasses, I could see that he wore contact lenses to change his apparent eye colour from blue to brown. Although Bob was quite slender, the figure before me wore padding, or possibly layers of clothing, to give the appearance of a more heavyset build. He'd also done something to darken his skin tone, and must have put padding in each cheek. The voice, however, was unmistakably Bob's.

"I'm impressed, Bob. Except for the voice, I'd probably pass you on the street without recognition."

He shrugged. "Tradecraft," was all he said.

"The real Avery. Is he OK or did you kill him?"

"No, he'll be fine. I used a fast-acting anesthetic, and choked him a bit to give it time to take effect, but he was breathing freely when I put the cuffs on him." He stepped aside so I could see and, sure enough, Avery's wrists were handcuffed together.

"You were a bit rough on him, don't you think?"

"Well, I was all alone here so I had to make sure I could arrest him. He was armed. See?" Bob lifted a snub-nose revolver, using his thumb and forefinger to hold it handgrip up, with the barrel pointing down towards the floor.

"I only just found out that he was the traitor everyone's been looking for all these years, so I had to get the jump on him right away. There was no time to call it in."

"How did you find him out?" It was amazing to me that I could carry on this conversation in a normal pace and tone of voice.

"Simple," he smiled. "I had suspected him all along, just like the FBI did." He nodded towards Vivian. "When I told him that I wasn't able to come out from Ottawa in time, he agreed to do it. It was our office that made all the travel arrangements for him, including his hotel reservation." Bob shrugged. "Once I knew that I was able to call the hotel and request a specific room. Then I had his phone tapped."

"Legally?"

He looked at me like I was stupid. "Of course I didn't do it legally. In this case, I thought the ends justified the means. When Avery here shows up in court – if it ever comes to court, that is – I think the judge will overlook such a minor transgression in this particular case. Don't you?"

I sighed. "I suppose so. Except for one thing. The traitor wasn't Avery, Bob. It was you. All along the way, it was you."

"You're crazy Alex!" Bob exclaimed. "Or maybe…." His tone changed to conciliatory. "Maybe you've been working too hard lately. Maybe you need to take a bit of leave and rest up."

Nice try, I thought.

"You might be right, Bob. But one thing I'm sure of is the identity of our traitor. Think back for a moment. Way back. All the way back 20 years, to the Avro Arrow incident. Our leak offered to sell the Arrow secrets to the British, and actually pulled it off over a complicated series of dead drops in which packages of documents were dropped off in return for envelopes of money. Naturally the British were keen to find out who their mysterious benefactor was. They tried, but they failed. As it turns out, they actually did get the evidence they needed, but they hadn't known what to look for, so they never even knew what they had."

"What do you mean, evidence?"

"Well, every time you set up a dead drop, they had operatives rush over and set up surveillance. At least, such surveillance as they could position on short notice. Since you tended to use crowded locations, they never actually spotted you pick up the money, but they took a huge number of photographs hoping to spot something in the crowds. As I said, though, it didn't do them any good."

"What's your evidence then?"

"Well. Surprise number one, is that they kept all those pictures, and then at some point in time they sent them home to be stored in the MI6 archives. Surprise number two, is that they're still there collecting dust after all these years. Surprise number three, is that I visited MI6 and they let me in to see those pictures, and I went through them too. They took thousands of them, and if you looked at them all there were several hundred people whose faces you could make out in some of them. And that's what I did. I went through every one looking to see if I could spot a familiar face. You see what I had, that MI6 didn't, was a knowledge of the twenty suspects and what each of them look like."

Bob didn't comment, but the look on his face made it clear that he knew what was coming next.

"Surprise number four was that I spotted one familiar face, Bob. It was yours. You were younger then, but it was you."

"Damn them! They promised not to try to identify me as part of the deal to get the documents."

"Yes. I'm afraid that spies tend to lie when it suits them. Surprising, huh?"

Bob growled, low in his throat, and surveyed our positions. Then, changing his grip, he pointed Avery's revolver at me.

As my revolver was already in my hand, I was able to point it at Bob at the same time.

"Standoff, Bob," I said.

"Not quite," he responded. With his other hand, he had reached into a pocket and he pulled out the remote-control device, holding it so we could see that the red light was on.

"Just tell me this, Bob. Why? Why betray everyone so many times, through so many years?" I didn't think he'd actually tell me, but he did.

"As I've told you before Alex, it's all just a game, really. Not at first. At first, we were all on a mission; a crusade; good versus evil, and all that. Then, later, it became somewhat of a game. A game for competitive people. Naturally, some play it better than others, and eventually you begin to wonder: Who's the best? And then you wonder: How would you even know? Eventually, the game became more important than the job, and I realized that the winner is really just the person that can fool most of the people, most of the time[76]."

"OK, but think, Bob!" I pleaded. "What comes now? If you shoot one of us, the others will come at you, and you must know how fast Silver can be."

Bob tilted his head as Silver had already begun to growl and silently begin a flanking maneuver.

"Tell him to stop, or I'll shoot Vivian," he said, in a very calm, serious voice. I believed him.

I told Silver to stop.

"Even if you manage to get all of us, the place is surrounded. You won't get past the dockyard."

"Nice try," he responded. "That's one of the oldest bluffs in the books."

I shrugged. "I'm actually telling the truth. I do that, you know. But, suit yourself. I've warned you. What happens next is on your head."

Thinking furiously, I saw Bob's eyes grow cunning as he decided on his next move. Keeping Avery's revolver pointed at me, he picked up one of the shiny projectiles and tucked it under his arm, behind his gun hand. "See this projectile? Just before Avery came in, I opened the access panel at its base and switched on the remote triggering device."

Next, he held up the little black box in his free hand. "And this is the remote control. You can see that it's live. The FBI was kind enough to send the instructions in case we had to turn it off. I turned it on instead.

"That makes it a 'Non-Zero-Sum Game.' If I lose, you all lose – our lives, in this case. Now then," he was back to feeling like he was in charge. "If you'll just step aside, I'll just take this remote control and walk out of here. Then I'll toss it away, leave the country, and never come back."

"Bob. Please," I tried once more. "The place really is surrounded – by MPs – and they're going to be inclined to shoot first and ask questions later. And even if you get by them, the CIA's going to be on your trail wherever you go. In fact, I wouldn't be at all surprised if there's a CIA agent waiting outside right now."

"You're bluffing again, Alex. You're a good chess player, but you're not yet in my league… and, even if you're right, I'm willing to take my chances."

I sighed, theatrically. "OK Bob, but just put the projectile and the remote control back in the crate. If you do, you can walk out of here. But you should know that, if I have to, I'll take you down to prevent you from stealing that weapon."

Bob had begun to take a step forward, but now he stopped and looked at me quizzically, with his head tilted to one side. "You'll take me down? Me? After all we've been through together?" he asked.

I shrugged. "I could ask you the very same question. Think Bob? Please! Leave the projectile behind and you can live."

"Silver! Stay!" I ordered. With my peripheral vision, I could tell that Silver, his senses on high, was positioning himself to spring towards Bob, aiming for his gun hand. Unfortunately, Silver was not in position to have been able to get at the gun in time, so I didn't want to take the risk of making the situation worse.

There was dead silence in the warehouse for a moment. Then, several things happened almost simultaneously.

Bob made his decision. He glanced at Silver, but kept his gun aimed at me and began to squeeze the trigger.

Vivian, screamed "He's going to shoot!" but she was too far away to physically interfere.

Jack didn't say a thing, but had begun to move. By the time I realized what he planned, it was too late. With a tremendous leap, he sprung right in front of me, just as Bob pulled the trigger.

The sound of a .38 Special round being fired in a confined space is unforgettable. Even in a firing range, while wearing hearing protection, it's loud. But for our unprotected ears, it was painful and dangerous; louder than a jet plane taking off; louder than a jackhammer.

The force of the slug drove Jack back into me, causing me to drop to the floor with Jack in my lap as I struggled to keep my gun lined-up on Bob. I'd been hoping to create an opportunity to use the anesthetic-dart-shooting pen that Emi had given me, but it was far too late for that now.

I don't know whether Bob had ever shot anyone before. Unlike me, many police officers go their entire careers with having to draw their gun, much less fire it in a dangerous situation. Whatever the reason, he froze for a moment, as if taking in the fact that he'd actually shot a fellow officer and the spy game was now more than an academic exercise. All I know is that in the instant it took for him to regained control of himself, I'd pointed my revolver straight at his heart.

Silver, worried by the distress he sensed in me and torn between my command to stay put and the danger he sensed in Bob, stayed where he was, vibrating, still growling, and poised to leap at a command from me.

"If I have to, I'll shoot you too," said Bob, but I could tell he realized that he had run out of options.

"It's still a standoff, Bob, and those sounds…" We could all hear the warehouse doors burst open, and the sound of running boots. "Those sounds are from MPs; the reinforcements you didn't believe me about."

I was distracted for a moment by Jack, who suddenly began to move around, which caused him to start coughing up blood. I couldn't even take the time yet to figure out where he had been shot because I had to keep my eyes on Bob. Silver was waiting for a command from me. Vivian, who was unarmed, had to stand her ground and wait. And me? For a moment, I suddenly felt separated from reality.

Time slowed down, and it was like I was detached from the current reality and was watching a scene from a movie, from outside my body even. Like a spectator.

Jack lay dying in my arms.

I saw myself looking angrily at Bob, with my gun pointed straight at his chest; my finger on the trigger; and tears streaming down my face.

I saw Silver stand nearby, looking so confused because for the first time in all the years we'd been together he didn't know what to do.

I heard Bob snarl: "Finish it, Alex. It's all over for me now anyway. You know you want to do it. Pull the trigger and get it over with."

I was distressed and angry, and I found that I wanted to do it. My finger began a well practised maneuver: a very slow, gradual squeeze.

Then, I seemed to hear another voice. It was a quiet but compelling voice. I don't even know why I could hear it with everything else going on, but somehow it penetrated through the mental fog, and I found myself angling my head, trying to make out the words.

"You can lower the gun now, Alex. We have him covered." Such a gentle, yet persuasive sound. "This isn't the Mountie's way. Your way.... Take a breath and let it go."

It was Don's voice. Was he finally here? I see myself risk a quick glance to one side. Yes, definitely Don, dressed as an MP Captain and pointing his own gun at Bob. A large, angry-looking .45 automatic. There are others with him.

Could it really be over at last?

"Let it go Alex..." I hear again. So softly.

Suddenly, I hear Bob snarl and point the gun at his own head instead. There is another deafening crack. The sound acts like a jolt, like when a film projector skips a sprocket, almost jams, and then gets realigned and carries on. Suddenly I'm back in real time. In my own body.

I see Bob drop his gun and collapse to the floor. I look dumbly at my revolver, ease my finger back, and lower the gun. I can feel that Silver has come over to rest his head on my leg. He gives a moan of sympathy.

That's when the shakes began.

Laurie Schramm

8 AFTERMATH

With reinforcements having finally arrived, plus a bewildered-looking Constable Williams, several tasks were quickly delegated.

Don detailed one of his MPs to radio-in for paramedics and to see if they could get a Navy helicopter in fast for a medivac to one of the big hospitals.

Vivian helped me to find and apply pressure to the holes in Jack's body. Bob's bullet had gone right through and, if it hadn't hit the heart, it certainly hit a major artery as both holes were bleeding like crazy. Jack was still coughing, but he'd lost consciousness.

Other MPs went to attend to Avery, who was still alive and had regained consciousness during the standoff. With his hands handcuffed, however, he hadn't been able to do much more than pull the black bag off of his head. The bag, incidentally, turned out to be constructed from black cloth that had been coated on the inside with some kind of extremely flexible and clingy plastic. That was why Bob had been able to so quickly restrict Avery's breathing, allowing him to be overpowered long enough for the fast-acting anesthetic to take effect.

Meanwhile, Don came up to ask Vivian and I some urgent questions.

"Are you OK?" he asked me, putting a comforting hand on my shoulder.

"No. But I'm not injured, if that's what you mean."

"Those projectiles. Is there any risk of them going off?" was his second question. "When Bob dropped the one that he was holding, my heart stopped for a moment."

It was probably the stress of the situation, but that sent Vivian into almost hysterical laughter. Unable to speak for a moment, she waved in my direction.

"No, it's OK Don." I said, tiredly. "The CIA made them up for the FBI, at my request. They resemble something the CIA is actually working on, but these ones are just fakes."

"Nobody tells me anything," Don complained. "So, it was all part of a sting then? A ruse?"

"A complete fabrication, from beginning to end. It had to be tempting enough to be useful as bait, and Bob thought he was going to be able to sell these new projectiles on the black market. It was also designed to provide Bob with an opportunity to frame Avery, so he'd take the fall for everything. We'd never have been able to pull it off without the help of the FBI and the CIA."

"And it worked!"

"Well, sort of, but at what cost?" I said, crying again. "God what a mess!"

As luck would have it, the navy had a helicopter airborne in the harbour area, and it was diverted to the huge dock outside the warehouse, which made a perfect landing platform, even for the huge Sikorsky. It was carrying a Search and Rescue Technician, who quickly examined Jack and got him hustled into the helicopter, which immediately took off with a deafening roar and headed for one of the big hospitals downtown.

When the paramedic ambulance showed up, Avery allowed himself to be examined but refused to be taken to hospital. He was amazed at the degree to which Bob had been able to replicate his appearance. He was wearing baggy pants, and a kind of padded vest under an oversize coat, to mimic Avery's heftier build. He'd dyed his blonde hair and eyebrows brown and added streaks of grey. He'd glued on a false moustache and heavier eyebrows, similarly coloured and streaked. He'd dyed his naturally pale face, neck, and hands just slightly to better match Avery's skin tone, and more.

"He's wearing contact lenses to change his eye colour," said Avery, inspecting the body closely. "And he's got pads in his cheeks to puff out his face."

I came over to see for myself, and glanced at the fake ID that Avery had retrieved from Bob's wallet. "Not bad. Wouldn't survive a close inspection, but from a medium distance it looks pretty good, and that's all he needed."

The paramedics took Bob's body away, and Don's MPs gathered up the crate and the two fake projectiles. It was just after dawn by the time we were walking out of the warehouse, and in the early morning light we noticed that we were being watched by someone who was sitting on a bench by the waterfront edge of the dock.

"Company?" I murmured.

Vivian followed my gaze, then did a double-take and said: "You do have a way with words, sometimes, Alex. Wait here, please."

As Vivian walked over to the bench, the figure rose. It was an elderly-looking man; medium height and build. He had scraggly, grey hair sticking out at odd angles from under a tired-looking hat, and wore a shabby-looking grey sport-coat with baggy pants. In one hand, he seemed to be clutching a rumpled brown paper bag of the sort that a suspicious-minded person might guess held a whiskey bottle. He stood hunched over when Vivian began speaking to him but, near the end, he straightened up and I was surprised to see that he was actually quite tall.

After a brief conversation, they shook hands, and Vivian walked back to rejoin us.

"Let me guess, CIA?" I said.

"CIA. They don't care about the dummy projectiles. In fact, he said we were welcome to keep them as souvenirs. What they *were* interested in was the identity of the traitor, and they sent him to observe."

"That and to make sure that we actually caught the right person?"

"They'd never admit that, but I wouldn't be at all surprised," said Vivian, with a smile.

"By the way," said Avery, "you didn't tell me the CIA projectiles were fake."

"No. Sorry about that. It was the same reason I didn't tell you that Bob was Gideon. I wanted to make sure your reactions were real when things unfolded. I am sorry you had such a close call with Bob, though."

"That's OK Alex. It was worth it to find the real traitor and to get my name cleared once and for all."

"While we're discussing your little surprises," Vivian chimed in. "Where did that remote control business come from? It wasn't the CIA. That access panel was supposed to be the way to set codes and a timer for the thing."

"I know, but I had a colleague put an addendum on your message with the arming instructions. Then, I slipped the remote into the crate when we were first selecting our hiding places in here. I thought we might need to stall for time because there would be no way to know how close Don and his MPs would be in the critical moments and I thought it might be handy to be able to make Bob think he had the upper hand for a while. It didn't work out as well as I'd hoped though. Which reminds me," I said, digging in my shirt pocket. "Here you are Don. It's actually the remote control for your garage door opener."

Even though the mission had succeeded, it had been a horrible day for me, and it got worse a few hours later when we learned the awful news that Jack had been pronounced 'Dead on Arrival' when the helicopter reached the hospital. It's always shocking when you learn that a colleague has died, at any age, and it made me feel worse that he died in my arms, and guilty that he'd died in his heroic move to save my life. He'd been a good colleague and friend. Silver and I attended his funeral later on, as did many other police officers from across Canada. Don came out for it, in full military dress uniform, and even Vivian flew back up to Canada for it.

Jack's buried at the RCMP Cemetery at Depot Division, Regina, where he and I had first met as fellow recruits in training. It's a peaceful place. Silver and I still go and visit him there when we're in Regina.

Stained-Glass Windows in the RCMP Chapel,
Depot Division, Regina

Laurie Schramm

9 EPILOGUE

Early November, 1981
Ottawa, ON

I thought I'd be sent on leave after my debriefing in Ottawa, to give me time to grieve and wind-down from everything that had happened, but no.

Staff Sergeant Avery Blunt was made acting Head of Section and, presumably on the orders of Uncle George, had taken some pains to make sure I was constantly being sent out on assignments, including assignments that would never have come to our section, or even the Security Service for that matter. They weren't exactly traffic duty, but it was obvious that they were trying to keep me busy and occupy my mind with current work as much as possible. I think they were just trying to be kind, and I can't say that they were wrong.

I thought I'd heard the last of what became known as the Gideon Case, but I was wrong about that too. It came up again one day in the third week of November. Silver and I were returning to Ottawa from a search for a missing child. The child had been found, unharmed, by one of the other search parties, but the important thing was that it all ended well, so I was feeling quite content when my police radio crackled and the dispatcher relayed a message that I was to proceed to a certain address and meet the officer on the scene.

I mustn't have fully had my wits about me as I remember thinking that it was interesting to be called to a house in the Rockcliffe Park area because that's where the Gideon Case had all begun for me – at Deputy Commissioner George MacLeod's house party. I hadn't

269

remembered Uncle George's address, but it all came back to me when I realized that it was his house to which I'd been called.

Standing on the front step of the house was Uncle George himself, the 'officer on the scene.' As Silver and I walked up the sidewalk to the front steps, I could see that Uncle George's wife, Mary MacLeod was standing there as well. Having saluted Uncle George and been hugged by Mary, we were invited in.

"I hope you don't mind being summoned like you were, but an opportunity came up on such short notice that there wasn't time for an informal invitation."

"It's no problem, Sir. We were returning from a child-search anyway. I'm just sorry that every time I come here, I seem to be wearing a soiled uniform."

He laughed. "Don't worry about that. If anything, it reflects the way you always seem to be on the job, getting things done."

"Did you find the lost child, dear?" asked Mary.

I smiled. "Well, Silver and I didn't, but another of the search teams did so it had a happy ending. That's the important thing."

Once I'd slipped my boots off, I was invited to join Uncle George in his study, just like I had been almost exactly a year earlier. As if he'd read my mind, Uncle George echoed the same sentiment.

"Ever watch the old *Mission: Impossible*[77] series on television?" he asked, as we walked through the house.

"Yes Sir. I used to watch them with my father every week. We almost never missed an episode."

"I enjoyed them too, never thinking that one day I'd be assigning an impossible mission to someone, but that's what I did almost exactly one year ago in this very room."

"He refused to bet on the outcome, too," said the familiar voice of Admiral White.

"It's great to see you again, Sir!" I said, walking over to shake his hand, followed by Silver who walked over, gave the Admiral a good sniffing over, then decided he recognized him and went to lie down on a rug.

"I'm sorry about Constable McDonald," said Uncle George, as we all found comfortable chairs to sink into.

"Me too, Sir. He was great colleague and a good friend, and he deliberately threw himself in front of a bullet that Bob meant for me. I'll never forget him."

"Good. There are two things you can do for him now. Honour

his memory and keep moving. I'm sure that's what he would have wanted."

I nodded. I agreed.

"Well then. I want to talk to you briefly about what people are now calling the Gideon Case. I read the report of your debriefing, of course, and I've spoken with Staff Sergeant Blunt and Deputy Director Wheeler in Washington. I didn't call you in right away because I wanted to give you some time to decompress and work through some of the grieving. You can blame me for making Blunt keep you busy with assignments, but I thought it might help you to be occupied."

"Thank you, Sir. I think it was the best thing to do."

"And you're feeling OK now?"

"Mostly Sir. I think," I hedged.

"Well, I won't pry any further. Now then, we'd like to hear about it in your own words, if you don't mind."

So, I told them my story, briefly, but holding nothing of any significance back.

"Amazing," said Uncle George. "A fine job. Well, congratulations on pulling off an impossible mission. You succeeded where everyone else failed. Admiral White here offered to bet a case of Scotch that'd you'd crack the case, but I wouldn't take it because I thought you'd pull it off as well. The few others that were in the know: Deputy Director Wheeler, his counterpart at the CIA, and 'C' at MI6 all thought it was a lost cause, that the traitor had covered his tracks too well, but they were wrong. They're all very impressed with you now though, I can tell you."

"Thank you, Sirs, both of you. I was very fortunate."

"Certainly, but you made your own luck. Took a few unconventional leaps while you were at it too. But they paid off."

"How did you ever get me into MI6 Sir? And how did you manage to get the CIA to play along?"

"As far as MI6 goes, that was Admiral White's doing, but our two nations' military intelligence services have a long history of helping each other out. Almost as long as the Mounted Police's relationship with the FBI, in fact."

"Once I explained everything to C," the admiral put in, "he was almost as eager as we were to get the matter solved."

"As for the CIA," continued Uncle George, "I can't take much credit there either. I just asked Director Wheeler to give it his best shot. I don't know how he did it, but Director Wheeler must have done some fast talking to get the CIA to play along."

"Well, it would all have been for nothing without their help. I just wish it hadn't turned out to be Bob that was the traitor Gideon. I knew I had to treat Bob like all the other suspects, but I really didn't want it to be him."

"You would rather it had turned out to be someone like Demeniak in A Section, hmmm?" He immediately threw a hand up. "No! Don't answer that. I shouldn't have said that out loud."

He saw the look on my face though, as I realized that I hadn't been entirely successful in preventing the corners of my mouth from curling up in a repressed smile.

"I suspect our thoughts are running on similar lines, but you did not hear me say that!"

"No, Sir. Of course not."

"Well, like you, I knew Bob had to be a possibility, but I didn't want it to be him either. He joined up when he turned 18 and had nearly twenty-five years in the Force. He would have been getting his fifth star[78] later this year. Back in 1959, he was a constable in the Security and Intelligence Directorate[79], the forerunner of the Security Service. The problem was that none of us suspected him any more or any less than the other 19 on the list."

"He was very good at his job, Sir, it's just that he turned those same skills and abilities against us."

"Yes," said Admiral White. "It's the old story of 'who watches the watchers?'"

"True, but it was worse than that," added Uncle George. "Ever since the 1950s and '60s, the intelligence thinking has been that there must be at least one traitor within, and a lot of effort was poured into trying to discover who it was. This was going on in intelligence agencies all around the world, including ours[80].

"Furthermore, the counter-intelligence thinking has tended to focus on the ideologically-motivated traitor, leading counter-intelligence officers – including ours - to overlook the threat from betrayals based on non-ideological motives and chase innocent, or even mythical, people. In Bob's case, it wasn't ideology, it was the challenge, and the money."

"And 'the game' Sir. I think the money was more like a way of keeping score. He was certainly too smart to spend it and be caught living an extravagant lifestyle."

"There, you see? 'The Game' became more important to him than the reason the game exists in the first place. That's why we needed someone – you, in fact - to take a fresh approach; be unconventional. Incidentally, what was the most difficult part of the case for you?" asked Uncle George, changing the subject.

"It was after I recognized Bob at one of the dead drops in two of the MI6 photos. When I came back to the office, I did my best not to reveal any hint of what I'd learned, especially to Bob himself. But the whole time I was afraid I would give out some kind of tiny sign and the jig would be up. Luckily for me, the look on Bob's face when I confronted him in Halifax showed that he'd had no idea. None at all."

"And then you set a trap for him. A huge trap."

"I'm just glad it worked. A lot more things could have gone wrong than actually did."

"Well. It's a huge relief to everyone who's in the know that you succeeded in closing off the leak, and Admiral White and I wanted to express our appreciation in person. Thank you."

"Thank you from me too," said the Admiral. "By the way, what did you think of your brief career as a Captain in the RCAF?"

"At first, it all seemed so bizarre, especially the part about being saluted. But later, once I was deep inside the role I was playing, it became kind of fun."

"Good," he said with a smile. "I hear that you impressed Lieutenant Moore and Sergeant Wilson."

"The feeling's mutual, Sir. I'd work with them again anytime."

"Well now," said Uncle George, bringing the meeting back to order. "The reason for calling you in here without notice was that the Admiral just flew in for another meeting today, and has to fly out again later tonight, so this was our window of opportunity. The two of us wanted to see you in person and together to offer our thanks… and our congratulations" His eyes twinkled.

"Congratulations, Sir?"

"Yes. You've just been promoted to Sergeant."

"Congratulations, Sergeant Houston," they both said, almost in unison. Mary, who'd been silent to this point, simply got up and came over to give me a big hug before the two men could approach and shake hands.

"Thank you, Sirs," I said. "But…."

"Just doing your job? Don't expect prizes or rewards? Hmmm?" said the Admiral.

"Something like that," was the best I could come up with.

"Well. It's not a prize. I suppose is a bit of a reward, to some extent. It's not everyday someone catches a traitor from within. But, at the same time, it's not specifically for the Gideon Case. More like for that and all the other cases of yours that came before it. Here's the promotion notice. It's effective today, so make sure your trip home is the last one you take wearing corporal's stripes."

I thanked him again.

"I also have a copy of a letter here that I'd like you to read later on," he continued. "It's the letter of recommendation for your promotion. It's rather lengthy, and it's signed by me, the Admiral here, Deputy Director White, and 'C' of MI6. You're not supposed to have it, so I'm not really giving you a copy, you understand."

"Yes, Sir. Thank you, Sir."

"Fine. As long as we're breaking rules, I think we should have one drink to celebrate, and then the Admiral's driver should be here to take him to the airport."

Later, as we walked from Uncle George's house to our truck, I looked down at Silver and said: "What do you think about it all, Silver?"

He looked up at me with his head tilted to one side, showing that he was paying attention and attempting to discern the gist of my words.

There was definitely a cross roads approaching. I was becoming too well known in too many places to continue doing much more undercover work, especially in anything involving foreign agents. At the same time, the Security Service had come under a huge storm of public controversy due its actions during the 1970 FLQ crisis[81]. In August, the McDonald Commission had recommended that the service be split-out from the Mounted Police and rebuilt as a civilian intelligence agency, thus separating policing and intelligence work into separate organizations. When the time came, I was pretty sure I was going to have to leave the Security Service in order to remain with the Mounted Police. My career goal had been policing, and none of my experiences in ten years as a police officer had changed that.

I knelt down on the sidewalk and looked Silver straight in the eyes.

"What should we do Silver?" I asked.

As he stared back at me with that mesmerizing gaze that he seemed to be able to turn on or off at will, an image floated into my consciousness.

I saw a First Nations human and a wild-looking wolf. It was a drawing of the first human-and-wolf bonding from ancient times, and I remembered that an elder in Skagway, Alaska had shown me that image. The elder that had originally instructed Silver and his sister when they were young. The elder had explained that, in the legend of their nation, the first human-wolf pair had become famous for noble deeds involving justice and the protection of the weak and the disadvantaged.

The next image, or sense perhaps, that entered my mind contained the words *We are pack.*

Throwing my arms around Silver's shoulders in a big hug, I nodded my head and said: "Pack."

"*Grruph,*" said Silver, sounding satisfied.

It was enough. When the time came, we'd figure something out, together.

Laurie Schramm

... Alex and Silver return in
"An Interrupted Mountie."

Laurie Schramm

BOOK 14 ENDNOTES

1. Adapted from the CIA's 'Moscow Rules." See A.J. Mendez and J. Mendez, *"The Moscow Rules: The Secret CIA Tactics That Helped America Win the Cold War,"* PublicAffairs, N.Y., 2019. The 'Murphy's Law' adage may have originated from mathematician Augustus De Morgan, who in 1866 wrote: *"whatever can happen will happen."* In modern usage, it generally means: *"Anything that can go wrong, will go wrong."*

2. From the 1854 poem *The Charge of the Light Brigade*, by Alfred, Lord Tennyson.

3. Hansard, "Announcement of Government Policy on Air Defence," House of Commons Debates, Official Report, Ottawa, ON, Friday, February 20, 1959.

4. With the passage of time, and the declassification and release of increasing amounts of formerly secret material, it appears that a number of factors were at play. Budget was a consideration, as air defence was consuming a large portion of Canada's military budget, and this included not only the Arrow program but also the Boeing Michigan Aeronautical Research Center missile program (BOMARC; an anti-missile missile), and the semi-automated ground environment program (SAGE; an air defence system that included radars, computers, and direction centres). The Americans, for their part, had a number of reasons for possibly not wanting Canada to build the Arrow, among which was anticipation that it would be the only aircraft in the world capable of the detecting and intercepting the CIA's U-2 spy planes (which they publicly insisted were weather-research aircraft).

5. See P. Campagna, *"Storms of Controversy: The Secret Avro Arrow Files*

Revealed," 4th Ed., Dundurn Press, Toronto, 2010.

6. The Department of Defence Production recorded three of the completed aircraft, and the one partially completed aircraft, as having been destroyed by July 7, 1959. Two more were recorded to be in the process of dismantlement, with expected completion within the same month. There seems to be some lack of clarity about the fate of the fifth completed Arrow, leading to speculation that it was spirited away and may still exist – somewhere. See endnote 5.

7. Although mechanical paper-shredding machines have been manufactured since the mid-1930s, they were used almost exclusively by governments until the mid-1980s, and were only more recently adopted into business and home use.

8. In the Security Service, at this time in history, B Section dealt with counter-espionage. See: J. Sawatsky, *"Men in the Shadows. The RCMP Security Service,"* Doubleday, Toronto, 1980.

9. At various times, in fact, several countries quietly expressed interested in the Arrow and/or its Iroquois engines, including France, the U.K., and the U.S.

10. In 1959, many hospitals were still refusing to allow fathers-to-be to go in past Admitting with their partners-in-labour. By the 1960s, most hospitals had begun to allow fathers into the delivery room during labour, and by the 1970s some were being allowed to remain for the actual birth.

11. A collection of documents produced by Avro Canada, subcontractors and the National Aeronautical Establishment are held in the archives of Canada's National Science Library. Among these are nearly 600 declassified documents that are available to the public. See: Avro Canada CF-105 Arrow Collection, National Science Library, National Research Council of Canada, Ottawa, ON.

12. A common term used to refer to a member of an intelligence service. Depending on the context, this could mean someone from the same country or someone from an allied country.

13. In real life, a complete set of blueprints did survive, having been taken home and hidden by one of the senior draftsmen on the project. CBC News announced their existence in 2020, and they were put on display at the Diefenbaker Centre at the University of Saskatchewan between January and April of that year. See: D. Shield, "Avro Arrow blueprints on display...." CBC News, January 6, 2020.

https://www.cbc.ca/news/canada/saskatoon/saved-avro-arrow-blueprints-ordered-destroyed-1.5416554.

14. A dead drop is any secret location that can be used to pass messages, documents, or other objects between two people without the need to ever meet face-to-face. The locations can be changed as often as desired, and a variety of methods can be used to signal when a drop has been made.

15. Ontario Provincial Police.

16. See: J. Starnes, *"Closely Guarded: A Life in Canadian Security and Intelligence,"* University of Toronto Press, Toronto, 1998.

17. Non-commissioned officers.

18. Joe Clark led the Progressive Conservate Party of Canada in three general elections, served one term as Prime Minister (1979-80) and two as Leader of the Official Opposition in the House of Commons (1976-79 and 1980-83).

19. Heavy water meaning water composed of deuterium and oxygen atoms rather than hydrogen and oxygen atoms. CANDU meaning CANadian Deuterium Uranium nuclear reactor systems, which use natural (not enriched) uranium fuel, moderated by heavy water.

20. Atomic Energy of Canada Limited, a federal Crown Corporation and the developer of the CANDU reactor technology.

21. In real life, Canadian passports were in high demand for Soviet espionage operations during the Cold War. The detection of fraudulent passport applications was made difficult when legitimate documents were obtained by people using faked identities. Post-second-world-war Canada was experiencing massive immigration, under cover of which illegal immigrants could, if they were patient enough, "assume the identities of deceased Canadians, acquire social insurance and Medicare numbers, establish work records, pay taxes, draw on social benefits, and so on, thus gradually filling out a profile that would be very hard to detect as false." See: R. Whitaker, G.S. Kealey, and A. Parnaby, *"Secret Service. Political Policing in Canada from the Fenians to Fortress America,"* University of Toronto Press, Toronto, 2012.

22. In real life, the RCMP did attempt to uncover a suspected Soviet mole during the Cold War. The operation was called Feather Bed, and stretched from the late 1950s to the 1970s, but there seems to be no public evidence it ever identified the mole, who was later identified by a Soviet defector (in 1985). See: J. Bronskill, "RCMP's Fruitless Cold

War Mole Hunt Included Senior Diplomats Ignatieff and Rae, Archives Show," *Toronto Star*, 22 March 2012.

23. See *An Indestructible Mountie* (ISBN: 978-1-9994940-4-9).

24. See *An Inseparable Mountie* (ISBN: 978-1-7772424-0-4).

25. See *An Intrepid Mountie* (ISBN: 978-1-7772424-6-6).

26. Counter-espionage. See endnote #8.

27. STU-I was the first of a series of digital, Secure Telephone Units (STUs) developed for the U.S. National Security Agency in the 1970s. The desktop telephone part looked much like a regular telephone, but it was connected to a sizeable cabinet containing racks of electronics. Subsequent generations, STU-II and STU-III were developed in the 1980s that approached the goal of a true desktop unit.

28. See *An Ineradicable Mountie* (ISBN: 978-1-7387599-2-7).

29. The Diefenbunker – Canadian Forces Station Carp - really exists. It was built in 1959 through 1961, opened in 1962, and remained operational until it was closed and decommissioned in 1994. It has since been designated a National Historic Site of Canada and reopened as a museum in 1998. *See* https://diefenbunker.ca/en/. For Alex's adventure involving the Diefenbunker see *An Ineradicable Mountie* ((ISBN: 978-1-7387599-2-7).

30. In the Security Service, at this time in history, the sections were denoted with letters A through L: 'A', for security screening, 'B', for counter-espionage, 'C' for administration, 'D', for counter-subversion (or anti-communism), 'E' for electronic surveillance, 'F' for files, 'G' for counter-terrorism (absorbed into D Section in 1976), 'H' for China, 'I' for physical surveillance, 'J' for bugging, and 'L' for informants. According to Sawatsky (See endnote #8): "*As far as is known, there is no K Section. For some reason the letters jump from J to L. One Security Service member theorized that K Section may exist but plays such a minor role that nobody knows about it. 'Either that,' he joked, 'or it exists and is very important'.*" Other accounts suggest that this section was for research. Since there is some mystery about whether 'K' Section actually existed, or it's purpose if it did exist, I have made it 'Special Operations,' hence very important, in these novels.

31. See *An Indestructible Mountie* (ISBN: 978-1-9994940-4-9).

32. The Cambridge Five was a ring of Soviet spies operating in the United Kingdom between the 1930s and '50s. Most of them held sensitive positions in MI5, MI6, or the Foreign Office.

33. J. Edgar Hoover was the founding Director of the U.S. Federal Bureau of Investigation (FBI) and served from 1935 to 1972. Hoover's main preoccupation was with communist subversion, whether real or perceived.

34. See *An Inseparable Mountie* (ISBN: 978-1-7772424-0-4).

35. See *An Intrepid Mountie* (ISBN: 978-1-7772424-6-6).

36. A cryptonym is a code word or name used to refer to something else without revealing its true identity. The something else, could be almost anything, including a person, word or phrase, project, or object.

37. The main organizational units within the Security Service were variously known as Sections, Branches, Operations, or simply Ops.

38. The 'Five Eyes' is an intelligence-sharing alliance among Canada, Australia, New Zealand, the U.K., and the U.S. It seems to have begun with a signals- and code-breaking alliance during the Second World War, and then expanded during the Cold War to include intelligence generally. It is still active in the present day.

39. This was the National Research Universal (NRU) reactor. A fuel rod ruptured, causing a fire and subsequent contamination of the reactor building.

40. In 1945, Soviet cipher clerk Igor Gouzenko abandoned his position with the Soviet Embassy in Ottawa and defected to Canada, bringing with him more than a hundred documents showing that a Soviet spy network was operating in Canada. This sparked an international crisis, because the network targeted people working in sensitive positions with access to military, scientific, and other secrets. The affair remained alive for nearly twenty years due to investigations, a Royal Commission, 21 arrests, and 20 trials leading to ten convictions in Canada and one in the UK.

41. This was the second Canada Cup. It had originally been scheduled for 1979 but went off due to disputes between Hockey Canada and the Canadian Amateur Hockey Association. Although rescheduled for 1980, this too collapsed due to Canada's boycotts in response to the Soviet Union's invasion of Afghanistan. Rescheduled a third time, it finally took place September 1–13, 1981.

42. The Montreal Forum (*Forum de Montreal*), the original home of the Montreal Canadiens, was arguably the most famous arena in hockey history. It opened in 1924 and was closed in 1996. Although the exterior of the historic building remains standing, it was gutted in 1998

and rebuilt to house movie theatres and a restaurant.

43. The 'nosebleeds' is a slang reference to the seats in the very highest, and therefore cheapest, rows of a hockey arena. In the old Montreal Forum, the nosebleeds were so high up that it was almost impossible to see the puck on the ice.

44. See *An Ineradicable Mountie* (ISBN: 978-1-7387599-2-7).

45. See *An Inseparable Mountie* (ISBN: 978-1-7772424-0-4).

46. See *An Intrepid Mountie* (ISBN: 978-1-7772424-6-6).

47. See *An Ineradicable Mountie* (ISBN: 978-1-7387599-2-7).

48. In August, 1980, when the Czechoslovakian team was playing in a tournament in Innsbruck, Austria, two of their star players, Peter and Anton Stastny (Šťastný), defected after the final game by driving to Canadian Embassy in Vienna, after which, with a police escort they made their way to the airport and flew to Canada where they joined the Québec Nordiques. A year later their oldest brother, Marian, defected as well, also to join the Nordiques.

49. See *An Inimitable Mountie* (ISBN: 978-1-0690565-0-4).

50. In real life, at the time of this story, Canadian Forces uniforms were not exactly as described due to a 1968 government initiative called unification, under which the various services were merged with unified commands, common rank designations, and common uniforms, the latter in rifle green. As time passed, some elements of unification were rescinded. In the late 1980s, for example the traditional air force and navy uniform colours were restored. In 2011, some of the more traditional command names were also restored, such as for the Royal Canadian Air Force (RCAF). In the fictional world of this novel series, however, unification never took place.

51. The RCAF's C-130H Hercules are four-engine-turboprop, tactical-transport aircraft. Designed to operate from low quality, short airstrips, they have been used for everything from troop and equipment transport, to search and rescue, and even air-to-air refueling operations.

52. Canadian Forces Base Trenton, located in southern Ontario, is home to 8 Wing, which provides tactical transportation worldwide and supports search and rescue operations over central and northern Canada.

53. At the time of this story, noise-cancelling headphones hadn't been invented yet. Amar Bose, the founder of Bose Corporation, invented

the first portable noise-cancelling headphone in 1989, and they only became widely available to the public in 2000.

54. Canadian Special Passports have a green cover and are issued to Senators, Members of Parliament, and government people in a non-diplomatic capacity that are travelling to a post abroad and/or on an official mission.

55. Several Boeing 707-347C aircraft were built for the RCAF and designated CC-137. Built in passenger and tanker versions, the former was used for long-range passenger transport, and particularly VIP transport, between 1970 and 1997.

56. In real life, the practice of referring to the head of MI6 as "C" dates back to Capt. Sir Mansfield George Smith-Cumming, RN, who became the head of the UK's Secret Service Bureau in the early 1900s and the first head of the renamed Secret Intelligence Service (MI6). Even before becoming head, he became known to insiders as 'C,' due to his habit of signing letters and documents (in green ink) with a C. Both the initial and the green ink became a tradition for later heads of MI6, for whom the C stands for 'Chief.' In fiction writing, the former intelligence officers John Le Carré called his MI6 chief 'Control,' while Ian Fleming called his 'M.'

57. Experts. Often scientists or engineers.

58. (a) Gideon was a prophet, judge, and military leader in both the Hebrew and Christian Bibles. (b) Gideons International is an Evangelical Christian association founded in the late 1800s, in the United States. They are best known for placing free bibles in hotel and motel rooms, the original idea for which seems to have been to engage traveling salespeople in evangelism. Since then, the Gideons have distributed billions of Bibles worldwide.

59. At the time of this story, MI6 (the UK's Secret Intelligence Service) had its headquarters at Century House, on Westminster Bridge Road in London. This building was used by them from 1964 to 1994. Its location was at one time an official secret, but ultimately became so widely known that it was declassified shortly before the service's headquarters moved to its present-day location.

60. The London Underground (also known simply as the Underground or by its nickname the Tube) is a rapid transit (electric train) system, only about half of which is actually underground.

61. In Ian Fleming's James Bond novels, Miss Moneypenny, was the

personal assistant for the head of MI6.

62. In real life as well, MI6 seems to be about the only part of the UK government that has been able to avoid having to transfer any their records to the national registry. See www.nationalarchives.gov.uk.

63. The M203 is a single-shot under-barrel grenade launcher designed to attach to a rifle. It was introduced in the 1970s, and can fire a variety of types of 40 mm rounds ranging from high-explosive, to star-shell, to CS (o-chlorobenzylidene malononitrile) tear gas grenades.

64. The RCMP's H Division is responsible for federal policing in Nova Scotia, and B Division for Newfoundland and Labrador.

65. The NATO M549 is a high-explosive, rocket-assisted 155 mm howitzer round. It has a maximum range of about 30 km.

66. *HMCS Assiniboine* (DDH 234), the second ship to bear this name, served in the Royal Canadian Navy between 1956 to 1988. She was the second ship to bear the name. A St. Laurent-class destroyer, she was converted to a destroyer-helicopter-escort in 1962 and spent much of her service as an anti-submarine ship patrolling the western North Atlantic.

67. 'The penny dropped,' is an old expression meaning that something has suddenly, or finally, become recognized or understood. It seems to have originated in Britain, in the late 1800s, when there was a proliferation of automatic machines that could be activated by the inserting (dropping) of a penny into a slot (including vending machines, gas meters, and almost-instant photo machines). In all cases, the desired action didn't happen until the penny dropped.

68. AIS, the VHS-radio-based Automatic Identification System, by which vessels are required to continuously broadcast their identity and position, wasn't developed until the 1990s. Similarly, although the first practical GPS (Global Positioning System) satellite was launched in 1978, it wasn't until the first large network of GPS satellites was launched in the early 1990s that GPS became fully functional.

69. The KH-9 (codename HEXAGON; also known as Big Bird) refers to a program of photographic-reconnaissance satellites used by the U.S. in the 1970s and '80s. Each satellite generally carried two main cameras. When rolls of film from the cameras were full, they were sent to one of four re-entry vehicles and jettisoned.

70. The RA-5C Vigilante was a reconnaissance version of the U.S. Navy's A-5 aircraft-carrier-based, all-weather, supersonic bomber. The RA-

5Cs were in active service between 1963 and 1980.

71. *USCGC Decisive* (WMEC-629) was a Reliance-Class, medium-endurance U.S. Coast Guard Cutter. At the time of this story, she probably carried a Sikorsky HH-52 Seaguard helicopter. She was decommissioned in 2023.

72. Georges Island is a small island in Halifax's inner harbour; almost directly offshore Pier 21. Located on the island is an operating lighthouse, which was originally established in 1876, rebuilt in 1917, and automated in 1972. Also located on the island is Fort Charlotte, which was constructed in 1750 and played various defensive roles up to an including the Second World War. Georges Island is now a National Historic Site.

73. On July 2, 1981, the *HMCS Assiniboine* ran aground in Halifax Harbour in heavy fog, requiring the aid from several tugboats to get free.

74. The Richmond Terminals, formerly the Richmond Yards, date back to the first railway in Halifax. This site is very close to where, on December 6., 1917, the out-bound freighter *Imo* collided with the munitions-freighter *Mont Blanc*, which was heading in-bound for the Bedford Basin. The collision yielded the massive "Halifax Explosion," which levelled approximately five square kilometres of the city. At the Richmond Yards, two of its piers were badly damaged and another two were completely destroyed by the blast. *See* D. Smith, "The Railways and Canada's Greatest Disaster: The Halifax Explosion, December 6, 1917," *Canadian Rail* 431(Nov./Dec.) 202–212 (1992).

75. A derivative of "There is no peace for the weary," or "There is no peace for the wicked," meaning that one must keep on working no matter how tired they are. The original quote is probably from the Bible: "There is no peace for the wicked" (*Isaiah* 48:22 and 57:21), referring to eternal punishment.

76. David Cornwell, a former MI5, then MI6 officer (better known as the author of espionage novels under his pen-name of John Le Carré) interviewed a close friend of Kim Philby, the long-standing MI6 officer and Soviet double agent who later defected to the Soviet Union. As a result, Cornwell/Le Carré concluded that: "What may have begun as an ideological commitment became a psychological dependency, then a craving. One side wasn't enough for him. He needed to play the world's game... when Philby was... living out the inglorious end of his career as an MI6 and KGB agent... what he missed most... was the

prickle of the double life that had for so long sustained him." See J. Le Carré, *"The Pigeon Tunnel. Stories from My Life,"* Penguin Canada, Toronto, 2017, p. 176.

77. The original *Mission: Impossible* television series was broadcast by CBS between 1966 and 1973. It featured the espionage exploits of a team of U.S. Government secret agents called the Impossible Missions Force.

78. Long service in the RCMP is recognized by the awarding of a star for each five years of service. The embroidered stars are sewn onto the left sleeve of the red- and brown serge tunics.

79. Prior to 1946, in the RCMP, domestic intelligence and security matters were handled by the Criminal Investigation Branch. Such work was moved to the newly created Special Branch in 1946, to which was added responsibility for counter-intelligence operations. In 1956, the Special Branch was renamed Directorate of Security and Intelligence. In 1970, it became the Security Service. The Security Service was later absorbed by the new and independent Canadian Security Intelligence Service (CSIS) in 1984.

80. In real life, there have been Cold-War-traitors within the RCMP Security Service. In the 1950s, there was agent 'Gideon,' a Soviet agent that was turned and run as a double agent, plus another officer that sold-out Gideon to the Soviets. The mid-1960s brought a very public case that led to the Mackenzie Royal Commission on Security. There have also been some unsuccessful mole hunts, such as operation 'Feather Bed,' that ultimately turned up no one, and operation 'Gridiron,' that landed on the wrong person. Similar things happened in the U.S. and Britain. See: R. Whitaker, "Spies Who Might Have Been: Canada and the Myth of Cold War Counterintelligence," *Intelligence and National Security*, 12(4), 25-43, 2008.

81. In the 1960s and '70s, there was a movement for Québec independence from which grew an urban-terrorist group called *Front de libération du Québec* (FLQ). With regard to the RCMP Security Service's activities in the events leading up to, and following the 'October Crisis' of 1970, it found itself under attack from two very different directions. On the one hand, a number of federal Cabinet Ministers – including the Prime Minister – complained that the intelligence gathered by the Security Service was inadequate, if not worse. On the other hand, the service was publicly attacked for going

too far in its efforts, some of which were labelled unethical and/or unlawful. In August 1981, a commission of inquiry into the operations and policies of the RCMP Security Service, known as the McDonald Commission, recommended civilianization, meaning a civilian security intelligence agency, separate from the RCMP and without law-enforcement powers, should be created. This was eventually accomplished in the *Canadian Security Intelligence Service Act* of 1984.

Laurie Schramm

An Interrupted Mountie

Adventures of the First Woman Mountie. Book 15

LAURIE SCHRAMM

Laurie Schramm

DEDICATION

To

Erma
the inspiration for the fictional character Marie O'Dwyer

and

Dr. Janusz Koziński, Ph.D., P.Eng., FCAE, FEC, FEIC, FRSC
the inspiration for the fictional character Sir Andreas Meyer

Laurie Schramm

BOOK 15 CONTENTS

	Dedication	293
	List of Characters	297
	Acronyms & Abbreviations	298
1	Preludes	299
2	Civilians for a While	309
3	VIPs	323
4	Cruising	341
5	In the Gulf	359
6	A Shadow is Revealed	383
7	It's Not Over Until It's Over	397
8	Aftermath	405
9	Epilogue	409
	Book 15 Endnotes	413

Laurie Schramm

LIST OF CHARACTERS
(IN ORDER OF APPEARANCE)

- Marie O'Dwyer, a cruise-ship passenger
- Tommy Jones, a pre-teen passenger
- Prince Albert Montenario, Principality of Montenia
- Hans, a bodyguard and friend of Prince Albert
- Crown Prince Michael Montenario, Principality of Montenia
- Sergeant Alexandra (Alex) Houston, RCMP Security Service
- Silver, an Alaskan Malamute; Alex's police-service-dog partner
- Major Don Harrison, Military Intelligence, Canadian Forces
- Captain Sandy Moore, Military Intelligence, Canadian Forces
- Staff Sergeant Frank Wilson, Military Intelligence, Canadian Forces
- Hank and Jenny Houston, Alex's parents
- Sophie Houston, Alex's younger sister
- Special Agent Vivian Rule, FBI
- Ginger Brandt, famous Canadian TV and film actress
- Deputy Commissioner George MacLeod, RCMP
- Rear-Admiral Peter White, Canadian Forces Security Branch
- Captain Noah Sorensen, MS Atlantic II
- First Officer (Navigation) Frida Haugen, MS Atlantic II
- Chief Security Officer Andrew (Drew) Harris, MS Atlantic II
- Edward Avon, a VIP passenger
- Alicia Avon, a VIP passenger
- Mitzi, a brown Pekingese, Alicia's dog
- Staff Sergeant Avery Blunt, RCMP Security Service
- Lorenzo Costa, a university student and passenger
- Bobby and Frankie, two other pre-teen passengers
- Jeremy Masters, a photojournalist for *Vogue* magazine
- Richard Jolliffe, a photojournalist for *British Vogue* magazine,
- Walter (Wally) Dolan, a photojournalist for *Elle* magazine,
- Sir Andreas Meyer, Diplomatic Advisor, Court of Montenia

ACRONYMS & ABBREVIATIONS

CO	Commanding Officer
ID	Identification
FBI	Federal Bureau of Investigation (U.S.)
INTERPOL	International Criminal Police Organization
NS	Nova Scotia
RCMP	Royal Canadian Mounted Police
Met	Metropolitan Police Service (or 'Scotland Yard,' U.K.)
MI6	Military Intelligence, Section 6 (or Secret Intelligence Service, the U.K.'s foreign intelligence service)
MP	Mounted Police (as in RCMP)
NYPD	New York (City) Police Department (U.S.)
PEI	Prince Edward Island
QC	Québec
SCUBA	Self-Contained Underwater Breathing Apparatus
TV	Television
VIP	Very Important Person

1 PRELUDES

May 8, 1982
Boston, Massachusetts

Shortly before 10 am, the cruise ship opened-up for the check-in and boarding of passengers for a cruise that would take them to Bar Harbour, Maine; Halifax and Sydney in Nova Scotia; Charlottetown, Prince Edward Island, then across the Gulf of Saint Lawrence and down the Saint Lawrence River to Québec City; and finally deposit them in Montréal eight days later.

About a third of the ship's passengers had already completed this itinerary in reverse order and were remaining on board to retrace the route back to Montréal, completing the circle. One of these, Marie O'Dwyer, was sitting out on her stateroom's verandah from which point she had a good view of the dockside activity, which was considerable.

Both the ship's crew of more than 500, plus a large number of dock workers, were all busy. Disembarking the departing passengers and their luggage, and cleaning the staterooms were all things that she had expected. This being Marie's first cruise, however, the range and magnitude of the dockside activities were unexpected, and she watched it all in such fascination that her knitting lay idle in her lap.

The outgoing luggage was taken out by a small fleet of motorized pallet-trucks bearing large wire cages that were full to the top with stacked bags. As the flow of outgoing luggage diminished, it was replaced by other outgoing materials: a staggering number of large bins and cages filled with garbage, many pallets loaded with flattened cardboard boxes and open-top boxes full of empty wine, liquor and pop bottles.

The returning pallet-trucks came loaded with an increasing flow of materials onto the ship; clearly fresh supplies of all kinds, including cases of frozen and unfrozen packaged or canned foods, cases that were visibly full of fresh produce and fruit, and cases of drinks of all kinds, from bottled water and pop, to wines and spirits.

As the return cruise was fully booked, some 800 fresh passengers – the other two-thirds of the ship's 1,200-passenger capacity - would be checking-in and boarding on this day. Some of the passengers had arrived early, of course, and nearly a hundred of these were lined-up outside Marie's field of view, at the entrance to the cruise-ship terminal building. As the first of the new passengers survived the processes of luggage check-in, registration and passport-checking, they – and their luggage - began trickling out of the rear of the terminal building. The luggage came out stacked in cages and transported by the pallet trucks, and ferried into the cargo holds, from which the individual pieces of luggage would be delivered by hand to the appropriate staterooms. The check-in process would consume the next four hours, while the luggage deliveries would extend well into the evening. None of that was visible to Marie who, in any case, was much more interested in the people themselves.

The passengers, for their part, formed-up into a new line at the entrance to the ship's gangway, well within Marie's span of observation, and she noted that the passengers were anything but uniform, spanning as they did all age groups. There were infants being cradled in their mothers' arms and toddlers in strollers, families with older children and young adults, the middle-aged, and a substantial proportion of seniors, some with canes, walkers, or wheel-chairs. As she gazed down at the embarking passengers, she had no trouble diagnosing some of their moods and reactions.

Some of the passengers had obviously cruised before, and seemed to take little to no interest in either the cruise ship or the various activities underway along the dock. Clearly, this part was just a repeat of a familiar routine for them, and some looked quite bored. Perhaps a cruise is just what they need, *she thought.*

For others, it was impossible to judge whether or not they were veteran cruisers as they were too busy with their own little dramas. In some cases, there were infants being fed from bottles, toddlers fussing in their strollers – some crying, some yelling, and some energetically attempting to climb out and escape. Not that this characterized all, or even most of the younger ones mind you. Indeed, many of them seemed remarkably well-behaved and a fair number were fast asleep. Among some of the families, Marie could see the signs of eager anticipation, while others seemed to be too busy arguing about this or that to even be paying much attention to anything else. Such a rich tapestry, *she thought,* like seeing a page out of each passenger's life history.

No sooner had she had this thought, than one of the young passengers caught her attention. She didn't know his name yet, but this was Tommy Jones, who was twelve years old and, with his family, was going on his very first cruise. Marie didn't have to be psychic to know it was Tommy's first cruise, his manner practically proclaimed it to the world.

For Tommy, the build-up to this cruise had been both exciting and excruciating. Exciting, because he'd never even seen a big ship in real life, living as his family did in Lexington, Kentucky, far from oceans and far even from the Great Lakes, so that the only boats he'd ever seen or been on in his whole twelve years of life to date had been small- to medium-sized, open powerboats of the sort that his uncles and grandparents used for fishing. Such boats were overloaded with six people in them. The fact that the cruise ship could hold nearly two thousand people, including passengers and crew, had sent his imagination soaring. At the same time, the waiting had been excruciating, but now they were finally about to board and his first sight of the ship upon stepping out from the terminal had made his eyes bulge and his jaw drop. Whatever he had imagined before, it sure wasn't a ship as large as the one that lay before him. Between the ship and its different-looking decks and the many things going on around him as he waited with his family to board, he hardly knew where to look next.

Marie smiled as she noted Tommy's expression and the way his head turned constantly as he tried to see everything at once and miss nothing. Marie was actually quite astute at reading people's expressions, but none of her skills and experience were required in Tommy's case, and she sighed contentedly as she watched him.

Meanwhile, inside the terminal building itself, another drama was being played out. This one had a rather large audience, which comprised the many passengers that were in a long line that snaked back and forth across the broad, open floor of the terminal until it finally culminated in the check-in counters of the cruise line. Here were lined-up several hundred passengers that had already seen what little there was to see in the building, most notably the almost endless-appearing and incredibly slow-moving line of which they were a part. Whatever these passengers' states of boredom and/or frustration, most of them were ripe for the diversion that was created by the appearance of a striking-looking, fashionably dressed, young woman that was being led by someone dressed in the uniform of the cruise line, and led right through and across the snaking line in which everyone else had to stand. The fashionable woman was accompanied by an unassuming-looking, and ordinarily-dressed young man who, by himself, would not have attracted any attention at all. But in this case, he did attract attention, partly because he was accompanying such a striking-appearing woman, and partly because the two of them were obviously being allowed to cut in front of everyone else in the huge, slow-moving line.

There must have been some people, of both sexes, that looked admiringly at the young woman, but a casual observer could possibly be forgiven for not noticing such looks in the face of the verbal comments being made by so many of the others in line. Some of the latter were in the nature of mutterings, while others were more in the nature of indignant outrage and clearly intended to be broadly heard by others, including, of course, the young woman herself:

"What the hell? Who does she think she is?"

"Some bloody VIP no doubt. Just what we need!"

"Get to the back of the line like everyone else!"

Some of the comments were less polite.

Before such comments could mushroom into a general groundswell, there was an interruption. It began with a commotion that for most of those in line was first heard, and then seen:

"Make way. Make way. Excuse us. Coming through."

"Hey, where do you think you're going? Get back in line like the rest of us."

"What's going on here anyway?"
"I wonder who that is," said a middle-aged man.
"Looks like a fashion model to me," said his wife.

Eventually, virtually all of the waiting passengers got their chance to observe three men jostling, if not actually elbowing, their way, towards what was assumed to be the VIP couple. Each of the three men was carrying an elaborate and expensive-looking camera mounted on a bracket that also bore a large flash- or strobe-light. The behaviour of the three men in their efforts to cut to the front of the line and pursue the VIP couple added insult to injury, and caused a rising tide of grumbling, complaints, and calls for someone to exert some control over the process.

The passengers' growing outrage was mollified somewhat a few minutes later, however, when the three photojournalists were seen being escorted by security officials back down the line and out of the building. These three, at least, were clearly not going to be treated like VIPs.

***

May 12, 1982
Enroute to Mount Nun in the western Himalayas
Ladakh Territory, India, near the India-Pakistan border

The Prince Albert Montenario, second-in-line of succession to the throne of the European Principality of Montenia, yawned as he was awakened by his friend, fellow adventurer, and bodyguard, Hans. It was time to face another day but Albert didn't need any prodding. It had already been an adventure, and the best was yet to come as they were planning to climb Mount Nun in a few days' time.

The pair had flown to Palam Airport[1] near New Delhi, India, and then taken a short two-hour flight to Leh. After completing some paperwork, because they had entered Ladakh territory, they met with their Sherpa guide and spent the day acclimatizing. The second day had included an acclimatization hike and a chance to visit Leh Palace. On the third day, there had been a three-hour drive to Kargil and on the fourth day, a four-hour drive to Tangol. Compared with their home country, which stood only a few hundred metres above sea level, Tangol village lies at 3,800 m

(about 12,500 ft.)

At Tangol they had their first good views of Mount Nun (7,135 m) and spent the night in tents. The following day was spent on further acclimatizing. Now finally, on Day 6, they would climb the moraine and make their way to base camp (4,600 m, 15,100 ft.), where they would spend yet another day acclimatizing. After that, they planned to proceed up to Camp 1 at 5,500 m (18,000 ft.), spend two days acclimatizing, then go to camp 2 at 6,500 m, then another two more days acclimatizing, and then wait for the right weather to permit an attempt on the summit at 7135 m, 23,400 ft. (4.4 miles up). That would be on Day 14 - if they were lucky.

It was dark outside. Although they had arrived on the early side of the optimum climbing season, their Sherpa guide had insisted that they depart early in the morning in order to cross a glacier and a couple of avalanche slopes before the afternoon sun had a chance to warm the snow-bridges on the glacier and the snow-covered mountain slope to one side. Once they'd climbed the moraine and followed it for several hours, it was time to cross the glacier, so they stopped to rope-up. They already wore their full-body climbing harnesses and helmets, but now it was time to clip themselves into one of their climbing ropes. Spacing themselves about 10 m apart, Hans tied himself into the leading end of the rope, Albert tied himself on using a figure-of-eight knot, while the guide tied himself into the back end. This arrangement was designed to have the most experienced climber – the guide – at the rear so that he could serve as an anchor should one of the others get into trouble, and the next most experienced climber – Hans – at the front selecting the precise route across the glacier.

Although the guide didn't allow them to stop while crossing the glacier, they did slow their pace from time to time and it was during one of such slow periods that Albert happened to look up and spot two figures high up on the looming mountain to one side.

"Looks like some skiers got up even earlier than we did" he called out to the guide. "Must be after some extreme powder skiing."

"Some fools," exclaimed the guide, looking up. "They're crossing the head of an avalanche slope. If the snow layers begin to slide, we could get swept away and buried. Pick up the pace. We need to get across. Fast!"

"They seem to be waving at us," said Albert, as all three men accelerated to the fastest pace their crampons and the snow-covered ice

would allow.

"Actually, it looks like they're throwing something," said Hans, who had also looked up and spotted the two figures.

"Why would skiers be throwing things?" asked Albert, as they were answered by two large explosions in succession. The explosions threw up large clouds of snow.

"Dynamite," yelled the guide. "Run!"

As Albert and Hans did their best to run, they heard a rumbling sound from the snow slope beside and above them.

"Head for the trees," yelled the guide, pointing to a stretch of trees up ahead. "We must reach those trees!"

No-one questioned the need to make haste as the volume of the rumbling sounds increased. As each climber did his best to run towards the trees, they couldn't help glancing to one side at intervals, so it was at about the same time that each of them noticed when the snow above them began to move downward.

The explosions had triggered an avalanche.

As the climbers made their best speed possible it was inevitable that Hans, in the lead, would not be able to choose their exact path with as much care as he had previously. As a result, he eventually led them onto a somewhat questionable-looking snow bridge that spanned one of the glacier's crevasses. To make matters worse, Hans wasn't able to choose his steps as carefully as he would otherwise have done, and just before he reached the far side of the crevasse his right boot punched right through the snow below him. Wildly throwing his weight onto his left foot, he tried to regain his balance so that he might extract his other leg, but in this case, his full body weight proved to be too much for the snow under his left leg and that boot punched through as well. Followed by his left leg. Followed by his entire body as an entire section of the snow bridge collapsed.

Albert heard Hans yelp, and saw him drop down through the snow bridge. Yelling "Hans has fallen through!" to the guide behind him, Albert was just able to halt his own momentum at the edge of the crevasse. With a large exhalation of breath, he was just thinking how fortunate he had been to have been able to stop in time when the weight of Hans falling straight down into the crevasse pulled him forward, causing him to lose his balance.

Ten metres behind Albert, the guide had acted quickly to stop and brace himself in the snow so he could attempt to halt any further slippage into the crevasse. Unfortunately, the sharp pull on the rope from Hans had caught Albert off-guard, causing him to fall headlong into the intact portion of the snow bridge. By this time, the front section of the rope was cutting into the newly broken edge of the snow bridge like a saw blade. Albert, lying prostrated on the snow bridge, watched in sick fascination as the rope ahead of him seemed to be getting shorter and shorter. Between the guide having braked and braced himself, and Hans now dangling straight down into the crevasse, the rope where it was tied into Albert's harness was now so tightly stretched it might have been made of steel. Between Hans' struggles to right himself down below and Albert's struggles to get back up on his knees, let alone his feet, the rope between them continued to saw through the snow bridge.

All of the snow bridge action had so far taken place in less than two minutes. It only took another minute for the rope to finish cutting through the snow before it reached Albert, who was then pulled down and over the edge of the broken snow bridge, at which point it completely collapsed. Now there were two climbers dangling vertically down into the crevasse, Albert near the top and Hans ten metres below him. This put a severe strain on the guide, who was also now being pulled slowly down the slope towards the open edge of the crevasse.

Two things prevented the guide from being pulled into the crevasse. One: he had driven his ice axe deeply into the snow and arranged his body to provide the maximum frictional resistance to being pulled forward. Secondly, the rope that had previously been so efficiently sawing through the snow bridge between Albert and Hans was now almost as efficiently sawing its way into the ice at the edge of the crevasse. Although this would make it very difficult to later pull the forward two climbers up, for the moment it was a god-send as the friction created by the rope's right-angle bend and it's being wedged in to the ice enabled the guide to prevent the two climbers from falling any deeper.

Meanwhile, the sound of the avalanche had become louder and louder as it rushed down the mountain slope toward the glacier — and the climbers. The guide, for his part, was still trying to figure out how he could possibly get the two climbers out of the crevasse when the avalanche overtook him. It tumbled him over several times, which had the effect of dragging Albert up and out of the crevasse, and Hans up several feet, but none of this did any of them any good because the avalanche also covered Albert and the guide with half a metre of hard-packed snow and ice. It also sealed-over the entire crevasse, leaving Hans to hang, helpless in a cold, pitch-black void.

When the avalanche had finally expended itself, an eerie silence descended over the slope and the glacier. For a moment, the only signs of motion were from the two skiers high up on the slope who, having watched the awful proceedings with a kind of grim satisfaction, began skiing back to whence they had come.

News of the avalanche would reach other guides and climbers by that evening and search parties would be sent out the next morning, but all the climbers at base camp knew full well that the chances of finding anyone alive were slim indeed. Search they did, of course. But, even with the use of avalanche transceivers[2], they were unable to find any trace of the guide and his two adventurers.

The village of Tangol, being something of a destination for mountaineers, had a telephone line and a single telephone. This was used to contact the listed next of kin of the two foreigners. In the case of Prince Albert, the call was made to his older brother, Crown Prince Michael Montenario, who immediately made arrangements to fly to New Delhi.

The Daily News

Thursday, May 13, 1984

Three Climbers Lost, Feared Dead in Himalayan Avalanche

2 CIVILIANS FOR A WHILE

Nearly a week earlier.
May 7, 1982
Loch Bòidheach Manor, near Baddeck
Cape Breton Highlands, NS

"I, Alexandra Houston, take you, Donald Harrison, to be my husband and lifelong companion. I promise to honour and respect you; to be your soulmate and best friend through all the joys and troubles of life. I will celebrate life with you, sharing our common journey and working out our differences, being faithful to you alone, as long as we both shall live...."

There was to be no patriarchy in our family, and to symbolize this, I spoke my vows first.

After a protracted engagement of almost exactly three years[3], it was hard to believe our wedding day had actually arrived and the ceremony was underway. I had met Don 1977, in the course of my second major undercover assignment. I had been sent to Nova Scotia to investigate a hiker's discovery, on Cape Breton Island, of a technological curiosity left-over from the Second World War[4]. When the discovery set off alarm bells in Canada's security and intelligence services, Don and I had been in and told to work together. Little did we know that it would be the first of many cases we would work on together, but that first case's several hair-raising and life-threatening experiences taught us a lot about ourselves and each other, among which was the fact that we made a great team. Now we were finally getting married, and we'd chosen the Cape Breton Highlands.

Despite barely achieving a high of 5°C (41°F), and the chances of rain being 2-in-3, it had turned out to be a beautifully sunny Saturday afternoon. We were somewhat immune to the weather, however, because to avoid the risk of rain, wind, and chill, our ceremony was being held in the great room of the Don's family's manor: Loch Bòidheach[5] Manor, in Cape Breton.

The great room had a high ceiling with exposed beams, a mixture of stone and heavy wood in the walls, and a massive stone fireplace occupying the bulk of one entire wall. The room was decorated with Scottish flags and banners, and even had two suits of medieval armor flanking inside of the entranceway.

Don's maternal grandparents, Jeremiah and Wilhelmina (Willie) MacLerie had bought the land and built the manor after his grandfather had become a successful business financier.

Over the years, much of Don's family had passed away: his grandparents, parents, uncles, and aunts, and one of his cousins leaving just two older sisters, a brother-in law, and some cousins. The latter were there for us now: his sisters Jane and Mary, Jane's husband Owen, his cousins Emily and Jennifer, and Emily's husband Jacob. Another cousin, Jack, had died the only other time I had visited the family manor and, even though it wasn't my fault[6], I suspected that his wife and another of Don's cousins, Grace, blamed me anyway. They had ignored our wedding invitation.

Standing beside Don were two of his closest friends and colleagues from the Canadian Forces military intelligence: Sandy Moore (recently promoted to Captain) and Frank Wilson (recently promoted to Staff Sergeant). I was a Sergeant in the Security Service of the Royal Canadian Mounted Police (RCMP) and Don a Major in military intelligence, both of us having been recently promoted. Although tempted, especially because of the promotions, Don and I had decided not to wear our uniforms. Sandy and Frank, however, were resplendent in their Air Force and Army dress uniforms, respectively.

On 'my side,' as they say, were my parents Hank and Jenny Houston, who had travelled out from Ottawa for the wedding. Standing at my side, were my younger sister Sophie, Vivian Rule (Special Agent, FBI), Ginger Brandt (the famous television and film actress), and Silver, of course, my Police Service Dog partner and friend. I had worked with Vivian and Ginger on multiple cases and we had become fast friends. We had invited another colleague and close friend, Constable Julie Sawyer and her RCMP Dog Service police-service-dog partner Scout, but they had been unable to make the trip.

We had kept the wedding very small at 25 people, which included two of my own cousins, a half-dozen friends from the university-student eras of our lives, and two rather notable guests that really stood out from the crowd. The latter two made quite an entrance as well.

Loch Bòidheach Manor

Shortly before the ceremony was due to begin, we heard an unusual sound that began low and then grew in intensity. I was hidden away, wearing my traditional white, but modernly-styled, dress, getting beautified by Ginger, who was very skilled with makeup and appearance, as you might expect from a professional actress. Meanwhile, in the role of typical groom, Don was nervously pacing outside, uncomfortable wearing his only civilian suit, and being slowly strangled by his tight collar and tie.

The first to hear the sound was Silver, of course. He swiveled his ears forward and gave a small "*Yip,*" as he paid attention, seeking to identify the sound. That got my attention, and soon I could hear it too.

"*Thump, Thump, Thump,*" it was the sound of a helicopter approaching. As the sound became louder and louder, Ginger and I went to a window to look out as it became obvious that it was a large helicopter. Before long, it resolved itself into the blasting roar and unmistakable appearance of a Canadian Armed Forces Sea King[7] helicopter.

When it landed, a crew member (the Tactical Coordinator) jumped out and stood smartly to attention, saluting as two older men got out. The first out was an admiral, resplendent in his dress uniform. I knew who it was, of course, but I had to look twice to recognize Rear-Admiral Peter White, head of the Canadian Forces Security Branch who, behind his back, we casually referred to as 'Don's admiral.' Although I'd met him many times, this was the first time I'd ever seen him in uniform and it was quite a sight.

The next out was a man I'd recognize anywhere: Deputy Commissioner George MacLeod, head of the RCMP Security Service. This was the man that had originally talked me into leaving the Metropolitan Toronto Police Force to join the RCMP, and after my first posting had more or less brought me along with him when he'd been transferred to the Security Service. This was also the man that I sometimes referred to as 'Uncle George,' although never to his face.

"I, Donald Harrison, take you, Alexandra Houston, to be my wife and lifelong companion. I promise to honour and respect you; to be your soulmate and best friend through all the joys and troubles of life. I will celebrate life with you, sharing our common journey and working out our differences, being faithful to you alone, as long as we both shall live...."

Standing beside us, Silver had been wearing his formal dog jacket that had been sewn in the style and colours of an RCMP shabrack[8] (horse blanket), complete with a yellow stripe around the border and the famous yellow 'MP' brand in the lower back corner on each side. For this occasion, we had attached our rings to it with safety pins, so that, when the vows had been exchanged, we could each reach down and unpin the ring we would be exchanging.

When that was done, the Justice of the Peace declared us married, and invited us to seal our marriage promises with a kiss. Then, we ended the ceremony with an adaptation of what may have originally been an Inuit poem[9]:

You are my partner
My feet shall run because of you
My feet shall dance because of you
My heart shall beat because of you
My eyes see because of you
My mind thinks because of you
And I shall love because of you.

After the ceremony, we exited the manor and traversed an arch of swords that were raised by Don's friends and even Uncle George and Admiral White. Following that was the inevitable torrent of confetti – which got absolutely everywhere in our clothing – and the traditional throwing of the bride's bouquet, and lining up for pictures out on the grounds. After giving people a chance to mingle and visit, we marshalled back into the manor for dinner. The main dining room was another large, elegant room with a high ceiling, lots of exposed beams in gleaming dark brown, and profusely decorated with Scottish banners and memorabilia. The dinner was a lively one, with the usual toasts, and a selection of speeches that were mainly designed to embarrass either Don or myself, or both. They all succeeded.

Following the dinner, Uncle George and Admiral White said good night and flew back to Halifax in the big Sikorsky helicopter. Almost everyone else was staying the night, so a dance had been organized for the rest of the evening. While I got red hair from my mother's side, Sophie got blond. At the dance, I couldn't help noticing the two blond heads that always seemed to be together. Apparently, Sophie and Sandy had discovered a natural affinity for each other such that they had proceeded to monopolize each other's company for most of the evening.

Several years earlier, the manor **had been converted into** a small but elegant hotel by Don's late grandmother, and its management had since been passed to Don's cousin Jenny. Accordingly, most of the wedding guests had booked rooms for the night as did Don and I. In our case, Jenny had assigned us one of the cottages, which were more modern, quite spacious, and dog-friendly.

We are pack, as Silver would say.

When we eventually retired for the night, Silver naturally followed us in, leapt up on the bed, and waited for us to join him so he could settle in for the night. He'd been doing this with me for years, of course, but now there would be three of us as Don had become a more formal part of our little pack.

You may be thinking that the title of this story refers to our wedding night.

Ha ha.

No, it does not. The interruption came later. Furthermore, while I can neither confirm nor deny any other guesses you might have about what may or may not have taken place later that night, anything that may have happened would have been accepted by Silver as one of the most natural things in the world. Right?

Silver and His Shabrack

The next morning, Don and I, and the remaining guests gathered for breakfast and present opening, after which we said our thank-yous and scrambled into my truck amid a second shower of confetti. When I started the ignition, Don and I were hit by a third blast of confetti. Someone had either gotten hold of my keys or else broke into the truck and dumped an entire bag of confetti into the ventilation ducts, then switched the blower motor to high so that simply starting the truck would create the confetti shower.

I'd taken some care to avoid anyone getting hold of my truck keys, so I naturally suspected one of Don's military intelligence friends of having the motive, opportunity, skills, and tools needed to circumvent the truck's door locks. The first people I looked at, as a result, were Sandy and Frank, who displayed such obvious expressions of angelic innocence that I didn't think I had to look any further to find the culprits.

Once we were finally on our way, we stopped just outside of Baddeck so we could get out of the truck and remove as much of the confetti as possible. We were only partly successful at this, and for the next year or so, every time I had to switch on the fan in the truck I was greeted by a few more pieces.

It took us about two-and-a-half hours to drive the scenic route south to the mainland and then west to the town Pictou, Nova Scotia, which is very close to the ferry terminal at a rural community called Caribou. Once there, we had to line-up and wait for about an hour for the next ferry, which would take us across the Northumberland Strait to the terminal at Wood Islands, Prince Edward Island (PEI).

I love ferry rides, especially when the ocean is calm, so I thoroughly enjoyed the crossing in the protected waters of the strait. It was a beautiful, sunny day, and Silver was allowed to stay with us, outside of the truck, as long as we stayed on the exterior passenger decks. That was perfect for us, since we wanted to stay outside enjoying the views anyway.

Once we had disembarked at the PEI terminal, it was another hour's drive northwest, through Charlottetown and on to our destination on the north shore of the island: the town of Cavendish. Cavendish is a very nice, somewhat touristy town and we had rented a quaint (meaning rustic) little cabin for a week-long honeymoon. Virtually next door was the famous Green Gables House (the inspiration for Lucy Maud Montgomery's *Anne of Green Gables* novels[10]), within minutes were a selection of beautiful red-sand beaches, and within about an hour's drive, more or less, was essentially everything else on the island.

Although we did plan to drive around the island, our top priority was to do almost nothing but lounge on the beaches. In fact, the very next morning found us lying on a beautiful, quiet, beach, enjoying the sand, water, and sun, and playing fetch with Silver. Since we were well ahead of the tourist season, it was a little cool, which we didn't mind, and very quiet, which we really appreciated. In fact, after nearly an entire day of lounging at the beach, I could feel the work-stresses being released from my body – a glorious feeling.

By the second day, I was feeling completely relaxed and I remarked to Don that I was almost, but not quite, getting ready to do things again.

"Like what?" he asked, as we were towelling off after a brief swim in the ocean. Silver, of course, had pointedly refused to go into the water, as he always did. For that matter, no other humans did either, probably because the air temperature was only 7 °C (45 °F), and the ocean temperature a brisk 3.5 °C (38 °F). It wasn't cold enough to stop us, however, although admittedly we only went in for brief periods.

"I don't really know," I replied, in answer to Don's question. "Maybe we should try a drive around the island; see some of the sights."

So, on our third full day on the island, that's exactly what we did. In fact, we circumnavigated the entire island, which turned out to be a beautiful drive, between the ocean and lighthouse vistas and the most neat and tidy looking farms I've ever seen in my life, all accentuated with the island's characteristic red-tinged earth[11].

On the morning of our fourth day[12], we were literally discussing what to do that day when there was a knock on our cabin door. Don got up to see who it was, opened the door and said "Just a moment please," and then looked back at me saying, "I think it's for you."

"For me?" I said, incredulously, suspecting that Don was joking. But I got up anyway and went to the door.

There were two uniformed RCMP Constables standing there.

"Sergeant Houston?" one of them asked.

"Yes?"

"We have a situation in Charlottetown. A cruise ship docked there has had a bomb threat phoned in. The bomb squad has been called in but there's no explosives-trained dog on the island, and not enough time to bring one in from the mainland. Our CO[13] asks if you'll come. He says there's a special reason for asking, but he didn't tell us what it is."

That sounded unusual to me, but there was no point in questioning the constables any further. I turned to look at Don, who nodded. He'd overheard the conversation and knew I'd want to go.

"Fine," I said. "Just give me a few minutes to change first."

The constables said thanks and that they'd wait outside.

Closing the cabin door, I went for the duffel bag I carried with me everywhere, which contained my tactical uniform. Although I worked in the Security Service, it wasn't unusual for Silver and I to get called out in our capacity as a police service dog team to search for people, evidence, or explosives. The duffel bag was heavy because, in addition to my uniform and boots it contained a lock box with my service revolver and a few other things that qualify as restricted or prohibited weapons in Canada. While I was in the process of changing, I paused when I happened to notice that Don was changing clothes as well.

Seeing me stop and look, he said "Want some company?"

I gazed at him for a moment, decided that there was no point in trying to explain the potential danger, which he knew very well, so instead I asked "Still have your usual assortment of identities with you?"

"Of course," he replied. "I carry them with me everywhere just like you and your duffel bag. My IDs have even been updated to refer to Major Harrison, or Lieutenant-Commander Harrison, as appropriate."

"In that case, OK. I formally request the assistance of the Military Police with regard to this incident."

By the time I was dressed, Don had changed into clothing that, while civilian, was at least practical.

"All set?" he asked.

"Almost. I think I'll just grab Silver's police vest to forestall questions about his presence on the ship." This was stored in Silver's own duffel bag. Different from the fancy shabrack Silver had worn at our wedding, this vest was basic black and carried attachment loops and patches on each side that said 'POLICE.' Once I'd retrieved the vest and a long lead, I said "Ready. Let's go."

When we exited the cabin, Don showed the constables his military police ID, while I asked "Are you going to escort us in?"

"Yes, Sarge," one of them replied. "We'll be going Code 2[14]."

"OK. I have a light in my truck, so we'll put it on and follow you in."

I still carried in my truck one of those magnetic base, red flashing lights that can be placed on the roof and then plugged into a cigarette-lighter socket. This, and a concealed police radio, were legacies from my very first undercover assignments six years earlier. With the light in position, Don, Silver, and I piled into the truck and we drove off, right behind the constables, who were driving a marked, highway-patrol car.

It isn't a long drive from Cavendish to Charlottetown – nothing is a long drive when you're in PEI – so we soon found ourselves parked near the cruise ship dock, which is right downtown, and escorted onto the ship, the MS Atlantic II[15], to see the captain. It was slow going against the flow when trying to board, however, because the ship was being evacuated as a safety measure and there was a steady stream of people making their way off.

Captain Noah Sorensen appeared to be in his mid-forties which wasn't exactly young, but younger than I expected, and I realized that my fanciful image of an older, white-haired cruise ship captain had come from watching too many movies and TV shows.

Captain Sorensen also introduced us to First Officer (Navigation) Frida Haugen and Chief Security Officer Andrew Harris. Like her captain, First Officer Haugen had a slight Scandinavian accent, and I discovered later that they both grew up in Norway. That was the only similarity between them however, as while the captain tended to speak quite formally and with some reserve, the first officer was younger, and seemed much more spontaneous and lively. The thought crossed my mind that I might be speaking with a future woman cruise ship captain[16]. Andrew Harris was a somewhat older, and very distinguished-looking man who was quite tall, heavyset, and spoke with a British accent. I later discovered that he was a retired Superintendent from Britain's Metropolitan Police Service (also known as 'the Met' or Scotland Yard).

"I'll let Chief Harris fill you in on the threat," said the captain.

"Since we're colleagues of a sort, you can call me Drew when we're alone, but not in front of the passengers or crew if you don't mind.... Right. Well then, a few hours ago, we received a phone call in which a muffled voice informed us that there was a bomb on board the ship and that it was scheduled to go off at 5 pm today. Now, our scheduled departure time is 4 pm today, and it's happened before that people that are running late phone in a bomb threat like this simply to delay our sailing, to give them time to make it to the ship. For that reason, we keep a very close eye on anyone that shows up late to board the ship. Of course, showing up late isn't proof that someone has made a bomb threat, but we investigate to the extent that we can.

"I don't want you to think that we're not taking this seriously," he continued, "I'm just saying that when this has happened in the past it's been a hoax."

"We noticed people disembarking when we arrived," I said.

"Right. We've instructed all passengers to leave the ship and we've laid on some special sight-seeing tours to give them something to do while we wait for five o'clock. The captain has also ordered most of the crew off as well, although, for the time being, we are continuing to load food, drinks, and other supplies, plus the luggage of new passengers that are joining the cruise here in Charlottetown."

"When we get closer to the threatened time, say about four o'clock," put in the captain, "then I'll have the rest of the crew off the ship and I'll be the only one to remain on board from then until a little after five o'clock. It's a tradition for the captain to remain. Then, assuming no bomb has exploded, we'll board the crew, then the passengers. Then, since the tide will still be favourable, we'll be off."

At this point there was a pause, and the security chief and first officer looked expectantly at the captain.

"Normally, when we get a specific-time bomb-threat like this we do everything we just said and then, when nothing happens, we resume our schedule. In this case, however, things are a bit different.

"We have a VIP couple on board."

Laurie Schramm

3 VIPs

"Ever heard of Alicia Avon?" asked Chief Harris.

"The name sounds familiar, but I don't know why," I answered.

"She's a fashion model, isn't she?" said Don.

"That's the one. A classic beauty, and a dead-ringer for the British actress Vivien Leigh that played Scarlett O'Hara in the old *Gone with the Wind* movie. Her face shows up on magazine covers and in cosmetic ads all the time. These days, she's been mostly working out of New York. The other thing about her is that she's unusually publicity shy. She's here on vacation with her husband Edward, and they've taken the Owners Suite on Deck 7. Our job, and the cruise line has been very clear about this, is to look out for them and their privacy as best we can."

"And we're here because there have been threats?" I asked.

"Very good," said the Chief, approvingly. "Yes, but I think you should hear about that directly from them."

Chief Harris led us to the Avons' suite, which was on Deck 7 of the nine publicly-accessible decks. His knock on the stateroom door was answered by a man, who the Chief introduced as Edward Avon (who he privately referred to as 'the husband'). He was of average height and build, with curly brown hair and lively-looking blue eyes.

As he guided us into the suite, the Chief explained who we were.

The suite itself was the largest of the suites on the ship at approximately 120 m² (1,300 ft²), including the spacious balcony. As

323

we entered the suite, my first impressions were of the sheer size of it, with its separate living/dining room, and secondly how bright it was, with its large, floor-to-ceiling windows.

"Military Police?" Mr. Avon asked, in surprise.

I explained that Don was my husband, that were we on our honeymoon, and that we'd used his credentials as an excuse for him to be able to come with us.

Hearing this, Mr. Avon was immediately apologetic, and we assured him that it was OK, and that we were each used to being called out on unusual assignments with little or no advance notice.

"All part of the job," I summarized.

This prompted him to ask more questions about our jobs, which we were happy to oblige. It was impossible not to find him likeable as he was charming, friendly, interested, and informal all at the same time, and invited us to simply call him Eddie.

As our introduction to Eddie was winding up, the bedroom door opened to the sounds of a small-breed-dog barking. First out was a brown Pekingese, who rushed over to within a few feet of Silver, then just stood there barking, its whole body vibrating with the effort. Silver, for his part, simply stood his ground and watched the smaller dog with interest.

"Mitzi! Enough!" said a woman's voice as Alicia Avon joined us, sweeping Mitzi up into her arms, from which vantage point Mitzi subsided into a series of growls and snorts.

Although I knew that Alicia Avon was a fashion model, I was somehow still surprised at how beautiful she was, with a full head of rich, dark hair, accentuated cheeks, and gorgeous hazel eyes, she really did remind me of the British stage and film actress Vivien Leigh. The second surprise was how beautiful she looked despite the complete absence of any discernable makeup. I will admit that I had the cynical thought that that might be part of the reason she was able to look gorgeous modelling any kind of makeup – because she didn't need it!

She was polite but aloof, at first, as we were introduced and I wondered whether this might be a defense mechanism against the constant media attention she received. To be fair, she did thaw considerably when her husband explained that we were on our honeymoon.

"Couldn't they have sent someone else?" she asked, sounding genuinely concerned.

"They could have," I explained, "but there are a limited number of police dogs with explosives training and none are permanently based on the island. That means we were the only ones that could have gotten here before the time mentioned in the threat." I further assured her that it was OK, and asked whether the couple could tell us what had been going on.

"I understand that you're concerned about the bomb threat?" I began.

"No," said Eddie.

"Yes," said Alicia.

"Yes," said Eddie, in a conciliatory voice.

After a pregnant pause, they said "yes," in unison.

Raising a questioning eyebrow, I looked from one to the other. "OK, why yes?"

With a bit of a sigh, Eddie said "We live in New York because of Alicia's modelling work. Along with her fame come fans, some of them quite ardent. Among the ardent fans is a man named Alf Regis, who has become completely fixated with her."

"A stalker," put in Alicia, in disgust.

"OK. Yes, a stalker," agreed Eddie. "Anyway, we were eventually able to get a restraining order against him, but that really sent him over the deep end. Since then, we've received a number of threats from him along the lines of 'If I can't have her, then no one else can either.'"

"You can't imagine," interjected Alicia, her initial reserve crumbling away. "It's been horrible, horrible."

"No," I replied. "I don't think I really can properly appreciate what it must have been like for you. Do you have any reason to suspect that this man is behind today's threat?"

"Not specifically," said Eddie. "It's probably a combination of our usual fears plus the fact that his last threat mentioned blowing both of us to bits."

"When was that?"

"About a month ago."

"Ok, and why did you first say you weren't concerned about today's threat?" I asked, looking directly at Eddie.

"Because it seems so improbable. Why go to all the trouble of tracking us here to Canada and then try to blow up an entire cruise ship when he's really just mad at the two of us, and all he has to do is wait for us to return to New York and then go after us there? I mean, imagine the size of a bomb that would be needed to destroy a cruise ship?" He looked meaningfully at Chief Harris.

"I'd prefer not to answer that, if you don't mind," was all that the Chief would say.

"Have you considered hiring a bodyguard?" I asked, trying another tack.

"Would a bodyguard be able to prevent a bomb attack?"

"I don't know. Maybe not. How about a private investigator to follow him then?"

"Yes. We tried that, but the PI hasn't been able to find him."

I looked at Silver, who was sitting beside me. Silver gave me a direct look, from which I sensed only sympathy. He wouldn't have understood all the words but he was very good at sensing moods and reading people. I looked at Don too, but he had his poker face on.

"OK," I said. "Thank you. Silver's trained to sniff out explosives. We'll go through the mostly likely areas of the ship with Chief Harris' help." I looked at the Chief, who simply nodded in agreement. "We'll see if Silver can detect anything. If he does, the bomb squad will be able to deal with it. If not, I can't give you any guarantees. Silver's very good at this, but if we don't find anything that's not absolute proof there's nothing there. OK?"

"Would you stay on the ship if Silver didn't find anything?" asked Eddie.

At this Don began to sit up straight and I knew that he was instinctively rising to my defense, but I waved him back with a gesture.

"That's a very good question. Would I trust him with my life, you mean?" I laughed. "You wouldn't believe how many times we've trusted and saved each other's lives in the past. Yes, I would stay on the ship if Silver couldn't find anything. No question."

This seemed to be enough for the Avons, who thanked us, apologized again for inadvertently interrupting our honeymoon, and saw us out.

When we stopped by Chief Harris' office to regroup for a moment, he said "Well, what do you think of them?"

"As people, you mean? Well, Alicia came across at first as haughty and reserved, but seemed to thaw and open-up as we talked. I suppose it's a defense mechanism for her. Eddie seems quite open and friendly, and he seemed amused rather than jealous of all the attention that gets paid to his famous wife."

"And their story?"

"It's fantastic," I said. "A thwarted stalker with a grudge I can understand, but to extend that to attempting to blow up an entire cruise ship sounds crazy. Even if someone blew out a hole below the waterline, there would be time to get the guests and staff off the ship before it sank if, in fact, it sank at all. Right?"

"Exactly," confirmed the Chief. "Even with multiple devices exploding in exactly the right places to overwhelm the pumps, and even if some of the watertight doors were left open or malfunctioned, there would still be time to get everyone off. Excepting, of course, any people unfortunate enough to have been caught directly in the blasts themselves.

"Don't forget," he continued, "this isn't exactly the Titanic, in open ocean far from shore, and with too few lifeboats."

"So, you think it's a hoax."

"I didn't say that. I don't think it's this stalker, but it could easily be the old trick of someone phoning-in a specific-time bomb threat to delay our departure. However. The cruise line says to pander to the whims of the VIPs, so that's what we're doing." He paused for a moment. "You don't have to, though."

I looked at Don, then back. "No. We're here now. We may as well do what we can. Can you get someone to guide us through the areas where luggage and stores come onto the ship"

He nodded. "I'll take you myself."

"Speaking of pandering," I said, cautiously, "I didn't think cruise ships allowed dogs on board unless they are service dogs?"

"We don't" said the Chief, "but when you pay as much as they are for the best suite on the ship, then you get some slack. In this case, the passenger list shows that little rat of theirs as an 'emotional-support service dog.'"

Something about the way he said this led me to believe that he was not telling us the whole truth, but a pregnant pause accompanied by my best penetrating look were no match for his ability to maintain an impassive silence and he didn't divulge anything further.

Fortunately, we didn't have to search the entire ship, just the areas in which cargo and luggage had been brought on board and/or stowed that morning. We had boarded the ship on Deck 3, which was one level below the deck with the lifeboats, and the fifth deck up from the waterline. As he guided us downwards, Chief Harris explained that between Deck 1 and the waterline were two more decks numbered 0 and 00. Below the waterline, there were two more decks. These off-limits-to-passengers decks contained hundreds of crew cabins, crew social rooms, the engine and mechanical rooms, storage areas, and so on.

"The Owners Suite you were just in is the largest of the passenger staterooms," he said, as he knocked on a door and then opened it when there was no reply. "This is a typical crew cabin."

We only peeked-in through the door, but the cabin was small and cramped, containing two bunk beds, a small but complete bathroom, a single closet sectioned-off for two people, and a desk/storage unit that held a small fridge and TV. There was no window or porthole.

"These are about 12 m^2 (130 ft^2)," he explained. "That's one-tenth of the size of the Owners Suite on Deck 7. The crew have their own kitchen and dining facilities, social rooms, and exercise area, so they don't actually spend much time in their cabins."

For our search, we began with the deck on which bulky materials were transferred on and off the ship. This was where luggage, food, and other supplies were brought onto the ship by motorized fork-lifts, either on pallets or in large cages. Chief Harris explained that, once onboard, these materials would be sorted and distributed to staterooms, kitchens, and storerooms as appropriate.

Silver didn't find anything among the pallets of stores that had been boarded but not yet distributed, nor in the main storerooms, food coolers, or freezers. We next did a general walkaround of all of the lower decks, which Chief Harris made into a kind of walking tour while Silver continued to sniff around. As a result, we saw the huge engines and generators, the heating, steam and air-conditioning plants, the desalinization plant (used to produce drinking water from seawater), sewage disposal plant, and so on, all amid mazes of piping and electrical conduit.

There were even huge storage rooms devoted entirely to more than ten thousand spare parts of all sizes and kinds. At one point we were introduced to the ship's chief engineer, who showed us his systems control room, which at first glance looked like a cross between a ship's bridge and a power station's control room. The waste handling systems and storage areas were equally large and impressive, as would befit a ship that produces a ton of garbage every day. Among other things, we saw cardboard being stacked into bundles in a bailing machine, and crew members separating out glass containers and feeding them into a glass-crusher. We were told that the various bulk waste bags, bales, and containers were dropped off at least once a week, if not more often, when docked in the various ports of call.

Following our below-decks activities, I paused in thought for a moment, then said "What's directly above and below, and beside the Avons' suite."

"How about the stateroom beside the Avons and the ones directly below it?" I asked.

"Not content to just go through the motions then?"

"Well. If we're going to search, we may as well do it properly." I smiled. "When I was with the Metro Toronto police, my Captain was fond of calling me the biggest pain in the butt in his division."

That provoked a smile! "Fine," he said, but he sounded more approving than disapproving. "Below the Avons' suite are staterooms; smaller ones. There are probably three of them below their particular suite. Above them are the fitness centre and spa."

"How about their balcony?" asked Don.

"We call them verandahs. In this case there's a solid exterior wall on the next deck up. If someone wanted to rappel down, they'd have to do it from two decks up. There are probably two verandahs directly below the one for this suite. On the Avons' deck, all of the verandahs on each side are connected by doors that are normally locked during each cruise. Their suite, however, is the exception as the bedroom is situated between the suite's verandah and that of the adjacent stateroom. There's only the one stateroom beside theirs.

"I'll ask the Purser to join us. I have master keys for almost everything on the ship, but the Purser will have a heart attack if we don't let him supervise us breaking into the passengers' cabins."

Later, under the Purser's watchful eye, I had Silver sniff around each of the staterooms that shared the Avons' wall (they called it a bulkhead) or floor (deck). It didn't take long, and we came up empty.

Finally, Chief Harris led us ashore so we could search the cages and pallets of materials that were still being loaded and/or were ready and waiting to be transferred to the ship. Again, Silver went around each cage or pallet, frequently standing up on two legs with his front paws stretched high-up on the sides of the containers so that he could get as close as possible to everything. It was after doing exactly this at the single baggage cage, that he lingered longer than usual in one spot and then promptly sat down on his haunches and gave me an expectant look. This was our one episode of excitement on the entire search.

"Can we get this cage unloaded?" I asked.

The Chief waved some baggage handlers over and had all of the pieces of luggage taken out and separated on the cement floor. After a few twists and turns, Silver found the suitcase he was looking for and sat down beside it.

"What'd you find Silver?" I asked, rhetorically, as we all moved over to see the case.

"What do you think?' asked Chief Harris, after a quick look.

"Well, false positives happen, but Silvers' pretty reliable. Even if he's right, it may not be a bomb though – in addition to explosives, he's also been trained to detect gunpowder and other explosive fillers in ammunition, gunpowder residues, and even the cleaning oil traces that are left on guns.

"So, it's up to you. They've apparently called the bomb squad, but I don't know how long they'll be in responding."

"Hmmm. Let's take a look inside the case. If we see anything that looks tricky, we'll stop and wait for help. OK?"

I shrugged. "We're on your turf, so it's your call as far as I'm concerned."

The Chief waved over one of the dock workers and asked for a wire cutter. When it was retrieved and delivered, he used it to cut the small travel locks off of the suitcase. First, he searched the two outside, zippered pockets. When he was searching the larger one, he gave a grunt, paused for a moment, then withdrew a small drawstring bag made of soft cloth, but which made faintly metallic clinking sounds as he lifted it out and opened it. Reaching in, he felt around, saying, "There's either a metal pen or…." Then his eyes widened as he brought the 'pen' out for a look.

"Well now, this is something you don't come across every day," he said with satisfaction as he held out a cylindrical grey tube about the length of a cigar but not as wide. As he turned it in his hand, I was able to recognize it.

"A pen gun[17]," I said. "I've only ever seen one in the RCMP Museum in Regina."

"A kid pulled one on me once, when I was a young constable on the beat in London," mused the Chief. "He even tried to shoot me with it, but fortunately, it misfired. Not loaded, at least," he muttered as he opened it up. When he turned the bag upside down, five .32-calibre cartridges dropped out and into his hand.

"Like I said, Silver's trained to detect gunpowder and residues, and so forth, besides explosives. Sorry."

"Don't apologize," said the Chief. "I'm impressed that he could find something this small in a case surrounded by others. I'm going to have to have a word with our security screeners though. This should have been caught when the bag was X-rayed."

I looked at him. "This is a prohibited weapon in Canada. It's not the kind of thing I can simply overlook...."

"Wouldn't expect you to. What do you want to do?"

"I'll take it for now, and I'll call for someone to came to officially seize the weapon and arrest the passenger that checked this case." As I said this, I pulled a plastic evidence bag from one of my cargo pockets and opened it so the Chief could drop the pen gun, cartridges, and cloth bag into it.

"Have whomever they send report to me and I'll take them to the boarding area when we re-embark the passengers. When the bag's owner goes through our security check-in, we'll have them without having to search for them."

So, that was the grand finale from our search. The Chief did open and search the insides of the suitcase but didn't find anything else of interest. No explosives after all, then, but one prohibited weapon. Finding such a small weapon in a sea of luggage and containers of all sizes and shapes seemed to raise our credibility with the Chief, if nothing else. I even thought that he might be upset that the pen gun got through his security in the first place, but he seemed almost pleased about that too.

"Not a problem," he pronounced. "Mistakes happen. The trick is to see them as learning opportunities, so we can improve."

"I doubt your passenger will admit much, but I wonder whether it was being smuggled aboard for offence or defense?" I mused out loud.

"An assassin, you think?"

"It seems unlikely, I'll admit, but something about this whole situation seems odd to me."

The Chief didn't say anything, and he had on his imperturbable facial expression, but I thought I detected a brief gleam in his eyes. More than ever, I suspected that he knew more than he was letting on, but all he said was "In my experience, it's best to trust your instincts."

"Hmmm hmmm," I said. "In my experience, still waters sometimes run deep."

That got through his mask, and I was rewarded with a brief smile, but nothing more.

I found a phone and called to request that someone be sent to arrest the passenger in whose bag we found the gun. After that, we headed back to the ship to see the Avons again.

"Have you considered that it wouldn't be difficult to place magnetic-explosive devices on the outside of the hull?" I asked, when we were about to walk up the gangway of the ship.

The Chief looked at me strangely. "What made you think of that?"

I pointed down toward the ship's waterline. "I'm also a SCUBA diver. If it was me, I'd consider it. An improvised limpet mine wouldn't be hard to build and I doubt you have the kinds of sensors that warships use to detect underwater demolition devices."

There was another pause, and I thought he wasn't going to answer, but he did.

"I hired a diver to do a sweep around the ship just before you arrived. It came out negative."

"So, you're more concerned than you've been letting on." It was a statement as much as a question.

"Let's just say that I'm a cautious fellow at heart," was his riposte.

Onboard the ship, we first reported to the captain. Having summarized our search, I concluded with "I can't tell you that there's no bomb on the ship. All I can say is that, with the Chief's help and guidance, we've searched the most likely areas and not found one."

The Captain glanced at the Chief.

"They were very careful. Even I was impressed," said the Chief to the obvious question. The he told the captain about the pen gun.

"Very well," said Captain Sorensen, "I'll have everyone re-embark and advise the Harbourmaster of our new estimated departure time."

We next went to see the Avons who, as the ship's VIP guests, had been the first passengers allowed back on the ship. As we approached their suite, I paused to look around. Deck 7 had two long passageways running the length of the ship, one on each side. More or less in front of the door to the Owners Suite, which was on the starboard side, was an access passageway leading to the staterooms on the port side. Forward of the suite was a solid bulkhead. Aft of it was another stateroom. Having searched there earlier, we knew what was directly above and below the Avons' suite, that there was only one adjacent stateroom, and we'd looked at the layout of their verandah.

As Don and I nodded our thanks, Chief Harris knocked on the door of the Avons' suite. After we'd 'run the gauntlet' of Mitzi's guard-dog routine, we got down to business and the Chief and I summarized our search.

"What about this passenger with the gun?" asked Alicia, nervously.

"Don't worry Ma'am, they will be denied boarding. We have the passenger's name and will detain him for the police," replied the Chief.

They all turned and looked at me.

"I have the gun with me here, and I'll give it to the officers that will be making the actual arrest."

"You see," said Alicia. "They've even followed us here!" she exclaimed.

They? I thought to myself.

"It's probably just a coincidence, dear," said Eddie, in a placating tone of voice. "Right Sergeant?"

"Frankly, I have no idea. We know essentially nothing about this passenger, yet. But, as the Chief said, he won't be allowed back on board."

Alicia still looked worried, but she and Eddie thanked us for searching and apologized once more for interrupting our honeymoon. With that, we took our leave and went back down to the gangway area to wait for someone to come and make the arrest. This actually took quite a while, but eventually two uniformed constables arrived at the security checkpoint, where Chief Harris and I briefed them and I handed over the evidence.

At that point, there didn't seem to be any reason to hang around any longer, so Don and I were saying our goodbyes to Chief Harris when First Officer Haugen joined us. She guided us to a quiet spot off to one side of the security checkpoint.

"The captain sent me to ask if you – all three of you – would consider remaining on board for the rest of the cruise until we reach Montréal."

"Did he say why?" I asked.

"He said to tell you that the Avons have specifically asked whether you could be persuaded to stick around for the rest of the cruise." She grimaced. "They went straight to the cruise line, so the captain only heard about it from the head office. You didn't hear this from me, but he's stressed and angry. Not angry with you, but with the Avons and the situation. His personal message for you is that he's very sorry to have to even ask this, but that he and the cruise line would be very grateful if you'd agree."

I looked at Don.

"It's up to you," he said. "As long as we're together, I'm content."

I looked over at the Chief, who was standing not far away trying to look inconspicuous. I had no doubt that he'd heard everything. "This is your turf Chief, as far as security goes."

He was able to hold his imperturbable expression at first, saying "My feathers don't ruffle as easily as all that. I think we'd all be grateful if you'd consider it." Then he gave a genuine smile. "If there is no real threat, then your presence will make the Avons feel better, which will make our lives a lot easier."

First Officer Haugen nodded in agreement.

"If there really is a threat, then the more help the better."

Trying to think it through quickly, I said "OK then. Three things. First, I need a phone link to shore so I can call my boss. Secondly, can you get us a stateroom that's really close to the Avons? Thirdly, we'll need to go back to our cottage to get our clothes and clear out."

First Officer Haugen was ready for this. "In reverse order, you should have time to get your stuff if you leave now.

"The ship is carrying about 1,400 passengers plus a crew complement of nearly 700, so it will take another hour and a half to re-embark the passengers and crew and to finish loading stores and luggage. The captain spoke to the Purser, and you can have the suite next door to the Avons – the one you searched earlier. It's not as huge as theirs, but it's very nice, and quite spacious."

She gave a bright smile. "We gave the couple that were in that suite a few inducements to get them to agree to switch staterooms, and they are very happy about it.

"If you'll come with me," she concluded, "you can use the phone in my cabin."

A few minutes later, seated at the First Officer's desk, I called my boss in Ottawa, Staff Sergeant Avery Blunt, to fill him in. To my surprise, he already knew most of the story.

"I was just about to try tracking you down myself," he said. "I'm glad you agreed to stay with the ship because the Force is also getting pressure to accommodate the Avons."

"Really? Why? And pressure from whom?"

"It's coming straight to the Commissioner from External Affairs[18]. They want us to provide a VIP security detail for the Avons for as long as they're in Canada. We can't get a team there before the ship sails, but if you stay on the ship, we can have a detail waiting if they want to get off the ship in Québec City, and we can have another one meet them when they disembark in Montréal."

"Sure, but why? With all due respect, I've never heard of a fashion model getting a VIP Security Detail."

"Me either, and I don't know the answer to your question. I don't even know if the Commissioner knows what it's all about."

"Well. I already suspected that the cruise line was being a lot more accommodating than seemed explainable, so I guess there's some consistency out there somewhere. In terms of on-board security, I already made a formal request for Don's assistance in his military police persona. Could you ask Uncle George to call Admiral White and clear it with him as well? I only did it so he could come along on the wild-goose chase, but this may be evolving into something more serious."

"Good idea. I'll feel better knowing that you'll have more backup than just Silver."

"Great. Two more things. Can you have someone check with the NYPD and FBI on this stalker character, Alf Regis? Secondly, can you get a background check on both Alicia and Edward Avon? We're running blind here. I don't think they're telling us everything, and I don't think we can protect them without understanding the nature of the threat and the motive for it."

"Agreed, but we both need to proceed carefully. If External Affairs finds out we're sticking our noses in, they'll go ballistic on us."

"Understood."

"Call me just before the ship sails, and I'll try to get some answers for you."

The next hour and a half were busy for us, as we had to drive back to our cabin, get our gear, make sure we had enough dog food to bring on board for Silver, and then check-out early.

***

Meanwhile, back at the ship, two young men had joined the line of passengers to re-embark. They had long hair and scraggly beards, were casually dressed in T-shirts and somewhat faded jeans, and looked exactly like what they were: university students. Their passports had shown them to be Italian citizens, and they were joining the cruise in Charlottetown, so their baggage was somewhere waiting to be loaded. Although the two knew each other slightly and, in fact, attended the same Swiss university, they had become separated by half a dozen people in line.

When the first young man went through the security checkpoint, there seemed to be some kind of delay, followed by the appearance of two police officers. Lorenzo Costa, the second student, was both close enough and tall enough to be able to have a reasonably clear view of the proceedings. He was able, therefore, to see that there was a brief discussion, followed by the first young man turning pale as a sheet and then being led away by the police. As he was being led away the young man walked rather woodenly, as if in shock — which he was.

Lorenzo knew why the other student was being arrested and he was both relieved and frustrated. Relived because it wasn't him that was being arrested, and frustrated because it meant the pen gun that he had slipped into his fellow student's luggage had been discovered. He had hoped that it was small enough to slip through security but reluctant to take the risk of having it found in his own luggage. Now that it was gone, along with the expendable fellow student, he would have to find another weapon of some kind on board the ship. What that might be, however, he had no idea.

***

While we were at our cottage packing up, I changed back into civilian clothes, stowed Silver's police jacket, and Don even changed into more touristy clothes. Then, we drove back to the cruise ship dock, put my truck into long-term parking, and went to check in.

We didn't have tickets, of course, so we had to ask the cruise staff to call Chief Harris for us, who came and met us himself to guide us through the boarding process.

This was just as well, because when we reached the security screening point at the top of the gangway, I was able to warn him that I was carrying enough metal to make his metal detectors go crazy.

"Just send it through and I'll take care of it," he said.

Sure enough, the metal detectors triggered screeching alarms, after which he did the hand-search of my carry-on luggage personally. He wasn't surprised to find my service revolver, ammunition and hand-cuffs, but his eyebrows did go up when I reached up under the legs of my Bermuda shorts to retrieve my double-barreled derringer from one leg and my military-looking lock-blade knife that were legacies from some of my earliest undercover cases. Given that each had been life-savers in the past, I normally had them on me when working in plain clothes and/or undercover.

It was with some amusement that I watch him struggle to maintain his trademark impassive demeanor, but he held it pretty well.

"Legacies of having an interesting career," was all I said, and he simply put everything back in my carry-on bag and told the security screener, who had watched it all with a horrified expression, that I was an undercover police officer, and to keep her mouth shut. She seemed shocked, but nodded her acquiescence.

Beyond security, the Purser himself was there to meet us, and escorted us to our stateroom saying that he had been briefed by the captain and to just ask for him if he could be of assistance in any way.

The suite he led us to was half the size of the Avons' but it looked luxurious.

"Quite a step up from our rustic cabin," Don observed.

It had floor-to-ceiling windows, a king-sized bed, a large sitting area, and a roomy bathroom. A glass door led to very spacious, private verandah that held two lounger-chairs, plus two regular chairs, and a medium-sized table. In one corner had been placed a decent-size square of artificial turf that must have been scented, because Silver immediately went to it, gave it a thorough sniffing, and then lifted a leg to pee.

I laughed. "I see you're used to accommodating dogs on the ship."

The Purser smiled, and said "It's unusual but not rare for us to have one or two service dogs cruising with us, so we try to be prepared. The artificial turf has been placed right over the verandah's drain, which is the low part of the deck, so it's easily cleaned. Your cabin stewards will wash it every day, when they service the room, and then spray it with a scent so that your dog will immediately recognize what it's for."

After getting settled in Don and I sat out on the deck, enjoying the opportunity for some quiet time. The ship was moored along the length of its starboard side, and since our stateroom was also on the starboard side, we were able to watch the various pre-departure activities of boarding the last of the passengers and stores.

Shortly before we were supposed to leave, a very late couple of passengers rushed from the check-in area, across the dock and toward the gangway. Seeing this, I jumped up from my lounger to get the binoculars that the cruise line had supplied with the suite, and tried to get a good look at the late boarders.

"A man and a woman, middle-aged maybe, they seem fit enough. Can't make out their faces, really. Nothing remarkable about their clothes or appearance," I summarized for Don as I was watching.

"Chief Harris will be watching them very closely and getting a background check done, so we might learn more from him later," said Don.

"Mmmm. It won't be long before they disconnect the service lines. I'd better call Avery while I can." I went into our suite and used the phone to place a call to my boss in Ottawa. Ottawa time is one hour earlier than PEI's, but I was still lucky to catch him before he left the office. When he came on the line, I said "We're about to sail and this is an open line."

"Understood. Two things. One. NYPD says the subject has been arrested for armed robbery and is being held without bail pending a hearing, so he will not be going anywhere anytime soon. Two. We checked with the cruise line and also with Customs[19] and found a discrepancy. The passengers you asked about are travelling on diplomatic passports from the Principality of Montenia. Ready for this? The names on their passports do not match the names given on the ship's passenger list. That's all we have so far."

"Wow. OK, thanks. Can you see if the West European desk[20] can come up with anything on them?"

"I've already asked, but nothing yet. Call me again tomorrow."

"Right. Thanks, Good night."

"Found something?" asked Don after I'd hung up the phone.

"Yes, but I don't know what it means. Apparently, Alicia and Edward Avon aren't their real names and they're travelling on diplomatic passports from the Principality of Montenia!"

Laurie Schramm

4 CRUISING

We continued to sit out on our verandah and watch as the crew cast-off and the ship headed out into the harbour. This being our first cruise, we were so enthralled that we ordered room service and ate it outside so we could continue to sight-see.

After dinner, the Avons invited us to join them on their own verandah for drinks. We readily agreed, but before we could leave Chief Harris showed up to check on us.

"I'm glad you're here Drew," I began, using his first name for the first time. "I found out that Alf Regis, the man the Avons had the injunction against, has been arrested for armed robbery in New York and is still being held pending a hearing. His full name is Alfonso Regis."

"Well, that takes one potential threat off our list. Anything else?"

"Yes, the Avons are travelling under different names from the ones on their passports."

He held his facial muscles well, but his eyes widened a bit. After a pause, he said "Yes. Well, that's quite right, in fact. That's quick work on your part, but I can't say I'm surprised. I did some checking of my own and discovered that you, Alex, are with the RCMP Security Service, and you, Don, are with Military Intelligence."

"May I ask why you think that?"

"One of the legacies of a career in The Met is that I still have a few friends in high places, in this case it was a friend in MI6."

"Hmmm. OK then, guilty as charged. Silver and I really are a Police Dog Service Team, but that's not my primary job. How about the Avons?"

"They are travelling incognito. Alicia Avon is her professional name, and Edward is using the surname Avon as well. Their real last name is Montenario. I had to be informed so that I could square things with your customs and immigration officers when they compared the passports with the passenger list.

"To answer your next question, the cruise line hasn't given me any additional information and ordered me not to ask any more questions."

"But....?"

"But I did some quiet checking on my own. Edward is the third in line for the throne, behind two older brothers. His father is the Sovereign Prince of Monteria. Kind of like a king, but they refer to him as the Sovereign Prince. That explains why the cruise line is willing to bend some rules for him."

"It also explains why our own Department of External Affairs is anxious about his security."

"Too right!"

"OK then, that's interesting but there's no reason to connect Edward's real identity with the stalker, the bomb threat, or the weapon in the luggage, is there?"

"None that I know of. Even if there were radical anti-monarchists planning something, Edward's a long way from the throne."

I decided to return to the bomb threat. "Do you have anything on the late-arriving passengers today?"

"Not yet. A middle-aged couple. Dressed like tourists, usual amount of baggage. Staying in one of the cheapest inner staterooms, but there's nothing wrong with that. At first glance, there's nothing remarkable in any way. The check-in and security-screening staff agreed that the man spoke with a bit of a European accent and manner but not strong enough to suggest a specific country. The woman didn't speak much at all."

"Not much to go on."

"No, but I've put out some enquiries. We'll see."

When we joined the Avons on their verandah, we were well out into the Northumberland Strait heading southeast, preliminary to steering north and swinging all the way around the eastern shores of PEI and into the Gulf of St. Lawrence. Being on the starboard side of the ship, we could see the coastline of Nova Scotia off in the distance.

I was able to steer the conversation to Alicia's background, and we learned some of her background and career history. It was interesting enough, but I had no way of judging how honest she was or wasn't being.

Don took a turn by asking Eddie about his background, to which he responded that he'd grown up in Europe, in a small place not far from Geneva, after which he'd been sent to England to study at Oxford, something he'd obviously enjoyed because it prompted some interesting stories about his university days. His anecdotes suggested that he'd studied a combination of political science and economics. After Oxford, he'd gone out and "knocked about the world a bit." This translated into having spent some time working on a merchant ship in the Mediterranean, then as a ranch hand in Australia, and later as a cowboy in Montana.

Although his stories were both entertaining and believable, Don gave me a few surreptitious looks that indicated he had a feeling that Eddie was being as selective with the truth as I suspected Alicia had been.

It was natural for us to exchange 'where did you two meet' stories. For our part, Don and I told the truth about our first meeting in Nova Scotia, but far from the whole truth. For their part, Alicia and Eddie told us about having met on the French Riveria when Alicia was there working on a photo shoot for a magazine and Eddie was there on vacation. No explanation was offered for how Eddie was able to afford to stay in such a place, and it seemed premature to try probing so pointedly into the details of his background.

When our conversation inevitably turned to the topic of threats, I asked if we could move inside their suite where there was less risk of being overheard. This surprised them, but they agreed.

Once inside, I told the Avons the news about her stalker being arrested and held in a New York jail. They already knew that Silver and I hadn't found any explosives, and Chief Harris and I had also reassured her that the pen gun we found had been confiscated and that neither it nor the passenger that checked in with it were on the ship. Nevertheless, Alicia still seemed apprehensive. Eddie, in contrast, seemed completely at ease and had been, in fact, the life of the party so far.

"Are you still worried about the reporters?" he asked her.

"No... yes, I guess I am really." She looked at Don and I. "I know it's silly, and I know that it comes with the job, but there are three magazine reporters that have been constantly following me lately. Sometimes they're asking reasonable questions, looking for good quotes, and trying to get me to pose for pictures, but other times they're obviously trying to get me to say something really stupid or to get a photo of me in an embarrassing-looking pose, and it's bothering me more than usual for some reason. That's why I'm planning to enjoy as much of the cruise as I can from right here in our suite."

Our conversation having been fairly superficial so far, I decided it was time to push things a bit. "I did learn a few more things just before we sailed." Alicia looked at me expectantly, while Eddie seemed to find something interesting to watch on the horizon.

"When I called my boss in Ottawa just before we sailed, he told me that the Commissioner is under pressure from our Department of External Affairs to take a hand in looking after your security. Now that's very interesting because it's so unusual."

The room went silent.

"My boss had one more bit of interesting news. He said that they'd done some quiet checking with the cruise line and Canada Customs, and it turns out that your names on the passenger list don't match those on your passports. Your diplomatic passports, that is, from the Principality of Montenia."

While I tried to maintain an expression of polite interest, no one said anything for a moment. Alicia had turned white as a sheet, while Eddie continued to be fascinated with something on the horizon.

Finally, he gave a sigh and said "OK, I guess there's not much point in trying to deny it. We really did meet on the French Riveria like we said. I had taken a ferry from Cannes to a little island called *Île Sainte-Marguerite*. It's pretty small and quiet – no cars, even. I was taking a brief vacation and I wanted somewhere quiet so I picked a quiet beach on the shore that was directly across from the mainland." He looked at Alicia, who picked up the story.

"A friend and I had gone to the same island for the same reason and ended up on the same beach. We'd noticed someone sunbathing over to one side but didn't really think anything of it. When we got too hot from the sun, we went for a swim. I'm not a strong swimmer, and I must have gone further out than I should have because when I got a severe cramp all the way up one side, I found that I couldn't touch bottom with my other leg. I yelled to my friend and did my best to tread water, but I mostly just thrashed around. My friend came over to help, but she's an even weaker swimmer than I am and her attempts to help just ended up getting my head dunked under the water. After getting dunked a few times, I was having trouble getting enough air in, and I think it must have been then that my friend began yelling for help."

"So, I'd been lying back in the sun," said Eddie, resuming the narrative. "I was probably even half-asleep when I heard a woman yell out. I could see two sets of heads and shoulders out in the water. One person started thrashing around with one arm like she was trying to tread water but having some kind of trouble. Then I heard another woman's voice yelling, and the second person I could see seemed to be trying to help the first, but apparently not very successfully as they both started splashing around. Then the second woman started yelling for help.

"I got up, ran into the water and swum out. When I reached them the second woman said that the first had a cramp and needed help. When I was able to get the first woman's attention, I told her I would come around behind her and take her back to shore. Considering she was sputtering and gasping a lot, I was impressed that she let me come around behind and put my hands on her chin, but she did. That made it easy for me to do a backstroke to the shore, dragging her – also on her back - with me.

"When we were ashore and got acquainted, it was Alicia's friend that informed me I was in the presence of a world-famous fashion model. For my part, I introduced myself as Eddie and explained that I was a vacationing cowboy from Montana, which was true at the time." Eddie laughed rather ruefully. "That was all Alicia's friend needed to know. She was on the hunt for a rich playboy type and essentially ignored me after that, but Alicia was different. We talked a bit, then arranged to meet for dinner later. Her friend didn't join us for that, and we talked some more and never seemed to run out of things to talk about – we still haven't, in fact. Anyway, we met often over the next few days, then continued a long-distance relationship."

"We'd still meet in-person when we could," continued Alicia. "Usually, it would involve Eddie travelling to wherever I was working and then we'd manage a day or two together.... I could never figure out how he could afford to travel so much, especially when it so often involved flying to far-off and expensive places. That was until he proposed." She looked at him and smiled.

"Yes, well, I'd been thinking about it a lot, and we'd even talked around the topic in general terms. When I couldn't stand it any more, I picked what I thought would be a romantic place and time...."

"Bullshit," Alicia exclaimed, then looked at Don and I. "We were having lunch in a sidewalk café, and he just blurted it out. We were talking about something unimportant, and right in the middle of it he stopped and asked if I would marry him."

"What'd you say?" I asked.

"I said that it was about time, because I'd just about given up hope, and yes. That's when he held up his hand and said there was a problem."

"I told her that before we took things any further, there was something she needed to know about me. Something that I normally kept hidden from almost everyone."

"I thought, axe-murder? Safe-cracker? Bigamist?" said Alicia.

"No," continued Eddie, "it was worse than that. I admitted that the Edward Montenario that sat before her was not actually American, but a citizen of the Principality of Montenia. That, plus that fact that the reason my last name bears such a strong resemblance to the name of my country is that my father is the Sovereign Prince of Monteria."

Alicia giggled, "You wouldn't guess it to look at him, would you?"

"I don't know," I said, looking him up and down. "Tidy-up his hair and put him in a formal military uniform, and I think he could look quite regal."

Eddie stood and gave me a formal bow, then straightened-up, looked at Alicia and stuck his tongue out.

"So, you're a member of the royal family but you obviously go to some lengths to hide that fact?" I asked.

"Yes. You see, I'm sort of a 'royal' in name only. As the youngest of three brothers, it's the oldest that is the heir to the throne, and the second-oldest that you might call 'the spare.' That means both my brothers have to prepare for the possibility of eventually succeeding my father. Assuming that my oldest brother assumes the throne, then there will still be a full life of royal duties for my other brother to look forward to, but not me. I don't have to prepare; I don't have to appear in public; I don't have to exist." He held up a hand. "That sounds like a complaint, but I assure you that it isn't. I don't want the royal life, I don't want to be in the public eye, and this way I get to do whatever I want, which is what I've been doing. In fact, I consider myself the luckiest of the family."

"Please forgive me for asking," said Don, "but where is Montenia?"

"Oh, well, it's not surprising you aren't familiar with it, although most Europeans are. We're a small country that's tucked in between France, Switzerland, and Italy. It's not far from Geneva, which you'll recall is what I told you earlier in terms of where I grew up. If you ranked the fifty or so European countries by size, then Montenia would be the 43rd largest at about 1,300 km^2 or, as the Americans would say, 500 square miles. That is, smaller than Luxembourg but twice the size of the Principality of Andorra.

"It's been governed by a constitutional monarchy since 1919, with the Sovereign Prince of Montenia, currently my father, as head of state. There is a Prime Minister, that's the head of executive government, and he or she is appointed by the Sovereign Prince from the members of the National Council, who in turn are elected by the people in each region. All legislation requires the approval of the National Council. Municipal affairs are managed by elected mayors who are, usually, non-partisan."

"Sounds interesting," Don acknowledged. "So, you're basically trying to keep a low profile then?"

"Yes. I'm sorry to put you two to all this trouble. It seems like there really isn't a threat to Alicia, and the only reason your diplomatic people are concerned is probably because my father has been quite ill lately. It looks like he's recovering, slowly, but people start getting nervous when the monarch gets ill."

"Well, thank you for telling us what's really going on," I said. "This whole thing has gotten us on a cruise ship for the first time, for free yet, and if nothing sinister happens over the next few days we'll just try to relax and go with the flow. Right Don?"

"I'm feeling pretty relaxed already," said Don, stretching out his legs and looking comfortable, but I knew it was an act.

Everyone laughed and we shifted to lighter-hearted conversations, but I knew Don better than that. He had a gleam in his eye that suggested he wasn't going off-duty anytime soon.

After chatting with Alicia and Eddie a bit more, we said goodnight and went for a walk with Silver on Deck 3, which ran the entire circumference of the ship. As such, it attracted most of the walkers, joggers, and runners, in addition to those passengers that were simply lounging comfortably in deck chairs and watching it all.

One of these was a grandmotherly-looking woman whose deck chair was positioned next to a bundle of large vertical pipes that ran all the way from deck to deck. It occurred to me that she'd probably chosen that spot precisely for the shelter from breezes that the pipes would afford, while still having an unobstructed view. She was holding knitting needles, and there was a bright-yellow something lying in her lap, but she seemed more focused on observing her surroundings than knitting.

Although I only looked at her for a moment, she noticed, and I was treated to a very bright-eyed look that called for a response.

"Hello," I offered. "I couldn't help noticing your brightly-coloured knitting."

"What do you think?" she asked, holding up a partially completed sweater that looked to be about right for a young toddler.

"I think you must have a grandchild somewhere that has a birthday coming up. Unless you're so well organized that you make your Christmas presents well ahead of time."

"Right the first time, and that birthday is coming up soon so I have to get this finished before the cruise ends. No rest for the wicked[21], that's me."

I smiled, raised my left hand in a friendly wave, and we carried on with our walk.

It was great to be able to see the views on each side of the ship, plus fore and aft, as we walked. Following our walk, Don left Silver and I sitting out on the verandah of our suite while he went off to try his luck at the casino.

***

Don's narrative begins:

As I left our suite and was heading aft, I glanced to my right and noticed two boys and a girl playing in the short passageway that connected the two main passageways that ran the length of the ship, one on each side. I'd seen one or more of these kids in that same space every time Alex and I had gone into or out of our suite, and it occurred to me that I had yet to see it vacant, which was odd. Odd enough to investigate, so I stopped, reversed course, and went back to talk to them. They looked to be eleven or twelve years old.

"Hi there, what are you up to?" I asked when I reached them.

"Just playing," one of the boys said. I could see that they were playing the board game *Clue*, which is a murder-mystery game.

"Sounds like fun, but you know there's a games room for kids and teenagers up on Deck 9, don't you?"

"Course," said the same boy that had spoken before and seemed to be the group's spokesperson, "but it's always full of teenagers!" He said this in the same tone of voice that he might have used to refer to bitter enemies, or perhaps bullies, or even murderers. I guessed from this that the teenagers had made the younger kids feel less than welcome.

"Ahhh. So, you needed to find some space just for yourselves then."

Three heads nodded in agreement.

"I see from the box that you're playing *Clue*. Do you like mysteries?"

The three heads nodded again.

"I don't suppose that you're playing it for real too, are you?"

Three guilty looks. *Aha*, I thought.

"You wouldn't, for example, be watching that stateroom door in the other passageway, would you? The one you can see very clearly from right where you happen to be playing?"

All three of them paled, and the two quiet ones stared fixedly at the deck.

"Yes. I thought so," I said, in as friendly a manner as I could. "Did someone threaten you into doing this, or are they paying you?"

"They're paying us!" said the quieter boy, speaking up for the first time, and in an awed tone of voice.

"Shut up, you idiot!" said the spokesperson.

"Look," I said, "it's OK. If you tell me about it, I promise not to tell your parents, or the ship's Captain, or even to try and stop you. You see, I'm working on a real-life mystery myself."

"You and that police lady?" said the spokesperson, "the one with the big wolf?"

"Yes, with the police lady. And that isn't a wolf, he's an Alaskan Malamute – like the dogs that pull dogsleds up north – and he's very smart. In fact, he's a police dog."

"Yeah. I saw him wearing a jacket that said 'Police' on it."

"You're very observant," I congratulated him. "I'm working with her too, see…" I showed them my military police ID. Each one of them gave it a close look and I was rewarded with three sets of eyes the size of saucers.

"We're here on a secret mission. I can't tell you what it is right now, but if you agree to help us, I promise to tell you all about it before the cruise is over. What do you say? Deal?"

They looked at each other for a moment, then the spokesperson said "You promise not to tell on us?"

"I give you my word as an officer in the Canadian Armed Forces," I said, very seriously, "and later, if you give me permission, I will tell your parents what a great job you did helping us out."

"OK then. A man promised us money if we'd watch that stateroom and go tell him when the woman comes out of it."

"Yes, I thought it must be something like that. How much?"

"He said two dollars every time she goes out and another two dollars if we can also tell him where she went."

My eyebrows went up and I smiled. "That's not bad. How much have you made so far?"

"Nothing," the spokesperson said indignantly. "They haven't left their stateroom at all since we started watching."

I chuckled. "OK. Let me make you a new deal. You agree that you should help the police?"

Three heads nodded yes.

"And you want to help solve a real-life mystery?"

Three heads nodded yes.

"All right then. On top of our original deal, I'll pay you another two dollars if every time you deliver a message to this man, one of you comes and delivers the same message to me as well. You can keep the money they pay you as well. OK?"

Three heads, carrying big smiles, nodded yes.

"OK. We have a deal. Let's shake hands and tell me your names. My name is Don, like it says on my ID."

"Tommy," said the spokesperson, Tommy Jones."

"Frankie," said the girl.

"Bobby," said the quieter boy.

"Fine. It's nice to meet you all. Now then, there's one more thing. You know what stateroom I'm in, but where were you supposed to find the man who's paying you to deliver the sighting messages?"

They gave me the number of a stateroom on Deck 1, the lowest of the passenger-accessible decks, and I went off in search of Chief Harris to find out who was in the indicated stateroom. As I suspected, it turned out to be one of the three reporter types that Alicia had said were always following her around. According to Chief Harris, they had boarded the ship in Boston and had begun pestering Alicia for comments and to pose for their cameras well before she had even boarded the ship. Since then, and made conspicuous by their 35mm cameras with large, professional strobe flashes, they had been lurking around the ship hoping to pounce on her whenever she left her stateroom. This particular reporter was an American man, travelling alone, named Jeremy Masters, and carried an international press card identifying him as a magazine journalist/photographer. The Chief also showed me his photograph. At the security checkpoint, Alex and I, and everyone else boarding the ship, had had to pose for a polaroid photo that the security people kept on file, and cross-referenced by name and stateroom number.

I recognized the man in the photo, as I had noticed the three reporters myself when Alex and I had been walking with Silver. Physically, they were a study in contrasts. One was tall and thin, with the kind of thin, pencil moustache that used to be popular with Hollywood actors. Another of the three was short and heavyset, with a wide, sunburned face, a cauliflower ear[22], and bushy eyebrows. Other than his height, it looked like he could have been a professional boxer. The third man, whom I now knew to be Jeremy Masters, was of medium height and build, very clean-cut, and expensively dressed. He had the look of a youngish, but successful, businessman or a rising politician.

The ship's casino wasn't large, but it had room for quite a few slot machines and an oval arrangement that included a roulette wheel and four blackjack tables. When I arrived, I discovered that the three photojournalists were sitting together at one of the blackjack tables. The right-hand seat facing the dealer, my favourite, was empty so I took it. This had the advantage of letting me see everyone's faces at the table, which didn't matter in terms of the game, but it allowed me to watch the expressions on the faces of the three I was most interested in.

Not surprisingly, some of the talk at the table was about our late departure.

"Anyone hear why we were so late sailing?"

"I heard they held the ship for some late passengers?"

"That's right. I saw a couple get on at the last minute, with a couple of crew members carrying their bags up the gangway behind them, instead of the way they usually load them."

"I heard there was a bomb scare and a policewoman with a dog came to search the ship."

"That's right," said Masters, "I saw them come aboard. That police dog looked like a wolf. I wouldn't want to run into him alone on a dark night!"

"Obviously, they didn't find anything or they wouldn't have let us back on the ship," said 'moustache man.' "The firm would never take the risk." He spoke with a distinctly upper-class-British accent and manner, which seemed somehow out of place for a fashion-magazine photojournalist.

"Too bad," said 'boxer man,' "a nice little explosion would have given us something to shoot and write about, unlike our precious fashion model." He had a baritone voice and spoke in a growly manner that remined me of an old-type sports broadcaster.

"What're you worried about, Wally?" said Masters. "Your magazine is paying for the cruise, and if you don't get any good shots or a story, you won't be doing any worse than the rest of us."

"Maybe so. At least we get to drink and play cards," he growled.

Conversation died out as the dealer finished shuffling the cards and began dealing out the first hands of a new shoe[23]. While my habit was to start at the minimum bet and then progressively wager more as long as I was winning, these three tended to bet high regardless of whether they were winning or losing, while also placing side bets on each others' hands. This meant that when they won, they won more money, but that a lot of money flowed out when they lost which, of course, happened the most often.

During the card-play, their comments were mostly about the cards. For example, it is common in blackjack to say something like 'nice hit' when a dealt card gives them a powerful hand, and even more common to complain when the dealer gets a powerful hand that overrides the table. Similarly, there was a considerable amount of pleading with the dealer to 'give us a break' and lose more often, all the while knowing full well that the dealer had no decision-making options in the game at all and was simply following the rules of play.

When it was time for the dealer to shuffle the cards, however, the men's conversations turned back to business. From their comments, I learned that all three were trying to get candid photos of Alicia and hoping to induce or trap her into revealing personal details about herself, all in the interest of writing a story about the day-to-day life she leads. They had apparently pounced on her when she and Eddie had been forced to get off the ship like everyone else, and then again when everyone was allowed to reboard, but they hadn't scored much in the way of candid comments or photos. Needless to say, if she remained in her stateroom for the rest of the cruise there wouldn't be any more opportunities until Montréal, our final destination.

"Be too bad if a fire alarm went off on Deck 7 in the middle of the night," growled Wally.

"Yes, and it would serve you right if you got caught and were thrown off the ship," said 'moustache man.'

"What's your idea then, Richard?" asked Masters, looking at 'moustache man.'

"I've secured a seat at the captain's table for dinner every night. That's where they'll be seated if they ever decide to try the main dining room, and I'll be able to listen-in at the table and try to steer the discussions into interesting directions."

"Has it worked?"

"Not as of yet, but we've three more nights and they're bound to tire of eating in their stateroom eventually."

"Hey, that's pretty smart," said Wally. "How about you, Jeremy. What's your angle?"

"Me?" replied Masters, "There's still time. I'll come up with something." He obviously had no intention of sharing with his colleagues the deal he'd made with the three kids.

As the evening, and the gambling, went on, it seemed that the three men didn't know each other well and had simply discovered that they were each on the trip for the same purpose, and that each of them, while being superficially friendly with the others, was working independently. After a few hours, Jeremy Masters was holding his own, and seemed to have roughly the same number of chips as when he'd started. The man named Richard, who I'd initially categorized as 'moustache man,' seemed to have lost about half of his original stake, while Wally, 'the boxer man,' had been wiped out and was frequently going back to his wallet for more money so he could stay in the game. For my part, I'd won for a while, lost for a while, and was finally back to about where I'd started. Judging that I'd learned about as much as I could by listening at the table, it seemed like a good time to leave, so I got up, wished everyone at the table good luck, and left the casino.

I'd no sooner exited the casino than I spotted Chief Harris walking towards me.

"Learn anything?" he asked, waving me to a quiet table in the adjacent piano bar.

I hadn't noticed him in the casino before, having been focused on the game and the three photojournalists, but he'd obviously spotted me and correctly deduced what I'd been up to.

"Not much," I replied, in answer to his question, and related my observations.

"Think any of them pose a threat?"

"Hard to say. If so, then I suspect it's just one of them acting alone and using a pretty noticeable cover. Jeremy Masters comes across a slick businessman-type. The tall one with the pencil moustache...."

"Richard Jolliffe. His Press Card identifies him as a photojournalist for *British Vogue* magazine. When I figured out what you were up to, I went and looked up the other two men in our files."

"Thank you. So. Richard Jolliffe then, is almost a stereotype of the old British upper-class, Eton and Oxford type, which seems out of place for a photojournalist. Such a jarring contrast is hardly inconspicuous, and I can't decide whether he's the real thing or is running a ruse that's so hopelessly amateurish that it's really quite clever."

"And the third?"

"Right. Wally...."

"Yes. Walter Dolan. According to his Press Card, he's a photojournalist for *Elle* magazine."

"They call him Wally. It's the same thing with him. He comes across as a former boxer with the manner of an old-time sportscaster. In his case, he can't help but look conspicuous. As far as the personality goes, he's either the genuine article or a good actor."

"That one, I was able to get some background on. Walter Dolan was a pretty good boxer in his day, but only got as far as working as a sparring partner for a professional boxer. He turned that into a steady job as a sports reporter and worked, for a while, as a radio announcer for boxing match broadcasts. From there he shifted to the fashion magazine, where he has a reputation for being the persistent, steady-grinder type that eventually gets his story, and photos to match."

"That's pretty impressive," I whistled, referring to the background the Chief had been able to dig up on short notice.

He nodded, accepting the compliment. "On him, I got lucky. Not so the other two. The people I was able to reach quickly gave me consistent stories about Dolan but had never heard of either Masters or Jolliffe. I think we'll want to keep an eye on those two."

I agreed and said goodnight.

When I returned to our stateroom, I was just about to fill Alex in on my evening's activities when there was a knock on the door. It was Tommy Jones, the unofficial leader of the kids I'd met in the passageway.

"Hi there Tommy," I said.

"You said to tell you if the lady next door went out, right?"

"Right."

"Well, she and her husband went out a few minutes ago. They're walking on Deck 3."

"Aha, and did you go report this to the man on Deck 1?"

"No. He's in the casino. I tried to go in there. I pretended that I was just going in to be with my parents, but a guy in a black tuxedo came up, asked to see my room card. Then he told me I wasn't old enough to go in there and kicked me out.... But you'll still pay us, right?" he said, hopefully.

"Right you are," I said, reaching for my wallet and extracting two Canadian-dollar bills, which I passed over. "Good work," I said, as he smiled and disappeared.

"Feel like a stroll before bed?' I asked Alex, after I'd closed the door.

"Sure, what was that all about?"

"Come on and I'll tell you on the way. Alicia and Eddie have gone for a walk. I think it might be worth checking to see if they're being followed."

Along with Silver, we made our way to Deck 3, the one that was best suited to walking around the full circumference of the ship. When we arrived, we could just see Alicia and Eddie walking arm-in-arm, with their backs to us, along the deck. That made it easy for us to fall in behind them, and we stayed as far back as we could without losing sight of them. As we walked, I told Alex about my meeting with the three children, who I referred to as my 'Baker Street Irregulars[24].' Then I filled her in on my evening in the casino and my chat with Chief Harris.

"You've been busy," she noted.

"All part of the service," I agreed.

Maintaining our distance from Alicia and Eddie, we strolled all the way around the ship without spotting anything unusual, and I was just beginning to apologize for wasting our time when Silver's ears stiffened, pointed forward, and he began a low but persistent growling.

Alex told Silver to be quiet and we increased our pace somewhat, while trying to see what was worrying Silver. As we closed the gap between ourselves and the Avons, as I still thought of them, it eventually became clear that Silver was closely watching a shadowy figure ahead of us. The figure was dressed in sweatpants and a kangaroo jacket[25] with the hood up and seemed to be hunched over somewhat. Between the colouring of the clothes and the evening twilight having dissipated, we couldn't really make out much in the way of details, except that the figure seemed to be trying to be inconspicuous.

As we slowed our pace a bit, in an attempt to observe without being observed, the figure occasionally disappeared from our sight – possibly by darting into one of the many doorways leading to the interior of the ship – only to reappear later as we all continued to walk along the deck. Silver, for his part, always seemed to know where the figure was, and all we had to do was follow the direction indicated by his upright ears and fixed stare, as he continued to emit low growls from far back in his throat.

We went on like this for almost an entire length of the ship, but just before the figure reached an unusually well-lit section of the deck, it disappeared. When we reached the last point at which we'd seen the figure there was a doorway that someone had wedged open, which was against the ship's rules, and beyond that a stairway leading both up and down. When we entered the stairway, we couldn't hear any sounds of footsteps, and Silver had relaxed and ceased his growling.

"If you go back to following Alicia, I'll go take a look in the casino. OK?"

Alex nodded, understanding what I meant, and as they went back out on deck, I ran up the stairs heading for the casino, which was two decks up. Decelerating quickly as I approached the casino, I did my best to calm my breathing and nonchalantly stroll in. There, at the same table as before, were the same three photojournalists, gambling away with the dealer's shoe still half full and looking for all the world like they hadn't moved in quite a while, certainly not in the previous few minutes.

Someone else on the ship was following the Avons.

Laurie Schramm

5 IN THE GULF

Alex's narrative resumes:

We caught up with the Avons when they returned to their stateroom, and told them about their mysterious follower.

"Could it have been one of the photojournalists that are on the ship hoping to corner Alicia?" asked Eddie.

"I had the same thought," answered Don, "and I went straight to the casino, where I found all three of them busily gambling. It had to have been someone else."

"One of the two people that boarded late then?"

"Possibly," I put in. "We just don't know."

"Should I be worried?" asked Alicia, somewhat rhetorically, as she sounded worried.

"We don't know that this person was up to no good, it's just that they were acting suspiciously. We'll continue to keep an eye out," I said. "One thing's for sure. Silver will let us know if we get close to the same person again, even if they've changed their clothing and appearance."

"Well, that's something," said Eddie, pouncing on any small bit of encouraging news for his wife's sake. "What should we do now?"

I didn't have anything very specific to suggest at that point. "I'd say just do whatever you would have been doing anyway, but be alert, trust your instincts, and maybe let us know next time one or both of you goes somewhere on the ship. One of us will come along but stay well behind you."

Don nodded his agreement.

Both Eddie and Alicia agreed to this and thanked us, after which we left them to turn in for the night and returned to our own stateroom.

"What do you really think?" asked Don when he and I were alone.

"I don't know," I mused. "Everything's contradictory so far and nothing makes much sense. I guess my main thought is that we're missing something. That there's something else going on that does make sense, but I don't know what it is."

"Well, we have a sea day tomorrow, so there won't be any more passengers coming on board, and I don't think Alicia and Eddie will stray far from their stateroom for a while."

Thursday, May 13, 1982
Cruising the Gulf of St. Lawrence

On cruises, a 'Sea Day' means that the whole day is spent at sea, without stopping at any ports. In our case, Don and I mostly stuck to our stateroom, out on the verandah enjoying the sea air and the views.

We did, however, go for morning and evening walks on Deck 3's promenade walkway that circumnavigated the ship, partly in hopes that Silver might spot and/or smell the new shadow we'd seen following Alicia and Eddie. Anytime we left our stateroom, Don let the 'Baker Street Irregulars' know where we were going. This was made easy by the fact that there always seemed to be at least one of them loitering around within view of the Avons' stateroom.

It was interesting to see people's reactions to Silver when we conducted these walks. Of the people that noticed the somewhat unusual sight of a dog on a cruise ship, there was a range of reactions including stares, curiosity, and mutterings like 'How come they get to bring a dog aboard?' 'Must be some kind of service dog,' and the like.

When we were stationary, like sitting outside in deck chairs, or inside in a lounge or coffee bar, we'd have people come up and ask. For those that seemed genuinely interested (and polite), we generally explained that he was a police service dog. This of course, caused most people to instinctively look toward Don, assuming that he must be the police officer. It didn't bother me, much, as I'd had enough years in the nontraditional role of policewoman to have learned to just let such things wash over me. (Well, most of the time at least.)

I say that, but it happened so many times that I was just on the verge of becoming irritated, when the exception occurred. We'd decided to sit down in a couple of deck chairs on Deck 3 to just relax and watch the passengers and the distant scenery go by, and there happened to be two empty chairs right next to the knitting, grandmotherly-looking woman that we'd met the previous evening.

"Hello! We meet again," I said, taking the chair beside her. "My name's Alex, this is my husband Don, and this is our friend Silver."

"It's nice to meet you again," she said pleasantly. "My name is Marie O'Dwyer." The she looked rather shrewdly at Don and I in turn, and pronounced: "Newlyweds – am I right?"

That caught us both off guard.

"Yes," I said, surprised. "Is it that obvious?"

"Perhaps not," she replied, "But I've noticed the pair of you before and you have a certain mutual attentiveness about you. There's something else, too but I can't put my finger on it. I've known lots of newlyweds in my time, and seeing you two brings those memories back."

"Well, whatever it is, you've got us pegged. We're on our honeymoon and this is our very first cruise."

"Me too." Then she chuckled. "My first cruise that is, not the honeymoon part, although I haven't forgotten my honeymoon by any means." She sighed then, and seemed to lapse, possibly into memories from the past, I imagined.

After a few minutes, she seemed to rouse from her reverie and turned towards me again. "Do you mind if I ask you another question?"

"No," I said, "Not at all."

"Well, I was just wondering which police force you are part of."

Caught off guard for the second time, I blinked for a moment, then found my tongue and asked a question of my own. "What makes you think I'm a police officer?"

"Well, I hope you don't mind, but I love dogs and of course I've seen you three walking around the ship before, and it started me wondering about...."

"Silver," I put in.

"Thank you. Yes, Silver. Well, he's a very handsome dog."

Silver raised his head at that point and gave her a piercing look of his own.

"It was obvious that he must be some kind of service dog," Marie continued, "so then I was wondering for which of you he or she was working. Then I realized it had to be you."

"Yes, you're right again, but why?"

She laughed. "He watches you constantly. Almost as much as your new husband Don does. When Silver gets up and moves around, he always comes back and sits closest to you. If you get up to go somewhere, even if it's only for a few moments, it's you he keeps an eye on. Same thing if you change direction while you're walking. He isn't always right beside you, but he always knows exactly where you are."

"You're very observant," I congratulated her, "but what makes you think I'm a policewoman?"

"I don't know, exactly," she said, with a puzzled frown. "In the first place, you don't seem like a person that needs a conventional service dog, but I can easily imagine you being with a police dog. My late husband was a policeman, so I've met many others in my time, and there's just something about your manner that reminds me of my husband and his friends. Maybe it's because while Silver is always watching you, you're always watching everyone else.… Oh, I don't mean that you're staring at people, or that it's obvious, but it's like you're maintaining a constant awareness of everyone else around you. Don's doing it too, but not so much. Now you Don…, you look like the leading man from a Hollywood movie but, if I had to guess, I'd say you have a distinctly military bearing about you."

"Guilty as charged," said Don with a smile, "and thank you for the compliment but I don't think I'd be a good enough actor to get into the movies."

"To answer your first question Marie, yes, I'm with the RCMP, Silver is a police-service dog, and he and I are partners… and friends. We've been together for 7 years now."

"A woman Mountie. How exciting! Are there many of you? Women Mounties I mean?"

"Yes and no. The Force has been training women officers since 1974, and there are about 350 of us now, but that's still only 2.5% of the total force[26] so, if you're looking for equality, we have a long way to go yet."

Our conversation shifted then, to women in nontraditional roles, and then to other things, and then we had to take our leave. After rising and saying that we'd enjoying meeting her, we moved off along the deck.

There was one more canine incident that day, but it didn't involve Silver. At lunchtime, Don, Silver, and I were sitting outside on our verandah when we heard the sounds of barking, followed by a huge crash, and followed in turn by several smaller crashes; all coming from the Avons' verandah next door. The latter crashes had sounded like glass breaking.

Naturally, we rushed over to the Avons' stateroom to see if anyone needed help. Their door being propped open, we were able to walk right in, where we were greeted by the sight of one of the crew down on hands and knees picking up pieces of broken glasses and plateware. Also on the floor was a large serving platter and the remains of what would have been the Avons' lunch.

Alicia was protectively holding Mitzi, their Pekingese, in her arms looking upset, while Eddie was clearly trying, somewhat unsuccessfully, to keep a straight face.

Apparently, Mitzi, possibly misled by the huge serving tray, had decided the crew member was a threat and got under the poor man's feet while positioning to take a bite out of his ankle. When he had gathered everything up and passed us on his way out the door, I was close enough to hear him mutter a few unprintable things about the evils of allowing dogs on cruise ships!

Nothing else unusual happened during the day, but we were surprised in the evening when we learned that Alicia and Eddie had accepted the captain's invitation to join him at his table in the formal dining room for dinner that night. It was actually a double surprise because, not only were Don and I invited as well, but guessing that we would not have brought dinner outfits, much less formal attire with us the Purser had included a note explaining where to go on the ship to get dinner-attire rentals, and that if we presented his note to the attendant, ours would be compliments of the captain and crew. Judging that being able to keep an eye on the Avons was important, we took advantage of their gracious offer. In the end, Don was fitted out with a dark suit, while I got a full-length black skirt with a nice, ivory-coloured blouse.

As we approached our table for dinner that evening, Don leaned over and said, *sotto voce* "The tall, slender man with the pencil moustache is Richard Jolliffe, one of the three photojournalists. He specifically arranged to sit at the captain's table each night in hopes that Alicia Avon would show up. This is going to be his lucky night."

I looked at Joliffe with interest. He wasn't just dressed in dinner attire; he wore a very elegant and expensive-looking tuxedo. We had just sat down and introduced ourselves, when Alicia and Eddie appeared and did the same. During the introductions, Joliffe explained that he was on assignment, working for *British Vogue* magazine, and very politely asked whether he could take a picture of Alicia with the Captain if he promised to put his camera away after that and not disrupt their dinner any further after that. His diplomatic approach worked, and Alicia and the Captain got up and posed together for the camera.

As the dinner went on, the topics of conversation around the table varied, as they often do in such circumstances and it was very enjoyable. Whatever else he might be, I observed that Joliffe demonstrated though his mannerisms and his conversation that he had the ability to play the diplomat role very well. In fact, he was so well behaved, and such an interesting conversationalist, during dinner that when a ship's photographer arrived seeking to take pictures of each couple, Alicia herself offered that Joliffe might as well take one of his own at the same time, which he did.

It wasn't all dining and conversation for Don and I of course, and Chief Harris was still on the job as well. While Don and I were keeping an eye on Alicia and Eddie, and the other guests at the captain's table, so was Chief Harris. Normally, around the ship, it was hard for him to be inconspicuous because he was always dressed completely in white, from shirt, belt and pants, to shoes, but he had the knack of being hard to spot when he wanted. At the dinner, for example, I happened to glance over to a quiet corner of the dining room and there he was, unobtrusively standing away from most people's line of sight, motionless yet observing, his facial expression giving nothing away. It was quite impressive. *I bet he was very successful at Scotland Yard*, and *I wouldn't want to play poker against him*, I thought to myself.

Following the dinner, Alicia and Eddie joined Don, Silver, and I in another of our walks around the promenade deck which was beautiful, with lights twinkling on the distant shorelines and a warm sea breeze. This arrangement made it impossible for us to keep much of an eye out for anyone following us, but I was certain that Chief Harris or one of his security staff would not be far away.

On our first loop of the deck, Don and I said hi to Marie, who was sitting in her usual spot, still with the same unfinished knitting in her lap.

When we had moved past and were out of her hearing, Don said quietly, "She'll not have missed who were walking with. What do you want to bet she's figured out we're working undercover here too?"

"Oh no. I won't take that bet," I replied. "If everyone was like her, we'd never be able to work anywhere undercover again! Maybe we should put her on the payroll too, along with your Baker-Street Irregulars."

The ship had begun to make its way down the St. Laurence River, and the entertainment director's evening broadcast over the ship's intercom included the suggestion that passengers willing to get up early in the morning might be rewarded with whale sightings as we approached the communities of Tadoussac, to starboard, and Rivière-du-Loup, to port. Near Tadoussac, he said, the Saguenay River flows into the St. Lawrence, and is the site of the Saguenay – St. Lawrence Marine Park, one of the best places in Canada to watch for whales.

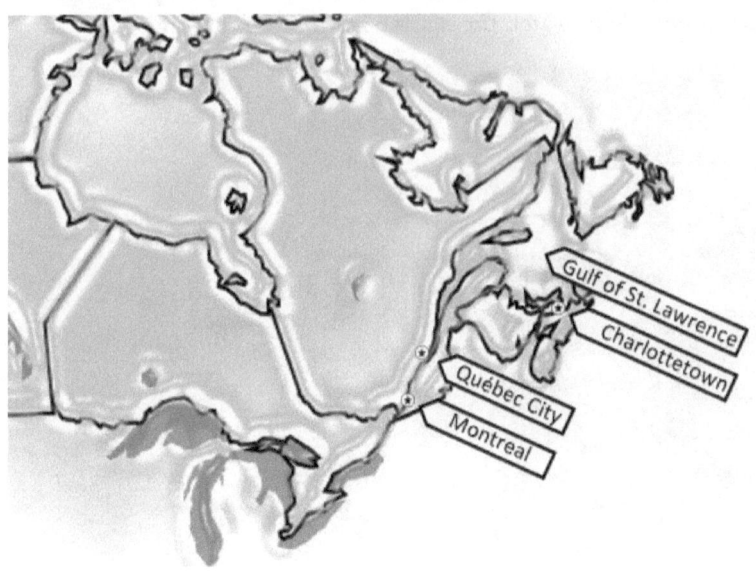

Friday, May 14, 1982
Approaching Québec City, QC

Don and I made the effort to get up at 5 am so we could watch for whales. Silver, for his part, decided it was too early for him and remained in our stateroom, snoozing, while Don and I made coffee and sat out on our verandah. Once settled, I read out several sections from a guide the ship had placed in our room. From it, I learned that some beluga whales and harbour seals live year-round in the estuary, and that many other species of whales, seals, and even birds travel thousands of kilometres to feed in this area, with the best viewing months being May through October. Perfect timing for us.

As we approached the Saguenay, we were rewarded with several seal sightings, although the distance was too great for us to judge whether they were Harbour or Grey seals.

For quite a while, we watched without success for whales, and then, just as we were passing the mouth of the tributary, we spotted a group of small, bright white whales: Belugas! A bit further along, we were rewarded with the sight of two whales with large dorsal fins at the surface. These appeared to be Minke whales. After that, we saw a few more seals, what might have been a couple of porpoises, but there had been no signs of really large whale species, like Fin or Blue whales. That was OK, it had been worth getting up early to have been able to watch the marine life that we did see.

A few hours later, it seemed like time to take Silver for a walk. Eddie and Alicia had left us a phone message saying that they planned to sleep-in that morning but would be up in time for the ship's docking in Québec City, so we went out on our own. When we left our stateroom, I glanced down the short passageway that connected to the port side of the ship and was surprised to see Marie O'Dwyer sitting on the deck playing some kind of card game with three children.

Noticing my glance, Don chuckled and said, "I see that Marie has met my Baker-Street-Irregulars. Come and I'll introduce you."

"Good morning, Marie," we both said, as we approached, then Don added, "These are three young people that have been helping me: Tommy, Bobby, and Frankie," pointing to each in turn.

"It's nice to meet you," I said. "My name is Alex and this is Silver."

"He's a real police dog!" Tommy said to his two colleagues, sounding very knowledgeable.

"We know that, you idiot," retorted Frankie.

As everyone was chuckling, I asked them what they were playing.

"Crazy Eights," came a chorus from all three.

Don added, "I see that you're corrupting these young people this morning Marie," looking pointedly at the small piles of nickels, dimes, and quarters beside each of the children, and the cloth bag on the floor by Marie that he correctly assumed contained a larger supply of loose change.

"Corrupting is such a strong word," said Marie, reprovingly. "I'm entertaining them and teaching them at the same time."

"She gives us the money to play with," said Bobby, "and when we're done, she gives it all back to us too – even if we lose!"

"Well, I guess we can't run you in for illegal gambling then," said Don with a grin.

"It's better than that," said Marie, adopting a superior look and tone of voice: "Give something, however small, to the one in need. For it is not small to one who has nothing[27]."

"Hmmm. Remind me not to get into a debate with you," said Don as we turned to head out for our walk.

"Next, she's promised to teach us how to play Blackjack" echoed Bobby's words as we walked down the passageway.

After a peaceful walk outside, we returned to our stateroom and basically just shifted to its verandah, from which we were in time to watch the ship's approach and docking at Québec City. Once again, being on the starboard side of the ship meant that we were greeted with a view of the majestic Château Frontenac, high up on the promontory of Québec, and situated within the fortress walls of Old Québec's Upper Town.

The Château Frontenac is one of Canada's 'grand railway hotels,' most of which were built across the country by either the Canadian Pacific Railway or the Canadian National Railway between about 1886 and 1958. I've always loved this hotel because of its location and its architecture, which is called 'Neo-Château' or 'Châteauesque' because it is a Canadianized château style that includes a blend of European baronial and château elements, including the wonderful towers and turrets.

As we disembarked the ship along with the Avons, and followed closely by the three photojournalists, we were met by a security detail that had arrived to watch over the Avons for the day. This was comprised of just two people, a sergeant and a constable, and was clearly not full security, making it obvious that HQ wasn't convinced there was a serious threat but had to do something. As the Avons walked off, with their security detail following behind, and the photojournalists following them Don, Silver, and I were temporarily freed of responsibility, so it seemed like the ideal time to do some sightseeing. This would be a day to explore the Old City!

Founded in the early 17th century, much of the city's historic character has been preserved, making it a notable tourist attraction. Adjacent to the cruise-ship dock is Old Québec's Lower Town, much of which still has cobblestone streets and large stone and heavy wood-beam constructed buildings, most have which have been converted into shops, restaurants and *boutique* hotels. Once we'd walked around this part of the city, we boarded a funicular railway car that took us directly up the side of the promontory of Québec, and over the massive walls of the old fortress.

At the top lie numerous attractions, all in the shadow of the Château Frontenac and within the walls of the fortress. This includes Old Québec's Upper Town, with everything from hotels and restaurants, to shops and museums, to churches and a 17th century monastery, to *La Citadelle de Québec*, which is still an active Canadian Armed Forces installation. Having explored some of these sights, we stopped at a sidewalk café for lunch, from which we noticed there were horse-drawn carriages taking people on tours. Encouraged by the positive recommendation of our server, we decided to take one of these tours ourselves.

Between our café and the Chateau was a broad, circular plaza that seemed to be the place to engage a carriage. As we walked across the cobblestones, we noticed that Alicia and Eddie must have had the same idea and were boarding a carriage of their own. It was with some amusement, then, that we watched the security detail get their own carriage and follow, then the three photojournalists did the same. The carriages must all have had the same standard tourist route, because once we'd boarded the next available carriage, we found ourselves following the journalists.

The driver of our carriage pointed out the major historic sights as he drove us along, first through the Upper Town and then out, beyond the fort, to the The Battlefields Park, within which is the site of the famous Battle of the Plains of Abraham.

Still out in front of us, highly visible on the plains, and still in their original order, was the procession of three carriages.

"They're not exactly inconspicuous," I commented to Don, as we had Alicia and Eddie looking like tourists out in front, then the carriages with the security detail and photojournalists, none of whom looked in the least like tourists, and then Don, Silver and I bringing up the rear. I'd brought my camera with me and, deciding that this was a 'keeper' moment, I was able to get a good photo of the three carriages in front of us.

It reminded me, for a moment, of the Keystone Cops from the old-time Hollywood silent movies but, thankfully, we didn't have any slapstick moments, nor any physical threats. So, although we felt that we had to remain vigilant, we were able to enjoy our sightseeing.

Following the carriage tour, it was time to make our way down the hill to Lower Town, as we were supposed to be back onboard by 4 pm for a 5 pm sailing. We weren't in a rush though, so we walked and window-shopped as we went. By the time we reached the ship I could see Alicia and Eddie standing in line waiting to go up the gangway, while their security detail stood discreetly off to one side, watching to make sure they got safely on board. When the sergeant noticed us, I gave him a wave, signalling that we were back to watching over them as well.

Looking at Eddie, I happened to notice him looking back. At

first, I thought he was looking at me but then realized that he was looking at someone, or something, that was behind us. Wondering what it was, but not wanting to look conspicuous, I dropped the small fanny pack that I often used instead of a purse. Reaching down to recover it allowed me to turn and glance behind. The only thing that caught my eye was a passenger waiting in line behind me that I'd never seen before.

With something like 1,400 passengers on the cruise, I had no illusions that I could recognize all, or even most of them, of course, but this one stood out. First, there was his manner of dress, as he wasn't dressed like a typical tourist. He wore an elegant but comfortable-looking mauve suit, with a shirt and tie in complimentary colours. The suit looked unusual to me, and struck me as possibly being a European style. Secondly, there was his manner of standing, which wasn't in the least casual. He didn't look nervous or tense, it was more that he stood erect; stately almost. Possibly a soldier or a diplomat, I thought. Third, he had an elegant-looking ebony or gloss-black cane.

In terms of physical appearance, he had sandy-brown hair that was well-trimmed but not military-short, and was of medium height and slender build. When he walked, it was with a slight limp, which explained why what appeared to be a middle-aged man would need a cane. Curious, I made a mental note to watch for him again when we were aboard the ship.

When we reached the security screening point, Chief Harris was there to greet us, or perhaps I should say, to meet Don.

"A couple of soldiers dropped by to deliver a bag for you Major," he said, addressing Don and motioning for us to join him off to one side. "We've already X-rayed it."

The 'bag' turned out to be a military-style duffel bag bearing a tag with Don's name and rank on it.

When Don opened the duffel and lifted up its main contents, we could see that it contained the working uniform of a Military Police Major.

"Boots and *everything*," said Chief Harris, with a slight emphasis on the word everything.

"You mean… ah yes." Don was feeling around in the bottom of the duffel. "There's a .45 calibre pistol in there too, isn't there?"

"That's what it looks like on the X-ray, ammunition too," said the Chief. "It's OK, but I would have appreciated getting a heads-up in advance about it."

"I'm sorry, Chief. I would have given you a heads-up had I known it was coming, but I didn't. This is as much of a surprise to me as it was to you and your staff.

"You mean...."

"Yes. It means that something new has happened and that someone thinks I might need this stuff. When we get to our stateroom, I'll make two calls. The first will be to my boss. The second will be to you. OK?"

The Chief smiled and nodded. We were on good terms again.

When we reached our stateroom, Don immediately dropped the duffel and went to phone his boss, Rear-Admiral Peter White, head of the Canadian Forces Security Branch, and whom we'd just seen at our wedding a week earlier. Don had called him when we were asked to remain on board the cruise ship in Charlottetown, just like I'd done with my own boss.

I'd gone out on the verandah while Don made his call, but went back inside our suite when I saw him hang up the phone. He looked thoughtful.

"Trouble?" I asked.

"Not exactly, more like worry. Eddie's oldest brother, the Crown Prince, died earlier today in a plane crash."

"Sabotage?"

"I don't know. I don't think anyone knows. The news just broke around Europe, but it hasn't been picked up yet in North America. Apparently, we got the news through our contacts in one of the NATO intelligence agencies. I doubt that your people, or External Affairs even, know about it yet, but I'm sure they will before the day's over."

"Do you think Eddie knows?"

"No idea, but I think I should go and tell him. He'll still have time to make a phone call or two before the lines get disconnected."

Don picked up the phone again and dialed another number.

"Chief? I know why that duffel bag was sent, and I have other news as well. How about meeting us at the Avons' stateroom? Right.

"He'll meet us there," Don said, after hanging up the phone.

The Avons were 'in' when we knocked, and as we followed Eddie into the suite, there standing by the verandah door was the man with the black cane that I'd seen in line behind us when we were lined-up to embark. He had sandy brown hair, was slender and, although he had changed clothes, he was still casually but somehow elegantly dressed.

"It's OK Andreas," he said, "they know who I really am," and he proceeded to introduce Don and I. While he was doing that, Chief Harris had arrived, so he was introduced as well.

"This is Sir Andreas Meyer. He is my father's diplomatic advisor and completely trustworthy."

Meyer gave us a formal bow.

"From the looks on your faces when I opened the door," continued Eddie, "I assume that you can guess why he's here?"

"Yes," I answered. "We're very sorry to hear about your news."

"Thank you," he replied. "As you know then, I've just learned that my oldest brother has died in a plane crash. He was travelling to the Himalayas to be there while the search was underway for my other brother, who was caught in an avalanche."

That was a shock. We'd only heard about the one brother.

"I think I'm having trouble coming to terms with it," continued Eddie. "I mean, I don't doubt the news, but I've lost one brother and maybe both of them. It's just hard to imagine it could be real. Does that make any sense?"

"It certainly does to me," I said. "As a police officer, I've sometimes had to bring the news of a family member's death to people. It comes as a shock, of course, and your body and mind both have to deal with it, which takes time. Everyone reacts in their own way, but it always takes some time."

"How, may I ask, were you able to find out so quickly?" asked Andreas. "I only found out about the plane crash this morning, and that was before the media outlets in Europe had found out about it. And it still hasn't made the news here in North America."

Don explained that he had only just learned about it, and that the news had travelled through the NATO intelligence services.

"Thank you. It took some time after the plane crash before the authorities were able to sort out who was who on the flight." He paused and looked at Eddie. "Would it be painful for you to hear me explain to these people what happened, Sir?"

"No," replied Eddie. "I'm not sure I properly took it all in the first time anyway. Please go ahead."

"Thank you, Sir." Then turning to us, he continued. "First of all,

Prince Edward's middle brother, Prince Albert, was attempting to climb Mount Nun in the western Himalayas. It appears that he, his bodyguard, and their guide were about halfway there when they were caught in an avalanche and covered and/or swept away. Upon hearing the news, Prince Edward's oldest brother, Crown Prince Michael, immediately booked a flight to India for himself and his bodyguard. The jetliner on which the Crown Prince was travelling crashed at Palam Airport in Delhi. It occurred during a heavy rainstorm, and the preliminary indications – preliminary only, mind you - are that the crash may have been caused by a miscalculated altitude, leading to a high rate of descent, a very heavy landing, and then the aircraft undershooting the runway causing a most rapid deceleration. Of the 112 occupants on the aircraft, 3 of 12 crew members and 16 of 100 passengers were killed. One of the latter, unfortunately, was the Crown Prince.

"You will of course be wondering how I came to be here so quickly. I happened to be in Ottawa discussing with your federal government the possibility of a new trade agreement that could be very beneficial to both of our countries. As His Highness has explained, I have the honor to serve as our Sovereign Prince's diplomatic advisor and I am sometimes employed as a kind of advance representative. In this role, I have been able to 'test the waters' as I think you say, with senior officials from your own government, and well in advance of anything that might be considered official on the part of either country."

"That seems very practical," I observed.

"Indeed it is." He smiled. "In any case, I was in Ottawa for such discussions, and therefore close enough to have been able to excuse myself and fly here in time to meet the ship."

"And now?"

He looked at Eddie for confirmation, who nodded.

"Now, His Royal Highness is second in the line of succession, after Prince Albert, who is still missing and…" he coughed politely, "and – please forgive me for saying this Sir – who is feared dead."

Alicia gasped, and there was a moment of silence before Meyer continued. "As such, there are responsibilities and things that Prince Edward will need to learn, and possibly learn very quickly. I am not the best person to help with such things, but, having been conveniently close at hand, I am here to offer whatever help I can."

"Don't let him fool you," snorted Eddie. "No one knows more

about royal protocol, diplomacy, or even how royals are expected to behave than Sir Andreas Meyer."

Meyer didn't comment, but I could see in his eyes that he appreciated the compliments.

"So, what happens now?" asked Chief Harris.

At a nod from Eddie, Meyer answered. "The Crown Prince's remains will be transported home, where he will lie in state, following which there will be a state funeral. Meanwhile, the search for Prince Albert continues and the local people will be doing all that can be done. On both counts, of course, things will take some time, so there is no need for His Royal Highness to rush back. I see no reason why he shouldn't be able to complete the cruise and then fly home in two day's time as originally scheduled. If that is your wish, Sir?" he said, the latter being directed at Eddie.

"Yes, I think that would be best. I would appreciate some time out of the public eye to get my mind around this, and Alicia will need some time to adjust to the changes this may create for us."

"What about security?" asked the Chief.

After another exchange of pointed looks and nods, Meyer answered again. "His Royal Highness was just informing me of how extremely pleased he and his wife have been with the efforts the cruise line, and you three in particular, have been making on their behalf. I also understand that there will be another security detail from your Royal Canadian Mounted Police to meet us when we dock in Montréal. A somewhat larger one than was assigned here in Québec City, I believe. They will stay with the royal couple until they board their flight home. Once we arrive in Montenia, we will be joined by two or three plainclothes officers of our own Directorate of the Police."

I noticed that Eddie made a face at the latter point. Meyer noticed it as well.

"Yes, Sir. I am afraid that you will now have to get used to having a small security team with you – bodyguards, if you prefer – at all times."

"In the meantime," said Eddie, "Alicia and I have two more days on this cruise and I intend to make the most of it. I would also like to continue to be just another ordinary person for the next two days, so, if I could only make one request of you three, it would be that you continue to simply refer to me as Eddie. I would make the same request of Sir Andreas here, but I know him well enough to know that no force on earth would be enough to compel him to do so."

Meyer gave him another formal bow, saying "Thank you, Sir."

"Before we get too casual about everything," I said. "Could you tell us something about the political situation in Montenia?"

"Certainly," said Eddie. "Sir Andreas, please correct me if I say something wrong or miss something important."

Meyer nodded in agreement.

"OK. Well, Montenia is called a Principality and it has a Sovereign Prince as its head of state, but it is no longer an absolute monarchy like it was in the old days. It is what is called a constitutional monarchy, because the Sovereign Prince only has certain authorities, and can only exercise those authorities within limits set by our constitution and the legal framework that supports it.

"The Sovereign Prince can, for example, make some senior government appointments and can influence some kinds of government decisions. For example, the Sovereign Prince appoints a Prime Minister from among the members of the National Council, who themselves are democratically elected by the people in each region, for five-year terms. The Prime Minister is the head of executive government, and all legislation requires the approval of the National Council. If we go down a level, municipal matters are managed by elected mayors (for four-year terms), and these mayors are usually non-partisan. So, you see, it is a mostly democratic system that preserves some elements of our country's prior history and customs.

"Coming back to the Sovereign Prince, much of his work involves the diplomatic side, and he often serves as a diplomatic representative internationally where his position enables him to listen and be listened-to without actually committing the government to anything. Sir Andreas here is often part of that process, and might be considered the advance representative that tests the diplomatic waters and prepares the way for the potential engagement of the Sovereign Prince. If matters go well, then the Prime Minister would get involved at the stage where actual commitments are being made, and trade agreements, for example, are normally authorized by the signatures of both the Sovereign Prince and the Prime Minister." Eddie looked over to Meyer, who nodded.

"Not precisely as I might have expressed it, Sir. But substantially correct."

"As far as politics go, the system operates the way it does because most of the people want democracy but they also like tradition. Most, but not all, of the National Council Members are either neutral or pro-monarchist, but there are those who would like to see the democratic part increase and the monarchist part become increasingly symbolic. My own opinion is that that probably mirrors fairly well the mood of the people at large. There are, however, factions that have rather strong opinions on all of this and that means that there are factions that either support or are against particular members of our family. If Sir Andreas will close his ears for a moment, I'll give you my take on the situation.

"My father's politics are generally viewed as being somewhat to the right of centre. Although he is generally well liked, some see him as being too stern, and suspect him of seeking to gain – or restore, if you like - more authority. Therefore, the radical left hates him and both they and the abolitionists want to dispense with him. The republicans – and by that term I do not mean the Republican party of the United States, but rather the people that want political power to reside with the public and their representatives rather than with the monarchy - want to at least neuter him. On the other hand, the royalists love him, and the radical right wants more power for elitist groups of their own definition, so they would be willing to support any royal willing to help or allow them to get it…. Sir Andreas, you look like you are feeling unwell."

"No Sir. I understand the necessity for this distasteful subject. Please continue."

"Michael then, my late oldest brother Crown Prince, had been viewed by some as one who would go further than Father and try to undermine or abolish all democratic institutions. I am not saying this was true, mind you, I am just expressing a point of view that seems to be held by many. That accentuates the kinds of feelings I have just described towards my father.

"Assuming that he is still alive my next-to-oldest brother, Albert - now the Crown Prince – well, his politics are generally viewed as being quite strongly to left and there are many that think he would seek to abolish royalty and democratic institutions alike and install a socialist system. Naturally the radical left espouses this thinking and loves him as a result. The abolitionists are in something of a quandary on this because, as much as they want our country to evolve beyond the monarchy, not all of them support socialism. The royalists, and the radical right all hate him, but each for their own reasons. The republicans, for their part, aren't too keen on him either but I doubt they'd resort to violence."

Eddie paused here, with a sympathetic – even apologetic – glance at Meyer.

"And you Sir," asked Chief Harris, "how do these groups view your prospects?"

"Frankly, I doubt they're even aware of my existence, much less my own political views."

"Ahem," said Meyer, in a weak voice. "On that point, Sir, I must respectfully disagree with you." Addressing the rest of us, he continued. "I must reiterate that I find this discussion coarse, oversimplified, and distasteful. However, I feel it is in the best interests of my Prince to alert you to the danger he may now face.

"Therefore, continuing in the language that His Royal Highness was employing, I would say that the groups he has mentioned are very much alive to his existence, have their own views on his probable political views, and that these views will now be voiced more often and with louder volume as more people become aware of his oldest brother's most unfortunate demise. I would say that His Royal Highness is viewed as being a political moderate, so much so that were he to become the Sovereign Prince he might very well seek to build on previous democratic changes and move the country, gradually of course, towards full democracy. As you will appreciate, such views would lead both the radical left and the radical right to fear him, although for diametrically opposed reasons. Of these, I would suggest that it is the radical right that would perceive that they would have the most to lose. The abolitionists and royalists would be unhappy, but not to the same degree, and I think they would adopt a 'wait and see' approach before landing on a position. The republicans would naturally be strong supporters and might even come to view him as a kind of latter-day spiritual Messiah."

"And all this, when I've only become 'the spare,'" sighed Eddie. Meyer didn't comment, but from his expression I judged that he didn't hold out much hope that Prince Albert would be found alive, making Eddie the Crown Prince.

"Well. It seems unlikely that any of these groups would be concerned enough, or organized well enough, to have been able to get anyone dangerous on the ship today," I said. "But we'll continue to keep an eye on things." Don and Chief Harris nodded in agreement.

"Thank you," said Alicia. "I'm still feeling rattled with all the strange things that have been happening lately. Just last night we heard some kind of scratching noises at our stateroom door, and I wondered whether someone might be trying to break-in."

"What happened?"

"Oh. Well, Mitzi heard the noises as soon as I did and raced over to the door with a torrent of barking. Eddie checked the door, while I got Mitzi calmed down, but there was no one there to be seen and we heard nothing more for the rest of the night."

"It might just have been some drunk staggering back from the casino who tried to get into the wrong stateroom."

"That happens pretty frequently," said Chief Harris. "Sometimes they even call us to report that someone's changed the lock while they were out, but of course it always turns out that they tried the wrong stateroom on the right deck, or the right location on the wrong deck."

That lightened the mood, but I could see that Alicia was still worried, and I felt uncertain whether it was due to her being jittery, or whether her instincts were sound and should be heeded. It seemed that we had little choice but to assume the second.

When we had a little time before dinner, I sat down and tried to write out a brief summary of what we had heard concerning the possible kinds of threats to the various members of Montenia's royal family. After Eddie's initial, rather flippant, summary, we had probed more deeply and eventually pried out of Eddie and Sir Andreas that some of the factions included people that nurtured such strong feelings of jealousy, restriction, anger and hate that there had been incidents of violent protest and even clashes between rival factions.

"Great," I said, when I showed my summary to Don. "If everyone knows that Eddie's father is seriously ill and at risk of dying then extremists from the various factions have reason to be watching all three brothers, if for no other reason than in case Eddie's older brothers decide to abdicate.

Excluding the Sovereign Prince, Eddie's father, my summary was:

	Michael	*Albert*	*Edward*
	Oldest, Crown Prince	*Middle, the 'Spare'*	*Youngest brother*
Personal Politics	*Very Right*	*Very Left*	*Centrist*
Radical Left: wants socialism	*Hate?*	*Love*	*Hate?*
Abolitionists: eliminate the royals	*Hate*	*Support*	*Dislike*
Royalists: want the status quo	*Support*	*Hate?*	*Dislike*
Republicans: want republic with only ceremonial royals	*Hate?*	*Disapprove*	*Support*
Radical Right: wants power for elites; willing to support royals to get it	*Supports*	*Hates?*	*Hates?*

"With Michael dying in a plane crash, someone will be investigating to find out whether it may have been caused by people from Montenia's radical left.

"If Albert dies, or has died, in the avalanche, then someone will be investigating to find out whether it may have been caused by people from Montenia's royalists, or the radical right.

"If the radical right or left, have people following Eddie, then either side could take a crack at Eddie if they get news of Albert's death."

"Seems like a stretch," said Don, "but history is full of examples of messy royal successions. It doesn't seem to change anything for us in the here and now though."

"No. It doesn't."

For dinner that night, Alicia and Eddie ordered room service and, with Sir Andreas as their dinner guest, had it out on their verandah. Don and I had opted to do the same thing, except on our own verandah and with Silver. We weren't too worried about Alicia and Eddie over dinner since Sir Andreas was with them, and also because we had figured out how to unlock the hinged dividing wall between their verandah and ours. This arrangement was intended to make it easier for the crew to wash down all the verandahs between cruises, but it also served our purposes very well by creating a way to get from our stateroom to theirs without having to go out into the passageway.

The May weather was perfect for dining and sight-seeing outside, and we made the most of it.

After dinner, Alicia and Eddie decided to go for a few turns around the ship on the Deck 3 promenade walkway. Don and Silver and I decided to accompany them, from a safe distance to the rear, but when we left our stateroom, Don immediately went over to have a word with the two out of three of his 'Baker Street Irregulars' that were loitering in the short connecting passageway to led to the port side of the ship.

"What was that all about?" I asked, when he caught up with Silver and I wearing a satisfied-looking smile.

"I just told them where we were going and paid them to keep an eye on both of our staterooms and to put one of those complimentary ship's postcards on our stateroom's message board if anyone, ship's crew or otherwise, tried to enter either one."

"That was a good idea," I said, impressed, "and you call me devious!"

Don didn't reply, but his quiet smile broadened a bit.

Our two turns around the promenade deck turned out to be just that, a nice walk in which we enjoyed the scenery that was visible from each side of the ship as it progressed up the river.

"What do you think of Sir Andreas Meyer?" I asked Don as we were walking.

"Interesting. He certainly has the manners and bearing of a diplomat. Look at his evening clothes. Mauve shirt, white pants and shoes, with a light-coloured linen jacket that looks perfect for summer wear. He always seems to be well dressed, but only a notch above everyone else so he looks elegant without being ostentatious. Although he's walking with a cane and a bit of a limp, he still seems to have the grace of a model. He could almost be a stereotype, and yet he seems very genuine to me at the same time. I can't figure him out. How about you?"

"He definitely has a diplomat's manner and a kind of aristocratic demeanor that's engaging rather than off-putting. I agree, he's either very genuine or one hell of a good actor."

After the second circuit around the ship, I was about to put it down as having been uneventful when I noticed Chief Harris standing, motionless, just inside an open doorway. When he caught me looking, he placed a finger alongside his nose, which I took as a signal to quietly approach.

"Nice evening, Chief," I said conversationally.

"Mmmm. Did you spot your shadow?"

"No, I didn't," I said, with all my senses snapping alive.

"Don't beat yourself up about it," he said, correctly interpreting my immediate flash of guilt. "Your shadow was dressed the same way as you described from before. I only got one glimpse of the face in profile, and my impression was of a male, but I might be wrong. He or she was very careful and kept well back of you when walking into the breeze and even further back when upwind of you, so even Silver didn't pick up the scent."

"Any idea who it might have been?"

"None at all. I couldn't intervene as long as they were just walking along and their only crime was looking furtive. The captain would have had a fit. I did, however, assign one of my staff to follow your shadow. If they return to their stateroom, we'll have the number before the evening is out."

Thanking Chief Harris I went and rejoined Don, and filled him in.

"I'm beginning to think that Alicia's tale about hearing scratching on their door might have been someone with a set of lockpicks," Don said.

"Could be…." I was about to speculate further when Silver stopped short, swiveled his ears up and forward, and gave a deep growl. For a moment, I couldn't see what had caught Silver's attention but then I spotted a figure dart through one of the large sets of double doors leading to the interior of the ship. Breaking into a run, all three of us headed for those doors.

The doors led to a corridor and also to stairwells leading up and down. Just inside the doors were two crew members with mops. To be doing so at that time of day probably meant that they were cleaning up some kind of spill, but it put the brakes on Silver's ability to follow any kind of scent.

"The ammonia in that detergent solution is going to saturate his olfactory receptors for a while. We can come back and try again in a while, but I don't think he's going to have much luck with so many people coming and going in this area."

"We're probably best off going back and catching up to the Avons then."

This only took us a few moments. As we resumed our following of Alicia, Eddie, and Sir Andreas, their stroll took us inside the ship and past the gift shop, where we noticed that a fresh crop of newspapers had been brought aboard. The Crown Prince's demise had become front-page news, and the media had also gotten wind of Prince Albert's mountaineering accident and possible death.

"Maybe it's time to raise the security threat level a notch," I mused.

The Daily News

Thursday, May 13, 1982

Crown Prince dies in plane crash

6   A SHADOW IS REVEALED

While Silver and I returned to our stateroom after seeing the Avons safely tucked into their own, Don had split off to try another reconnaissance in the casino. When he returned a couple of hours later, however, he didn't have much to report.

"Our three photojournalists were rooted to their chairs at one of the blackjack tables again," he said. "I was able to stand behind them and watch the play for a while, and then a seat opened up and I sat-in at their table with them. While I was there, they didn't discuss the plane crash or make any connection to the Avons at all, not out loud anyway. Masters and Dolan did complain a lot about Jolliffe, the British-sounding one getting those pictures and a few quotes at the captain's dinner table, and about the two of them not getting any further ahead at all, but that was about it."

He paused in thought for a moment. "The only thing that struck me as unusual was that Jolliffe didn't respond to them. He didn't tease them; and he didn't defend himself or commiserate with them. In fact, he seemed distracted and thoughtful."

"Do you think he's a threat?"

"I've no idea, but I can't shake the feeling that he isn't entirely what he pretends to be."

***

Very late that night, Lorenzo Costa, one of the two university students that had been late boarders in Charlottetown, had been lounging in a deck chair with a ship's blanket covering up to his chin. He was on the normally well-travelled Deck 3, and had been waiting for a quiet time when the promenade walkway was unoccupied. He had watched while the last diners and floor-show patrons had taken a last stroll around the ship, and was waiting to make sure that no one else was about. When he judged that the walkway was as unoccupied as it was ever likely to become, he cast off the blanket and got up. He was wearing sneakers, dark grey sweatpants and a kangaroo jacket with the hood up, just like he had been while following the Avons earlier in the cruise.

Checking again to make sure there was no one around, he casually walked over to one of the ship's lifeboats which, like all the others, was suspended in a cradle above the deck. At each end of the lifeboat were support frames for the davits – essentially small cranes – that were used to swing the lifeboat out and then lower or raise it to or from the water below. The crane arms themselves had been swung inboard and were arranged parallel to and above the length of the lifeboat. There was just enough light for him to be able to climb up one of the support frames and then, using one of the davit arms for support, clamber into the stern of the lifeboat.

Once in the stern, he crawled to the entrance hatch, which wasn't locked of course, and quietly entered the lifeboat. Once in, he pulled out a small flashlight that gave him just enough illumination to be able to hunt around for the lifeboat's emergency equipment. Mounted near the boat's wheel and engine controls he found what he was looking for: a waterproof case with a stenciled label. It read 'FLARE GUN.' Taking down the case, he opened it to reveal a standard Very-pistol flare gun and several wide cartridges marked either flare or signal. He took one of the flares and loaded it into the gun. As a replacement for the confiscated pen gun, it wasn't much of a weapon, he thought, but it should suffice. With it, he should be able to maim, if not kill, which would still make the desired political statement.

May 15, 1982
Cruising the St. Lawrence River

Saturday was another sea day; this time along the St. Lawrence River to Montréal. Being well into the river meant calm sailing for the remainder of the cruise, which was a relief for the passengers that had been experiencing mild seasickness earlier on.

The scenery had changed as well. Extending from the banks on both sides of the river is a large plain called the St. Lawrence Lowland, much of which comprises farms. The farms adjacent to the river are particularly eye-catching, because they are laid out in long, narrow strips arranged parallel to each other and perpendicular to the river. When these plots of land were originally established, under the French seigneurial[28] system, this design provided river-water access for the greatest number of farms. Seeing them now, they looked beautiful in their assorted shades of green and brown.

Around mid-morning, the Avons called to say they wanted to go for a walk. Don, Silver, and I joined them, or perhaps I should say that we followed them, as we kept well back. They were also joined by Meyer, who seemed to have attached himself to Eddie. The two of them had a lot to discuss, I supposed. Eddie seemed to know him, and accept him without question. Although I didn't sense anything false about him, I did have to wonder whether he was who and what he seemed to be. I certainly hoped Eddie was right about him.

Neither Don nor I spotted anyone looking or behaving like our shadower, Silver didn't seem to react to anyone either, and they had Meyer with them this time, so we were able to relax just a little and had a very nice walk.

As we approached the spot where we had previously met Marie O'Dwyer, she gestured to attract our attention so we took a moment to sit beside her.

"Good morning," she began, "I hope you don't think me too much of a busybody, but I noticed something suspicious last night and I don't know what to do about it. I thought perhaps you could give me some advice."

"I'd be happy to try, if I can," I responded. "What did you see?"

"Well, it was very late. I don't sleep very well anymore and last night was particularly bad so I decided to try sitting out here for a while. It was really quite calm and beautiful. The ship just seems to glide along now that we're on the river, which is so much nicer than all the rocking and pitching we got when we were out on the open ocean, and it was a clear night.... Anyway, I was just sitting here in my usual spot, when a person came along that made my spine tingle because I couldn't escape the feeling that they were up to something."

"What made you think that?"

"At first, it was because the person seemed to be almost creeping. When he was just about to pass that second lifeboat there," she pointed to one of the five lifeboat-tenders that were hanging from their davits just above eye level along the side of the ship, "he stopped and looked around, as if to make sure that no one was watching.

"Well, I was watching, of course, but that late at night I think I must have been in quite deep shadow sitting here beside these big pipes. On top of that, I was wearing quite dark-coloured clothing, and his manner made me feel just a bit alarmed, so of course I didn't move at all.

"Anyway, he didn't seem to notice me, or see anyone else for that matter, and then he did the most remarkable thing. He climbed up one of the davits and then crawled into the back end of the lifeboat."

"That certainly sounds unusual," I offered. "Do you know what he was doing int there?"

"No. Not exactly. It was so quiet out here that I could actually hear the sounds of him moving around, and I thought the lifeboat might have swayed a bit, but it might have been just my imagination. He was only inside for a few minutes, maybe five; not more than ten, and then I saw his head stick out from the back end again – the stern I guess it's called – and I figured he was checking to make sure there was still no one else around. Then he climbed back down and skulked off that way," she said, pointing towards the bow of the ship.

"Well, that certainly sounds unusual," I agreed. "You've been saying 'he.' Are you sure it was a man?"

"Oh yes, he walked the way a man does. He seemed fairly athletic, the way he climbed in and out of the lifeboat, and I would say he must be quite a young man too."

"How was he dressed?"

"That I could see from when he first walked by me: grey sweatpants and a darker grey kangaroo jacket. He had the hood up too, so I couldn't see much of his face, just a bit of pointed nose sticking out. Oh, and there was some hair sticking out: dark hair, so it must have been either dark brown or black."

"OK. What is it that you wanted our advice about?"

"Well, whether I should tell someone about it? Report it I mean, like to someone in authority among the crew."

"Ah. Well, yes, I think you're right that someone should be told. How about this, Don and I can report what you've told us to the ship's chief of security, and if it's OK with you we'll also give him your name, in confidence. That way if he has any other questions, he'll be able to find you. If he does, he'll be discreet about it though, and make sure not to cause any embarrassment. Would that be all right with you?"

"Yes, thank you, it would put my mind at ease, and don't worry about me – at my age I don't embarrass very easily anymore."

"OK then. The Chief of Security is a man named Andrew Harris. Is there anything else you can tell us about last night?" I asked as Don and I rose from where we'd been sitting.

"No, I don't think so... yes, I almost forgot. When the man climbed down to the deck from the lifeboat, I noticed that he was carrying something under one arm. It must have been a satchel, or a box, or something like that. It was about this size." She spread her hands out to indicate a dimension of about ten inches (25 cm).

"Now that's interesting," said Don. "I think Chief Harris is going to want to know what that was. Don't be surprised if you see a crew member come along and go up for a look before long."

"Thank you, Marie," I put in. "We can't tell you the details just now, but it's possible you'll have helped us prevent a crime."

"That's a nice thought. Maybe I'll get some time off of Purgatory[29] for it," she replied, with a smile.

Taking our leave of Marie, we caught up with the Avons and accompanied them through the rest of their walk, then went to report Marie's news to Chief Harris.

"Any idea what someone might want to steal from a lifeboat-tender?" Don asked Drew after we'd related the story.

"Not really," he replied. Those boats are stocked with emergency ration and drinking water, but I wouldn't have thought they're worth stealing. I'll have one of the crew go through the lifeboat with an inventory list and see if anything's missing, but it might not be a case of theft at all. It's more likely that someone's brought something like drugs aboard and hidden them there before trying to smuggle them off the ship at one of our ports of call. We've seen that trick tried before."

Apparently, it was going to be an eventful day as there was another security lapse that afternoon. We found out later that Meyer had gone down to the ship's gift shop to get something that Alicia wanted. Shortly after that, Eddie had apparently gone off on his own too.

We were lounging in our stateroom when there was a knock on the door. It was one of Don's 'Baker Street Irregulars,' there to report that Eddie had left the Avons' stateroom and was browsing through the ship's various store. The ones that sold jewelry and watches, and the like. Leaving Don to go watch over Alicia, Silver and I rushed down to the promenade deck, which also housed the ship's gift shop and other stores. The promenade deck itself was quite crowded, it being mid-afternoon, but I was eventually able to spot Eddie up ahead and moving away from us. At the same time, I heard Silver give a low growl, but he seemed unfocused, as if he had caught a scent of concern but couldn't judge the direction with so many people moving around us.

I did my best to keep an eye on Eddie while trying to get through the crowd and catch up to him, so I was fairly well positioned to see a sweatsuit-clothed figure approach him from behind. The figure certainly resembled our shadow.

With my progress being impeded, I took the risk of calling out to Eddie, which made both he and the shadow turn around and look back. Seeing me, but not knowing why I'd called out, Eddie – who was beside the ship's rail - stopped dead in his tracks. This, in turn, caused the shadow to crash right into him.

As Eddie seemed to be apologizing, the shadow seized the opportunity and pushed Eddie up and partway over the ship's rail. As the two of them hung there for a moment, both of them off balance, I quickly knelt, unclipped Silver from his harness and told him to go.

Silver, who had by then identified the shadow person as the one he'd been concerned about all along, needed no urging and took off at full acceleration which, for a large dog, was considerable.

Eddie and the shadow struggled. Eddie was trying to get off and away from the ship's rail while the shadow was trying to push him the rest of the way over it. Before their struggle could be resolved,

Silver drove his shoulder full force into the shadow, pushing him off of Eddie and forward. The shadow was nimble, if nothing else, and managed to get rebalanced and veer into the crowd before Silver could make another attack.

As I reached Eddie and was making sure that he was all right, Silver was still trying to get at the shadow, who was scrambling through the crowd. The shadow was just barely able to get through an open passageway door, and close it, before Silver could get a grip on him with his jaws, leaving Silver standing there barking at him in frustration.

I called him off. Our priority was Eddie.

When we were all gathering together once more in the Avons' stateroom, several things stood out. Our shadow person was clearly after Eddie, not Alicia, and Eddie had learned a lesson: his carefree days were over.

"Pretty brazen too, to attempt something like this in broad daylight," added Chief Harris, who had heard about the incident from crew members and come to join our debriefing.

"Or pretty desperate," added Don. "After all, this is the last day of the cruise."

"Yes, and there's more. I had a crew member check the lifeboat that your Ms. O'Dwyer told you about and there is something missing. There was a box containing a Very-pistol and flares."

"Uh-oh," I said. I didn't want to mention it out loud in front of the Avons, but Don and Chief Harris knew exactly what I was thinking: that our 'shadow' mystery person may have been the passenger that tried to smuggle the pen-gun onto the ship, and that he had now found an alternative weapon.

Even without this knowledge, Eddie was suitably repentant, and accepted Meyer's diplomatic but firm 'suggestion' that neither he nor Alicia leave their stateroom unescorted. That seemed to satisfy Meyer and Chief Harris, but I was more worried than ever.

As Don, Silver, and I headed back to our own stateroom, my mind was running scenarios. For me, at least, the threat level had just moved up another notch.

Nothing else unusual happened for the rest of the afternoon, and Don, Silver, and I spent it lounging outside on our verandah, while Eddie and Alicia – accompanied by Meyer – did the same, except on the Avons' verandah.

I had expected that Eddie and Alicia would want to have their last dinner at the captain's table in the main dining room, but they decided on room service instead. I took this to mean that Eddie was more shaken up by the incident on the promenade deck than he had been letting on. Whatever the reason, it certainly made security easier.

For our part, we had our last dinner outside on our verandah while the ship continued cruising past the northern shore of the St. Lawrence River. As we had left open the connecting door between our two verandahs, the Avons were able to observe when we had finished eating and invited us over for an after-dinner drink. Being more-or-less on duty, Don and I decided that a small drink each would have to suffice.

We had a nice, wide-ranging chat and, although Eddie avoided the topic of the royal succession, it seemed to me that he was beginning to take life just a bit more seriously than he had been before the news of his brothers reached us. Watching him, I found myself hoping that life as a royal wouldn't completely dampen his natural playfulness and zest for life. As I was thinking this, I happened to notice Meyer watching me rather closely and, when our eyes met, he gave me a slight nod as if he knew exactly what I was thinking and agreed with me.

After a while, we said good night and took our leave, and a couple of hours later everyone settled in for the night.

It must have been well after midnight when there was a scratching sound at the door of the Avons' stateroom.

Once again, Lorenzo Costa, had waited until it was very late at night before making his move. It was quiet in the passageways, and even the kids that always seemed to be playing in the corridor across from the Avons' stateroom had long since been packed off to bed. Withdrawing his two chosen lockpicks from a pocket he moved to the Avons' door. He was more confident now, as he had learned from his previous unsuccessful attempt on their door and had been practicing on his own stateroom door. It still took some trial-and-error work, but it wasn't long before he felt the tumbler move and he was able to open the door.

Putting the picks away, he withdrew the Very-pistol from where he had tucked it into his waistband at the small of his back. He knew that he would have to move quickly before the Avons' Pekingese heard him and began a cacophony of barking. As he silently crept over the threshold, he heard not the high-pitched barking of a small dog, but the low, menacing growl of a much larger dog....

Don and I had arranged to keep watch in shifts, and it began on his watch. The last thing I remembered was lying down on the stateroom's couch while he took up position in a chair, some distance away. I had probably only just fallen into a deep sleep when I was woken by Don's hand on my shoulder. When I opened my sleepy eyes, he had his left hand on my shoulder and the index finger of his right held up against his lips to signal silence. Seeing me nod, he stood back up and pointed towards the stateroom door. I realized that there was a scratching sound at the door at the same time as Silver began to growl. I immediately put a hand on the back of Silver's neck and whispered for him to be silent. I knew that he wouldn't actually remain silent, but he did heed me enough to avoid barking.

As Don moved back over to the other side of the stateroom, he withdrew his big, Colt .45 automatic and took up position. I grabbed my .38 service revolver and took a position, with Silver beside me, along another wall so that we were arranged in a triangle, with the door and soon-to-be intruder at one vertex. In this way, if there was any shooting, Don and I would not be aiming in each other's direction.

They're in for a surprise, I thought with a grim smile, as the stateroom door opened.

With my left hand I gave Silver a warning grip at the top of his neck. He understood, but I could feel him begin to vibrate.

Someone crept in through the door. In the dim light it certainly looked like our 'shadow,' in terms of height, build, and clothing. Whomever it was seemed to be holding a very fat pistol of some kind in their hand, and it took me a moment to realize that it was an older style flare gun, a Very-pistol.

"Stop! Police!" I called out, causing the figure to swing toward me.

"And think twice before you try anything! We have you covered," called out Don from his position. The figure then looked toward Don but kept the pistol pointed toward me.

Time slowed down.

"Drop the gun!" I commanded.

The figure hesitated, and I allowed a moment before repeating the command.

"Drop the gun. Now!"

As the figure looked back to me, I could see that it was a male face with a short beard. He looked like he was calculating his odds, so I tried pushing him a bit.

"You can't win this. You can't outshoot the two of us, and the Avons aren't even here. We traded staterooms with them for the night, so why not just drop the gun so we can talk?"

I could see that he was thinking furiously, and I could even see from his body language the exact moment that he made his decision, I just couldn't tell what the decision was.

He decided to hedge his bets. He made a lunge forward, swinging his aim towards the suite's bedroom as he did so. As he began running towards the open door to the verandah, he fired the gun towards the bed. It had been loaded with a flare, not a smoke cannister, and it took off like the rocket it was.

I released Silver, which he correctly interpreted as permission to pursue and he sprung towards the man at the same time as he leapt through the open doorway. The flare must have had a three-second delay, as it ignited in the bedroom at the same time as the man – with Silver and Don, who was closer than I, in hot pursuit – vaulted across the verandah and over the rail.

There must have been a splash, but I certainly didn't hear it. I was too busy grabbing the phone and telling the ship's operator that we had a fire in our stateroom and needed help.

The flare had landed at the head of the bed and was so intense that the pillows and bedding caught fire immediately. When the responding crew members reached our stateroom, we had turned on all the lights and both Don and I were throwing water on the bed using what equipment we could. There were no fire extinguishers in the ship's staterooms so, in Don's case it was an ice bucket and for me it was a medium-sized flower vase. We weren't trying to put the fire out; we were just trying to contain it. Within minutes, a crew member with a proper fire extinguisher, followed by another with a fire hose arrived and put the fire out properly. By that time Chief Harris had arrived and, with him, we retired to our own stateroom to get away from the smoke and talk to Eddie, Alicia, and Meyer, the latter of whom had stationed himself on our couch as an additional protective measure.

When we had related everything that had happened, Chief Harris got up and went to the phone to call the captain and brief him. When that was done, he came back, and plopped down tiredly into a chair.

"Well, the Captain says he can't do the usual 'Man Overboard' thing because this part of the river is too narrow for the ship to turn around. Confidentially, I don't think he wants to anyway, not for an attempted murderer anyway." Alicia gasped at that, but she must have realized that you don't break into someone's room in the middle of the night and shoot off a high-intensity flare just to scare them.

"What will he do then?" asked Eddie.

"He's calling the Coast Guard right now, and they will alert the police forces on both sides of the river. If this guy didn't get sucked down into the propellor..." There was another gasp from Alicia, who was having a bad time of it. "Excuse me, Mrs. Avon. If this man survived the fall, and if he can swim, he'll turn up somewhere."

He looked at Don and I. "Did you get a good look at him, his face I mean?" We looked at each other, then nodded. "Yes, good enough, I think."

"Fine. Then we can go through the security photos and, once you've picked him out, I'll notify the authorities of his name and so on."

"I think we'll find that he was one of the last to board in Charlottetown, and I wouldn't be surprised if that pen gun we found actually belonged to him," I ventured.

"As opposed to the one that was arrested?"

I shrugged. "They may have been working together, or our shadow may have slipped the pen gun into the other's luggage making the one we caught an unknowing accomplice. It would be interesting to see how the arrested one reacts when shown a picture of tonight's marauder."

"You think this fellow from tonight is the one that phoned-in the bomb threat?" asked Eddie.

"It's beginning to look that way," said Chief Harris.

"If you wouldn't mind giving me this person's particulars as well," ventured Meyer, "I will forward them to our own national police force. It could be that he's associated with one of the extremist factions that His Royal Highness was describing for you yesterday."

"Good idea."

Leaving the Avons under the watchful eye of both Meyer and one of Chief Harris' security staff, Don and I went with the Chief to look through his passenger files. It didn't take long.

"That's him," I said, looking at the second photo the Chief brought out.

"I agree. No question," confirmed Don.

"These two were among the very last bunch to board in Charlottetown, and the first one is the guy that was arrested for having the pen gun in his luggage," said the Chief. "They're both listed as students at the University of Geneva. The second one – your intruder from tonight - is Lorenzo Costa. According to their passports they are both Italian citizens. The first student's permanent address is also in Italy, but Costa's permanent address is listed as being in Montenia." There was a pause while he copied all of this out for Meyer.

When we returned to our stateroom, we found that the Purser was there as well.

"We were just about to have a look at the other stateroom," said Meyer. "Perhaps you would care to join us?"

We agreed and the whole group of us trouped next door. What we found was jaw-dropping. There was almost no odour of smoke, courtesy of the large fans that we'd seen several crew members taking away down the passageway. The bed and bedding had all been removed and replaced, and the only real evidence of the fire was the scorched wallpaper at the head of the bed.

"How did you manage this?" I asked the Purser.

"We have a large crew and we have spares of everything," he explained with a smile. "Everything scorched was removed, then everything that was soaking wet, then the water itself, then everything else was replaced from our spares inventory. Even the bed. Meanwhile, those large fans you saw were blowing gale-force to get rid of the smoke and help with the drying. The only thing we couldn't do tonight was replace the scorched wallpaper, but we'll get that done tomorrow morning."

After suitable congratulations and thanks from the Avons, the

Purser and the last of the crew departed. Then the Avons insisted on moving back into their original stateroom, assuring us that the threat was long gone and that, in any case, Meyer was insistent on sleeping on their living room couch. Without any real reason to argue the point, Don and I agreed and returned to our own stateroom in hopes of getting a few hours of sleep before dawn.

"That was a bit tense back there for a moment," said Don as we were settling. "I could hardly believe it when I realized that the kid was holding a Very pistol! Not your typical assailant's weapon."

"Assuming that it was his pen gun that we found, then I suppose it was the best he could come up with on short notice. Especially after his earlier attempt to push Eddie over the promenade rail failed yesterday."

"I suppose. Do you think he actually intended to kill Eddie with it?"

"Who knows? Maybe he thought that just injuring him would make the news and serve as a sign of rebellion from whatever cause he was attached to. At least our trick with the 'musical staterooms' worked and he ran into us instead of the Avons."

"Yes. That was a shock. I could see it on his face. He recovered quickly, however, and he was nimble enough to loose-off a shot at the bedroom – assuming that the Avons must be in there - and then still make it to the rail one step ahead of Silver's jaws, all of which was pretty impressive."

"Well, the threat has come and gone now, at least," I said, with a contented sigh.

I was wrong, of course.

Laurie Schramm

7 IT'S NOT OVER UNTIL IT'S OVER[30]

If you want a thing done well, do it yourself!

Various (see Endnote 31).

It was natural for the rush of crew members responding to the reported fire on Deck 7 to draw a number of spectators from among the passengers. These latter gathered in the narrow passageway that ran from port to starboard, the same one that usually seemed to be inhabited by children playing games. At the back of this gathering, Richard Jolliffe was able to position himself so that he was not very noticeable yet had a good view of peoples' comings and goings, and could raise his camera and take a picture from time to time.

As a result, he was in a position to observe Security Chief Harris leave the stateroom with the fire, followed by the red-haired policewoman, her police-service dog, and the military-looking man that he'd previously seen somewhere else aboard the ship. With them out of the way, Jolliffe was able to step into the Avons' stateroom for a look. When he did so, he was both surprised and angry to find that there was no sign of the Avons, nor of the student, Lorenzo Costa. There were only a large, blackened portion of the bed and linens, all still smoking, a scorched area on the wall above the bed, and some crew members poking around to make sure the fire was out.

Damn students, *he thought to himself.* Can't count on them to do anything right. *He'd already learned of Costa's loss of the pen gun and his botched attempt to push the Prince — he knew full well who Eddie Avon really was — over the rail. Now it appeared that Costa's latest improvisation hadn't worked out any better than his previous plans.*

At that point, his thoughts were interrupted by a crew member who had spotted him and politely, but firmly, asked him to leave. He'd nodded, raised his camera and took one more picture — for show — and left the stateroom.

As he re-entered the long starboard passageway, he was just in time to see the door to the policewoman's stateroom open and the Purser walk in. While the door was open, he could see the prince, his wife, and 'that bureaucrat Meyer,' as he thought of him.

Aha, *he thought.* So that's where you've been all along. Someone's been very clever. *Now he understood Costa's failure. Apparently, it was time to take a hand himself.*

If you want a thing done well, do it yourself[31], *he thought to himself as he walked away, thinking.*

***

May 15, 1982
Montréal

We were awakened by the dawn sun. It was Sunday morning, and a quick look out our windows showed that, sometime in the early morning, we had reached Montréal. We had no sooner dragged ourselves out of bed, ordered breakfast via room service, and were seated out on our verandah to eat when Eddie appeared on his verandah. When we invited him to join us, he grabbed a chair and brought it over.

Accepting only a cup of coffee, he chatted while we ate, mostly about the events of the previous night. As he was doing so, he was interrupted by Meyer, who had come out to their verandah as well.

"Excuse me for interrupting, Sir, but this note was just delivered by one of the crew," he said, handing over a small envelope bearing the cruise line's crest and the ship's name. Inside was a notecard. "There has been a problem with your credit card. Would you kindly drop by the front desk by the Front Office on Deck 4 so we can resolve this before you disembark the ship this morning."

"We probably went over the pre-authorization level. I'll go down and get them to run my card through again," said Eddie, getting up from our table.

"I will accompany you, Sir, if you do not mind?"

"I really don't think it's necessary, but come along if you wish."

"Thank you, Sir."

As they crossed from our verandah to the Avons', so Eddie could get his wallet, Don noticed me frowning.

"Something wrong?" he asked.

"Maybe... no... I don't know. Does it seem odd that the cruise ship would only discover a credit card problem at the end of the cruise? The Avons must be pretty wealthy, and Eddie is probably independently wealthy as a prince in his own right."

"You know what they say, 'It's not how much you earn, it's how fast you spent it.'"

"True. And I suppose they may just have hit a pre-authorization limit like Eddie said.... Stay here and finish your breakfast, I'm going to take Silver and follow along. It's better than sitting here worrying about it."

I was already dressed in my standard morning garb, a loose-fitting top and sweat pants, so I only paused to grab my little .38 Special derringer and my wallet with my badge in it, called to Silver and went to the door. Opening it just a sliver, I could hear when Eddie and Meyer walked out of the other suite. They didn't pass our door, so they must have gone to the large stairwell that was in the short connecting passageway across from their door. I gave them ten seconds, signalled for Silver to remain by my side, and cautiously stepped out.

I didn't move too quickly, as I knew that Eddie would automatically adjust his pace for Meyer's slower gait with his cane. Chancing a look around the corner of the stairs, I was fortunate to see them disappearing around the corner to the next flight down. We continued like this downwards for a while. There were two sets of stairs for each deck level, and we had to go from Deck 7 to Deck 4.

It happened when Eddie and Meyer had reached Deck 5, which was usually the busy one due to the presence of most of the ship's shops, lounges, and the casino. They must have been just working their way through the crowd to get to the next flight of downward-leading stairs, when I heard Eddie exclaim "Hey! Watch where you're going mister." Followed by Meyer's voice "Step back, Sir! He has a knife."

As the sounds of scuffling permeated the air, I took the rest of the stairs two at a time and rounded the corner in time to witness an amazing sight.

A number of murmuring and exclaiming passengers hastily stepping back to create a kind of arena space in which Eddie was standing still and holding one arm as if it had been hurt. Immediately in front of him, Meyer had positioned himself as Eddie's defender and had changed his grip on his cane so that he held it like a sword. Facing Meyer from only a couple of feet away was the British photojournalist Jolliffe, except that instead of his usual camera, he was holding a large knife. It looked like a chef's knife with something like an eight-inch blade and Jolliffe looked like he knew how to use it.

As I paused to survey the whole area, Jolliffe moved from side to side, like boxer or a street-fighter testing for a possible opening. Meyer was in motion as well, but his movements were different, more like those of a dancer or a martial-arts practitioner. Both men looked like they had been in fights like this before, and I was further surprised to see that Meyer's limp seemed to have disappeared.

Taking out my badge in one hand and derringer in the other, I called out "Police! Stop it now!" This got the crowd's attention and the fighters', although Meyer and Jolliffe only gave me a glance and each shifted slightly away from me as they recalibrated their thinking. Meyer was faster, and was able to close in by half a step and give Jolliffe a solid whack on his right hand with his cane. Unfortunately, Jolliffe was holding the knife in his left hand, but you could tell that the blow hurt. At the same time, I ordered Silver to go for the knife hand. He was ready for that, and bounded in.

Seeing that he couldn't win, Jolliffe smoothly flipped the knife so he was holding the blade near its tip, threw it at Eddie, who fell as he tried to dodge the knife. Meanwhile, Jolliffe dove into the crowd heading away from Silver and I.

I had raised my derringer and was taking aim when Jolliffe was swinging his arm back for the throw, but he was faster than I could settle my aim and, in any case, there were too many innocent people standing behind him for me to risk a shot with such an imprecise weapon.

My priority, and Meyer's, were the same and we both went to check on Eddie, who was picking himself up off the floor. As he stood up his big, easygoing smile was back on.

"Are you quite well Sir?" and "Are you OK?" came simultaneously from Meyer and I, to which question Eddie held up the knife. A knife covered in blood.

"Did you actually catch it out of the air?" I asked, amazed.

"Only because he didn't take the time to throw it properly," replied Eddie with a grin. "It hit me right here" – indicating a spot on his chest that was just about directly over his heart – "but it hit me with the haft, not the point. All I had to do was grab it when it hit me. Thanks to you two, I might have a small bruise over my heart; nothing worse." Then he took another look at Meyer, who was trying to inconspicuously hold his left shoulder with his right hand while supporting his cane under his right arm. "Sir Andreas, you're bleeding!" Sure, enough, Meyer was bleeding enough to saturate the arm of his jacket, and blood was beginning to pool on the deck beside him.

"His knife struck me in the shoulder when he first lunged at you, Sir."

Chief Harris then arrived, as did Silver, the latter holding a bloodstained shirt in his jaws.

"Looks like Silver did some damage," said Eddie, with satisfaction.

"Yes," I said, kneeling down to check Silver for injuries and not finding any. Then I looked at the bloody shirt. "It's Jolliffe's entire shirt," I said, "I'm guessing that Silver didn't get a complete grip and that Jolliffe somehow slipped away, sacrificing his shirt in the process. Well, I'm sure the Chief's staff will be able to track him down. A man with no shirt and dripping blood is going to be a bit conspicuous."

Chief Harris waved a crew member over and gave instructions to escort Meyer to the Infirmary on Deck 1. "If you'll excuse me, I'll see to tracking Jolliffe down immediately."

Agreeing, Eddie, Silver, and I accompanied Meyer down to the ship's infirmary. There were no other passengers there when we arrived, so the doctor was able to look at Meyer's shoulder right away. He also looked quite closely at the knife. "Nice and sharp. Probably stolen from one of the kitchens. It looks clean enough, other than the blood, and the cut looks nice and clean. Whomever it was, they didn't cut anything vital, so we'll just stitch it up and I'll put you on a course of antibiotics just to be on the safe side. Right?"

Meyer didn't answer because he was looking at Eddie in horror. "Sir! There's blood seeping through your hand where you're holding your arm!"

"Yes," agreed Eddie. "I'm seem to have picked up a little scratch in the fight as well. Go ahead doctor, deal with him first. My arm will keep."

It didn't take long for the doctor to deal with Meyer's arm, after which he took a close look at Eddie's arm. "Yes. Nice and clean; not too deep. Very similar, in fact. Same treatment for you then."

We stayed with Eddie and Sir Andreas while the former's stitching and bandaging was completed and then all of us returned to the Avons' stateroom, where Don was already sitting with Alicia. After the usual exclamations and explanations, our conversation turned to Jolliffe.

"Will he be able to get away?" asked Alicia.

"Not likely," I said. "Silver probably put a nasty gash in his arm and there should be a trail of blood on the deck, judging by the amount that was on his shirt. If they don't find him soon, I imagine the Chief will call and ask us to have Silver follow the trail. Besides, they know what he looks like and what stateroom he's in. The Chief will have alerted his staff at the gangway and everywhere else on the ship. I don't think he'll be at large for long."

Any further questions were held off by the ringing of the Avons' phone, which Eddie got up and answered. It was obviously Chief Harris calling. After listening for a while, Eddie thanked him and hung up. "That was the Chief. They found him in one of the crew areas, trying to bandage his hand and steal some crew clothes. The Chief's been trying to question him about his motive and affiliations but Jolliffe isn't talking yet. The Chief has called the Montréal police, and in the meantime has him under guard in the brig."

"The brig? You mean they have a jail on a cruise ship?" asked Alicia.

"Oh yes," said Meyer. "Cruise ships generally have a small jail, just in case. It's normally located on one of the crew-only decks. The Chief probably doesn't want to lock him in his stateroom for fear that he might try to jump off the ship, like that student did."

"By the way, I'm curious," I said, turning to Meyer. "When you were fighting with Joliffe you seemed to be very proficient, and I noticed that your limp was gone. Is it possible that you actually came on board to serve as a bodyguard for your Prince, rather than as a diplomatic advisor?"

"Yes, well," he gave a discreet cough. "I came aboard to offer whatever assistance to His Royal Highness that might be within my power. I admit that the cane and the limp are only for show. That cane, by the way, looks like ebony but it is solid titanium, very light, very well balanced, highly dangerous in trained hands, and perfectly legal in all countries.... It can be an advantage, don't you think, to be underestimated by one's adversaries?"

"I do indeed." Even I was beginning to speak like Meyer.

"Everything that I previously told you was true, however. Let us say that I am *also* a diplomatic and protocol advisor."

"Well, I'm impressed, Sir Andreas," said Eddie, "I had no idea you had these other, hidden talents and I always assumed that your limp came from that United Nations peacekeeping action you were part of."

Meyer bowed his head in acceptance of the compliment. "That was the UNEF II[32], Sir, to which we contributed a small force to help supervise the withdrawals of Israeli and Egyptian forces following the Yom Kippur War. My leg was injured in the peacekeeping activities, and I did have to use a cane for a period of time. Although I was fortunate enough to make a complete recovery, the experience provided me with the idea for the deception, which I have employed ever since entering your father's service."

When everything had settled down, Don and I went to say goodbye to Chief Harris, after which we went back to changing clothes and getting ready for disembarkation. Don went off to find the 'Baker Street Irregulars' to thank them for their help, and to see whether they wanted him to speak to their parents about how helpful they had been. They did, and Don was particularly effusive in his praise of Tommy. Don, Silver, and I also went out in search of Marie O'Dwyer, and found her in her usual deck chair. It didn't look like she'd make any progress on her knitting, but she said she'd had a wonderful first cruise and was pleased when we explained what we'd been doing on the ship and that it seemed like it was going to end well.

When it was time to go, we accompanied Eddie, Alicia, and Meyer off the ship. There was no subtlety about our approach this time: we weren't there to follow the couple at a discreet distance, we were there to guard them for short time it would take to disembark and clear customs. For that reason, this time we went in uniform. Don had on his military-police operational-dress uniform, which involved a beret, combat shirt, and combat pants in olive-drab[33], a military police brassard, and combat boots. This, coupled with his web belt and .45-bearing-holster, made him look quite formidable. I was wearing my standard tactical uniform, with its thigh-mounted holster. Silver had on his black, police-service-dog vest.

When we passed through customs and immigration, we handed the Avons over to a new and larger security detail, and exchanged thanks from them, good wishes from us, and good-byes.

8 AFTERMATH

Don and I were each given permission to resume our interrupted honeymoon so, along with Silver, we flew directly back to PEI where we collected my truck and were able to get a different cabin, but at the same place in Cavendish. The next several days consisted of not much more than going for walks, going to the beach and relaxing.

Don had been assigned to a temporary position at National Defense Headquarters in Ottawa, which was going to give us some time to decide how to handle our two-career marriage without having to live apart, for a while. Nothing was ever said, but we both suspected that Don's convenient assignment was the result of some kind of back-room deal between my deputy commissioner and Don's admiral. We were very grateful for that, as we had some major decisions to make.

We hadn't been back in Ottawa long before we received a very nice letter of appreciation from a grateful cruise line, who offered us a complimentary cruise. Of course, as public servants we couldn't accept such an expensive gift, but we did thank them and promised to take a cruise with the line some other time at our own expense.

At about the same time, we received a very nice, and elegant, letter from Sir Andreas Meyer, expressing his personal thanks for our work and giving us some of the latest news. Crown Prince Edward Montenario, who had been known to us as simply Eddie, and his wife Alicia returned home safely and he immediately began studying – while having to perform - the Crown Prince role. Presumably under Mayer's tutelage. Apparently, Eddie, as I still thought of him, took charge of the arrangements for both brothers' funerals as well as assuming various other duties in order to lessen the burden on his father, whose health had not been improving.

About a month later, we received a variety of news from Montenia.

Regarding the death of Prince Albert, it was later learned that another climbing party had witnessed the two people that had thrown the explosives that caused the avalanche. That made it murder, and it was suspected to be the work of a Montenian extremist group. After further investigation the Montenian authorities, working through INTERPOL[34], were able to identify the two. They were found to be linked to a far-right political group that was in turn supported by a group of rich nobles – some of the elites that Eddie had mentioned to us earlier. The two men themselves, however, had gone into hiding and the Montenian authorities were still looking for them, aided by a Red Notice[35] from INTERPOL.

As to the death of Crown Prince Michael, the investigation by India's transportation authority concluded that the plane crash was indeed caused by a miscalculated altitude, leading to a too rapid rate of descent and a heavy landing that fell short of the runway. The root cause was therefore put down to human error. I don't know that this was widely believed, however, as the coincidence of timing seemed just a bit beyond the bounds of reasonable probability. In this case the Montenian authorities suspected factions within the radical left and the abolitionists – possibly even the two groups setting their differences temporarily aside to work together - but no individuals were ever conclusively suspected, and even a second investigation in the plane crash failed to turn up evidence of tampering with the aircraft. As far as I am aware, the real story remains somewhat of a mystery.

Lorenzo Costa, the student from the cruise ship, was found and rescued by the Coast Guard, who turned him over to the RCMP. The original bomb threat had been recorded on tape, and when it was played for Costa, he broke down and admitted that it had been him. He had needed a diversion, he said, in order to buy enough time to get to the ship before it sailed. He had met a fellow student on the flight from overseas, and had taken the opportunity while standing in the cruise ship's check-in line to slip the pen gun into the student's luggage, where we had later found it. Based on his sworn statement, the charges against the fellow student were dropped, and then transferred to Costa.

Although Costa admitted to the gun, and to the subsequent attack with the flare gun, the investigators were never able to get him to admit to working for any specific organization or cause, much less to the obvious link between himself and Joliffe. The investigators concluded that he was more afraid of Jolliffe and whomever else he was working for than he was of Canadian justice.

Although Joliffe really was an accredited photojournalist for *British Vogue* magazine, this turned out to have been a cover. Close inspection of his passport showed that it was a counterfeit. That triggered a closer look into his identity and background, which led to the discovery that his real name wasn't Richard Jolliffe. Under his real name, he was well known to the Montenian authorities as a kind of for-hire *agent provocateur*[36]. There were already warrants out for his arrest in Montenia and, in an attempt to plead for asylum in Canada and thereby avoid deportation, he claimed to have been blackmailed into hiring Costa to kill Eddie and, through his lawyers, offered to plead guilty to charges of assault on Eddie and Sir Andreas if he could remain in Canada and not be sent to Montenia. As to who had blackmailed him, he named several members of the Montenian nobility. The Montenian authorities, meanwhile, had accused him of simply being a paid agent of the nobles and had made a formal request for his extradition. The last I heard the case was still in the hands of our immigration authorities.

The other thing that the Montenian authorities turned up, was that the identified nobles had been holding secret meetings with a cousin of Eddie's to whom no one had previously paid much attention, because he'd been so far down in the line of succession. By questioning each of the nobles individually, and in the face of being exposed by Joliffe, one of the nobles eventually broke down and admitted that their group had made an arrangement by which they would support the cousin's claim to the throne (in case of Eddie's unfortunate demise) in return for the cousin's support of their wealth and positions in Montenian society. When this news came out, it only remained to attempt to determine whether Joliffe had been hired, blackmailed, or possibly both.

I still don't know the answer regarding Joliffe, but the whole experience felt like either the result of a series of unbelievable coincidences or else the result of an amazing web of factions and plots. Perhaps reality really is stranger than fiction sometimes.

Laurie Schramm

9 EPILOGUE

Several more months later, we learned from the news that Eddie's father had died of natural causes and that a period of national mourning and a state funeral were being arranged. Shortly after that, we received two more letters, both from the Palace in Montenia. The first was richly embossed on expensive paper and, in extremely formal language, invited Don, and Silver (!) and I to attend the coronation ceremony as special guests of the royal family.

The second letter was in a similarly elegant envelope, but inside was a handwritten note, on plain paper, in which Eddie pleaded with us not to be put off by the formality of the occasion and that we would count it as *another* personal favour if we would please make every effort to attend. On the back side of the note, it read:

P.S. If you are able to come and be with us for this, everything will be at our expense: travel, accommodations, etc. etc., everything.

P.P.S. I know that, as good public servants, you would not normally be in a position to accept our offer to cover all of your costs. Be advised, then, that we are making a special diplomatic request of your Department of External Affairs, that you be permitted to participate and honour us in this way (and accept our gift of transportation and hospitality). Unless you really don't want to come, be assured that we will bully your government into giving you an exemption from the rules about accepting gifts, and into pleading with you to agree. Our trade agreement with Canada is a good deal for both countries but it hasn't been signed yet. When we make this casual observation, Ottawa will understand and act accordingly.

P.P.P.S. Sir Andreas wanted to send you a note about all this but I over-ruled him, fearing that he would express it in such convolutions of diplomatic protocol-ese that you might fail to grasp the essential message.

Unsurprisingly, since the coronation invitation was made officially and through proper diplomatic channels, the Department of External Affairs practically begged us to accept, which we did.

... Alex and Silver return in
"An Inveterate Mountie."

BOOK 15 ENDNOTES

1. Palam Airport, 16 km from New Delhi, was expanded and renamed to Indira Gandhi International Airport in 1986.
2. Avalanche transceivers, devices that can be used to either emit or receive a radio signal became commercially available in 1971. The radio signal they emit is converted, when in receiver mode, to a tone that is audible to the human ear and becomes louder the closer one is to the transmitting unit. When used in grid searches, they can be effective in locating transmitters that have been buried in an avalanche. They are widely used by backcountry skiers and snow and ice mountaineers.
3. See *An Intimate Mountie*, 978-1-7387599-0-3.
4. See *An Indestructible Mountie*, 978-1-9994940-4-9.
5. Pronounced 'lok bôé-yhach.'
6. See *An Intimate Mountie*, 978-1-7387599-0-3.
7. Sikorsky CH-124 Sea Kings are twin-engine, anti-submarine warfare helicopters that were used by Canadian Forces for over 50 years, and which were usually housed on and deployed from destroyers and frigates of the Royal Canadian Navy. Sea Kings were a familiar sight to people in Canada's Atlantic provinces in those days, partly because they frequently assisted with maritime search and rescue operations.
8. Dating back to at least the 18th century, the shabrack (or shabraque) was originally a large cloth placed over, or under, the saddles of European cavalry. At some point it became traditional

to add a border of contrasting colour, and to display a crest or other symbol in the lower-rear corner. The RCMP shabrack, which is placed under the saddle, seems to have originated in 1887, at about the same time as "MP" was registered as the horse brand of the North West Mounted Police. It is black with yellow trim and displays the MP brand, topped by the Royal Crown, displayed (also in yellow) in the lower-rear corner on each side.

9. This poem is variously referred to as either based on an old Inuit poem or else the non-Aboriginal poem included in the American author Elliott Arnold's Western novel *"Blood Brother,"* which was originally published in 1947. The latter interpretation is clearly incorrect as the poem in *"Blood Brother"* is very different. In the absence of a definitive source, I personally prefer the Inuit attribution.

10. The Green Gables house is now a national Heritage Place, managed by Parks Canada. The house and farm, which belonged to relatives, provided some of the inspiration for Lucy Maud Montgomery's famous *Anne of Green Gables* novels, in which the fictional village of Avonlea was drawn from real-life Cavendish.

11. 'Charlottetown Soil,' the predominant type of soil in Prince Edward Island, has a distinctive red colour, which is due to its high iron oxide content.

12. This coincides with the day of the avalanche described in the Prelude chapter.

13. The Commanding Officer for L Division. Normally a Chief Superintendent.

14. Code 2: Respond as quickly as possible with limited use, as necessary, of emergency equipment, but complying with the provisions of the Motor Vehicle Act.

15. The name and ship in this story are both fictional. However, in real life the White Star Line operated a transatlantic ocean liner called *SS Atlantic* until it struck a reef and sank off the coast of Nova Scotia (just south of Halifax) in 1873. It remains a popular wreck for exploration by sport SCUBA divers.

16. In real life, the first woman to become captain of a major cruise ship seems to have been Karin Stahre-Janson of Sweden, who was appointed captain of the *MS Monarch* (Royal Caribbean International) in 2007.

17. A firearm that resembles a wide-bodied pen, usually of small- to moderate calibre. They are single-shot weapons, that are cocked

and fired using a simple spring-loaded bolt. Some pen guns are designed to fire blank cartridges, signal flares, noise-makers, or even tear gas cartridges.

18. The federal department that manages diplomatic relations and promotes international trade, development, and humanitarian assistance. At the time of this story, it was known as the Department of External Affairs, but has since been renamed several times and is now (officially) the Department of Foreign Affairs, Trade and Development, but is commonly referred to as Global Affairs Canada.

19. Canada Customs later become the Canada Customs and Revenue Agency. In 2003, the customs function was consolidated with others in the present-day Canada Border Services Agency.

20. By this point in history, the Security Service had created 'desks' to cover potential international threats. These were 'regional desks,' and were organized along geographical, rather than ideological lines. One of them covered Western Europe and the Pacific. See S, Hewitt, "Cold War Counter-Terrorism: The Evolution of International Counter-Terrorism in the RCMP Security Service, 1972–1984," *Intelligence and National Security*, **33**(*1*) 67-83, 2018.

21. This phrase comes from an old proverb, generally attributed to Hebrew origin and translated into English in about the 16th century. The original English-biblical meaning meant that sinners were doomed to eternal torment in hell. The 20th century, however, saw the emergence of an irreverent, humorous meaning that the wicked and/or lazy must work harder than others. A related offshoot is the expression 'no rest for the weary.'

22. A cauliflower ear is one that has become thickened and/or deformed as a result of one or (usually) more direct blows to the outer ear causing a build-up of fluids. It is commonly associated with boxing.

23. In casino blackjack, the 'shoe' is a tray that holds the shuffled cards, usually six or eight decks worth. The cards are held at an angle, and the shoe allows the dealer to remove them one at a time when dealing. This arrangement speeds up the game, by enabling multiple rounds to be played before shuffling, and it also reduces the opportunities for the dealer to cheat.

24. In Arthur Conan Doyle's fictional Sherlock Holmes stories, the famous detective sometimes enlisted the help of a group of street urchins that had the ability to "go everywhere and hear everything." See A. Conan Doyle, *A Study in Scarlet* (1887), and *The Sign of the Four* (1890).

25. A kangaroo jacket is a kind of hooded sweatshirt, usually made from the same kind of fabric as sweatpants. The classic style is made like an anorak, with no zipper up the front, and having a single broad pocket accessible from the left and/or right sides. In some regions they are called hooded sweatshirts (or hoodies), while in Saskatchewan they are called bunny hugs.

26. In 1982, in real life, women represented 2.5% of a total uniformed complement of RCMP officers of all ranks of 13,269. Calculated from data presented in Solicitor General, "Annual Report," Supply and Services Canada, Ottawa, reports from 1974/75 through 1981/82; and in L. Comeau, "Women's Struggle to Gain Equality Status in the RCMP," M.A. Thesis, Carleton University, Ottawa, 1990.

27. "Give something, however small, to the one in need. For it is not small to one who has nothing. Neither is it small to God, if we have given what we could," is attributed to St. Gregory Nazianzen, a 4th-century Christian Father.

28. Under the French seigneurial system, lands for development (*seigneuries*) were granted to people as a reward for services provided to the king. Each *seigneurie* would have a manor house and a mill, surrounded by these narrow strips of farmland. The *seigneur* would own and maintain the mill, and the *habitants* would operate the farms, in return for which they had to pay taxes to the *seigneur*. This system was established in Québec in the early 1600s, and lasted for over two hundred years, being abolished in 1854.

29. The phrase "You'll get time off Purgatory for that!" is a typically Catholic expression intended to console someone by implying that their contributions and/or sacrifices will be recognized and rewarded by God, thus reducing their time spent in Purgatory after death.

30. Attributed to the great American baseball player and coach, Yogi Berra, speaking to a reporter during the New York Mets' 1973 pennant race. See Allen Barra, *Yogi Berra. Eternal Yankee*, W. W. Norton & Company, NY, 2009.

31. The proverb 'If You Want Something Done Well, Do It Yourself,' and its variations have been attributed to a variety of people including Henry Wadsworth Longfellow and Napoleon Bonaparte, but it actually seems to date as far back as the 16th century, if not earlier.

32. The Second United Nations Emergency Force (UNEF II) was assembled to supervise the ceasefire at the end of the Yom Kippur War, plus the buffer zones and redeployments of the combatants. UNEF II was active between 1973 and 1979.

33. At the time of this story, the original unification of the Canadian Forces' three services was still in effect. The services returned to more individually distinctive uniforms in the late 1980s.

34. INTERPOL, the International Criminal Police Organization is an inter-governmental organization with nearly 200 member countries. It is headquartered in Lyon, France. Commonly referred-to as Interpol, the organization enables the police from member countries to share and access data on crimes and criminals.

35. An INTERPOL Red Notice is a request to law enforcement agencies around the world to locate and provisionally arrest a person or persons pending extradition, surrender, or similar legal action. Extracts of the Red Notices are published at the request of the member country concerned and where the public's help may be needed to locate one or more individuals, or if the individual(s) may pose a threat to public safety.

36. An *agent provocateur* (inciting agent, in English) is someone that actively entices one or more others into committing a crime.

An Inveterate Mountie

Adventures of the First Woman Mountie. Book 16

LAURIE SCHRAMM

inveterate

adjective: having a long-established, ingrained habit

The Canadian Oxford Dictionary, Oxford University Press, 1998

Laurie Schramm

DEDICATION

To Dr. Joe Muldoon, Ph.D., M.B.A., B.Sc., with whom I made so many enjoyable trips to the fascinating, real-life Gunnar Mine, Mill, and Townsite on the north shore of Lake Athabasca.

Laurie Schramm

BOOK 16 CONTENTS

	Dedication	423
	List of Characters	427
	List of Acronyms and Abbreviations	428
1	Preludes	429
2	A New Assignment	459
3	Rick Gets Inserted	475
4	Vivian Gets Inserted	493
5	The Scientists Arrive	503
6	Vivian's Treatment	513
7	Call to Action	535
8	Convergence	551
9	Epilogue	565
	Book 16 Endnotes	571

Laurie Schramm

LIST OF CHARACTERS
(IN ORDER OF APPEARANCE)

- Harland Walker, a United States Senator
- Dr. Ernst Wildersbach, owner of Athabasca Outfitters
- Lisa, a radiation-therapy technician
- Robert Johnson, a mysterious American
- Ben Delorme, a fly-in fishing-camp guide
- Sergeant Alexandra (Alex) Houston, RCMP Security Service
- Silver, an Alaskan Malamute; Alex's police-service-dog partner
- Major Donald (Don) Harrison, Military Intelligence, Canadian Armed Forces
- Deputy Commissioner George MacLeod, RCMP Security Service
- Rear-Admiral Peter White, head of the Canadian Forces Security Branch
- Staff Sergeant Avery Blunt, RCMP Security Service
- Special Agent Vivian Rule, FBI
- Richard Cooper, CIA operative
- Alistair Hughes, camp cook, Athabasca Outfitters
- Dexter Sherman, a computer consultant and sometime hacker

LIST OF ACRONYMS AND ABBREVIATIONS

AECL	Atomic Energy of Canada Limited
AI	Artificial Intelligence
CFB	Canadian Forces Base
CIA	U.S. Central Intelligence Agency
CPIC	Canadian Police Information Centre
ESP	Extra-sensory perception
FBI	U.S. Federal Bureau of Investigation
HQ	Headquarters
MI6	British Secret Intelligence Service
RCAF	Royal Canadian Air Force
RCMP	Royal Canadian Mounted Police
SUV	Sport Utility Vehicle
U of A	University of Alberta
WATS	Wide Area Telephone Service

CODE WORDS

Sparrow	The first CIA operative, Robert Johnson
Hawk	Captured or killed
Cat	Richard Cooper
Mouse	Vivian Rule
Dog	Alex Houston
Guns	Don Harrison
Turtle	Dexter Sherman

1 PRELUDES

Sunday, November 9, 1981

The driver of the large tractor-trailer unit yawned. He'd risen early, and had picked-up the trailer from a factory in Mississauga. It was now several hours later. The sun was just rising, traffic was light, and he was looking forward to delivering his cargo. The manifest listed it as a prototype Amelior-8 manufactured by a company named Accelerated Nuclear Inc. He'd never heard of either, and had initially balked at the idea of transporting some kind of nuclear device, but had relented when it was explained to him that the device was neither a nuclear reactor, nor a nuclear weapon, but was simply a new device for treating cancers using electrons and X-rays. He'd heard of X-ray machines of course, but he didn't know what electrons and X-rays were, but at least the machine wasn't a bomb or a weapon. That and the bonus he'd been offered, "as an expression of the shipper's appreciation for his assistance in getting the device to the Toronto General Hospital for testing and evaluation."

He yawned again. Time for coffee, *he thought. When the highway signs next displayed the food and fuel images, he took the off-ramp and parked at a large truck-stop. He didn't take any particular notice of the medium-grey van behind him that took the same off-ramp and parked a short distance away in the same parking lot. There was no particular reason why he should have noticed that the driver of the van got out at about the same time he did, and entered the coffee shop just behind him.*

Intending to get his coffee in a to-go cup, his first stop was the bathroom. The bathroom was empty as he headed for one of the urinals, only dimly hearing the sounds of another person entering the bathroom. He'd just begun to relieve himself when he felt someone brush-up against him from behind, followed by an extremely sharp and intense pain radiating from one ear to somewhere inside his head. His body slumped almost immediately, as he lost control – and consciousness – and was only prevented from falling by the man behind him, who had placed an arm under each of his armpits.

The man from behind – the van's driver, in fact – dragged the truck driver to the one large toilet stall and arranged the body so that it was seated on the toilet and slumped against the near wall. Having stepped back to reassure himself that the body looked as normal as was possible in the circumstances, he searched for and removed the man's key ring. Then, he used damp paper towels to clean up the small amount of blood that had trickled from the truck driver's ear. With all that accomplished, he left the stall and, with the help of a tool designed for the purpose, locked the door from the outside and left the bathroom.

Once out in the parking lot, the van driver waved to another tractor unit that had previously been following the van. As it started up, the van driver opened up the target tractor, disconnected and jacked up the trailer, then climbed into the cab and drove it to another spot in the lot. The driver of the second tractor unit swung over and backed up close to the unattached trailer, then got out to lower it onto the fifth-wheel plate, making sure that the king-pin engaged properly, then got out to connect the electrical and compressed-air lines. When all of this had been completed both the van and the tractor-trailer unit, with its stolen trailer, drove out of the parking lot and turned back the way they had come, heading northward toward Barrie.

After about an hour's drive they reached Barrie and proceeded to a truck stop with a large, drive-in truck wash of the self-serve, wand-wash type. It wasn't busy so early in the morning, so the driver was able to drive the entire unit right in. As the big door was closing, the truck driver exited and climbed up behind the cab, where an extendable ladder was attached. By the time he had freed the ladder from its attachments, he had been joined by the van driver who helped him extend the ladder and set it up beside the large trailer. The van driver had brought with him a duffel bag, from which he extracted the first of many cans of aerosol, quick-drying paint. Taking a couple of cans with him, the truck driver climbed the ladder and crawled up onto the roof, after which the van driver mounted the ladder but only to a point near the top of the trailer. Both men began painting the trailer.

As the van driver painted one side, he worked his way down the ladder, then moved the ladder over by a few feet, and repeated the process, something he did over and over again until he covered the entire side of the trailer. By this time the truck driver had finished painting the top, so he climbed down the ladder, after which both men began painting the other side, one working from the ladder on the upper portions while the other worked his way around the entire rest of the trailer painting as much as he could reach from the ground.

Within an hour, the entire trailer had been painted in a flat, medium-grey colour that completely hid both the colours and logos that it had formerly displayed. As a final touch, the van driver removed a licence plate from the duffel bag and replaced the trailer's original plate. When this was done, the two men placed the original licence plate and all of the empty spray cans into the duffel bag, which the van driver took back to the van. The truck driver then raised the truck-wash's large exit door and drove the truck out.

The van driver took one more walk around the tractor-trailer, inspecting it in the early morning sunlight, made a satisfied-sounding grunt. It was far from a professional-looking paint job, but once it had picked up some dirt and grime from the highway travel it would look like any other drab trailer. He gave the truck driver a thumbs-up signal.

Both vehicles then drove back onto the highway, heading toward Sudbury, after which they would take the Trans-Canada Highway, heading for Western Canada.

It was another hour before the dead body was discovered in the bathroom of the first truck-stop, 30 minutes before the police and ambulance arrived, and another two hours before anyone realized that the trailer had been stolen. By the time the police had been alerted and begun to search for the trailer, the thieves had reached Sudbury, nearly 450 km away. But it was worse than that because no one knew what direction the

Laurie Schramm

trailer went, and no one knew that it had been repainted, nor that it had its licence plate switched.

***

The Daily News

Sunday, November 9, 1981

Miracle Cancer-Treatment Device Stolen from Accelerated Nuclear

432

Seven months later,
Sunday, June 6, 1982
Saskatoon, Saskatchewan

In terms of physical attributes, Harland Walker looked like the stereotypical, or even Hollywood conception of a senator hailing from the Southern United States. He had a solid build, was reasonably tall, and had a full head of snow-white hair, a white moustache, and a white, pointed, goatee beard. He spoke with a southern accent and he even walked with a cane, although he was perfectly capable of walking without it. Conveniently enough, he really was a U.S. Senator and he was shrewd enough to emphasize, rather than diminish, his resemblance to the stereotype.

The one somewhat jarring note, as he disembarked from the jetliner on which he'd arrived, was his clothing, which bore no resemblance whatsoever to the senatorial stereotype. This was because he was dressed in the khaki 'bush-attire' that he regarded as an appropriate outfit for someone heading for a fly-in fishing trip. The only exception was his trademark white Stetson hat. It wasn't his best hat to be sure. It was in fact his oldest and most heavily worn Stetson, but it meant that anyone glancing at him for the first time would immediately be put in mind of the classic southern-gentleman image.

When the Customs and Immigration official asked about his purpose in visiting Canada, he declared himself to be on a fly-in fishing trip to Lake Athabasca in northern Saskatchewan. He presented a brochure from a fly-in fishing camp known as Athabasca Outfitters, plus his booking receipt/travel itinerary but the official merely examined his passport, then returned it and wished him a good trip. The senator's itinerary showed that he would be connecting to a small plane to fly to Prince Albert, then to a plane to Uranium City, and then to a float plane that would take him to a fishing camp on Lake Athabasca. He further volunteered that he had no fishing gear with him as everything was to be supplied once he reached the camp.

Although unfamiliar with the name of this particular fishing camp, everything else aligned so perfectly with the stories of dozens of American fishers that patronized Saskatchewan's northern fishing camps that the official had no qualms whatsoever about welcoming the visitor to Canada and passing him through.

Accordingly, three plane trips later, the senator found himself landing on Lake Athabasca itself. When the float plane had taxied to an old-looking wharf and he had disembarked, he was met by a distinguished-looking man who identified himself as Dr. Ernst Wildersbach.

"Welcome, welcome," said the latter, shaking the senator's hand enthusiastically. "How was your trip? No trouble with Customs and Immigration I trust?"

"No trouble at all," replied the senator, "I'm just tired from all the travelling."

"Of course, of course," said the doctor. "If you're not too tired, we'll offer you a nice hot meal and then show you to your cottage. Tomorrow, we'll show you everything – explain everything – and then we can begin."

"I must admit that I am extremely curious about everything, but I agree that some food will be all that I can remain awake for."

"Fine, fine. I will lead you to the dining hall and then I will have one of my assistants show you to your cottage. Don't worry about your luggage, it will be waiting for you when you get there. I must apologize for not spending more time with you this evening, but I assure you that you will have my fullest attention in the morning."

"And the treatment?" the senator tried but failed to keep a slight note of desperation from his voice.

"Absolutely, absolutely. I will show you everything. We will take some X-rays, then I will explain everything, and then we will begin the treatment immediately after that. Tomorrow morning without fail." The doctor led the senator to a pickup truck, motioned for the senator to get in, and then he himself took up position in the driver's seat.

Feeling somewhat reassured, the senator got into the truck and settled into his seat. As they drove around the metal-clad warehouse-type building that stood in front of the dock, they almost immediately passed a towering structure that had been the site's most eye-catching feature when the float-plane had circled the site before landing on the lake.

"What is this place anyway?"

"Ah, yes. There's quite a story here. We're using a ghost town. All the structures you're going to see here are part of an abandoned uranium mining operation left over from the cold war[1]. It was built in the 1950s to provide uranium for your own country's nuclear weapons program. The big

tower is the headframe for the hoist that serviced the underground mine. If you look to your right, you will see what looks like a small lake."

"It looks artificial," said the senator, noting that it was oval in shape and appeared to be nearly a quarter mile long. His estimate was close; it was actually a thousand feet (300 m) long.

"That's very observant of you. They began with a large open-pit mine, then did the underground workings later. When everything was shut-down in the 1960s, they blasted to create a connection between the underground workings and the bottom of the open pit, then they blasted a channel between the pit and the lake, and voilà, *the open-pit and underground workings were completely flooded up to the level of the big lake itself, which is what you see now.*

"The buildings you can see to our left were warehouses and mine maintenance shops, and up ahead you can just see the mill where they processed the ore to produce yellowcake uranium concentrate. It was all very self-contained. Behind the mill there's a huge acid plant – they made their own sulphuric acid for the mill here – and there's a concrete plant too." The doctor turned left. "That building on our right was the powerhouse, but the generators were salvaged long ago so we have had to bring in our own diesel generators. Ah. Here we are. This is the original cookhouse. You can just see some of the large bunkhouses behind it."

"I thought you said I'd be staying in a cottage," said the senator, sounding surprised and possibly a bit grumpy.

"I did. I certainly did. The bunkhouses are all quite derelict now and I suspect that the upper floors may be quite unsafe. There is much more to the site than you've seen so far. They built an entire townsite here: a department store, community centre, hospital, school, and a nice little collection of small houses, some of which we have fixed up quite nicely. When I mentioned a cottage, I was referring to one of the fixed-up little houses. You will find it quite comfortable. Quite comfortable."

"Why was it shut down?" asked the senator, still thinking about what he had seen on their short drive.

"Mined out the entire orebody. They kept the mill running a little longer, to process the last of the mined ore. By the early 1960s, Canada, the U.K., and the U.S. all had more than the uranium they felt they needed, so the uranium price began to fall. By the mid-1960s the uranium market had crashed, causing most of the local mines to close. That meant

they couldn't even process ore for other mines, so they shut down the mill here, and the entire community left, virtually overnight. At its peak, the town had about 850 people. By 1964 it was a ghost town. Later on, you can borrow one of our vehicles and drive around it as much as you like. It's all quite fascinating, really."

"How did you manage to take it all over?" asked the senator, still trying to get his mind around the doctor's story.

"I leased it from the provincial government, of course. It was just sitting here abandoned and in the middle of nowhere. The government had a loan program aimed at entrepreneurs and start-up businesses, so..."

"You borrowed the capital on the promise of new jobs and increased tourism and used the money to pay the same government for the lease," finished the Senator with a smile. This was something he could understand.

"Exactly, exactly."

"And do you actually run a fly-in fishing camp here?"

"As far as anyone knows, yes. We have fishing gear and boats, and some of our staff are knowledgeable enough to be able to take people out fishing. Our boats go out every day," he said with a wink, "although normally it's just our own people going out to fish and keep up appearances. But we do take our patients out as well, if they are interested. You will be welcome to go out yourself if you wish, in between treatments. The fishing is really quite good. Quite good."

"And no one knows anything about what you really do here?"

"No, no. Dear me, no," he said, then immediately contradicted himself, "The staff know, of course, and our agents and former patients know, otherwise our word-of-mouth business would very quickly become extinct."

"Just like the old uranium mine," observed the senator.

"Exactly, exactly. A very apt comparison," he chuckled.

"But why, doctor? Your agent explained the services you provide, and supplied patient references — which I checked out quite thoroughly — but he was quite vague about the need for secrecy. Kept insisting that it was the only way to keep the waiting lists short and provide rapid access to the treatments. But I'm not so easy to fool as all that. There's more to your story than exclusivity isn't there?" He gave the doctor a penetrating look from under his bushy white eyebrows.

"Well, you're right. Absolutely right. Yes indeed. The part our agent

told you about is partly true, of course. Secrecy and premium prices enable us to maintain next to no waiting time for our treatments, which enables wealthy patients such as yourself to avoid the long waits that everyone else has to endure in America, Canada, and most other countries around the world for that matter." He gave the senator a shrewd look. "But there is another reason. Our state-of-the-art radiation machine is unlicensed, so we can hardly admit that we have it, much less that we are using it to treat cancers and save lives."

"Unlicensed! But... but..." the senator began to sputter.

"Now, now. Calm yourself, senator. There is no cause for concern. No cause for concern at all, I assure you. Our radiation treatment machine has been fully tested and is completely safe as long as it is being used by trained professionals, which is what we have here. And it's not experimental, dear me no. Our unit is what is called the production prototype, meaning that it is the same as the ones that will soon be rolling off assembly lines but this one was very carefully built by hand. To the exact same specifications as the future production ones will be, but carefully built by hand. Everything has been done excepting only that the regulatory approval process is very slow. I don't have to tell you how slowly the wheels of government machinery move." He looked the senator in the eye. "No. I can see that you do understand. The regulatory process takes years when anything nuclear is involved, and it takes even longer when new technologies are developed. But otherwise, all the testing and certifications are complete. I will even show you the documentation tomorrow. Please. No more question for now. Let us go inside and I will introduce you to the dining room staff. As I said earlier, I promise to be available to answer any and all of your questions tomorrow after breakfast. Then, we will only proceed if you feel completely satisfied."

"And if I don't?"

"Why, my good sir, if you do not feel completely satisfied then we will take no further steps. We can assist you with new travel arrangements and you may leave whenever you wish." He paused, for effect, then smiled. "You can even go fishing first, with one of our guides, if you like."

The two men walked into the dining hall. "This is our main dining room. You'll find a meal schedule in the house you've been assigned to. The house will have a fully functional kitchen stocked with a few necessities like coffee and snacks but, for anything substantial, everyone eats together here in the dining room. It's all very friendly and informal." Then, after introducing the senator to one of the dining hall staff, the doctor took his leave.

A good, hot meal left the senator somewhat mollified, and when he was later guided to one of the nearby houses, he was surprised to see that it was very comfortably appointed, which provided a confidence boost.

Early the next morning, Dr. Wildersbach met the senator as he was finishing his breakfast. "How are you feeling this morning, Senator? Ready for your first treatment?"

"I sure am. In fact, I'm feeling finer than a frog hair split four ways"

"Fine. Fine," said the doctor, struggling to understand the expression but pleased at the Senator's obvious enthusiasm. When you're ready, we'll walk over to the hospital and take some X-rays. Then we'll begin."

A short while later, the X-rays having been taken and developed, the doctor put one of the films up on the lighted viewing box that was mounted on the wall. "If you look right here," he pointed to a rather fuzzy spot on the upper back and slightly to one side of the spine, "that's the location from which your surgeon removed the cancerous tumor." The senator nodded. He'd been shown something like this before.

"Our job now," continued the doctor, "is to attack the little bits of growth that have been left behind. For that, we'll be using the Amelior-8, which is the very first of a new generation of machines that will be produced by Accelerated Nuclear Inc. once they receive regulatory approvals, as I mentioned to you last night." The senator nodded again.

"The machine is what is called a medical linear accelerator[2], and what it does is accelerate electrons to create high-energy beams that can destroy cancerous tumors with very little impact on the nearby tissue. In your case the main tumor was quite close to your spine, so we can treat it with just an electron beam. If it had been deeper inside your body, then we'd have had to convert the electrons into X-rays but there's no need for that in your case.

"What we're going to do is treat you once a day until we're sure that we've completely removed all of the cancerous cells."

"My own doctor said that this could be done in as little as four weeks," the senator said, hopefully.

"Well now, that's possible. Yes, certainly possible, but I can't promise

you that. You have to understand that it might take a little longer, but I'm quite confident that it won't be more than six weeks."

The senator nodded. He'd been told this as well. *"When will you be able to begin?"*

"Right now, of course. Right now," said the doctor, nodding his head. *"Yes. Yes, just follow me and we'll go down the hall to our treatment room. This was the original mine hospital, you know,"* he explained, as they proceeded out and down the hallway. *"It had seven beds, a resident doctor, and four nursing staff, making it just the right size for us here. All we had to do was renovate some of the rooms and add the dedicated power generator that you probably heard running when we walked over here."*

As the doctor led the way through a new doorway, the senator could see that they were in a small control room where a young woman immediately stood up from a computer display to greet them.

"This is Lisa," introduced the doctor. *"She's the technician that will be operating the machine. Lisa, you have the prescription for the senator's treatment: electron beam treatment of 180 rads at 22 MeV."*

"Yes, doctor."

"Fine. Fine. Senator, I will leave you in Lisa's capable hands, and I will come back and check on you in a little while." So saying, the doctor took his leave.

"Come with me Senator," said Lisa, *"and we'll get everything set-up for you."* She led him into the treatment room and had him lie face-down on the treatment table. *"Comfortable? Fine. As you can see. I'm moving the table and rotating the gantry so that the treatment beam will be aimed exactly where we want it. There. Now I'm adjusting the treatment field size – that means the area that we want to be targeted by the electron beam... there. Now, I'm going to leave the treatment room and sit down at the computer console. You'll just be able to see where I am if you look through that little window in the wall. OK?"*

"Yes, fine."

"Great. Now then, when I get there, I will switch on the intercom so we can speak to each other." Lisa left the room, closed the door and settled-in at her computer terminal, from which position she could also control the intercom.

"Senator? Can you hear me?"

"Yes," came the Senator's surprised sounding voice. *"In fact, I can*

hear you very clearly."

"Excellent. I will give you a running commentary on what I'm doing while you just lie there and relax and try not to move your body."

"I'll try." Came the reply.

"Fine. The machine and computer are on, and I am just typing in your name and the machine settings: that means the gantry rotation, field sizing, and a few other mechanical details. The computer will check to make sure that the data I enter matches the settings I just made manually when I was in there with you. It will only allow me to proceed if they match perfectly. That's for your safety, you see."

The Senator could actually hear the clicking sounds as she pushed the keys on the keyboard. Lisa, meanwhile was reading the lines as they came up on her display:

```
PATIENT NAME: WALKER, HARLAND
DATE: 82-JUN-07      TIME: 09:30
OPR ID: LISA


TREATMENT MODE: X ENERGY      BEAM ENERGY (MeV):22

                            ACTUAL PRESCRIBED
GANTRY ROTATION (DEG):         0.0        0.0    OK
COLLIMATOR ROTATION (DEG):   359.2        359    OK
COLLIMATOR X (CM):            14.2       14.0    OK
COLLIMATOR Y (CM):            27.1       27.0    OK
WEDGE NUMBER:                    1          1    OK
ACCESSORY NUMBER:                0          0    OK
```

"OK. Everything is looking good... Oops. I made I typing error. Just a moment." Lisa had noticed that she'd accidentally typed 'x' (for X-ray) when she had intended to type 'e' (for electron) mode. This was because most of the treatments involved X-rays, and she had gotten used to typing this. On the other hand, she'd been operating the machine for some time and was used to quickly making changes using the system's editing features. Using the 'cursor-up' key, she edited the treatment mode entry from 'x' to 'e'.

```
TREATMENT MODE: ELECTRON      BEAM ENERGY (MeV):22
```

Checking to make sure that the other parameters she had entered were still correct, she hit the return key several times to pass through them while leaving their values unchanged. The next line on the display read:

```
SYSTEM: BEAM READY      OP. MODE: TREAT      AUTO
```

"OK. I've fixed the error and rechecked everything else." Lisa then hit the one-key command B, for beam on, to begin the treatment.

```
TREATMENT MODE: E ENERGY      BEAM ENERGY (MeV):22

                              ACTUAL  PRESCRIBED
UNIT RATE/Minute:                0        200
MONITOR UNITS:                   8        200
TIME (MIN):                    0.04       1.0
```

The machine switched on, but only for a few seconds, after which the display showed 8 monitor units delivered, which was a severe underdose considering she had set the machine to deliver 200 monitor units. She had become quite used to the machine's eccentricities, however, which caused it to halt or pause from time to time without warning. In this case, she interpreted the machine's underdosing as just another unexpected pause and did what she always did in such cases: tap the P key to resume treatment. The machine promptly shut down with messages reporting that treatment had been paused and a MALFUNCTION 66 error code.

```
TREAT: TREAT PAUSE      REASON: MALFUNCTION      66
```

At the same time, she heard a scream from inside the treatment room. Getting up and rushing into the room, she found the Senator scrambling off of the table and attempting to stand up.

441

"Are you all right? Let me help you," she said as she grabbed one of his arms and steered him to a nearby chair.

"What in God's name was that?" he gasped. *"There was a thump and what felt like a huge electric shock to my back, and it felt hot, very hot."*

"Just sit right here and I will go get the doctor. It will only be a moment." Forcing herself to appear calm and professional, she walked out of the room and turned the corner. Then, out of sight of the Senator, she ran to the outer hallway and along it looking for Dr. Wildersbach.

The machine, meanwhile, sat quietly continuing to display the malfunction message. A typed sheet taped to the side of the computer monitor held a listing of malfunction error codes. For MALFUNCTION 66 it read *"dose input error,"* which the machine's operating manual explained meant that the dose delivered had been either too high or too low. Unbeknown to either Lisa or Dr. Wildersbach, the prototype machine had some programming bugs, one of which was that some of the machine settings — such as the orientation of the bending and focusing magnets - changed fairly slowly, whereas the prescription data could be edited very quickly — more quickly in fact, than the machine was programmed to check for such changes. This sometimes led to mismatches between the computer values being displayed and the machine settings actually in place. In some cases, this led to inadvertent but severe overdosing[3].

When Lisa returned to the treatment room with Dr. Wildersbach, he immediately examined the senator and discovered a skin burn spanning the area treated. They moved him to a bed in the one hospital ward that was still being maintained, all the while assuring the senator that he had simply had a bad reaction to the treatment, and that it would clear in time.

"Does this mean you won't be able to continue the treatments?" the senator asked.

"No, we should be able to do another one tomorrow, as scheduled. You just rest quietly here for now and I will come and have another look at you later this afternoon."

When Dr. Wildersbach examined him that afternoon, however, the 'burn' looked much worse. He didn't admit this to the senator, however, and instead told him that they would like to keep him overnight in the hospital, but that they would resume treatments the next day, as planned. Then, he went to run some diagnostics on the machine itself.

"What do you think doctor?" asked Lisa, after he had checked all of the machine settings.

"The damn thing has done it again. It delivered a massive dose instead of the one I prescribed."

"But I assure you, I made sure everything on the display was reading exactly as it should before pressing the 'P' key to proceed."

"I know. I know. And nineteen times out of twenty, the machine delivers exactly the dose that has been selected, but in one time out of twenty it delivers something different: either too much or too little radiation. Someday, Accelerated Nuclear is going to discover that either there is a bug in the computer software, or else an intermittent electrical fault in the linear accelerator, and fix it. But, for now, this machine is all we have to work with."

"Do you think the senator is going to die like the others?"

"I don't know yet, Lisa, but it's certainly possible. Yes, certainly possible. We may have to console ourselves with the thought that we are able to save the lives of most of our patients, but not all of them."

In fact, the senator had indeed received a massive overdose, concentrated in the treatment location but extending to his spine.

Over the weeks following the accident, they continued with his treatments knowing that they would probably only make matters worse. As a result, the senator began to experience pain in his back, then in his shoulders, and eventually in his extremities. Within four weeks, the senator had extreme difficulty moving his limbs and became unable to walk. The doctor concluded, correctly, that the senator had developed radiation myelopathy of the cervical spine, but did not admit this to anyone, much less the patient, who died in week four.

Although they had not lost a large number of patients due to treatment malfunctions, they had developed a procedure for dealing with them. The doctor had two specific, highly-trusted orderlies for such work, whom he called in to remove the body. The first stages of this removal were conducted with the utmost dignity and decorum, with the body encased in a standard body-bag, placed on a gurney, and covered with a clean sheet. The orderlies then took it from the building and drove it to a location beside the flooded mine pit, but on the far side and well away from the normally travelled roads. There they placed the body bag into a rowboat that was moored there.

Later that night, the two orderlies returned to the boat bringing with them a heavy chain from one of the machine shops. Then, they rowed out to the centre of the flooded pit, wrapped and secured the chain around the body bag, then carefully eased it over the side and into the water. The body bag went in without a sound and immediately sank the 110 m (360 ft.) to the bottom. In Dr. Wildersbach's judgement, the odds of anyone going SCUBA-diving in a pit filled with radioactive water, much less to a depth of 110 m, were low indeed.

All patients admitted for treatment were sworn to the utmost secrecy, but of course some violated this by, for example, telling a spouse where they were going. This is what had happened in the senator's case. When, therefore, enquiries were made about the 'senatorial fishing-guest' who had gone missing, the staff explained that the Senator had indeed come for a most relaxing fishing expedition, had declared himself to have had a very good time, and had been flown by seaplane to Uranium City, and from there by a chartered plane to the Prince Albert airport, then by commercial aircraft to Saskatoon, and finally connecting to a U.S.-bound flight.

What no one admitted to, was that it had been a member of the staff, dressed in the senator's clothes, made-up to resemble the senator in appearance, and carrying the senator's passport and other documents, that had made the flights – even to the extent of boarding the first flight cross-border in to the U.S., in this case to Denver. Once in Denver, the staff member, who had a change of clothing in his carry-on bag, changed his appearance back to normal, discarded the senators clothing and documents, and boarded a return flight to Canada under his own name.

When a worried senator's wife hired a private detective to attempt to locate her husband, he found – as he was intended to - that the trail went cold in Denver.

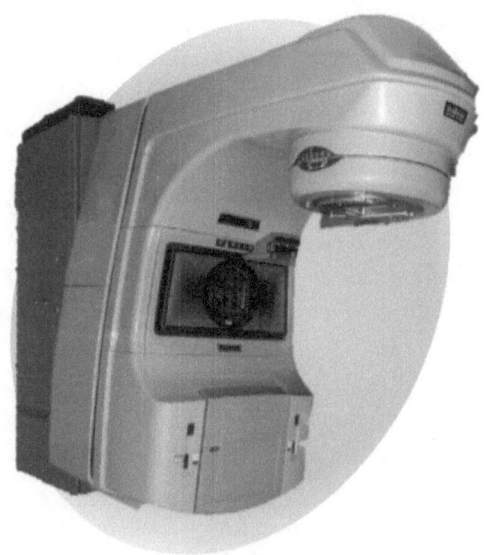

Sunday, July 24, 1982
Saskatoon, Saskatchewan

One of the first arrivals at the airport this Sunday morning was a Boeing 737 in the livery of one of America's largest airlines. The big jet touched down without incident and taxied to the terminal building. Among the passengers that disembarked and made their way to Canada Customs and Immigration was a man with brown hair and eyes; with average looks; was of average height and build; and he looked - ordinary. So ordinary, in fact, that if you passed him in the street nothing about his appearance would catch your attention. This was one of his skills: looking so unremarkable as to be virtually invisible in a crowd. He had many other skills as well.

His American passport identified him as Robert Johnson. That wasn't his real name, but it was a common enough name. The names Robert and Johnson were the second most common first and surnames, respectively, in the United States. Not the absolute most common, however, that would be James Smith, but even that could have attracted the attention of an unusually alert customs and immigration official, and Robert Johnson did not want to attract anyone's attention just yet.

When the official asked about his purpose in visiting Canada, he declared himself to be on a fly-in fishing trip to Lake Athabasca in northern Saskatchewan and offered to present a booking receipt/travel itinerary.

He certainly looked the part. Although Robert Johnson's trip to Canada resembled that embarked upon by Senator Harland Walker a month and a half earlier, there were some notable differences. Although his clothing was the kind of wilderness-adventure clothing common to visiting American tourists heading for a northern hunting- or fishing-camp adventure, the tourists' clothing was generally brand-new, or at least in excellent condition. Johnson's clothing, on the other hand, had clearly seen better days as it showed every sign of hard use – faded, stained, patched, frayed in places, and almost threadbare. Almost, threadbare, that is. A very careful examination would have shown that it was still as strong and functional as it had been when purchased new. Similar descriptions could be applied to his luggage, which looked equally travelled and worn: a backpack and duffel bag – both in camouflage pattern – and a long cylindrical case with a shoulder strap, of the kind used to carry fishing rods. Everything about him seemed so commonplace that, having looked him over, the official simply stamped and returned his passport without even hesitating, then wished him a good trip.

Johnson, and several other similarly clothed and equipped passengers from the same incoming flight, had a short wait then boarded a twin-engine turboprop plane to fly to Prince Albert. From there, the other passengers transferred to different planes, presumably on their way to some of the many fly-in fishing camps that are distributed around Saskatchewan's north which, contrary to the Saskatchewan stereotype of endlessly flat prairie, almost completely comprises lakes and forests. Johnson himself was scheduled to fly directly to the former Gunnar uranium mine site on a dedicated charter aircraft, rather than connecting through Uranium City, but he had some time before the flight.

Having collected his baggage, he carried it with him into the terminal's one 'Family Washroom.' After locking the door, he changed clothes and also changed the appearance of his baggage, in the latter case by the simple expedient of unzipping the close-fitting covers that encased his backpack and duffel bag. With their covers off, the backpack and duffel bag were revealed to be a medium-brown khaki colour, and both of them in excellent condition. Even the fishing-rod case had a zippered cover removed, revealing the standard black plastic of a traditional, shoulder-slung map case. Tucking the zippered covers into the duffel bag, he re-entered the terminal proper. Anyone chancing to look at the man exiting from the family washroom would have seen a man in the summer uniform of a government conservation officer, complete with crested, dark-blue baseball cap, and wearing sunglasses.

In the unlikely event that he encountered a real such conservation officer in the brief time he'd be spending in the air terminal, he had a cover story involving being sent out to conduct a series of surprise fisheries and wildlife compliance checks (including selected fly-in fishing camps) plus environmental inspections related to such things as shoreline alteration, unlawful dumping, and so on. He would then express extreme surprise that the local conservation officer had not been notified in advance, offer his apologies and suggest that the real officer 'take it up' with the head office in Regina. That would, of course, take some time and the fly-in fishing camp at Gunnar had no telephone service.

As it turned out, no one questioned his assumed identity and his charter float plane eventually arrived to pick him up and fly him directly to the Gunnar site. It was late afternoon when they crossed Lake Athabasca, landed, and taxied to the Gunnar dock. While the pilot was busy tying up the plane, they were met by a man dressed like a local and who identified himself as Ben Delorme one of the camp's fishing guides. But, quickly assessing his manner and the way he carried himself, Johnson figured him to be more like a guard than a guide. He'd expected something like this and launched into his cover story.

Delorme asked them to wait and stepped away in order to be able to speak to someone on a handheld radio.

VHF radio, Johnson thought to himself. He was able to overhear a few of the words, enough to verify that Delorme was relating his story to someone with more authority. It wasn't long before Delorme came back.

"Spoke to the owner. He's just up near the town and will come right down. It will only be a few minutes."

"Fine," replied Johnson, stepping over to select a sturdy-looking wooden crate to sit on, from which position he took out a cigarette package and waved it towards Delorme in offering. Delorme, for his part, seemed surprised but didn't hesitate to approach and take one. Having lit cigarettes for each of them, Johnson leaned back and relaxed, noting as he did that Delorme stepped back to smoke his. Johnson nodded approvingly, Delorme had placed himself between the dock, where Johnson was relaxing, and the rest of the site — just like a guard would.

Ten minutes later a pickup truck rounded the corner of the warehouse and approached the men. An older man got out of the truck and walked over.

"I understand you're here for some kind of surprise inspection. Have we done something wrong? My name is Dr. Ernst Wildersbach, by the way." He put a hand out to shake. "Retired doctor that is, I'm the owner of Athabasca Outfitters. We have a lease on the old Gunner mine-site, as I'm sure you know."

"Yes, I do, and no you haven't done anything wrong. At least, nothing I'm aware of. It's the Ministry's policy to conduct a certain number of surprise fisheries and wildlife compliance checks every season. We probably do about a third of them each year, so each operation only gets checked once every three years or so. That way there's a regular pattern, and paper-

trail, of inspections without having to burden each operator every year with the inconvenience of having us trapse around sticking our noses into everything every year. Of course," he added deprecatingly, "the rare operation that flaunts the regulations gets checked much more regularly, but we don't want to interfere with the good operators which, to be fair, represent the vast majority."

"Very reasonable. In fact, a surprisingly reasonable attitude for a government regulator to take. No offense, mind you."

"None taken. Call it a balancing act. The government wants operators like you to run your businesses here, the tourism business is an important part of the economy, but we have a job to do as well."

"Fine, fine. But what's happened to Mike, our regular conservation officer?"

"Nothing, as far as I know." Johnson affected surprise. "The Ministry is experimenting with having dedicated officers do these inspections. In fact, these inspections are the only thing I'll be doing during the tourist season this year. I started on the May long weekend, and I'll be doing them until just after the Labour Day Weekend in the fall — all over the province. I guess someone higher up thinks that the local officers are at risk of becoming too complacent about their assigned areas, or something like that. Anyway, your regular guy will do spot checks, but my job is to look the whole operation over in a single sweep. In this case, it's a bigger job than usual because you've leased the entire site even though you're probably only using pieces of it."

The doctor nodded. "That's right. We greet our customers here, feed them in the dining hall, house them in some of the smaller houses, and run the boats out of that little marina that's near where the curling rink and school used to operate. We also use this warehouse for storage and the old machine shops for repairing our boats and vehicles."

"Makes sense to me," said Johnson, "but I'm afraid I have to look over the whole operation, including the head-frame, mill, acid plant, community housing and buildings, tailings areas, and even the shoreline."

"That will take some time," said the doctor.

"Actually, it won't be too bad. Most places I just need to peek into and move on, and the parts that you are actually using won't need much more than quick glance. This is the first time I've visited this particular site, but I have the original Gunnar Mines maps and descriptions from

1957 to guide me."

"You're certainly welcome, but I'd like to have one of my staff act as your guide. I'm sure you can find your way, but some of these buildings are on the verge of collapse and it would be unfortunate and embarrassing for both our company and your department if you got injured while you were here. Besides, my man can chauffeur you around wherever you need to go, and he'll have a portable radio with him so he'll be able to call for help if you should find you need anything. We're not full up with customers right now, so we can spare someone without interfering with business."

"That's very good of you," said Johnson, *who'd expected nothing less.* Now for the tricky part, *he thought. He made a show of looking at his watch.* "I wonder..." *he said hesitantly.* "I was supposed to arrive here this morning and be finished by about now, but I had some unexpected delays. I can get the plane to fly me to Uranium City and find a place to stay overnight, unless..."*

"Nonsense. There's no need for that at all. We can put you and your pilot up for the night, and then you can start your inspection first thing in the morning."

"Well, if you're sure..."

"Certainly, certainly. Always ready to cooperate with the government. You'll find the food here is excellent, especially if you enjoy fresh fish." He chuckled. *"We have a nice little two-bedroom house I can put at your disposal, if you and your pilot don't mind sharing?"*

"I'll talk to him, but I'm sure he'll agree. I'll offer to pay him double, and I think the thought of the extra money will make the decision for him."

"Fine. Fine. Talk to your pilot then bring your gear up to the truck and I'll drive you to the houses. Ben here will give you a hand." He looked meaningfully at Delorme who took his cue and began sauntering down to where the plane was tied up.

With their bags loaded into the truck, Johnson and his pilot climbed in with the doctor, who drove them to one of the houses that was within easy walking distance of the dining hall. Along the way he gave them the same description of the mine-site and its history that he gave all visitors to the site. In this case, however, he also drove by a small cove, pointing out that the mining company had constructed a small dock and barged in sand to make a beach for the staff to enjoy and launch small boats from. He *explained that it provided some shelter from the big lake and that the pilot was welcome to move his aircraft there if he wanted. The pilot said he'd like to take a closer look at it before deciding, and Johnson offered to walk down with him after they'd settled their baggage in the house.*

By this time, it was shortly before dinner would be served so the doctor suggested they take their look and then head for the dining hall.

"I may not be able to join you for dinner," he cautioned. "But I will certainly meet you after breakfast and make sure that you have anything you might need for your inspection." With that, he took his leave. As the two men carried their luggage in to the house, Johnson noted without surprise that Delorme, who had followed them in a separate truck, was parked not far away.

After a few minutes, the two men walked the 150 m (500 ft.) from their house to the marina so the pilot could look it over. There were a couple of beach chairs on the sand beach, several canoes stacked over to one side, and two small motorboats tied up at the dock. Over to one side of the small bay was another float plane, which was moored to a buoy and also secured by two ropes to trees on the shore. There was a second, unused, buoy not far away.

"What do you think?" Johnson asked the pilot.

He shrugged. "The weather forecast for tonight and tomorrow was clear, but the weather can change quickly on a lake this big. I think I'd feel safer moving the plane over here and using a three-point mooring arrangement like they've done with the one here."

"Take a look over my shoulder. Do you see a truck parked up the way behind us?"

The pilot looked up, then gave an exclamation of surprise. "Yes. Keeping an eye on us, I suppose?"

"Hmmm. Not very trusting, are they? See if you can get him to drive you back to the other dock so you can get the plane. If he's reluctant, make up some story about a forecasted storm brewing just out of sight and that you want to get the plane over here as soon as possible. He'll call in for instructions on his radio. See if you can overhear the conversation, will you? Meanwhile, I'll see if I can get one of these boats started so I can help you tie-up to the buoy and bring you back here. Do you have ropes in the plane."

"For tying up to the shore you mean? Sure. I've got ropes and cargo

straps. We'll be able to jury-rig something." The pilot walked up the hill *from the marina and spoke to Delorme. There was a delay, after which the pilot walked around the truck and got in. The truck drove away.*

Dragging one of the chairs up from the beach, Johnson placed it on the dock in a position from which he could look out over the lake, but easily glance back up the hill to the road. Settling himself in, he lit another cigarette and made a show of looking out over the lake. Within a few minutes, he heard the sound of a truck approaching and then shut off. Being careful to only turn his head very slightly he was just able to discern that another pickup truck had parked such that the driver could keep an eye on him.

Oh no, my friends, you don't catch me out as easily as all that, *he thought to himself. He contentedly tipped his baseball cap down lower on his face and dropped his chin down towards his chest as if having a snooze while he waited for the plane to arrive.*

Later that evening, having secured the float-plane and having enjoyed a good meal in the dining room, the two men had walked back to their house for the night, followed at a discreet distance by one of the company's pickup trucks.

"They're not very good at this, are they?" asked the pilot, who knew Johnson was up to something, but not what.

"No. I've been watching them, and they seem like hired muscle that mostly do odd jobs around here. They're probably tough enough, and maybe even good in a fight, but they're not professionals."

"And you are?"

Johnson smiled grimly. "That's the kind of question you're being paid not to ask," he reproved.

"Sorry. What's next then?"

"Next, we wait for twilight." The two men entered the house and turned on all the lights. After an hour or two, they switched all the lights off.

"I'm going to watch for a while," Johnson said to the pilot. "Don't be surprised if I disappear for an hour or two. If anything happens to me just remember: you know nothing. You were simply hired to fly me here, wait around, and then fly me out. Nothing more. In the worst case, they'll make up some story about me or invent some kind of excuse to get you to fly out

of here: take it, and when you get back to civilization, phone the number I gave you. It's toll free. When someone answers, tell them you have a message from Sparrow. The message is: 'Hawk,' repeat that back to me."
The pilot did so, twice. "That's it. Try to get some sleep. With luck, I'll see you in the morning."

For the next hour, Johnson prowled from room to room, pausing to the side of each window and silently watching for a while before moving on to the next. Within the first half hour, he had identified two watchers by the occasional lighting of their cigarettes. There was one watching the front, and another watching the back. Not bad, but not very original, *thought Johnson, who went to change into dark grey shirt and pants, and then applied black camouflage face-paint and put on a black wool toque. From his duffel bag, he withdrew two sheathed knives, one of which he attached to his left forearm, under his shirt sleeve, and the other to his right calf, under his pant leg. The knives were identical, double-bladed throwing knives, the kind that are exceptionally dangerous in the hands of a trained professional. Johnson was a trained professional.*

Checking the luminous hands on his watch showed that it was close to midnight. Twilight, *he thought, and went to a side window that he'd previously opened. Moving carefully, he silently slipped out the window and lowered himself to the ground where he crouched, listening. Hearing nothing unusual, he crept silently towards the trees and melted into the forest.*

Johnson knew that at such a high northern latitude, he would have only two hours of semi-darkness before it began to get brighter again. That meant he had to budget his time. There were several roads with similar houses on them, all accessible from the forest. Most of these he passed by with only the glance that was needed to verify that they were still in a state of abandonment and disrepair. Only a few, all of them close to the one he and the pilot shared, had been fixed up for guests but quick glances through the windows with the aid of a shielded penlight showed them to be currently unoccupied. Except… he had begun to turn away from the last window on the last house, when something made him turn back for a second look. It was a bedroom, and the bed had been made-up, but it looked like there was something pushed back under the bed. Whatever it was, it wasn't visible unless someone deliberately looked under the bad, or viewed it from a shallow angle, as he was doing.

Johnson crept around to the back of the house and tested the door. It was unlocked. Once again, he stopped and listened carefully for a few moments, as indeed he had been doing regularly on this excursion. Hearing nothing concerning, he opened the door and crept quietly to the indicated bedroom, reached under the bed, and withdrew a small, brown, well-worn leather briefcase of the kind that was then popular with civil servants and politicians. Opening the single clasp released the strap that held closed the expanding top, he opened the case. It contained a bottle of bourbon whiskey, several paperback novels, a notebook and pen, and a travel folio. Opening the folio, he used his penlight so he could scan the documents. They were the fishing-camp booking and travel documents, and business cards, of one Harland Walker.

Careless of someone, *thought Johnson, as he replaced everything in the case and put it back where he had found it. Then he got up, stretched, and noiselessly made his way out of the house and melted back into the forest. Checking his watch, he noted that he had time for one more stop. He decided on the hospital, which was only about 200 m (650 ft.) away. Pausing to get his bearings – he had previously memorized the mining company's maps and surface plans showing the locations of all of the significant structures on the site – he headed for the hospital, following game trails to the extent possible. Soon, he came upon the west side of the hospital, but crept around to the back.*

Sensing that there was no one around, he crept along each wall, pausing only long enough to shine his penlight into each window. The hospital was clearly in use, but nothing appeared to be out of the ordinary. If there's anything interesting, it will be on the inside or else on the second floor, *he thought, debating whether to attempt to enter the building or not. He checked his watch. There was just enough time left for a quick reconnoitre.*

Concerned that this might be the one building for which the doors and windows were alarmed, he looked higher up. On the outside of the building, there was an old-style steel fire escape from the second floor – the kind that had a section of the ladder suspended by springs so that it was well above the ground. From around his waist, he unwound a length of woven rope that was quite thin but extremely strong. He next searched around for an oblong-shaped rock. Finding one, he tied it to one end of the rope then experimented with tossing it up and toward the lower rungs of the suspended ladder. His aim being quite good, it only took three tries before the launched rock flew between two of the rungs, struck the side of the building and then fell to the ground. After untying the rock, he took both lengths of rope in both hands and tied them together so that the rope formed a loop that ended about two feet off the ground. Holding onto the ropes, he placed one foot into the bottom of the loop then slowly stepped up so that it carried his entire weight. With a scraping sound, the ladder came down two feet. As it did so, he extended his arms fully upward, grasped the ropes, and pulled down bringing the ladder all the way down. Then, having retrieved the rope and wrapped it around his waist, and having stood quietly for a few minutes to listen, he began to climb.

When he reached the top of the fire escape, he used one of his knives to open the simple latch on the window, slid the window open, and crawled in. It was dark inside, but he could tell that he was in a dormitory room of some kind. Using his pencil flashlight again, he confirmed his first impression: that it was not in use and had not been for many years. Carefully stepping around the debris that was scattered on the floor, he did a quick survey of the other rooms, discovering the entire floor to be a dormitory, with bunkrooms, washrooms, a laundry room, and a simple kitchen. His briefing hadn't included enough detail for him to know that this was where the nurses and other single women had been accommodated during the mine and mill's operating years.

There was a centrally-located staircase, which he descended. Finding himself in a hallway that appeared to run the entire length of the building, he surveyed this as well, locating the examination and treatment rooms, a seven-bed patients' ward, several offices, and what he took to be the doors to supply rooms. The first one he checked was, in fact a combination supply room and dispensary, while the other opened onto a small room containing a small desk bearing a computer and monitor, and another door bearing a radiation safety sign, and above which was mounted indicator light. Nodding to himself, he went in and opened the inner door. This latter room had no exterior windows and was pitch dark. His pencil flashlight revealed a large stand bearing a padded surface that was obviously meant for a patient to lie on. The stand was fitted with several mechanical levers and gears, which he took to be the means of moving the patient-bearing top up or down and left or right. To the left of the table was a tall, imposing machine that stood at a slight angle from the vertical. It was obviously some kind of radiation treatment machine that could rotate in a circular arc above a patient's body. Johnson nodded to himself, he had expected something like this, but they'd had to make sure.

Switching his flashlight off, he glanced at the luminous hands of his watch. Time to be leaving. This time he simply walked to the back door, carefully scanned all around the door's perimeter to check for alarm switches and, finding none, he unlocked and opened the door, then stepped out.

'Find anything interesting? asked a male voice as a blinding white light stabbed into his darkness-accustomed eyes. As he instinctively threw a hand up to shield his eyes while he tried to locate the source of the voice. he sensed - more than heard - something come close behind him. He was very quick to turn around, but whomever was behind him was faster. He felt, and even heard, something hard hit him at the base of the skull, and he was just beginning to feel the wave of pain when he collapsed, unconscious to the ground.

***

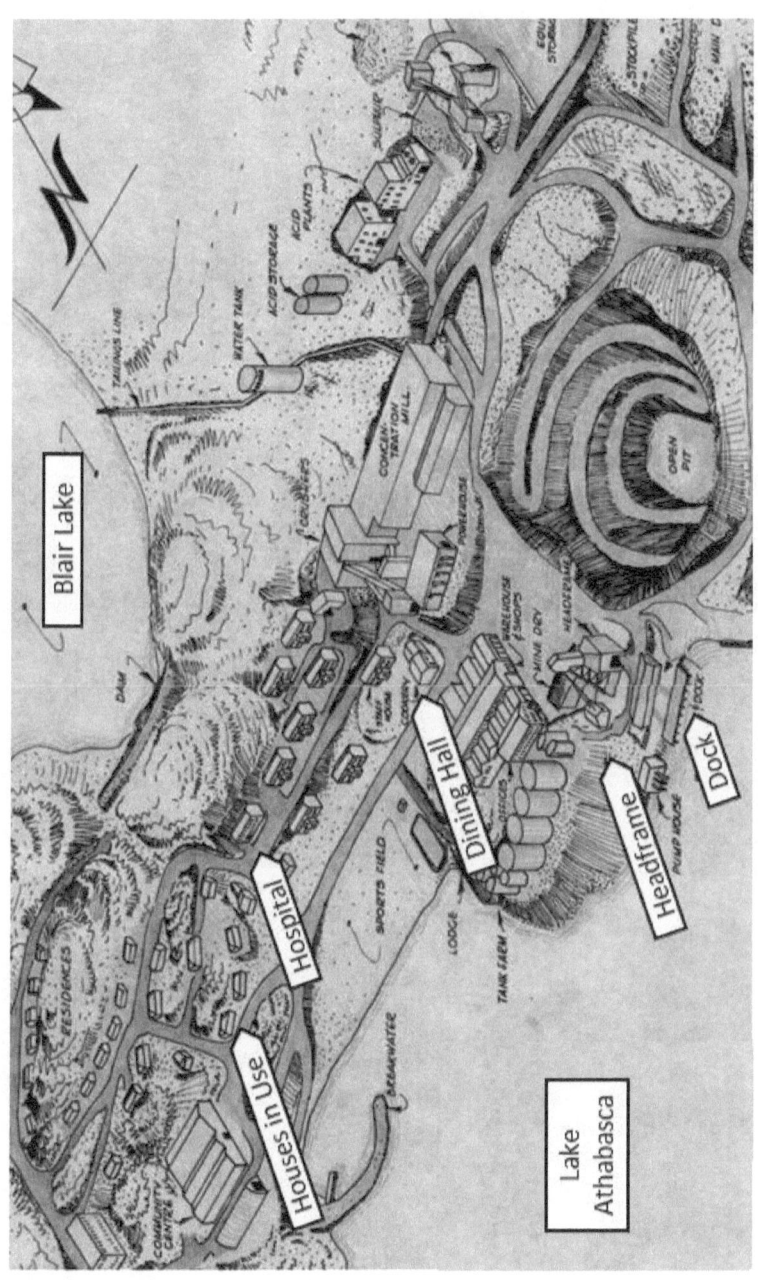

Laurie Schramm

2 A NEW ASSIGNMENT

Wednesday, July 28, 1982
RCMP Headquarters Building
Ottawa, ON

"He'll see you now," said the inspector who served as Executive Officer to Deputy Commissioner George MacLeod, the head of the RCMP's Security Service.

We must look like an unusual trio I thought as we rose from our chairs. My name is Alexandra Houston and, at the time, I was a Sergeant in the Security Service. Next to me was Silver, a large Alaskan Malamute; my long-time Police Service Dog partner and friend. Next to Silver was Major Donald Harrison, who served in military intelligence in the Canadian Forces and who was also my husband. It still seemed strange to think of him as my husband as we'd only been married for three months. After the wedding and honeymoon, Don had been assigned to a temporary position at National Defense Headquarters in Ottawa, which was giving us some time to decide how to handle our two-career marriage without having to live apart. We appreciatively suspected that Don's convenient assignment was the result of some kind of back-room deal between Deputy Commissioner MacLeod and Rear-Admiral White, the head of military intelligence. We were very grateful for that, but we'd thus far made no progress on how to reconcile our careers. On this particular day, we'd been summoned to the Deputy Commissioner's office and I couldn't help wondering whether fate was about to take a hand.

As the inspector stood aside, we made our way into the office of the man that had persuaded me to join the force in the first place, and who I sometimes referred to as 'Uncle George,' although never to his face. After taking a few steps inside, we stood to attention – even Silver – and in the momentary silence I noticed that, seated at his meeting table, Uncle George was accompanied by Admiral White and Staff Sergeant Avery Blunt, my immediate superior.

Uncle George told us to relax and, with a wave, indicated we should join them at the meeting table. "We all know each other too well for formalities," he said, as Don and I took our seats and Silver found a place to lie down nearby, "so let's get right to it." He nodded meaningfully at the admiral, who took over.

"We have an unusual situation, or, more correctly the CIA has a situation, and the Americans have asked for our help."

"That's odd, isn't it Sir?" asked Don, "They've always preferred to go their own way and keep their own counsel."

"They have gained that reputation, yes, but as I said the situation is unusual. Let me try to summarize what we think we know." He leaned forward over the edge of the table. "Several days ago, a private pilot made a phone call from the Fort McMurray Airport to a highly confidential number at Langley[4]. He said that he was relaying a message from Sparrow, and the message was 'Hawk.' That was the whole thing, a message from Sparrow comprising the single word 'Hawk.'"

"Sounds like secret-agent stuff from an old movie," I commented.

"So it does, but it set off alarm bells in the CIA. Apparently, they'd sent an undercover operative to snoop around one of the old, abandoned, Cold War uranium mine sites on the north shore of Lake Athabasca."

"Do you know which one?" I asked, suddenly more interested.

"We thought that would interest you. Yes. It was the old Gunnar mine," put in Uncle George.

"A fairly isolated mine and mill site. It was so remote they even had their own small townsite. I visited it once years ago, when I was stationed in the area."

"You will naturally be wondering what sparked the CIA's interest," resumed the admiral. "Back in June, a U.S. Senator flew up there, ostensibly for a fly-in-fishing vacation with an operator called

Athabasca Outfitters, which has leased the site from the provincial government. There used to be a commercial fishing co-operative using part of the site but it closed last year. Apparently, the provincial government was more than willing to have another company have a try at building-up some local business in the area. In any case, the senator never returned home and, after a few days beyond his expected return, his wife hired a private detective to attempt to locate her husband. He discovered that the senator began his trip home but disappeared after landing in Denver.

"As you can imagine, that didn't do much to alleviate the senator's wife's concerns, so she called the FBI." The admiral paused to allow for the obvious questions, but Don and I remained silent so he could tell the story in his own way. With a nod, he continued.

"Right. The FBI took her call seriously and did some investigating. When they checked the Denver airport's security tapes, they showed the senator's wife some images of the man that presented the senator's passport to a U.S. Customs and Immigration officer. The wife insists that, although there's a superficial resemblance, the man in the photo is definitely not her husband. As they investigated further, the FBI learned that the fly-in-fishing operation is only a cover, and that the real reason the senator went there was for secret cancer treatments that would enable him to avoid the usual long waiting lists back home. Apparently, the availability of these cancer treatments is strictly word-of-mouth, but the FBI found a friend of the senator's that had gone for such treatments himself, and who had recommended them to the senator. It was only because of the senator's disappearance that this friend opened up to the FBI at all, since he'd apparently signed some kind of nondisclosure agreement that had stiff penalties for any violation of its terms.

"Obviously, something about this business is illegal or there'd be no need for such secrecy, or the remote location, or the fishing-camp ruse. The physicians might be unlicensed, or the treatments might be unusually risky and unlicensed, or something else, we don't know. But. Some people must think they work or there would be no word-of-mouth referrals and not many people would pay the outrageous fees being charged…. You with me so far?"

Don and I nodded.

"Once the FBI learned what I just told you someone, somewhere, decided that the CIA should send an undercover operative in to investigate." The admiral held up a hand to stave off the obvious question. "As you already pointed out, such an act is odd. The CIA routinely have operatives here in Canada, working in cooperation with our own intelligence personnel, but it's rare for them to send one in undercover, and without telling us. Of course, there's no way for us to know for sure how often, but we think it's pretty rare. They're our allies after all. It's not actually illegal, as long as they don't start breaking our laws, but any such clandestine operation of theirs on our soil could cause a major diplomatic embarrassment, so they wouldn't do it lightly."

"So why would they take the risk?" put in Uncle George, rhetorically. "I asked the FBI that directly. It turns out that Senator Harland Walker serves on the U.S. Senate Select Committee on Intelligence, which has oversight on the CIA, and which makes him important enough for them to want to find him quickly and quietly, if possible."

Wow! I thought. "You think they're worried that he defected to the Soviets?" I asked.

"That, or that the Soviets kidnapped him and are trying to extract intelligence from him."

"So, they sent someone in to follow the senator's trail," said Don.

The admiral nodded. "He flew the same route for most of the way, then chartered a float plane to get him to the Gunnar site. We don't know how he got access to the site, but he'd instructed the pilot that if he disappeared to phone a certain number and say he had a message from Sparrow, which was the code-word 'Hawk.' Obviously, Sparrow was code for the operative, and the FBI managed to pry out of the CIA that Hawk meant that he'd been captured or killed."

There was silence for a moment, before the Admiral continued. "As you can imagine, the message set off even louder alarm bells at the CIA, and I'm told off-the-record that the President's National Security Advisor instructed the CIA Director to do what should have been done in the first place: enlist the FBI's help in getting us to investigate. A request along those lines came to both our services and was copied to the PMO[5], who advised the Prime Minister and granted approval for a small, joint team to go in and discover what happened to the senator and CIA operative, if possible, and in any case to get to the bottom of what's going on up there.

"The Deputy Commissioner and I want you two to be a part of

it. I don't know whether the fact that you're now married to each other changes anything, but you've each been highly successful at unusual assignments in the past, both on your own, and when you've worked on them together." He paused in order to gauge our reaction.

I looked over at Don. He didn't say anything or visibly react, but there was a gleam in his eye that I understood very well.

"Is that what you meant when you said joint team – police and military intelligence?" I asked.

"Not entirely," Uncle George smiled. "Our American friends naturally want to be in on this too. The idea is to have you two – and Silver, of course – from our side, matched up with two representatives from the American side. The FBI want to send Special Agent Rule. Partly, no doubt, because she also has worked well with you two before so you know and trust each other." He shifted a bit uncomfortably in his chair.

Here it comes, I thought.

"In comparison, the fourth member of the team," he cleared his throat, "will be somewhat of an outsider. The CIA will be sending one of their operatives. At this point we don't know who it will be. So that's it. I think we've told you essentially all of what little we know." He looked at Don and I in turn.

"Will you do it?"

I turned to face Don again. He was still keeping his face carefully neutral, but the sparkle in his eye was still there and as he looked into mine, he slowly winked. We both turned back to face Uncle George and the admiral and said, in almost perfect unison, "Yes Sir."

"Fine, fine," said Uncle George. I could imagine him rubbing his hands in anticipation of getting the operation underway. "As of now, you're both relieved of all other duties. You'll have until tomorrow morning to hand-off anything current to others. Staff Sergeant Blunt will serve as your point of contact. You'll have to figure out a way of maintaining communications when you're in the field, and he'll act as a relay for new information any of us may be able to obtain. He'll also be responsible for getting you whatever you may need operationally, including additional team members if you need them. Choose wisely, but in principle you potentially have access to anything either of our two countries can provide in terms of intelligence and police and military assets. Once the four of you have met and discussed it, you can choose your own leader. Any questions?"

"When will that be, Sir? I mean, when and where will we meet Vivian and the CIA operative?" I asked.

"They'll both be on tomorrow's morning flight from Washington. I suggest you meet them at the airport and take it from there."

***

The next day found us waiting at the airport when the morning flight from Washington landed. Scanning the passengers as they entered the terminal building, it was quite a while before Vivian came in. It was Silver that spotted her first, of course. As his ears perked up and he rose from his sitting position, he gave a yip and looked up at me.

"Yes, Silver, it's Vivian. Let's go meet her." Vivian was brunette, a bit taller than I am and more slender, with large brown eyes. Her manner wasn't always serious, but she tended to be very aware and intent. *The kind of person that doesn't miss much*, was my first impression when we'd first met five years earlier, and experience had confirmed that impression. We'd all worked with her before and become close in the process, so it was a warm reunion. As she knelt down to hug Silver, I asked whether she'd met the CIA operative before.

"No," she replied. "I don't even know who it is, only that the operative will have been briefed on us and should have been on the same plane."

"Isn't that taking secrecy a bit far?" asked Don.

"You'd think so, wouldn't you? But there's a lot of paranoia and the 'need-to-know' doctrine has become so embedded in the CIA's culture that we often joke that they don't even tell themselves everything they know.

"Seriously, they've had some nasty security breaches over the years, and our two agencies haven't cooperated with each other much since the '60s[6]."

"Great. Whomever this is could turn into a big liability if they're the sort that isn't willing to work with us," I grumbled.

"I've had the same thought, but they're not all cast in the same mould. I've met a few that I would trust to have my back when the going gets tough. We'll just have to wait and see."

As we watched the last of the passengers from Vivian's flight come into the terminal, we were about to give up when a man near the very rear of the crowd broke away and began walking in our direction. The first things I noticed about him were his curly dark hair and beard. His hair was long enough to project out from under the beret he was wearing, and his beard was quite bushy. Beyond that, he was deeply tanned, dressed in a tee-shirt, faded jeans and sneakers, and had a backpack slung over one shoulder.

As he continued walking in our direction, a few more things become clear. I was surprised to see that he appeared to be quite young. *Not teenager young, but not into his thirties yet either*, I thought. Given his manner of dress, he could pass for a graduate student at almost any university. *Correction*, I thought as the silk-screened image on his tee-shirt came into focus. It was Che Guevara[7]. This fellow could pass for a counterculture activist at any college or university. He even looked a bit like a young Guevara.

As he approached, Silver was staring at him intently. With my hand on his shoulder, I could feel that he wasn't sensing anything dangerous, so I assumed it was curiosity. Still, I would have liked to have known what his first impressions were.

When he was close enough for us to speak without having to raise our voices, he stopped, looked at each of us in turn and said "Special Agent Rule, Sergeant Houston, Major Harrison, and Silver. I've read up on each of you, and it's a pleasure to meet you in person. I'm going to be known as Richard Cooper on this expedition. Please call me Rick."

We responded in turn, with greetings, handshakes, and invitations to refer to us as Vivian, Alex, and Don, respectively. He had the relaxed, friendly manner of a mature university student, but there was no mistaking the intent look he gave each of us when we shook hands.

"The usual protocol is to avoid trying to pet a police dog but, since we'll be working together is it alright for me to introduce myself to Silver?"

"Yes. Just don't make any sudden movements until he gets to know you," I replied, surprised and pleased that he would think to ask first.

He grinned. "Might take a bite out of me and ask questions later you mean? I'm not surprised. I bet he can look quite fierce when his fur is up too."

"You got that right. He nearly scared the life out of me when we first met: I thought he was a wild wolf at first."

"Ah, but now you're famous, aren't you Silver?" he said as he knelt fully down on both knees, lowered his head in a submissive gesture, and then gazed directly at him.

Silver, for his part, gave him that penetrating stare that I knew so well, and held it for what seemed a long time but was probably only about twenty seconds.

"He's reading me like a book. Isn't he?" Rick said to me without taking his gaze away from Silver.

"Probably," I said. "What did you mean about being famous?"

Rick reached out and gave Silver a gentle rub on one ear, while Silver surprised me by not only accepting it but leaning in to enjoy it. Rick looked around, but the crowd of deplaning passengers had disappeared and there was no one nearby. He looked up at me then. "Not famous in the usual sense, but famous in some parts of the intelligence community. I understand that you've met Captain Emilis Matulis, Assistant Military Attaché at the Soviet's embassy here?"

I nodded.

"I've read up on your adventure together. Must have been a surreal partnership for you, but a great success. Anyway, reading between the lines, I bet he told you that the Soviets have an entire program on ESP: extra-sensory perception?"

I nodded again. This was all supposed to be secret, but there seemed to be no point in trying to deny it, and I suspected he was partly testing me as well.

"So they do, and so do we[8]," continued Rick. "I've read both files, and there's a section in each of them on Silver, together with estimates of his abilities. I imagine that MI6 and others are at least aware of the high points." He leaned back and stood up then. "What do you think, do I pass?"

I smiled. "Let's see." Dropping to one knee, Silver immediately turned to look at me. "What do you think of him?" I asked, looking directly into his eyes.

We can't literally read each other's thoughts, of course, but the image that formed in my mind was interpreted by my brain as: *I like him.*

I gave him a pat on the head and stood up. "I think you've been accepted on probation," was all I said.

"Works for me," he nodded, seeming satisfied. "I'm probably not what you were expecting?"

"No," said Vivian. "I've only met a few operatives from Langley and they were all older and very inconspicuous-looking."

"Yes. That's kind of our standard. People that can fit into any kind of crowd without being noticed. They tend to be kind of stuffy and uptight. Sometimes I get partnered with colleagues so that our adversaries focus on me and I lead them on wild goose chases while my colleague does the real work unnoticed."

"Dangerous," put in Don.

"Very," he said with a big smile. "I think I've become addicted to adrenaline."

"So. If you're the CIA's black swan, does that mean you're not strictly need-to-know either?" asked Vivian, doing a little probing of her own.

"Sometimes yes, sometimes no. I understand the principle and I know why it's important, but it's no substitute for intuition and independent thought."

That got a rise out of all of us.

"Isn't that an unusual attitude to have in a secretive, para-military organization?" I asked.

"It is," he said, flashing another brilliant smile. "That's probably why I'm always on the edge of being fired and my boss calls me the biggest pain in the butt in our section."

I couldn't help but laugh in surprise, which had everyone staring at me. "That's exactly what my Captain used to say about me when I was on the Metro Toronto force many years ago and, in a way, it's what led to me joining the RCMP[9].

"And have you changed much?" he asked, looking shrewd for a moment.

"Not so you'd notice," said Don before I could reply.

"Did your outfit and appearance cause you any trouble with Customs and Immigration?" asked Vivian.

"Like suspecting me of being a revolutionary or even an anarchist you mean? Not really. It did prompt the officer to ask about me politics. I said that I only wear this get-up because it helped me meet girls on campus."

"And they bought that?" I asked.

"You could say that. The officer laughed and wished me luck."

There was some shaking of heads, a pause, and then Vivian brought the meeting back to order.

"Well, Rick. Welcome to the pack. What do you say we get

started?"

"Grruph!" said Silver.

Being a cautious bunch, we spent the afternoon at RCMP HQ in a meeting room that was regularly swept for bugs – electronic eavesdropping devices, that is.

First, we compared notes to ensure we were all working from the same information. Rick had been able to discover the name of the pilot that had taken the first CIA operative to the camp on Lake Athabasca, so that gave us one good lead.

Vivian had been able to interview the missing Senator's widow, and from her learned the identity of the friend that had referred the senator in the first place. From the friend, she had learned that the specific medical treatments for which he and the senator had gone there were radiation treatments. "Given the remote location, and the fact that it's probably not even on the power grid, I suspect they have an unlicensed radiation therapy machine up there," she concluded.

"I wonder where you'd get a thing like that," I said. "You wouldn't want to leave witnesses or a paper trail, so maybe you'd either try to buy one on the black market or else steal one yourself?"

"We have people that follow the black market," said Vivian. "I can make some calls."

It was agreed that she would make her calls, while I checked on the possibility of a stolen radiation therapy machine, and Rick and Don would make some calls in an attempt to locate the pilot.

CPIC, the Canadian Police Information Centre[10], was housed in a nearby building so, rather than calling them, I walked over thinking that I'd be able to more clearly describe what I was looking for if I was there in person.

One of the databases maintained by CPIC covers things that have been reported stolen, like vehicles, boats, or bicycles, for example. When I got there, I waited for someone that could help me and explained what I was looking for. When the operator accessed the appropriate database and typed in some keywords, the mainframe computer delivered the search result in less time than it had taken to explain my request. Having thanked him, I had a smile on my face as I walked back to our meeting room.

When we next gathered to compare notes, everyone had news. Don and Rick had discovered the name of the air-charter service in

Fort McMurray, Alberta, for which the pilot worked. At first, this seemed like an odd place from which to book a charter to fly to the Uranium City area, but Don explained that at slightly more than 360 km (225 miles), Fort McMurray was actually the closest city to the Uranium City area, not Prince Albert or Edmonton, each of which was nearly twice as far away at 730 to 765 km (about 450 to 475 miles). Rick added that his lost colleague would have gone in under-cover and might have chosen a charter service from a different province to reduce the risk of having his cover blown. In any case, it was agreed that someone should travel to Fort McMurray and interview the pilot in person.

Vivian reported from her experts that there were no medical radiation therapy machines on the black market and probably never would be due to their size, complexity, and need for specialized, periodic maintenance. There were however, people that would be willing to steal one for a fee but that fee would be so high that it would probably be more cost-effective in the long run to simply buy one legitimately so it would have maintenance support.

My news was that CPIC had an entry for the reported theft of a prototype medical linear-accelerator called an Amelior-8. It was stolen the previous November 9, from a semi-trailer at a truck-stop about an hour's drive south of Barrie, Ontario. The machine was built in Mississauga, and was on its way to the Toronto General Hospital for evaluation and clinical trials. "I phoned the manufacturer, a company called Accelerated Nuclear Inc., and they explained that this thing was a fully functioning production prototype. They say it can deliver focused beams of either X-rays or electrons over a range of energy levels. Their claims to fame are that the machine is the most compact ever built and that it is completely automated. A computer does all the work. All a person has to do is aim the thing at the target area, key-in the treatment requirements for the computer, and then the computer takes it from there. They say the machine is worth a million dollars."

Don gave a whistle. "That's serious money all right."

"And convenient," said Vivian. "All packaged up on a semi-trailer ready to go. You steal it, take it some place out of the way, set it up, and it can almost run itself. All you'd need is a physician with flexible ethics and patients willing to pay big money to skip the waiting lists[11]."

"That and a source of power," said Rick, "but a remote site would already be on diesel power. Worst case scenario, you just buy or steal another generator for it."

"So, we may have an unlicensed physician operating a stolen, unlicensed, radiation-therapy machine to treat rich cancer patients that are in a hurry. If that's the case what happened to the senator?" I mused.

"We talked to the senator's family physician," said Vivian. "The cancer wasn't life threatening; in fact, they'd already operated to remove the cancerous tumor in his upper back. The radiation treatments for which he was on a waiting list were simply to kill any remaining cancerous material. So, if he died when he was at the camp, it seems unlikely that it was from natural causes."

"Maybe there's a problem with the radiation machine then," said Don. "It's a prototype after all, and you said it's computer controlled. Maybe it sometimes breaks down, or goes out of alignment, or the computer doesn't work properly, or something."

"Could be," said Rick. "If it was something like that, then they'd have known that the senator would be missed, and that there was a chance someone could have found out where he'd gone. Just the possibility would have made them extra suspicious of strangers like my colleague."

"Right, and since he was sent in to investigate…" said Don.

"Yes. He'd have had a good cover story but he would eventually have begun to snoop around," agreed Rick. "If they caught him snooping somewhere he shouldn't have been, in the middle of the night, say, and without a plausible excuse, then they might have decided on direct action. I think I should go find this pilot and see what else we can learn from him. They'd have had to make some excuse to get rid of him, and in any case, he should be able to tell us something about my colleague's cover story and the size and layout of the operation."

"Did the company say anything about the computer that runs this machine?" asked Vivian.

"Oh yes, they were very proud of it. It's a PDP-11," I said, consulting my notes, "and they said that it not only controls the machine, and the radiation dosage levels, but it takes care of all the safety checks as well."

"So," said Rick with a snort, "an almost completely roboticized medical treatment machine, and only a prototype, meaning that it basically works in the lab but hasn't been demonstrated in a real-world situation yet, or even in regular, repetitive use I'll bet. Call me old-fashioned, but that sounds like an accident waiting to happen."

That brought a few chuckles.

"Rick, you're the youngest one in this room. Are you telling us that you're afraid of computers?" asked Vivian.

"I'm not afraid of them when they're doing actuarial calculations for insurance companies or keeping track of financial accounts for banks, but putting them in charge of people's safety makes me nervous. Look, how many of us took computer science in college or university?" Everyone put a hand up. "OK, so we all know what they can do. Do you all remember how many lines of code we had to write to get the computers to do pretty simple things?" Everyone nodded. "And when we did our programming assignments, how often did the computer stop running part way through executing the programs we wrote because of some stupid little error or typing mistake?"

"All the time," I volunteered. "Sometimes, I'd have to fix an error, re-run the program until it stopped when it hit a later error, fix that, re-run it, and so on and so on, twenty times before the program would finally execute to completion and produce results. Even then, it didn't always produce the right results because of another error that didn't stop the program from running but which made the computer do something I hadn't intended."

"Exactly," said Rick, "and I bet we all worked on programming big, mainframe computers. Right?" Nods all around. "So now imagine a radiation machine that can send a high-energy beam or electrons or X-rays into your body, but it's completely controlled by a new generation small computer, and that computer hasn't been tested on any real patients yet, much less the number of patients that would have to be clinically tested before regulatory approval is granted." He paused, to let that sink in. "Now then, how many of us would be willing to take a chance on this new and unproven machine if our cancer wasn't immediately life-threatening and we had the option to wait six months or whatever and get it treated by a fully-tested and proven machine in a real hospital?"

No hands went up.

"Of course, even if you're right, the people going up there might not know that its unproven," I said.

"I'm sure you're right," said Rick. "And maybe I'm wrong about what's really going on up there."

"Maybe the machine is fine and the doctor is unlicensed," said Don.

"Maybe they're using the machine for some kind of completely new and experimental procedure," said Vivian.

"Who knows?" agreed Rick. "But it must be something like that or there'd be no need to set up in secrecy in such a remote location."

"That brings us back to something we probably all had in mind to begin with," said Don. "We'll need to get someone in there to find out what's really going on."

I was about to make a suggestion when I noticed that Vivian had been waiting for an opportunity to speak. "Vivian?" I asked.

"Yes. I have an idea," she said with a cunning-looking smile.

"This is difficult to talk about, but some time ago I had a bout of breast cancer and had to have a lumpectomy operation to remove the malignant tumor. The cancer has been in complete remission ever since, but...."

"You're suggesting you go in as a patient?" I asked.

She nodded. "That's what I propose, yes. I thought of this when I was interviewing the Senator's widow and when I interviewed the friend that had referred the senator in the first place. The friend was upset and angry, and I had no trouble getting him to agree to make a referral for me too, should it become necessary for me to go in undercover. The arrangements are made through a kind of agent in Uranium City, and I asked him to make the referral for me as a contingency. If we don't want me to go in, it can easily be cancelled."

"Don't you need to show medical records for that?" I asked.

She nodded. "I also took the precaution of having a copy of my medical records and X-rays adjusted by a radiologist consultant that the Bureau often uses. The records now show a recent test indicating some re-appearance of the cancer in some nearby lymph nodes, and the senator's friend will advise the agent that I'm both widowed and wealthy enough to pay."

"Please don't take offense at this, but are you up to the challenge?" said Rick. "This won't be a routine undercover surveillance operation, and you know what's likely to happen if you're found out..." he raised his eyebrows meaningfully.

"Thanks, but unless someone has a better idea, I don't see how else we're going to get someone on the inside. I've also been thinking that there are a few adjustments that can make me appear a little older in ways not easy to detect. That should help me avoid suspicion. If the physician is 'old school,' and if I turn on the rich-widow-charm he'll never suspect a woman anyway…"

As the day wore on, we brainstormed on other sneaky methods that we could use to reconnoitre the area and to infiltrate the camp itself, but no one came up with a better idea than Vivian's and we decided not to land on any more specific tactics until we'd learned more.

It was decided that Rick and Don would fly out to Fort McMurray and interview the pilot, while Vivian, Silver and I would fly to Edmonton and establish a staging area. We figured that it would be a lot closer to the Gunnar mine site than Ottawa but not close enough to be seen and potentially remembered by anyone from the fly-in camp on Lake Athabasca.

3 RICK GETS INSERTED

Friday, July 30, 1982

As planned, Vivian and I flew to Edmonton to set up our base of operations at K Division headquarters, where we were given two offices and a small, nearby meeting room to use.

Meanwhile, Don and Rick had flown to Fort McMurray to track down the pilot that had flown the original CIA operative. As they later related to us, they found him almost immediately, lounging between flights at the air-charter service for which he worked. Don identified himself with his military police ID and said he was conducting a sensitive national security investigation. That seemed to be enough for the pilot, who was happy to tell them what he could.

The pilot said that his passenger identified himself as Robert Johnson, a government conservation officer, and had said he wanted to conduct a surprise inspection at the Gunnar fly-in fishing camp on Lake Athabasca. Johnson hadn't been very specific, but he hinted that he was looking into reports of illegal moose and black bear trophy-hunting on the part of some of the visitors that were ostensibly there to fish. Johnson hadn't shown him any kind of official identification but was in uniform and the pilot hadn't had any reason to doubt his identity.

The pilot said that he been contracted to pick up Johnson in Prince Albert and fly him to Athabasca Outfitters, a fly-in fishing camp that was based out of the former Gunnar uranium mine site on the north shore of Lake Athabasca, which is what he had done. They had crossed the big lake without incident, landed on the water and taxied to the old Gunnar dock, which was showing its age but still serviceable. They were met by one of the camp's fishing guides, who used a handheld radio to call someone who seemed to be the boss, and owner, of the outfit. The boss identified himself as a retired doctor, Dr. Ernst Wildersbach, and the pilot gave Don and Rick a description of him.

According to the pilot, Johnson gave Wildersbach a slightly different description of his reason for visiting, in this case calling it a routine, surprise fisheries and wildlife compliance check. The pilot assumed that this was to avoid making them unduly concerned. Johnson said that he wanted to glance over the whole operation, and Wildersbach offered to provide a guide for this purpose. Johnson agreed, and then claimed that he'd arrived much later than planned and asked whether they could be accommodated for the night and do the inspection the next morning. This was a surprise to the pilot, who had picked Johnson up at the pre-arranged time and delivered him to the camp exactly on schedule, and who had personally made a reservation for the two of them to stay in bed-and-breakfast accommodations in Uranium City that night. Despite his surprise, the pilot said he'd kept his mouth shut and simply followed Johnson's lead.

"They put us up in a small two-bedroom house that was still in pretty good shape. It had power, but I could hear generators running so I think the whole site operation is powered by diesel generators," said the pilot. "When we were alone, Johnson said he'd pay me extra and we were always going to be staying somewhere overnight anyway, so I was quick enough to agree.

"When they drove us to our house, we drove by a small cove where the original mining company had built a small dock and even made a sandy beach. The cove was reasonably sheltered and I later moved the aircraft there for the night. I did notice that there was another aircraft there, a Twin Otter[12]. It was well moored and looked like it hadn't been flown in a while.

"After we'd had supper, we returned to the house we'd been assigned. Johnson told me was going to 'watch' for a while and not to be surprised if he disappeared for an hour or two during the night. I could tell he was up to something, of course, but he reminded me that I was being paid extra not to ask too many questions. Then he did a funny thing that made the whole situation seem even stranger. He told me that if anything happened to him, I was to remember that I knew nothing about him, and that they might tell me some kind of story aimed at getting me to fly out without waiting for him. In that case, I was to accept everything they said and simply fly out. Then, when I got back to 'civilization,' I was to phone a toll-free number he'd given me and give them a bizarre message."

"Yes," said Rick, "he told you to say that you had a message from 'Sparrow,' and that the message was one word: 'Hawk.'"

"That's right," said the pilot. "That's exactly what he said, and then it all played out just like he said too. He never did return to the house, and the next morning I pretended to have slept through the night and not to have heard or noticed anything. Wildersbach himself came to tell me that Johnson had risen early and one of the guides had taken him out by boat to tour the other fly-in fishing camps in the area, that he'd be gone several days, and that I should go ahead and fly home. He would arrange to get a message to me when he wanted to be picked up again. Well, I wouldn't normally have accepted that at face value, but since it was almost exactly what Johnson said might happen, I went along with it and flew back here to Fort McMurray. When I got here, I made the phone call, exactly as he'd asked. What the hell is going on over there?"

Don jumped in at that point, saying "That's what we're trying to find out. There's something odd going on there. Johnson was sent in to snoop around and now he's disappeared. That's why we're here. We want to find out what's going on and what happened to Johnson."

"That's not the whole story," said the pilot.

"No. It's actually hardly any of the story," laughed Don, "but it's all that is safe for you to know. Can you give us a description of each of the people you saw there?"

He did so.

"Thanks. Is there anything else you can tell us?"

"I can do better than that, I can show you." The pilot reached into the lower drawer of a desk and removed a thin zippered document case.

"Johnson left this behind on the aircraft. I didn't mention it when I phoned because he told me to stick to the words that he'd given me, but I did open it later. It shows the whole site."

Taking Don and Rick to a chart table, he opened the case and withdrew a thin set of papers and began spreading them out. "The big one is just the standard hydrographic chart of the area. You can see where the camp is here on the Crackingstone Peninsula." He pointed to the location. "Now, the others are more interesting. These drawings show the layout of the entire mine, mill, and townsite at the time when it was operating, and it looks like they were made by the Gunnar Mining Company itself."

"Can you show us which buildings seemed to still be in use?" asked Don.

The pilot pointed to the warehouse building by the dock, the house in which they'd slept, the dining hall and the hospital. "Those are the only ones I can be sure of," he said. "You can see that the house we were in was quite close to the dining hall."

"Can you tell us more about the dining hall?" asked Rick.

The pilot described what he remembered, saying that it seemed to be the same dining hall from the original mining operation days, rustic, but cleaned up.

"Any idea how many staff working there?" Rick continued.

"In the dining hall you mean? Looked like just the one cook. In the wall between the eating area and the kitchen, there was kind of a full-length open window with a broad ledge along which the various platters and bowls of food were placed. The cook was able to fill and arrange them from the kitchen side and we, on the other side, were able to go along it with our trays, selecting the food we wanted. I went up to it several times, and I only ever saw the one cook doing everything. When we were leaving, we took our dirty dishes and cutlery back, and it was still just the one guy washing up the dishes by himself."

"Can you describe the cook for us?"

"Middle-aged, grizzled, prematurely balding. Looks a bit like the stereotype of the ship's cook on a fishing boat or tramp steamer, but I have no idea whether he's ever been one."

"Did you talk to him at all?"

"Not really. He explained what was on the menu when we first arrived. That was simple as there weren't many choices available: one main, a couple of choices of vegetables, a couple of salads, bread, and so on. Then, when we brought our dirty dishes back, I asked if he'd like a hand cleaning up but he said no, that there wasn't much to do and he was going to finish it up and then go visit the 'Angler' for a drink. By that he meant the Northern Angler camp, which is another fly-in fishing camp that is quite close-by. I've flown people there myself many times. Anyway, from the looks on the faces of two of the guides that were sitting nearby, I took that to mean he was a regular drinker over there. Some of the fly-in fishing camps have a reputation for a bottomless open bar, which means they get visited a lot by some of the locals in the area. The most notorious is the Northern Angler which, as I said, is quite close to the Gunnar site where the Athabasca Outfitters camp is."

"How do they communicate with the outside world?" asked Rick, "radio?"

"That's right," said the pilot. "Some of the camps are just on Marine VHF and they get messages relayed by other boaters and other camps in the area. Some of them though, like the Angler, have a ham radio base station from which they can cover a greater distance, but they still rely on messages being relayed, or telephoned, by other ham operators."

"Can you connect to them?"

"We can call the ones with ham radios directly, yes. For the others we have to go to ham operators that also have Marine VHF, which is most of them, and get our messages relayed. Why?"

"Can you call up this Northern Angler Camp and see if they have room for a guest?"

"Sure, for when?"

"Soon. Tomorrow even. And for at least a week, if possible."

The pilot agreed to try and went off to the charter company's radio room. When he was gone, Don asked Rick what he was thinking.

"I'm thinking that I could go in now and do a little drinking with the cook from Athabasca Outfitters – the one we're interested in at Gunnar."

"Intel gathering?"

"Sure, but I'm thinking that if he's a heavy drinker it wouldn't take much to make him get a little sick too." He grinned.

"Hmmm. You mean it would be quite a coincidence if he was too sick to go back to cooking at the camp for a while."

"You're quick, Don, I'll give you that."

"OK. Suppose he happens to become temporarily incapacitated. That gives us a chance to substitute a cook of our own, but who? And how would we get one up there in a hurry?"

Rick's smile turned crafty. "It would be me, of course."

"You? You realize it would mean commercial-style cooking for whatever number of people happen to be in the camp?"

"Sure, but you're looking a man of many talents." Rick gave him a boyish grin. "At one time, in my notorious youth, I was a cook on an ocean-going trawler. That meant feeding about twenty people or so but spread out across the six watches[13]."

Don shook his head in wonder. "Talk about having hidden depths. Are you sure you want to take the risk?"

Rick nodded his head. "It's kind of why I'm here. It's not so much that I was picked to come – I volunteered."

"Volunteered? You somehow strike me as ex-military, and you know what we say about volunteers?"

"Someone who misunderstood the question?" He laughed. "Well, you're right. I spent some time as a Ranger in the army.

His grin vanished. "Before I was recruited to the CIA, I was in the military and each of our services has a version of 'leave no soldier behind, dead or alive.' You Canadians probably do as well." He looked at Don, who nodded. "Well, the man calling himself Johnson was a colleague and a friend. He may not be alive, he may not even be up here, and even if he is we may not be able to rescue him, but someone has to try."

"I get it," said Don, putting a hand on Rick's shoulder. Well, the only question now then, is whether the fishing camp is fully booked or not."

They didn't have long to wait before the pilot returned, saying "You're in luck. They're not actually very busy right now so they'd be glad to have a paying customer show up on short notice. They're still on the air so if you come with me, you can give them your name and a credit card number to hold your place. Then, I can fly you in tomorrow, if you like."

"Sounds like your cue all right," said Don as Rick got up to go with the pilot.

When the booking had been completed, Rick and Don huddled to clarify their next steps and it was agreed that Rick would leave the next day for the Northern Angler Camp, from which he would try to infiltrate the Athabasca Outfitters camp at Gunnar. Don, for his part would fly to Edmonton, bring Alex and Vivian up to date, and work with them on their own means of getting to the area. Assuming that Vivian was able to get in as a patient, they would try to have her bring a concealed radio of some kind to give to Rick.

"OK," said Rick. "We don't know what she's going to look like when she gets there, possibly similar but older-looking, so let's agree on some simple recognition words: 'Cat' for me, 'Mouse' for Vivian, 'Dog' for Alex, and 'Guns' for you."

"Fine. We'll see if we can find a way to insert Vivian as well, and Alex and I will be lurking somewhere close by, but you're going to be on your own out there for a few days."

"Situation normal," smiled Rick, "but if I can get in, I'll keep a low profile and gather what intel I can until Mouse shows up."

The next day they flew out, but in different directions, with Don flying southwest on a commercial flight to Edmonton, and the charter pilot flying Rick northeast to the area of the two fishing camps. In Rick's case, it was only about an hour's flight and when they were close, he was able to have the pilot circle over the Athabasca Outfitters/Gunnar site so he could enhance his mental map of the layout, then on to the Northern Angler Camp.

At the latter camp, Rick threw himself into the role of 'just another American customer.' In contrast to the university student/rebel image he'd portrayed when flying to Ottawa, he was this time playing the dedicated fisherman. While in Fort McMurray, he had had both his hair and beard cut fairly short, and he had acquired typical outdoor adventure clothing including a couple of lightweight, ripstop-nylon[14] shirts, long- and short pants with cargo pockets at the thighs, and a baseball cap sporting the logo of a famous brand of fishing gear. In this guise he was accepted at face value, checked-in, assigned a comfortable room, given a tour, and was able to arrange to go out fishing with a guide in the afternoon.

The fishing was good, partly because the local guides knew all the best locations, and Rick returned with several lake trout and northern pike. He'd been quite proud of one 42-inch (1.1 m), 36-pound (16 kg) lake trout in particular until the guide told him about the largest one ever caught in Lake Athabasca: which weighed-in at an incredible 102 pounds (46 kg)[15]. Nevertheless, he'd had an enjoyable and productive outing consistent with his cover story, plus the luxury of having the guide clean his fish and even package and freeze them for him.

The camp's dining room was like everything else in the camp: nice but rugged rather than luxurious. The food, on the other hand, was great, and Rick lingered over his meal so he could eavesdrop on the conversations among the other guests.

Near the conclusion of the meal someone stood up to welcome the recent arrivals, like himself, and to remind them about the lounge and games room and that the bar would close at 11:30 pm.

Rick divided his evening time between exploring the camp facilities, walking along the dock and shoreline, and making the occasional foray into the lounge and games room to check for non-clients. The only people that ever seemed to be in the latter were clients, however, so he eventually gave up for the day.

Patience is a virtue, he thought to himself, although it was not a virtue that came easily to him. The next day comprised an early morning fishing trip to a different location than he'd been taken to the day previous. This time he was able to catch several arctic graylings. The afternoon brought another trip to yet another fishing spot, where he was able to catch several walleyes. After spending most of the day out on the water he was famished when it came to suppertime, which comprised another great meal featuring fresh fish one of the guides had caught that day. After eating, Rick went for a walk around the camp and spent some time just sitting outside looking out across the lake, before wandering over to the lounge and games room for a look around. A quick scan of the inhabitants produced only the recognizable faces of his fellow guests, so he casually walked back outside and resumed his seat by the camp's dock.

As a beautiful, peaceful evening descended he was just beginning to doze off when he heard the sound of a motorboat approaching.

Finally, Rick thought.

In due time a boat arrived at the dock. It looked very much like the ones already tied up nearby, except that this one was painted in the different colours and had the name Athabasca Outfitters stencilled near the bow. A grizzled, older man climbed out of the boat and Rick had time to examine him while he was busy securing it at the dock. The charter pilot had been able to give him only a general description of the Athabasca's cook, but Rick was reasonably confident that this was be the cook in question.

"Howdy," said the man when he'd straightened up, turned toward the lodge and caught Rick's eye. "Get out fishing today?"

"Sure did," enthused Rick. "Caught a couple of nice-sized lake trout and a couple of respectable northern pike!"

"Good for you," said the older man and, with a friendly nod, he walked over to the main lodge building.

Meanwhile, Rick made a show of dozing off again although he was in no danger of falling asleep any time soon. He was going to give it some time before making a move. In fact, it was more than an hour before Rick judged that it would be entirely normal for a tired customer to head for the bar before turning in. When he did enter the lounge and games room, he spotted the grizzled older man sitting alone at a small table in the corner that was quite quiet as a consequence of being as far away as possible from the part of the room where most people were playing games and chatting.

Rick made a show of walking by the various games that were being played and then sauntered over to the corner table.

"Mind if I join you? It's quieter over here," he said, giving a meaningful tip of his head toward the games area, then he reached out a hand to shake. "My name's Rick Cooper."

"Be my guest," was the reply. "Alistair Hughes. You're the fellow that caught the fish." It was a statement rather than the question, but Rick answered anyway.

"That's right, although I have a feeling that everyone that comes up here catches fish."

"Pretty much. At least the ones that want to." He went ahead and answered the question that was obvious from Rick's expression. "What I mean is, some people just come up here to get away and relax. Oh, they might go out with the guides once in a while, and even go through the motions of fishing, but they leave just as happy whether they catch anything or not."

"I hadn't thought about that," said Rick, truthfully, "but I guess that makes sense. Me, I'm here to fish and relax, but in that order. How about you?"

"Not me. I don't catch them, I cook them."

"You buy them, you mean?"

"Well, that too, but what I mean is, I'm the cook at the other fishing camp. The one that's just around the peninsula from this one."

"Really! The cook. Been working there long?"

"Just since the beginning of the season. They only just opened over there."

"Well, it's a small world. I worked as a cook once – for a year it was."

"You don't say. Where was that?"

"Let me go get a drink and I'll tell you about it." After getting up, Rick turned back before leaving the table. "What are you drinking? I'll get you fresh supplies."

The camp had an open bar that was tended by one of the fishing guides. "I see you've met the competition," he said when Rick approached, but there was no malice in his tone or expression.

"Alistair? I guess so. Says he's the cook over at the other camp. He must like your camp better than his."

The guide snorted. "More like he likes our prices better. We have an open bar, even for the locals that drop by, but he has to pay for his drinks at his own camp. Our management thinks it's good policy to have the locals feeling kindly disposed towards us and it livens the atmosphere up somewhat."

"He's a regular then?" Rick asked, as if guessing.

"Oh yeah. He's like the definition of a regular. Be careful if you decide to have more than one or two drinks with him – he's apt to get boisterous when he gets drunk."

"I'll bear that in mind. Thanks," said Rick, borrowing a tray on which to put the four drinks he'd ordered, two for himself and two for the cook.

Returning to the table, Rick passed over the drinks and explained about having spent a year as ship's cook on an ocean-going trawler.

"Better you than me," said Alistair. "I get seasick just being out on the lake here when the weather gets rough. And it's worse when I've been drinking."

Rick looked pointedly at Alistair's empty drink glasses that had been pushed to one side on their table.

"Why do I do it then, you're wondering?"

"No, no. I'm far too polite to ask," he said with a smile.

"Well, I'll tell you anyway. The pay's good, but there's nothing else up here to do. Someday I'll pack it in and go somewhere else, but I need to save up some money first."

Rick nodded. "Makes sense. It was the same with me and my ship's cook job. After a year was up, I'd saved almost everything I'd been paid and went on."

"What did you do then?"

"Well, there's a story there. I didn't want to get another job as a cook so I changed direction completely and..." Rick went into a lengthy description of his next job, how he'd landed it, and some of his experiences. It took some time, because it was quite an adventure and, perhaps surprisingly, he told the complete truth – at least about that phase of his life.

As the evening wore on, they exchanged more stories and had several more drinks each, although Rick always volunteered to get them so Alistair was unaware that, early on in the evening, Rick had switched to non-alcoholic drinks for himself.

When the bartending guide announced Last Call for drinks at 11 pm, Rick went to the bar to get one last nightcap drink for each of them. While there, he unobtrusively dug a small prescription-pill bottle from his pants pocket, tapped out a small, white pill and pretended to pop it into his mouth. "Touch of sinus congestion," he said to the guide. "Came on when I was flying in this morning."

When the guide turned to serve another customer, Rick dropped the pill into Alistair's drink. It dissolved almost immediately. As they finished their nightcaps and continued to trade stories, Rick watched Alistair with heightened interest. The latter was already flushed and sweating to some degree, but these were both enhanced within about fifteen minutes. When the announcement that the bar and lounge were closing, Rick got up from his chair saying "I could use some fresh air before bed anyway – I'll walk you down to the dock."

"Sounds good," said Alistair who rose rather unsteadily, then quickly made a grab for the back of his chair. "Must have had a couple too many. I'm feeling dizzy."

"Do you need a hand?"

"No. I'll be fine once I get to the boat."

As they walked to the dock, Alistair's gait was slow, unsteady, and erratic and he was beginning to feel nauseous, so he was in no condition to notice that Rick didn't seem at all intoxicated.

"You feeling OK?" asked Rick at one point.

"No," said Alistair with a groan, and clutching his stomach. "I think I'm going to be sick. It's strange. I haven't gotten sick from drinking since I was a kid."

"Maybe you've caught a flu bug or something," said Rick sympathetically.

When they reached the Athabasca Outfitters boat, Alistair bent down to untie the mooring rope and immediately dropped to his knees and violently threw up the entire contents of his stomach. Although almost everything was vomited right away, he continued with dry heaves for some time, then collapsed to a sitting position on the dock.

"Whew," he gasped. "I don't think I'm going to be able to survive the trip back."

"Tell you what," said Rick, in a concerned voice. "I'll take you back. Just give me a minute to go tell one of the guides so they know what's happened to me."

Alistair just nodded and remained sitting while Rick jogged back to the lodge. When we returned a few moments later, he found Alistair in the same position, with his head down, and moaning.

"OK. Will you be able to direct me if I drive?"

Alistair nodded and Rick helped him into the boat then got in himself, pushing off from the dock as he did so. The motor started up immediately, and they headed out. The Athabasca camp wasn't far away, but as they progressed out of the relatively sheltered water near the Northern Angler camp it became increasingly clear that the weather had worsened while they'd been drinking and the lake had become quite choppy. As they made to round the point of the peninsula, they were even more exposed and the swell had their little boat hammering into one wave after another.

This is going to make him feel even worse, if that's possible, thought Rick to himself, and indeed, Alistair was huddled on his seat with his head down and his hands gripping the boat, still retching with dry heaves.

Once they'd rounded the point, Rick could see the massive headframe[16] from the old Gunnar mine and he simply headed in that direction until Alistair waved one arm and pointed to the small marina where they should dock. When they neared the small dock, Rick shut off the motor, clambered over Alistair, and grabbed a mooring ring. Then he got out of the boat, tied it up, and reached down to help Alistair out of the boat. Even in the dim light he looked paler than he had when they left the other camp.

As they walked up the slope from the water, everything was quiet. Rick could hear a generator running somewhere, and there were a couple of makeshift streetlamps on which provided just enough light for them to see the roads and structures. Rick had to hold onto one of Alistair's arms now for him to be able to walk, and the latter used the other arm to give directions to his house.

About halfway there, they encountered a man that Rick guessed was one of the camp guides. He took one look at Alistair and laughed. "Well, you must have outdone yourself tonight, Alistair!"

"We met in the bar at the Northern Angler camp," explained

Rick. "I think he's got something more wrong with him than drinking too much. I don't think he'd have made it back if I hadn't brought him."

"OK," said the man, pointing to one side. "His house is right there. If you wouldn't mind helping him get there, I'll go get the boss – he's a doctor."

"Sure. I'll wait." Rick helped Alistair to his house, where the latter collapsed into a living-room chair.

It wasn't long before the man returned with an older man that he introduced as Dr. Ernst Wildersbach, the owner of the camp. Wildersbach had brown eyes, dark hair, thick eyebrows, mustache, and a short Van Dyke-style beard.

Must have to dye his hair to keep it that dark, thought Rick, as the doctor began checking Alistair over while at the same time asking him about his symptoms. When this was done, he stepped back and gazed thoughtfully at Alistair.

"What do you think doctor?" asked Rick.

"I'm not sure. No. Not sure at this stage. The nausea and vomiting, stomach pain, weakness and dizziness suggest possibly a stomach flu or food poisoning, and he's flushed and sweating but he's not running much of a fever. He might have the Norwalk virus[17]. He says that he didn't eat anything when he was over at the Northern Angler?"

Rightly taking this to be seeking confirmation, Rick answered. "I don't think he did. Not while I was with him anyway."

"Hmmm. Well, the virus can be spread by either food or person-to-person contact. Embarrassing for us if he caught food poisoning from his own food, but no one here has reported feeling unwell yet. Time will tell."

"A virus and a severe hangover. I wouldn't want to be in his place tomorrow morning."

"Tomorrow morning. My God! Someone has to cook breakfast for our guests and staff!" He turned back to face Alistair. "What about it. Do you think you'll be up to cooking breakfast tomorrow?"

"Arrrgh," said Alistair, who was holding his head in both hands. "I wouldn't count on it." Then he looked up, wincing in pain from the sudden movement. "The way I'm feeling, I may not even survive the night…. Maybe you could get Rick here to cook for me for a while – he's been a ship's cook."

As the doctor turned to look at Rick he summarized his

experiences as a ship's cook, repeating the essentials of what he'd told Alistair earlier in the evening.

"A year as a ship's cook you say, and for a crew of twenty?"

"About that. Sometimes a few less, sometimes a few more."

"Hmmm." The doctor took a long, thoughtful look at Alistair, who looked worse, if anything. "Why don't you stay on here overnight. It's much too dark for you to go boating in unfamiliar waters. In fact, I'm surprised you made it here without incident. No. No. I think you should stay here in one of our guest houses for the night."

Rick made a show of hesitating. "Well...."

"It's the least we can do to show our appreciation for your Good Samaritanism."

Rick made a show of considering the offer, then shrugged. "I am kind of tired so, OK, I accept. Thank you."

"Fine. Fine. Let's Alistair into bed, then come with me and I'll take you to one of our guest houses."

As the two men walked to a nearby cluster of small houses, Wildersbach said, "You know, I'm not at all sure that Alistair is going to feel up to cooking tomorrow. What would you say to staying on here for a day or two and take over the cooking while he recovers?"

"Work here you mean?" said Rick, in a surprised voice.

"Yes. Yes. But just for a day, or two. It would help us out tremendously, and when you're not busy in the kitchen, you can still get out with one of our own guides and boats and get some of the fishing done that you came here for." Seeing that Rick was considering it, he added "We'd pay you of course. We wouldn't expect you to work for free. If you don't mind my asking, what kind of money were you making as a ship's cook?"

"Oh. Well, when I first started, I was getting $4.50 an hour, but by the time I'd been doing it for a year I was getting $9."

"How about if we consider it like overtime and pay you double: $18 an hour?"

"Canadian or American?"

Wildersbach smiled. "I meant Canadian, but I'll pay it in American if you'll do it. What do you say?"

Rick hesitated, then seemed to come to a decision. "All right. I'll do it. But only for a couple of days, OK?"

"Fine. Fine. Here we are at a house you can use. Why don't you go inside and relax for a moment. You'll find a complete set of fresh linens and towels and things inside." He stepped back and looked at Rick consideringly. "We should have something that will fit you well enough. I'll have someone bring you some toiletries and a change of clothes. After breakfast tomorrow I'll have one of our guides take you over to the Northern Angler so you can get your gear."

Within an hour, Rick was settled into bed for the night.

Good old '796[18], he thought as he drifted into sleep. *Works every time.*

Rick rose early the next morning, made his way to the dining hall and looked everything over. The kitchen was well laid out and well stocked, so he put a large urn of coffee on the percolator and began assembling things for breakfast: juices, fruit, breads, and jams, etc. There were toasters on the dining-room side of the broad serving window so people could toast their own choices of bread, and there was a selection of cereals for which he put on a large urn of hot water to heat for those that wanted porridge. For the hot dishes, he began preparing hash-brown potatoes and, while these were cooking, he started on sausages and bacon, all of which would eventually be placed in large warming trays and put out to sit along the serving window. When people came in to eat, he planned to cook them eggs to order as they went by the serving window.

Everything went well, with Rick constantly having to answer questions along the lines of 'What happened to Alistair?' It was near the end of the breakfast period when a nurse came in to ask for a breakfast tray for their new patient.

"Sure," replied Rick. "Do you think he's up to eating solid food this morning?"

The nurse made it very clear that no, she did not, but that it wasn't up to her. The doctor wanted him to try.

"OK," said Rick cheerfully. "How about juice, dry toast, and some fruit for now? If he can keep that down, I can supplement it later."

The nurse though that would be entirely appropriate, and waited while Rick assembled a tray. As he handed it to her, he said "I just put on a fresh urn of coffee to perk. When it's ready, I can bring him a cup if you like?"

She thought that would be fine, thanked him, and left with the tray.

Rick really had just put on a fresh urn of coffee that he'd planned to keep available for people for the rest of the day. When it was ready, he poured a large mug two-thirds full then made up the rest of the volume with brandy from a bottle he'd discovered in the kitchen's huge pantry. After that, he dropped in one of his little white pills.

When he'd carried the steaming mug of coffee to the small hospital, he asked the nurse if he could take it to Alistair himself so he could try to cheer him up, and was told that would be fine as long as he only stayed a moment. Thanking her, he went to the room she indicated.

"How are you feeling today? Any better?" he asked, as he entered the room. It was set up with two beds but Alistair was the only patient.

"Not worse anyway," Alistair grumbled. "Slept like a log, but woke up with the world's worst hangover!"

"Did you eat any of your breakfast?" Rick asked, casting a glance at the food tray, which was obscured by a crumpled white napkin.

"Not much," was the reply. "Don't like fruit but had a sip of the juice. Tasted terrible! I did eat the toast, but only to make the nurse shut-up and go away."

Rick chuckled appreciatively. "How about some nice hot coffee? I just made it fresh."

When Alistair seemed to hesitate, Rick immediately placed the forefinger of his left hand alongside his nose and said, "I think you should try it. It's my own special coffee."

Alistair's eyes brightened immediately as he guessed Rick's meaning and he reached out for the mug. After taking a first, cautious sip, he took a second, deeper drink, then sat back against his pillow and gave a contented sigh. "Rick, you are a lifesaver!"

"Best cure for a hangover," Rick whispered confidentially. "But not a word to anyone or I'll never be able to bring you another one."

Alistair responded by taking another sip and them mimicking Rick's finger-alongside-nose gesture, saying "Just between us cooks."

"Fine," said Rick. "I'll come back and check on you a bit later. Who knows, you might need another coffee."

Rick had been back in the camp kitchen for perhaps twenty minutes when Dr. Wildersbach came in for a cup of coffee. Rick was just on the verge of striking up a conversation with him when the nurse ran in saying "Doctor, he's vomiting up his breakfast." As the doctor went out with the nurse, Rick went back to cleaning up the kitchen and dining room. A passerby would have heard him whistling while he worked.

When Rick returned to his accommodation that morning, he found that his duffel bags had been retrieved from the Northern Angler camp and were there waiting for him. Taking them into the bedroom, he very carefully opened each one, paying particular attention to the clothes piled at the tops. Then he stepped back and looked out the window for a moment. It was Rick's habit to always place strands of coordinating-coloured thread on top of the articles in his bags so he could easily determine whether they had been searched in his absence. In this case, the threads were gone.

Well, well, he thought. *Not a very trusting bunch I'm staying with! Good thing I didn't bring anything incriminating with me.* He reached into his pocket and brought out two amber-coloured[19] prescription-pill containers. *Except these, of course.* But he wasn't worried about the pill bottles. In addition to the standard size, shape, and colour of the containers themselves, they each had authentic-looking pharmacy labels giving the names of himself, the prescribing doctor, and the pharmacy. The label on the bottle containing the PP796 pills indicated that the pills were captopril, a common blood pressure medication that was normally formulated into small white pills that looked very much like the ones in Rick's container. The second pill container had a similarly authentic-looking label but contained a very different kind of pills.

I'm in! thought Rick. *Now all I have to do is lie low, keep Alistair in the hospital, keep my eyes and ears open, and wait for Mouse to show up.*

It was Tuesday, August 3.

Laurie Schramm

4 VIVIAN GETS INSERTED

Meanwhile, two days earlier (Sunday, August 1)
Edmonton, AB

Our plan was to have Don and I pretend to be research scientists doing some kind of fish-health or limnological research[20] on the lake, which would give us an excuse to loiter around in the waters near the Athabasca Outfitters camp.

In this regard I had contacted Dr. Alan Grey, my old analytical chemistry professor at Carleton University (where I had originally trained as an analytical chemist) and asked if he would 'hire' me back as a Research Associate, and then send me out to Northern Saskatchewan to collect the appropriate samples for a fictional research project. He knew about my current job and, in fact, I'd done something like this once before, with his help, and it had been quite effective[21]. Just like before, Dr. Grey found the idea quite amusing and said he'd be glad to play along in this latest 'cloak and dagger' affair of mine. With his help, we decided that I'd go out to collect samples for a study of possible connections between radioactive metal concentrations and tissue health in the Lake Athabasca fish population. All Don and I would have to do was catch samples of the fish species, dissect them, and freeze them in sealed bags that could be shipped back to the university for analysis. So, it was settled that Alex Houston, B.Sc. would re-enter the world of science for a while.

Dr. Grey had also agreed to contact a chemistry-professor colleague of his at the University of Alberta (U of A), whom he knew well enough to ask for the use and/or donations of an appropriate collection of lab-ware, reagents, and sample bags and bottles. Accordingly, Vivian and I had taken an unmarked police SUV and driven to the U of A Chemistry Department.

There, Dr. Grey's friend had assigned a research associate (who managed her lab for her) to guide us around and help us find what we needed. We did far better than I'd expected, and came away not only with the lab- and sample-ware I'd asked for but also the loan of a stereo microscope and a compound microscope[22].

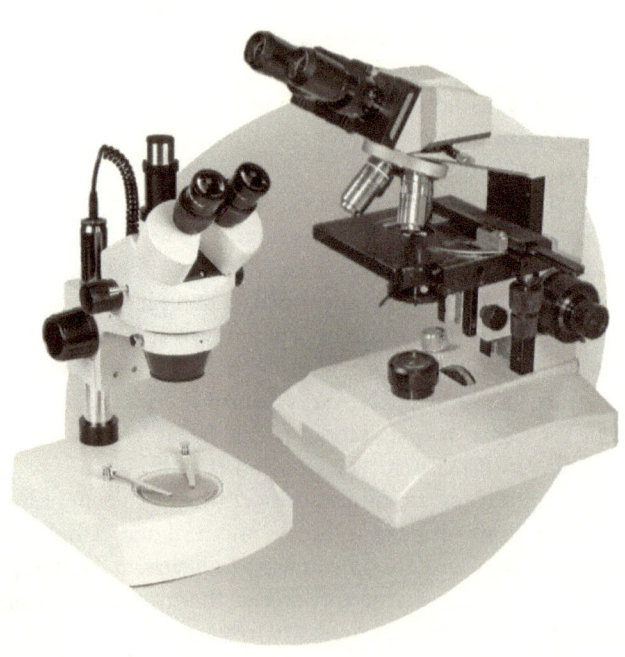

For communicating with each other, I had signed out five Motorola MX300 hand-held VHF radios plus a base station, all of which had crystals for the standard and tactical frequencies, plus the relatively recent feature of DVP voice encryption[23]. The base station was to be installed on whatever kind of boat we were able to rent for use on Lake Athabasca.

Beyond that, we had a lot of shopping to do, but most stores were closed on Sundays, so we had to wait a day[24]. At mid-day, I drove to the airport to pick-up Don, who was flying in from Fort McMurray. On the way back from the airport, Don summarized what he and Rick had learned from the charter pilot and explained about Rick seizing the opportunity to fly straight to the fly-in fishing camps and attempt to infiltrate the Athabasca Outfitters camp. When we got back to our temporary office space at K Division headquarters we were in for a surprise.

When we walked into our meeting room there was an older woman waiting for us, dressed for the wilderness with a kind of safari-style outfit comprising khaki shirt and pants, low hiking-style boots and a bush hat. Don and I stopped in our tracks for a moment, but Silver just calmly walked up to her to smell her clothes and accept a pat on the head. I did a double-take in the same instant that I realized why Silver was being so friendly.

"Vivian! I hardly recognize you," I said, looking her over. "You've dyed your hair grey and done it up in a bun, and under those old-style cats-eye glasses your eyes look grey too. Contact lenses?"

Vivian nodded. "The contacts change the colour and they also make me near-sighted. The glasses don't change my colour, but they correct my vision back to normal. That way if someone picks up my glasses and looks through them, they'll appear real. There are some distortions though, so it's a bit disconcerting to have my vision change twice like that, but I'm getting used to them."

"Very ingenious," I said. "And what have you done to your skin?"

"You like it? I've tried to keep it simple and understated. I've made my face paler with a bit of light foundation and some touches of green concealer rubbed into spots on my forehead and cheeks. I've added hints of wrinkle lines to my smile line and chin using a fine brush and a darker concealer, then brushing them over with a wide brush and a lighter concealer, and using a sponge to soften the edges. It's supposed to be subtle and easy to repair and easy to reproduce each morning. Anything more exotic and the doctor might catch me out."

"You've done something else to your face too," I said, holding her at arms length and peering at her.

Vivian opened her mouth in a wide smile. "Tooth overlays that change my facial profile just a bit, and with a few imitation gold fillings consistent with being from the previous generation. They're just like dentures, really, except that my real teeth are under them."

"Amazing," said Don.

"Think it will work?" she asked.

"Well, you'll never fool Silver like this, but beyond that I think you're good to go."

Another thing we got done, despite it being a Sunday, was finding and booking the rental of a houseboat that was docked at Fond-du-Lac, a remote fly-in community on the eastern shore of Lake Athabasca. It being prime summer-vacation season we had to take the only one left, which was probably larger than we needed, but the operator explained that it was seldom rented out due to its relatively high rental rate. From the description, it sounded like there would be lots of room for us to live and also operate a modest floating-laboratory operation, and we were assured that we'd also be able to rent a motorboat we could use for fishing and sampling.

The next day, Monday, was shopping day. We had two unmarked police SUVs assigned to us, so we divided up tasks and Don went off in one while 'the girls,' Vivian and I, took the other.

For his part, Don started out at CFB Edmonton (commonly known as Namao[25]), where he signed out duffle bags filled with camping gear suitable for use on a houseboat, such as sleeping bags, a cooler for extra food, and even fishing tackle. From there he went off to grocery-shop for the non-perishable food. Fresh food we planned to purchase when we got to the lake.

Vivian and I started out at camera shops in search of used camera gear of the sort that a reasonably serious amateur photographer might carry around. We had no trouble finding a Nikon 35mm SLR camera and compatible wide angle, normal, and telephoto lenses plus film and a selection of lens hoods and filters. It took a bit longer, however, to find a suitable camera bag that could hold all the gear and in which we could also hide the relatively bulky handheld VHF radio I had. In the end, we had to buy a brand-new one which we 'weathered' by taking it to a commercial laundromat and washing a few times on a high-temperature cycle and substituting bleach for detergent. After that, we put the camera bag into a dryer, added a pair of running shoes, kept tumbling the bag until it was not only dried but well pummelled. It came out looking respectably shabby and I later was able to take advantage of the Velcro™-tabbed dividers to create a hidden compartment at the bottom-rear of the bag in which to place the police radio. The camera and lens compartments were then arranged beside and above it. It wouldn't stand-up to a careful search, but we thought it would pass a casual one.

After that, we shopped for a few other things like disposable Styrofoam coolers for packing the fish we planned to catch for shipping back to a lab for analysis. With so much gear assembled, we had to charter a plane to fly it, and Don, Silver and I to Fond-du-Lac, where we had rented the houseboat.

On the following day we parted. Don, Silver and I flew to Fond-du-Lac, while Vivian stayed back. The next day, she would fly to Fort McMurray enroute to the Athabasca Outfitter camp as their latest patient.

***

Wednesday, August 4

Vivian had an uneventful airline flight to Fort McMurray, met the same charter pilot that had been interviewed by Don and Rick, and flew with him to Lake Athabasca. In contrast to the commercial jetliner from which she had just disembarked, the charter flight was in a Cessna 206 bush plane fitted with amphibious floats[26]. Never having been in a small airplane before made the next flight a completely different flying experience.

On the negative side, the seats were less comfortable, there was no in-flight service, and the ride was quite bumpy with a few patches of frightening turbulence. The noise would have been deafening as well, had not the pilot invited her to sit in the right-hand seat up front and provided her with a set of headphones that screened out most of the noise and allowed her to listen to the radio communications and occasionally converse with the pilot himself.

On the positive side, they flew at a vastly lower altitude than had the jetliner, so she had an excellent view of the terrain over which they flew, which was principally composed of forests, rocky patches and lakes. The pilot directed her attention forward when the huge expanse of Lake Athabasca came into view[27], and again when they were close enough to the lake to experience the amazing sight of the broad sand dunes adjacent to the southern lakeshore[28]. As they flew over the sand dunes, she had the surreal experience of feeling like she was momentarily flying over a portion of the Sahara Desert that had somehow been magically transported from North Africa to northern Canada. After that, it was almost an anticlimax to fly across the lake itself and land close to the abandoned Gunnar mine and mill site, home of the Athabasca Outfitters camp.

When the pilot had taxied to the main wharf, Vivian's introduction to the camp mirrored that received by Senator Harland Walker almost exactly two months earlier. Upon disembarking, she was met by the distinguished-looking Dr. Ernst Wildersbach.

"Welcome, welcome," he said. "How was your trip? No trouble I hope?"

"No, everything went fine," Vivian replied, "I'm just tired from all the flying. Something about air travel really wears me out."

"Of course, of course," said the doctor. "Everyone says the same thing. If you're not too tired, we'll offer you a nice hot meal and then show you to your cottage. Then tomorrow, we'll show you everything, explain everything, and after that we can get straight to your treatment."

"That's music to my ears. I can certainly stay awake long enough to eat!"

"Fine, fine. I will lead you to the dining hall and then I will have one of my assistants show you to your cottage. Don't worry about your luggage, it will be waiting for you when you get there."

"Oh yes, that reminds me. There's another fly-in fishing camp near here isn't there? One called the Angler, or something like that?"

"Yes. Yes. The Northern Angler camp is very close. Why do you ask?"

"The charter company asked me to try to deliver a camera bag to one of their guests that they took there on Sunday – someone named Richard Cooper. Apparently, it was accidentally left behind at the airport."

"Richard Cooper. Richard Cooper. Would that be a Rick Cooper by chance?"

"I suppose so. I really don't know."

"Well, there is a Rick Cooper who is a guest over at the Angler, but he's helping us out over here right now doing temporary duty as our cook. Our regular cook has taken sick, you see, and we've been most fortunate to have Rick fill-in for us. I must say," the doctor added, in a confidential tone, "that the standard of cooking has improved as a result, so you're in for a special treat. Yes, a special treat."

"Well. That's fine then, isn't it. Let me just collect the camera bag from the pilot and we can see if it belongs to your new cook." As he did with all those who came for radiation treatments, Dr. Wildersbach led Vivian to a waiting pickup truck, they both got in, and as he drove, he gave a running monologue pointing out some of the features of the long-abandoned uranium mining operation. As they bounced along the rough roads, Vivian made appreciative sounds and comments, and before long they ended up at the original cookhouse, now renamed.

"This is our dining hall," the doctor said as they walked inside. "You'll find a meal schedule in the house you've been assigned to. The house will have a fully functional kitchen stocked with a few necessities but for full meals, everyone eats here." When they walked over to the broad, open window across which the food dishes were set out, they could see that there was a man working in the kitchen.

"Good afternoon, Rick. What's on the menu for tonight?"

"Hi Doc," said Rick, with a wave. "I'm making up a special baked Walleye. It just came in from one of the guides. It'll get lightly breaded and seasoned, then very gently baked. I'm trying to outdo those pan-fried fireside meals that the guides make for your clients for lunch out in the field. I'll be serving it with baked beans and fried potato wedges, plus a nice assortment of salads."

"My goodness, if you can better the guides, we'll never let you go! Rick, I'd like you to meet our newest arrival: Vivian Rule."

"Nice to meet you Vivian," said Rick. "Please excuse me for not shaking hands but, as you can see, they're covered in flour," he said, holding up his arms to display white, flour-coated hands and wrists.

"No problem," said Vivian. "But you might want to clean up anyway, because I brought you something." She held up his camera bag.

"My camera gear!" he exclaimed. "How did it come to you?"

While Rick went to the big sink to wash, Vivian explained about the charter air service finding it left behind. "I was going to ask the doctor whether he could radio the other camp so you could come and get it, but it turns out you're right here."

"Well that's a happy coincidence," Rick said as he walked over to the window and accepted the bag. Then he opened it, making sure that the doctor had a good view of the contents, and took out the camera body and one of the lenses. Putting the two together, he removed the lens cap and experimentally focuses on the far corner of the dining hall. "Everything seems to be intact. Not even a mouse got in! Thank you for bringing it for me."

"My pleasure. I'm glad there was no mouse. I saw a cat sniffing at the bag in the air terminal, so I wondered," she quipped, providing Rick with the second code word. "I was coming to this camp anyway, so it was no trouble at all."

"Since you have a little time before supper, I'll show you where you will be staying," said the doctor.

"See you later," added Rick, closing up his camera bag.

With a wave to Rick, Vivian followed the doctor out of the dining hall and back in to the truck. From there they drove a short distance past several larger buildings, that the doctor explained were abandoned bunkhouses, to where a half-dozen, well-spaced, small houses were located. "These have all been very nicely fixed up for our patient-guests, because they are right beside the hospital," he added. Then, having ushered Vivian into one of the houses, he handed her the key, saying "I think you will find this a bit rustic but quite comfortable. Yes, quite comfortable. I have some other things requiring my attention right now, but I may see you at supper this evening. In any case, I will come and collect you at breakfast in the morning.... You did bring the X-rays and medical report with you?"

"Oh yes, I brought everything you asked for. It's all in my luggage."

"Fine. Fine. We'll review those in the morning and I will show you everything and explain everything, and then we will be able to begin the treatment. Tomorrow morning without fail" and, so saying, he took his leave.

After a brief rest, Vivian walked to the dining hall for supper and was surprised, intrigued, and more than usually on her guard when the doctor came to her table and asked if he could join her. She naturally agreed, and found him to be an engaging and entertaining conversationalist. Their wide-ranging conversation continued well past the conclusion of their meal, and it occurred to her that the doctor seemed to be showing an unusual level of interest in her. *Romantic interest?* she wondered. *Real or feigned then?*

When they eventually rose from the table, the doctor, who by that time had insisted she call him Ernst, invited her to go for a stroll before turning in for the night.

They continued their conversation as they walked down to the lakeshore and she showed a suitable level of interest in hearing about his career in Europe. This allowed him to brag a bit, and her obvious appreciation for his anecdotes of trials and accomplishments seemed to have the desired effect.

After sitting at the marina for a while, enjoying the view of the lake, the doctor – Ernst – walked her back to her house, thanked her for the pleasure of her company and took his leave.

Interesting but dangerous, thought Vivian, wondering which was more likely, that the doctor was playing games with her or that she had found a weakness she might be able to exploit.

Oh well, at least I made it in and met Rick already! thought Vivian. *Now all I have to do is see what I can learn and hope to survive the medical treatment.*

Laurie Schramm

5 THE SCIENTISTS ARRIVE

Meanwhile, a day earlier (Tuesday, August 3)

Don and I had flown to Fond-du-Lac, in the northeast corner of Lake Athabasca, to board the houseboat we'd booked. Our float plane had docked very near to where the houseboat was tied up so that, after signing the rental and payment paperwork and borrowing a hand-cart, we were able to quite easily transfer all of our gear from the plane. It was time-consuming, however, so by the time we were finished there was just enough time to do some shopping, for which we left Silver behind on the boat.

Fond-du-Lac, is a remote, fly-in settlement of the Fond du Lac Denesųłiné (Dene) First Nation. It is one of the oldest, most northern communities in Saskatchewan having been originally established around a Hudson's Bay trading post in the late 18th century. The community's population is about 900 people, most of them of Dene or Métis descent, large enough to support a well-stocked combination grocery- and department store that was the successor to the original trading post. We were able to buy all of the perishable foods we wanted, and lingered for a while to take in other features of the store like their displays of handmade fur hats, mittens, and moccasins. There was also a very nice bakery, from which we purchased an assortment of wonderful-smelling baked goods. We were even able to buy a good supply of dry ice that we would use to keep our fish samples frozen.

After hauling the groceries back to the houseboat, we again left

Silver behind and went in search of a late supper. The community had a couple of places from which to choose. We ended up at the dining room of a lodge and were treated to a very nice homestyle meal. After that, it was late enough that we simply left the houseboat tied up where it was and spent our first night there.

Wednesday, August 4

The morning brought another travel day for us, and for Vivian as well. While Vivian was spending the day travelling to, and getting herself established in the Athabasca Outfitters camp, we set out on the lake to navigate our way westward towards Uranium City. I say navigate, and we had brought along a hydrographic chart[29] and sought advice from the locals, but all we had to do really, was to head west and follow the north shore.

Don and I took turns unpacking and setting up our gear, including creating a realistic-looking research setup, but that left lots of time to just sit and enjoy the scenery. I'd mentioned that it was a large houseboat. Officially it was listed as "sleeps 16," but it would more realistically be up to twelve if you didn't count the ability to fold-out the sofa bed or convert the kitchen table. In any case, there was lots of room for us and our gear.

We'd also rented a twelve-foot, aluminum-hull 'zodiac-style' hypalon™ inflatable boat[30] and 40 hp outboard motor. The boat could either be towed behind the houseboat or else secured on the top deck. To facilitate this, there was a swing-out boom and electric winch that could be used to (separately) raise and lower the boat and motor.

I'd never been on a houseboat before and found it very relaxing. Of course, being a large (over fifty feet, 15 m, in length) and heavy craft, its 'cruising speed' was eight knots (about 15 km/h, 9 mph). The upside was that time slowed down for us and we could enjoy the trip.

I particularly liked sitting up on the flying bridge, where there was a 360° view. The north shore featured alternating patches of tree-less rocks and clusters of black spruce and jack pine; in one place I spotted two moose placidly foraging, in another a black bear, and in still another I watched a muskrat approach the shore and smoothly slip in to the water. In the air, we spotted a much wider range of birds including several species of ducks, some loons and herons, some ruffed grouse, a couple of hawks, an eagle and, of course, quite a few Canada geese. Silver was well used to being in boats – even on this very lake[31] – so he was quite content to simply lounge on the upper deck where he too could look around.

At a speed of eight knots, it took a little over five hours to reach Uranium City, where we put in to take on fuel and spread our cover story about being biologists on a research cruise. From there, another two hours put us in the vicinity, but out of sight of, the Athabasca Outfitters camp. There are quite a few islands in the vicinity, and we picked a spot among them that was well sheltered, but neither overly conspicuous nor hidden, and tied up there for the night.

Thursday, August 5

We knew that the guides in the fishing boats would see us, of course, but we thought that it was better to let them come to check us out than the reverse. Besides, we had some fishing to do in order to add realism to our story. So, in the morning, we pulled out and anchored a short distance away to do a little fishing and Don actually caught two northern pike, which we filleted and dissected. I took a couple of samples from one of them to create examples we could put under our microscopes. I'd also cheated by purchasing some frozen fillets at the store in Fond-du-Lac to form the beginnings of our 'research collection.'

If things had gone well by this time, Rick would be in place as camp cook, and Vivian established as a patient.

We didn't think it would be very long before someone from Athabasca Outfitters dropped by to play the innocent passerby as an excuse to see what we were up to, but were surprised that it happened within hours rather than days. It was just after lunch when a fishing boat motored up to the stern, and a male voice called "ahoy there."

"Good morning," I said, when I reached the stern. I noticed, as I did so, that the boat had the name Athabasca Outfitters stencilled near the bow.

"Ben Delorme. I'm one of the guides at the Athabasca Outfitters fishing camp just over there on the mainland," he said, waving an arm in the direction of the camp. "I just thought I'd drop by to say hello and ask if there's anything you need."

"We're fine for now, but that's very good of you," I congratulated. "Would you like to come aboard for a cup of coffee?"

"That would really hit the spot," he said, and he tied up his boat and clambered out.

"I'm Alex and this is Silver," I said, as Silver approached him for an investigative sniff. He'd put out a hand to sniff, but he immediately snatched it away when Silver began a menacing growling.

"Silver!" I said, in an admonishing tone, at which he reduced his grows to a low level but didn't entirely stop. I noticed that his hackles were up a bit. "He's just trying to defend me," I said, by way of explanation.

With a wave, I turned and led the way to the galley – it looked more like the kitchen in a motorhome than a boat's galley – with Silver following along behind, still with a low series of growls that, were he human, would have been like grumbling under his breath.

"This is my husband, Don," I said when we got there.

"Ben Delorme," he said, shaking hands with Don. "One of the guides at the Athabasca Outfitters fishing camp just over there on the mainland."

"He came to see if we need anything and I offered coffee," I said. We already had a pot of coffee on the range, so I poured three cups while Don asked him some questions about how their fly-in fishing season was going.

"We have a few guests right now," he said, "but it's been slow this year."

"Are you two some kind of scientists or something?" he asked, noticing the two microscopes we had set up on what would otherwise be the dining table, and the obvious array of glassware and other paraphernalia that surrounded them.

"That's right," I said. "We're part of a research project to study the uptake of radioactive metals by the fish in the lake, especially those caught near the abandoned Gunnar uranium mine site on either side of the peninsula. We've already caught some *Exos Lucius*, that's northern pike, out here and later on we'll move to the other side of the peninsula and try to get some *Coregonus clupeaformis*, lake whitefish, in Langley Bay.

"We're especially interested in uranium and some of the elements from its decay series, like radium, and lead[32]. We're not just going to measure the uranium content, because the different radioisotopes can migrate into the environment at different rates. After we've dissected the fish, we put samples of the muscle, liver, and bones in these plastic bags and keep them frozen on ice. They'll all be analyzed later, but you can see what the tissues look like under these microscopes."

I showed him a sample of fish tissue under the stereo microscope, then a stained sample, that was mounted on a cover slip, under the higher magnification of the compound microscope.

"Very interesting," he said. "How many fish do you need for this?"

"We're trying for at least a half-dozen of each species from each location, in order to have statistically representative results when the analyses are done."

"OK. And what are you trying to prove?"

"Not so much prove as learn. We think that the tailings are virtually certain to have spilled over into Langley Bay, and that rain and melting snow will be leaching additional material and washing it into the bay with each successive season. The solid particles will be gathering in the sediment, and from there the radionuclides can get into the water, and therefore into the fish. That should mean that the fish in the bay would have greater concentrations of radioactive metals in their tissues than the same fish out in the lake proper, like where we are right now, and even those should have higher concentrations in them than fish in other lakes and rivers that are not close to uranium mine tailings[33]. Depending on what we learn, it could provide a reason for the government to begin cleaning up these old uranium sites, and it's possible that the fish aren't actually safe to eat."

"Oh. The boss won't want to hear that!"

"No. I'm sure you're right, but your customers should be fine since they'll only be taking a few fish to eat. The local residents, on the other hand, have been here eating the fish for decades since the mine and mill closed. That might be a different story."

"Oh. Well, I suppose that wouldn't be so bad then."

"By the way, do you think we could get permission to catch some samples from the flooded-mine pit? The radionuclide levels in the fish might be even higher in those fish[34]."

"I don't see why not. I'll mention it to the boss. Drop by sometime, the boss is a doctor so he might like to meet you and hear about the fish anyway."

"Thanks, we'll do that," said Don.

I walked with Delorme back to the stern of the boat, with Silver trailing us and looking unhappy, and saw him off.

"What do you think?" I asked Don when I returned to the galley.

"He probably really does serve as a fishing guide, but he has the manner of a guard, or maybe ex-military, about him. He wasn't obvious about it, but when you were explaining the scientific stuff, he took a good look at everything."

"Yes, and Silver's senses obviously had him concerned too. It's a good thing we hid the radios and base-station antenna down in the engine compartment. We might as well bring out the base station and get its antenna up. We could get a call from Rick anytime now."

The rest of our day was uneventful and we had a leisurely afternoon and enjoyed a gorgeous evening twilight over the lake.

Friday, August 6

After breakfast, we took the inflatable boat and went to Athabasca Outfitters to ask for permission to collect some fish from the flooded open-mine pit. We were met by Delorme, making us wonder whether he had been watching for us, but he was civil enough saying, "I already spoke to the boss about your request. He's too busy to come himself, but says you are welcome to go ahead. If you'd like to hop into my truck I'll drive you to the pit."

We loaded Silver and our fishing gear into the back of the truck, then got in ourselves and he took us the short distance to the flooded mine-pit. Circling around it, he drove to the far side of the pit, where the remnants of forest bordered it, and where there was a rowboat beached and tied to a large tree. He said he'd come check on us later in the day, but that he wasn't sure when that might be. We thanked him, and said we'd be fine to simply walk back to the dock when we were done.

We spent the morning out in the pit fishing. Although we fished from the boat, we didn't fish too far from shore because most of the fish we caught were from less than about 25 feet (7.6 m) down. In five hours, we caught six northern pike (*Esox lucius*) ranging between 51 and 66 inches long (1.3-1.6 m) and six common suckers (*Catostomus commersoni*) that ranged between about 30 and 46 inches in length (76-117 cm).

With the fish in hand, we rowed back to shore and beached the rowboat where we had found it. After tying it up to a metal ring that was attached to a heavy chain, we followed the chain back to where it was secured to a large tree.

"Look at this," said Don, inspecting the robustness of the method that had been used to secure the chain. The fittings were heavily rusted. "They didn't just bring the boat here for us, they've been tying it up here for some time."

When we walked back to the water's edge, we took a careful look at where we'd pulled the rowboat while pretending to be checking to make sure we hadn't left anything behind. Sure enough, there were a number of grooves on the beach showing where it had been pulled up on previous occasions.

"Why keep a boat here?" wondered Don out loud.

"I don't know," I replied. "I doubt anyone would swim or catch and eat fish from the pit that you'd have to assume was radioactive, especially when there's a massive lake within sight that's bound to be cleaner and have healthier fish in it."

"No," he said, thoughtfully, "you wouldn't want to risk taking anything out, but you might want to put something in it."

"You mean like disposing of things you don't want found, like deceased patients, you mean?"

"Maybe. Or possibly even someone that you caught snooping around just that little bit too much."

"It's an idea. I don't see how we're going to search it though. It's probably several hundred feet deep[35]."

With these chilling thoughts in our minds, we gathered up our fish and fishing gear and walked the roughly half-mile back to the dock on the lake where our inflatable boat was tied up. Once we'd loaded the boat, pushed off, started the motor, and were out on the water, Don said, "Good thing we weren't obvious about snooping around where that rowboat was."

"Oh?" I asked.

"We were being watched all right, but from a distance, with binoculars probably."

"Must have been, or else Silver would have sensed it."

"I think that must be why they kept their distance. I only noticed when we were walking back to the dock. When I stopped to tie my bootlace, I peeked back and just caught the movement of someone hiding behind the headframe."

"I'm surprised you caught them with the old shoelace trick!"

"It was probably just a fluke and I happened to glance back just when they were changing position."

"Well," I said, "we assumed we'd be followed and watched. We were right."

"Yes, but it doesn't give us any clue what they're up to here."

"No. I think that's going to be up to Rick and Vivian."

"It's nice to be out on a mission together though," he said.

"Always!" I said, which was immediately seconded by a "Grruph!" from Silver.

Well, I thought as we motored back to the island at which we'd tied-up the houseboat, *we're in place with our cover story established. Now we watch and wait.*

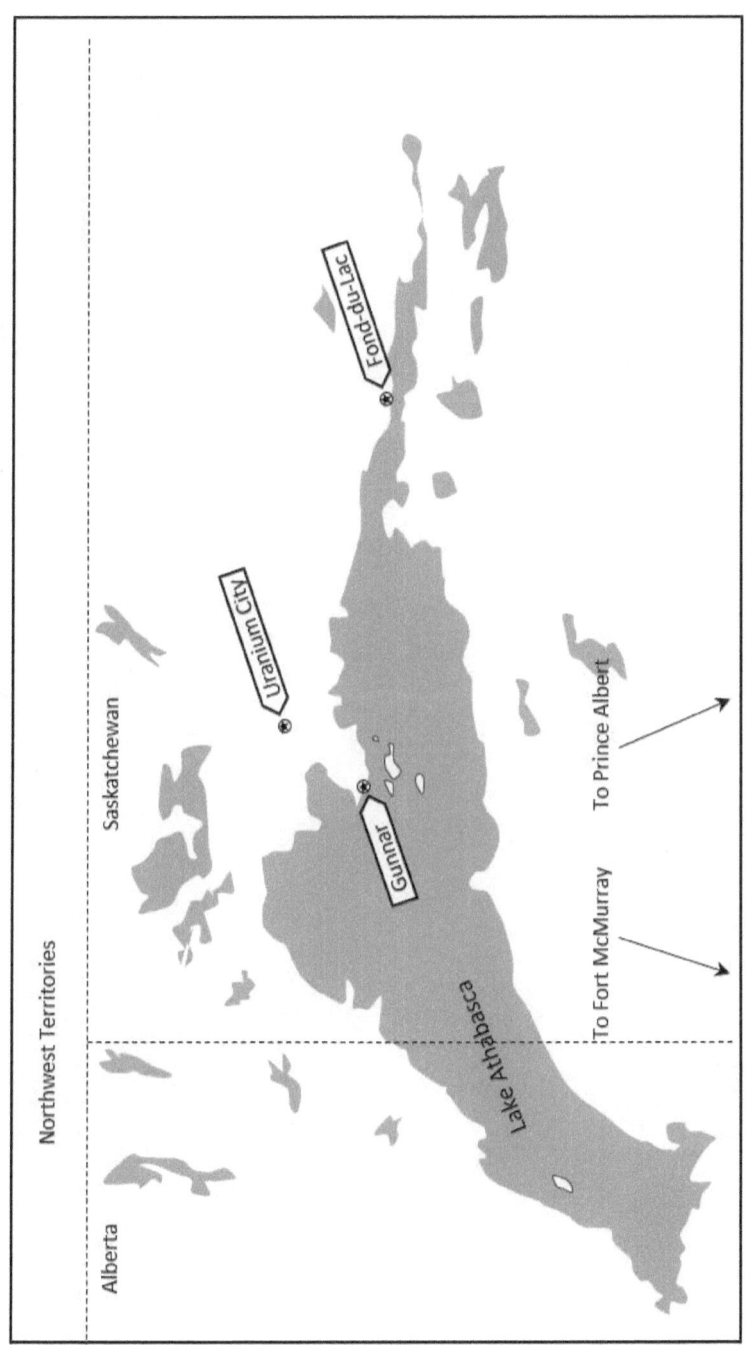

511

Laurie Schramm

6 VIVIAN'S TREATMENT

Meanwhile, beginning two days earlier (Wednesday, August 4)

While Alex and Don were setting out in their houseboat Rick had promptly hidden the VHF radio in the attic of the house he was staying in. Beyond that, he'd been kept busy with his cooking duties. He had also continued with his morning visits to Alistair to check on his condition and to bring him fresh cups of coffee. Although he was still adding PP796 to the coffee, he had reduced the dosage to half a pill, which was enough to give Alistair the same symptoms of nausea, weakness, and dizziness, but with less stomach pain. Plus, he was able to eat some simple food like plain toast, without vomiting. As a result, the doctor seemed to be encouraged by the apparent improvement in Alistair's condition and convinced that further bedrest would lead to recovery. Rick's aims were to keep Alistair out of commission and the doctor concerned yet content, but he was under no illusions that he'd be able to get away with it for much longer.

His role as camp cook had gone well, particularly since he tended to prepare somewhat different dishes than had Alaistair. The staff and guests had viewed this as a pleasant change and had become quite friendly except for Delorme, who seemed to be the doctor's right hand and effectively his head of security. It didn't seem like Delorme had any friends or wanted to be friendly with anyone, although Rick found him to be civil enough. After his first few days as cook, Rick had learned to distinguish between the real fishing guests and the pretend fishers who were really there for medical treatments. The former talked constantly about boats, the outdoors, fishing, fishing gear and, of course, the fish they'd caught, the ones that had gotten away, and the ones they still hoped to catch. These guests were always the first up, the first in his kitchen for breakfast, and the first to finish-up so they could get out on the water with the guides.

The pretend fishers, on the other hand, tended to sleep in, show up last for breakfast, and generally talked about anything but boats or fishing. Although, to be fair, some of them did seem genuinely pleased to be in the wilderness rather than their big cities. Rick made an effort to engage these guests in conversation whenever he could and they seemed to simply assume that, as a staff member, he must be in on the racket so they spoke to him openly when he showed interest and concern, so he had no trouble learning about their medical problems.

By visiting Alistair each day with his mug of special coffee, Rick was also able to observe where the other patients were examined and treated, although he had been careful to seem unobservant and oblivious to such things.

When he wasn't busy with planning meals, cooking, serving, and cleaning up, he alternated between going out fishing with one of the guides and going for walks around the abandoned mine site. He had even specifically asked for and been given permission for these explorations, although with a warning that some of the houses and structures might be in danger of collapse and that there were almost certainly chemical and radiation hazards in and around the mill and acid plant buildings[36]. He wasn't interested in the latter buildings, but did survey the entire site, discovering as he did so a little neighbourhood of small houses that were located some distance away from everything else at the tip of the peninsula. Among the other houses, dormitories, and buildings he learned which few were in use, another few that remained abandoned but seemed structurally sound, and those that appeared to be completely unsafe.

One of Rick's mottos was 'check your six[37],' and it was something he practised religiously. As a result, on his first two strolls around the site, he was fully aware of being followed, but he'd expected that. The man following him the first time wasn't very good at it, but Rick ignored him and played the innocent but curious visitor. The second time, it was Delorme following him and Delorme did know how to shadow someone. Here again, Rick was careful to give no sign of being aware of his follower and stuck to his casual sightseeing plus some extended periods of just looking out over the lake. After that, even Delorme seemed to lose interest in him and he was unable to detect followers on subsequent walks, although he remained careful and vigilant anyway.

In addition to the various buildings, and their layout, Rick also explored some of the game trails that abounded in the nearby forest. On one of these explorations, he was following a game trail when it crossed an obviously human-made but long disused and heavily overgrown gravel path. In one direction it seemed to lead to the open pit mine. Curious, he followed it the other way, into the forest. Before long, he encountered a low building. His first thought was that it was an old trapper's cabin, as it was a one-room structure made entirely from squared-off, heavy baulks of wood that were joined at the corners with classic, full-dovetail notches.

The windows were boarded-up and there was a large, heavily corroded padlock on the front door. When he went up and gave the lock an experimental tug, it immediately opened together with a mini-shower of particles and flakes of rust. Opening the door showed him nothing but pitch blackness, but he had a small penlight in his pocket. The penlight provided just enough illumination for him to gingerly step inside and look around. The shack was mostly empty, but it was immediately clear that this was no trapper's cabin. Strewn around on the floor were the remnants of small wooden crates. When he picked up one of the empty crates and held it up to the light, he could read the stencilling. On the ends, it read: "FORCITE," and on the sides: "MADE IN CANADA BY CANADIAN INDUSTRIES (1954) LIMITED."

He whistled softly. *No wonder they built this shack so far away from the mine*, he thought to himself. Replacing the empty box, he began methodically search the entire shack. He was looking for any surviving sticks of forcite[38] and, if possible, blasting caps and fuses.

Beyond the old explosives shack, the only noteworthy things Rick spotted on his strolls were the repurposing of one of the old buildings for storage, the repair and upkeep of the docks, and the rowboat tied up on the flooded open-mine pit.

For some reason he couldn't identify, the flooded pit interested him. From the maps and documents obtained by his fellow CIA operative, and delivered by the charter pilot, he knew that the pit was shaped like a tall, narrow funnel. Underneath, the miners had mined underground as they continued to follow the ore body to greater and greater depths, with a maze of underground workings that had been serviced by the hoist and massive headframe. When the mining had ceased, the company had blasted the thin shoulder of granite separating the pit from the lake, causing everything to be flooded - the open pit and all of the underground workings alike. He wondered what lay at the bottom of the pit, knowing that in many such mining operations a wide range of equipment and materials would be simply bulldozed into the pit at closure; he wondered whether there were fish still living in the lake, and if so whether they had become so afflicted with genetic mutations as to be unrecognizable; and he wondered why anyone would keep a rowboat stationed there.

On one of his fishing trips with the most friendly and outgoing of the guides, he had tried innocently asking about the possibility of radioactive fish, and had been told that no one was worried about the fish in the big lake, but no one was willing to chance fishing in the flooded pit.

Other than their meeting and handoff of the camera bag, Rick hadn't seen much of Vivian beyond the level of attention he gave each of the guests when they came to the dining hall to eat. He did notice that the doctor had joined her for supper on her first night, and that afterwards the two had gone off for an evening stroll. He also noticed that on her second day, she had taken her lunch tray and sat down with the kid that always seemed to eat alone while covering his table with a mound of computer printouts. The kid had removed his headphones when she spoke to him, cleared a space for her tray, and then went back to his printouts. Rick was amused to see that Vivian hadn't let that pass, and somehow managed to engage him in some kind of discussion.

I wonder what's so interesting that those two have gotten together, he thought.

***

Also on Thursday, August 5

Vivian began her first full day at the Athabasca Outfitters camp

516

with breakfast, where she smiled at Rick and exchanged a few of the same kinds of friendly comments with him that she would have with any other cook in similar circumstances. Knowing Rick's true identity, she was pleasantly surprised at how good her breakfast omelet tasted and was genuine in her praise when she left.

When she reached the small hospital, she was led to the doctor's office where he greeted her, inquired about her accommodations and meals, and then got down to business. After taking some time to read the copy of her medical file, which she'd brought with her as previously instructed, he slipped the X-rays from her file onto the backlit, wall-mounted viewing and had a close look at them as well.

"Well, well, your initial treatments went very well indeed and the new appearances of the cancer in your lymph nodes are at a very early stage. In fact, I'm surprised that your specialist even discovered them, but it's well that he did so because the earlier we can catch and treat them the better the success rate."

"That's what I was hoping for Doctor, and that's why I wanted to get the treatments as soon as possible rather wait for months and let the cancer spread."

"Very wise. I think that's very wise indeed, and since you were able to come here so promptly, I'm very confident we'll have no trouble whatsoever clearing everything up in just a few treatments.

"Nurse!" he called out, and the nurse promptly came in from the adjoining office.

"Would you take Mrs. Rule to the treatment room and get things ready while I work out the course of treatments that we'll use?"

"Yes Doctor," she said, and indicated that Vivian should follow her.

It was only a few steps down the hallway to the treatment room, but they first entered the small control room where a young woman was watching someone who was working at a computer display terminal.

"This is Lisa," introduced the nurse. "She's the technician that will operating the machine. Lisa, the doctor will bring you the prescription for Mrs. Rule's treatment in just a few minutes. He'll also bring the X-rays and show you the two locations he's going to want you to irradiate."

"That's fine. Dexter here just needs a moment to print out some more of the computer program."

As the nurse nodded and left, a male voice said "There. I'm

sending the last part that I need to the printer. It will only be a minute."

It was a young male voice, Vivian thought, and, sure enough, after pressing a few more keys on the keyboard, a thin young man with prominent glasses and a shock of unruly hair straightened and then stood up. As he did so, the dot-matrix teleprinter[39] beside him began to make a metallic, mechanical sound as its print-head began racing back and forth, alternating printing lines of text from left-to-right then right-to-left. It was printing on continuous fanfold paper that was drawn up from a box on the floor, fed through the machine by a tractor-feed mechanism that meshed with holes that perforated each side of the paper. The printed sheets were fed to a basket behind the printer in which the pages re-folded themselves into a neat stack.

"Dexter this is Mrs. Rule, our next patient," said Lisa. "Mrs. Rule, this is Dexter Sherman, our computer consultant." Although she said it with a straight face, her eyes twinkled as if to communicate that she found it amusing that their computer consultant was probably only eighteen or nineteen years old. Dexter smiled, nodded, and shook hands before turning to watch his printout being generated. He was strongly introverted and not comfortable conversing with strangers so there was an awkward silence for a few moments, but the printing was soon completed and he was able to gather up the printout, add it to several other stacks of similar printouts that were strewn on the desk nearby, and left without saying anything further.

"He's a computer-nerd[40] and he's running diagnostics for us; apparently some kind of kid-genius about computers," said Lisa by way of explanation.

"Oh. Alright," said Vivian.

Lisa led her to the inner treatment room, showed her the machine, and got her settled on the treatment table. By the time that was done, the doctor had come in with Vivian's X-rays and some written notes. After greeting Vivian, he put her X-rays up on a set of wall-mounted light boxes and showed Lisa the target zones for the treatment.

"I want you to set-up for the 10 MeV electron-beam treatment, and deliver a 200 rad dose to each site."

"Yes, Doctor."

"Excellent. Excellent. Now then, Vivian," he said, taking one of her hands in his. "You have nothing to be concerned about. I will leave you in Lisa's capable hands, and I will come back and check on you in a little while."

"Thank you Doctor," she replied.

When he'd left, Lisa moved the treatment table and rotated the gantry so that the first treatment beam would be aimed where she wanted it, then said, "The machine has been aimed, now I'm adjusting the beam width so we just hit the first part that we want to be targeted by the electron beam…. There. Now, I'm going to leave the treatment room and sit down at the computer console in the next room. There's an intercom we'll be able to use to speak to each other. OK?"

"Yes thanks," said Vivian, doing her best to hide her nervousness.

Lisa went to the next room, closed the door, sat-down at her computer terminal, and switched on the intercom.

"Mrs. Rule. Can you hear me?"

"Yes."

"OK. I will provide a running commentary so you know what I'm doing out here. You just lie there and relax, and I'll tell you which times you'll need to try very hard not to move your body."

"Alright."

"Here we go. The machine and computer are on, and I am just typing in your name and the machine settings. The computer will now check to make sure that the data I entered matches the settings I just made manually when I was in there with you. It will only allow me to proceed if they match perfectly. That's for your safety."

There was the sound of clicking as Lisa pushed the keys on the keyboard. She was reading the lines as they came up on her display. Eventually, it read:

```
SYSTEM: BEAM READY     OP. MODE: TREAT     AUTO
```

"OK. Everything looks good. Hold still now." Lisa then hit the one-key command B, for beam on, to begin the treatment. There was a brief mechanical sound and then the room suddenly went black and silent. There was a squeal, but it came from Lisa rather than Vivian.

Vivian only had a moment to consider what might have happened before a Lisa came into the room waving a flashlight in front of her.

"Are you OK?" she asked.

"Yes, fine," said Vivian. "What happened?"

"Power failure," Lisa replied. "The generator probably went on the blink again. It only happens rarely, but it does happen, I'm afraid. Let me help you up off the treatment table."

After assisting Vivian, she led her out of the treatment rooms, down the corridor, and to the hospital entrance.

"Wow. It's nice the see daylight again," Vivian commented, squinting through the door.

"Yes. I have to go find the doctor and let him know what's happened. Are you OK to walk on your own, or would you like my help?"

"I'm fine now dear," said Vivian in her most grandmotherly voice, "you just go on about your business and I'll go back to my house. Do you think the power will be out in the dining room too?"

"It should be fine. The hospital and dining room are on separate generators."

"In that case, I think I'll just walk over there and get myself a nice cup of tea."

When Vivian entered the dining hall, it was empty except for some sounds emanating from the kitchen and one table in a corner that was completely covered with heaps of computer printouts with Dexter buried in the middle of it all, alternately holding up sheets of fanfold paper to read and making notations on a pad of paper.

She first went to the kitchen's serving window. "How's our master chef doing this morning?"

"Oh, hi!" said Rick, looking up from where he'd been crouched by a low cabinet searching for some kind of cooking utensils. "I'm doing just fine, thank you." He rose, walked over to the window, and looked around the dining area to see who was there, then in a low voice said "I couldn't help noticing that you met our new computer consultant."

"Dexter? Yes, we were introduced just this morning when I went for my first treatment, and we had breakfast together."

"Ah. I'm not supposed to know about the medical treatments, but there aren't many secrets from the staff around here. How did it go?"

"It didn't. There was a power failure just when it they were about to start. Everything's on hold now until they find out what's wrong and get the generator fixed. They're expecting to have it back on this afternoon."

"Umm hmmm. Are you a betting woman by chance?"

"Me?" she said, surprised. "Well, within reason I suppose. Why?"

"Because I'll bet you it doesn't get fixed quite that easily. I happened to be walking by the hospital this morning and noticed that the generator sounded a bit rough and was producing quite a bit of smoke."

"And?"

"And I wondered whether it might have a bad batch of diesel fuel in it."

"Is that common?"

"Well, it happens, you know. There could have been too much water or sludge in the tank, someone might have mistakenly topped the tank up with gasoline instead of diesel, that kind of thing."

"You seem to know a lot about it."

"Not really, I've just picked up some little bits of experience here and there over the years," he said, putting on an innocent expression.

"Hmmm. Remind me never to play poker with you. I don't think I'll bet against you now either. OK then, smarty-pants, how long do you think it will take them to fix the generator?"

"They might have some mechanically-minded people in a camp like this. I'd say tomorrow afternoon at the earliest."

"Sounds like someone has either accidentally or deliberately bought me a little time then."

Vivian had been fixing herself a mug of tea while talking. As she made to walk away, she lowered her voice even further, saying, "Glad you're here Rick."

Rick smiled and reached over to put a small dish of fresh doughnuts on her food tray. "All part of the service."

Walking over to where Dexter was seated, Vivian noticed once again that he had a lightweight pair of headphones on. Judging from the sounds, he was listening to some kind of noisy music. Realizing that he'd never hear her if she said anything, she simply pulled out a chair and sat down right across the table from him.

He saw that almost immediately, sat up and looked at her while lifting the headphones from his ears. That made the type of music, at least, quite clear.

"Heavy metal?" she asked, looking meaningfully at the headphones.

He blinked. "Yes," he said, looking confused.

"Well don't look at me like that. I may be old but I'm not dead!" She smiled. "Black Sabbath?"

"How do you... I'm sorry, I mean yes, it's called *War Pigs*[41]."

"Good choice," she said, then smiled again. "Do you mind if I join you?"

"Uh. No. Not at all," he said, looking up and blinking a few times through his glasses. Then he switched off his Sony Walkman and set it, and the headphones, aside then pushed some of the printouts to one side so there was room for her tray, which she was still holding. In doing so, a few piles of paper from the far side of the table slipped of and fell to the floor but he didn't seem to notice. In fact, he immediately put his head down and returned to his reading of printouts and making notes on the pad of paper.

Vivian studied him over the brim of her mug of tea. Her first and second impressions of Dexter were that he fulfilled most of the stereotypical characteristics[42] of a computer scientist: male, pale and thin, wearing glasses, probably very intelligent, obsessed with computers and programming to the exclusion of other interests, lacking interpersonal skills and socially awkward.

"May I ask what you are doing?" she said.

"Me? Oh. You mean with all this?" he looked up and pointed to the piles of printouts. "Debugging."

"What does that mean?"

Dexter paused in thought for a moment, as if considering how to phrase an answer she could understand. Then he pushed his glasses higher on the bridge of his nose. "They think there's a problem buried somewhere in the computer program. Sometimes when they tell it to have the machine use a certain energy level or duration, it doesn't do it."

"You mean it refuses?"

"Oh no. A computer can't normally refuse a program instruction. It's more like it doesn't turn the beam on, or not high enough, or not for long enough."

"So in that case the patient doesn't get the treatment. Why were they going to treat me this morning then?"

"I think it's because it doesn't happen very often. They told me that it almost always follows the commands the operator types into the terminal, but once in a while, like maybe one time in twenty, say, it doesn't do it."

"I see," said Vivian in a thoughtful voice. "Does it ever go the other way then?"

"The other way?" Dexter sounded confused.

"I mean does it sometimes turn the beam on too high, or for too long?"

"Oh. I'm sure not. They would have told me, wouldn't they?" He sounded horrified. "I mean, they wouldn't keep treating people if that were the case. I mean, do you know what could happen to a person if the energy level was really cranked up?" If possible, he looked even more horrified, as the implications took hold in his imagination. Then he seemed to get a grip on his thoughts and shook his head. "No. I'm quite certain they would have told me."

"I'm sure you're right," she said, not believing it, then tried changing the topic slightly. "So what are you doing about this 'bug' as you call it?"

"I'm going through the computer program line by line so I can figure out what the original programmers have done. It's not really all that complicated, but as you can see," he waved at the piles of printouts, "there are an awful lot of lines of code – I mean many, many lines of text giving the computer instructions."

"Yes, I can see that," she said, bending over to peer at some of the typed lines on one of the pages. "How did you ever learn to do this kind of thing and where did they even find you? There can't be all that many people around that can do what you're doing."

"I don't even know for sure," he said, thoughtfully. "Someone came to one of the meetings of a computer club I belong to at Stanford. It's where a bunch of us computer hackers get together to learn about the latest developments in computers and to talk about our projects."

"Projects?"

"Right… ah, do you know what a hacker[43] is?"

"I think so. Someone that builds or modifies their own computers or writes their own computer programs?"

"Exactly!" he said, sounding relieved. "In my latest project, for example, I designed a telephone interface board that plugged into one of the expansion slots on my computer and allowed me to interface with the phone system and generate phone company tones. Then I wrote a program that made my computer do the dialing and search for phone numbers that had computers attached to them. It was fun, but then a friend of mine that had done essentially the same thing carried it too far and had his computer making over a hundred calls an hour. That got the telephone company upset, and when he started using it to find WATS[44] numbers, with which he could make free long-distance calls, he not only got in to more trouble with the phone company, but the FBI too[45]. That's when I started being a lot more careful in what I was doing."

"The FBI you say? Yes, I can imagine that might be scary," murmured Vivian.

"Right. I wasn't trying to do anything wrong. It was just the challenge, you know?"

"I do know. So, someone came to your club you were saying?"

"Oh, right. Yeah. This guy came and said they were acting as the agent for a company up north that needed someone to go up and debug a computer program on a PDP-11 computer. It would be a summer job, they said, with good pay and room and board included. I needed a summer job but hadn't quite gotten around to doing the applications, and we were already into summer, so I put up my hand."

"And here you are," said Vivian. "Are you enjoying it?"

"Oh yes! Their problem isn't easy to diagnose so it's fun, and also good experience for me. If I succeed, then I might be able to get a similar job back home…. By the way," he said, shifting the subject abruptly, "is it weird that they're paying me in cash?"

His question caught Vivian off guard, but she recovered quickly. "I don't know about weird. It's unusual, certainly, but it's not illegal."

"OK. That's good."

"And how are doing in your debugging task?"

"Well, it's complicated because there are sometimes a lot of things going on at almost the same time. For example, there are bending magnets that are used to shape the beam and once the instruction is given it takes about eight seconds for the machine to move the magnets to where they're supposed to be so a flag is set to indicate that's happening. During that time, the computer is busy doing other things, so it has to go back once in a while to see if the flag has been cleared. Then it has to check to see if there are any other change requests, before moving on to the next task. Does that make any sense?"

"I suppose so. What's the problem?"

"I don't know yet, but there's only a limited amount of memory available to store information and there are a lot of things to keep track of, so the programmers made a whole bunch of these logic sequences, and a whole bunch of assumptions. Then, based on those, they wrote a whole set of user instructions so that the user would only type in certain instructions, in a certain order, so that none of the assumptions would be violated."

"And?"

"And everything looks fine! I mean, if you do what the manual says to do, and in the sequences that the manual says to use, then the program works and the machine does exactly what it should."

"So what are you working on now then?"

"Well, I'd asked Lisa to tell me everything she could about what she'd done differently each time there'd been a problem and she said nothing. But then I sat in on some treatments she was doing and I noticed that she'd developed a way to quickly make changes when she entered something wrong. She uses the 'cursor-up' key to edit the entry, then, instead of re-entering all the other treatment information, she just hits the return key over and over again to get back to where she was before. That leaves all the other values unchanged."

"OK, is that a problem?"

"Well, you wouldn't think so, would you? I mean the terminal screen will show that all the entered values look correct, but that's not how the manual says to make changes, and I'm wondering whether doing it her way violates some of the assumptions the programmers made about how long it takes for the mechanical tasks."

"Like moving the magnets you mentioned."

"Right. So I'm trying to imagine I'm the computer, and Lisa's making her quick changes, and I'm trying to change beam energies and move magnets to keep up with the instructions I've been given."

"I can see why you're having to concentrate so hard. I think I'd better stop distracting you so you can get on with your work then, but thank you for explaining it to me."

"You're welcome," he said, looking directly at her and blinking a few times. "You know, you're the only person that ever asked me about it."

"Tell you what. If I see you again tomorrow, I'll come and ask you how you're doing."

When Vivian left the dining hall, she went for a short walk that took her behind the hospital, which enabled her to observe a man on his knees and bent over part of the large generator that was located by the back wall of the building. He seemed to be dismantling part of it. Based on the number of components lying on the ground beside him, and based on the stream of swearing and muttering she could hear, the process was not going well.

Smiling to herself, she continued on to her house, where she changed clothes and then went back out, this time to explore around the abandoned mine and mill facilities.

At supper that evening, the doctor once again came and asked if he could join her.

"Of course, Ernst. Please do," she replied. By tacit agreement, they referred to each other formally when in the hospital but were otherwise on a first-name basis.

The doctor began by apologizing for the disruption caused by the failed generator and confidently predicted that everything would be back in working order by the next morning. Vivian allowed herself to be soothed and they were soon discussing other subjects.

Once again, the doctor invited her for an after-dinner stroll and they walked along a different route this time, one that took them away from the larger buildings and in the opposite direction from the mine and mill facilities. This took them along an old road that was obviously not often used, and culminated in an unusual scene at the end of the peninsula.

"What do you think of this Vivian?" he asked.

"Why, it's like a little suburb!" she exclaimed, taking in the series of quaint, small houses that were arranged there, each with its own front and back yards – although small ones – and most with the bent and rusting remains of children's swings and toys in their yards. "They even have little white picket fences around them. These must have been for the families."

"Yes. The more senior staff were allowed to bring their families with them. It would have been a way of encouraging them to come and work in such a remote area, I imagine. And you can see that they've located them where there are very nice views of the lake, and as far away as possible from the mining operations."

"It's beautiful."

"Yes. We'd have fixed up some of these houses for our little camp except that it's better for us to be close to the dining hall and hospital and, of course, the docks and so forth."

They walked to the water's edge and stood for a moment taking in the evening view over the water.

"You could almost imagine yourself retiring to a place like this," said Vivian.

"You think so?" asked the doctor, startled. "You really feel that?"

"Yes I do Ernst, why the surprise?"

"Because I feel that way myself. Yes I do. And you're the first person to come here and react the same way. The fishing fanatics come to fish and relax for a while but then rush home. The medical patients come here to hasten their treatment, and then they want to rush back to their normal lives. The staff are here for the money, and only the money. Even our fishing guides are tired of fishing and tired of having to deal with our guests. But I...."

"Yes, Ernst. What about you?"

"It's so different than anywhere I've been before. I feel that I could stay here – live here – even if we shut down the business and everyone else left...."

"Wouldn't you become lonely Ernst?"

"Yes. Probably so. Probably so. There are people around though. Nice people really. And interesting. They've all come to get away from something, but they share an attraction for living in such remote and peaceful country. Of course, if I had someone to share it with...."

"Like me you mean? Isn't that a little sudden Ernst? We've only just met you know."

"Yes. Yes. Of course. I apologize. I wasn't meaning to rush you or anything. It's just that it feels so natural to be talking to you about anything, and I feel that I can relax when we're together. Well, you know what I mean."

"I like you too Ernst," said Vivian. "But let's not rush things, OK?"

"No. No. Absolutely not. But I do wonder. Vivian, your treatments are not going to take very long, and I'm expecting complete success. Yes, complete success. And after that, you'll be flying back to wherever home is."

"Virginia."

"Ah. Virginia. I've never been there. Well. Well, after you've returned home would you permit me, that is, could I come and pay you a visit some time?"

"I think that would be very nice Ernst. I will make sure you have my phone number and mailing address before I leave."

The doctor lapsed into a contented silence, and they automatically began retracing their walk back to the house in which Vivian was staying. After saying their goodnights, the doctor moved on and Vivian stood in her living room for a moment, reflecting. *Well, well*, she thought. *It's been a long time since I played the part of a siren on a case.*

Friday, August 6

At breakfast in the morning, Vivian ordered another omelet and when Rick came to the serving window to hand it to her, he said "Careful, the plate is just a bit warm."

Reaching out to take the plate, she detected what felt like a piece of paper underneath so she was careful to place the plate on her tray in a way that didn't dislodge whatever it was. As she walked across the dining room, she held the tray firmly with her left hand and used her right to explore under the edge of the plate. There was a piece of paper there. As she walked, she slipped the paper into her hand, crumbling it up as she did so. When she'd selected a table, she put her tray down and strolled over to the ladies' washroom.

Alone in the washroom, she opened up the paper and smoothed it out. On it was written a brief note:

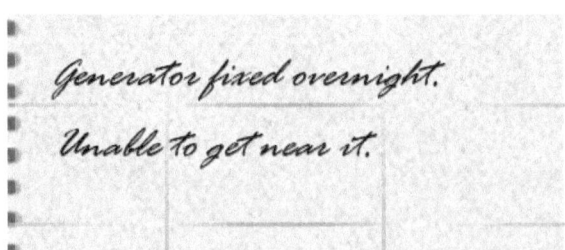

Generator fixed overnight.
Unable to get near it.

After reading it, Vivian tore it into small pieces and flushed it down the toilet.

She considered Rick's note as she ate her breakfast, and decided that she'd go ahead and take the risk. Later that morning, as scheduled, she presented herself at the hospital and went through the same steps as the previous day. Once again, Lisa provided a running commentary as she entered and checked all the computer settings:

```
PATIENT NAME: RULE, VIVIAN
DATE: 82-AUG-06      TIME: 09:45
OPR ID: LISA


TREATMENT MODE: ELECTRON      BEAM ENERGY (MeV):10


                             ACTUAL PRESCRIBED
GANTRY ROTATION (DEG):         45.0    45.0      OK
COLLIMATOR ROTATION (DEG):    359.2    359       OK
COLLIMATOR X (CM):             14.2    14.0      OK
COLLIMATOR Y (CM):             27.1    27.0      OK
WEDGE NUMBER:                     1      1       OK
ACCESSORY NUMBER:                 2      2       OK
```

"OK. Everything looks good." The next line on Lisa's display read:

```
SYSTEM: BEAM READY      OP. MODE: TREAT      AUTO
```

"Stay still now. I'm going to begin." Lisa hit the one-key command B, for beam on, to begin the treatment. The machine switched on, and Vivian head a low, metallic buzzing that lasted for a full minute.

On her display, Lisa read the computer's summary:

```
TREATMENT MODE: E ENERGY      BEAM ENERGY (MeV):10

                        ACTUAL PRESCRIBED
UNIT RATE/Minute:         200       200
MONITOR UNITS:            200       200
TIME (MIN):              1.01      1.0
```

"Perfect," she said to Vivian over the intercom. "Everything looks good. I'll be right there to help you up."

"Is that it?" asked Vivian, as Lisa approached.

"That's it. How do you feel?"

"I feel fine. In fact, I didn't feel anything at all."

"That's good. Some patients feel like the treatment area gets warm, but your dose wasn't large enough for that. The computer's happy though, and Dr. Wildersbach will be happy too. I'll take him a printout of the results, and he'll see you later about next steps."

Thanking her, Vivian left the hospital, walked over to the dining room to get some tea, and then took it with her to drink down by the marina. As she approached the dock, she spotted Dexter sitting on a wide bench, staring vacantly out over the water.

"It's nice to see you outside and not buried under stacks of computer printouts," she said, when she was close enough.

Startled, he gathered his wits and looked up at her. "Oh, hi. Yes. I'm sitting here, well, because I don't actually know what to do next."

"You mean you've solved the problem?" she asked, sitting down beside him.

"Not solved, no. But I know what it is."

"Would you like to tell me about it?" she prodded. "I probably won't understand anything you say but sometimes when you have to explain a problem to someone else it helps you rethink it."

He blinked, considering. "That's pretty smart. Yes, alright, thank you. Let's try it. I found two problems, actually. The first is in the program itself. Remember what I told you I was doing yesterday?"

Vivian nodded.

"OK. Well, I was on the right track. If an operator needs to make changes the programmers specified a certain way to do it, and they assumed that the operators would follow their instructions. Lisa, on the other hand has used the machine so often that she's learned shortcuts so she can quickly fix typing mistakes. But depending on the mistakes, and the actual keystrokes she uses, it can throw off the assumptions the programmers made about allowing time for the machine motions to happen, so after the mistakes are corrected the display will show that everything is OK, and the program will act like everything's OK, but it might not be OK. Does that make sense so far?"

"I think so, yes. You mentioned yesterday that if something like that happened, the machine might deliver too little radiation, or deliver it over too small or too large and area where it was focused."

"Yes, and I was right…. But you were right too."

"Me?"

"Yes. You asked whether it could lead to overdosing, and it can. In fact, using Lisa's method to correct a single mis-typed setting could lead to the machine delivering a radiation dose that's a hundred times too high. So, if the prescription was for a 200 rad dose over an area of one square centimetre, then the machine could actually deliver a dose of 20,000 rads[46]. Depending on where it was aimed, I think that kind of dosage could seriously injure or kill someone, don't you?"

"I don't know anything about science or medicine, Dexter, but from what you say, I wouldn't be at all surprised…. Didn't you say there were two problems?"

"Yes, it was Lisa who told me about the other one, although she doesn't think of it as a problem. She said that this is the very first of a series of new machines that aren't even on the market yet, and that one of the big features of this machine is that so many of actions are now automatic, including all of the safety features. She said the idea is that having the computer control almost everything is supposed to prevent human errors and therefore eliminate mistakes in the treatment."

"That sounds good."

"It does, but look, I'm taking computer courses at Stanford and spending as much time as I can in their AI Lab[47]. It's probably because I spent so much time working on PDP-10 computers that I got this job, the PDP-11 they have isn't much different from what I'm used to. Anyway, what I was taught was that if you try to automate machines that can cause real harm or damage, then you need to build-in mechanical safeguards so that if the program accidentally tells the machine to do something really stupid, then the mechanical safeguards prevent it. OK?"

"Yes, that seems sensible to me."

"Right. Anyway, according to Lisa, with this machine the developers took out all the mechanical safeguards. I guess they figured that since they'd built lots of safeguards into the program, there was no longer a need to duplicate them with mechanical ones."

"So," Vivian said, thoughtfully, "everything leads back to the program. Can you fix it?"

"Fix it!? No. Well, maybe, I suppose. But it would take, like, forever."

"Have you told the doctor?"

"No. That's why I'm out here thinking. You see, I'm afraid to tell him what I've learned."

Vivian gave him a close look. "Let me guess. You're afraid that there have been accidents in which people have been badly hurt, or worse, but the fact that they've insisted that the mistaken doses were too low to be harmful means that they're trying to hide the fact."

He nodded, looking miserable.

"And that if they find out you've discovered their little secret; they might not be willing to risk allowing you to go home and tell people about it."

He nodded looking a shade paler and, if possible, even more miserable. "It's worse than that, he whispered. "I've actually changed the program and I'm afraid they'll find out."

"What do you mean?"

His words came out in a rush now. "With the generator fixed, I knew you'd be going back for treatment this morning. I was afraid. I mean, what if there was a mistake today and the machine malfunctioned in the bad way. It could have hurt you, or killed you even! When they came and told me last night that the generator had been fixed, so I could go back to working on the program, I couldn't do it, but then I couldn't sleep. So, I got up and went back to the hospital late last night. No one worries about that – I do it all the time – they just think I'm weird and ignore me. Anyway, I added a few lines to the program so no matter what prescription gets entered the machine only puts out a very low dose. Not enough to hurt anyone, but so the machine still makes all the same noises people like Lisa and the doctor are used to hearing."

"You did all that for me?" said Vivian, startled.

"Yes you, and any other patients of course, but mainly because I couldn't stand the thought of you getting hurt when I could have done something about it. So…."

"So you did something about it. Good for you! And, thank you," she said, putting a hand on his arm. "I appreciate what you did.

"You know," she continued thoughtfully, "you look so much like the stereotypical computer nerd that I bet people assume that you're very naïve. But you're not naïve at all are you?"

He smiled weakly. "I know that I'm very introverted and awkward around most people – except you for some reason – maybe that's because you remind me so much of a favourite aunt I have. Anyway, I do pay attention to people, and I've seen things growing up that taught me that people aren't always what they seem, including not being as good as they seem."

"Hmmm. How are you at lying?"

"What?" he said, startled.

"Lying. Can you do it convincingly? Would you be able, for example to keep burying your head in your computer printouts for another day or two, pretend that you're still making progress, and that you think it's just going to be a case of adding a few commands to the program so it does a better job of checking that the machine settings really do match what Lisa enters on the keyboard? And NOT let on what else you've learned?"

He thought about it for a moment. "Yes, I think I could do that," he said. "But what good would that do? After the day or two goes by, they'll expect some kind of results."

She gave him a direct look. "Do you trust me?"

He paused for a moment, considering, then gave a definitive-sounding "Yes."

"OK then. Just keep on with what you've been doing and if anyone asks, make it sound like you're making progress and are optimistic about fixing everything soon and don't let on that you suspect the system of being able to hurt people."

"All right. Ummm. It was you that said I'm not naïve, and no offense intended, but if you think you can help me you must be something more than just an ordinary, but nice, widow."

She gave him a brilliant smile, lowered her voice for effect, and said "I am indeed, and I promise to tell you all about it later."

Laurie Schramm

7 CALL TO ACTION

Leaving Dexter on the bench, Vivian walked up the hill and made for the dining room. It was not yet lunchtime so there were only two men having coffee in one corner of the hall. They looked like guides.

Vivian walked over to the serving window and, in a voice that was just loud enough for the men to hear, said "Rick, could I make a special request for dinner tonight?"

"Probably," said Rick, as he approached the window.

When he got there, Vivian made sure her back was turned towards the two men and leaned in towards Rick. In a much lower voice, she related what Dexter had just admitted and her concern that he was not likely to be a good enough actor to fool the doctor if questioned.

"I think we'll need to have him extracted," she concluded.

Rick nodded, thinking quickly. "Do you know about the little suburb of houses near the point?"

She nodded. "Yes. The doctor and I walked over there last night. That's probably as good a pickup point as any."

"I'll go try to get Alex and Don on the radio and arrange it for just before twilight. If anyone hears a boat near there, they'll assume it's one of the Northern Angler's boats heading back to their camp."

With a curt nod, Vivian turned away and, in a louder voice, said "Thanks Rick. See you later."

"No problem, I just have to dig out a few supplies."

As Vivian walked out the front door and headed for her house, Rick walked out the back door, heading for his. On his way, he was

535

careful to make sure he wasn't being followed and that his house wasn't under surveillance, then went in and retrieved the police radio from its hiding place in the attic. Turning it on, he said "Cat calling. Cat calling." After waiting twenty seconds or so, he repeated the call.

There was a lengthy pause, and Rick was just about to try again when the radio crackled.

***

"Dog here, go ahead Cat," I replied from the houseboat, having heard his call and gone inside.

The code words were really just a means of making sure no one had stolen one of the radios. With the proper words having been spoken, Rick switched to plain English, relying on the radios' encryption for security.

"We need an extraction. There's a computer whiz kid here that helped us, and now Vivian thinks he's in danger of being found out. Can you pick him up at the little collection of houses located near the west end of the peninsula? They should be marked on one of the site drawings Don has."

"Wait one," I said, which was a shorthand way of saying 'Wait just a moment.'

Don had come inside in time to hear Rick's request and was reaching for a file of documents. Flipping through it, he pulled out a surface plan of the site as it had been in 1957.

"Got it. What time?"

"Uncertain, but assume just before twilight. Can you bring a handheld, in case things change?"

We knew that every moment Rick was on his radio increased the chances of being discovered, so I simply replied, "Will do. Out."

"His name is Dexter. Out."

"We'll have to take the inflatable," said Don. "If we all go, I can stay with the boat and keep watch while you and Silver get the kid. Silver should be able to help find him and sniff out any threats."

"I agree. We'll need to pack a few things."

***

When Vivian walked into the dining hall an hour later, it was just beginning to fill up. She noticed that Dexter was sitting by himself at a table surrounded by piles of computer printouts, as usual. This time, she ignored him completely and simply went to the serving window to select her lunch. As she was ladling soup into a bowl, she happened to glance up and see Rick standing to one side in the kitchen, watching her. When their eyes met, he gave a slight nod and tapped the side of his nose with his right index figure. Without giving any indication she'd even seen him she took up her lunch tray and went to sit at an empty table some distance away from everyone else. If Dexter even saw her come in, he gave no sign of it.

When she had finished her lunch, she took her tray to the clean-up area, dropped it off and walked to the door. As she did so, Dexter raised his head, spotted her and gave her a hopeful look. She didn't say anything, but as she passed by, she looked him straight in the eye and casually winked, then continued on out the door.

That's all I can do for him right now, she thought. *We'll have to see what happens next.*

In fact, nothing much happened for the next several hours, until late in the afternoon when Dr. Ernst Wildersbach entered the dining hall and walked over to Dexter's table.

"Still at it, I see," he said.

"Yes sir," replied Dexter, looking up at him and pushing the bridge of his glasses up on his nose. "I think I've found the problem and I'm just working out the changes I'll need to make. There are quite a few lines of code that will have to be changed." For illustration, he held up a sheet of computer printout on which several lines of code had been circled, with new lines hand-printed in the margin beside them.

None of this was comprehensible to the doctor, but he would never have admitted that. Instead, he went on offence. "Well hurry it up, can't you? It's taking too long. Why, if I didn't know better, I'd suspect you were just wasting time while you rest here using up my accommodations and my food and money!"

"N-n-no sir," stammered Dexter, who had turned white and recoiled. "I would never do that."

"Well, see that you get it fixed. I want it finished tomorrow, even if you have to stay up all night, understand?"

"Y-y-yes sir," replied Dexter as the doctor stormed out.

A short time later, Vivian returned to the dining hall hoping to have a quiet chat with Rick. The lunch patrons were long gone with the sole exception of Dexter, who was sitting in his usual place. The only difference was that, although he was surrounded by the usual pile of printouts and hand-written notes, he wasn't working on them but was simply sitting there looking dejected.

"What's the matter Dexter?" she asked. "You look pale and troubled."

He looked around to make sure they were alone, the replied "The doctor was just here chewing me out for not being finished yet. Then he yelled at me and said that I had to be finished by tomorrow, even if I had to work all night."

"So why not just tell him you're finished. It will take them some time to discover what you've done."

"I could say the words, but I don't think I can fool him. When he was here just now, I tried lying about my progress, but I could feel myself turning pale and I kind of seized-up and started stammering like I used to do when I was younger. I think he might have interpreted it as me being intimidated by him, which I am, but I think he'll catch on if I try to keep it up."

Vivian looked at him consideringly, then came to a decision. "Yes, you're probably right at that.... Still trust me?"

"Yes," he said immediately.

"OK then. Is all this," she pointed at the table, "the whole program and all of your notes?"

"Yes. Everything."

"And is there anything back where you're staying that you absolutely can't live without?"

He considered it. "Just my passport, I guess."

"OK. Pile all this up in some kind of order, then leave it here and go get your passport and come straight back here. Got it?"

"OK. If you say so."

"I do. And Dexter, just walk casually, don't rush. Imagine you're just taking your time strolling there and back as if you don't have a care in the world, and for heaven's sake don't furtively look around to see if anyone's watching. Just act oblivious to everything. OK?"

"OK. Whatever you say."

"Good. Do it now. I'll be here waiting for you."

After Dexter had finished sorting out the paper, he left the dining

room as instructed. Vivian then went to the serving window to find that Rick had been standing right there on the other side, but to one side where he would be hidden from the sight and anyone not standing close by.

"Trouble?" he said.

Vivian nodded. "The doctor's getting cranky and Dexter's rattled. I think we need to get him out now. He'll be a perfect witness if any of this ever goes to trial and I don't want him disappearing on us."

Rick nodded. "I got through to Alex and Don. They'll be at the point just before twilight. Around 9:30 or 10 pm, say."

"That's a long time to wait but it will have to do. Is there a way he can get there through the woods, so no one will see him?"

"Yes. I'll take him so he doesn't get lost and I'll find a nice house to break into so he can hide. I can make sure we're not followed, too. Is he going to need all that stuff?" he asked, looking at the piles of paper on the table Dexter had vacated.

"Yes. He has the whole computer program printed out and he knows why it doesn't always work, and he knows it's capable of injuring or killing the patients."

Rick gave a low whistle. "No wonder you want to spirit him away. We've got them."

"Almost. We still don't know what happened to your colleague or the senator."

"No, but we have a pretty good idea. Anyway, it turns out that the camp's 'Lost and Found' department is right here in the kitchen. If you grab his stuff, I'll liberate a backpack."

By the time Dexter returned, Vivian had stuffed his papers into a backpack while Rick had filled the rest of the space with bottles of water and pre-made, bagged sandwiches from one of the kitchen's fridges. Vivian waved Dexter over and made introductions.

"Rick, this is Dexter. Dexter, this is Rick. You can trust him. He's going to take you to a house way out at the point and you're to stay hidden until this evening when someone will come for you. Can you do that?"

"I think so," he said. "How will I recognize them and how will they know where I'll be hiding?"

"They won't know, at first, but it will be a woman with red hair and a dog that looks like a wolf. The woman's a Mountie, and the dog's a police dog. The dog will find you."

"A real Mountie?" he asked, "like in the movies?"

"No Mountie is like the Hollywood versions, although now that you mention it, this one actually comes pretty close, and she's real all right. Stick with them and they'll keep you safe. OK?"

Dexter looked at her, then at Rick, then pushed his glasses up on the bridge of his nose. "Who are you people anyway?"

"For now, just think of us as two people that are helping you. The woman's name is Alex. She'll answer all your questions once she gets you away from here. Rick and I will catch up with you in a day or two." She looked at Rick. "All set?"

"All set," he replied. "Dexter, all your papers are in here, plus some food and water." He handed it over so Dexter could put it on. To Vivian, he said "If you need it, I hid my camera bag in the attic of my house."

"Right. Thanks. Dexter: go with Rick and do what he says."

"OK Mrs. Rule. Thank you."

"Come in through here Dexter," said Rick, opening a door that was located beside the broad serving window. "We're going out the back way." To Vivian, he said, "I'll see you at supper."

Rick led Dexter to the back door of the dining hall, then said "We'll split up for the first part so if anyone spots either of us they won't think anything of it. I want you to walk down the road to the hospital, just like you do all the time. If anyone challenges you, you're on your way to the hospital to continue with your programming. If they search your pack, the food is in case you need to work late on the program just like the doctor told you to do.

"Next. When you get to the hospital, walk right past it, turn right and follow the road to the small lake that's back there. I'll meet you there."

"OK."

"Good. Off you go then."

As Dexter walked the familiar route to the hospital, Rick let him get almost out of sight before setting out himself on a route that took him past the buildings that were being used as dormitories and even the ones behind them that weren't in use at all, as evidenced by the profusion of broken windows. As he passed the latter buildings, he increased his walking pace and made a sharp turn around the last building so he could peek back to see if anyone was following. When he was satisfied, and moving quickly then, he entered the nearby woods and followed a series of game trails that took him past the rear of the hospital. As he neared Blair Lake, he was relieved to see Dexter walking towards him. Being well hidden in the trees, he startled Dexter by calling out to him when he was only a few feet away.

"Phew. You scared me there for a moment," said Dexter. "I didn't see you at all."

"Sorry. Come crouch down beside me here for a moment. I want to see if you're being followed."

Dexter did so and tried to emulate Rick, who was intently scanning the buildings and roads that were within their view. After a while, he became restless and began to fidget.

"Stay still," Rick admonished. "One of the so-called guides is crafty and knows how to shadow a person. If he's following you, he isn't dumb enough to be obvious about it."

Wrapping his arms around his chest, Dexter hugged himself tightly and focused on holding still.

After what seemed like forever, Rick looked over at him, smiled, and said "Good job. Staying still and remaining vigilant doesn't come naturally to most people. It's a skill. I think the coast is clear. Let's get moving." With Rick in the lead, the two men walked roughly northwest, following an obviously much-used game trail that ran alongside the lakeshore. After about a quarter of a mile (400 m) however, Rick changed course to southwest, saying "From here we cut through the forest until we come to a kind of suburb of small, abandoned houses." Although their destination was only about 1,500 feet (450 m) 'as the crow flies,' they had to walk at least three or four times that distance by following game trails. Just when Dexter was beginning to feel like they'd never get out of the forest, he almost tripped over something. It was a white picket fence, or at least it had been at one time, and it surrounded a little house and backyard, with the remnants of a children's swing set and a scattering of old, rusting metal toys.

"We've arrived," said Rick. "Let's head for the houses that are closest to the point." Moving around the house, they followed the old road in a counter-clockwise direction until they found themselves at a house that actually looked out from the point with an almost panoramic view of the big lake.

As Dexter watched, Rick went all the way around the house, testing windows and doors as he went. When he arrived at the back, he found the door was unlocked so he walked in. A quick check of the rooms showed that the house hadn't been used in a very long time.

"This should be as good a place as any to hide out," he said to Dexter. "You've got food and water, so all you have to do is lie low and wait for evening. You'll hear a small boat of some kind approach. They'll have to find a place to beach, so it might not be right in front of you but it shouldn't be far away. You're looking for a woman with red hair and a dog."

"What if they don't come?" asked Dexter, in a worried voice.

"If they don't make it, stay here and stay quiet. Either Vivian or I will come back, but it will be very late at night. OK?"

"OK."

"I have to leave you now so I can get back and get everything ready for tonight's supper."

"What are you? You can't be just a cook."

"For now, let's just say that I also cook. I promise to tell you more in a few days," and with that, Rick left.

When suppertime arrived, Vivian walked into the dining hall and immediately went to get a tray and get her food.

"How are things with you?" she asked, when Rick came to the serving window to explain the evening's meal options.

"Just fine, thank you" he said. "Just another day in the great Canadian north."

Satisfied, she made her meal choices and went to a table. Once again, she was joined mid-meal by the doctor.

"How are you feeling after your first treatments, my dear?" he asked.

"Fine, I think. I don't actually feel any different at all."

"No. No, that's as it should be. The dosages we used were low. We'll do another set every day for the next four days, then give you two days of rest, and then we'll reassess where we are."

"Did you have a busy day besides treating me?"

"Yes. Yes. In fact, we have two other patients beginning treatment. One of them is going to be a difficult case. Quite urgent, really, and we're going to have to use very high energy treatments, but let's not dwell on my problems."

Vivian allowed him to deftly shift their conversation to other topics.

Saturday, August 7

Vivian's next treatment had been scheduled for 10:30 am in the morning. Her guess that they'd had another patient in before her was confirmed by the fact that the doctor and Lisa were discussing it when she walked in.

"And he didn't notice anything, you say. Nothing at all?" Dr. Wildersbach was saying.

"No doctor. I asked him more than once," Lisa replied.

"That can't be right. We need to hit that spot hard and at the intensity and duration I prescribed he should have felt the area heat up. The machine must have...." he broke off, having seen Vivian walk in. "Where is that infernal kid anyway? If he's changed the program without my approval, I'll skin him alive!"

"He hasn't been in yet today doctor. Normally he's already in here working before I arrive but there was no one here this morning. I thought he might not be feeling well, so I asked one of the guides to go check on him. When he came back, he said that Dexter wasn't in his room and that he hadn't shown up for breakfast either."

"That's odd. Very odd. And this is a fine time for him to disappear, just when we're in the middle of...." He glanced at Vivian again and didn't finish the sentence, but his anger was clearly rising.

Taking a step towards Vivian, he caught her arm with one hand, saying "Vivian. You were talking to him yesterday. How did he seem to you?"

"Well, he was buried in all those printouts and notes like usual, and he's not really a people person, so we just exchanged a few pleasantries, but he seemed distracted to me."

Dr. Wildersbach reddened, tightened his grip and shook her arm. "You were talking to him for more than just a minute. It must have been more than a few pleasantries. What else did he say?"

"Ernst! You're hurting me! I don't even remember what we talked about. I was just trying to be nice and draw him out a bit, but it didn't work. He said that all he's been doing here is checking the computer program for you and he hasn't time to do anything else, no fishing, no anything else really."

With an effort, the doctor took a deep breath, regained control of himself, and released his grip on Vivian's arm. "Apologies. My apologies. I shouldn't have gotten excited and taken it out on you. I've been under a lot of stress lately and didn't sleep well last night, but that's no reason to take it out on you. I apologise."

"It's OK Ernst, I understand."

In a calmer voice, he said "Did you see him at any other time yesterday?"

"I don't think… wait a minute. Yes I did. It was later in the afternoon. I saw him walking down the main road. You know, towards all those mine buildings and that big, tall scaffold-like tower."

"The headframe, you mean."

"Yes, I guess that's what you call it. I don't mean that he was necessarily going to it, only that he was walking in that direction." Vivian paused, then continued. "You don't think he would have gone exploring inside those buildings, do you? They look dangerous to me, with those roofs looking like they are about to collapse and who knows what machinery and chemicals falling apart inside."

"Hmmm. Hmmm. Maybe you're right. Those buildings are too dangerous to enter, but he's young enough to have done something stupid like that. I suppose I'll have to get some of the guides to go search for him." Muttering to himself, he stalked out of the hospital.

"Does he get angry and flare-up like that often?" Vivian asked Lisa.

"Oh no, not the doctor," said Lisa, but her eyes and facial expression said something entirely different. She seemed to be struggling with something for a moment, then she leaned closer and lowered her voice. "I shouldn't be telling you this, but we lost a patient this morning. I think that's why he's so upset."

"That makes it easier to understand. Thank you for telling me."

While Lisa went ahead with her treatment, Vivian was feeling very relaxed and composed with this second one, knowing that Dexter had changed the computer program to ensure she only received a safe dosage. When it was over and Vivian left the hospital, she tried to walk like she was just out for a casual stroll, but her destination was the dining hall. The dining room was empty when she got there, and she found that Rick was in the kitchen with the beginnings of lunch preparations.

"Things are heating up," she said. "They had a patient die this morning, which seems to have put the doctor in a foul mood. On top of that, he's become suspicious that Dexter might have altered the computer program and he's now organizing some of the guides to search for him."

"Good thing we got Dexter out last night then. I think I'll take a fresh mug of coffee over to my friend Alistair in the hospital. I might be able to find out whether the body is still there. If it is, I'd like to know what they ultimately do with it."

"Me too," she agreed.

That same day (Saturday, August 7)

It was quiet when Rick entered the hospital with his trademark mug of special coffee for Alistair. He was only putting a third of a pill in each mug now, to ensure that Alistair was continuing to show 'improvement' without yet feeling quite well. In fact, when Rick asked him about his recovery, he said that he was doing better eating more, and holding it down. "I think another day or two and I'll be able to return to the kitchen. That will put you out of a job I'm afraid."

"That's OK," laughed Rick. "I enjoyed it, and I still got lots of fishing in, but it's about time I went back home."

"I'm going to miss your special coffees."

"Well, you're very welcome. At least as chief cook you know how to make your own when the need arises.... By the way," he added, as if it has just occurred to him. "I heard a rumour that a patient died this morning."

"We're not supposed to know about that kind of thing," replied Alistair, "but yes, and it's been happening about once a month. The patient that died is in the next room." He indicated the direction with a tip of his head.

"Really, one a month. What do they do with the bodies, ship them home?"

"No. It's odd but they don't ship them out and no family members ever come to collect them." He waved Rick closer to his bed and lowered his voice to a whisper. "I don't think they even tell the relatives, or anyone else, when a patient dies."

"Really? Why? And what do they do with the bodies then?"

"I don't know the answer to either. I've heard the guides complaining sometimes though, when the doctor and Delorme aren't around. They get told to carry the bodies off and dump them somewhere, but I don't know where."

"Stranger and stranger," said Rick. "You think they just dump them in the lake?"

"Could be. It's deep enough if you go out a ways and from the complaints I heard it seems like they only take them out at night when it's dark."

"Sounds like a plot for a horror movie. Evil doctor conducts gruesome experiments and the bodies are dumped in the lake."

"I don't know, and I don't want to know. And you heard nothing from me, right?"

"Right," said Rick. "Well, I have to get back and make sure I'm ready for the lunch crowd. Enjoy your coffee."

Alistair raised his mug in salute as Rick left.

Meanwhile the previous day (Friday, August 6)

It was a relief to receive the radio call from Rick since it had been over three days since I'd seen Vivian and over six since Rick had flown to the fishing camps, and we readily agreed to extract the 'whiz kid.' There wasn't a lot to plan or prepare, so we mostly just had to wait, Don's joke about us having to 'standby to standby[48]' had worn thin, and I'd become impatient.

When it was time to go, we all got into the inflatable boat and Don piloted us to the pickup site. This involved motoring among the many small islands that lie off the southwest point of the peninsula. When we emerged from between the islands, Don headed along St. Mary's Channel as if we were just another motorboat heading for the Northern Angler fishing camp, which would take us around the Crackingstone Point and into Black Bay. Of course, we were headed for the point itself and, at the last minute, Don turned us to starboard, and we began looking for a safe place to land.

Having beached the inflatable, and tied it to a sturdy-looking tree, Don selected a position from which he could keep watch and guard the boat, while Silver and I made for the small community of houses near the point that was shown on the Gunner Mining Limited's drawings we'd reviewed.

I didn't have to give any special command to Silver. The mere fact that I was creeping along stealthily and looking around told him all he needed to know. As we approached the houses, I was just trying to decide how to go about our search when Silver's ears perked up and he began staring at the house that was nearest the point.

"Is there someone there, Silver? Let's go see." With Silver at my side, I walked up to the front door and knocked. Glancing down at Silver, I could see that he didn't look concerned - he obviously wasn't sensing danger at the moment – so I simply knocked on the door and called out "Dexter? Police."

There was a scuffing sound and a young man's voice said "This door's jammed somehow, but the back door is open."

"OK," I said, "we'll meet you there." When we reached the back door there was a young man waiting for us. He was wearing a backpack, and he looked and sounded scared.

"You're Dexter, I presume?" He nodded. "Hi. I'm Sergeant Alex Houston, RCMP, and this is my partner, Silver." I took out my wallet and showed him my badge. "We're working undercover. That's why we're not in uniform. Are you ready to get out of here?"

"You bet I am," he said.

"OK. Stay close behind me. We're not going to move quickly, partly so no one trips in this low light and partly because I want Silver to be able to hear or smell the approach of anyone that might be unfriendly. When we get to the shore, we'll be met by a rather large man, but it's OK, he's with us. Come on."

Although I was being cautious, our short walk back to where we'd tied up the boat was uneventful, except that Dexter nearly jumped out of his skin when Don suddenly, and quietly, materialized out of the gloom from where he'd been watching.

"Sorry about that," I said. "Silver didn't react because he knows Don's scent. This is Don. Don, this is Dexter. We can all get better acquainted when we're away from here."

"Right. Hi Dexter, pleased to meet you," said Don. "Let's push the boat out a bit so you three can hop in."

In a few moments we had untied the boat, pushed it off the beach, and Dexter, Silver, and I had climbed in. After giving it a last push-off with his legs, Don scrambled in as well, and made his way back to the motor, started it, and put it in reverse so we could back away. When we were clear, Don headed us back into the channel, from which we retraced out route back to the houseboat.

When we reached the houseboat, Dexter asked Don whether he was a Mountie too.

"No, he said, I'm just another part of the team," and so saying, he produced his military police ID and badge. "What's in the backpack?" he asked, changing the subject, "it looks full."

Dexter explained what he'd been doing at the camp, ending with the fact that he had a complete printout of the computer program plus his notes on the bugs in the program and how they could affect the machine settings.

"There you go," I said, "some kind of intermittent machine malfunction was one of the things we'd speculated on. It was Rick's thought that it might be caused by problems in the computer program."

"Why was Vivian so insistent that I bring everything with me?"

"Well, probably because it's the way she thinks. She's a Special Agent with the FBI, and she's thinking ahead to a potential court case."

"Wow, FBI too, plus RCMP and military police. What's Rick then?"

Don and I looked at each other for a moment. "What did he tell you?"

"He admitted that he's more than just a cook, but didn't explain what he meant. He only said that he'd tell me more in a couple of days."

"Hmmm. We should leave it at that for now. He is working undercover and with us, though, as you've already figured out."

We spent the next hour or so getting as much information as we could about the camp, the various people in it and, of course, Rick and Vivian.

"Know anything about a guide called Delorme?" asked Don at one point.

Dexter nodded. "Not much, but I used to visit my uncle's ranch a lot back home. If this was a ranch, then I guess Delorme would be the foreman, because he's the one that gives everybody orders, and he's the one that the other guides complain about when he isn't around. One of them claims Delorme was a mercenary fighting in South Africa before he came here."

"Hmmm," said Don, "that certainly matches my first impression of him: ex-military."

From everything Dexter had told us, it seemed unlikely that his disappearance would be discovered until the next day, but to play safe, Don and I decided to alternate watches overnight. We knew that we could count on Silver to alert us to anyone's approach, but we thought it best to have at least one person that was more or less fully awake in case prompt action was required. Dexter was amused to see us flip a coin to determine the watches. I drew the first watch (20:00 to midnight), Don the middle watch (midnight to 04:00) and then me again for the morning watch (04:00 to 08:00). That also meant Don had to cook our breakfast in the morning.

Dexter's amusement was short-lived however, and he sobered up instantly when he saw us dig out our travelling gun cases, unlock them, and load our pistols. Although Don settled and fell asleep almost immediately, the sounds of constant tossing and turning suggested that Dexter was having trouble settling. After about an hour, I noticed that Dexter had quieted down and that Silver wasn't beside me anymore. Curious, I got up and crept quietly inside the houseboat and along to peek in the open door of the small cabin we'd made available for him.

"Hi," said Dexter, when he saw me.

"Everything OK?" I asked.

"It is now. I was worrying about everything, especially Vivian back there at the camp, and Silver must have sensed it because he came in here, jumped up on the bunk, and stretched himself out right beside me. That was cool, and it was comforting having him lay here with me, but the interesting thing was when I noticed him staring at me."

"Oh?"

"Yeah. You're going to think I'm crazy, but as I looked into his eyes, it was like he was trying to tell me to relax – that everything was going to be OK."

I smiled. "Well, if you're crazy then I am too, because he does that kind of thing to me all the time. I don't understand it, but I love it…. Good boy Silver!"

Leaving the two of them, I went back to my watching position up on the roof of the houseboat. It wasn't long before I heard Silver scrambling up the steps and felt him nestle in beside me.

"How's Dexter doing?" I asked him, not expecting a response, but the sounds of snoring coming from down below gave me my answer anyway.

"Well done, Silver," I congratulated, giving him an ear rub.

It was a beautiful night, although at this latitude[49] (59°23' N) and this time of year, there was no true nighttime. Nautical twilight[50] began around 22:20 and astronomical twilight was just setting in –

and my ability to make out the horizon was fast disappearing - when Don relieved me at midnight. It was back to nautical twilight when I relieved Don at 04:00. The sky had changed from a dim, bluish-cast to distinctly light, and I could see the horizon and make out shapes on our boat and the nearby shore. Although I was sleepy, it was actually quite a beautiful time to just sit out and feel alone in the world while watching the sun rise up above the horizon.

8 CONVERGENCE

Saturday, August 7

As it turned out, our caution had been unnecessary that night. I didn't hear any boats come remotely near us. Our morning was similarly uneventful, but all that changed right after lunchtime, when we received a radio call from Rick.

"They had a patient die this morning," he began, "and I've been told that the guides take the bodies away and dispose of them when that happens. If so, I want to know how and where, so I'm planning to follow them if I can. I'm guessing that the quietest times are either mid-afternoon when the customers are out fishing and the patients are being examined or treated, or else late at night."

"Do you want us to come in as backup?" I asked.

"Yes. I'm not confident of my ability to keep eluding Delorme, but I think you should wait for my call."

"Agreed. We'll be ready. Out."

The prospect of providing backup for Rick, and possibly Vivian as well, forced us to make a decision on whether one of us should remain behind to guard Dexter. In the end, we decided that we should put Dexter into hiding on the island to which the houseboat was moored. With this in mind, we filled his backpack with some essentials including several flares, so that, if something happened to us, he could attempt to signal a passing boat or the regular supply barge from Fond du Lac. We also gave him one of the handheld police radios with instructions to listen-in only, and not try to call out except in case of emergency. I wrote out a list of our agreed-upon code names, then added one for him: 'Turtle.'

"Turtle?" he asked, sounding a bit offended.

"Well," I said, "there's no point in giving you a code-name like 'Hacker' or 'Whiz-Kid,' is there?"

"Ah. Good point," he said, sounding mollified and even a bit pleased.

It turned out to be a good thing that we made our preparations for Dexter promptly. Don and I both expected that we'd be waiting until late at night, but it was only about an hour later that we received another call from Rick.

"They're on the move," he reported. "A truck just pulled up to the rear of the hospital and two of the guides loaded what could have been a body, wrapped in a sheet, into the back. I'm in the woods behind the hospital.... Wait one."

There was a minute or two of silence, then: "OK. They're heading east, so probably towards the old dock, the flooded pit, the waste rock piles, or the tailings area. I'm going to follow them. I'll collect Vivian on the way if I can. My next messages may be very short in order to minimize the chances of being overheard."

"Roger that. We'll head for the shipping dock. Out," I replied.

***

When the guides had driven away with the large bundle in the back of their truck, Rick emerged from hiding and walked directly to Vivian's house and gave her the latest news. She decided to join him and the two of them were walking toward the dining hall when they noticed a truck parked by one of the nearby dormitory buildings.

"What do you think?" asked Vivian.

"In a remote place like this, I bet they just leave the keys in the vehicles. There's no risk of theft here."

Rick was right. When they reached the truck, the keys were in the ignition, so they simply climbed in and drove off in the direction Rick had seen the guides go.

***

Leaving Dexter on the little island as planned, Don, Silver, and I had taken the inflatable boat and headed straight for the shipping dock. As soon as we got out of the boat and had a chance to look around, we noticed a pickup truck parked by the one of the old buildings that had been cleaned-up and converted to storage. While Don went to have a look at the truck, Silver and I went to see what was going on in the storage building.

When we went back and met up with Don, he said "Anything happening in there?"

"Sort of," I replied. "One of the staff is just inside the door taking a nap."

"That's a help," Don chuckled. "We're in luck here too, the keys are still in the ignition." Opening the door, he got in and waited while Silver and I went to the other side and climbed in as well.

As we drove off, my portable radio crackled to life.

"Mouse calling. Mouse calling." It was Vivian.

"Dog here. Go ahead Mouse."

"We've borrowed a truck – black in colour - and are trying to catch up to the two guides. They are in a red truck."

"We've borrowed a truck as well. It's white. We are currently positioned by the headframe."

Suddenly Rick chimed in: "We have their dust in sight ahead of us, Dog. Wait one."

There was a pause while Rick attempted to close the distance and see which way the guide's truck would turn. "They're veering north around the pit," reported Vivian.

"Roger that. We see them crossing our line of sight as well," I confirmed. "We'll move around the southern side of the pit and hold."

Don drove along the narrow path that was all that was left of a former service road that ran between the mine's open pit and the huge waste rock pile.

After only a few minutes, Vivian came back on the radio. "They've passed the turn-off to the tailings… now they're passing the acid plants… now turning south. They're either heading for the east side of the pit or the waste rock pile."

I gave a double click on my radio to confirm that we'd received the message.

"My money's on the pit," said Don. "I bet that's why the rowboat is tied up there."

"I think you're right," I agreed, as Don started the truck and moved us a bit closer to the east side of the pit.

***

Unbeknownst to us, Rick had come to the same prediction as Don and was explaining to Vivian about finding the rowboat tied up at the flooded pit.

"I don't suppose you're armed?" he asked Vivian.

She shook her head. "No."

"Here." Rick passed over a six-inch chef's knife in an improvised sheath that he'd made out of cardboard and duct tape.

"Thanks. What about you?"

"I have a smaller one in my boot, and I also have a few of these." He reached down to his right-side, pant-leg cargo pocket, opened it and extracted a stick of dynamite.

Vivian raised her eyebrows. "Remind me not to mess with you in future. That must be pretty old. Do you think it's stable?"

"I doubt it. These sticks are called forcite, which used to be common in the mining industry. I know it's supposed to be waterproof, so that helps, but I don't think it will take much to set them off. Anyway, these are the only weapons we have, so they'll have to do."

After a few more minutes, Vivian got back on the radio. "They've turned. We're going to hold up until we see whether they take the next turn or not.... OK. They've turned again – Rick says it's the pit for sure.

"You have jurisdiction here. Do you want to move in and have us stay back?"

"Yes please. We're moving now."

***

With Rick and Vivian keeping watch, Don drove around the side of the pit and down the same short road that Rick and Vivian saw the guides take. Sure enough, they were parked exactly where we'd parked when we'd fished there, and Don immediately stopped the truck so we could try to assess what they were doing. I was surprised to realize that had only been the previous day. So much had happened that it seemed further away than that.

We had a fairly clear view, and it appeared that each of the guides was walking along the fringe of the trees, stopping and bending over once in a while as if looking for something. It wasn't long before one of them straightened up from one such exercise, holding something in both hands.

"Rocks," said Don. "You know what those are for."

I was already thumbing the transmit button on my radio. "Bingo. They're collecting rocks. We'll be moving in shortly."

Vivian gave a double-click in response.

We'd no sooner completed this exchange than the other guide had picked something up and was walking toward the first, who was out of our sight behind their truck.

"Let's go," I said, and Don and I opened the doors of our truck, climbed out, along with Silver, and left the doors open rather than risk the sounds associated with closing them. By this time, both guides were out of sight behind their truck. Using only hand gestures and eye movements, Don and I quickly agreed to approach from opposite side of their truck, so he veered to the left and the forest side, while Silver and I veered to the right on the side of the flooded pit.

When I had swung around enough to see the guides again, they were both kneeling down, working on something to do with the large bundle, and completely oblivious to us. I looked across at Don, who nodded, and kept on walking toward the guides. I was just about as close as I wanted to get, and was about to speak, when one of the guides suddenly looked up, saw me, and jumped to his feet.

"Hey! Who are you and what are you doing here?"

"Police!" I called. "Both of you get up and put your hands in the air."

The one that was already standing put his hands up, looking apprehensive, but the other guide snarled something I couldn't make out and drew a large knife from a belt sheath as he stood up.

"I don't think so," he said, beginning to walk towards me and holding the knife in an offensive position. "Why don't you just turn around, missy, and get out of here while you still can?"

Everything he'd just done set off alarm bells in Silver's head, who snarled and immediately moved ahead and to the right of me so he could take up a flanking position in a maneuver the two of us had carried out so many times before, in so many other dangerous situations, that I hadn't had to give him any kind of signal or instruction. What I did do, was take out my snub-nosed .38 Special revolver and point it at the guide, saying "Police! Drop the knife, stand still, and raise your hands. That's your second warning. You won't get a third."

"Everyone knows Canadian police don't shoot first! Why don't you just put that away and leave us alone. Otherwise, I'm going to come over there and take that little pea-shooter away from you."

"I think you've been watching too many movies, friend," said Don's voice from behind the guides. "Trust me. She'll shoot you if you make her."

"Bullshit," the man said and came toward me with is knife up, in a fighting crouch.

"Silver!" I called, and made a motion with my hand.

In almost the same instant Silver exploded toward the guide from the side, like a coiled spring. It was amazing how fast he could accelerate for such a big dog.

His movement caught the guide off guard and he was slow to react. By the time he had turned to face this new threat and decided how he wanted to hold the knife, Silver had advanced close enough to spring and threw himself into the air. The results were that Silver was able to encase the guide's knife hand in his big jaws, his momentum and weight threw the guide off-balance, and the two of them dropped down to the ground – with Silver's jaws firmly attached to the guide's hand which was still holding the knife and, for the moment, incapable of letting it go. By that point, the guide's initial scream of agony had morphed into a series of moans.

While Don came up and handcuffed the first guide, I told Silver to release the second, allowing the knife to drop to the ground while the guide cradled his injured hand. With Don watching the guide, I moved in and picked up the knife. The guides' truck had a small first aid kit, enabling us to dress the second guide's wounded hand and then we handcuffed him as well.

With Don and I each taking a guide by the arm, we walked them over to the water's edge where the large, sheet-wrapped bundle had been placed in the bow of the rowboat. It was certainly about the right size for an adult body, and was secured by several lengths of rope tied around it at intervals along its length. Tied to two of these ropes were mesh bags that appeared to have been made from sections of fishing net. Inside each bag were the rocks the guides had been seen collecting by the trees.

Before touching anything, I ran back to our borrowed truck, moved it closer to the rowboat, and retrieved the camera that I had brought with me. I used it to capture shots of the bundle in the rowboat from several angles. When that was done, we took a closer look at the boat. There wasn't much doubt about what was in the wrapped bundle, but I took out my knife and cut one of the ropes so I could partially unwrap the sheet at about where I thought the face might be. I'll skip providing a graphic description and just report that it was a human male that had clearly been dead for some hours. After Don had taken a look as well, I re-wrapped the exposed part and secured it with the cut piece of rope.

"I didn't know what was in there," protested the first guide. "We were just following orders."

"Shut up you idiot," snarled the second guide, whose attitude had not been improved by having Silver lacerate his hand.

"We'll take statements from each of you later," I said. "We have a few other things to do first." Standing up, I made a radio call to Vivian and Rick. They would have been watching the action, so all I had to do was tell them about the body, and confirm that the guides were in custody.

"What next?" asked Vivian.

"I think our priority now should be to find the doctor, before he hears about all this and tries to slip away. After that, we can radio the Uranium City RCMP Detachment[51] for help."

Up until that point, all four of us had avoided Uranium City for fear of inadvertently making anyone suspicious of us being anything other than the cover-story images we'd tried to project, but the need for secrecy would most likely be gone once we had the doctor in custody.

Vivian responded with a double click, and I suggested they wait where they were and we would go to them. First though, we loaded the two guides and the wrapped body into the truck's open box. With the two guides in a sitting position, hands manacled behind them, we passed a sturdy-looking rope between their arms and the cargo hooks on each side of the box. This gave them enough slack to shift position but not enough to get up or out of the box. This wasn't the absolute safest position for them to be in, but we didn't want them together in the back seat of our truck either. When we were loaded, I radioed Vivian that we were on our way.

Once we'd met up with Vivian and Rick, we decided to drive to the area where the hospital and dining hall were, to begin searching for the doctor. With Rick and Vivian in the lead, we drove past the acid plants, and their truck was just passing the flooded pit and the turn-off to the headframe and main dock, when a shot rang out and the front-right corner of their truck suddenly sagged.

"Must have taken out the tire," said Rick, struggling to retain control. Fortunately, neither truck had been moving very quickly over the broken and rutted road, so he was able to resume control and immediately threw the truck into reverse and stomped on the gas.

In our truck, Don had braked hard and immediately shifted into reverse when we heard the shot, so we were already backing up when Rick began to do the same.

Meanwhile, right after the first shot, there was another loud crack, then another, and then another. One of these hit the front passenger-side tire of Rick's truck, one missed the truck completely, and the last one struck the windshield and went right through creating a small hole with a wide fragmentation fringe.

Somewhat ironically, the loss of the second front tire made it easier for Rick to keep the truck moving in a more or less straight line, although the rapidly collapsing tire created much more drag. Since he had the accelerator floored, though, the truck kept on moving backwards until he judged them to be out of the line of fire.

"Sniper somewhere around the bend," said Vivian over the radio. "Went for the front tires first, then the windshield. Good shot too: three hits out of four rounds!"

"Can you judge the direction?" I asked.

There was a pause while Vivian and Rick consulted. "When the first shot came, we were pointed toward the headframe and the south end of the warehouses and mechanical shops. Rick thinks the round that came through the windshield was angled sharply down because the slug dropped right down in front of the dashboard, so the shooter may be on a rooftop or even the headframe itself."

At this point, both trucks had stopped and Don and I had run up to speak to Vivian and Rick. Don and I had brought a pair of binoculars with us from the houseboat so, after a brief conference, we decided to try an experiment. Taking one of the handheld radios, and having left Silver with stern instructions to remain with Don, I crept through some low bushes that had grown up around the edge of the flooded pit, and then switched to a crawl, with my chest on the ground and using my arms and elbows to slither and shuffle forward until I had a clear view of the mine's headframe and the warehouse and mechanical shop buildings. Then I stopped and radioed back. "I'm in position, go ahead."

At that point, Rick put his truck into the lowest forward gear and started forward, while Don in his truck followed immediately behind. This time, however, before rounding the bend in the road by the pit, Vivian opened the passenger-side door and jumped out, then Rick slipped over to the passenger side and jumped out as well. When he saw Rick jump, Don closed the distance between the two trucks, hit the gas and turned the steering wheel hard right. When Don's truck hit Rick's, it struck the passenger-side corner of the bumper, forcing Rick's truck to turn left. With the latter still being actively pushed, it turned the corner and its front end came into the view of the shooter.

Four more shots rang out in fairly rapid succession.

"Semi-automatic; could be a hunting rifle," said Rick, who had jumped onto the passenger-side running board of Don's truck when the latter had stopped and then reversed again at the sound of the first of the latest volley of shots. Vivian had taken the opportunity to jump into the box of Don's truck at the same time. "I heard another crack," continued Rick. "I think he put another round through the windshield of what's left of our truck."

"The shooter is up high in the headframe," I reported over the radio. "Must have a scope, because I saw some reflections."

"Rick and Don think it must be Delorme," said Vivian, who had retained her radio. "Rick figures he must have seen the two of us take the truck and become suspicious, but he may be unaware that you and Don are here."

"Your truck has stopped moving and it's gone quiet," I said, "I think it just stalled. I'll stay put and see if he comes out for a look."

"Roger," replied Vivian.

Nothing happened for what seemed like a very long time, but was probably not more than ten minutes. Then I saw a truck emerge from between the headframe and the other buildings.

"Truck emerging from near the headframe," I reported. "You might want to back up so you're out of sight if the shooter goes to investigate Rick's truck."

There was a pause, then "We agree. Reversing now."

With what I assumed was the shooter's truck coming straight towards me, it seemed safest for me to stay put and trust in the bushes to keep me hidden, although I'll admit to taking my gun out – just in case.

As it turned out, I needn't have worried because the truck turned left and went around the mechanical shops. I doubted the driver could hear my voice over the sounds from their truck at that point, so I got on the radio. "Truck has turned left, is ignoring Rick's truck, and heading west along the main road…. OK. It's passing the dining hall now and still heading west."

"We're coming around the south side of the pit now and will pick you up," said Vivian.

By that time, I'd changed position so I could better see down the length of the main road, although I still kept low to the ground to avoid being spotted in the truck's rear-view mirror.

By the time the truck carrying Don, Rick, Vivian, Silver, and the two guides rolled up to me, I was standing upright, still observing through the binoculars.

"Truck just took the branch road leading to the hospital before I lost sight of it," I said.

"They didn't bother to see if we were alive or dead!" said Vivian.

"Probably didn't care," put in Rick. "I still think it has to be Delorme. By now he knows Dexter's gone missing, he'll have guessed that Vivian and I have been working together, and he saw us following the two guides with the body. Even if we're still alive and uninjured, our truck's out of commission so he has time to report to the doctor and get a decision on whether to come search us out or make a run for it. Anyone disagree?"

None of us disagreed. A very short conference followed, with the result that Rick took over the remaining operational truck and he and Vivian dropped Don, Silver, and I off at the main dock where we'd moored our inflatable boat, then they drove off towards the hospital, with the two handcuffed guides still secured in the truck box.

Our plan, of course, was to split up. For one thing someone, probably Delorme, had a rifle and was a good shot, so we didn't want to be caught all together in one place. For another, we still didn't know whether the doctor would choose 'fight or flight' and, for the moment at least, the inflatable was our only other available transport. So, while Rick and Vivian drove the main road, Don, Silver, and I went in approximately the same direction but by water, aiming for the marina where there was a Twin Otter bush plane moored – the one that the charter pilot had told Rick and Don about eight days earlier. That plane was just the kind of thing that could be used for a quick getaway.

Our inflatable was roomy enough for our needs, and quite stable in choppy water, but whatever else it might be, it wasn't designed for speed, nor did it have a huge outboard motor on it. As a result, we were just rounding the bend in the shoreline by the former mine's tank farm when Vivian came on the radio.

"They didn't waste any time," she said. "By the time we reached the hospital, Delorme had already been there and he and doctor had left. We were just beginning to search for them when we heard the first engine start-up on that bush plane they have near the marina. We're driving to the marina now and have the plane in sight and – damn, I can see the second propellor beginning to turn. I don't think we're going to be able to stop them, but we'll see if we can grab a boat."

"Roger," I replied. "We have them in sight too. If we can get to the end of the breakwater in time, we may be able to block them in."

As we headed for the breakwater at full speed – which, as I've said, wasn't all that fast – we could see the plane begin to turn, driven by the one engine that was fully up to speed.

"This is going to be like playing chicken," yelled Don.

Soon, we were indeed pointed head-to-head and, as the second engine came up to speed the plane was clearly moving faster. Rather than the sedate pace at which a seaplane would normally taxi out from behind a breakwater, in this case the pilot had the plane moving as rapidly as possible.

"We're too small and light to stop them!" yelled Don. "We're going to have to hope they aren't willing to take the risk of ramming us and turn aside."

As we got closer and closer, however, the plane just kept on accelerating and it became clear that they were desperate enough to risk a collision. The only slight concession the pilot made was to turn the plane slightly to their starboard side in hopes they could squeeze between us and the end of the breakwater. I had just enough time to wonder whether the water there would be shallow enough to ground one of the floats when Don judged that we had gambled and lost, and threw the motor over in a hard turn to our starboard side.

The sight of the plane, with its twin roaring engines, bearing down on us was heart-stopping, and I had only enough time to reach for Silver's collar with one hand and a life-jacket with the other when the plane's port-side float hit us just back of the bow, causing our boat to flip over on its side, spilling everything into the water.

For the next few moments, I had thoughts only of getting my head above water and getting Silver supported by the life-jacket I'd grabbed, before he was lost to panic. For those of you that haven't followed all of our adventures, I should explain that Silver had a lifelong terror of being immersed in water due to a terrifying experience he'd had as a sled-dog when his whole team, dogs, sled, and musher, had broken through the ice when crossing a river, and all had been plunged into the icy water and nearly died[52]. Unfortunately, this wasn't even the first time Silver and Don and I had been rammed by something and sunk, although the previous time we'd been in a larger boat and had been rammed by a submarine[53], the experience from Silver's perspective must have been just about the same. In any case, when I surfaced, I still had a grip on both lifejacket and dog, and I was able to get the former underneath the latter, who had the instinct to dog paddle but I didn't like the look of terror in his eyes. Don had swum over to us by that time, and pulled us to the overturned inflatable so I could use one hand to hold the grab-rope that ran around the boat's perimeter.

From this vantage point, Don and I watched the next developments play out. The bush plane had continued out into open water and was just beginning to turn into the wind when a speedboat came flying around the tip of the breakwater with Vivian at the helm and Rick looking over to see if we were OK. We could see, but not hear, him say something to Vivian who immediately cut the engine power, but when they saw us waving them forward, she pushed the throttle all the way forward and they accelerated away in pursuit of the bush plane.

"That doesn't look like one of their fishing boats," I said to Don.

"No. It's large and a lot more powerful. I think it must be for making trips over to Uranium City, or even for water skiing. I think she's going to catch them."

Indeed. While we watched, the speedboat was already approaching the plane when we heard its engines roar, as the pilot – presumably Delorme, I thought – began his takeoff run. In the speedboat, which was by this time on a parallel course and level with the plane's cockpit, I could see Rick waving at the pilot in an attempt to get him to abort. Then Rick abruptly sat back down and I thought he must have given up, but then suddenly he was standing again with his left hand holding on the windshield frame and his body twisting as if he was preparing to throw something.

"Oh my!" was all I had time to say before, with a convulsive jerk, we saw him throw something at the plane.

There was a sudden flash, followed by a brief but loud roar, after which the plane's left float seemed to suddenly disintegrate. *Rick had lighted and then thrown a stick of dynamite.* As that thought penetrated, we saw the plane sharply tip over on its port side. Then, when the wing tip hit the water, the drag on the wing and the momentum of the plane conspired to twist the plane even more sharply to port and then, listing at a steep angle, it began to settle in the water.

Still at the helm Vivian, for her part, had put the wheel over an instant after Rick had thrown the dynamite, which was not a moment too soon as the plane's wing tip very nearly hit the stern of their boat as they were turning away.

With the plane, still at a steep angle, wallowing in the waves, Vivian piloted the speedboat around to the plane's starboard side, where the front door had been thrown open and the doctor was struggling to get out. That he had to struggle in this was explained by the fact that he was using one arm to protectively cradle some kind of case that he held against his chest. Nevertheless, Rick was able to guide him safely into the speedboat.

As we later learned, in their haste to get away, neither Delorme nor the doctor had fastened their safety belts before taxiing out, so when the plane was so abruptly corkscrewed around and down in the water, both of them had been driven headfirst into the plane's windshield. The doctor, intact but bleeding heavily from a cut on his forehead, had insisted that Delorme was dead and that they should hasten to get away from the plane before it sank, carrying them with it but Rick, not believing him, left him in care of Vivian while he climbed into the plane himself to check.

Rick had found Delorme lying against the door, half in and half out of the water. He had been stunned by the impact of his head against the windshield and was just beginning to regain awareness of his surroundings when Rick reached over to help him get out. Once Rick and Delorme were safely in the speedboat, neither Rick nor Vivian said anything about the doctor's insistence on abandoning his assistant as they didn't want to set the two men to fighting with each other – yet – but Vivian made a mental note to use the episode to create a rift between the two when it came to getting statements from them later.

Abandoning the listing plane, Vivian next piloted the speedboat over to where we were. Since Don, Silver, and I were in no danger, and so very close to shore, Rick simply grabbed the inflatable's bow line, tied it to a cleat on the stern of their boat, and they slowly towed us back to the marina.

9 EPILOGUE

I arrested the bedraggled, but intact, Dr. Ernst Wildersbach and Ben Delorme, of course. The doctor was surprised to learn that Rick had been a plant, and he was stunned about Vivian. Delorme hadn't suspected Vivian but had always had a bad feeling about Rick.

The bag that the doctor had been so carefully clutching turned out to be a leather briefcase. It had opened up during his rescue, spilling out bundles of money. When we put the money back, we found that the briefcase had been packed full with cash in both Canadian and American currencies. I seized that as well, counted the money, and wrote him a receipt for it.

We asked the doctor about the dead person in the bundle, but he refused to say anything at all beyond demanding to see a lawyer.

Being about 25 kilometres (16 mi) away from Uranium City, our handheld radios were out of range, but the base station we had on the houseboat had more than enough range. So, leaving the others to watch our prisoners, Silver and I borrowed the speedboat so we could get to the houseboat, retrieve Dexter, and radio the Uranium City RCMP Detachment. With their help, we were able to put together enough boats to transfer the prisoners to the detachment where they could be held.

There were a number of subsequent investigations, of course, but I was only involved in the first one. The Uranium City Justice of the Peace issued a search warrant so we could go back and search the doctor's office and hospital for files related to the patients treated. The files we found showed that, in the eight months they had been operating the radiation-treatment machine, they had treated about eighty patients, most with multiple treatments. Of those, about one treatment in twenty malfunctioned and produced damaging radiation doses that quickly, or slowly, led to six patient deaths.

An attempt was made to recover the bodies from the flooded pit using grappling hooks which failed due to the repeated losses of the hooks, presumably due to their tendency to latch onto old machinery or timbers, some of which may have been disposed of from the surface when the mine closed. The second attempt, using commercial divers breathing specialized gas mixtures[54], was much more expensive but ultimately mostly successful. The divers were able to recover five bodies and reported seeing the other two, but the latter were too enmeshed in unstable-looking machinery to be safely recovered. Of the five bodies recovered, one was identified as being that of the senator and another that of the first CIA operative that had been using the name Johnson.

Ultimately, four of those that were recovered were sent to next of kin. The CIA refused to identify the operative known to us as Johnson, but Rick assured us that the body would be returned properly, if quietly, once it had been shipped to the U.S.

When it came to the trials, Wildersbach and Delorme pleaded not guilty to the various charges, but four of the other guides avoided stiff penalties by testifying against both of them. Given the guides' testimonies, Dexter's testimony regarding the computer-controlled aspects, the written records we found, and the bodies, Wildersbach was found guilty of practising medicine without a licence, operating the radiation treatment device without the required licenses and, of course, multiple offences related to the 'indignity or neglect of a dead body' section of the Criminal Code. It also turned out that Wildersbach was in the country illegally, although he wasn't to be deported until he had served his sentences in Canada. Delorme was found to be an accessory and sentenced accordingly.

As far as the original theft of the Amerior-8 machine and murder of the truck driver in Ontario, we suspected that the two men involved were probably Delorme and Wildersbach, with Delorme committing the murder, but the Ontario Provincial Police had been unable to find enough evidence to bring charges against anyone, and our own search of the hospital and residences at the Gunnar site hadn't produced any evidence linking the two men – or anyone else, for that matter – to those two particular crimes, and to this day they remain 'unsolved.'

Along the way, Accelerated Nuclear Inc. was notified of the discovery of their Amelior-8 machine, and also of Dexter's analysis and diagnosis regarding their faulty computer program. I didn't ever hear whether they went to the effort and expense of transporting the machine out, but they were so impressed with Dexter's work on the program that they offered him a full-time job at their headquarters in Mississauga, which he accepted. Although his advanced training, a standing, permanent-job offer, and a clean record should have been more than enough to get approved for a Canadian work permit, I like to think that recommendation letters from the RCMP, Canadian Forces, FBI, and CIA probably didn't hurt his chances either.

... Alex and Silver will return

BOOK 16 ENDNOTES

1. In the early 1950s, a combination of cold-war security concerns and industrial technological advances led to uranium exploration in northern Saskatchewan, among other places, leading to several good quality discoveries. One of these, the Gunnar uranium deposit was discovered at the southern tip of the Crackingstone Peninsula on the northern shore of Lake Athabasca in 1952. Gunnar was considered to be the richest uranium strike in Canada at the time, and was unique in the region because it could be initially developed with a low-cost open-pit mine, as opposed to an underground mine which, in Gunnar's case, was developed later. Located about 40 km away from Uranium City, the site was considered to be too far away for routine services, so the company built a mill and a dedicated community in addition to the mines. When the Gunnar mill construction was completed in the fall of 1955 it doubled Canada's uranium production capacity. In 1956 the Gunnar mine was the largest uranium producer in the world. By the end of 1963, Gunnar's reserves were gone and the entire operation was simply shut-down. By this time Canada, the U.K. and the U.S. had more than enough uranium for their needs, and almost all of the other nearby mines were closed as well, leaving the entire Uranium City area to fall into decline.
2. In real life, and in the mid-1970s, Atomic Energy of Canada Limited (AECL) developed a very similar machine called

Therac-25 that inspired this part of the story. Costing a million dollars each, at the time, the Therac-25 was a compact, medical linear-accelerator, controlled by a PDP-11 computer, that could deliver either X-ray photons at 25 MeV or electrons at various energy levels.

3. In the real-life inspiration for this story, eleven Therac-25s were installed in North America for which six accidents causing serious injury and/or death occurred between 1985 and 1987, after which the machines were recalled to make extensive design changes that included hardware safeguards against software errors. See: N. Leveson, "Medical Devices: The Therac-25," in *Safeware: System Safety and Computers*, Addison-Wesley, 1995.

4. 'Langley' refers to a community in Fairfax County, Virginia, that is home to the headquarters of the U.S. Central Intelligence Agency.

5. Prime Minister's Office.

6. In the 1960s and '70s, according to investigative journalist Edward J. Epstein, "Mutual suspicion between the CIA and FBI of each other's moles and sources became so intense that in 1971 [FBI Director] Hoover broke off relations with the agency." The CIA's preoccupation with moles, traitors, and compromised sources eased later, in the 1980s, when much of the agency's focus shifted to electronic-intelligence gathering which, at the time, was judged to be secure. See E.J. Epstein, "Deception. The Once and Future Cold War," G.B. Putnam, N.Y., 1989 and "The War of the Moles," *New York Magazine*, 13 March 1978, pp. 12-13, https://www.cia.gov/readingroom/docs/CIA-RDP81M00980R002000090048-9.pdf

7. Ernesto 'Che' Guevara was a Marxist revolutionary and guerrilla leader in the Cuban Revolution against the dictator Batista in the 1950s. In later years, and especially after his death in 1965, his visage became a common countercultural symbol of rebellion.

8. During the Cold War, both the Soviet Union and the United States conducted extensive research programs into possible existence of, and possible military uses of ESP. See for example: A. Jacobsen, *Phenomena: The Secret History of the U.S. Government's Investigations into Extrasensory Perception and Psychokinesis*, Back Bay Books, Boston, 2018; and Martin Ebon, *Psychic Warfare: Threat or Illusion?* McGraw-Hill, NY, 1983.

9. See *An Inconvenient Mountie*, ISBN: 978-1-9994940-0-1.
10. The Canadian Police Information Centre (CPIC) is Canada's national police database. When the author worked at CPIC in 1971 (before its launch), we referred to it by spelling out the acronym's letters – 'C-P-I-C' - but after the system became operational in 1972, people in the field began to refer to it as 'seapick.' See: B. Sharp, "*Cop*," Friesen Press, Victoria, BC, 2014.
11. At the time of this story, medical linear accelerators were just beginning to become widely available. In 1976, for example, there were only about 336 in operation worldwide. See: S.G. Laskar *et al.*, "Access to Radiation Therapy: From Local to Global and Equality to Equity," *JCO Global Oncology*, **2022**, *8(August 12)*, 7 pp., doi.org/10.1200/GO.21.00358
12. The de Havilland DHC-6 Twin Otter is a twin-engine, short-takeoff and landing aircraft developed in the 1960s and still in production (now by Viking Air). Easily switched from wheeled-, to float- or ski landing gear, they are ubiquitous in Canada's more northern and remote regions and one of the most famous of Canada's 'bush planes.'
13. On a merchant ship, these are usually the First Watch (20:00–24:00), Middle Watch (00:00–04:00), Morning Watch (04:00–08:00), Forenoon Watch (08:00–12:00), Afternoon Watch (12:00–16:00), and Dog Watch (16:00–20:00).
14. Ripstop nylon contains crosshatched coarse, strong, yarns at intervals so that tears will not spread, and is often coated to make it water resistant or waterproof. It originated during the Second World War, sometime after nylon was adopted as a replacement for silk in parachutes. Ripstop nylon began appearing in consumer products for campers and hikers in 1980, and would still have been regarded as state-of-the-art at the time of this story.
15. The largest known lake trout, at 102 lb. (46 kg), was caught in a gill net in Lake Athabasca in 1961. There is a photo of it in the article at: BCLSS, "Lake Trout (Salvelinus namaycush)," BCLSS Newsletter, 13(1) April, 2010, BC Lake Stewardship Society, https://www.bclss.org/news/lake-trout#:~:text=The%20largest%20known%20lake%20trout,)%20(Mathias%2C%202009).
16. The headframe is a tall structure that sits directly above the main

shaft of an underground mine and contains the hoisting mechanisms for raising and lowering miners, mining equipment, supplies, waste rock, and the mined ore.

17. Generally termed the Norwalk virus at the time of this story, this common cause of gastroenteritis was renamed norovirus in 2002.

18. PP796 is a triazolo-pyridine compound discovered by ICI Pharmaceuticals in the early 1970s. Originally intended to be used in the treatment of asthma, it was found to have a strong emetic effect in humans. A dose of 5-8 mg causes nausea and induces vomiting, accompanied by dizziness and sweating and flushing. At this dosage, vomiting occurs within 30 mins. The half-life in humans following single oral doses is between 1.5 and 3.5 hours. Due to its strong emetic effect, PP796 has been included in formulations of the herbicide paraquat, most commonly Gramoxone™, since 1976. It is included as a safety measure because paraquat is highly toxic to humans, the idea being that if a person accidently ingests the formulation, the PP796 component will cause them to almost immediately vomit. Although paraquat was banned in 2007 by the European Union, formulations of it are still widely used in about 100 other countries (but not Canada since 2023).

19. The ubiquitous amber-coloured plastic containers for prescription medications came into widespread use in the early 1970s. The amber-coloured plastic blocks UV light that would otherwise potentially degrade the medication.

20. Limnological research focuses on inland water systems, such as streams, rivers, and lakes. It can involve any or all of the physics, chemistry, and biology of these water bodies.

21. See *An Indestructible Mountie*, ISBN: 978-1-9994940-4-9.

22. Stereo microscopes have binocular eyepieces and produce a 3D (stereo) image at relatively low magnifications, such as 10X to 40X. They are usually set-up to provide reflected-light illumination, but some can be used in transmitted-light mode. Compound microscopes commonly have either single- or binocular eyepieces and produce high- to very high magnifications of small samples placed on a microscope slide. They can be used in reflected or transmitted light modes, sometimes using illumination of wavelengths outside of the visible light range, and typically produce magnifications in the

range 40X to 1,000X.

23. The Digital Voice Protection (DVP) algorithm for the encryption/decryption of voice communications was developed by Motorola in the mid-1970s (it is also known as VULCAN, Motorola's internal codename).

24. It wasn't until 1984 that municipalities in Alberta were able to allow, or continue to prohibit, retail stores opening on Sundays.

25. Although CFB Edmonton is close to the city of Edmonton, it is also just south of the hamlet of Namao and was formerly called RCAF Station Namao. For many years, the base continued to be referred to by its older, short-form name: Namao.

26. The Cessna 206 is a single-engine, six-seat, aircraft with fixed landing gear that can be equipped with floats, amphibious floats, or skis, used in commercial air service as well as for personal use. It has been a popular choice as a bush plane, among other things, since its introduction in 1962 and it was still in production at the time of writing.

27. At 7,850 km² (3,030 sq mi), Lake Athabasca is the 20th largest lake in the world by surface area. In terms of lakes within, or bordered by Canada, only the Great Lakes, Great Bear Lake, and Lake Winnipeg are larger.

28. The Athabasca sand dunes extend for about 100 kilometres (60 mi) along the southern edge of Lake Athabasca and represent one of the most northerly active sand dune formations on Earth. Some of the individual sand dunes are as much as 1,500 metres long and as tall as 30 metres.

29. Canadian Hydrographic Service chart CHS6310.

30. Zodiac inflatable boats became famous in the 1960s and '70s due to their ubiquitous appearance in the underwater documentaries made by the French oceanographer and filmmaker Jacques Cousteau (who also co-invented the first successful open-circuit SCUBA breathing apparatus). The inflatable tubes in Zodiac boats, and their similarly-designed competitors, were made of synthetic rubber compounds, one of which was DuPont Hypalon®. In addition to being strong and flexible, these materials have very good resistance to heat, ultraviolet light, and gasoline. Dupont stopped making the Hypalon material in 2010.

31. See *An Inconspicuous Mountie* 978-1-9994940-2-5.

32. Ignoring the radioisotopes with half-lives of less than 22 years,

the uranium decay series is: uranium-238 → uranium-234 → thorium-230 → radium-226 → lead-210 → lead-206 (which is stable).

33. In real life, the movement of mine tailings into Langley Bay (adjacent to the Gunnar mine and mill site) really has led to high radionuclide concentrations in the resident whitefish and, to a lesser extent, the pike. See, for example: D.T. Waite, *et al.,* "The Effect of Uranium Mine Tailings on Radionuclide Concentrations in Langley Bay, Saskatchewan, Canada," *Arch. Environ. Contam. Toxicol.,* **1988**, *17*, 373-380.

34. In real life, they are. At the time of writing, radionuclide levels in the flesh and bone of fish caught in the flooded Gunnar open-mine pit are one to two orders of magnitude greater than levels in fish caught from an uncontaminated area of Lake Athabasca. The fish have been accumulating the radionuclides from materials being mobilized in and/or washed into the pit.

35. In real life, the Gunnar open-pit mine was mined to a final depth of 328 feet (110 m) below the level of the lake.

36. When active, the mined uranium had been crushed and processed using an acid-leach process for which the sulphuric acid needed was produced on-site from sulphur that was barged in from Alberta. For more details see: L.L. Schramm, *Gunnar Uranium Mine. Canada's Cold War Ghost Town,* Amazon.com Inc., 2016, ISBN: 978-0-9958081-2-6.

37. 'Check your six' was originally an Air Force term for 'watch out behind you,' based on looking for enemy aircraft to the rear at the 6 O'clock position. It was later broadened to other services, and broader meanings (including off-duty situations).

38. Forcite was a 'gelatin dynamite,' comprising 30 to 80% nitroglycerin mixed with cellulose, sodium or potassium nitrate, and a hydrocarbon like tar (to make it waterproof). It was commonly used in mining operations up until about the end of the 1970s.

39. At the time of this story, the printer would likely have been something like the DECwriter III, capable of printing 180 characters per second in draft mode; about 300 lines per minute on 9⅞" paper.

40. The relative popularities and meaning of the terms nerd and geek have changed over the decades. Those characterized as nerds or geeks have stereotypically been male, intelligent,

socially awkward, and dedicated to the point of obsession with a specific field or topic. In general, where a distinction is made, it is that geeks are fans and students of their subjects whereas nerds are practitioners of them.

41. Black Sabbath, although already a hit in the 1970s, was one of the top heavy-metal rock groups in the 1980s. Their anti-war song *War Pigs* (1970) is often cited as the best of their many hits.

42. See: S. Cheryan *et al.*, "The Stereotypical Computer Scientist: Gendered Media Representations as a Barrier to Inclusion for Women," *Sex Roles*, **2013**, *69*, 58–71.

43. Originally, the term computer hacker referred to the early computer nerds, for whom the term 'hack' was applied to neat hardware or programming tricks; but it later changed to the modern meaning of someone that acts to subvert computer security.

44. Wide Area Telephone Service (WATS) was a flat-rate, long-distance telephone service plan for businesses in North America, by which they were given a special number and an included number of hours. WATS was introduced in 1961 and operated until the early 1980s.

45. For a real-life example, see: S. Levy, *Hackers: Heroes of the Computer Revolution*, Anchor Press/Doubleday, N.Y., 1984.

46. This kind of thing actually happened to several patients in the real-life Therac-25 case. See N.G. Leveson and C.S. Turner, "An Investigation of the Therac-25 Accidents," *Computer*, **1993**, *26(7)*, 18-41.

47. The Stanford Artificial Intelligence Lab (SAIL) at Stanford University, sometimes called the 'AI Lab,' was founded in 1965, it was merged into Stanford's Computer Science Department in 1980, but then re-emerged as a stand-alone in 2004.

48. 'Standby to standby,' like 'hurry up and wait,' is military sarcasm referring either to having to wait for long periods of time because of logistics or command indecisiveness, or to the military's tendency to perform tasks quickly and then be idle.

49. At $59°23'$ N, Alex would only have been about 795 km (500 mi) south of the Arctic Circle.

50. Twilight is caused by the scattering of the sun's light in the upper atmosphere despite the fact that the sun's geometric centre lies

below the horizon. At Alex's location and time of year, the twilight sequence would have been approximately as follows: civil twilight (21:30-22:20; sun's centre 0-6° below the horizon), nautical twilight (22:20-23:50; sun's centre 6-12° below the horizon), astronomical twilight (23:50-02:50; sun's centre 12-18° below the horizon), nautical twilight (02:50-04:20), civil twilight (04:20-05:20), and sunrise at about 05:20.

51. At the time of this story, the Eldorado uranium mine was still in full operation, and Uranium City had a six-person RCMP Detachment, but it didn't last much longer. The Eldorado mine, among others in the area, closed in 1982, causing an economic collapse that forced most residents of the community to leave. See: "Dennis Lars Schneider," *Pillars of the Force*, Friends of the RCMP Heritage Centre, Regina, SK, accessed 26 July 2024, https://mpvirtualpillars.ca/listing/auto-draft/

52. See *An International Mountie*, ISBN 978-1-9994940-6-3.

53. See *An Indestructible Mountie*, ISBN 978-1-9994940-4-9.

54. Although fictional, this would have been technically feasible as commercial divers can perform very deep dives breathing gas mixtures such as Heliox (a mixture of oxygen and helium, but no nitrogen) and a rebreather (which provides mobility by avoiding the need for surface-fed hoses). A diver with a Heliox rebreather would be able to operate at the maximum depth of the pit, which is about 110 m (360 ft).

ADVENTURES OF THE FIRST WOMAN MOUNTIE

Individual Novels	Collections
Bk 1: *An Inconvenient Mountie*	*Adventures of the First Woman Mountie. Omnibus Volume 1*
Bk 2: *An Inconspicuous Mountie*	
Bk 3: *An Indestructible Mountie*	
Bk 4: *An International Mountie*	
Bk 5: *An Inseparable Mountie*	*Adventures of the First Woman Mountie II: The Second Omnibus*
Bk 6: *An Indispensable Mountie*	
Bk 7: *An Inexorable Mountie*	
Bk 8: *An Intrepid Mountie*	
Bk 9: *An Intimate Mountie*	*Adventures of the First Woman Mountie III: The Third Omnibus*
Bk 10: *An Ineradicable Mountie*	
Bk 11: *An Incommunicado Mountie*	
Bk 12: *An Instructive Mountie*	
Bk 13: *An Inimitable Mountie*	*Adventures of the First Woman Mountie IV: The Fourth Omnibus*
Bk 14: *An Inside Mountie*	
Bk 15: *An Interrupted Mountie*	
Bk 16: *An Inveterate Mountie*	

www.laurieschramm.ca

Laurie Schramm

SUMMARIES

An Inconvenient Mountie (**Book 1**). 1975. Alexandra Houston is asked to join RCMP as its first woman Member - as a pilot project. She accepts, hoping it will fulfil her dream of doing "some real policing," while not realizing that she should be careful what she asks for. Her first posting is to a remote part of Northern Saskatchewan, where no one is used to dealing with a female Mountie and her adventures in small-town policing are compounded by crises, crime, and mystery.

An Inconspicuous Mountie (**Book 2**). 1976. Alex and her dog Silver are training to work as an undercover team. Meanwhile, trouble is brewing north of Fort McMurray, Alberta where not everyone is happy with the development of the massive oil sands mines and tensions are running high. Before their training is complete, a pipeline is bombed, and new threats emerge. As Alex and Silver are sent in, this time they need to be ... inconspicuous.

An Indestructible Mountie (**Book 3**). 1977. A hiker on Cape Breton Island discovers a strange installation hidden in the forest, on an oceanside cliff. Word of her discovery reaches the RCMP Security Service, where it sets off alarm bells, and Alex and Silver are sent in. As they investigate, a technological curiosity from the Second World War turns out to be the centre-piece of something current, and sinister. This time Alex and Silver will need to be... indestructible.

An International Mountie (**Book 4**). Alex finally gets a break from a series of hair-raising assignments and heads for Alaska on vacation. While there she hopes to investigate Silver's origins and hike the famous Chilkoot Trail. Meanwhile, a young Girl Guide gets lost in the wilds of Alaska and experiences, first-hand, the meaning of the Guides and Scouts motto: *"Be Prepared."*

An Inseparable Mountie (**Book 5**). Called away from vacation in Alaska, Alex and Silver are inserted into an unfolding mystery in northwest British Columbia. Second World War artillery shells seem to be washing up on a beach and having disturbing effects on the kids that find them. These catch the attention of Military Intelligence as well, and Canadian Forces Lieutenant Don Harrison joins them in a search that will take them into danger once more.

An Indispensable Mountie (**Book 6**). 1978. When a Soviet nuclear-powered spy satellite veers off course and explodes over Canada's north, a military search operation is launched to recover the radioactive pieces. But there is a search within the search, as Alex and Silver are sent in undercover to discover whether one of the satellite's top-secret components may have survived. As they search a virtually uninhabited wasteland, they soon discover that aircraft malfunctions and the Arctic cold are the least of their problems.

An Inexorable Mountie (**Book 7**). Alex boards a cross-Canada train to look for security vulnerabilities in advance of an upcoming VIP trip. At least, that's her cover assignment. In reality, Alex and Silver are after bigger game. As they roll through the Atlantic Provinces, Central Canada, and the Prairies, Alex notices some strange behaviours on the part of several of her fellow passengers. These evolve into break-ins, intrigue, and a growing certainty that quite a few people on the train besides herself are not who they seem to be.

An Intrepid Mountie (**Book 8**). When Alex and Silver experience a chance encounter with two suspicious characters on the front lawn of Canada's Parliament Buildings, Alex decides to do a little digging. The results take them from the Pacific coast of British Columbia to the Atlantic coasts of Newfoundland and Labrador, on the trail of a professional agitator whose appearances at organized protest events seem to coincide with a trail of violence, injuries, and death.

An Intimate Mountie **(Book 9).** No sooner does Alex get engaged than she and her fiancé are invited to a family funeral and reunion at a lodge on Cape Breton Island. There, Alex learns about an ancient family curse, experiences suspicious events, and hears about still others from family members. Following a near-death experience, she begins investigating in earnest. When one of the lodge staff is found murdered, she has to move quickly if she is to figure out what's been going on and identify the killer before another murder takes place.

An Ineradicable Mountie **(Book 10).** 1979. When a young American woman experiences two attempted kidnappings in two successive days, Alex and Silver are assigned to protect her from some surprisingly persistent and well-informed pursuers while the woman's father concludes secret international negotiations. To buy time, they hide out in a secret, underground military installation, but their location is soon discovered and they find themselves under siege. With stealth and secrecy gone Alex realizes that, this time, she may have to shoot her way out of trouble.

An Incommunicado Mountie **(Book 11).** Alex, her fiancé Don, and Silver make a late-fall visit to a brand-new ski lodge high up in the Canadian Rockies. After only a short period of hiking and mountaineering in this idyllic setting, their vacation is threatened by a snow-storm that cuts off both power and access to the lodge. While they and a group of university students wait out the storm, a suspicious death puts Alex on the trail of a murderer.

An Instructive Mountie **(Book 12).** When Alex and Silver are called to the scene of a train derailment in Central Canada, the horror of the devastation is magnified by their discovery that it was intentionally caused; and by a bomb. The bombing turns out to be the first of many, leading Alex and Silver across Western Canada as they try to figure out where the next strikes will occur - and how to stop them.

Laurie Schramm

An Inimitable Mountie (Book 13). 1980. The chance discovery of a sunken cargo of Second World War-era uranium ore in Canada's Gulf of St. Lawrence puts Alex and Silver on the trail of a clandestine theft and black-market operation led by someone that doesn't hesitate to kill in order to avoid exposure. The first death appears to be accidental, but Alex is suspicious. After the second 'accidental' death, Alex is convinced she's investigating not only a mystery, but two murders as well.

An Inside Mountie (Book 14). Alex is drawn further into the shadowy world of espionage and betrayal when she is asked to hunt for a security leak that is buried somewhere inside one of Canada's intelligence services. But which one? If it's within her own service, the 'leak' may already be aware of her assignment, in which case the hunter could become the hunted.

An Interrupted Mountie (Book 15). Alex is just beginning a PEI honeymoon with her husband Don when she is asked to respond to a call for bomb-threat assistance at a cruise ship. With time pressing and no other police-dog-service team available, they agree to try to help. A routine search transitions into a request for them to join the ship for the rest of the voyage as a makeshift, undercover protective-service detail for VIP passengers. What at first seems to be a pleasant and straightforward task becomes complicated when they learn that the VIPs are not who they seem to be, and may be under threat from several different kinds of people, for quite different reasons.

An Inveterate Mountie (Book 16). Alex, Silver, and Don are sent on a covert mission. Someone has been using a fly-in-fishing camp on a remote northern lake as a cover for sophisticated but unlicensed, secret cancer treatments enabling wealthy patients to get treated while avoiding long waiting lists. When a powerful U.S. Senator goes for treatment and never returns, the CIA sends a covert operative to investigate. The alarm bells really go off when a charter pilot phones an unlisted CIA number to relay a codeword meaning that the operative had been captured or killed, forcing the U.S. Government to ask for the Canadian Government's assistance.

584

ABOUT THE AUTHOR

Laurie Schramm comes from an RCMP family, grew up while living in the RCMP Barracks (Depot Division) in Regina, Saskatchewan, and spent several summers working as a civilian for the RCMP while in high school and university. Early personal influences included not only the real-life RCMP culture but also Hollywood's versions via such classics as Rose Marie, and Susannah of the Mounties. Many of the events described in these novels are based on, or inspired by events from the author's real life, although not necessarily within an RCMP context.

For more information, see Laurier L. Schramm on **Linked in**

and:

www.laurieschramm.ca

Laurie Schramm

Laurie Schramm

www.ingramcontent.com/pod-product-compliance
Lightning Source LLC
Chambersburg PA
CBHW031020030726
47497CB00004B/933